Terri Rags

ROOTS of INDIFFERENCE

ISBN: 1-4392-0354-7
ISBN-13: 9781439203545

ACKNOWLEDGEMENTS

My gratitude goes to my daughter, Juli Jacobson, for her computer savvy, mediating and organizational skills. To Joan Baker, my friend and mentor, whose suggestions and encouragement helped me, complete this novel.

⌘ ⌘ ⌘

This book is dedicated to all the wonderful people of the Lower Rio Grande of Texas, who contributed and shared their stories throughout the years. It's through their eyes, their lives and their struggles that made this book possible.

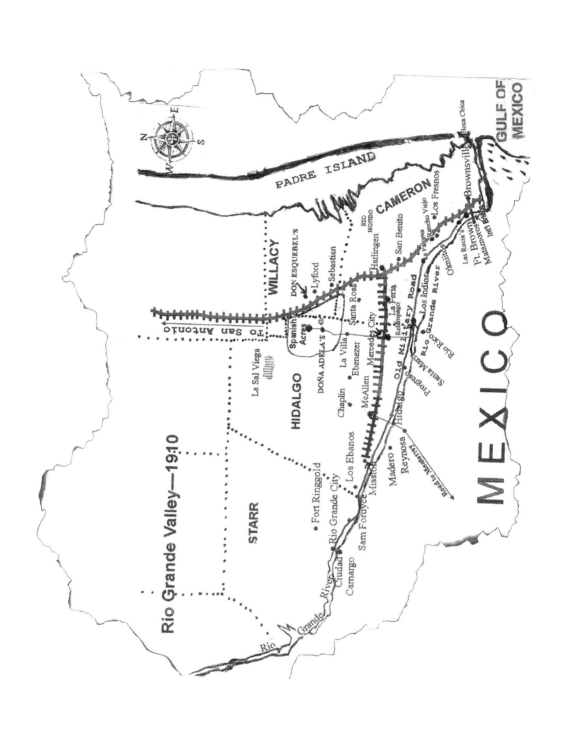

Rio Grande Valley—1910

ROOTS of INDIFFERENCE

"To everything there is a season and time to every purpose under the heaven…"
Ecclesiastes 3:1

PROLOGUE

Mercedes, Texas – 1980

Above—the heavens were busy conspiring with the semi-tropical weather that was always stifling and humid, as it had been for thousands of years in the region of the lower Rio Grande Valley of South Texas, a region disturbed by winds that blew forever with pestering vapors. But the constant sea breeze coming from the Gulf of Mexico was a Godsend, a ruffled blessing that created the balance and tempered this hot, torrid land that slumbered in annoying, sweltering heat. Skies remained vitreous, bleached-out, blue enamel.

Below— amidst earths' plain—natives stirred with cleverness and savvy.

⌘   ⌘   ⌘

On a sultry September afternoon, a weary, homeless, old man, arrived by bus, halfway between heaven and hell to the quaint little town of Mercedes, Texas. The "Queen City" of the Valley, as it was called, sat peacefully in the heart of Hidalgo County and basked in the dormant heat. It was a friendly, welcoming community that seemed to cast a synthetic, magical spell on all outside visitors and whispered from its ghostly corners, "Stay awhile—visit me. Join us! Glad you're here! Welcome to great Texas hospitality!"

Fred Juelson had soulfully journeyed all day by bus, struggling with old age and ill health as he crossed the International Bridge from Matamoros, Mexico, into the border town of Brownsville, Texas. He then waited hours for transportation and took the lower Rio Grande Valley transit bus that traveled to the other small towns along the border.

Many years had passed since the old man had set foot on Texas soil. Several miles north of Mercedes was the town of La Villa, and just north of that patch of ground was the place where he was born. The land called *Los Burritos* was part of the *Ojo de Agua Tract* region. This was the original land of his forefathers who had struggled and sacrificed to build the great Juelson cattle empire. And now, coming home at last had revived many disturbing memories filled with immense sadness. One thing Fred was certain of—he had come home for his final time. First, he must pay his respects to his sister Victoria's grave, and second, he must decide upon his final resting place.

The long journey had taken its toll on the still formidable-looking, eighty-year-old man. The spirit of the wretched past was showing its ugly face—karma coming full circle, and, like the salmon swimming against the stream, returning to the place of its birth, he was coming home to die. Too exhausted to continue to his destination, he found comfort on a wooden bench in a small park, where he could rest and regain his thoughts. He placed his heavy old suitcase and a rope-bound cloth bag on the ground next to his feet. They contained all of his worldly possessions—written papers portraying the accumulation of his lifetime accomplishments.

In his youth, the old soul had been a giant of a man at six-foot-five. Now, his huge shoulders were slightly bent from the long years of service as a humanitarian and a physician, a "buggy doctor," as he was called by many of his patients. He was grave and serious in spite of his shabby, faded and wrinkled shirt and gray suit. He wore an old, greased-lined, beige Stetson that hid his receding hairline and baldness. Large dark circles under his kind, gray eyes gave him a look that was gaunt and hollow.

Fred had been a man of many talents, considered a "jack-of-all trades," quick with his tongue, conversant on any known topic. He was fortunate enough to have been well educated, and he attended the finest private schools and medical colleges, and was tutored in music and fine arts. He came from a rich and prominent family in South Texas, and his early childhood was lavished with luxury, the prodigy of his family's pride. His adolescence had been conflicted between the love of music and the intrigue of nature, and he was sympathetic to the significance of life, always asking and inquiring.

Who would have believed that this charismatic man so dedicated to his profession would sink to the level of his current condition? It was hard to believe that he was now only a shadow of his former self, an unknown, merely existing, resembling more a panhandler than a doctor.

Fred Juelson had become but a memory to this forgotten, illustrious, racially mixed people. An intelligent instructor of medicine, he had struggled arduously against injustice and discrimination on both sides of the Rio Grande. He had been a sentimentalist, especially for the less fortunate, those who were unlearned, humble, hungry. He had become a loner, but rationalized his own solitude in his unusual manner of restlessness and turbulently odd pattern of life. The time had come—he was aware of the alpha and the omega's circle of life.

His past years had brought out bitter resentments that churned within his tormented spirit. All he had now were his cherished but clouded memories, and hard truths and lessons in life. Old age and death were coming with stealthy steps. It was only a matter of time, as the clock kept ticking, and before long, he would become soil of the earth. Until then, his roots would be impossible to define. In his long, epic journey, and somewhere along his long-lived life, he had forgotten—God.

Gasping for breath, Fred pivoted and began gazing at the town that once had held his future. Bitter feelings churned in his stomach, leaving a hollow sensation of desperation and loneliness.

West of the park were young boys playing ball and making a lot of noise. He leaned his head back and closed his eyes, withdrawing into himself. He tried to concentrate on the events that had caused him to leave Mercedes and the Rio Grande Valley so many years ago. Too many memories, marked with poignant disappointments, were like dirty water under the bridge.

His thoughts wandered back to his family, his sister Victoria, and his cherished early childhood.

From out of nowhere, a rock flew through the air and hit the corner of the wooden bench, startling Fred, breaking his concentration. A frightened, black mongrel dog, lean and hungry, came running toward him. Its ribs were showing and its tongue hung out from thirst. Patches of raw skin, bloodied and infected, marred its coat. His tail wagged occasionally, showing his friendliness and desire for affection, but later draped between his legs, indicating signs of defeat. Cowardly, he lay on the ground shaking while observing the old man. The boys had stopped playing, and one was throwing stones and cursing at the animal.

Fred, angered by this injustice and being very sensitive to any hurt animal, found that his blood boiled. He used all his strength, held on to the edge of bench with his left hand that steadied him, and stood, partly stooped, displaying his lean-built body. Trying to keep his temper in a masterful restraint, he pointed his index finger. "Hey, *Cabrón!*" he yelled at the boy throwing the stones. "You damn bully, leave the dog alone! Why don't you pick on someone your size?"

Two of the boys began to laugh and mock and made faces, using insulting words toward the old man.

"Get away from this park! Go home and help your mother!" Fred shouted again and stood his ground. *"Cobardes!"* he called them. "Go home and do your homework! Get smart! Get intelligent! You stupid *pendejos!"*

The laughter continued until one of the boys picked up the ball and said, *"Chale ése!"* They decided that the old man meant business. *"Oye bató,"* repeated the other one. "Let's go!" As they left, one of them pointed to his head and circled his finger, indicating that the old man was crazy.

By now, the black dog sniffed the ground, trying to find a morsel of food.

Fred managed to sit back in a comfortable position on the bench and looked down at the shaking dog. He fumbled in his ragged cloth bag and brought out a piece of dried bread, then patted the ground with his right foot, getting the dog's attention. "Come, come," he cooed, showing the animal the food.

The bewildered dog looked puzzled and stood for a moment and wagged its tail again and cocked its head to one side, not accustomed to any kind gestures. It had been abused and mistreated by people and was not quite sure of the old man's intentions. Fred repeated, "Come, come."

The dog hesitated, coyly standing inches away, and watched the old man.

"You little shit," said Fred out loud, knowing that the animal was hungry. He threw the piece of bread on the ground close to his feet, but kept a close watch on the dog from the corner of his eye.

Startled and shaken by the incident with the ornery boys, Fred's hands began to tremble and his legs shook. He had been cursed with incurable Parkinson's disease many years ago. The last four years the illness had become incredibly worse and had gained an irrevocable hold on him, leaving him miserable and chronically fatigued. The man who had tried to cure everything from man to beast to fowl could not even help himself. No medicine had helped so far, not even the miracle drug, *el dopamine*. What could cure the fatal disease eating the cells of his brain?

It took a long while before his tremor completely stopped. His breathing became easy and calm. He whimpered with a sharp pain. *The signs of old age*, he thought, and began realizing that his main worries now were only in liniments, creams for his pains, and aching bones. Age was cruel and unfair, getting old was to suffer. If he had only known this when he was young, foolish and uncaring of protecting his body in his early years. He was lucky he still had most of his teeth and could hear fairly well, but sometimes he couldn't remember where he put things. His eyes fogged with tears.

He was still angry at the boys' thoughtless stupidity in hurting the small, defenseless dog. *What does the immature younger generation know about life? These young boys have no respect, especially for their elders.* Calling him crazy! What did they know of the sacrifices it took a person like himself, who overcame discrimination and the hatred prevalent in the Valley in its early years? If they only knew his grandfather, who was one of the pioneers in the region, and how he had struggled to build a life here. And his father, who had fought for human rights until the day he died. Fred noticed that the boys had completely disappeared from the park. The little black dog stood close by his feet, watching him. The old man pushed the dried bread, with the toe of his shoe, nearer to the dog, but it wagged its tail, stood cautiously and never moved toward the bread. The old man gave out another loud wheeze and turned to scrutinize the town.

⌘ ⌘ ⌘

Mercedes was an old town, even as old as Fred. It was a special town because there was nothing special about it. No monumental statues, no skyscrapers, no hotels or motels, no historical or sacred, consecrated grounds, no recreational areas, nothing to attract travelers. Like scores of small border towns, it was the quiet, picturesque, carbon copy of a postcard scene, which offered a natural unseen beauty. Tall arcades of palm trees, nestled in citrus trees and various types of tropical shrubs, sweltered in the summer sultriness'.

Typical of other small border communities, Mercedes proudly displayed its distinctive water tower, perhaps the tallest structure in town, glaring silver in the blazing, scorching sun and imbued with the spirit as well as the name of the town. The humdrum atmosphere in

Mercedes was peaceful and slow-paced. The residents never hurried, taking one day at a time. Most of the natives were related in one way or another, either through marriage or kinship. It was a town sweltering in heat, passion, and malicious, slanderous gossip. The natives made life as interesting as possible by engaging in rumors, prying into other people's lives, making jokes and laughing at one another's problems. The laughter was therapeutic and a pastime habit. They would invent names as a joke, christening the individual with an attached nickname identifying and branding the person for a lifetime. They would giggle and tittle-tattled about their adventures, marriages, and miseries. They spent the hot afternoons behind closed shutters, supposedly taking a siesta, but keenly watching their next-door neighbor's actions.

At dusk, it was not uncommon to view the older women sitting inside screened porches, talking about worldly issues and gossiping about hushed-up family secrets. Holding a cold drink, they would fan pesky flies or annoying mosquitoes. Old men scratched their crotches and rubbed their testicles. They spat on the ground, passed gas, talked about guns, dogs, women, and their daily dealings, and told stories of the old times and of their hero, Pancho Villa.

The balmy, breezy nights were special for the young people, almost adventurous and intriguing, becoming a bewitching enticement. There was a strong impulse in human sensuality when the young became impatient, and passion came on strong, taking priority. The coming of the full moon brought romantic energies and thoughts of tantalizing adventures. One thing was clear: no one lacked for love or affection. It flourished. No one knew for sure if the water had anything to do with the romantic encounters or if it was the sultry air, the throb of Spanish guitars, the tangy, spicy foods, or the smell of the tropical vines. Love lived everywhere. Young girls with pangs of adolescence were restless with inquisitive appetites and longing. Boys coming of age savored the camaraderie in an overheated state, preferring the nights when they were stirred by agonizing thoughts, and searching for any female's warm affection.

The local habitants lived and died from generation to generation with their quintessential ways, and their ethnicity taught them to become better patriots and peaceful, loving citizens. A handful of hyperactive individuals stubbornly pursued their dreams elsewhere and moved away, usually to the northern states to find better jobs in larger cities. They had learned, as they aged, that all the riches, money, and all the materialism in the world, could not replace the close relationship of the family bond. Many succeeded there and returned only to visit.

⌘   ⌘   ⌘

In the early days there were large *ranchos*, owned by American citizens of Spanish and Mexican descent, and for hundreds of years the vast land with thousands of acres had belonged to them and their families. In all those years, the land had stood idle and undeveloped in spite of many hurricanes and weather conditions that changed the environment and the land; however, unwanted vegetation proliferated, producing millions of cactus, mesquite, chaparral, and formidable shrubbery, lacing skyward.

But then in the early 1900s, something exciting happened along the Texas border. A great change came among the peaceful natives, snowballing into a bombshell. Crafty-minded, intelligent white men brought the railroad and the vision of opportunity into the *terra firma*. In 1905, the railroad developers began manipulating and lured the owners of the *ranchos* into selling their land, hiring cheap Mexican laborers to clear the mesquite and cacti and obstinate bushes. The white man envisioned great dreams, reflecting on their greedy wallets and fortunes. The rattlers, tarantulas and cockroaches were not pleased with the earth-shattering project, they protested—but it was progress.

Fred was seven years old when the town of Mercedes was established. First it was called Mercedes City as an early township. Now, as he gazed around, Fred analyzed the old town. Few of the palm trees that had been planted in the early years remained; those that did remain were tall and translucently wispy. The streets from east to west were named after each state of the union. The stores and mercantile buildings faced each other on a two-block main street. Two of the original drug stores that had competed in business against each other still stood. The new Hidalgo Bank was built on the corner of Texas and the old Highway 83 where the old but grand Mercedes Hotel had once stood. He viewed Texas Street, the two-way, one-traffic light that had been the main drag of the community, especially on Saturday night's payday for many of the laborers and agricultural workers in the vicinity, who came into town to spend their money on groceries and commodities.

The old railroad depot north of the park and across from Highway 83 stood empty; its faded-out grooved red tile roof still remained, surviving many harsh years of hurricanes and torrid heat. A stubborn magenta bougainvillea vine clung to its brick side, while many unattended pink and white oleander bushes surrounded the grounds. The outskirts of the town were fertile, alluvial soil, dedicated to flatland agriculture, where cotton was raised on hundreds of acres; other fields raised citrus, melons, tomatoes and a diversity of vegetables.

North of the railroad depot across the tracks stood rotten, faded, boarded-up and empty packing-plant buildings, reminiscent of the early '40s, '50s and early '60s. From these, millions of cartons of citrus, tomatoes, melons, and vegetables had been shipped to all parts of the United States. Mercedes had been the mecca of this enterprise.

Across the tracks, lived the majority of the Mexican people in heavily populated *barrios*. The railroad tracks that had served very effectively were a grim reminder of the early prejudice land planners had in dividing the town—an intimidating barrier to segregate the Mexican and Anglo population. *El barrio Mejicano* was a one-block street with a barbershop, the Mexican theater, a Mexican drug store, two grocery stores, a gas station, and small novelty shops. Homes in the *barrios* were surrounded by brick fences with wrought-iron entrances and a flourishing array of colorful flowers and tropical plants. There also drab shacks with peeling paint and bare yards full of junk. North of the tracks, there were always more children, more dogs, and loads of laughter. Occasionally, strong *corridos* music would be heard from the *cantinas* along north Main Street, with the loud laughter of unemployed men playing pool, drinking beer, and bragging of their past romantic conquests, displaying their *machismo.*

Large flatbed trucks, heavy with loads of picked cotton, rumbled onto Texas Street, heading to the gins north of the town, leaving a trail of diesel fumes and dust. A large canal came from the Mercedes pumps located south of the town and supported the area with water. To the far west, Highway 83 passed a bridge over a large levee, which led to the town of Weslaco.

Fred was surprised since his long absence to see the many changes in the town's landscape. Viewing Highway 83 earlier from the window of the bus, he thought the towns and the area looked ghostly. He had seen so many faded-out advertising signs, decaying, old, unpainted, boarded-up buildings, and vacant gas stations. He also saw the skeletons of old antique cars and shells of old trucks, left to the corruption of the elements. Vendors, who once had "ma and pa" small-shop groceries, had now gone by the wayside, becoming victims of the new federally built highway just north of Mercedes.

The afternoon had already reached its final peak. The day had become a pewter-haze of heat waves, undulating along the hot pavement, giving the town an aloof, sleepy illusion that seemed to hang over the entire area. The sun was a bright glow, dropping slowly down, touching its rays over and beyond the few remaining palm trees. The old man was glad that he had not come during the hottest time of the year, known to the locals as the *canícula.* Those dog days had come and gone, along with their natural eternal misery—Texas dust.

⌘　⌘　⌘

Fred looked toward the west, but it was to the west that he would have to struggle a quarter of a mile to the house where he had lived after his twelfth birthday. The mansion had been left to his only sister, Victoria, who was now dead. It was a house that, if its walls could speak, would tell of its own private skeletons in the closet. Had he not been sick and disoriented by age, he would have come earlier, if only he had known sooner of his sister's ill health. He had received the message of her passing almost a month ago. *Oh God,* he thought, *it has been an exhausting trip and so many memories linger among the ethereal corners of this town.*

Regressing back in his mind, it was political motives and certain so-called citizens who had incriminated him and sealed his fate, completely destroying his life and his dreams for the future. *Dear Lord,* he thought, *it has been so many years.* He shuddered to think of that moment in time was the turning point in his ambitious career. He had been caught in a circle of political injustice and a spider web of conspiracy, creating a devastating impact on his family, especially his diplomat father— Ambassador of Goodwill, and Senator—who was left with a searing emotional scar that could never be erased. Because of his racially mixed blood and his upstanding character, Fred fled from the United States into Mexico, where he had remained for so many years, where questions were never asked.

His homecoming was to pay his respects and visit Victoria's grave. His beloved sister had been beautiful, and yet so cunning in her own ruthless manner, but she had stood by him and fought for his name and dignity throughout his absence. It was Victoria who always seemed to understand his odd pattern of life. She comprehended his prodigal habits and unpredictable behavior. The Juelson's matriarch was dead, and Fred's future now was bleak.

⌘ ⌘ ⌘

Overtaken by a tremendous nostalgia, Fred's mind now regressed back to an era in time, a different dimension, and crossing over among the constellations of his youth. His weary eyes stared at the swaying palm trees as tears welled and blocked his view. He began experiencing a fuller unity with his soul and slowly went into a deep, sleeping trance.

In his vision, he became as a child of ten, seeing the many joyous seasons of his youth. A strong pang of remorse ran throughout his soul, with unspeakable words going back to his childhood at Spanish Acres, his roots, the kingdom of his dreams. He remembered everything so vividly, registering the miracle of his existence, paralleling himself with other known organisms in this vast universe.

The dawn of each day, with its innocent mornings, were like no other, as the gentleness of the early sun's rays crept over the great gulf of flatland, swirling mists and uncovering the earth. Out in the cactus brushwood there was a sense of serenity, of oneness with the earthly universe, and it laughed with the joy of discovery. The blinding glare flirted with Fred's shadows, embraced his perceptions, then laughed at his smiles; and yet, millions of atoms stirred in awe of the vast stillness. His clouds were always little desires of white cotton candy.

But how great were the sunsets, like nowhere else. The sun at dusk was like the gentle kiss of twilight. And at no other place on earth did the evening star shine so large and bright.

And then there were the long, hot summers, dog days, lazy days, wading in the creeks: heavenly bathing and swimming in the *resaca*, and jumping from a long rope into the water; running wildly barefooted through the cool, soft earth; chasing baby raccoons and watching them play; listening to the cooing of the morning doves and the singing of the playful mockingbirds—all etched indelibly in his memory. He remembered the longstanding, asinine jokes that brought tears of laughter to his eyes, and digging in burrows for tarantulas and throwing them to each another—shocking! He remembered playing with lizards and horny toads, and the simplicity of tadpoles in the streams after an early spring rain. The rhythmic singing of the cicadas was always a mystery, with their wide blunt head, droning their songs and laying eggs that would not hatch for thirteen years.

But it was always amazing to him when the miracle of the fireflies came in the spring. The little fairies, he called them, sparkling love potions in a fantasy world of lost enchantment, radiating like the Fourth of July, like burning lanterns illuminating the darkest firmament, only for the sake of love and courtship. How wonderful were his memories full of foolishness, friendship, and exciting exploration. He was captivated by the multicolors of the rainbow. Why did the flowers bloom? Why did the moon shine at night? His world was full of magic, mysteries, and beautiful miracles. He was a knight in shining armor, the time of his innocence. Ivanhoe was his hero, the cathedral of his adolescent. Hell! With a pocketknife and a horse he could conquer almost anything. He was an important king in those days, chasing dreams in the kingdom of his youth, reveling in the happiness of his infallible life—innocent and unworried. He was rich in those days, and no child could have asked for more. And as for Hell, it was a fictional fable.

It had all been so long ago. But the visions and memories he possessed and treasured would live with him forever. He became as a child again, remembering, regressing back and back...

When I despair, I remember that all through history

The ways of truth and love have always won.

There have been tyrants and murderers and for a time

They can seem invincible, but in the end they always fall.

Think of it, always….

Mahatma Gandhi

CHAPTER 1

Spanish Acres - 1910

The summer had been extremely hot and had come early like a young she-witch in heat, lingering and passionately cursing all that she touched. It had been an elongated dry season, with strong tide-winds off the Gulf continually blowing, contributing to the miserable, unbearable heat. Little rain was in sight, especially in the thorny, parched thickets of South Texas, the region where the majestic Rio Grande River divided two countries, carving its way from the northern Rocky Mountains and meandering in its long journey south. It was the river that had defied the times and the elements—magnificent as it was, ultimately dropping down below sea level, crashing its white breakers and disappearing forever into the immense Gulf of Mexico.

The ranchers in the adjoining areas speculated with great concern that perhaps a long drought was at hand. They had not seen a drop of moisture for several months and the countryside depended on water. The lower Rio Grande Valley was a fertile land that God had given and now had seemingly forgotten, always holding humanity at bay amidst untamed animals, insects, scorpions, rattlers, mesquite, and cactus.

The new century was welcomed with its new technologies, but at the same time overwhelming to the population with the coming of electricity and automobiles, making people nervous. It ended the horse-and-buggy era, and it was feared blacksmiths would be put out of work. The Industrial Revolution had begun and it brought the concept of western thought, controlled by a money-oriented universal view. Orville and Wilbur Wright had made their first successful airplane flight, and the construction of the Panama Canal had just begun. William H. Taft had just been elected President. Haley's Comet had appeared brightly on the horizon as an appalling warning sign. The Mexican people, with superstitious awe, saw it as an evil message— "a bad omen," they would say, gazing toward the heavens. They gossiped in anticipation, making the sign of the cross and remarking: *"Dios mío!* What is this world coming to?"

The year had been interspersed with sparks and whispers from stargazers, witches, great prophets, and psychics predicting an upcoming event—a war so devastating that the whole world and all of mankind would be affected. The mood was now becoming threatening, and folks gazed toward the heavens for signs. What was this great prophecy?

⌘ ⌘ ⌘

On a hot, blistering day in the latter part of August of the same year, *Don* Federico Juelson was heading back to his ranch called Spanish Acres, the famous cattle ranch known throughout the land as one of the most prosperous in the region, several miles north of the village of La Villa.

The intensity of the white rays was beating down on him, as if dozen of cactus needles pierced throughout his entire body. It had become a day of wilting heat, worse than any other so far. The sky had become an almond silver haze, with almost no color. It was an unusual day for this part of the country, for there was no wind. Rivulets of perspiration poured down his back and forehead, and his bronzed face glistened as his soaked jacket clung to his flesh. The strong daily breeze that had been there as long as he could remember did not exist today. He kept thinking that perhaps it was a great cosmic, solar turbulence in the dense air, and he became conscious more of a puzzle that stirred his imagination as though by some weird tide—it was eerie. There was no doubt, the day was strange. There was no breeze, only the awed silence. But, nature did funny things; nature was unstable, lacking consistency in this part of the country, and often gave no reasonable logic. Stillness always came before the storm.

"*Vámonos, muchachos!*" he commanded. "The sun is already at high noon, and it's too hot for branding. Turn the mavericks loose. We'll finish up tomorrow." *Don* Federico mounted his horse, turned his head, and gave his foreman an order. "Have some of the boys ride up to the southeast side and check to see if the barbed wire is still holding on that fence that needs fixing. I do not want any trouble with *Don* Esquibel because of my livestock getting onto his land."

Roy Dale nodded, tipped his hat in acknowledgment, and then replied, "We'll shore do, *patrón*."

The air was becoming oppressive, and without the breeze, the heat was unbearable. *Don* Federico's beautiful black stallion, El Chulo, moved restlessly under him. "J.D., come on boy!" he called out for his five-year-old German shepherd wandering in the jungle of dense cacti. The odor of smothered mesquite embers lingered in the stillness amidst the silence of the vast desolate, prickly undergrowth, along with the stench of burned cowhides hanging heavy in the stagnate air. The branding irons and the water wagon were left standing for the following day.

Half an hour on the trail back home the *Don* stopped for a moment and grabbed his water canteen. He rested long enough to wipe the sweat off his forehead, took several sips, and got off his horse. He then took off his Stetson, filled it with water, and gave some to El Chulo. The magnificent animal had been given to him as a gift several years ago by his wife's parents living in Monterrey, Mexico. He then patted his horse's neck as a sign of reassurance and rubbed his forehead. "It won't be long, boy. We'll be home, soon," he whispered. El Chulo snorted, nodded his head and stomped the ground with one hoof, as if he understood what was being said.

While *Don* Federico mounted his horse, J.D. appeared out of nowhere, stood at attention for a moment, and then barked. The black and tan dog wagged his tail and stood still, as if waiting for a command from his master. His bright eyes and pointed ears always displayed a cheerful disposition. His quick, boundless energy and his curious wit were always getting him into mischief. He barked again.

"Okay, I hear you," answered *Don* Federico. "Where you been? Chasing rabbits, I suppose. Well, that's okay. Head for home, boy! Let's go home, boys!" he said loud and clear. J.D. gave a sharp yelp and jumped yards in front of him, taking the narrow path that lead to the hacienda. *Don* Federico adjusted his gauntlets, took hold of the reins, and tapped his horse with his stirrups. "C'mon let's go!" he shouted. "Let's head for home!"

It had been like this all of his life—the hardest weather in the world, with only two seasons. The hot summers were like opening the ovens of Hell, devouring everything that lived with their scorching heat. The other season was the short winter months, which were much different from winters up north. In this region, it poured rain. But amidst it all, there was a special, magnetic, scenic beauty that only the eye of the beholder could capture. The lowing of the cattle, the flash of a fleeing whitetail deer, the howling of a lonely coyote, the dangerous confrontation with the *javalinas* or wild boars, and the twittering of the mockingbirds never tired him. And in the early spring, when the *arroyos* ran swift and full with runoff, the blooming of the cactus flowers was a magical, botanical splendor.

Thousands of longhorn and whiteface cattle roamed, carrying the brand "J." It was, perhaps, the only good thing that could be produced in this torrid area. Many called it, "The hind-end of all creation." Although *Don* Federico's heart was saddened by the memory that both his parents were now dead, this piece of land was now his legacy and birthright, his own private world.

The dispute over the southwestern boundary had caused the war between Mexico and the United States, which was terminated with the signing of the Treaty of Guadalupe Hidalgo in 1848. An ordinance of secession was passed on February 1, 1861, but Texas was restored to the Union on March 30, 1870. When all of the squabbling ended and the dust had settled, the boundary line became the Rio Grande River, which divided the two countries, the beginning of '*roots of indifference.*'

Don Federico's father, George Albert Juelson, was half Scotch Irish. The other part was shrouded in mystery that was never disclosed. Eloquent, arrogant, and proud, George Juelson would never talk about his licentious past and would get violently angry, and downright quarrelsome when questioned. Nobody dared to ask him; nobody would talk about his background. All that was known about his father was that he had been a general in the northern states, had grown tired of the military actions and abhorred the government rules, orders and regulations.

George Juelson had left the Cumberland Gap area of the U.S. before the Civil War had broken out. He wandered into Texas with a Saratoga trunk full of money in search of adventure after hearing wild tales of the south border region. Stories about the Alamo, and his heroes, Daniel Boone, Sam Houston, and Stephen Austin had always intrigued him and became his siren call. He was a visionary, skillful, and with his intelligence would no doubt have a great destiny. Ah! It was those brilliant early mornings and those luminous evenings, the freedom of vast virgin spaces, land unconquered—this meant everything to him.

Southern Texas was truly a man's country. "A place where you could be your own man, and do what you pleased," George Juelson would say. "Hell! You could even belch, fart out loud, and take a shit out in the middle of the open spaces, and nobody would give a damn," he exclaimed. Heaven's country with good Mexican-American people—and wasn't this part of Texas attached to the United States? That in itself was playing your cards right.

It was not long after George Juelson settled in this strange untamed world that he began courting the pious, aristocratic Maria Elena Ballon. Within two years they were married. She was twenty years his junior and came with a drop or two of sophisticated Spanish blueblood. From her dowry, given to her by her grandparents, *La Señora* Ballon drew several land grants just north of the Llano Grande. The majority of the land covered many acres north of La Villa in Hidalgo County and into adjoining Cameron and Willacy County.

Coming into a wealthy landowner's family, Maria Elena Ballon was born on a large ranch north of Brownsville and had studied at the Convent of the Incarnate Word Academy. Her great-grandfather, Antonio Ballon, was a nobleman, a military man under the Spanish conquistadors. And by serving the King of Spain, he was awarded allotments of large tracts of land called *porciones*. Antonio Ballon's family helped colonize the area in 1800, and they owned thousands of acres in the early days.

George Juelson had acquired other parcels of land by wild gambling, which he enjoyed doing as a hobby, and by buying cheap land. Many had called him an entrepreneur because of his aggressive nature, and his shrewd instincts in building a cattle empire and a name for himself and for his future children. He was a man not weighed down by tradition or confined by religion, and it was one of the many reasons he had left the northern states to begin a new, excitingly different life and to be free.

The trail in front of *Don* Federico had become hazy. He found himself on top of an undulating hill and riding down from the sloping hill, he began dodging limbs, riding side to side, back and forth, trusting his horse to traverse the right track, evading the deep *arroyos*. The heart of mesquite country, the area was called the great *brasada* by the Mexican *vaqueros*. It was an uncivilized jungle full of an armada of dense *cejas*, thorn thickets; the *retama chino*, the wild currant; the *argarita;* and *ocotillos*. The prickly pear grew as tall as a man on a horse, alongside *el chaparral prieto*, rattail Spanish dagger, *Junco*, and so many more that required minimal moisture.

A man unfamiliar with the terrain and not knowing his direction could easily become distracted and lost. Many a *vaquero* had lost his life in the thorny area, and for days, sometimes months and years, their bodies were never found. In late 1882, the remains of a Catholic

ROOTS OF INDIFFERENCE

Oblate priest, Father Kerelum, were found by some of the *vaqueros* rounding up stray cattle. It was apparent that the old priest had gotten disoriented, had poor eyesight and lost his way in the untamed and harsh *brasada*.

The prideful *Don* Federico began dodging cow dung, being careful that his horse avoided the piles of the dung many of the Mexicans used for fuel. Occasionally *el patrón* would come upon a clearing where wild Johnson grass grew in abundance and had turned marigold brown and brittle from the lack of rain.

Don Federico shouted to J.D., who would occasionally run in front of the horse's legs. The dog would become excited, abruptly run wildly, chasing a rabbit under a small brier of *nopales*. "J.D.! C'mon boy, go find the dirt road!"

It was not long after that the *Don* was able to get on the curved dirt road, headed for home. His arms felt strained from the constant controlling of the horse's reins. Hypnotized by the dry conditions and the hot weather haze, his solitary thoughts were then broken by the plaintive cry of a gray hawk circling over his prey, as sounds of the horse's hooves hitting the solid dirt road echoed. He noticed from the direction of the Gulf a purple canopy of clouds, wrapped in silence.

Roy Dale, his head foreman, had appeared from the undergrowth. Catching up with *Don* Federico, he began riding side-by-side, humming the song *Red Wing*. Roy Dale smelled of leather, cows, tobacco, and sweat. His face was caked, almost unrecognized by the white clay dust that covered his clothing, hat, and boots. *Don* Federico chuckled at the man's appearance.

"Like them mavericks?" Snickered the *Don*.

"Hell yeah! I can't live without 'em, gotta love 'em leetle doggies."

As the two trotted up the dirt path, they could see the tall metal windmills, but the hacienda was still obscured, hidden out in the middle of the vast *brasada*.

"Why, it's hotter 'en Hell," mused Roy, chewing his black tobacco, looking sideways from his horse toward *Don* Federico, and then spitting. "Seems dat in de las' days, it'd be like 'tis. Wunder if we're not gunna git no mo' rain? I 'member when I was growin' up in the Cimarron Strip in Okie, we had sim'ler weather to whut we're havin' now." He then mopped his face with an old faded bandana, which he always wore around his neck. He turned his head, again emptying his mouth by spitting into the dry, gray thickets.

Don Federico Juelson was now in his fifties, his face darkened, tanned by the brutal sun. His hair had streaks of white on both sides of his temples. He was not a tall man, but his presence created the impression of a man with prestige and power, and pedigree was in his blood, a true gent of the old school. He was distinguished looking, proud of his education and his wealth, and proud of his mixed-blood heritage. He rode his horse with pride, radiating always a spirit of resilience.

"Ah! I suspect that a storm must be brewing out in the Gulf of Mexico," he finally remarked. "Remember last year when we had so much rain, some of the cattle died? It's been so dry now and we need the water. Remember ten years ago? It was the same year you came to live with us. That was a tough, hellish year. Many of the cattle died from screwworms and we couldn't get to them fast enough to save 'em. Father's main reason for hiring you was to help us with the calves, bulls and the horses. That same year, we had the *chubasco*, the hurricane that killed many of our cattle and also killed many poor innocent people as far away as Galveston. Be a good idea to get Miguel and the boys to round up as many cattle for the buyers in San Antonio, and get them shipped out as soon as possible. We must have at least a thousand head to be shipped. Better to be safe than sorry, for I fear that we're getting another storm in the next few days. Something sure is brewing up in the Gulf. Damn! We sure need the rain."

"Good idée" agreed Roy. "We'll git them fetched up for ya'. Why ol' Manuel, talked jus' dis mornin' of a full blown *chubasco*. Said dat his bones was a hurtin' 'em. I reckon 'em never wrong."

Roy Dale was one of his father's favorite cowhands. George found him in San Antonio and took the liberty of hiring Roy for his hacienda. He had been a young cowpuncher and a trail hand, driving cattle back and forth into Abilene, Kansas. A rare character, different from the ordinary cowhand, he was a half breed, half Irish and Cherokee Indian, with sandy-red hair and beautiful blue eyes, making him handsome in a special way, even though slight of build. His brown skin had the healthy glow of a man who had spent many years making his living outdoors. His walk had a skipping step, and he had a peculiar, courtly manner, always tipping his hat with respect, especially to the ladies. He was a natural storyteller, talking with a slow drawl. He could not read or write, but held a doctor's degree in animal veterinary understanding, according to *Don* Federico's thinking. He had never married, using the excuse that his work had prevented him from ever wanting the kind of responsibility that came with marriage. Roy had never found true love—at least, not yet.

Don Federico had learned much from Roy and held him in high esteem, especially within the last year, ever since his father had passed away and he had acquired his father's debts and responsibilities. With Roy's help, he understood more about the hardships and the daily routine and the arduous work that it took to run a *rancho*.

As J.D. was running several yards in front of the horse, his ears perked up. He began barking.

They halted their horses at the sound of hooves pounding the soft dusty road ahead. "Sum one's cumin'," Roy said.

J.D. kept barking.

"That's enough barking, J.D.!" shouted *Don* Federico. The dog yelped and recoiled, but seconds later began running faster up the dirt path to meet the person who was coming.

Don Federico paused, trying to scrutinize the figure coming toward them up ahead. "Looks like Victoria!" He became apprehensive, since his daughter was supposed to be taking music lessons from Miss Bell. "It's too hot for anyone to be out riding a horse that fast. Something's wrong, I can feel it!"

"Dat Miss Bell sure's a fine music teacher, but she shore is a skinny ol' maid," Roy said, laughing. "I git da feelin' she'd like to git into mah flanks."

"She would make someone a fine wife! A well-educated person and knows her music too. She came highly recommended. But I do think she's got her eye on you. Every time she sees you, she becomes nervous, frustrated, and forgets what she's doing." said *Don* Federico. Both men laughed.

Victoria Juelson was *Don* Federico's oldest child and only daughter. Almost sixteen, her beautiful brownish hair was flowing in the wind as she rode her horse toward the two men, leaving behind a thick cloud of dust.

"Papá, Papá!" she hollered, trying to catch her breath. "Mother needs you quickly back at the hacienda. There's trouble! *Don* Esquibel is there with some of his *vaqueros*. *Don* Esquibel's cowhands found a Mexican girl in the bushes close to the *Resaca*, and they brought her over to our place. She's bloody all over her body and looks terrible! We don't know if she is going to live or die!"

"Where is the girl now?" asked *Don* Federico, dismay evident in his voice.

"We put her in Roy's bunk for the time being, since it was the closer bedroom downstairs," she said, giggling. "All of the other ladies agreed. They said you wouldn't mind sharing your bedroom with a lady. Aside from the bloody face, the girl is a real pretty one, too."

"Well doggies! I swanee bee!" replied Roy in complete frustration. "In mah bunk, in mah room," he said over and over again.

"*Bueno, Hija!* We're on our way. Tell *Don* Esquibel I'll be there soon," answered *Don* Federico. Frowning, he looked at Roy and the two exchanged glances in total bewilderment.

Victoria turned her mare around. "Mamá sent Manuel with the wagon to get *La Señora* Adela. They should be coming soon," she said, before she hurried up the road.

"Oh, hells bells!" Roy said. "Gonna git lots o' hocus pocus," he said. He began laughing. "With dat ol' hag, dat *bruja* Adela, yus gonna git more suspense comin' yo way, *patrón*. Waal, now! Yus gonna git some more bullshit from ol' man Esquibel," he snickered.

"You'd think he had enough brains to take care of her in his own home," *Don* Federico snorted. "He wanted an excuse to snoop around. Nosey old buzzard! Damn! It will be another problem to worry about, another person in the house, not that it matters anyhow. We got plenty of room, but a sick girl—"

Riding his horse at a lope, *Don* Federico wondered if his boys had gotten into another hassle with *Señor* Esquibel's cowhands. He hated confrontations with the cantankerous old man, who was always finding something wrong with his property, or with *Don* Federico's cattle getting onto his land. A lonely old alcoholic, he had lost his wife three years ago after years of beatings and abuse, leaving him with several sons and many grandchildren.

Over a year ago, there had been a dispute, a fist-fighting, bloody incident, and a lot of gossiping in both families. One of *Don* Federico's cowhands, a blacksmith, got in trouble at *Don* Esquibel's home with a young kitchen helper, creating problems for everyone.

The cowhand was caught red-handed, with his pants down, by the woman's husband, who almost killed his wife in a harsh beating. The matter caused a lot of resentment between the two families from both ranches, and *Don* Federico finally had to let the man go. He hated the thought of adulterous relationships, and had informed the blacksmith when he was hired that it would not be tolerated. A woman's place was to run the household and be a wife, a companion, and a mother; women were to be treated with respect. Both ranchers had settled their differences very gracefully, months after his father's funeral. Traditionally, each took care of his own problems on his own property. But the incident had left harsh feelings between the families and the *vaqueros* on both establishments.

There was also a strong possibility of not being able to trust *Señor* Esquibel. Rumors from his own workers had floated around in past years. It was said *Don* Esquibel had stolen some of *Don* Federico's bulls and bred them to his own cows. Rumors like this were hard to prove, but in this part of the country, a man caught stealing could be hanged, with no questions asked. The border ranchers settled their own feuds. It was a strict code of honor. Rustlers stealing cattle and getting caught would face grave consequences. But *Don* Federico was a peaceful man, never letting the loss of one or two cows come between him and his neighbors.

Don Esquibel, in his own right, was actually a rich man, even though it did not show in his appearance or way of living. He owned several acres on the east side, past the railroad tracks adjoining his spread in Willacy County, where he raised longhorn cattle and hundreds of white goats. Blanca, the white nanny goat, an adored pet with a bell around her neck, had been given by *Don* Esquibel to *Don* Federico's oldest son, Fred, on his fifth birthday. *Don* Esquibel would sell the meat and cheese from his goats in return for other commodities. He lived very modestly, in an old hut, with several rooms attached to the shanty, plus a big bunkhouse for his workers and a barn fenced by walls of upright, cut mesquite trees.

"The devil is loose," *Don* Federico said.

"Yep," replied the foreman. "Wunder what the hell's goin' on?" he mused. "I shore hope dat none of the leetle doggies have gotten onto his land."

Don Federico spurred El Chulo faster and became silent, his face showing concern. Then he replied, "Probably some stupid, irksome problem, something to do with his cattle. You know how the old fart is!"

Roy started to laugh, "landsakes! No need gitt'n too riled-up, now," and turned his head to spit.

As the dirt road curved, they came upon the iron-gate entrance to the enormous two-story, Spanish Acres mansion. The letter "J" stood high above the entrance, suspended in mid-air with barbed wire displaying the emblem. Tall prickly pear cactus stood on each side of its stone walls. From the entrance, *Don* Federico viewed movement. Several of his workers and *Don* Esquibel's cowhands were leaning on the stone walls; others were talking, sheltering themselves from the wilting heat inside under the high arches and the verandas next to the big mansion.

Roy hurried his horse, saying, "reckon I'd bet'er git, now git," and broke into a faster gait and left *Don* Federico's side. J.D. followed.

Don Federico dismounted, giving his horse to one of the stable boys. "Pepito, where is *Doña* Francisca?" he questioned. The small boy stood shyly, grabbed the reins of the horse, and pointed to the back of the house toward the kitchen area.

Approaching the group of men, the great *Don* sensed some kind of turbulence. Some of the men spoke, some greeting him with respect, tipping their hats, while others looked soberly confused. He shouldered his way through the crowd where he spotted *Don* Esquibel coming toward him, gripping his sombrero.

"*Buenos días, Don* Federico," he said in a sharp tone. "I am sorry to bother you at this time of the day, with the heat being so terrible, and you so busy with your cattle, but—"

"Yes, yes, go on," replied *Don* Federico, breaking the conversation with annoyance and mopping his forehead with his handkerchief. He extended his hand, with apprehension, but in a gracious gesture. "It's been over a year since my father's funeral when you paid your last respects, and we had that serious talk about our workers' dispute." He took his hat off and wiped his forehead again.

"Yes, you are right," *Don* Esquibel said seriously. "I'm concerned about the young Mexican girl, *Señor!*"

Don Federico, puzzled and sweaty, wiped his face and replied, "Is she from Spanish Acres?"

"No! At first my boys and I thought she was from your place, since she was found on your property. It took us about an hour bringing her here, and we listened to her crazy talk, trying to decide where she was from. We finally understood that she was from across the river, the village of Rio Rico. My *vaqueros* found her between the fences, but inside your property," he insisted.

Don Federico was annoyed that the old fart kept saying *inside your fence, on your property.*

"What happened to her?" questioned *Don* Federico, raising his eyebrows, "and why bring her here?" He wanted some kind of accountability from the rebellious old fool.

"We are all frightened of the situation," answered *Don* Esquibel as he moved closer to *Don* Federico, and whispered, "*Señor*, may I please talk to you in private?"

"Yes, of course. Let's go into my library where it's cooler inside and we can talk more privately." He began taking off his gloves and jacket. He ordered the servants out in the hall to bring them something cool to drink and some water and clean towels to wash up.

Don Federico headed in the direction of his library. *Señor* Esquibel followed down the long, marble, corridor, past the elegant, formal living room. On one huge, white wall was a colorful oil painting of George Albert Juelson, dressed in his general's uniform.

Inside of the library, hundreds of leather-bound collections of Texas law books caught the eye. The attractive appearance of the room was enhanced with elegant, dark mahogany and oak furniture. Carved wood was on the fancy desk, with a marble top and designs on the chairs made of solid leather. On one side of the wall was the mounted head of a wild boar. A large glass hutch was filled with silver and gold embossed rifles from Mexico, and several knives and antique guns were displayed inside another glass case.

Don Federico closed the French doors. "This should keep out the noise of barking dogs and people talking," commented the *Don*, as he politely offered *Don* Esquibel a seat and some of his imported wine and Cuban cigars.

"No, thank you," answered *Don* Esquibel, "but I will take something cool to drink."

Two heavyset, gray-haired women, Ophelia and Olivia, knocked and politely walked in. One held a pitcher of lemonade and two glasses, the other a basin of water and towels. They greeted *Señor* Esquibel with warm words, asked about his family, then excusing themselves, left the room quietly.

"Well! What is all this about? The story sounds very mysterious to me," *Don* Federico inquired with a suspicious frown, serving his guest a glass of lemonade. He then washed his face and dried it as he took his seat on the other side of his desk.

"It's been so hot, and we sure need water," said the *Don*, making himself comfortable.

"*Señor*," the old man began, now clearing his throat. "Apparently, from what we have gathered, the girl told the *vaqueros* her name is Soledad. She was screaming and delirious in her speech. Supposedly, armed *bandidos* abducted her from a small village across the border. She had repeatedly been raped by all of them. Not only did they force themselves upon her, but they beat her around the face pretty bad. She is almost unrecognizable. She also mentioned that sometime during the night, she managed to escape into the wilderness, not knowing where she was or where she was going, while the *bandidos* were busy with the redheaded *gringa* woman."

"Redheaded *gringa*, did you say?" *Don* Federico leaned forward and interrupted, raising his voice in question. "What happened to *la gringa*? What does she have to do with what you're talking about?"

"*Señor*, she is dead!" answered *Don* Esquibel, with terror evidenced by his high-pitched voice. His hands kept fumbling with the brim of his sombrero, nervously turning it around and around as it rested on his crossed legs. "Soledad spoke little, trying to make us understand, since her jaws are so swollen." He cleared his throat. "Armed *bandidos* came and raided their peaceful village in the late afternoon. They were demanding money for guns and rifles and other ammunition that they were bringing to three strangers who had mysteriously showed up in the village. All of the villagers were shot and killed, including the children. Those that fled to the bushes close to the river were also killed. Soledad never had a chance to escape. The *bandidos* caught her while running away and loaded her onto their horses and crossed the river into Texas where the men abused her."

"How did the *gringa* woman get involved?" *Don* Federico was trying to decipher the story, as his interrogation was getting nowhere. *Don* Esquibel had been drinking and was inebriated, excited, and had gotten the information secondhand from a delirious girl. Now *Don* Federico was presented with a story that was developing into a sensational incident that could cause both races much concern.

"The *gringa* woman was in the wooded area, picking some mesquite wood, close to *El Ranchito De La Feria*," said *Don* Esquibel. One of the *bandidos* moved in on her, and she was taken by force. They already had Soledad with them, according to what Soledad said. I think she said that she counted at least four *bandidos*, who raped both of the women. After raping them, two left." He went on, "What seems so strange, was what Soledad said." He rubbed his chin as though deep in thought.

"What was that?" *Don* Federico asked, focusing intently on Esquibel.

"The main man that raped her was a big, husky white man, from this side of the border, pretending to be a bandit. He spoke bad English words and with bad broken Spanish.

After he was finished with her he handed her to the others. They were all pretending to be Mexicans, dressed in colorful serapes and Mexican sombreros. She heard him talking about *Los Rinches*. They said they were going to have a "picnic" with the Mexicans. They had all laughed mockingly," the *Don* said. "This in itself will stir evil within the region and the two countries." He was obviously frightened.

"*Los Rinches!*" replied *Don* Federico. It was the hateful slang word used by the Mexican people to describe the Texas Rangers, who were deeply despised. "*Los Rinches* are inhuman, especially when they deal with any problems with the Mexican people." *A white man*, he thought, rubbing his forehead in thought, as his elbows rested on the desk. "Something strange is going on at the border and more horrible than we suspect." He bent over his desk, got closer to *Don* Esquibel's face, and looked straight into his eyes. "Too many horror stories are being told on both sides of the river, where the white man can kill Mexicans with no repercussions. The rape of a Mexican woman happens, probably every day, and it's taken with a grain of salt, a diversion of animal lust. No one does anything about it, since women have no say and no authority. But, what happens when a Mexican man rapes a white woman, or worse, kills her?"

"Lynching, of course," replied *Don* Esquibel.

"That's exactly what I mean! You can bet that *los Rinches* will have their work cut out for them, blaming the Mexicans for this incident. It seems like several white men from this side of the river are doing something illegal, and have a cover-up for this murderous event. The Rangers will be on someone's trail, pointing their fingers at somebody's ass, and the Mexicans will be the targets. The Mexican people are going to suffer for the murder of the *gringa*, especially the honest people who are just trying to survive. This is going to create more deaths, more shootings and lynchings, especially when *los Rinches*, the sons-of-bitches, justify it because they're enforcing the law. Those arrogant Rangers who think they have been appointed by God himself to bring justice into this land are going to play havoc with the Mexican men in this area. How can anyone prove that the *gringa* woman was killed by a white man?"

"At this time, Soledad does not know that the *gringa* woman is dead." *Don* Esquibel's eyes studied Federico with interest while he continued. "She kept crying, saying to us to go find her, to go find the *gringa* woman who needed our help, and it is best she doesn't know at this time. The *vaqueros* found the redheaded *gringa* a half mile down on your property by the *resaca*. The horrible, bizarre way in which they killed her made several of the cowhands sick. They had never seen anything like it."

"How did the *gringa* woman die?" *Don* Federico demanded. His apprehension turned to worry, since it was on his property that the body was found. He had been distinctly reminded of this fact several times.

"They stabbed her, all right, but in a way you would never think! The *bandidos* spread her thighs and stuck a wooden spike into her genital organs, sitting her on it. She probably bled to death! Blood and flies all over," he said, making a terrible face.

There was a long silent moment. *Don* Federico sat back in his leather chair, feeling as if his entire soul had left his body. His thoughts were now spiraling as rage and hatred overtook him. He raised both of his hands in disgust and got up again from his chair and walked to the window. He stood for a while glaring out the large window toward his great cattle empire. Then he rubbed his chin again and chewed the inside of his mouth, a nasty habit when confronting a major problem.

He walked back to his desk. "Goddamn!" he cursed, facing *Don* Esquibel and leaning on the desk. "This problem is worse than I thought. This will stir a total state of confusion among the whites and the innocent Mexican-American families." He straightened himself up and began pacing the floor. "Killing a Mexican individual is like killing a rattlesnake in this part of the country, and nothing is ever done for justice. But killing a white woman is bad news. The situation on both sides of the river and the hatred among the whites and the Mexican-American people who have lived here for years will develop into a civil war, where no one will be safe." Cold shivers ran up and down his spine. "Where is the body of the *gringa*? What did your boys do with her body?"

"Why, my boys would not touch the white woman. They left her there as she was found."

"Left her there?" roared *Don* Federico, glaring at the old *Don*.

"Why, yes. They were afraid. Terrified. Finding a dead *gringa's* body, in that condition, the whites would have accused them of the killing. The whites shoot first and talk later. So no one was going to pick her up and take any chances. They are frightened. Do you understand, *Señor*?"

"Yes! Yes! I understand your logic," replied the *Don*, very agitated and disgusted at the American system of injustice. "She must have a family somewhere! They must be concerned. I'll have Roy and some of my boys who know the area ride out and get the body. We'll wait until it gets cooler, later on this afternoon. I will try and make some arrangement and return her to her family. That's about all I can do for now. I'll be going over to Harlingen to get some supplies and have some unfinished business with the head of the Texas Rangers, my father's supposed best friend. Remember him—Bernard Hanson?"

"How can I forget? He is a brutal son-of-a-bitch," replied *Señor* Esquibel. "That bastard killed one of my wife's cousins three years ago. *Los desgraciados*, the Texas Rangers, suggested that he was shot in the back escaping. The white people who are now in control of the region have put the patrolling *Rinches* in charge, giving them the authority to do what they please. Think of what happened to Jacinto Trevino over by Los Indios last May. His cousin was being horsewhipped by a white man and later died. Jacinto shot the perpetrator and fled into Mexico. If the *Rinches* had caught him, they would have tortured and lynched him."

"I know," answered *Don* Federico. "And it looks like it's going to get worse," he added, becoming more inflamed. "While I'm in Harlingen, I'll try to find out if they have gotten wind of this incident. I'll need to get some supplies. We are completely out of coal oil and grain, giving me an excuse to ask questions while I'm there. We'll try to get the *gringa's* body to her family as soon as possible. I'm sure her family is looking for her by now."

"I understand!" *Señor* Esquibel replied in agreement.

"When Soledad heals and feels better, I'll ask her about what took place. I'll be able to get a clearer picture of what actually happened. Something is not right!"

Don Esquibel began talking about the unrest in Mexico. "My son is already heading back to Texas after finishing his engineering studies in the State of Tamaulipas."

"Has it been that long? It seems like it was just yesterday that José left to attend school."

"From his letters, things are getting very bad in Mexico, especially in politics. There's a lot of talk of a revolution. I fear for all of us on both sides of the Rio Grande."

Don Federico, being a man of innate justice, began worrying about the body of a dead woman lying out in the wilderness. He needed to get Roy and some of the *vaqueros* to go out and get her. He walked around to *Don* Esquibel and extended his hand in gratitude. "I'll have my boys get in touch with you on my next decision. It's been nice seeing you again, and has been my pleasure. It's too bad it was under these unfavorable circumstances. Feel free to visit Soledad any time you want. And, yes! I'm afraid that this is not the last we are going to hear about the unrest in Mexico. If there is a revolution, we are all going to suffer, being so close to the border." He paused for the moment. "And also, *Don* Esquibel, let's keeps this incident between ourselves. Please inform your cowhands not to repeat anything until I have more information and can get the truth straight. I'm afraid there's more to this story, and we are all dealing with a dangerous situation. The less said the better."

"Of course," replied *Don* Esquibel. Again, they respectfully shook hands, and the old man departed, disappearing with his *vaqueros* waiting for him under the hacienda's cool arches.

A loud commotion, marked by the sound of barking dogs and loud voices, could be heard from the outside entrance to the house. It was Manuel with *la Señora Doña* Adela, the herb woman, called *"La bruja de la brasada."* The healing doctor of the region, she carried a large, colorful bag made of maguey threads, which was full of magic herbs and oils.

There was always an eerie feeling of awe about *Doña* Adela. Her crude mannerism and barbaric disposition gave the impression that she was a woman not to be trifled with. There was always the stench of herbs and oils and the necklace of rattlesnake tails hanging around her neck. With the heat of the day at its peak, she was wearing a long, black cape the same length as her dark shirt. Her hair, which at one time had been jet black, was now snow-white, and pulled back by some kind of homemade rope. In her left hand was the crooked black cane that she relied on to keep her feet steady. Made out of a lightning-struck ebony tree, it made her feel lucky.

La bruja's wrinkled face resembled someone who had died and been dug up. Resurrected from the grave, and her crooked and feeble hands were arthritic and dotted with age spots. The old woman never changed—she always looked the same. Perhaps it was because she was a full-blooded *Tejas* Indian with high cheekbones and very dark skin. She had numerous remedies for the sick, including the "evil eye" methods—stomach sickness liniments, called *empacho* among the Mexican people, with solutions and potions of magic. From the wicked to the do-gooders, all would consult her for fortune telling and the rituals that she performed. Going into a deep trance, she could foretell the future with amazing, unerring accuracy.

La Señora Francisca loved her because the old woman was reliable. She was the only one within a thirty-five-mile radius who would help her with the needy, sick people in this region. There were few doctors, and none if you were a Mexican. The majority of doctors were white, and the white doctors did not attend to the needs of any Mexican person, nor anyone with a Mexican last name.

Doña Adela was a walking wealth of spiritual knowledge. She was a shaman with impressive ability and would scare the pants off any individual who did not know she possessed mystical powers. Most mysterious were her large, light-colored eyes, so light that they had no color—crystal clear, like the eyes of a cat.

The stories that were told about *la bruja* were grandiose and imaginative and became more monumental among the natives in the region as time passed. Many years prior, when *Don* Federico was in his early twenties, completing his studies in Mexico City, he had returned to a scandalous rumor that had spread throughout the region, about a man who had died from fright after seeing *Doña* Adela.

Apparently a Mexican man in his early forties had wandered close to the *resaca* as it was getting dark, trying to find his prized goat. The man did not realize that he was trespassing, because in those early times the *ranchos* did not have fences. The man got lost in the thickets of the *brasada* as he pushed forward into the dense jungle hell, determined to find his lost animal.

He finally came to a clearing where he heard someone talking. As he got closer in the shadows of the night, he noticed the silhouette of a woman without any clothes on. He hid behind a mesquite tree and watched, with his eyes wide open and his heart almost leaping out of his chest. He noticed that the woman was in the middle of a ritual, performing witchcraft and talking in an unknown tongue. With a full moon on the horizon, he witnessed the spectacle as she lifted her arms toward the sky, offering a plate of food to the Moon Goddess.

Time slipped away, and the Mexican man could not recall how long he stood and watched the devilish performance, but in an instant, *Doña* Adela had transformed into a black wolf and began howling at the moon. Her eyes were like two bright lights, and she knew that he was standing behind the tree, because she turned her head in his direction and then lunged toward him like a wild demonic spirit.

His family found him the next morning in a state of *espanto*—fear—wandering among the mesquite in a state of shock. He had peed and shit his pants without even knowing that his lower extremities had become weak—not knowing and not caring. The Mexican man was in a delirious state for a week, with scratches all over his body. His heart gave up and he died shortly after. His tale created much fascination among the Mexican cowhands and ranchers and was enlarged upon in years to come.

The cowhands would converse and laugh about it, but not take any chances. They respected *la bruja* with her super powers. West of the *resaca* was considered sacred grounds. And no *vaquero* in his right mind would dare get close to that acreage. However, there were those who desperately needed immediate help with personal problems, matters of love, money, or revenge. Or, in worse cases, they wanted someone dead.

ROOTS OF INDIFFERENCE

"*Buenos días, Señora* Adela," said *Don* Federico, walking up to greet her with a glass of lemonade in his hand. "Seems like another hot day with no wind!" he said.

"Ah! *Gracias,* no day is hot enough for me. As old as I am, I need the warmth," she replied, taking the glass out of *Don* Federico's hand. "What's all this about? A girl being beaten and raped," she said. It brought out many years of old wounds and memories filled with pain, which she herself had experienced so many moons ago, when she was very young and innocent. "Manuel told me a little of what happened, but Manuel is getting old and gets excited very easily, just like me."

Don Federico began. "I just came in from branding. *Don* Esquibel's workers brought her here. I don't know the full story yet, but we are gong to find out. Most of the women are with her, out in the kitchen area. By the way, *Doña* Adela, did you see or hear any strange noise last night? Anything that might have caused any kind of suspicion, or something that just did not seem right, out in your area?"

"The dogs barked part of the night," she replied. "I think that perhaps a wild cat of some kind was nearby. I had some of my *manzanilla* tea and went to bed and fell asleep. My eyes are not as sharp as they used to be. Why?"

"The injured girl who was raped was found in the direction of the *resaca,* close to your home."

"No! I did not see anything. I was too tired last night. I took my usual brew, which makes me very sleepy, and rubbed liniment on my aching bones. I had a very peaceful sleep."

He studied her for a minute and decided not to question her any further since he believed she was totally unaware of the incident. He changed the subject. "Lunch is being served. Come! Let's head over to where all the women are attending the injured girl. I was told she is in Roy's room over by the kitchen. I'm hungry enough to eat the hind-end of a steer!" said *Don* Federico.

Doña Adela cackled loudly, with much enjoyment in her laughter, and spoke: "You all owe me some dry beef for this visitation. Or better, half a hog." She laughed again. "I will need Manuel to get some goods when he goes to *el mercado* in Reynosa."

Don Federico smiled. He reached for her maguey bag. "Let me help you with this load." He took the bag and began holding onto her left arm. "Come," he said, "Let's go see about the girl."

The coming of *Doña* Adela was an exciting, uplifting event for the people of Spanish Acres, fostering good hope and wellness, for she was an herbalist and a healer. Many lived in the isolated areas of the smaller *ranchitos,* and the majority was completely isolated from the civilized world and still living a primitive Mexican lifestyle. Many lived and died in the shadows of their own environment and never sought outside help, so visitors were always welcomed.

Don Federico and *Doña* Adela stepped out from the marble tile into the passageways of the cobblestone patio, past the main water fountain and iron cages filled with dozens of tropical birds. Hundreds of blooming vines in multi-colored splendor clung to the stuccoed side of the mansion.

J.D. was playing with their new dog, King, a black year-old Doberman pinscher pup given to *Don* Federico and his family as a gift from Ricardo Del Calderóne's family, Victoria's future in-laws. Blanca, the she-goat, stood dumfounded in the middle of the patio gazing at the spectacle that was *Doña* Adela.

The sounds of the ebony cane hitting the hard stone floor echoed as it steadied the old Indian woman. She let go of *Don* Federico's arm and stood still for a moment, as if in deep thought, staring sideways at the great *Don* because of the crooked condition of her aged body. Then she closed her eyes and lifted her head toward the heavens. Her facial expressions were twisted, resembling a dark, dried prune. Her left hand lifted skyward, and then it opened, as if reaching for something in the air.

And then, she began prophesying: "I feel something! Something dark! I'm picking up something—something evil!" Her eyes squinted, her wrinkled mouth moved. "This girl has a connection, something in regards to your father. There is something evil in this message— evil roots. I see guns, ammunition, and plots of injustice. I see the crossing of water, horses, and important men in high positions. There are lies and deceitfulness, murders, and tyrants who seem invincible. This girl was meant to be here for a reason. She comes with news, important information that you need to know."

"My father?" replied *Don* Federico in complete bewilderment. "He's been dead for over a year." He chuckled nervously, as if the old woman were going mad.

The ancient one fixed her gaze on *Don* Federico with her clear-colored eyes. "You need a *limpia*, with *yerba buena*, spearmint, and one of my readings now, and you need one bad," the old witch said, pointing her crooked finger at him. "Everything I say will come true. I have never been wrong, and I was never wrong in telling your father the truth, even though he disagreed with me so many times. But everything came to pass. Your father should have listened to me! I kept telling him about his enemies. Friends, he would say, and all the while, they were using him. He would never believe me when I told him who they were. He was surprised. It caused his death. You need a reading! You are also in danger!"

"Oh! No!" *Don* Federico laughed and waved his hand, dismissing the thought. "I don't believe in that mumbo-jumbo stuff." He was scholarly, educated, and was inclined to scoff at anything involving witchcraft. But he was outnumbered by the rest of the people in the region who were not scholarly or educated and believed in *la bruja's* prophecying. This was one subject he was prone to avoid and preferred not to pursue.

"You wait," the old woman said with confidence. "You will come and see me for a reading in the near future. What I have to tell you, I should have told you a long time ago, after your Papá died, but the time has never been right. You will want answers—answers that only I can tell you." Her eyes looked weird—almost demonic. "I will tell you when we're alone and no one can hear us. For what I have to tell you is going to surprise you. You will know the real truth."

"We're alone now! So tell me." *Don* Federico demanded, frowning and now curious.

ROOTS OF INDIFFERENCE

"No! Not now. I have a service to do in healing the injured Mexican girl. What I have to tell you—you'll be better sitting down. It's a very long story and I'll wait until it's more convenient. When I can sit and talk more comfortably."

"Okay!" answered *Don* Federico, reluctantly. "At this point, he was willing to say anything, just to calm the old woman down. He knew that the greeting committee from the kitchen would be showing up at any time. He did not want to hurt her feelings in not responding to a reading. After all, she was doing the family a great favor and a great service to his wife by attending, with great effort, the injured, dying girl.

Don Federico felt a great concern overtake him. The hairs on the back of his neck stood up as a cold chill overtook his body, and it seemed his thoughts were already infected with evil. A Pandora's box of gripping doubts was becoming his worst nightmare. He got the impression that the old woman was hiding something. She had knowledge of his father's previous adventures, for old man George had consulted her many times and spent many hours with her when he needed her advice. The land where *Doña* Adela lived had been given to her by George Juelson in gratitude for her generous, benevolent, loyal service to him. The question was, just what service was she giving his father? Fortune telling and warning him of problems was one thing. This in itself had been a mystery. The elder Juelson was a man who was not easily cross-examined. He had a violent temper and to interrogate him about his risky, speculative ideas or to question any of his whereabouts would have meant instant retribution. And now, *Doña* Adela's hints were leading into a precarious subject, which was more than *Don* Federico wanted to know.

When *Don* Federico was just a young boy in his early teens, he knew that his father had engaged in unethical dealings, years after his mother had passed away, and he became fully aware of his father's other secret romantic encounters. Now *Don* Federico's bright mind leaped to an uncomfortable conclusion that he was almost afraid of hearing. A chill of suspicion hit him. His appetite, which was normally insatiable after being out in the *brasada*, had diminished. He decided perhaps he should be paying a visit to the two-seater outhouse and checking his underclothes.

Señora Adela continued walking in her faltering, uneven steps, hanging onto her cane as she rambled on and on about the strange weather and what she had seen in her vision of things to come.

The loud squawking sounds of the colorful Mexican parrots, the toucan birds, and barking dogs attracted the attention of *Doña* Francisca along with the house servants, kitchen helpers, daughter Victoria, son Fred, and the youngest sibling, Carlos. They joined with other ladies as they heard *Don* Federico and *La Señora* Adela approaching from the courtyard into the open-air kitchen. A servant from the kitchen area walked up and took the empty glass from *la bruja's* hands, kissing it in the old Mexican tradition of respect, while others supported the old woman's arms.

La Señora Juelson, the attractive *Doña* Francisca, graciously approached *Doña* Adela. She was wearing a long, white skirt and high-collared blouse with a marcasites brooch and earrings to match. She warmly hugged the old *bruja* and greeted her. She was known for her benevolence, love, and maternal nature towards all the people who lived at the hacienda. Everyone knew her for her small talk, called *consejos*, not considered gossip. She was the voice of knowledge and talked quietly with infinite patience and a certain honesty, and always with an air of sincere humility and wisdom.

She was taller than the average Mexican woman, with a slender silhouette combined with dignity and grace. Her eyes were large and as black as her hair, which was pulled high on top of her head. She thanked the old woman for the act of kindness in coming to her aid. Letting go of *Doña* Adela, *Doña* Francisca stopped, distracted with an annoying cough. The coughing did not stop and she was gasping hard, coughing so hard she almost lost her balance. She finally managed to find a white handkerchief within her long sleeve and brought it toward her mouth.

"Mamá," cried Victoria, coming to her assistance and consoling her, patting her on her shoulders. "Are you all right? You need to sit down. Can I get you some water?"

When the wheezing stopped, *Doña* Francisca made a wry face and dismissed it with the wave of her hand, pretending that it was nothing to worry about. "I'm perfectly fine, *Hija!* Just a little cough! Dry throat! I'll be well in a couple of days." She then turned towards *Don* Federico and kissed him on the left side of his face, whispered softly in his ear, then said, "Federico, I'm glad you hurried. The body of a dead women lying out in the jungle wilderness—*Dios mío!* What is going to happen?" *Doña* Francisca stopped abruptly and began coughing again.

Don Federico stood speechless, still traumatized from the visit of *Don* Esquibel. The incident of the young girl still needed to be confronted, and he was increasingly disturbed about the hellish suspicions of his father's adventures. "There is nothing to worry about, *Corazón*," he finally said. He then kissed his wife on her forehead and changed the subject. "*Querida*, I still do not like the sound of that cough. We need to take you to Reynosa and have Dr. Cantu examine you. I sure don't want anything to happen to you, *Corazón!*"

Doña Adela stamped her *huaraches*, and, in her blunt authoritative way, glared at *Doña* Francisca. "*Dios mío*, you've still got that nasty cough. The medicine I sent you a month ago has not helped. When I get back to my *jacale*, I'll make a stronger tea for you." The old woman looked around and kept talking. She sauntered on and then abruptly stopped, casting a glance at Roy, who was leaning against the stone wall. He held a tortilla in one hand and a bowl of chili in the other, watching the procession going by.

"Haven't gotten married yet?" she questioned him. "No!" she answered herself, in a scolding and insulting tone. "You're too lazy to go out and find a wife. Instead they come for you, and find you here at Spanish Acres." She kept her balance with the help of her cane, and shook her crooked index finger at the foreman. "But, she's already here!" The old *bruja* cackled, feeling sure of herself. "She has come here for you! You'll have a partner soon! You'll be married soon! You'll have responsibilities."

Roy, who had a hungry-dog appetite, stopped eating and stared at the old women in amazement. *What the hell does she mean, "soon?" She's crazy! The idiotic old hag! Crazier than a shit-house rat,* he thought to himself.

The scrawny music teacher, Miss Bell, who was also watching the confrontation, glanced at Roy and then smiled with delight. *Perhaps there's a possibility*, she thought. *Miracles do happen!*

The revered *bruja* kept talking as she staggered around the group. As she passed each individual she would point her finger and prophesy what she was feeling at that exact moment. Everyone crossed themselves and whispered among themselves, *Dios!* Help us!

CHAPTER 2

As the sun began setting toward the west, a blood-hued twilight formed in August's torrid dusk. The dark shadows of the night came, swallowing a horizon relentlessly weighed down by vermilion colored clouds. It gradually changed as the dimness snuggled in, slowly overshadowing the Spanish mansion, and the great *brasada*.

The cowhands and the workers clustered together in the eating area, amidst the light of the kerosene lamps and hurricane coal oil lanterns, drinking black coffee and smoking their hand-rolled cigarettes. Many were sitting in silence, with a dazed expression, as doom weighed heavily upon them. They were afraid to think of what had happened out in the *brasada*. The atmosphere had taken on an air of deep irredeemable gloom; nervous tension engulfed them all, a feeling unfamiliar to the usually happy, tranquil natives.

Roy and several of the cowhands from *Don* Esquibel's *vaqueros* had volunteered to retrieve the body of the dead *gringa* mainly out of curiosity and respect. They had all waited until late in the evening, when the heat and earth had cooled down, and headed to the area of the *resaca*. They had returned tired and hungry and above all—empty-handed.

"Where's the body?" the residents asked, including *Don* Federico, *Doña* Francisca, and the entire household.

There was no body, only the evidence of a struggle and blood on the dry, dusty ground, and flies.

"There is nothing more we can do now," said a disappointed *Don* Federico to his workers and their families. "We'll have to round up over a thousand head of cattle in the next couple of days to be shipped out before the weather changes and a *chubasco* is on the way. I'll send another party of workers out into the *resaca* again tomorrow, if possible. Maybe they'll find something. People don't just vanish."

"A wild cat got her," suggested one of the *vaqueros*, his voice full of concern.

Don Federico was getting worried. "In time, she'll be found." The tone of his voice was mixed with rage and irritation; he was sorely disappointed in the events that were unfolding. He turned his back and went into the library, closing the door. A glass of brandy would surely relax his nerves, and a Cuban cigar would calm his anxiety and help him contemplate the day's drama.

The night was an indelible darkness. Out in the sweltering heat of the undergrowth, the rhythm of the bullfrogs near the several waterholes throbbed. As the wind energized ever so slightly, the windmills cranked and turned, and the chirps of crickets pulsated into the darkness.

The Mexicans from the hacienda were ignorant and without formal education, but they understood nature and went by their instincts. Even the singing cicadas and the barking dogs could sense the oncoming waves; for that matter, there had been warning signs of an oncoming storm—many storms. A hurricane was indeed brewing in the Gulf of Mexico, but internal complications had also stirred the poor in Mexico into what would become a long and deadly rebellion.

Lying in bed, *Don* Federico was full of tormenting thoughts. The mosquito netting from his canopy bed had been put aside, lying partly between the floor and the edge of his resting place. He wanted some breeze that would cool and comfort him from the heat, and yet there was no comfort. His arms were folded, resting under his head; his eyes stared fixed toward the high ceiling, thinking that perhaps this had been one of his most trying days. Too many things were starting to cloud his mind. What had happened last night out in the wilderness? Where could the body be? What was the old *bruja*, Adela, insinuating? *Don* Esquibel talking about a revolution kept thoughts spiraling over and over again and again in his mind. He was concerned about his wife's consistent coughing, an unhealthy cough. He worried about his children, wanting the best education for them—the only solution to escape the bias and prejudice that had become so prevalent in this area. Why did there have to be so much hate between the two struggling races along the border?

Don Federico was well versed in the human unrest on both sides of the river. He had tried to forget the oppressing misery that dwelt within the souls of the hard-pressed Mexicans. He was a peaceful and fair man, but in the last several years a sense of rage and hatred had over-shadowed him, the result of so many injustices against the Mexican people, including the mysterious death of his father.

His thoughts reflected on the history of the Rio Grande Valley and the influence brought on by Mexico. President Díaz of Mexico dominated his country with an iron hand as a dictator, although he had opened his country to foreigners with money to invest, and had put Mexico on the map of international commerce. Other countries were now calling her, "Mexico, the treasure house of the world." But, in all of his years on the throne, Díaz did nothing for the poor villagers. He reduced the population to a condition of serfdom even worse than the repressive regime that existed under the Spanish or the French rule. The common villages of the Mexican Indians were seized and turned over to the rich landowners. These *hacendados* reduced the Mexican Indians to a total state of slavery, bound to the soil with unjust cruelty and left without hope.

Don Federico, being a man of innate fairness, felt sympathy for the poor peasants. Their nature had become indifferent, if not hostile, to such laws. To the Mexican, time—yes, time—meant that tomorrow would always come. The word *mañana*, to which they were all accustomed, was now a hopeless tomorrow. Had the Holy Catholic Church not told them never to worry about tomorrow? But the poor struggling Mexicans had become virtual slaves, with no land to grow their crops. When was *mañana* coming? The prosperity that had put their great country on the map had been at the peasants' expense, with hundreds toiling in the hot burning sun for the benefit of the rich landowners. The millions of aggrieved *peóns*, who were the foundation of the country, had suffered under the feudal policies of Díaz and his cronies' greed. For the poor Mexicans to rebel and take up arms was their only hope, their only chance for survival. A revolution would bring changes.

As the influx of the white man mingled with the ageless customs of Mexico, it fomented resentment from the native dwellers, who for centuries had owned both sides of the Rio Grande River. The white man rapidly made trouble between the two cultures, settling all matters with guns and the whip. The Mexican-American natives who had lived on the Texas side had become used to their Mexican traditions and customs, but the new habits and ways of thinking and doing business introduced by the Europeans created a racial issue. The dominant power of the white man over the Mexican-American people, who took life freely and were mostly illiterate, not only suppressed them, but made them feel inferior. This began the sowing of the '*roots of indifference*,' the seeds that germinated trouble between the races in the coming years. One was ambitious to clear the land with zealous demands, and hungry to become rich; the other hostile, proud and fearless, and perhaps too confident about their land.

Like a magnificent, gnarled and aged tree, whose roots stretched far and wide across the Rio Grande River, the Treaty of Guadalupe Hidalgo, splitting the two countries, was like the sudden severing of a massive organism. The natives were ripped from their Mexican heritage, creating problems which would last throughout the coming generations. The Mexicans had families and relatives living on both sides of the border, and any incident would automatically affect them all. The native citizens of the Rio Grande Valley considered themselves the true Texans, and they sometimes referred to the English-speaking strangers as foreigners.

The Europeans, many of whom called themselves "greenhorns," being unfamiliar with frontier ways, represented many diverse cultures. Later, the Mexicans called them *Anglos*, which distinguished them from the rest of the residents. The word *Gringo* came years later because of their songs. One, especially was, *Green Grow the Lilacs*.

Don Federico remembered when he was a young boy, how the so-called *gringos* had looked at him and his mother and had made rude remarks about his parents' mixed marriage. However, the great *Don* was more than Mexican-American, for he was cultured, with a great education and social advantage over most men in this area. On this tormenting night, he was a man who neither laughed nor smiled, feeling drained and empty. In this region, his word was law, but still deep inside him was a man sensitive to the world's common problems. Changes were coming. They were in the wind—they were in the milieu and worried whispers. Unable to sleep, he got up and paced the floor in his chambers. How he hated aggression and the appalling quicksand of injustice, which was so common in this region.

It had been more than a year, he remembered, since President Díaz had met with President Taft of the United States. He, with *Doña* Francisca, her mother and her diplomat father, José

Hinojosa, had attended the ceremonial event in El Paso, Texas. How could he ever forget the President of Mexico, the old, dignified Indian President, articulate, eloquent, and charming, his uniform displaying his prized two-dozen medals across his chest, in an effort to outdo President Taft and his White House staff. Later that evening, in the city of Juarez, sixty guests had sat down with the two Presidents to a delightful state dinner for which the Mexicans were hosts. The table, as he remembered, was serviced with gold plates from the presidential palace in Mexico City. How elegant! How magnificent! Such splendor! He had met Díaz in Mexico City many years back. Federico was engaged to marry *Doña* Francisca at the time. And President Díaz was glad to see *Doña* Francisca again, the daughter of his retired cabinet member, *Don* José Hinojosa, the wealthy diplomat from Monterrey. The President of Mexico had promised them that properties were secure in Mexico, especially for a rich, wealthy investor like her father, *Señor* Hinojosa.

Thinking back, *Don* Federico's instincts told him that nothing was secure in what the president had said over a year ago. Anything could happen, and soon, for there were strong rumors and talk all along the Texas border of a political overthrow in Mexico.

Don Federico was not a religious man. God was for the poor, the destitute, and the afflicted. For those who had outgrown it, like himself, the well-to-do, wealthy, and well-fed, there was only the God concept. However, *Doña* Francisca was extremely religious. She had the Holy Catholic Church wrapped around her body and soul, for it was her faith, with the help of myriad saints, which had brought her safe through all of the chaos of raising her children in this untamed wilderness. *La Señora* was educated in a convent southwest of Monterrey and she loved to take care of the poor and the needy. Everyone respected her and loved her for her sincere humility and gentle kindness. In turn, Spanish Acres was always full of stranded people who would come, work, and stay for days at a time, or months, and sometimes never left.

Why think of religion now? Don Federico thought. *Religion has not helped matters at all. As a matter of fact, it had been the religion that had taught the Mexican-Americans to be humble and silent.* Never were people so dreadfully superstitious and church-fueled, for fear of losing their souls. But man had brought out the evil in himself—fighting the good verses evil. But evil did exist, and it surfaced commonly every day. How the silence of the night tormented his soul. He had so many unanswered questions!

It was early morning before he got any sleep. But in his sleep, he dreamed that he was lost in an unknown land. A foreign land—wilderness—strange people, his father's ghostly presence, instructing him not to listen to what people were telling him, to go by his own conscience and instinct.

CHAPTER 3

Two days had come and gone, and the following morning was full of noisy activity. Every small child from Spanish Acres who could scream or yell had walked under *Don* Federico's upstairs bedroom window. Every dog in the vicinity and even Blanca's bell kept clamoring, ringing as the children played. *Just listen to the noise*, thought *Don* Federico, walking over to the window, looking down and realizing that he must have overslept. He wondered where the loud pounding was coming from earlier that had actually woken him.

Downstairs, coming from the parlor he heard the music from Beethoven's *Moonlight Sonata* drifting throughout the upstairs balcony. Victoria's playing of her piano was sweet to his ears, even though she played the same tune over and over again, trying to perfect it. Quickly dressing, he hurried downstairs and met Mamá Maria coming halfway up.

Maria, the head servant, was more like his mother than a servant. She was a friend who had been with the family since before he was born at Spanish Acres. She had nursed him with patience and love, cared for him throughout his manhood, given him advice, and continued to be loyal, knowing, yet keeping, many of the family's hush-hush secrets. She was a mixture of Mexican and Indian blood, born on a *ranchito* close to Mission, Texas. Mamá Maria came from a starving family of ten. *Don* Federico's father had taken a business trip to Mission, where he discovered them and took pity on them. He gave them money and brought the young Maria to Spanish Acres to serve the family.

Mamá Maria was a short, broad-hipped, heavy set, dark-skinned woman with high cheekbones reflecting her Indian heritage. She took care of the household needs, from the kitchen to linens. She knew every inch, every step, every nook and cranny in the large hacienda, which had over twenty guest bedrooms. Nothing escaped her piercing eyes. Burdened by past calamities and sickness, she walked with a limp because of the arthritis in her hips and knees, her heavy steps hammering the tile floors.

Maria had been married to Manuel for over fifty years, never bearing him any children. While she saw to the needs inside the hacienda and gave orders, Manuel did everything outside from carrying mesquite wood for the open-kitchen stoves, to performing odd jobs, and running errands for everyone. He also kept the grounds clean and watered the gardens for the vines to bloom, and to please *Doña* Francisca.

"*Ay! Hijo*," she said affectionately. "You slept late this morning," speaking in her half-English and half-Spanish lingo. "I brought you some black coffee."

"*Gracias*, Mamá Maria, and, yes, I did sleep late—had trouble sleeping." *Don* Federico glanced at his pocket watch, knowing that clocks obeyed no rules in Spanish Acres. "Rough night!" he answered, taking the cup from her hand. "I hear Victoria playing her piano. Where is everybody this morning?" he asked, as they both made their way to the dining room for his breakfast.

"*Señora* Adela left early this morning, and *la Señora Doña* Francisca went to check on some of the children who are sick from *empacho* in Spanish Quarters. Fred is playing outside and Carlos is in the kitchen with Manuel. *Los vaqueros* had breakfast real early this morning and left with Roy to round up the cattle." She then took a deep breath and said, "*Dios mío*, everyone is frightened."

"We are too far from the border and there is no need to worry," *Don* Federico said in a calm, reassuring voice.

"Ay! *Hijo*! Of course not," she said to please him, but not so sure herself. She clasped her hands over her large breasts and then wiped her hands on her red striped gingham apron.

"Good! Now, tell me how the Mexican girl is doing this morning. What's her condition today? Is she getting any better? Has she eaten anything?" He was full of concern.

"The girl ate a little warm *atole*, oatmeal. Olivia is sitting and watching her at this moment." Mamá Maria's speech slowed and began to reveal more confidence.

"That's good! That's one good thing that has happened this morning. I'll have to talk to her about what happened out in the *resaca* and get a clearer picture of what took place. I'll wait until she's feeling better and wants to talk. *Don* Federico abruptly changed the tone of the conversation. "Have Manuel get the mules and wagon ready. I'm going to Harlingen to get some supplies. I'll also need to take care of a matter with Mr. Hanson from the Texas Rangers. And I'll need to get things for Victoria's fiesta coming up in the next couple of months. The money that we get from selling the cattle will help in the celebration."

"Be careful with the *Rinche*," cautioned the old servant. "So many cruel stories are being told by the *vaqueros* how he hates the Mexican people." She paused for a minute, thinking, but kept walking. "Anything to do with Soledad, or the dead *gringa*?" she questioned.

"No." he said calmly, not wanting her to become concern. "We have got to have things arranged before we take Victoria to school in Mexico." His voice became more authoritative. "I don't want anyone talking about Soledad's incident, or the dead *gringa*. We know that there is a dead body out in the *brasada*, but there's nothing we can do about it. I don't want any of the women gossiping. I have already told *Señor* Esquibel to keep his cowhands quiet until I investigate the matter more fully. I'm going to probe ol' Hanson's thoughts and pulse, and maybe he'll mention something about any incident happening the days before. I also need to discuss my father's gold mine in Monterrey and see what Hanson plans to do about the working conditions, since we became partners. I need to know what Hanson's responsibility is in helping to run the gold mine. Frankly, I think it's too much of a bother, if you ask me."

ROOTS OF INDIFFERENCE

"*Si*," replied Mamá Maria attentively, nodding her head, as she ordered the kitchen helper to bring in *Don* Federico's breakfast as soon as possible. "I'll get Manuel and have him get the mule team ready. He must be already out in the barn." She hurried outside.

Ophelia came in with a basket of corn tortillas, a plate of fried eggs, fried potatoes, mashed beans and strips of pork bacon, and placed them at *Don* Federico's place at the head of the large mahogany table. Already there was a big pitcher of fresh orange juice from the citrus orchards outside. Olivia entered the kitchen, coming from Soledad's room with a tray of dirty dishes.

"What was all the pounding this morning?" *Don* Federico questioned one of the ladies as he started to eat his food. "Sounded like someone was using a hammer on one of the buildings, and so early!" He looked up at Olivia and waited for an answer. She hesitated, brought her hands to her mouth and burst out laughing.

Ophelia began laughing too and related the story to *Don* Federico. "Last night, the *vaqueros* were telling ghost, spirit, and demon stories from around this area. And poor Pablo—you know how he believes everything you tell him, and how scared he gets. He went to the outhouse after eating, and while sitting in the privy, one of the barn cats meowed and began scratching the outhouse door. Well! Poor old Pablo forgot what he was doing and stormed out, taking the door and all—with his pants down around his ankles, wailing and yelling. Everyone laughed so hard that they had to use the latrine themselves. Pablo must have not slept at all, because early this morning he found a hammer and was trying to fix the hinges on the door. He was so embarrassed; he left to see about rounding up the herd without eating any breakfast."

"Well! Did he get it fixed?"

"No!" replied Ophelia, laughing. "It's slanting sideways, and it screeches every time you open the door." Both women exited into the kitchen chuckling.

"Damn!" said *Don* Federico, "I'll get Manuel to fix the damn shithouse door."

The music from the sonata stopped and Victoria appeared from the parlor. "Did I hear you talking about me? Papá! I hope it's not important."

"Yes, *Hija*," answered *Don* Federico. "We are starting to make plans for your future." He continued talking while eating his breakfast. "Going to school in Monterrey will take a lot of planning from your mother and me, and your mother insists that the convent school for young girls in Monterrey is better at training you in manners and in social behavior, to be a lady of refinement like your mother. Your mother and I feel better since your grandmother and grandfather live in Monterrey and close to the convent. Your future in-laws, the Del Calderónes, can come to see you while you're there too. You will need to grow up as a social lady and learn how to act in society. Here in Spanish Acres, things are done too liberally. After all, once you finish your courses and studies we'll have to make other plans. Your wedding to Ricardo will take much planning."

"Why can't I pick my own husband?" Victoria argued. "In this new century, women are starting to decide for themselves who they will marry," she stated defiantly, stroking her long, dark hair and breaking into a coy smile, testing her father.

"Foolishness and nonsense!" thundered *Don* Federico, failing to see the humor, and in no mood for sarcasm. "You are talking unintelligently. You have been promised to marry Ricardo. We have always wanted the best for you and what is best for your future. He comes from one of the finest families in Monterrey with high social ties, good blood, and he can give you a comfortable living." *Don* Federico hurried to finish his food.

Victoria rebelled, defying her father's immutable word that was law. "He's too old for me!"

"The Del Calderónes have been planning your wedding for a long time and are looking forward to the event. They have been social acquaintances of your mother's family for years. Yes, I agree, he is much older than you are, but in marriage it doesn't make any difference, when he's stable in property and money. We can not change the promise."

Frustrated, *Don* Federico began to explain his reasoning. "Do you want to be an old maid? Just look at Ophelia and Olivia! Poor old maids that my father took pity on them so many years ago. Do you want to live like them? You need to get an education, get married, have children—that's the cycle of life. Women have no rights in anything, except household duties and taking orders from their husbands. I don't want to hear any more of this foolishness."

Victoria countered his declaration. "I don't want to live in Mexico! And besides, I don't want to take orders from a strange husband that I don't even know!"

"As long as you live in this household, you'll do as we say! And let this be the last time you speak that way and talk in that tone again, young lady! How dare you question our orders! Is that understood? All of a sudden women are starting to question things and are thinking for themselves—they want liberation—bullshit!"

Victoria stood as in a trance, the teasing quickly ended. Stubbornly resisting her father's harsh demands, she clinched her hands so hard they were sweating. *Such nonsense!* She thought. Why couldn't she find her own husband? And besides, she could not stand the famous Del Calderónes—so overbearing, so demanding, thinking that they were so rich that they could buy any young bride and be able to control her. Marrying a man she did not love, because it was planned through family traditions was ridiculous. Arranged marriages were nonsense!

She was going to be sixteen soon and felt she was old enough to say what was really on her mind. Could women not think for themselves? She had an intelligent mind, and besides, women got married for love. Already Victoria had the physical attributes of a full-grown woman. She was tall and slender, with a small waist and full, rounded breasts. Her long, dark-brown hair had a tint of gold from the sun and the hours she had spent outdoors. Her features were delicate, with a small nose, a delicate, sensual mouth, and sparkling hazel eyes. The workers and *vaqueros* in the hacienda called her by her nickname, *La Borrada*.

On the edge of tears, she stared at her father without saying a word, red faced, feeling humiliated, knowing that no matter what she did, it was never good enough. However, Fred, her younger brother, could do no wrong because he was a boy. Her father viewed her as less, a woman who had no rights. His commands were law, and on Spanish Acres you did what he said. She had no other choice. She was trapped.

ROOTS OF INDIFFERENCE

It was at that moment that Roy and Fred walked into the dining room. With tears running down her face, Victoria glared at Roy and Fred, then turned, brushed her cheeks, and walked away.

"Whoa—Wa's a goin' on?" Roy asked, sensing tension. He had walked in on a family dispute.

"Have we got all the cattle rounded up?" questioned *Don* Federico, angrily changing the subject. His priority now was getting the cattle loaded in the train's boxcars and on their way to San Antonio. "The sooner we get them loaded and shipped the better! We must have at least a thousand head. We need to hurry, because the sky this morning looks like we might get some weather."

"Al-reedy started," said Roy. "I left ol' Miguel Garcia and de others roundin' up all of 'em. By *mañana* we ought to be in good shape, *patrón!* We gits a good load o' cattle this time."

"Well done! Good!" responded *Don* Federico, delighted with the progress. He wiped his mouth with a cloth napkin as he finished his breakfast and stood up. "Roy!" he commanded, "you and Fred get ready. We're heading to Harlingen and getting some supplies. We're low on bag balm for the cattle, coal oil, tobacco for de-worming the horses, and I need to do some bartering with the beef for other supplies. Fred, get yourself ready, and you better wear your riding hat. I thought you would like to come with Roy and me to get away from the ranch for a while, and maybe it will keep you out of trouble."

Fred was only ten but looked older than his years. The future depended on this prodigy child, and only the best was expected of him when he grew up. Extremely tall for his age, he was already five foot, six inches, with beautiful brown hair and gray eyes. Thin as a post and full of nervous vitality, he was smart as a whip, but his awkward gait appeared clumsy, and mischievous, he was always getting into trouble. He pulled pranks on everyone he could get a laugh out of, and he loved to search for the mysterious things in nature. He was fascinated with animals, humans, plants, and anything that lived—anything that was warm and breathing. He loved life as a whole, with all its curious fascinations, and especially horses, which he called, "God's work of art."

"What's keeping Manuel and the wagon?" *Don* Federico wondered aloud, looking at his pocket watch and pacing back and forth from the dining room to the kitchen. An hour had already passed since he had commanded the wagon and mules. Not having enough sleep had made his disposition most undesirable. His word was law, and he insisted everything be done in order. "That Manuel gets slower by the minute!" he hollered. "You'd think he was pulling a wagon full of rocks."

Being quick and restless, Fred hurried out to the stable and peeked through a small opening between the cracks in the wood. He could see Manuel singing and taking several sips of tequila from one of his many hidden bottles he stored in all corners of the stable where he worked.

As usual, Manuel's stomach hung out of his pants, his shirt was undone, and his shoes untied. His graying hair, what little was left, stood straight up, wildly pointing in all directions. Preparing this wagon was a tedious job to Manuel, but with a smile on his face, he accepted the task. It was all in a day's work. With one hand he would scratch himself and then rub his head, while the other hand stayed glued to the bottle.

Fred being Fred, he could not resist being the mischievous, little devil that he was. Sneaking in behind Manuel without being noticed, he pretended to be *Don* Federico. He lowered his voice in a deep growl and yelled out as loud as he could, "Man-uel!"

"*Ay! Ay! Ay!*" cried Manuel as the tequila sprayed in all directions, down his face, his stomach and onto the front of his pants. Trying to juggle the bottle with both hands and catch his breath, he was not fast enough—the bottle hit the floor with a crash. Pieces of glass flew everywhere.

Fred laughed so loud he could be heard by all who were in the outdoor kitchen.

"What's taking so long?" demanded *Don* Federico, striding toward the barn. "What's so funny?"

Fred moved quickly and, with his feet, began covering the broken pieces of glass with the straw that lay on the barn floor.

Glaring at Manuel, *Don* Federico noticed the wagon waiting outside and could smell the tequila. "What are you two up to? What's so funny?" he questioned.

Using his quick wit, Fred replied, "Manuel has been running around all morning with the fly of his trousers unbuttoned and exposing himself."

Manuel moved outside and wagged his head and began moving faster, adjusting the harness to get the team of mules ready. He fastened the whiffletree to the wagon, while his eyes fixed on *Don* Federico, with a guilty smile exposing what few teeth he had left. He said, "I'm getting too old and sometimes I forget to put *it* in!"

"Well, Manuel," replied *Don* Federico, "we've got many loose women here, and they would surely take advantage of your condition." He was trying hard to keep his composure, repressing a grin, and then joined in with a hearty laugh, which was a rare occurrence. "You being such a desirable *hombre* could get you in trouble with Mamá Maria," he teased.

Roy already sat on his horse, waiting at the entrance of the stable, and caught the drift from Manuel. *Why! Dat ol' coot*, he thought. *He's been at it again...a drinkin'*. He could smell the strong odor of liquor yards away.

"*Sí Jefe!* The wagon is ready," said Manuel finally, as he rambled on with a thousand unnecessary explanations about a *chubasco* coming. He could feel it in his ol' bones. He could smell it in the wind. And from the way the birds were flying this morning, a storm was brewing in the Gulf.

Finally, the trio was on their way. *Don* Federico drove the mule team with Fred sitting next to him. The boy was getting old enough to learn about the business of the ranch, and he was picking up on how men talk. Roy rode his horse alongside the wagon, and all three were still laughing about ol' Manuel, and about last night's outhouse incident with Pablo.

The sky had become somewhat overcast, with fleecy cumulus clouds forming far out on the horizon. The temperature was ten degrees cooler than the day before, but the humidity was nearly one hundred percent, keeping it sultry and oppressive.

ROOTS OF INDIFFERENCE

The road to La Villa led straight south. It was the same old *La Sal Vieja* Road that for years, people had traveled to get salt rocks for human consumption and for their cattle. There was nothing but large prickly-pear cactus, mesquite, tall undergrowth, and chaparral on both sides of the dirt road. *Doña* Adela's house stood several hundred yards from the road, hidden among the *brasada's* undergrowth and sheltered by many tall cottonwood trees. It was a gray, strange looking place, blending into the environment as though part of it.

"Too bad I didn't get a chance to visit with *Doña* Adela," commented *Don* Federico, as he cleared his throat. "I get the feeling she is not saying everything she knows. Sure wish we could find the *gringa's* body." Then there was a long silence, with only the wind and the sounds of mockingbirds and blackbirds calling to each other.

A swirling, dusty whirlwind came from nowhere toward them. The team of mules started to spook, as well as Roy's palomino. An eerie feeling overtook the three of them, a strange electrifying feeling of dread. It was as if evil existed there in *Doña* Adela's domain, evil that stirred unexplained phenomena.

Don Federico's eyes shifted to Roy, riding alongside. "Last night, while I lay tossing and turning in my bed, a thought came to me and it's galling me. Why does *Doña* Adela's son, Roberto, keep popping into my mind over and over again? Where was he when the killing took place? Think about it! He must have seen something, the way he roams the *brasada*, prowling around. He knows every cactus and mesquite tree there is in this wilderness. I'm gonna have to talk to him if we can find him, and I'll bet we'll come up with some answers. I'll bet he knows something! It seems like *Doña* Adela is afraid of something. Maybe she's trying to cover for him."

"B' dang! Ya' might be right, *patrón*! I hadn't thought of dat!" Roy replied.

Don Federico handed the reins to Fred and began to relate some of the experiences he had had with *Doña* Adela. "When Victoria was only a year old, back in the late 1890s, she became deathly ill one night with a temperature of over one hundred. Francisca, being familiar with the old Mexican superstition of the "Evil Eye," sent one of the workers to fetch *Doña* Adela. After viewing the baby, the old lady claimed that Victoria was suffering from that affliction. She ordered a fresh-laid egg to be brought in. She began rubbing it all over Victoria's little body, and within a few minutes the child was perfectly fine. No fever. She was completely well, laughing and giggling as if nothing had ever happened. I couldn't believe it!" *Don* Federico exclaimed.

"Later, *Doña* Adela took an egg and opened it in a glass of fresh water. Right before our eyes, on the surface of the yoke, was the face of a man who had sold us some goods and yards of material earlier. I remembered he couldn't get his eyes off Victoria, wanting to hold her. She was a beautiful little girl with her curls and lace and all. According to the custom, you're supposed to touch the person you're possessing. Francisca, being very careful, would not let the salesman touch her. I think these beliefs exploit people, put fear into them, but that's the way life is here and nobody questions it."

A horrible sensation overcame Fred as he felt a cold chill all over his body, and he moved closer to his father. He gazed toward the old *jacale*, and in the tops of the cottonwood trees were hundreds of blackbirds gawking, hunched together, as if watching them go by. Behind the thick undergrowth, he caught a glimpse of the humped silhouette of a figure watching them.

Periodically, the foreman and *Don* Federico exchanged talks about the good ol' days and how it had been in the early part of the region. Roy would bring up about his life as a young boy when he lived in Oklahoma and the Panhandle of Texas. There were few men more respected than his father, thought Fred proudly, as he listened to the interesting stories being told, while he handled the reins of the mules.

Two roads intersected on the outskirts of La Villa, creating a small clearing in the primeval cacti infestation, and a few little huts squatted in between the heavy thickets of chaparral. The small village boasted a small, open stable, one windmill, a water trough for the horses, and one wooden hut that served a few specialty cold drinks. Hard liquor was brought out only on Saturday nights, since it was hard to buy and shipped by wagon from across the border in Reynosa. When the *vaqueros* got their monthly pay, and on Saturday nights, the area became a rowdy, rip-roaring spot, with live music, card playing, and secret gambling. Women of the night would show up, giving the local workers many hours of pleasure. It was one of Roy's favorite spots, and he would tease the married *vaqueros*, saying "Dis da place to tear up a pea patch, by dang!"

An hour had passed. After watering Roy's horse and the mules and having a cold drink themselves, the three resumed their journey into Harlingen, with Fred once again taking the lines. *Don* Federico informed his son, "If you go straight south on this road, you'll come to the town of Mercedes City, where your Aunt Emma, Felicia, Jaime, and John live, but by turning left here, we'll be in Harlingen within a few hours."

"I'd like to see Jaime and John!" Fred said, thinking of his twin cousins. "I haven't seen them for several months. Don't care to see Aunt Emma, she's so bossy. But I do miss the boys."

"Gaw'd dang! Ya' had to brin' her name up!" roared Roy, then he snickered, trying to juggle his chewing tobacco and the reins of his horse. "Dat thar wimmin can talk the hind-end legs off a burro. By golly, that's all we'll need," he said, laughing.

"I'm surprised we haven't seen Emma show up lately," said *Don* Federico. She normally made her monthly calls to Francisca, bringing her new style of crocheting, new material, or a new recipe that someone invented. He continued, "Emma never did like the idea of Francisca residing so far away from her guidance. That's because Emma can't tell her what to do every single minute of the day. She resents the idea that Francisca is living out in the mesquite jungle with a bunch of old women, old men, and ensconced on a cattle ranch instead of having the opportunity to be a refined lady. She has always fancied Francisca enjoying the life of a sophisticated woman drinking tea at social parties. Emma thinks she is so cosmopolitan. Maybe among the stiff-necks of Monterrey, but not in Mercedes City."

"She calls Spanish Acres the wilderness," replied Fred.

"Bah!" *Don* Federico frowned and adjusted his hat. "What does she know about wilderness? That reminds me, I do need to go to Mercedes City in a couple of days. Need some supplies from Milton's Mercantile. I also need to see about the property my father bought several years ago, when old man Dominquez was selling his land, almost giving it away for a few cents an acre."

"Can I come with you, Dad?" Fred asked. "I want to visit with the twins."

"Fine, son, we'll see about it! I know one thing. We will not be staying overnight at your Aunt Emma's house. There is nothing pleasant at their home. You have to take your shoes off before entering and you're afraid to touch anything—it's an uncomfortable place. She hates the smell of my Cuban cigars, nobody laughs, and it's a very dull and dreary place, as though you're in a high-class palace. Their new three-story house reminds me of a funeral home. I can't stand her retired judge husband either. It's like he's trying to judge you, with those beady eyes peering from behind his bifocals."

"What was Mercedes City," questioned Fred, "before it was a town?"

"The area was called *Mesquito* by the Mexican *vaqueros* and Indians who roamed the region in the early years, hunting for wild boars and deer. It was established and renamed four years ago by a rich syndicate. One of them was a friend of your grandfather George, named Yoakum, a very eloquent and a very persuasive promoter. However, your grandfather did give some of his land and money for the building of the railroad from Brownsville up to Sinton. The township was named Mercedes City after Mercedes Dominquez, who had originally owned and controlled most of the area. Later the American Rio Grande and Irrigation Company claimed a town site, bringing the railroad across from Harlingen straight up along the border."

The ride was now becoming hot and tiresome. There was a long silent pause as the trio continued toward the town of Harlingen. Roy suddenly began riding faster, and *Don* Federico took the reins from Fred and slapped the mules into a trot. The eastern sky was producing heavy, dark clouds. A light drizzle of occasional rain and gusty winds made the mules snort and toss their heads.

Out on the horizon several Mexican men were busy clearing the land and burning the mesquite and cactus in a large pile. They were on the outskirts of the town that for years had been nicknamed "Six-Shooter Junction." Turning the mules, *Don* Federico headed them southeast. It was a shorter route through the thorny jungle to the "Hub of the Valley."

"Ah, yes," said *Don* Federico with a remorseful sigh. "This is the "Valley of Tears." In the late ninetieth century, a plague killed many people here. That's why the Mexicans gave it that name."

"Da feces from dat shit house rats cause dat, an' there's plenty of 'em here," said Roy.

Don Federico continued talking. "It's amazing how the so-called investors have seen the potential value of the land, and they are trying to change the name to the "Magic Valley." The only magic is the money. The white investors have been buying the land from the Mexican-Americans for pennies, then they specify where they can live. They advertise all over the United States that this is paradise and offer free transportation to prospective buyers."

Clearing his throat, *Don* Federico continued with his impromptu history lesson. "In 1903, the first major railroad was started, linking us with the rest of the United States, and opened the way for the white men to come in and start buying cheap land. For the Mexican-Americans, the image became that of a foreign land, instead of the mother country that it had been for hundreds of years. The investors imported cheap wholesale laborers from Mexico to clear the land and start irrigation ditches, paying them in Mexican pesos. Many people from the northern states came. The majority stayed, but some did not like the heat in the summer and left. Many of the investors wanted to build large sugar plantations, those that came from Mississippi or Louisiana, intent upon making the Mexican people into the Negro slaves of old—just with a different language and a different color."

Fred and Roy listened intently while *Don* Federico continued.

"What the white people don't realize, or perhaps have ignored, is that the forgotten Treaty of Guadalupe Hidalgo spelled out the rights of the Mexican-American people who lived in this area. But how many people can read?"

As they entered the town of Harlingen, called by the white investors "Mexican Acres," because it was mostly inhabited by Mexican people, *Don* Federico went on. "The Mexicans are not allowed to buy property or live south of the railroad tracks after the town was designed. The railroad divided the town, like the rest of the communities in the Valley. This is called 'redlining' and it separates residential areas. The city is controlled by rich, biased individuals running everything. Congress passed the Fourteenth Amendment in 1868, after the Civil War, prohibiting states from violating laws of equality. But I guess it applies to all the other states except the southern states, like Texas, where they segregate the Mexicans, or the poor Indians and black people in places with 'Jim Crow laws,'" he said facetiously.

Don Federico paused only long enough to wipe the sweat from his forehead. "Crooked lawyers triumphed in passing laws that disenfranchised Mexican people, and reinforced violence with their own terror tactics. They made up their own little laws to benefit themselves. The Mexican people are not supposed to mix with the white people, especially in any public places nor public schools, railroad cars, recreation areas, eating facilities, hospital rooms, or sleeping quarters. They can clean and cook for them and be their slaves, now that's all right," he said sarcastically. "This is the type of thing that creates racial issues and hatred. No Mexican can cross over into the white side of town, especially at night. In all the small Texas towns, signs are posted, intimidating Mexicans and Negroes. They are not to be found roaming at night. Under this makeshift system of southern laws, they can be shot with no questions asked!"

CHAPTER 4

The Mexican people lived in the north section of Harlingen, where the streets were dusty, dirty, and uneven, with dry potholes full of trash. Harsh winds of clayish dust blew in annoying clusters. In one-room shacks, the Mexicans lived in rough, appalling poverty. Other *jacales* were made of scrap lumber, the walls framed with tarpaper, unfit even for animals to tolerate. There were other better looking shanties made of thatched mesquite mixed with plastered mud, with roofs of dried palm leaves. Jungles of cactus and mesquite and thorny undergrowth surrounded the *jacales*, sheds, and shacks; no planted tree could be seen. Hand-washed clothes were scattered on uneven gray, dry, mesquite fences; some were strewn up on chaparral brushes. Mangy, unfed dogs paced the dirt road, while many ragged children played barefooted in the dusty streets.

The contrast became obvious as they crossed over the tracks to the white area of town—it was cleaner and greener. They passed the Paso Real Stagecoach Inn, close to the large sugarcane mill that one of the pioneers of the town had started. Posted there, true to *Don Federico's* word, were posters saying "No Mexicans Allowed." This meant Mexicans could not enter the eating places or use any facility, especially the white's outhouses or any of their drinking fountains.

From a distance, the group could see the Lon C. Hill house, built in 1905, which was the first home in Harlingen. Hill was a promoter and responsible for the development of the town. The community had over three hundred residents already incorporated into the town that same year. In the white district, there were small shops, mercantile stores, a bank, horse stables, corrals, blacksmith shops, and two hotels. Horsetrading was conducted all along Jackson Street, and the railroad depot was at the Van Buren intersection. The headquarters of the Texas Rangers, or *Los Rinches*, was located in the middle of Main Street, and next to it stood the sheriff's office. Patches of mesquite, undergrowth and cactus were scattered in between the newly built structures.

Large wagons with heavy, hundred-pound barrels, and others with hay and goods were being pulled by horses and mules. Busy women, hurrying along in drab, dark dresses, shopped at the various stores, while others wearing gingham-checkered clothing held onto shopping baskets, with sun bonnets hiding their faces from the elements. Many of the local white ranchers did their business here because it was centrally located, and groups of towns-people were on hand for the daily arrival of the train at the junction of the Missouri and the Southern Pacific railroad. Heavy cargo, baggage and express trains going up the Valley were being unloaded onto wagons pulled by horses or mules. Behind the railroad depot, many pistol-toters used the wall for target practice, making for a rowdy scene. They were hard-looking *hombres* wearing large, faded Stetsons and silver belts, and armed with pistols hung on their hips in double holsters.

"I'll tell ya' whut ah thin' 'bout Bernard Hanson," said Roy, as they got closer to the Rangers' building. "He's a damn dangerous *hombre*. Meaner den a rat'ler! Ever since yore father died, he was dat *hombre* in question. As fur as I'm concerned, I don't want any part of 'em. I don't put no stock in any lawman. His name fit's 'em all right, with a big 'B' fur bastard."

There was a long pause, then *Don* Federico gave a loud sigh and narrowed his eyes. "It's been more than a year since Dad died so mysteriously. Nobody can convince me that it was just a heart attack! Bullshit! The bruise on the back of his neck suggested something else. We didn't notice it until days had passed and Dad was being dressed for his funeral. As a matter of fact, it was Mamá Maria that brought it to my attention—a dark, purplish discoloration on Dad's neck, like a thin, sharp cut."

Don Federico cleared his throat and continued. "Dad got Hanson to go in partnership with him in the gold mine in Monterrey. How the devil he convinced my father is beyond me. Ol' Hanson must've had something on my dad's head. Frankly, I don't like the man myself, but I'll have to deal with him until we settle an agreement. He's the typical individual brought in when the whites began infesting this area, with all of the racial hatred toward the Mexican people. Yes, there have always been skirmishes here and there, for as long as I can remember. Hanson was a hero when he came back from fighting in the Spanish-American War. He was with Teddy Roosevelt when the Rough Riders were organized to fight in that war, helping the Cubans. Yes! I agree with you, Roy! I think he's a very dangerous man. The hair on the back of my neck stands straight up when I see him. But I have plans, and if everything goes well, ol' Hanson will have lots of explaining to do."

Don Federico struggled for breath as the wagon approached the hitching rail next to the wooden porch of the Texas Ranger office. "Fred, take the wagon over to Lozano's Mercantile Store, give ol' man Lozano this list, and tell him to put the supplies on my bill. I will barter with him later on the half dozen cattle he bought from me a week ago." He glanced toward the heavens. "We'd better take care of things pretty quick. The sky is getting darker, and the wind is trying to pick up. This conversation shouldn't take me very long!"

Roy nodded and touched the tip of his hat as a signal of approval. *Don* Federico took a deep breath as he climbed up the steps to the wooden porch, trying hard to hold onto his composure. He had decided to play it safe, cut the nonsense short, and get down to brass tracks. The final decisions on the gold mine had to be resolved. He entered a small, crowded room filled with the pungent smell of tobacco.

The office was a mess, like the man at the desk. Rifles and guns lined the shelves, mixed with photographs of rough-looking Texas Rangers on the wall. Dusty filing cabinets stood open with papers piled high. Two flags stood beside his desk: one of the state of Texas, and the other of the United States. *Don* Federico wondered if Hanson was trying to appear as an intimating government official. An old, blue, enamelware coffee pot stood simmering on top of an iron stove, and, by the strong smell, it had been boiling for many hours. The sharp sound of the tapping of a telegraph could be heard in the background.

Hanson's legs were crossed on top of his unorganized desk, displaying his leather boots with fancy gold metallic stars attached to them. He was leaning back in his chair, enjoying one of his cheap cigars. The sight of *Don* Federico surprised him, as if seeing a ghost, and he dropped his legs hard to the wooden floor.

He was a brute of a man, weighing at least two hundred and fifty pounds, with cold, dark pig-eyes. He had come from the debased school of tainted, unlawful teaching and "unscrupulous excessive maleness," as it was called. Rumor said he drank hard, smoked dozens of cigars a day, gambled, and aside from getting enormous pleasure in killing, took joy in women, especially the Mexicans, whom he preferred. He could get away with almost anything, for he was the law, and with his badge and two six-shooters, he could cover his tracks very easily. He had the majority of the whites fooled, convinced that he would restore law and order, and he did so in his brutal public acts that were effective against the Mexicans. Those around him felt manipulated by his power and control, responding only to his greedy, evil needs.

"Well!" exclaimed Hanson, moving his cigar to the opposite side of his mouth. "What the hell brings you to Harlingen? Is it the hurricane from the Gulf coming in our direction? It's amazing when the weather turns, what it brings in." He cocked his head toward his assistant, a young rookie named Smith. There was obvious sarcasm in Hanson's voice. The assistant eyed *Don* Federico from his small desk in the corner and snickered.

Haughty and uncultured, Hanson failed to offer *Don* Federico a seat. The *Don* found a chair that was stacked with papers. He moved them to one side and sat on the edge, turning to face Hanson.

"Yeah," said Hanson, jokingly. "Why don't you sit down somewhere?"

By the strong, foul smell of alcohol, *Don* Federico sensed that the brute was drinking cheap whiskey, and he noticed the bottle in the debris on top of the desk. Hanson took a few sips and offered some to *Don* Federico.

With the courtly manner of a Spanish *Don*, Federico waved it away. "No! Thank you! It's too early for any drinking."

"You're more accustomed to the expensive kind!" retorted Hanson, displaying his ill manners. "You're more used to the good stuff—brandy, scotch, or even champagne. Your father enjoyed the best of everything. And surely it's rubbed off on you. You rich sonsabitches have everything!" he replied scornfully, exposing his brown, stained teeth. Leaning back heavily on his chair, he lifted his legs and returned his boots to the messy desk, unconcerned.

Invoking his father's name associated with a dirty word provoked *Don* Federico and sent the blood rushing to his head. Trying his best not to let his temper get the best of him, he said flatly, "Leave my father's name out of this, Hanson!" He stood up and harshly pushed the chair with his boot, giving it a quick shove to one side, causing several papers to slide to the floor. He adjusted his gun belt. "My father is dead and gone. Nothing is going to bring him back. I'm here strictly for business! I don't like this any more than you do."

He put his hands on the desk and leaned toward the Ranger. "I need to know what your plans are about the gold mine in Monterrey. Since you and I have unfortunately become partners, and nothing is being done about running it."

"Whoa! What the hell ya' mean—'plan to do about it'?" yelled Hanson. He was inebriated by this time, and his face reddened with agitation. The atmosphere in the room became tense. "I don't plan to do a goddamn thing about it!" he said, coughing and clearing his throat. His eyes widened, and it appeared as if fire and brimstone were coming out of them. "Matter of fact, the dividends have been real good this past year."

"Dividends from the gold mine?" questioned the *Don*. "Without you lifting a finger and doing anything about it? Well, how nice! How convenient it was for you!"

"I just got lucky," Hanson bragged.

The young rookie Ranger sensed the atmosphere was about to explode into a real fracas. He calmly put down the papers he was reviewing, stood up, and walked out into the dusty main street.

"I'll bet," said *Don* Federico, shaking his index finger in Hanson's face. "Tell me, Hanson. How did you come to own a piece of my father's gold mine? How did you pull that off?" he demanded.

"Well! Hell!" stammered Hanson, knowing he was getting cornered. His actions became suspicious. "Your father had a habit of doing a lot of bragging. Shooting off his mouth about his sonabitchin' money, all the land he had, and his goddamn cattle. He bragged about other properties he had in Mexico and here in Mercedes City. While the four of us were gambling, playing serious poker at the Mercedes Hotel, your father began flaunting his great wealth. The three of us took him up on his word. We told him to put up or shut up."

Hanson paused to take another sip of the cheap whiskey. "Your father was drinking very heavily and began betting up to a thousand dollars a hand. He began losing, but kept betting. He was a poor loser and didn't want to stop. He kept betting, drinking, and boasting more than ever, and he kept the cards coming for a long time. I tried to stop him, but he wouldn't listen. You know how stubborn he was, never wanting advice from anyone. Your father was a very determined man in anything he did. It was past midnight, and by that time he had lost several thousands dollars, the majority of it owed to me."

Don Federico stood listening, never commenting or interrupting, and glared at Hanson, trying to believe what he was saying. Then he spoke. "So Dad gave you part of the mine for his recompense? How convenient! How lucky you are!"

"Hell! He owed me the money. It was his damned idea! Your father signed a piece of paper, witnessed and signed by the other two men, giving me a partnership in the gold mine. He promised that the dividends coming from the mine would more than pay the bill." He coughed, took several puffs from his cigar, put it down, and then continued. "Lawyer Parker has your father's handwritten document in his office. He witnessed the whole damn thing." Hanson paused for a moment, as if catching himself in giving out too much information. He picked his words carefully. "I was his confidant," he said convincingly. "He relied heavily on our friendship. There's a lot more that you do not know about your father—there's more, but maybe it's better this way."

"You mentioned Parker. Who else?" asked *Don* Federico, narrowing his eyes and now furious. "Besides you, Parker, and my father, who else was involved in this shark playing game?"

"I thought you knew all this time!" gasped Hanson, with a surprised expression. His crafty, beady eyes were dead set on *Don* Federico's actions, and he felt forced to answer. "Your own relative from Mercedes City," he said. "Judge Howard Ale."

"Howard Ale?" The name hit *Don* Federico like a lightning bolt. Emma's husband! It was all coming together as the completion of a great puzzle.

"Shark game?" replied Hanson coldly. "You're not suggesting the game was rigged?" The Ranger glanced at *Don* Federico with a suspicious look, feeling that he might be catching onto their con games.

Astounded over the discovery of Howard Ale's involvement, *Don* Federico ignored the question. He began pacing the floor. "I would like to get this settled before taking my family to Monterrey in January. I'd like to sell my part—you buy me out— or vise versa," he replied, eyeing Hanson with suspicion.

"Going to Monterrey, eh?" commented Hanson, leaning forward. He began pulling the cigar out of his mouth and looked interested. Like a shark exposing his true nature, he was no longer hiding his cunning and deviousness. He was an opportunist, taking the side that benefited him the most.

"Yes! My daughter Victoria is going to school south of Monterrey. Francisca will be visiting her family, while I go and see about the gold mine. We plan to spend Christmas and the New Year in Mexico with my wife's parents. While I'm there, I'll inspect the mine, during the first week of the New Year. I would like to establish a commitment between us and square things up before then."

"What the hell is your big rush?" growled Hanson, putting his cigar back into his mouth and holding it between his stained teeth. "There's money to be made in the gold mine! January!" said the Ranger, getting up from his desk. He slammed his boots down on the wooden floor and, in deep thought, he brushed his dark beard with his right hand and walked toward the front of the office to the window facing the busy street.

Don Federico sat down again on the edge of the chair and studied Hanson as he stood facing the window. He was waiting to see if the man was going to take any responsibility in the partnership of the mine. A missing ornament on one of Hanson's boots caught his eye. They were custom-made boots, but one of the gold metal stars was missing from his right boot. He found it odd and distracting.

Hanson finally spoke. "Normally, it's been pretty peaceful around here during the winter months. But, hell! In the last couple of weeks, there have been several skirmishes from across the river, affecting all of us. I'll have to make some kind of plans and leave one or two of my Ranger's to take care of business."

"Since we are both accountable for the outcome of the gold mine, maybe we can set up an agreement, a contract, as to who is going to do what with it!" remarked *Don* Federico impatiently.

"I may not have the time!" Hanson thundered. "Several days ago, Sheriff Anglin and several of my boys were notified of a disturbance by the border in that shit-hole of a village, Rio Rico, across the river. Found four men and several women with children all slaughtered—everything was destroyed. It was a hellacious mess. Nothing was left standing in the area. All of the crappy huts were burned down and nothing remained except the smell of the dead bodies. With the help of some *Federalist* officials from Matamoros, they ended up putting kerosene on the bodies and setting fire to the whole goddamn mess. An old man, who had been to see some of his relatives on the *Rancho de la Manteca* returned hours later. He was hysterical and had inspected the bodies and mentioned that one of the young girls was missing, possibly had escaped. I would sure like to know what happen to her so we can get some more information as to what took place in that shit-hole."

I bet you would, thought *Don* Federico, recalling the poor girl, Soledad. He remained silent, letting Hanson do all the talking, hoping he might incriminate himself.

Hanson immediately changed the subject, becoming vague, uncomfortable and edgy about the Rio Rico massacre. "I'll let you know what I plan to do." His mouth was tight with rage, either from the border incident or because the *Don* was questioning him, pinning him down, and forcing him to take some responsibility for his newly acquired foreign mine. "Mes'kin bandits!" he ranted. "Yes, that's who they were. Assassins! Greasers! Bastards," he kept repeating. Being an alcoholic, Hanson turned red-faced when angered, highlighting his coarse, pockmarked skin and red-veined nose.

"The Mexican *Federalists* will bring justice to whoever did this, having jurisdiction in Mexico, not in the United States." *Don* Federico replied, livid over Hanson's persistent dirty digs.

"Justice, you said justice? Hell! I'm the justice here! If I had gotten my hands on the sonsabitches I would have blown their heads completely off." Hanson boasted, swinging his hands and repeating over and over all the terrible things he was going to do to get even, as if he had to account for that incident.

Don Federico got the impression that Hanson was feeling remorse. There was more to his story that wasn't being told. The *Don* kept silent and narrowed his eyes. He was known to be a tough negotiator. His facial features became expressionless, displaying a cool head. Still sitting next to Hanson's desk, he kept his distance, and yet his eyes never left the brute's sight. He had gotten the information he wanted, especially the disappearance of the young girl Soledad. Apparently the Rangers suspected there was an escaped witness, who, unbeknownst to Hanson, was staying at his place. *What about the other woman involved, the gringa! Had anybody reported her missing?* He wondered.

"You still haven't said what you're going to do about our gold mine. That's the main reason I'm here. There's going to be problems here on the border and in Mexico."

"Here you go again!" roared Hanson, like a demon. "Is that all you have on your mind?"

"There's talk going on all along the border of a Mexican Revolution. This means trouble for any investors in that country, especially Americans. If we want to settle the gold mine between us, we need to do it as soon as possible," said *Don* Federico becoming frustrated and getting nowhere with a solution. He was talking to an idiot who had gotten lucky by using his father's friendship and did not understand the seriousness of the coming problem.

"Revolution, hell! There's always something going on across the river. That doesn't scare me. I can handle any situation or, for that matter, any goddamn Mes'kins that come along, here or across the border. You pick the place! I don't need any help with the gold mine, and I haven't seen the day that I couldn't take care of myself. There's an awful lot of money at stake in that mine." His conversation skipped back and forth between the two different subjects at hand.

"Hanson!" yelled *Don* Federico, interrupting his blathering. "Regarding my father's partnership, I'm willing to sell out. Or else I'll buy you out." He could sense the Ranger going into one of his hellacious rages.

"You must be out of your shittin', cotton-pickin' mind," shouted Hanson, raising his arms dramatically, and moving his cigar to another position in his mouth. "Me, sell out? I haven't received all of the money your father owed me. This damn job doesn't pay worth a shit. So having the gold mine has made it very beneficial for me." He walked back to his desk, leaned forward, and looked straight into *Don* Federico's face. "What you need to do, Juelson, is surrender the gold mine and put it in my name. Or I'll tell you something even better. You might wanna give me some of your land in return for the difference. I'll make it real easy for you. As a matter-of-fact, the land over by the *resaca*, where the crazy old woman and her lunatic son live—I sure would like to have that piece of ground."

I'll bet your ass you would! *Don* Federico remained silent, glaring at the man he felt was responsible for his father's death. There, of course, had been no evidence and no one to pin anything on. No one would talk, and there was no way to prove anything. Hanson had been the last person seen with his father, and the Ranger claimed his father had a massive heart attack in an angry card game. But how could he explain the thin cut on the back of his father's neck, similar to that of a Mexican stiletto? The rumor had been that his heart gave out because the stakes of the game had gotten too high. But his father did not have a heart problem. That was the mystery.

"I'll need to check into what you've been talking about," answered the *Don*. "I'll need to get some of the facts straight. I'm going to Mercedes City in a couple of days to get supplies, and it will give me a chance to talk to Howard Ale. He had information on Father's doings, since he kept him up on legal things. This will give me time to think about what you said regarding the gold mine." *Don* Federico spoke evenly, but felt his temperature rising. "This will give me some time to put things together, do some investigating. And as for me to give you part of my land that my dad worked so hard for, Hanson—this is out of the question. It'll be a cold day in Hell! That land by the *resaca* doesn't belong to me. My father gave *Doña* Adela and her son that land, and she is to stay there until she dies. Then the section will come back to me, and when I die—well, the rest is none of your business."

"Right!" yelled Hanson. "You got a lottta balls coming in here, telling me what I have to do." His voice got progressively louder. "What you need to do is kill that old bitch and get rid of that crazy boy she has and give me the goddamn place. That should solve some of the problem with us." Hanson continued spewing his venomous words, as cigar smoke and spit spurted out of his filthy mouth.

"It's real white of you to think that killing innocent people could solve our problem," answered *Don* Federico, glaring at the brute. "You know and heard my intentions, and I'm making a gentleman's request. It's up to you now. What are *your* intentions in this partnership, and what's *your* responsibility in running the gold mine? If we are partners, I need to know what your plans are. There's a lot of work in running a gold mine, especially without any experience and in a foreign country."

"At this time, I don't plan to do a goddamn thing about anything," roared Hanson.

"Well, that's fine with me. And as far as I'm concerned, we may never talk again, and never would be too soon for me. I'll let my attorney from Brownsville do the talking for the both of us and settle my father's business. This conversation has gotten nowhere, and we are wasting time." The *Don* felt like he was holding a bad poker hand with unpredictable cards and it was time to fold and walk away. He began walking toward the door.

Hanson's face was a portrait of anger; his eyes stared transfixed, glaring with a cunning hatred as he watched *Don* Federico depart.

Bastard! The *Don* thought. *This is not the end of this story. If he thinks he's going to swindle me out of the gold mine, he's got something else coming.* It irked him that this illiterate bastard had been befriended by his father. However, he could see why they had become friends—they were very much alike: his father with his ambitious, ever-expanding enterprises; and Hanson, a gambler with a powerful desire for manipulation and control. But they were opposites in that his father was a man well respected and loved by all who knew him. *How dare Hanson? Who the hell does he think he is?*

The missing gold metal star on Hanson's boot was starting to disturb him. Deep in his subconscious mind, he visualized some poor Mexican man trying to save his land, being kicked in the ribs by Hanson's boot, and the star dropping on his property. A knot of anger twisted and formed in his stomach. The great *Don's* mind raced, stunned by what he had heard about his father's adventures. He would get to the bottom of the story. Being an honorable man of justice with an innate sense of fairness, he would get things straight.

As *Don* Federico stepped out the door, he came face to face with a drunkard coming to visit Hanson. Thomas White was a small man, middle-aged, white-haired, and wearing faded overalls. He had drifted into town over a year ago and had been hanging around the local saloons.

"Wouldn't happen to have a quarter for a drink?" asked the drunk.

Don Federico reached into his pocket and pulled out a silver dollar. "Have four good whiskey shots on me!" he replied loudly, looking the man square in the eyes. Then, in a soft whisper, he addressed the man. "Have you found out anything?"

"Got the information you need. I'll get in touch with you later," the drunk whispered hoarsely.

Tom White saluted him by taking his hat off and nodding. Talking loudly, he glanced beyond *Don* Federico to see if anyone was watching them from inside the Ranger office. "Thank you so much, sir! Top o' the mornin' to you, mister," he said, as if they were complete strangers, then winked at *Don* Federico.

Hours passed as Roy and Fred had amused themselves by looking in the shop windows and discovering such things as mannequins wearing nothing but colorful, striped underwear. They were like two innocent children being led into the maddening world. This was the new style coming into a world of outlaws, cowboys, and *vaqueros*, amidst the mixed cultures and new modern ideas introduced by the Europeans.

"I wunder if by displayin' dos' damn get-ups dat they inten's for us to become re-la-tives to the rat'lers," snickered Roy.

"We'd become cousins to the snakes," agreed Fred, laughing.

"I wouldn't git caught dead in dat…dat…git-up!" Roy chuckled. "Sum' good-lookin' ol' gal might see me in dat and call me a sissie!" They both laughed.

Fred had immensely enjoyed the day. He had bought Victoria a beautiful silver music box, which would go well on her elaborate dressing table. He couldn't wait to see her look of joy and surprise when she opened her present. Most of all, he couldn't wait until the whole blessed ceremonial event would take place for her birthday. All kinds of people would be coming to her fiesta: people from all the *ranchitos* in the Valley; his grandparents from Monterrey; relatives from Brownsville from his Grandmother Juelson's side, which he had not seen in over a year. Other relatives he couldn't wait to see were John and Jaime from Mercedes City. Families from across the river would also join them in Victoria's birthday celebration.

Over a year ago, everything had been postponed by the death of his grandfather, George. How he missed him. The entire immediate family went into mourning for a long time, wearing only black clothing. Mirrors were draped in black cloth for over three months. The wakes! Those long agonizing prayers that followed one rosary after another, saying the same thing over and over again on bent knees after the funeral, for days that followed. *This year, it's gonna be different!* Fred decided. He told Roy, "Victoria is going to be sixteen, and everything is going to be so much fun. I can hardly wait."

Crossing the main dirt road, *Don* Federico met them halfway on Jackson Street. "Men!" he ordered. "Let's get the team and wagon and let's get goin'. The clouds to the Southeast look very unfriendly," he said, pointing to the dark, cloudy sky. "Manuel was right. He is always right. There's a hurricane on its way, and we had better hurry home. The wind is picking up and getting worse."

"Reckon we need to git. It's a gittin' to weathered-up."

Roy tried to strike up a conversation with *Don* Federico, but saw the sullen and bitter expression on his face. His instincts told him that something had gone wrong, and there were things bothering the great cattle baron. He looked like he had been pistol-whipped.

"How da thing' go for ya'?" The amiable foreman asked the question in passing conversation. *Don* Federico did not answer right away. He was already chewing the inside of his jaw. It was a sign of deep thought and problems.

"We'll talk about it when we get home," replied *Don* Federico, somberly drained. "We must hurry home and get the supplies inside. Looks like the weather's changing and a hard storm is heading our way." Then he went silent.

Moving quickly with their heavy load, they took the shortest possible route straight north of Harlingen and then turned west. Eventually they would arrive at the entrance to Spanish Acres by way of an uneven, dirt pathway that had not been traveled for many days. Old tracks from past wagon wheels were engraved in the hard dirt road; the land around it was covered in dry grass, and rough mesquite and untamed brush spread their heavy branches, shadowing both sides of the road. Very little was said, for their main goal was to get home before dusk. The wind was rising fast and talk had now become virtually impossible.

Roy began trail-blazing in front of *Don* Federico's wagon. He was familiar with the wild, harsh terrain and the shortest route, and he kept pace far ahead of the wagon. The mules snorted and wheezed when the wagon's wheels sank and hit the rough potholes. *Don* Federico and Fred held onto their hats and bounced in uncompromising positions on the hard wooden wagon seat, struggling to stay in the wagon. Tumbleweeds skittered and dry native Johnson grass rattled. The dust devils whirled, coming toward them from all directions.

Occasionally a jackrabbit jumped from the bushes out into the dirt trail, staring for a moment, and then hopped on, hiding in the thick bramble. Small, white-tailed deer always alert to movement, darted about in front of them, taking refuge in the impassable underbrush.

Hours passed. They came upon the *resaca* and hurried on. Soon, out in the far distance, they could see the familiar metal windmills of the hacienda, standing tall in the dust-laden air. The cacti, scrubs, and undergrowth had come alive in the late afternoon with creatures sensing the tension in the foreboding and volatile weather bearing down upon them. Hundreds of black tarantulas, out of their burrows, were crossing the dirt road, knowing instinctively that a storm was coming and that they needed to run for cover.

CHAPTER 5

Meanwhile, *Doña* Francisca had left the hacienda at the break of dawn and strolled to visit the hired hands' families, as she did daily. With her great devotion, acting from strong commitment, the lady of the hacienda would bring them medicine, mostly herbs and commodities from the hacienda's storehouse. With her deep religious convictions, she would start her day in prayer, attending the small chapel of *La Virgen de Guadalupe.* It was a small shrine, next to the water fountain in the main courtyard, built for her in the early days of marriage to *Don* Federico. Saying her morning invocations had always consoled *Doña* Francisca, giving her strength and courage for the coming day. There was always something going on in the hacienda, and each day had become a trying one. She would then attend to her household duties full of zest, giving Mamá Maria orders for what she expected for the noon and evening meals.

Mamá Maria in turn would delegate to each of the servants or women's helpers what needed to be done in the household. There was so much to do, and each day seemed to bring in more work. Food preparation took much effort and a great deal of time. The basic household duties ranged from rendering fat, called tallow, from the cattle, to the making of candles and soaps from it. They spun yarn for their own clothes, did hand washing and machine sewing, chopped wood for the stoves, and cleaned the house and grounds continually.

Doña Francisca had brought to the region pride, and most of all, a gracious, inbred culture and humility. All were symbols that characterized her austere, aristocratic customs. Early this morning she had said her farewells to *Doña* Adela, who had stayed for two nights, but had left at the break of day with more pressing emergencies at her *jacale*, taking with her slabs of dry pork and beef that were common bartering payment for her loyal service.

The dusty dirt path to the neighborhood workers' living section ran a quarter of a mile north of the big house and then angled into a big bend called Spanish Quarters. *Doña* Francisca passed the high arches next to the open-kitchen's water pump with large washtubs used for pulling water in buckets to the kitchen and for doing the regular washing. Fresh eggs, cold milk, cheese, slabs of bacon, and leftover unprepared foods were kept underneath, below the kitchen in a large, cement room built for storage next to the cool water pump, where they would remain cold and fresh.

She continued on, bypassing the stables where the well-bred horses were kept. Two large barns, several corrals, and high silos of grain stood next to the smokehouse filled with half slabs of pork and beef. Next to the barns was another large shed where the three different carriages were kept. There were two open-post canopy blacksmith shops with straw roofs to keep out the rain and the sun, where always the hot embers were kept burning for use in any emergency. The side walls were full of harnesses, bridles, yokes, and branding irons, with water gourds hanging on all four corners.

Most of the land had been cleared around the hacienda, except for a few cacti and chaparrals that persisted under hard, unyielding conditions. There were several big, tall cottonwoods next to the corrals, as well as ebonies, and many lilac hedges along the pathway that had been planted during the early development of the hacienda. To her right was a large natural pond, bringing water into the household, and also attracting many small animals to drink and quench their thirst. Around the ponds were many sabino trees, a swamp cypress. There was also a large, bald Montezuma cypress brought back from Mexico City when *Don* Federico was born. It was an old Mexican tradition when a son was born to plant a tree. These were grown close to the pond, as they required a lot of water. Miles beyond the pond were tall wire fences that separated Spanish Acres from *Señor* Esquibel's property to the east.

In turn, *Doña* Francisca, in her early years of marriage and with so much enthusiasm, had helped brighten the dreary scenery by transporting from Monterrey several kinds of citrus, avocado, papaya, and mango trees that were planted throughout the immediate area of the hacienda.

Doña Francisca had decided to walk this morning, instead of bothering poor ol' Manuel as she usually did to travel by carriage. *The weather is changing*, she thought. *Perhaps it might rain.* Rumors were that a *chubasco* was coming this way. She would welcome the cool fall days, as the hot summer, *la canícula*, had stayed so long. The sky looked like a gray blanket covering the heavens. It was a land of hard secrets— the difficulty in finding the location of precious water. In every direction were big metal windmills pumping water into large aluminum tanks that brought the cattle in to quench their huge thirst. Far beyond, the land swelled toward the quiet morning and shimmered in the undergrowth blending with the ashen color of the earth. Sounds of the bawling cattle continually echoed.

Doña Francisca had not slept well for several days. Besides her annoying cough, millions of thoughts were going through her mind. Could it be possible that Mexico was spiraling into war? The thought of her parents living in Monterrey worried her. Her father, a retired diplomat for President Díaz, was still doing cabinet counseling in the government and could easily be at risk. There were other worries, too. One concerning her was her husband's gold mine in Monterrey and the land he had inherited from his father, and its buying power in Mexico. There were problems with the mine and *Don* Federico needed go see about the situation. Another worry was Victoria's schooling—was it a good decision at this moment in time to be studying in Mexico? The coming of the injured Soledad into their household had bothered *La Señora* as well. What would happen to the young girl? She felt a deep compassion for Soledad and her unfortunate situation. *Doña* Francisca worried about the dead *gringa*, too.

ROOTS OF INDIFFERENCE

Why wasn't the body found? Whatever happened to her? And why was the body left so close to their land in the first place? Was it some kind of a warning sign?

A quarter of a mile farther on, *La Señora* passed the little, unpainted, wooden school building, in which she taught the children of the hired hands three times a week, with the help of Victoria. Around the bend, and snuggled in between a jungle of undergrowth, cacti, and shrubs, were the rough-hewn, unpainted quarters where most of the *vaqueros* and hired hands lived. While a few were single, the majority had families with several children, but all shared the tribulations of everyday life. Between the quarters were gardens: large stalks of corn; large, colorful squash, called *calabazas*; tomatoes; several varieties of chilies; big striped watermelons; and cantaloupes. The land with water could grow anything. It made for an inviting environment rich in abundance.

Elena Garcia greeted *Doña* Francisca in the middle of the dirt path with a big "*Hola*" and a smile, while carrying her youngest child on her left hip and a load of dry mesquite wood for her stove on her right. Elena and her husband Miguel were the second oldest residents in the working quarters. Miguel was the main *vaquero* on the ranch and had been with the Juelson family since he was a young man, always in charge of taking the cattle every year to San Antonio. The couple had a large family, including Yolanda, their oldest daughter, who worked and helped with chores in the main house.

Elena was perhaps in her late thirties, but looked fifty, as her hair was turning salt and pepper gray; she was short and heavy, with sagging breasts and large hips. Her face was brown and coarse from the tormenting rays of the sun, and she looked more Indian than Mexican. Her pleasant attitude and her robust vitality made everyone love and respect her, overlooking her rough appearance.

"How's the young girl doing this morning?" questioned Elena, concerned. "Nobody in the quarters slept last night. The men stayed up all night around the campfire outside talking into the wee hours. Most of the talk was about the body of the *gringa* and what happened to her. The women are worried sick and concerned about a revolution in Mexico. We are in a state of panic, since we live so close and have relatives across the border."

Doña Francisca, who was very private in her personal life, searched for words. "Soledad is going to be fine. *Señora* Adela said it will be at least a couple of weeks before we know the results of her injuries. She still has several bruises on her body, but it's her face, and especially her eyes, that are the worst. That's what bothers me! The scar will remain, not only in her body, but in her soul. And as for the revolution, only God knows!"

"Ay! *Dios mío!*" moaned Elena, walking back toward her house. "Those *malditos gringos* are going to blame the Mexican *vaqueros* for the death of the *gringa*. By the way, have they found her body yet?"

Concentrating on her own personal matters and with a troubled, anguished look on her face, *Doña* Francisca only answered, "No!" She began to cough, covering her mouth with her handkerchief.

"Say! I made fresh tortillas, and they are still warm," Elena said, walking up to the steps of her humble abode. "Let's have some hot coffee and *agarita* jam with them!"

It wasn't long before the rest of the women in the quarters had joined them in discussing the present circumstances of the *gringa* and the young girl called Soledad. It became a social henhouse of chatter concerning the present weather, the revolution across the river, *Señora* Adela's predictions, and the sharing of medicines and herbs. It was as if the woman could control and cure with a flick, all diseases and world situations. The women from the quarters had a cutting wit and made fun and laughed at themselves and their daily routine of life.

Children outside in the dusty dirt yard were playing catch with a ball and could be heard yelling and shouting with glee. Suddenly, there was a hushed wind that stirred, and the commotion from the little ones went silent. A sharp, loud, penetrating screech from one of the children came from outside the quarters. The women ran to the screen door and tried to see what was causing the disturbance.

"What is it?" questioned Elena, standing at the screen door and trying to count her children. The rest of the women stood behind her, with their necks stretched out, trying to figure out what it was all about.

"The dog!" yelled one of the children, pointing to the animal.

"What dog?" Yelled Elena. She flew out the door and toward the petrified child. It was not hard to see that one of the neighborhood's mangy dogs had gone mad. It was the same animal that had disappeared weeks ago.

The other mothers ran outside and grabbed their little ones and fled with them inside their own homes and watched the scene from inside.

Elena's nerves were like steel. She kept getting closer to her three crying children, trying to reassure them that everything was going to be all right. "Calm down!" she said, waving her hands as she approached the rabid dog. One of the women, from behind her screened porch, threw Elena a straw broom that landed on the ground next to her. Elena, watching her steps, managed to look down and pick up the broom and began using it as a defense, nudging the dog to distract it from the children.

"Don't let the dog bite you!" cried one of the women hysterically, who had come out of her home and was standing a few feet behind Elena.

"Don't get too close to the dog! The dog is sick! If he bites you, you will die!" yelled another from inside her screen door.

The comments and suggestions had not helped the panic-stricken, frightened children, but had only confused them into a state of chaos. Even in their innocence, they knew that something was wrong with the dog. He was not friendly as other animals were and was not acting normally, as he kept growling, showing his teeth and snapping at anything that moved. The three startled children were bunched together and kept moving backwards. The children were trapped; behind them and on both sides were walls of prickly-pear cacti preventing them from any way out, as they stood cornered, frantically yelling and crying.

Doña Francisca had walked outside the screen porch and stood bewildered. She felt helpless. Trembling, she put one hand up to her mouth, not able to speak, in fear and concern for the children.

ROOTS OF INDIFFERENCE

The dog swayed erratically, advancing toward the children. Apparently the loud noises upset him, and he was attracted to the movements of the frantic children. The beast's mouth was open, and there was a white, frothy mass of saliva flowing from his drooling tongue. He would occasionally rock, moving from side to side, showing his big teeth, and then snapped furiously, growling and staggering toward the children. His eyes rolled back in his head, as if he were going blind. The yelling from the ladies continued, driving everyone into a state of panic.

From out of nowhere came the thunderous crack of a rifle, loud and echoing throughout the *brasada*. There was a long pause—a hushed silence. The mangy dog gave out a loud yelp, twitched a bit, and then lay dead, sprawled in the dirt, as a mass of white foam mixed with splattered blood flowed onto the ground from his mouth.

Elena's first thought was to run and hug her children. The other mothers rushed to their children, their eyes searching the surroundings for the hero who had saved the day.

It was Victoria!

She sat on her palomino, rifle in hand, a stunning vision for all to behold. She was radiant and beautiful, with a bandana tied across her forehead, holding her long hair away from her face. The way she carried her rifle seemed to symbolize the heroic pioneer women of the frontier. Victoria had been well taught, just like her father, who could shoot the eye of a rabbit a hundred yards away. An attitude of pride slowly erased her smile, then a determined look hardened her features, suggesting that she realized she could do anything a man could do—ride, shoot, kill. Her expression reflected the hatred that *Doña* Francisca had seen so many times in the faces of the Mexican people whenever they were being unjustly treated.

Giving out a sigh of relief, *Doña* Francisca rushed toward her daughter. *La Señora* felt as if every drop of blood had been drained from her body. Her knees quivered as she took one step in front of the other, not knowing whether to laugh or cry, or do both at the same time. How immensely proud she was of her daughter.

"Is the dog dead?" Victoria questioned the excited gathering of woman and children. Her expert hands skillfully held the reins, controlling her horse, which was still skittish after the loud report of the rifle.

"*Sí, sí*" were the cries of the people.

"*Sí, Hija!*" replied *Doña* Francisca, stunned and beside herself with excitement.

"Victoria! Victoria!" shouted the older children in admiration. Their screams and tears had turned into smiles and laugher. The smaller children clung to their mothers, looking relieved.

"I was on my way to exercise my horse, when Mamá Maria and the other servants in the household heard the screams. Mamá Maria thought it would be a good idea to get my rifle and check to see what all of the commotion was about, or if anybody needed any help. She thought it could have been a rattlesnake under the cactus."

"It was a good thing! The saints are with us!" commented a shaken Elena, whose face was as white as the ashen ground. With a sigh of relief, she hugged her children close to her.

Hearing the crack of a rifle, the *vaqueros* from the nearby pasture rushed over, looking frightened and worried about their families. "It's a good thing you carried the rifle," said one. "I only carry a small pistol, and it wouldn't have reached that far."

Another *vaquero* showed up and spoke. "We better bury the dog away from this place. It's safer. It must have been bitten by a rabid animal. We don't want such a contagious disease to spread to the other dogs in the quarters."

Doña Francisca, in between her coughing fits, gazed up at Victoria with poignant concern. "If you must ride out, stay on the main *La Sal* road up to *Doña* Adela's place and ride back. Make sure you have enough bullets for your rifle," she suggested. "With all of the killing and commotion going beyond the hacienda, you never know when you're going to need it. There are so many wild boars, wild cats, and especially, the rattlers. All those evils! *Dios!* Better stop by the kitchen and have Yolanda ride with you. At least then I won't worry so much."

Yolanda! Victoria thought. "Mamá, Yolanda is busy in the kitchen helping Mamá Maria," she snapped. "I'll be all right, and besides, Yolanda is too slow. By the time she gets a horse saddled, with the slow help of Manuel, I could have ridden there and back. I don't want her with me," she said stubbornly, putting the Winchester in the scabbard on her saddle. "I want to exercise my horse before it starts raining. I should be back in a couple of hours."

With a hard twist of the reins, she kicked her palomino toward the pond and then southeast into the deepest part of the *brasada*, heading toward *Doña* Adela's region. Her horse galloped briskly through the meadows where the expensive thoroughbred horses had been taken to pasture, attended by the working *vaqueros*. As she rode by, she waved. The *vaqueros* commented, "There goes *La Borrada*."

Victoria followed a narrow track, surrounded on both sides by thick mesquite. She entered the impenetrable jungle, swarming with cacti, mesquite, and chaparral. Concentrating on maneuvering her horse, her mind wondered about the poor injured peasant girl. How she had survived running through the wilderness of the *brasada*, and at night, was a complete mystery. Soledad had a strong will and was showing possibilities of a good recovery. She shuddered at the thought of the dead *gringa* out in the *resaca*.

There was something refined and yet forbidden, almost an unbridled innocence in her surroundings. It was a hard land, a land of imperfections, undomesticated and unknown elsewhere in the world. It was an unmolested land, violated only by the wild animals and insects that lived and roamed within its environment.

Victoria nudged her palomino into a jogging gait and followed a thin path so often taken by many who lived at the hacienda. It was a shorter route to the *resaca*. She rode with sureness and with a certain refinement that radiated her mood, contrary to the gloomy, dreary day. Dark clouds were rolling in from the Gulf and a strong, humid breeze had begun to stir, bringing in a sense of premature excitement. It was a day that one would only find in South Texas. The wind blew steadily, tossing her long hair flowing out behind her, and the world belonged only to her. This was the land that her grandpa George Juelson had conquered, and like Texas, she and the land were wild, untamed, and beautiful.

ROOTS OF INDIFFERENCE

The palomino would occasionally snort and whinny, taking her deeper into the rough, tangled undergrowth, the potholes of the jungle *brasada*. The cadence of her horse's hoofbeats blended with the dry leaves, tangled twigs, and cracked ground on which he trod. Victoria cautiously checked side to side for signs of rattlers lying close to the fallen trees, for it was during the fall season that the serpents were beginning to shed their skins and become blind, striking at anything that moved. Throughout the mesquite trees, the mockingbirds chirped among themselves.

Coming into a clearing, the horse crossed a dry *arroyo*, then continued trotting in a straight path. The gait became hypnotic, a pleasant harmony of music to her ears, which gave Victoria an urge to elevate her head toward the heavens. It gave her a sense of connection between the immediate and the remote. She began playing a spiritual game, with the first drops of rain falling softly against her forehead. She could already smell the wet, clayish earth.

Life was comfortable; life was good. She had the reassurance of her mount, which kept going straight without her guidance. She spread her hands towards the sky, and felt the light drizzle of raindrops coming toward her. *What a blessing*, she thought. *The rain feels cool and comfortable since the weather has been so hot and sticky.* High above her and out on the horizon, she noticed a flock of geese, flying west in their familiar V shape. She closed her eyes. She felt hypnotized by the land, and her mind began to drift—drifting into the unknown abyss. She resembled a Comanche queen with her headband, her face turned skyward, and her arms stretched out toward the firmament, performing some kind of personal spiritual ritual. *This is my land, and one day I will own all of this. All of this will be mine!*

Victoria lost track of time, but she knew she was getting closer to the marshy area of the *resaca*. Her nostrils began picking up the peculiar smell with which everyone who lived in Spanish Acres was familiar—the black, greasy, disgusting odor that bubbled and reeked on the other end of the water's edge. But it was at the *resaca* where large bullfrogs, possums, raccoons, and other animals lived. Snakes in particular were known to hibernate and crawl underneath the large rocks close to the banks.

The chattering of all living creatures and the chirping of the busy mockingbirds in the mesquite distracted her as she gazed up among the gnarled trees. Along the edge of the *resaca* were low shrubs, a mixture of common trees, with tall cottonwoods, laurels, and some dark ebony that encircled the watery marsh. She approached the *resaca* slowly, while steadying her restless horse, which was getting edgy. Suddenly, without warning, the palomino spooked and snorted, rearing up and bucking Victoria out of the saddle.

Everything happened so fast, Victoria found herself face down on the ground, dazed and confused. Seconds went by before she realized that her legs were lodged on top of the worst kind of cactus in the Southwest, the prickly pear, and she knew instantly that she was in trouble. She tried to twist her body, but felt the agonizing pain of the needles, already tormenting her legs. Her hands were free, so she pushed and pulled her body away from the deadly cactus, as the needles and thorns scraped her legs. She could hear her horse only yards away, breathing hard and standing next to a lonely sabino tree close to the *resaca*. She heard the rustling of the wind as the rain picked up, steadily sprinkling the dampened earth and briers. Lying on the muddy ground, she lifted her head and glanced toward the palomino. "You stupid horse!" she exclaimed in anger. She felt like an imbecile and remembered how many times her parents had told her to watch her riding. Her hands dug into the damp earth as she pushed herself upward, trying to grab a large mesquite branch lying next to her.

As she struggled to get up, two strong arms encircled her bosom, lifting her up, helping her to her feet. Surprised and frightened, Victoria turned around and began pulling down her ruffled riding skirt.

There stood the most devastatingly handsome man she had ever seen. *It must be the devil,* she thought at once. He must have transformed himself into a beautiful man and was waiting for her alone out here in the desert jungle. Traumatized, gasping for words, and out of breath, she said, "Who are you? Where did you come from?" All the while, her eyes were glancing at the rifle on her horse.

He laughed out loud with pleasure, finding her predicament very comical, and answered gallantly, "Why, my horse brought me right to you!" He nodded at his chestnut mare. "I've been traveling all morning and my horse was thirsty. I hope you don't mind if she drinks out of the pond. I hope you weren't hurt by the fall!"

"No, not at all," said Victoria, grimacing, yet her bleeding legs were throbbing in excruciating pain.

"*Mí perdón, Señorita,* I hope you aren't hurt!" he repeated. He grinned, and then began talking nonchalantly. "Apparently this must be the only place that has water. I have been traveling this morning for miles in this region and decided to take a rest." He turned to retrieve his horse.

While the stranger was busy with his horse, Victoria hopped on one foot toward her own horse, trying hard to hold onto her skirt and her composure, even though the pain was becoming agonizing. Within an instant, she managed to reach the scabbard holding her rifle. She pulled it out and twisted around, pointing the rifle at the stranger. Sucking in her breath, she cried out as loud as she could, "If you take one step closer, I'll blow your brains right out of your head!"

"Wait a minute!" he shouted. His hands went immediately up in the air in an attitude of defeat. "I was only trying to help you," he explained. "I'm just a lonely traveler, delivering a message. Are you hurt?" he said politely, coming toward her, grinning. He brought his arms down, unconcerned that she meant business. "Here! Let me help you!" he said.

"Don't come any closer! I mean it!" Victoria yelled at him.

"You need to get those needles out of your legs." He paused and then continued, "If you don't, you'll be coming down with a hellacious fever and infection. And I doubt if any doctor around here can save you." The stranger took several steps forward and faced her at close range, eyeing her up and down, making her flush slightly.

Victoria stood baffled, rain and perspiration running down her face and neck. Her arms trembled from holding the heavy rifle. She stared at the tall, well-built man, not quite knowing if he was for real. His beautiful olive completion glowed. His thick eyebrows and long eyelashes were as black as his wavy hair. His small trimmed mustache was shaped and curved around a delicate, perfect mouth that displayed his seductive grin and his beautiful teeth. His dark, teal-green eyes were overwhelming, almost irresistible, sparkling like two precious emeralds.

"Delivering a message—horse feathers! I'll bet you were!" Victoria replied, confused and indignant. "Where did you come from?"

"I'm your knight in shining armor, and the wind and my horse brought me right to you." He said it in an amusing tone, making a joke. He then pulled off his hat, shook the rain from it, and bowed to her teasingly. He straightened up and continued with his conversation. "I'm looking for an important man, and I'm unsure if this is the right direction. I have confidential papers to deliver on a very important mission. It's a matter of life or death! I stopped at a crossroads," he said, pointing to the south. "There was a small gathering of little huts, then a *ranchito*. An old man and his wife told me to come straight north and that I shouldn't have any trouble finding him."

The stranger proceeded to put on his hat, becoming more at ease, even though the rifle was still a threat. He eyed it apprehensively and then returned his gaze to Victoria and continued to speak. "The old *viejo* told me that the man I'm looking for owns all of the land north of here and that all I had to do was to ask anybody in this part of the country. But, I see that people in this region are unfriendly." His eyes wandered over Victoria's body, studying her, undressing her, as if taking each piece of clothing off her, one at a time.

"We don't take much liking to strangers in this part of the country. Too many unanswered killings! Who's the man you're looking for? She demanded. What's his name? The man who owns all of this land is my father."

"Well! Let me guess! And you're his daughter!" he replied in a sardonic manner, widening his eyes, and displaying his charming smile once again.

"*Don* Federico Juelson! That's his name!" she blurted.

"That's the man, the one I'm supposed to talk to." The emerald eyes shone with delight. "He's the man I need to get in touch with and give this information to as soon as possible."

"Horsepuckie!" she exclaimed. "A likely story! You wouldn't have known if I hadn't told you. My name is Victoria Juelson, and my father's family has owned all of this land since before the turn of the century." Her tone of voice cooled down a little, and she found herself becoming a little more trusting. Her legs were now beginning to throb painfully, and she grimaced with pain once again.

The stranger understood. "You better see about your legs, *Señorita!*" he said with concern. "You need to have someone take those embedded spines out of your skin, for in a couple of hours you'll be running a high fever. Trust me! I know what I'm taking about!" His eyes traveled with delight very slowly over her body, enticing, luring, penetrating deep into her soul.

"It's very kind of you, Sir! But I think I can manage by myself! I must go! My parents will be waiting for me. It's late. I've been gone too long. They'll be worried. The rain's coming down faster. I've got to get home as soon as possible."

The stranger came closer and reached out for her as she struggled to get on her horse. "Here! Let me help you," he said, trying to convince a stubborn young girl of his honesty and good intentions.

"Don't come any closer!" ordered Victoria. "Just because I'm hurt doesn't mean I can't shoot to kill. I can still pull the trigger with one hand. Now stand where you are!" she stammered awkwardly. Turning her back to the stranger, she began mounting her horse with one hand, while holding onto the rifle. But the rain had made the saddle leather slick, and she slipped, falling to the wet ground and crying out in pain.

"This is totally ridiculous!" the stranger said. "Here, I'll help you!" he insisted. "I'll ride in with you to the hacienda." He reached down to grab her, but hesitated for an instant, becoming aroused by sudden and uncalled for fantasies.

Victoria's hair and clothes were dripping wet. She had just realized that her blouse and long skirt were clinging to her body, exposing every curve of her petite, hourglass figure. Her hands and arms were covered in mud. The pain in her legs was getting worse, and she could feel the pressure already from the spines doing their evil deed.

"Dispénseme," he said coming toward her, ignoring the rifle. "Please, Señorita. Let me help you on your horse. That's the least I can do. I'm not afraid of your rifle. I'm not here to hurt you or anyone. I have traveled a long way, all the way from the state of Chihuahua, and I'm tried and hungry. My horse and I need some rest, and I need to talk with your father. If he is your father as you say he is, I need to get this message to him as soon as possible. It's from the future president of Mexico. So please allow me!" He had become more serious and his talk was becoming more convincing.

Victoria did not answer. She stared up at him from the wet ground, feeling a surge of surprise, excitement, and a strange sensation she could not explain. She felt his strong arms around her as he picked her up. She was in a total state of trance and did not speak, still clenching the rifle, hypnotized by his awesome power and the suspense, forgetting who she was. In one quick motion, the stranger grabbed the rifle out of her hand and threw it to the ground, then pinned her against her horse.

He pressed his body against her and grabbed her wet hair at the back of her head, making her look straight into his emerald eyes. He was so close that she could feel his heartbeat and his heavy breathing. His mustache was touching her face and rubbed against her lips.

His eyes were wild as the wind and penetrated deep into her hazel eyes. "Look, Señorita," he demanded in a harsh voice. "I don't know what kind of joke or game you are playing, but in the part of the country where I come from, people who point rifles at other people better use them, or be prepared to get killed. All I'm asking is to get this message to your father, as quickly as possible! You need to get back to your house and take care of your legs, and stop this nonsense. You're behaving like a spoiled girl who gives orders and everyone bows to your command. But you need to listen and understand me."

His green eyes wandered down to her lips, then down to her neck and heaving chest, and up to her lips again. Victoria's white cotton blouse had lost most of its buttons and was clinging to her torso, revealing her tantalizing breasts to the eyes of this stranger. For a split second, the stranger had tempting thoughts. He felt a wild, irresistible desire, seeing such a beautiful girl expose herself through her thin, wet clothes, and for a moment he almost forgot his important mission. For one instant, his manly intent was to ravish her, to throw her on the ground, and with great passion, lustfully kiss her breasts, to show her how a real man makes love. "I could kiss you, and perhaps take you, here and now, since we are out in this wilderness—nobody can see us—but this is not the right moment," he whispered into her ear, rubbing his cheek against her face.

The passion dissipated quickly. He came to his senses and began to regain his composure, knowing that any wrong move would jeopardize his assignment, making a big difference in his undertaking. He ordered her to pull her skirt up and away from the affected area so the material would not touch the spines on her legs.

Victoria mumbled and struggled in defiance, but the stranger still had her muzzled and pinned down. She tried to speak, but then, in an unexpected motion, he gently released his pressure and let go of her hair. His right hand went directly over her mouth. "Don't say anything!" he instructed her. "Don't you scream! I just want to help you! Just do as I say! You devilish hellcat! Now! Spread your legs!" he commanded.

Oh! God! Thought Victoria, *I ignored my mother's orders.* She began to tremble uncontrollably as she squirmed with tension, sensing the stranger was in complete control of her. She felt a haunted, hollow feeling—a feeling of being trapped. *What's going to happen? Oh, Lord! I disobeyed my mother!*

The stranger stood facing her and slowly moved down in a crouched position. He then reached between her legs and grabbed the back of her long skirt, bringing the fabric forward and wrapping it up front and around her legs and knotting it below her knees. The touch, the warm feeling between her legs, had given him a titillating sensation of raw emotion that only a man could understand. *Dios! Beautiful face, gorgeous legs, and full, rounded breasts,* he thought to himself. Gently and with tender, trembling hands, he picked Victoria up, set her in her saddle, and handed her the rifle. He took a deep breath and blew it out. *God, help me! They make tough women in Texas! God help the man who tries to tame this girl!*

"Come!" she ordered, looking down at him. "I'll take you to my house. Just follow me! Try and catch me!" she teased, like the spider enticing her prey. No one at the hacienda rode faster than Victoria. She kicked her palomino into a gallop and took off down the path, feeling a wonderful sense of freedom and relief.

"Wait! Wait for me!" yelled the stranger, but his voice was lost to the wind. Feeling hopeless and drained by his unexpected emotions, he was, at the same time, captivated by the defiant young woman he had found out here in this wilderness. He stood mesmerized and intrigued, realizing that the man he was searching for had such a beautiful creature for a daughter. He took in a deep breath. *What a girl! What an afternoon!*

As she raced away, Victoria turned her head and looked back at the handsome stranger who looked surprised and stood stupefied, like the cat that let the mouse get away. *He must be kidding me,* she thought, halfway smiling, as if she were escaping from an evil encounter and outsmarting the opposition. If her parents found out she had run into a complete stranger out in the cacti jungle, and he had touched her legs and fondled her breasts, her father would surely kill him. *What was he planning to do, anyway?* She wondered. *Taking the spine needles from my legs was out of the question.* That would not be lady-like and was forbidden at Spanish Acres. Men could not be that intimate with ladies out in public. *The nerve of him saying that I was a spoiled girl. Bah! I am not a girl— I am a woman!*

The afternoon was ending and the skies were getting darker. It started to rain harder, with gusts of rain hitting her face. The rain was going to be a blessing. To the west in a lovely sunset haze on the southeast horizon were numbers of heavy, treacherous-looking clouds heading toward Spanish Acres. Lightning flared; the wind and rain were becoming stronger.

Who is that stranger? I never did ask his name, thought Victoria. So handsome, so powerful, and no one had ever talked to her in that way, except her father, when he was angry. She was in awe, enchanted, perhaps, and dazzled. *But, Dios! He is so good looking!* So different, more charismatic than any other men she had known. What was it about him that was so intriguing? What kind of magical voodoo did he possess? His eyes were expressive, beguiling, so beautiful and magnetic. From the moment she had looked into his eyes, she had experienced a carnal flow of emotions so strong and thrilling, so different, that she had almost forgotten the agonizing pain in her legs. She felt embarrassed at how he stared at her body. And yet, looking down at herself, she realized that she had exposed her breasts to a total stranger. *He never intended to hurt me. He was only trying to help,* she repeated, trying to convince herself. *I wonder how long will he be staying at Spanish Acres?*

She would need to tell Mamá Maria and her Mother about the encounter as soon as she got back, but she could not come to the reality of explaining what really happened. On the back of her running horse, she felt as though she were sailing along on a cloud, and with a wonderful secret. *I wonder what he wants with my father. I should have been more polite. But after what happened several days ago, no decent girl is going to take any chances.* Then a horrible thought overcame her. *What if he's somebody really important? And I acted so rudely!* The big windmills of Spanish Acres soon came into view in the distance, and then the hacienda, and the oncoming rain. She must hurry!

CHAPTER 6

Victoria arrived at the hacienda in agonizing pain. Her clothes and hair were soaked, and her bleeding legs and ankles were already red and swollen. Manuel took her horse as she dismounted. He had been pacing the hard, stone courtyard outside the kitchen, waiting for Victoria's return, since he was in charge of the horses, and Victoria's horse had not returned to the stables. Victoria told Manuel to inform her father that a courier was looking for him and was making his way toward the hacienda with important information. Manuel nodded and disappeared with the wet horse into the stalls. She then stormed inside holding her skirt away from her bleeding legs.

She was taken immediately upstairs to her bedroom, where the diligent hands of Mamá Maria and *Doña* Francisca began working on dislodging the imbedded cacti spines. They had been worried out of their minds from her long absence. Not being there for the evening meal, Victoria was brought a plate of food by Yolanda, who then stood by silently watching.

Victoria laid face down crossways on the bed, with only a soft white towel wrapped around her torso. Her bottom remained covered by her silky pantaloons, while her bare legs protruded out from the edge of the bed. Her wet clothes had been stripped and taken to the washroom. She was lucky to have been wearing her high-buttoned kid boots, for they had protected that part of her skin, but the thickness of her ankles showed collateral damage from the horrible painful spines.

"Hold still, *Niña!*" demanded Mamá Maria, as she hovered over Victoria's legs with a magnifying glass and tweezers, as if she were a precious diamond ready to be cut. "And what took you so long in getting back?" she railed. "We were all sick, worried out of our minds, wondering what had happened to you! We were getting ready to send Roy and the other *vaqueros* out to find you!"

"Mamá please don't pull so hard," pleaded Victoria. "It hurts like the devil. Ah! Ah! Ay!"

"Well, *Hija!* That teaches you to pay attention to where you are going, young lady! Riding out and staying so long is almost unforgivable. I wish that you had taken Yolanda with you and listened to my instructions. You mustn't be riding by yourself. How many times have we told you that?"

Yolanda remained silent but chuckled to herself, like the cat that ate the canary, treasuring all of the verbal thrashing, since she had always resented Victoria for being the spoiled rich girl that she was.

Doña Francisca was in an unusually serious mood; the incident with Soledad had triggered a delicate nerve, especially with regards to her only daughter. "Young girls must not be roaming around this untamed region unescorted, and furthermore—" Her words got caught in her throat and she began coughing. When she could speak, she continued, "All it takes is one minute and you could be dead."

"*Por Dios*, Mamá," Victoria snapped. "This is our land! I was just exercising my horse. I haven't taken him out for several days." Her mother's words "young lady" triggered resentment in Victoria's mind. "The stupid horse bucked me off, probably thinking that he was stepping on a rattler. A young man, a messenger wanting to talk to father, he said, who was resting by the *resaca*, rescued me. He helped me up from the cactus patch and put me back on my horse." Victoria was trying to sound diplomatic. "He was very polite and talked about coming from Chihuahua to visit with Father on an important issue."

By the exchanged glances and the expressions on the two women's faces, especially her mother's, which looked like she was going to faint, Victoria knew immediately that a sermon was at hand. Her head was on the block. Now where was the swinging ax?

"Victoria!" exclaimed *Doña* Francisca, in a high-pitched voice. She always called her *Hija* maternally, and was always so sympathetic and always harmonious to all of the household and her needs. But when her mother raised her voice and used her given name, Victoria's instincts immediately told her she was headed for a long lesson on morals and proper conduct. "You know better than to become friendly with strangers! Have you forgotten what happened to Soledad?" *Doña* Francisca scolded her. *La Señora* pivoted her head and caught Mamá Maria's eye, both in a state of astonishment. The two looked at each other and shook their heads. Yolanda stood like a statue, rolling her eyes.

Turning over, Victoria had some quick explaining to do. Using her charm and salesmanship ability, which she had inherited the genes from her grandfather George, she continued. "But, Mamá it wasn't what you think!" Her eyes lit up. "The nice gentleman helped me, and we need to thank him when he shows up. He is headed this way and should be here soon. I left him in a hurry because of the pain in my legs. The gentleman is some kind of an emissary, bringing Father an urgent message from somebody real important in the state of Chihuahua."

Their conversation went on, with the two women asking questions about the stranger. What did he look like? What was his name? As if it had mattered. Questions becoming like the Spanish Inquisition. All that she would say was, "He was so handsome, so strong," and "I don't know!" Victoria straightened herself up. She glanced at Yolanda, who stood bored stiff, unconcerned, but absorbing it all, rolling her eyes and resting on her wide tamale hips first one side and then the other. Victoria wished she had not mentioned the stranger, but she was glad she had not given full details of what had really happened, or she never would have heard the end of her sinful actions. It would be her own private secret, not telling anyone about the exciting, adventurous, scandalous event.

A commotion of barking dogs and people talking and scurrying about suddenly arose from the downstairs entrance of the hacienda. *Doña* Francisca walked to the French doors that led onto the balcony and began closing them, as a streak of lightening flashed across the horizon. She stood for a moment coughing and caught sight of a man on a horse approaching through the front arches. "I see someone coming! Go get Manuel to help him with his horse," she ordered Maria. "We'll need to put him up for the night. Thank God. Looks like we are going to get some rain, so much needed for the cattle and all of the ranchers." She stopped for a moment to cough again, became confused, found her handkerchief, wiped her mouth and then put both hands holding her head, as if losing her bearing on which priority was first. She then said, "Never mind, Maria, just stay with Victoria, while I walk downstairs and see about our guest."

There was a hard knock on the big front doors. *Doña* Francisca had stepped outside the hall as the howling wind was banging the windows and roof, and other noises could be heard coming from the outside due to the wind, which had gained velocity.

"Yolanda!" *Doña* Francisca ordered, stepping back into Victoria's bedroom, "Come downstairs with me and get the west room ready for our company."

Yolanda was stiff, like a wooden puppet, never saying a word as she followed *Doña* Francisca.

"*Bueno,*" Mamá Maria replied as she continued to talk and doctor Victoria's legs. "I'll be finished soon. You'll be good as new again," she said in a loving tone.

"That stuff stinks! I can hardly stand it!" Victoria fired back impatiently, referring to the alcohol Mamá Maria was using. Her excitement had not diminished from her recent experience. She was anxious to get up, get dressed in her newest gown, and join her mother and the visitor downstairs.

"It only stinks for a little while. This liniment is what the *vaqueros* use, given to me by *Doña* Adela, for poisonous snakebites. A potion made from Spanish dagger thorns. It will take the redness and the swelling from your legs. It prevents you from getting a high fever. You'll feel better in the morning. You'll see what Mamá Maria tells you is true, *corazón!*"

Doña Francisca and Yolanda hurried downstairs. Already they could hear *Don* Federico's greeting to a young man, who was trying to shake the rain from his clothes and hat. *Doña* Francisca began coughing and attracted *Don* Federico's attention. "Ah!" He glanced up at the ladies descending the stairs. "Let me introduce you to my wife. *Querida!* This is Juan Alvarez, who comes all the way from Laredo, bringing us word from our dear friend, Madero."

Don Federico apologized, having to excuse himself from the handsome gentleman. It was raining hard now, and there were things he had to take care of in the barn and he needed to give Roy his orders. He promised to return as soon as possible and disappeared into the long halls, talking to Manuel, giving him instructions concerning Juan's horse and what needed to be done for the following day.

"*Cómo está usted, Señora* Juelson? Juan Andreu Alvarez at your service." He bowed formally and graciously extended his hand to *Doña* Francisca, smiling. Then he noticed Yolanda, who was standing behind *Doña* Francisca. "And who is this beautiful young woman, one of your daughters?"

"This is Yolanda Garcia," introduced *Doña* Francisca, "one of our helpers, and yes, she is like a daughter to us—she has lived here all her life. Yolanda is going to get your bedroom ready, your food, and get you comfortable for your stay at our place."

"I was not expecting to stay overnight, but—how marvelous." Juan smiled at *Doña* Francisca, admiring her beauty. He was not expecting such generous hospitality from a family he was not acquainted with and in a strange land, especially Texas. However, Madero had talked very highly of the family, and in his travels he had met many kindly people.

Yolanda stood in awed amazement, as if seeing a pictured prince. She stood frozen in place and could not contain her excitement. She had dreamed about a man like him and had wished for him in so many of her potions that *Doña* Adela had given her. He was the perfect man—the perfect knight, who every young girl dreams about in her everyday thoughts and wishes. In all of her life, she had never seen such a handsome man.

"Word from Madero," replied *Doña* Francisca, composing her thoughts. "The last word we've heard from him was that he was in prison in San Luis Potosi, sometime in the early spring." *La Señora* turned to check on Yolanda, who stood as if she were cemented from her waist down and had not moved. "Yolanda!" she said, pointing to the kitchen and bedroom area. "Go get the food and get the bedroom ready. Thank you."

Juan answered, "*Si, Señora*. Madero has been freed and is on his way to San Antonio. He was released on bond, but had to stay in the city of San Luis Potosi, in danger, while the Federalist Troops in Mexico were watching him all the time. He left word with me to get in contact with your husband, *Don Federico*." Juan was a little nervous, but smiled, displaying his friendly disposition and likeable demeanor. "I was to bring him to San Antonio, where we'll be staying with our friends."

The conversation went on for several minutes, discussing the political situation in Mexico. The artful *Doña* Francisca started with her own small talk, going into a lengthy discourse about the weather they were having. She was a master in obtaining information in her own sweet and unassuming way. As soon as *La Señora* ascertained the visitor's status, she would immediately zero in with common questions, such as: Where is your family from? Where are you going to school? What do you plan to do with your life? Normally these were the three most important questions that would establish frankness in their communications. Knowing the family prominence was important, and after those answers were established, she could proceed with her normal conversation. Rank was important, because it determined on which level of the hacienda he would sleep.

Yolanda glanced sideways and fluttered her eyes at Juan. She slowly disappeared toward the kitchen area, shocked and still dazzled, blinking her eyes, and with a smile on her blushing face. *Qué mango!* She thought.

ROOTS OF INDIFFERENCE

Don Federico returned after seeing to Juan's horse and having the servants take care of his wet jacket. He was apologetic and kindly cut in on the conversation. "Let's go into the library where we'll be freer to talk." He turned to *Doña* Francisca "*Querida!* I don't think that Juan has eaten anything. Please see that the servants prepare him some food. He'll be staying the night, or for that matter, as long as he wants." He then addressed the young Alvarez. "It's too bad that you had to come to our hacienda when the weather is so stormy. We have seen better days. But come! Please make yourself comfortable." *Don* Federico graciously pointed and ushered the young Alvarez down the long corridors to his library.

Doña Francisca politely excused herself and ordered one of the other maids in the kitchen to help Yolanda prepare the guest his bedroom and his dinner. The young women were huddled around the long halls, talking and giggling among themselves, including Yolanda, making remarks about the handsome, young Alvarez. "Now, girls he's only our guest. Remember! Only the best for our guests!" she said. "Get to work!" Between her talk and laughter, she coughed. "Yolanda! Please make sure that he has plenty of fresh water in the porcelain pitcher, and clean towels. Take the basin and clean it, and also check to see if the urinal under the bed is clean." She then headed for the upstairs bedrooms. In her quarters, she grabbed her embroidery basket and walked down the long hall to check on Victoria's welfare and to have a talk with her.

Victoria had already gotten herself washed and dressed in a more elaborate, low cut, blue lace dress and was sitting facing the mirror, while Mamá Maria was gently combing and trying to dry her long hair. Before *Doña* Francisca had a chance to sit down, Victoria's eyes lit up. "What's his name?" she questioned. She became all nervous and excited before her mother had a chance to say a word.

"His name is Juan Alvarez, and he comes from across the border. He mentioned Monterrey. He is very well educated, has excellent manners, and speaks excellent English as well. I do not know how affluent his family is, but if he is studying to be a physician, as he indicated, they must have wealth. Most families in Mexico normally do not have money to send their sons to medical schools in Guadalajara, so I presume they do. He is caught up with the Mexican revolution against Díaz. Such a foolish man! He is so handsome. He has now joined with Madero to lead the war. He wants your father to go with him to San Antonio to visit with Madero, who is there now having a convention. I personally do not like it. I think that with all this talk, there are going to be problems."

"That's him! The same man I saw at the *resaca*," replied Victoria all aroused. Her eyes sparkled like fireworks. Then her expression went from joyous to concern. "War? Did you say war, Mother? What about Madero and Father? Will I still be going to school in Monterrey?"

"I'm afraid so. I think that Madero will eventually become president. Our friend, President Díaz, is getting too old. Your grandfather has retired from the Mexican political government, and I'm glad he is out of office. He is no longer having to deal with so much corruption and is now enjoying ranch life with his prized bulls outside of Monterrey."

There was a long pause in their conversation, like the silence immediately before an explosion.

"Victoria!" said *Doña* Francisca. Her tone of voice rose, becoming more firm and serious. She had gotten herself comfortable on the red velvet French chaise next to the armoire beside Victoria's bed, and began embroidering, looking up over her glasses. She continued, "Have you forgotten our little *consejos*? Have you forgotten that you have been promised to marry Ricardo Del Calderóne, when you turn eighteen? You're betrothed!"

"Yes! Mamá," Victoria answered, with a fleeting look at Mamá Maria, and seriously concerned.

"Your father informed me that you were joking to him about not getting married! It upset your father terribly that he had to talk to me about your conversation with him. Ricardo has been studying in Paris, France, to get the education to better himself and for your welfare. It will benefit you to have a husband like Ricardo, with an education to make a good living. So when you become his wife, you'll become a lady of charm and society living in beautiful Monterrey."

"Mother—," Victoria started to say something.

"Let me finish, young lady. Your father and I are better judges of your future and are sending you to school so that you can achieve, and learn good manners, and be presentable to others in what you do and say. That is very important in our society. You should not get so excited about other young men, because they are handsome. I have noticed your actions, and that bothers me, but that is very common with girls your age who are very impressionable— but that is part of nature—part of growing up. You'll get over that as time goes on. You are making a big to do about our guest and becoming very emotional. It is most embarrassing. He is a man we know little about. That shows improper manners on your part, and is all the more reason to be educated, so that you can get acquainted with socially important people."

Doña Francisca went into long detail about the importance of being a lady and having good proper manners. She talked about the importance of morality and avoiding unacceptable behavior, all reflecting her own tranquil attitude. "Men don't like silly young girls, gossiping and giggling all the time." She started to cough. "They like intelligent adult women." She began coughing again. "Women should stay in their place." She began wheezing, got up, pulled her handkerchief from her blouse and held it against her mouth. She couldn't say another word, and sounded as though she was strangling in her own phlegm. She left the bedroom, went into her chamber, and closed the door.

"Mamá, are you all right?" was all that Victoria could say. Startled, she stood up, briefly studied her reflection in the mirror, and then turned to Mamá Maria. "Mother is seriously sick—more than she is letting on, Mamá Maria!" But Victoria's concern for her mother did not detract totally from her enthusiasm about the stranger. She was inquisitive about downstairs where the excitement was luring her, wanting to see more of the handsome revolutionist. "I'm going downstairs," she said, thankful that her mother's disturbing coughing had stopped her from nagging any further about her actions.

ROOTS OF INDIFFERENCE

"Ay! *Hija!* I would not pester your father at this moment. He is in a serious conference with *Señor* Alvarez. And you know how your father hates the idea of anyone interrupting him when he is busy. I don't think he wants your opinion in any kind of political matters. Better go and play the piano and practice your lessons, or stay in your room. I had better go and check on your Mamá. Her cough is getting worse. I wonder if we could get the young Alvarez doctor to examine your mother later."

As Victoria walked halfway down the curved stairs, with her long, taffeta gown swaying in waves, she could hear voices coming from her father's library. When she reached the marble tiles at the bottom of the stairs, she looked both ways, hoping that nobody was watching. She slowly sashayed closer, trying to get a glimpse of the stranger through the crack in the door, which was not tightly closed. She could see her father standing and pacing, making motions with his hands, like he always did when he got excited, banging on the desk and looking angry. Somehow or other, it looked like the two men had the Mexican revolutionary problems under control. Cautiously, she peeked through the opening between the two French doors.

Little brother Fred, in turn, had gotten word from Yolanda, who had quickly told the other servants, who were described by Mamá Maria as developing into a hornet's nest, gossiping that there was an important guest in the house, and that *Don* Federico and the stranger were discussing revolution and war.

And as for the saying "curiosity killed the cat," inquisitiveness and prying ran extremely strong in the family line; Fred had to see for himself. For war, guns and those destructive things were his main interest. He had played the game so many times with his toy tin soldiers: plan strategy, divide, and conqueror—victory was his motto!

He had ventured from the main living room and was on his way to his bedroom, when he caught a glimpse of Victoria's actions. Silently, he hid behind one of the pillars that held the arches of the antechambers, occasionally spying on Victoria from behind the pillar. He had to put his hands over his mouth to conceal his mischievous laughter. Victoria in turn was fascinated by the activities going on inside the library. She was bent over, getting a better view and swaying her behind, tapping to her own rhythm. Unfortunately, Victoria did not know that Fred was watching her, or that Mamá Maria was standing quietly in the middle of the stairway observing Fred. Fred's naughty thoughts were undeterred. He was full of impulsiveness and seemed to be possessed by a devilish, playful spirit that had invaded his restless mind. Fart for brains. So much for his mother's constant Catholic preaching, there were times he certainly could have grown horns and a tail for being ill-disciplined.

As the saying goes, "boys will be boys." Fred decided to take things into his own hands. *That will teach her,* he thought, *to be listening to other people's conversations.* Without any foresight or consideration as to the disastrous consequences that it would bring, he bowed down, put his hands over his head with his fingers resembling horns like a bull, and ran as fast as his feet would take him, ramming right into Victoria's rear end.

Victoria crashed! There was a loud scream coming from Mamá Maria, who was an eye-witness to the incident. "*Dios mío!*" The cry resounded through the long corridors. "That devil child!" she cried, meaning Fred. Victoria sprawled, face down, looking like a dismembered rag doll on the library floor, broken glass and all.

"What is this?" *Don* Federico yelled, humiliated and in horror, choking and gasping for breath and wanting immediate answers. "What in the world? What's happening? Victoria! What's the meaning of this?" He stood by the door, his mouth open and his hands in the air, appalled. In the background, he caught a glimpse of Mamá Maria grabbing Fred by his right ear and shoulder. Fred was fighting her, trying to escape, but she held onto him to show *Don* Federico who the main culprit was.

"I'll beat your hind-end off royally, young man," roared *Don* Federico in anger, as he struggled to take his belt off. "Go to your bedroom! I'll be right up! You better have a convincing explanation, young man!" Frustrated, with flushed face, he turned his attention to the handsome courier. "Excuse us, Juan. I need to go and take care of the delinquent children—family crisis. Seems that my children need a cultivating lesson in manners," he said, pointing to his belt.

Juan's first instinct was to rush over to Victoria's side and assist her. The whole place was a state of confusion as servants and workers ran to help. Some stood in the foyer, looking into the library with their mouths open, dumbfounded. Their chatter, turning to laugher, became contagious. Fred's screams were heard throughout the house, as *Don* Federico was following him upstairs, talking loudly and disciplining him on his rude behavior, especially when guests came to visit.

"I'm going to die. I'm going to die!" cried Fred.

"Not at this time," replied Mamá Maria, wryly.

Roy appeared, attracted by the commotion, eating corn-on-the cob, barefoot, and looking loutish. "Waal now, doggies!" He grinned. "His gonna git his britches tan. Sounds like a good butt lickin'. Dat shit gonna be all over!"

Juan sauntered toward Victoria and grabbed her by the waist and pulled her up toward him. He whispered in her ear. "Damn! This business of you falling on the ground all the time has got to stop. We have to do something about this! I'm getting tried of picking you up! And what is that horrible smell?" And saying that, he was halfway grinning, and if the truth were known, he would have hysterics, but he was too mannerly and polite and could never be disrespectful.

Victoria felt her face flush as she pushed away from him. She almost slapped him for what he said. She was mad and terribly embarrassed. She wished that the ground would swallow her up, body and soul. Out in the entry, servants stood stunned, watching her. She hurried as fast as her feet could carry her, with tears running down her cheeks, as she tried to straighten her ruffled skirt and ignore the crowd. Mamá Maria followed. Victoria turned to see Yolanda coming from the kitchen. Yolanda had one hand overt her mouth to hide her grin, and the other hand held Juan's plate of food. "Well! What of it?" Victoria hollered at Yolanda. "What are you laughing at?" If looks could kill, Yolanda would have been dead!

ROOTS OF INDIFFERENCE

Don Federico returned shortly, breathing hard and in a sweat. He wiped his forehead, slumped into his leather chair, and apologized to Juan several times. "Please excuse my children," he kept repeating. "Please excuse Fred's thoughtlessness. He is extremely impulsive and needs discipline. He'll be going soon to a military school close to Austin, Texas. Victoria is still very young and needs to learn much in life. We are sending her to *El Colegio De Santa Maria* in Monterrey, in January, where she will start her schooling. My children get very restless, so they play jokes on each other."

"How old is Victoria?" Juan asked, somewhat bemused, while eating his food. "She looks much older than what she probably is!"

"Victoria is going to be sixteen in November. We are planning a big celebration. We missed her fifteenth birthday last year, on account of my father's death." He went into an elaborate discussion about his doubts of how his father had died and how he was not convinced that it was natural causes. He then decided to change the subject. "You are more than welcome to come and join us in the celebration. We hope you will be around so that you can share in our big fiesta."

"I just might do that!" commented Juan, and with these words a radiant joy spread over his face.

"You'll be staying with us until the storm has passed," suggested *Don* Federico. "If we get too much rain, it's almost impossible to leave—mud will be clear up to your knees." He began laughing. "While the storm continues, it will give me enough time to get things organized and give out orders on what needs to be done here on the ranch. I can prepare myself to go and visit with my friend Madero. It will also give me the opportunity to visit with my only sister, Josie, whom I haven't heard from in a long time. Also, while I'm in San Antonio, I'll be able to buy gifts for my family. We need many things for Victoria's celebration!" He paused and studied Juan Alvarez. "Now! We can continue our conversation about Madero."

"Thank you," replied Juan, with great satisfaction. He had finished eating and put his plate away, washed his hands on the damp towel at his place, and continued his talk about Madero and how the man was in great danger. He talked about the old ways and of old man Díaz. "We are on the brink of a great catastrophe if things don't change."

"I just finished reading the book *Barbarous Mexico*. It's quite shocking about the Yacquis Indians' slavery. Imagine! Slavery existing in this free world and in Mexico! Several months ago, one of my *vaqueros* got a Sears and Roebuck catalog, and inside was a hidden piece of paper written by the famous journalist, Ricardo Flores Magón, who told about the injustices people were experiencing in Mexico, and how he had escaped. He is now living in the United States, in fear of being killed. It's very disturbing."

"Everything is true and much worse," answered Juan enthusiastically, trying to convince *Don* Federico to join the group of men to fight for justice and human rights across the border. "Ricardo Magón has been writing the truth about Díaz for quite some time. He took exile in the United States after fleeing Mexico because of the realities he has witnessed and experienced. He continues writing *El Regeneración.* The majority of people here in the United States do not know the real truth. He wants the people to open their eyes and see what's happening in our country. Díaz has had the newspapers suppressed, announcing only what is pleasant and only what the rich investors want to hear. That's another reason on his suppression keeping the news from getting out of the country. The poor people are struggling. There are too many injustices. Madero knows firsthand the conditions and problems of our country. I left medical school to follow him, because I know he wants to do the right thing and unite our country. With Díaz, nothing will ever change. Do you see now why we have to have a revolution? To change our country and give democracy back to the people. It is our only solution for a great change."

There was a long silent pause but the two men agreed that the country of Mexico needed change. *Don* Federico said, "Well! Is Díaz going to win the election this time around? This will be his eighth time, you know. Does Madero think he can get enough people to back him?"

Juan got up and began pacing the floor. *Don* Federico eyed him sharply and listened carefully. "As you know, the running mate of Díaz is the despised Ramon Corral. The people hate him because of the Indian slave trade he has in Veracruz, killing many of them, taking control over their land. Rumors are that Corral has about a year to live, since he is dying from venereal disease. Díaz and Ramon Corral are the hated *Científicos*, who believe only in themselves. To hell with the poor, they say. Now, the *Mestizos*, crossbred like myself, are the true Mexicans. We have a sense of our Mexico. The credit will have to come to us for having created a common people out of the many diverse groups on Mexican soil. Survival has become a matter of luck and miracles. Many say that the *Mestizos* have low traits and no personal ambitions or scruples. Now, you know, *Don* Federico, that is not true! Sure, many say that we are lazy, but what are the Mexican people supposed to do when they are so controlled and exploited?"

Juan spoke with eloquence and tenderness that only a *Mejicano* could speak. He continued, "Madero wants to give unity to his people, who since time immemorial have been divided by language, race, culture, and class. Díaz, in turn, tries to impress the foreigners with his big lavish celebrations. Just last month, all of the foreign guests were invited to visit Mexico, all expenses paid. The party cost twenty million pesos, more than twice what Díaz has spent this year on education." Juan's conversation went on. He talked about the terrible atrocities that were being committed in jails and how the people were treated so brutally. He talked about the poor whose brown bodies sweltered in the hot sun, and worked in the coal mines and silver mines, and others who cried for warmth in the cold, all for lack of knowledge and not being educated. Regardless, they were all slaves, reviled and despised.

Frowning, *Don* Federico was silent for a long time, his two hands clasped on his mahogany desk. "You're correct. The newspapers are not reporting any wrongdoing in Díaz's regime. However, rumors are seeping in from natives across the border, and the book I just mentioned does speak of much cruelty. Ironically, we live this side of the border, and Díaz is doing a good job in keeping it concealed from the masses." *Don* Federico was impressed with the enthusiasm of this young gentleman, whose sparkling eyes were so intriguing, and who seemed to want so much to change Mexico for the betterment of its people.

ROOTS OF INDIFFERENCE

He thought of his own life and of the lives of prominent men and women he had known in Mexico. What would become of Francisca's parents? "Things have to change all right, but it will be a terrible, bloody revolution. Those who are secure and comfortable are going to fight for those privileges they have had for so many years." He sighed. "Yes, I'm afraid there have been signs. Haley's Comet, which scared the people of my ranch and some of my cattle, brought rumors of an unforeseen future, wars, and great famine. What concerns me now, is that I will be contributing to the Mexican Revolution. Many lives will be lost. My wife's parents are getting old and have lived very comfortably on their land and have plenty of money to live the rest of their lives in Mexico. What will happen to them if war is declared?"

Juan stared at *Don* Federico and answered with much uncertainty, "I do not know, but we need a new government and everything needs to change!"

"Any money that I give out after this meeting must be kept confidential." Tapping his finger on his desk, he looked Juan straight in his eyes. "This meeting is not to be disclosed to anyone. Understand? I want you to give me your solemn oath that this conversation never took place—the money or talk of Revolution. If word gets out that I was contributing to the war in Mexico, my name in this part of the country would be dishonored. I will be called a traitor and run out of the area. I would never be able to face my family or friends."

"You have my word, *Don* Federico," replied Juan, leaning forward from his chair and shaking the great *Don's* hand. "I'm also taking a big risk with my family and my life, coming into the state of Texas and demanding money from total strangers for the cause of war in Mexico!"

"You are doing what you think is right and just. I would probably be doing the same thing, if I were in your shoes. I hate aggression, but sometimes a person has to do what is right and take the first step. Just the thought of you leaving the medical profession and risking your life is very noble."

Juan kept talking convincingly, for he was a true Mexican and a true *Mestizo*, like he had said. "On April the fifteenth of this year, Francisco Madero was nominated for president by the Anti-Reelections party. Some of the members should be with us in San Antonio, including Madero's two brothers. Madero has been a regular reader of Ricardo Magón who spoke against the tyranny of the Díaz's administration, and has been an earlier contributor to Magón's liberal party. Madero is our man to bring us out of these conditions. When he becomes president, he will be the answer to all of our prayers and give the Indians back their land."

"I have known the Madero family for a long time. Francisco went to school with me in the Military College at Chapultepec. He was sent later to Paris to learn about bookkeeping and become a banker. His father, *Don* Evaristo Madero, traded in Texas with my father in cattle, bulls, and fine wines. His is considered one of the most important families in Mexico. *Don* Evaristo later went into banking and years later became the governor of the state of Coahulila. Madero's wife, Sara, was a Pérez before she married Madero. They have married recently. My wife Doña Francisca knows her family very well."

"Madero spoke very highly of your family. That's the main reason he wants you to join us in San Antonio. He mentioned that if there was one person he could rely on, it was you." Juan was a classical Mexican—a Mexican actor when playing the game of salesmanship and intrigue, and he reached the height of ideal Latin originality. He spoke very sincerely, with tears in his eyes, of human suffering. Becoming serious, Juan radiated his well-bred, gallant nature and was eager to explain the Revolution to *Don* Federico. "Gustavo and Raoul, Madero's older brothers, are busy trying to collect as much money as possible. They need your support to buy ammunition and rifles. We got word that a shipment of American rifles has already been transported from a village of Rio Rico to Reynosa."

"Rio Rico!" snapped *Don* Federico, his mind triggered by the named village. Angry, he frowned and got up from his desk. "There was a massacre in that town, several days ago. There's a young girl from Rio Rico staying here, who was brought to my hacienda after being savagely raped and beaten." The conversation took a different twist. "Who sold the rifles?"

"To tell the truth, I don't know!" answered Juan, much surprised. "All I know is that some Texans are becoming very rich in selling us the goods from this side of the border. Contraband! We were pleased with the merchandise, but we do not know anything of the incident you mentioned."

"That's a real mystery!" *Don* Federico retorted. "I wonder who would have access to guns and would sell them for a better profit?" He questioned seriously, while rubbing his chin and pacing the floor. He related the incident concerning Soledad and the missing *gringa*, and gave him detailed information on what had happened until now. "With your medical knowledge, I wondered if tomorrow you'd be so kind as to see the young injured girl. I know she needs medical attention. As for the money to give to Madero, I'll have to wait until Manuel returns back from shipping and selling my cattle in San Antonio."

"I'll be more than happy to check on the girl," commented Juan. "I did not bring my medical supplies with me. But I'll see what I can do to help. I find the story very strange. And the body of the *gringa* has never been found? That's very bizarre indeed!" He got up, yawned and stretched. No longer puzzled, he understood Victoria's reluctance about strangers in their land.

"Come!" *Don* Federico said, getting up from his chair and then pointing to the hallway. "We have said enough for one night. I know you must be tired. Let me get one of our girls to show you to your room." Moving out into the corridor, *Don* Federico yelled, "Yolanda! Please, show Juan to his room." He turned and addressed the young Alvarez, who was already showing signs of weariness. "We will talk some more tomorrow. You're tired and need some rest, and with the weather like it is, I don't think we are going to San Antonio for at least a week. The wagon and mules cannot travel in the mud."

Juan kept eyeing Yolanda with delight. She had appeared like a ghost from the long passageway. Yolanda, who normally moved slowly and required a large dose of cayenne pepper to coerce any productivity from her, was standing out in the hall with her hands full of clean towels and a pitcher of water. Her eyes locked on Juan's face, but she quickly shifted them to the floor when she noticed the *Don* watching her. She had never persuaded herself to shuffle her feet so quickly and with so much delight. She turned around with a smile, mocking the other captivated girls who were glued in place, watching her disappear upstairs with the handsome Juan Alvarez.

As slow as she was, she was known for her unvirtuous actions. At eighteen, Yolanda had already conquered many of the workers' hearts on several ranches on different joyous feast occasions, gratifying each and every one of the cowhands in pleasurable measures. She was also known for her steady patience. She spoke very little, only listened and kept her thoughts to herself, but she knew and heard everything that was happening. She was a chameleon; she was here, and she was there, spiteful, like a black widow spider, with four eyes on the back and front of her head, trapping her victims in her coiled web.

Juan was pleased. His mission had been a successful one. He would stay in Spanish Acres until the storm passed, feeling a warm comforting bond of union with the family. Then, *Don* Federico would go with him to the great city of San Antonio to see the "Apostle Madero," the liberator of Mexico, the founder of the great reform movement. *Gran Hombre!*

Don Federico returned to his leather chair in the library, contemplating what Juan had just brought to his attention. He began to collect his thoughts. And in the back of his hidden memory, the thoughts of *Doña* Adela kept rolling back and her words were becoming more vivid, more real. *The girl is here for a reason! She was sent here. The connection is with your father!* He remembered her also saying something about guns, ammunition. *What does all this mean?* This was insane! Could it be possible that a group of men from this side of the border were smuggling weapons across the river into Mexico? Anything was possible! And a large amount of profit on smuggled goods was also feasible. The border was known for corruption and everything that was evil—liquor, prostitution, slavery, and murders. Even small children from Mexico were being sold to families in the United States who could not have children. But, who had access to government things?

His mind was being overloaded with questions: the matter of the gold mine; the death of the *gringa* woman; his father's mysterious death; the cattle and his ranch; his wife's persistent cough. And then there was Soledad—what was her destiny? Victoria's schooling in Mexico was becoming questionable. And yet, as his mind was heavy with worry, he thought of himself giving money to fight the Revolution. Was this any different from the people who were buying and selling goods in a clandestine way and doing things illegally? The main thing was that he knew Madero was honest, wanting to change a country that for centuries had known terrible injustices. He would ponder on this all night long, as he tossed and turned in his bedchambers.

The weather kept getting worse. The rain had become a gully-washer and gradually soaked the earth and ran from the bottom of every ravine, as the range animals began drifting toward higher ground. The *resaca* and the *arroyos* that were usually dry carried torrents of water as the heavy downpour continued all night.

The windmills whirled and rattled, lacking the oil that sustained them. The cattle out in the jungle *brasada* and pastures bawled, while the bullfrogs croaked, and the crickets chirped. A nightmarish glow hovered above the land, and alarm had touched every human face: some with joy because of the prior lack of water, and others for the unforeseen future. But all through the night the foul weather persisted and hammered the skies with luminous colors. Lightning strikes flashed across the heavens with an uncanny persistence as if King Lucifer were being turned loose from the pit of Hell to continue his destructive force, as a million demons screamed in the depth of the night.

The storm kept getting worse.

CHAPTER 7

When morning came, the sun struggled to peek through several dull gray, scattered clouds that still remained hanging low in the sky. The rain had eased, and although the storm was gone, a heavy fog lingered. Only a soft breeze coming from the east blew steadily.

For the first time in months, Juan had slept in a comfortable bed with all the amenities fit for a king. He had been sleeping soundly until awakened by noises coming from the hall outside his bedroom. The ride from Laredo had been long and dangerous, while hiding and sleeping outdoors and in unwelcome places. For the moment, he didn't know what to expect. All he knew was to follow orders and go by the instructions he had been given a week ago. While gazing at the ceiling and the beautiful furniture and accommodations, he heard a hard knock on the door that startled him.

"Yes! Who is it?" he answered.

"Yolanda, *Señor!*"

"Ah! Yolanda, please come in," he replied, pulling up the sheet and hiding part of his face, playing with Yolanda and revealing only his shining green eyes.

Yolanda peeked in slowly. "*Buenos días,*" she said, exposing a forced grin in spite of her haughty nature. In her hands was a wooden tray with fresh brewed coffee, sugar, and a small pitcher of cream. "*La Señora* asked me to bring you some coffee."

"Ah! *Muchas gracias*, I can sure use some," he answered, as he straightened himself up in bed and gazed toward Yolanda with a cheerful smile.

Yolanda put the tray on the table next to the bed and walked over to the window. A brilliant light dispersed as she pulled the velvet drapes and opened them.

Juan brought his hands over his face protecting his eyes from the bright light and then spoke. "The storm must have left, since the sun is out!"

"*Sí, Señor*, it brought much water. The *vaqueros* have been out early this morning fixing fences and the part of the barn roof that was torn off, and repairing some of the roofs on the homes in the Spanish Quarters. Many of the cattle got frightened by the lightning last night, stampeded, and tore down fences and one windmill."

"Is *El Señor* out with the *vaqueros* also?" Juan questioned, while pouring cream into his coffee and staring at Yolanda's figure intensely.

"*Si*, Señor, he left very early this morning with Roy and the other *vaqueros*. They are checking on his cattle and other livestock in the west pasture."

"What time is it? I must have slept late!"

"Everyone has been up for a long time and had their breakfast early. *La Señora* was worried about you."

He answered surprisingly, "Worried about me?"

"She thought maybe you weren't feeling well. You have traveled from a great distance and with the rain and all, getting wet last night you might have gotten a *resfrío*," she said.

"No, *gracias!*" I feel rested. Thank you! I'll be fine as soon as I get up." He was sensing her emotional reactions and acting curious about her age and if she were married. May I call you *Señorita* or *Señora?*"

"No, I am not married," she replied. Her face reflected a glow and a small grin as she moved her body in a rhythmic motion toward him and rolled her crafty, dark eyes. "*La Señora*, wants to know what you want for breakfast, eh?"

"I'll be down as soon as I get up, shave, and clean myself," he replied, glancing at the washbasin where the white porcelain pitcher stood. He brushed his chin with his left hand, still gazing at her with admiration. "Anything is fine with me."

"Ah! You are a guest in this house, *Señor*. You can have anything you want! All you have to do is just order it!" She said it with her low, enticing voice, moving her large, firm hips side to side, like a snake in heat.

Juan raised an eyebrow. Their eyes locked, almost bonding, and then he reacted to her obvious, blunt invitation. "Anything?" he answered, electrified, catching his breath, not believing what he had just heard. He placed the cup on the stand. He lifted the bed cover up and held onto it with his left hand and patted the mattress. He moved over, making space for her to come to him. His green eyes bored into her, sizing her up and down, a wolfish smile on his face.

Yolanda paused, breathless. She was mesmerized by his eyes, while her face set in a coquettish, luring smile. She flushed as she came forward and bent down deliberately in his direction, exposing her firm, full bosom from the low-cut peasant blouse she was wearing— and picked up the urinal. Unhurried, and knowing that Juan was already aroused, giving him time to fantasize about what he would be missing, she turned toward him with a seductive look and said, "*La Señora* and everyone is waiting for you downstairs."

"But wait. When will I see you?" he asked. "When will you be coming to my room?"

"Soon, very soon," Yolanda said, as she opened the door and moved on down the hall.

"*Ay! Caramba!*" voiced Juan with glee, overwhelmed by the hospitality. This was indeed a lovely place out in the heart of a desert and in the middle of nowhere. He got up and slowly walked to the iron window balcony. Viewing the sky, he saw the storm was gone, with only a few clouds adorning the heavens above the rain-soaked landscape. Puddles of water were in all directions, while elsewhere it looked like a lake, with lonely mesquite, cactus, and undergrowth bushes reflected in the water. The hacienda was large, and the area that had been cleared for it was huge. There must have been at least twenty or more *vaqueros* working on the south side of the range. He could hear several of the cows bellowing in protest, since they stood up to their knees in mud. A rooster crowed with astounding clarity. The dogs would occasionally bark. Violin music was coming from downstairs.

He wondered what everyone was doing so early in the hacienda. He tried to picture in his mind where everyone fit in the large mansion. He wondered what Victoria was doing. A lovely creature with such beautiful eyes and yet, so very young, he kept thinking. She was probably going to get more beautiful as she got older. But oh, what a temper she had! She had spirit, the kind of a sudden ardor of youth he liked. It was amazing what could be achieved with wealth, influence, and power. Perhaps one day, he would have it all. He kept hearing the constant pounding coming from all sides of the hacienda. His mind also wondered about the dead *gringa*—not being able to find her body was strange. He kept thinking about the young girl who had been savagely raped, and having to examine her and see about her condition. His mind was a jumble of thoughts, and he was developing an appetite.

Yolanda tiptoed downstairs quickly. She had been gone too long from her kitchen duties, and her mind was also full of thoughts as she circled around the long tile corridors, headed toward the outhouse to empty the urinal. Her heart pounded with excitement at the thought of Juan being interested in her enough to arouse the man. It only proved to herself that men were all the same. *The asses! Bastards!* She thought. She hated every one of them, except for her father and her two brothers. She wanted to destroy every single man who walked the earth. She was a man-hater. *Men*, she thought, *are evil—they would screw a snake, if it stood up to them.*

Her mind raced back to when she was eleven years old and just starting to develop into adulthood, when a cowhand, who no longer worked at Spanish Acres, violated her. He would force her to have sex with him in the barn, while she was milking the cows, or would catch her, raping her out in the dense jungle undergrowth, while she was gathering wood for the earthen stoves. He would violate her every chance he got, catching her alone. He would force her to have sex in different positions, also orally and anally, introducing her to a world of shame and guilt.

Being so young and innocent, she was unable to tell her parents because of the embarrassment and the scandal that it would bring to her mother and father. Working with *el patrón* was difficult because of his strict rules with his workers, not tolerating any trouble, and work was hard to come by, especially in this area. That *vaquero*, in a lustful passion, would also sneak into the kitchen quarters while she was sleeping alone, covering her mouth so she couldn't scream. He sodomized her many times, and for three years satisfied his desires. By then, she knew all there was to know about satisfying a man. Luckily, by the good grace of *Doña* Adela, who knew her problem and had kept it a secret, she was given a vinegar potion that kept her from getting pregnant.

She was glad the vaquero was gone. She had never hated anyone like she hated him. *May he rot in Hell*, she kept telling herself. *The filthy pig!* Her thoughts wandered towards the foreman, Roy. She had been in love with him for years, and on many occasions they had had a sexual encounter. But Roy never spoke of love or any commitment of marriage. She also thought of the many nights she had pleased *el Señor* George Juelson in his bedroom chambers. This was also a secret that only *Doña* Adela knew, and if the truth ever came out, she and her family would be thrown off Spanish Acres in disgrace. *El Señor* George Juelson was kind and had promised her land and had given her a legal document, but then he died. She missed him terribly.

Yolanda's passion for the handsome Roy was starting to lose ground, especially when she saw him peeking into Soledad's quarters where she lay sickly. The other servants remarked that Roy had been asking about Soledad. But, it was because he was worried and concerned, like everyone else had been. Everyone was nervous and agitated with fear. Yes! That had to be the reason, she kept telling herself. So many times Roy had played his guitar, singing only for her, in the courtyard. Things were getting too complicated, and she had to get things ready for *el patrón*, traveling to San Antonio.

"Maria!" Yolanda cried as she approached the huge dining area. "The guest will be right down. I have to go empty this," she said, showing Maria the urinal.

"*Bueno*," Mamá Maria replied. "As soon as you empty the urinal, wash it clean and place it back in the bedroom. Clean the bedroom, and make sure you open the windows so that it airs the room out. Then come down into the kitchen so you can help with the guest's breakfast." In the kitchen, the women's skillful hands went swiftly into action.

Juan hurried out into the hallway and stood, unsure not knowing which way to go. He kept hearing pounding coming from the downstairs. He remembered the direction from which he had come to his bedroom last night, but the mansion was enormous. He could have taken the long hall, and then walked down the side cement steps that led down the long corridors into the kitchen area, but instead, he decided to go through the main area of the house. Walking down from the middle on the main stairs, he stood observing the beauty of the mansion, amazed at the magnificent decor. He could hear music coming from the parlor of the house and echoing along the massive columns of solid, whitewashed stone supporting the upstairs structure. The floors were inlaid of pure white Italian marble throughout the house. Oriental and Persian carpets lay on the marble steps as a protection for the slick, glass-like floors. There was imported fine china, and enormous crystal chandeliers hung from the ceiling. Massive, dark French and Spanish furniture were in use throughout the hacienda. Golden framed mirrors and splendid paintings decorated the walls, while large vases graced each corner. Luxurious velvet drapes covered the French windows that led to the outside courtyard, patios, and fountains.

Juan found his way by the aroma wafting down the long tile halls and finally, after several twists and turns, was soon comfortably seated in the dining room next to the bustling open-air kitchen area as servants hurried in and out of the kitchen. The huge, dark oak table was adorned with a white Spanish lace tablecloth and set with fine china plates. It would easily seat over twenty guests. The tableware was pure silver, and the glasses were fine crystal. The chairs were large and dark, carved with Spanish designs.

In front of him, a platter of food was set that could easily choke a dog: two fried eggs, and fried *frijoles*, fried potatoes, and a large beefsteak weighing over a pound and sizzling hot, stood waiting for him. Whipped hot chocolate with cinnamon sat beside a cup of coffee and a large pitcher of orange juice. There were little trays of homemade sweet pastries, called *empañadas*, along with a tangy tomato sauce mixed with green chilies. On the side was a platter of warm corn tortillas, wrapped in white cloth.

"What a meal!" Juan retorted. "I can't eat this much. Yes, I'm hungry, but—"

"*La Señora* ordered this for your breakfast this morning!" Ophelia interrupted in her gravelly voice, solemnly pouring steaming coffee into his cup.

"Excuse me, *Señora!* I don't want to be nosey, but what's all the loud pounding I kept hearing from the upstairs room?"

A smile appeared on the old lady's face and she began laughing. "Manuel and some of the helpers are busy killing insects and snakes that have crawled in from the water. The storm brought in many bugs—they are everywhere! They have killed several large, black tarantulas on the walls, and many scorpions and centipedes are inside the house. Some of the *vaqueros* have already killed several rattlers." After imparting this information, the servant departed, giggling, leaving Juan to finish his breakfast.

Black tarantulas, scorpions, centipedes, rattlers—delicious, especially with my breakfast, he thought. "Ah, delicious!" he said softly under his breath.

After his breakfast, and while still sitting at the table, Juan caught a glimpse of *Don Federico* and Roy talking as they came from the kitchen. There was much activity going in the hacienda, as dogs barked continually. Women around the kitchen area chatted with one another, dishes rattled, and occasional giggles erupted, interwoven with music coming from the far end of the house.

The music abruptly stopped. Fred and Miss Belle presented themselves, found chairs, and sat next to him. Juan was delighted and asked Fred, "I love the music you were playing. Chopin, Beethoven, Mozart? There is nothing more beautiful than the sound of the violin. Is that what you plan to be when you grow up? Becoming a violinist? By the way," he turned, addressing Miss Belle, "you are a wonderful teacher."

Miss Belle smiled and replied, "Thank you!"

"No!" Fred answered. "My father wants me to be a lawyer, but I want to be a doctor."

"Ah!" Replied Juan, amused at the young boy's comment. "A very noble profession, but it takes long hours of studying the human anatomy…long hours of dedication…long diligent hours, healing and taking care of people. It's a big commitment. I'm taking a sabbatical at this time, while taking care of political matters for my country. But as soon as Mexico gets on its feet, I will continue for at least two more years and get my degree, before I can set up my practice and become a physician."

Olivia and Ophelia entered from the kitchen area and one of them spoke. "I just made some fresh coffee. Or can I get you anything else?" she said, addressing Juan and Miss Bell.

The plain, mousy looking Miss Belle held up a cup and replied, "Yes! Thank you."

Juan nodded his head, and Fred requested a large glass of orange juice.

Don Federico walked in with Roy and smiled at Juan and asked, "Did you have a good rest, *Compadre?* How was your breakfast?" He yelled to the kitchen crew, "Bring some coffee!"

Juan stood up graciously and shook *Don* Federico's hand. "Wonderful! The best rest I've had in months, and the breakfast was outstanding and delicious! *Gracias!* Your hospitably is extraordinary. I'll be seeing about your patient as soon as I've cleaned up and washed my hands."

"Ah! There's no hurry!" *Don* Federico answered. "Take your time. Rest and enjoy our hacienda and our hospitality. You'll be here for at least a week, or two, since nobody can get out. The roads are soaked with mud and are impassable."

He turned to Roy. "The *vaqueros* and I have a lot of work to do, especially getting the young mavericks to higher ground. There are fences to mend, posts to fix. The damage the wind and water did last night made a mess, especially to the shit houses. Don't forget that! Not only that, but go around killing snakes, insects and tarantulas. They are everywhere!"

"By golly, dat mud is slick'r than snot on a door knob," commented Roy, looking at his boots, his jeans, and jacket, with both hands lifted up in the air. He had mud clear up to his chin. "It's nothin'—we've seen it worse!" Everyone began laughing, for the weather had now become the main topic.

Doña Francisca walked in from the kitchen with Manuel. Both of them carried large baskets of eggs, vegetables, and homemade cheese. She was surprised but glad to see everyone laughing and having a good time in the dining room. While departing into the cooking area, she started to cough and then regained her composure. "*Buenos días*, Juan. Have you had breakfast?" she asked, very cheerfully.

Juan stood up and responded with a gracious "yes" and "*gracias*," again. *Doña* Francisca smiled and headed into the kitchen, while Mamá Maria took the basket from her hands and said, "This cheese will make excellent enchiladas for the evening meal."

While the chattering and commotion was going on, Juan kept his thoughts to himself and listened to the men converse and, discussing their plans for the day and the following weeks. *The majority of family is here, except for the hot-tempered beauty, Victoria.* His eyes kept wandering to the entrance of the kitchen, hoping and desiring for her to show up. He noticed that Yolanda had come from the kitchen wearing an apron and was scurrying around the dining room, picking up the dirty dishes. He became aware that Yolanda's eyes would occasionally travel in his direction, and then would glance toward Roy.

Doña Francisca returned from the kitchen area. "The roof of the schoolhouse is leaking, and the terrible pounding from one of the helpers fixing the roof made it impossible for Victoria and me to teach. We could not hear a thing." She coughed. "We're sending all the children home."

So that's where she is, thought Juan. *Soon the gorgeous beauty will be walking in the door.* His neck strained looking toward the door in anticipation, while his heart skipped a beat.

In the meantime *Doña* Francisca, coughed again, and in her refined manner, turned to Juan and asked him, "How long have you practiced medicine? It is not every day that we have a doctor who comes to the hacienda and visits us. *Don* Federico said he mentioned to you about the injured girl. We will be eternally grateful while you are staying here, if you would be so kind as to check on Soledad."

"No problem. It will be my pleasure," replied, Juan smiling. He stood up and rolled up his sleeves. "I'll need some alcohol, hot water, some clean towels, and soap to scrub and wash my hands and arms. I also need someone's strong hands to assist me."

There was a stir and giggles coming from the kitchen as one of the helpers replied, "He is going to examine *la muchacha!*" Another spoke, "Lord, I wish he would examine me! I would not mind him touching me! He's so handsome. What a *mango!*"

Doña Francisca walked into the kitchen as the young girls and women were watching and listening to what Juan was saying. "Goodness, girls!" *La Señora* interrupted. "Let's get the water boiling. Yolanda! Go and get the big bottle of alcohol, iodine, and chloroform from the storehouse, and Mamá Maria, you will come with me to assist the young doctor," she ordered. Her presence made everyone scramble like cockroaches when the lights came on.

Coming from the soaked, muddy path was Victoria holding her ruffled skirt up to avoid the wet ground. She caught glimpses of Juan outside the kitchen area, with his sleeves up, scrubbing his arms and hands with soap over a porcelain water basin. Juan glanced toward her, straightened himself up, and grabbed a towel to dry his hands and also to catch her attention. *Ah!* Thought Juan, *she is like an angel. A swan when she moves with each step. Her long legs are so beautifully shaped.* His eyes, shining and expressive, were fixed on Victoria, pulled like iron to a magnet, while his mouth displayed his normal wolfish smile. "*Señorita,*" he said. "Your legs, are they any better today?" Mockingly, his eyes sized her up. "No broken bones from yesterday's fall?"

Victoria quickly let go of her skirt, letting it drop to the ground. Her cheeks flushed becomingly and she quickened her steps. "They are fine!" She forced a smile and then looked at the ground, watching her steps, avoiding the potholes filled with water. "*Doña* Adela's potion worked marvels on them," she replied. She hurried into the kitchen as quickly as possible, almost taking the screen door and all, in a storm of embarrassment. After her mother's lesson in moral behavior and the commitment she had in being wed to Ricardo Calderóne, she mustn't let on how he was beginning to affect her.

She stood and pressed herself against the kitchen wall and closed her eyes. *What is it about him that makes me so flustered and so nervous? His glance makes me so very uncomfortable, the way he looks at me, almost undressing me with his lovely eyes.* She sighed.

Children ranging in different sizes and ages from six to ten years were coming along after Victoria, having abandoned the leaking schoolhouse. Little Carlos met Fred outside and all scattered to play with the rest of the other children, catching the abundance of croaking frogs that were on the patio and in the courtyards. Some of the other children who were barefooted began playing hide and seek and splashing in the puddles of water; others began chasing Texas lizards, the horned toad.

Outside of the hacienda, the dogs began barking. One of the *vaqueros* rode his horse fast and entered under the main high arch of the hacienda and yelled, "Someone's coming up the road. We have company!" Other workers fixing the outhouse asked, "*Quien son?* Who is it?" All looked dumbfounded.

Don Federico and Roy heard the commotion and walked from the patio out to the front of the mansion. They stopped at the edge of the road, close to the entrance gate, and watched the stranger approach. He was riding his horse at a high speed in spite of the muddy road's adverse conditions. The dogs began barking uncontrollably and paced back and forth on the watery path, attracting everyone's attention.

"That's enough!" commanded the *Don* to J.D. and King and the other dogs. "Get back to the house!" he shouted.

"*Oiga!*" said the stranger, addressing the two men. "I'm looking for El Meester Ju'son!"

Frowning with an intense curiosity and suspicion, *Don* Federico replied, "I'm he!"

"I have a note from a *gringo* who is waiting to talk to you at the crossroads of La Villa road. I also have some of your mail." The stranger paused long enough to settle his snorting horse and opened his vest. Slowly he handed *Don* Federico a small, white piece of paper and handed him his mail. "I was paid to deliver this message to you, meester." The brown-skinned stranger quickly turned his horse with "*Arriba! Ándale!*" And headed down the road in the direction he had come.

After reading the note, *Don* Federico looked at Roy. "It's from Tom White," saying it with intensity and a nervous eagerness in his voice. "Maybe I'll get some answers and get to the bottom of my father's mystery!"

"Dat drunk from Six-Shoot'r Junction," snickered Roy, then laughed so loud that his voice echoed. "Do ya' want me to go with ya', *patrón?*"

"No! I'd better go by myself. He probably has plenty of personal information regarding my father's death. And besides, Tom White is no drunk, he just pretends to be one. He is doing me a big favor, with pay of course! Do you remember the detective, the one I hired over a year ago?"

"Yep, I vaguely 'member, somethin' like dat," said Roy, "Whut of it?"

"Well! He's the detective. I'm getting to the bottom of my father death."

"No!" Roy stumbled back in the rough rocks in surprise and glanced at *Don* Federico, then paused, spitting into the weeds. He was flabbergasted that Tom White was a detective and not a drunk.

Within an hour, *Don* Federico had El Chulo saddled and loaded and trotting south toward the crossroads. There, in the midst of the mesquite and the cactus-ridden muddy ground, was Tom White, sitting on his gray mare. He was dressed in a colorful disguise, a big Stetson hat and Mexican poncho wrapped around him clear up to his eyes, making him look like a fat toad.

"Sorry to have you ride all the way to this clandestine place, but I had no choice. I think that the whole bunch in Harlingen is starting to get suspicious. My job is finished and I need to go back to San Antonio. I did not want anyone to see us talking," he said nervously, and looking spooked.

"I understand!" responded *Don* Federico, calming his jittery horse. "Have you got the information I need?"

"Plenty," Tom replied. "Your intuition about Hanson was dead on! Shit, I've about become an alcoholic in doing this investigation, but in the long run, it will pay off for you. It's been a good mission and assignment for me and thank you for hiring me. What it boils down to is this: the whole deal was blackmailing your father, understand? A set-up including bribery and extortion, or however you want to call it! I've heard Hanson laugh several times when your name was brought up, and he bragged with his so-called partners of killing your father for the gold mine and whatever they could get out of him."

He paused again, letting the news sink in. "There's more! Better watch out for rigged papers on your land, where the old witch woman lives. Do you realize that Hanson has had an investigation going on with a corrupt scoundrel, a geologist claiming the possibility of finding oil in the area? Just think, *Amigo*, black gold, here on your land!"

"Yes! There's talked of oil," *Don* Federico replied, fretful but not extremely concerned. "Hanson brought up to me about my father signing the gold mine over to him. He mentioned that my father owes him money from gambling! Frankly, I think its bullshit, if you ask me!"

"Oh, man! Oil! Just think!" White was all excited, changing the subject from Hanson back to oil. "It's the upcoming thing," he said. "People in Oklahoma and in the Houston area are becoming wealthy discovering oil. Just think, with the production of the Model-T, the airplane, machinery, and so many things that run on oil." He took a deep breath and changed the subject again. "Speaking of Hanson," he said, "he has more devious ideas! You are supposed to be next! I suggest that you give him that goddamn gold mine. Frankly, it's not worth it. You can get your ass wrung out down there."

"The oil will have to wait, for now. You spoke of blackmail, but with whom?"

"Your father sought affection in any woman's arms and was lured into having an affair with the wife of William Smith, the young Texas Ranger rookie, the skinny dude who patronizes and kisses Hanson's ass. Well! The bitch's name is Della Mae, the redheaded one, with big blue eyes, and heavy breasts."

"Yes, that Ranger was working in the Ranger's office, but left when our conversation got heated."

"Well, that's his wife. And in the last couple of days he has been looking for her. She's disappeared. They have a very stormy relationship, fighting all the time for money. Apparently, he never did make much, and she never has enough."

Astounded, *Don* Federico's eyes narrowed into an icy steel gaze as he tried to absorb Tom White's information; this was turning into a nightmare. "No! It's not possible! Not my father—" said the *Don*. At the same time, he was thinking she was perhaps the missing redheaded woman found and left in the *brasada*, but being unsure, he preferred to keep this information to himself, since no corpse had been found.

"Yes! Mister Juelson, it's all true. I'm sorry you had to hear this from me. But you paid me to find out all these things. Your father got mixed up with a rough bunch. Your father's so-called friends, like Hanson, are killers by trade and instinct, nothing more. Murderers if you ask me! Hanson is the biggest mother of them all, with no remorse or conscience, and he is the one who planned it. Money, my friend, greed, that's what it all about, it's called, *roots of evil.* Your father was drunk and signed a piece of paper, and that same night was *accidentally* killed? He was caught in bed with the redheaded bitch—a set-up. They were all in on it! They could all see dollars signs in front of their eyes. They bribed him to sign the document. What's real hilarious is—"

"What's that?"

"Your father knew long before he was killed that something was going to happen to him. Instinct, perhaps! He was starting to suspect and read between the lines with his so-called friends. Your father designed a payment method from the Monterrey, Mexico bank, on a one-time dividend to his blackmailers, and made them think that he was dividing the gold investment for the rest of their lives. They didn't realize what your father's plans were, because the gold mine is yours legally and in the country of Mexico? C'mon," he laughed. "He outsmarted the bastards! Smart ol' dude, but he paid with his life. He was clever, but not clever enough, especially when you're dealing with an outright murderer like Hanson." He paused and cleared his throat. "When you left Hanson's office yesterday, he was drinking heavily and laughed and bragged that down in Mexico you were going to get your "Alamo" at the gold mine. He was going to meet you there with his group."

"Very cleverly planned," *Don* Federico's voice quivered in an unnerved fashion. "But not clever enough! Thank you, Tom, for your job well done. Where can I send you the money that I still owe you?"

"Mail it to my post office box in San Antonio. I have already sent a telegram to the United States Deputy Marshals, in Austin, explaining everything. There's a bunch of contraband going over the border, and with the information on Hanson, and his sonsabitching bastards, if he gets caught—you know how cunning he is—he needs to be locked up forever in a federal prison."

"I'm much obliged!" *Don* Federico replied. His thoughts spiraled, creating a knot in his throat as he thought of his dead father's adventurous romances.

"The federal marshals should be able to take care of the rest. You'll not be seeing me again. Not unless there is an indictment and the federal boys need me to testify in Brownsville. I'm packing my bags, tonight, if possible! And I'm heading up north, where I belong. It's getting too goddamn dangerous, especially this close to the border and the corrupt Texas Rangers."

"Thanks again!" *Don* Federico said.

"Come and visit me, whenever you're in the San Antonio area. Here's the package with all of the information you'll need. I have explained everything, and my seal is on those documents."

"I will, my friend, and thank you again for your kind service. I'll never forget this." He reached for the large, heavy envelope and shook Tom White's hand. "As soon as the area dries up, I'll be in San Antonio within a week or two and will come to see you."

"Good! *Adiós, amigo!* As the saying goes! See you sometime in San Antonio! Be careful in Mexico! There are jackals there, too!" Tom White extended his hand again.

ROOTS OF INDIFFERENCE

"Hasta la vista, mí amigo. I will."

Don Federico sat on his horse for a minute watching Tom White heading back through the potholes filled with water and the dense jungle of mesquite, until he disappeared among the hostile cacti.

The redheaded woman was probably the young Ranger's wife, and he probably did not know she was dead. *Don* Federico's thoughts kept going back to what *Doña* Adela had told him. On his way home, he would stop and talk with her. The old *bruja* was right—he needed a reading. The old woman was never wrong.

⌘ ⌘ ⌘

At the hacienda, *Don* Federico sat somber, with elbows on the desk, head in his hands, while examining Tom White's documents detailing all speculations on Hanson and what Tom had heard. *Doña* Adela had told his father of his coming fate. *La Bruja* had also disclosed a family secret that was hard to swallow. A painful, shocking secret that he would have to keep, and not reveal to anyone.

A soft knock surprised him, and he glanced toward the door. *"Amigo,* Juan! Come on in. Take a seat," he said, smiling. He stood up and showed Juan a chair. "What did you find out on the injured girl?"

"A beautiful creature indeed," Juan informed him. "But she's in bad shape!" he said, shaking his head in disgust. "Soledad has serious injuries. Besides having a bad head concussion, she has several broken ribs. *La Señora* and *Doña* Maria helped me wrap bandages round her chest. I also took the liberty of examining her on the inside, and it would be very unlikely that she could ever have any children. The muscles inside her uterus are stretched and ripped and she is torn from the inside out. She would have serious complications having children." He concluded, "It's too bad, a nice woman, and seems so kind— she would make someone a good wife."

"Well! She can stay here for as long as she wants and get healed. Time will tell! Time is always the best healer," *Don* Federico added, looking distraught and bitter. Their conversation went on for over an hour, with many medical and political issues.

Outside, the rain and mud had prevented the *vaqueros* from completing their daily routine, and the responsibilities of fixing windmills and repairing fallen fences were impossible. They were unable to get some larger groups of cattle out that were deep in water and mud in the dense jungle of the *brasada;* many were in low gullies, ready to calve and unable to extricate themselves. They needed to get to them real soon.

The previous dry season had brought in many blowflies that attacked the baby calves and colts. Weimer's screw-worm medicine was bought by the case and mixed in large buckets with the black, greasy, sticky oil coming from the *resaca* area. The medicine was then applied to the newborn's navel, saving the little animal's life. Without it, the fly would implant its eggs, which in less than a week became larvae, which turned into screwworms, embedding themselves into the body of the animal, eating it alive from the inside out. That was a cruel part of nature that had to be watched.

Meanwhile, the men sat around telling stories and singing out in the middle of the courtyards and patios where it was cooler. Roy brought his guitar and, joined by Juan, Fred, and the older workers, all began singing the beautiful song, *El Abandonado*. They continued to sing, *Aya en El Rancho Grande*. Several joined in the singing in a strident Mexican barbershop harmony. The few who didn't sing enjoyed the music, and sat around smoking cigarettes and visiting amongst themselves. Manuel managed, to no one's surprise, to find several bottles of tequila and mescal and began distributing to everyone. It was after the last song that one of the *vaqueros* spoke up, since it referred to the workers and how tough they all were. "Ah! Yes! The Mexicans are tough *hombres*—we can endure anything!"

Roy immediately broke in. "If ya' think that the *vaqueros* are tough *hombres*. Let me tell ya' a story of the *gringos*, living up North." His voice became louder and boastful, then got serious.

"At thirte 'n, I was already workin' on one of the *ranchos* in Okie. A *muy macho hombre* came and skidd'd into our camp one day. He had been ridin' all day comin' from the hard plains. His horse was a mount'in lion. His bridle was barbed wire. He was using two rat'lers—one fur his quirt and the other was wrapp'd 'round his neck. Takin' his hat off, he den took a big slug o' sheep-dip. 'Boys!' he said. 'I hate to drin' and run, but shit! There's a tough man chasin' me!'"

The *vaqueros* rolled on the floor amidst the rest of the workers' uproarious laughter. The intake of liquor had helped.

"Ah! Very funny! Very funny! Compadre! That Roy is a real *hombre*! Eh!"

"*Puro Corazón*, all heart" said one.

Another replied, "Of course, it must have been the devil himself!"

Another one said, "The devil is everywhere!"

One commented, nearly choked with laughter, "That *hombre* Roy, got a head on him—he picks up *la lengua pronto*, the language quickly."

Juan, sitting next to Fred, found it not only amusing, but also compatible to his way of life and dreams. He found it interesting that the people here in Texas were no different than the *Mestizos* from Mexico: simple minded, down to earth, hard working people, and unlearned like everyone else.

He viewed his surroundings—the large open arches and verandas; the beautiful flowering vines, with a variety of colors; the enormous fountain; the floor of cracked stones filled in with Spanish tile and cement. The beauty of it all brought a melancholy into his deep thoughts because it was so romantic, especially at night. And always, surrounding the rancho on all sides was the fascinating jungle full of wild animals and insects, cacti, and mesquite that adorned the incredible, sprawling, vast landscape. *Los Americanos* were shrewd individuals. With a little thought, they became wealthy overnight. *I want a beautiful home and estate like this one, and a beautiful wife to share my life, and many children.* For now, his dreams would have to wait.

ROOTS OF INDIFFERENCE

The whole patio was aglow with singing and chattering. The dogs were busy barking, playing with Blanca, and children were amusing themselves with hide and seek, laughing and making noise.

The women from the kitchen brought out several pitchers of fresh lemonade, since the weather had become so muggy and humid. Roy began strumming his guitar to *Cielito Lindo*, a favorite song, from the Spaniards into the New World.

Victoria and Miss Belle, distracted by the outside music and noise, decided to step out in the courtyards and join the rest of the crowd. Miss Belle's heart fluttered, skipping beats as she watched Roy, playing his guitar and singing those beautiful Spanish songs. The next song was *Clementine*, and he looked directly towards the skinny schoolteacher, who was obviously in a state of embarrassed bliss. He followed it up with *El Corrido de Gregorio Cortez*, the famous ballad being sung along the border.

Juan's eyes sought out Victoria's presence. He immediately stood up and sauntered toward her like a slow, approaching storm.

Uttering an exclamation of disgust mixed with joy, Victoria stood paralyzed. She caught his form from the corner of her eye. *Here he comes! Dios!* She said to herself. Her face blushed too scarlet with shame remembering yesterday's incident and last night's humiliating catastrophe. She had not been able to sleep, and hated herself for being so childish and silly. How could she explain being so stupid? Glancing up, she looked into the most beautiful, bewildering eyes that the light of day had changed into a teal blue-green. He stood there with obvious longing as their eyes locked. "*Señorita*, how are your legs?"

"You asked me already this morning! Amazing! They are fine. And guess what?"

"What?"

"No fever!" She said it sarcastically, but broke out in a nervous laugh.

Juan understood her and laughed also. He admired her aloof manner, her proud behavior, and her sharp comment, so he decided not to proceed further in that discourse. He began chuckling with her and realized how young, beautiful, and spoiled she was. He was also aware of his own handsome looks and charm. A master artist of people's feelings, he began playing with her emotions. Wanting to begin a more direct conversation, he said, "Your father was telling me that you are going to attend the convent school south of Monterrey." Expressing himself in a more jovial manner, his smile always displayed a pleasant attitude. He was captivated by her delicate features, her hazel eyes, and her hourglass figure. He wanted to put his arms around her waist and felt a great urgent desire to kiss her.

"Yes! I am," she answered nervously. She batted her eyes and smiled charmingly. She became aroused by his presence and recalled her mother's incessant reminder of being gracious at all times, regardless of the situation. "Why do you ask?"

"Monterrey is my home, where I grew up. My family still lives there, at least my mother and sister. My father died several years ago. I know the area like the palm of my hand. The convent is miles away, high in the mountains, one of the finest in the region, especially for wealthy girls. Of course, who needs training in sarcastic remarks and sharpening of their tongues?"

It took a couple of seconds before Victoria's brain registered his comment. The conversation took on a cat and mouse game. She laughed contemptuously. Becoming angry, she spurted out, "It's a small world. Then you must know the Del Calderónes?" She glared at him, flushing slightly.

"Of course," he replied, annoyed at hearing the Del Calderóne name. "All of the people in Monterrey are well-acquainted with their name. The Del Calderónes are wealthy, politically powerful people living in several fancy villas with thousands of acres stolen from the poor *Mestizos* they killed," Juan retorted angrily. "They have become rich on the soil stained with the blood of the *peóns!* The old man is a controlling, ruthless general, at whose hand my father was killed. This was one of the main reasons I decided to leave my medical profession and enter into the Revolution with Madero to bring justice to Mexico. President Díaz will have to be removed, if Mexico is going to survive its internal strife."

Juan's face had flushed, and he became bothered by the stern hatred that was evident in his voice; his eyes flashed. "Is that where you'll be spending your weekends while going to school—with them?" he asked irritably. His voice then softened, aware he had shown a part of his forbidden nature from the other side of his mask. "How do you know the Del Calderónes?" he asked with some contempt.

"The Del Calderónes have been close friends of my mother and her family for many years, being *'compadres,'* when they baptized Fred. And No! I will not be staying with the Del Calderónes," she answered, realizing that she had hit a nerve with him by repeating their name. She understood that *El General* was part of the hated Díaz regime. "I'll be staying with my grandparents who also live on the outskirts of Monterrey." She began to soften her conversation, recognizing that it was a man's world. "I don't know anything of politics! All I know is that Monterrey is where I'm going to school, and I have heard that it's very beautiful, with many sights to see."

"You are absolutely right! My humble apology for talking polities. Women do not comprehend government laws or understand what Madero is trying to do to reform the country of Mexico." He bowed, displaying his gracious manners. He became more at ease, appreciating that she was young, unable to grasp his manly desires and his worldly ambitions. "Monterrey is one of the most beautiful cities and the air is very clear. And it sits at the foot of *El Cerro de la Silla*, Saddle Mountain. While you're there, you must see Horsetail Falls—it's very romantic."

Juan continued as their conversation took on a lighter tone. "I've heard you're a fair shot with a rifle! Some of the *vaqueros* were talking about you killing the mad dog yesterday morning. They said you were the children's hero."

"Why, thank you," she replied, very pleased with herself. "I was raised with a rifle and cut my teeth on one. Around here you need to protect yourself," she said, looking directly into Juan's eyes.

"You mean you truly would have shot me?" He was surprised and began laughing out loud. "I did not know that I was in mortal danger, in the presence of a serious, down-to-earth killer. I could have gotten killed!"

They both laughed heartily.

"We all want to thank you for checking on Soledad and taking care of her. Everyone was talking, including Mamá Maria. She can't stop talking about you and what a hero you've become. She needed medical care. *Doña* Adela did what she could, but she is no doctor."

"Who's *Doña* Adela?" Juan asked, looking curious. "Whoever she is, she did a darn good job, recognizing that Soledad's ribs were broken and her insides torn."

Victoria was shocked at what he just said. The expression on her face turned from jovial to aghast. She brought her right hand to her mouth. *Horse feathers! Did he say her insides were torn? How did he check her insides—perhaps it was just doctors' talk?* She replied, "*Doña* Adela is a *curandera*, who lives a mile west of the *resaca*."

"A *curandera*—how interesting," he said. And how long has she been doctoring people?"

"Long before I was born. She has taken care of the hacienda's people and the rest of the Mexican people living in this region. She doctors them and reads cards and tells fortunes."

"She can predict the future?" Juan raised his eyebrows, becoming very interested in what Victoria was saying. "I have always been intrigued and fascinated with fortune telling. Maybe *Doña* Adela will read for me. At this very moment, my whole life is at stake, and perhaps she could tell me what's coming up in my near future, especially here in Texas. The *gringos* do not like Mexican strangers bringing in messages from Mexico. I ran into some real cowboys with pistols and rifles in the town of Rio Grande City and had to sleep in an abandoned barn." He was dramatic and apparently had theatrical training. "I would also like to get her formula for the lotion she put on your legs. You never know when I'll need to use it, or perhaps save someone's life with it. Can you take me there?" His eyes narrowed, and he appeared pleased that he had gained Victoria's approval.

"My parents have given us strict instructions not to ride too far outside the hacienda," she answered nervously. She remembered her mother was taking a nap in her upstairs bedroom. And from her room, if she caught a glimpse of them conversing too long, Victoria would be headed for another long talk about her unbecoming boldness and lack of morality.

"Perhaps tomorrow?" he proposed with enthusiasm, as his eyes brightened and became wide with excitement. "You and I, and we can even take Fred along for a ride out in that direction. My horse needs the exercise. Who's going to know where we're going? This is a large area. And besides that, you'll be with me and your brother!" He sounded very persuasive.

Before Victoria could answer, she noticed her father had walked out from the library and begun mixing with the crowd. He seemed more cheerful than earlier, but still projected a gloomy authoritarian face. The music had stopped. Roy was not playing his guitar, but was sharing sips of tequila with one of the friendly neighbors. Miss Belle had returned to her piano and paperwork in the parlor. Yolanda had gotten tired of spying on Roy and Miss Belle, and decided to drift into the kitchen where she was needed, because Mamá Maria was already yelling at her. Love and hate were all around and emotions ran high, and in general, people were frightened.

"Juan!" exclaimed the great *Don*, taken by surprise. "I need your attention please!" He approached the couple from behind. He cleared his throat. "I'm pleased that you're socializing and talking to my daughter, making her acquaintance, and you're enjoying your stay with us. The ladies in the kitchen have just announced we'll be eating within the hour. Enchiladas are on the menu. But I need to talk to you and Roy in the library, for a minute, if I can get Roy's attention."

Juan took in a deep breath and felt guilty, not knowing what was coming. He felt the same feeling of being caught with your pants down in an intimate moment with your best friend's wife. His concern turned into an air of uneasiness and his thoughts began spiraling. Was he showing the *Don's* daughter too much attention? He did not want to make any waves, at least not at this moment. Shaken and apprehensive, he answered, "*Sí, Señor!* I'll be in right away."

The sun had slanted to the west and could be only partially viewed between the clouds.

Occasionally, a gentle drizzle of rain would sporadically fall, increasing the humidity and making the weather uncomfortable, sticky and sultry, but it never bothered the singing carried on by the inebriated group.

In the library, Roy and Juan found a seat and faced *Don* Federico across his desk. The *Don* leaned forward and began telling the men the information he had gotten from Tom White. The news did not surprise Roy, for he knew Hanson and the stories that were being told by many workers who had come and gone from the hacienda. There were reports of his charging the Mexicans for being drunk and disorderly. Hanson would throw them in jail and then demand large amounts of money to free them. Many of the desperate Mexican people would be forced to sign documents and divide their land to gain their freedom. Old judge Parker, handy in writing up legal records, received payment under the table. The property where Hanson lived had come from that arrangement.

Juan already felt the liquor taking effect and realized there would be no repercussion in his actions, so he asked about Hanson. He understood that corruption and extortion was no different across the border, but in Texas, it was more sugarcoated, in signed documents, making them look legal.

Then, in a lengthy conversation, *Don* Federico told Juan about his problem with the gold mine in Monterrey. Since the Revolution was coming, he would make plans to take a trip to the mountains.

"It's too dangerous!" voiced Juan. "Highwaymen are stationed all over those mountains. The last word is that the mine has been abandoned. Bandits got their hands on the gold and killed the workers."

"Perhaps, you're right." *Don* Federico countered, looking distraught. "I have been looking at this document for over three hours and have decided not to do anything with the gold mine. But, I do need to inspect it while I'm there. If a war comes, it will have to wait until everything clears up. Everything that I suspected, Tom White has confirmed. On these documents about Hanson, he was right. Those bastards have been planning to get part of my property, even before my father's death."

"Lardy me," answered Roy.

"This leads to another problem that needs to be addressed, Roy. Tom White informed me that several people have been looking around in the area where *Doña* Adela lives. Apparently a geologist, a friend of Hanson, thinks that oil exists in that area. There is indication that the black, smelly, stuff from the *resaca*. The grease that we apply to the windmills and the axles on the wagons and buggies, has become valuable. Those men have been snooping around, without our knowledge, suspecting the area contains plenty of black gold."

"Law me! Ya' mean dat black stuff dat we put on doggies' bellies—has become valuable? Waal, hush my mouth! Shit is gonna hit the windmill's fan!" shouted Roy, excited and smiling from ear to ear. "*Patrón*, yore gonna git rich! Yippee! Damn! Ya' lose one gold mine and discover another one!" The liquor had taken effect. Roy was feeling his oats.

"Hanson would like to get his hands on that section. I need to start putting the *vaqueros* on guard around that area, especially at night. We'll wait until the land starts drying and the water recedes, then we can decide what we have to do."

"Shore, *patrón*," Roy said.

"It's the only good news I've had today. As a matter of fact, it's been the only good thing that has come my way, considering all of the other distressing information. First of all, I'll have to start checking if the information is true, and then hire an engineer and people who know about drilling oil and what it takes to get an enormous project like this going. Any undertaking like this will take lots of *dinero* and several months of preparations and planning."

Juan cleared his throat, stood up, and reached into the pocket of his white shirt. "I don't want to change the subject," he interrupted. "But, you need to take a look at this. I meant to give it to you earlier, but it slipped my mind. This was clenched in Soledad's left hand. Could it be a clue of some kind? She didn't talk and I couldn't get any information from her." He laid the object on top of the desk.

Roy moved in more closely on *Don* Federico's side of the desk, picked up the object, and observed it in the light. "Wha' da' hell is it?" he said, looking puzzled.

"Looks like a piece of metal of some kind, a star-shaped ornament, maybe brass or copper. Looks like it was ripped from something, but who?" All three were befuddled and glanced from one to another.

"As soon as Soledad gets better, I will try and have a talk with her," *Don* Federico replied, and then he paused. Instantly, he knew where he had seen the missing piece. "I'll need to speak with her— that's vital to this investigation." He stood up and spoke, ignoring his thoughts. "For now, my friends, let's go down to the dining area where the ladies have prepared us a wonderful meal."

Don Federico remembered that he needed to get some supplies for his horses, but with Juan's unexpected arrival and the urgent trip now to San Antonio, he now needed to change plans.

"Roy," he ordered, "head over to Milton's Mercantile in Mercedes City after the ground dries, and get the horse supplies. Have him put it on my bill."

Roy nodded his acknowledgement by tipping his hat.

"Come!" *Don* Federico addressed the two men, already strolling under the arches and heading toward the kitchen. "I'm getting hungry!"

CHAPTER 8

The storm had finally left, and the reconstruction of fixing roofs and fences and cleaning up the area around the hacienda had become a regular routine. The rounding up of cattle and horses from the deep gullies and undergrowth became customary. Weeks passed. The land had started to dry, and the water had begun to vaporize. The weather was still humid during the day, but had become much cooler at night, as the days were starting to get shorter. The rain had indeed been a blessing to every farm and *rancho*.

Miguel Garcia had arrived from his long train trip from San Antonio, bringing *Don* Federico a large leather bag with the profits from his cattle. There would be plenty of money to celebrate Victoria's sixteenth birthday and to donate to Madero's cause. Miss Bell had returned to her home, with pay, leaving Victoria and Fred assignments, until her return the following month for more music lessons.

During the third week in September, the curious *Don* Esquibel and his son, José, came to visit Spanish Acres. José was perhaps the only educated son of six children in *Don* Esquibel's home and had been studying engineering at Cuidad Victoria, Mexico.

The *vaqueros* were skillfully roping and riding some of the wild mustangs that had been rounded up after the hurricane in the large corral, several yards away north of the kitchen area. *Don* Federico sat half-straddled on top of the wooden fence while Juan perched beside him. Fred and Manuel were standing beside the *Don*, looking through the wide opening between the corral posts. They were all admiring Roy's masterful skill in roping.

"José!" said *Don* Federico. "How are things in Cuidad Victoria, *amigo*?"

"The day I left Cuidad Victoria, which was two days ago, the press had just released the election of President Díaz. The people, especially the peasants, were all in an uproar."

"Because of President Díaz's election?" asked *Don* Federico.

"No, because of his choice for a running mate, *El Señor* Corral. This man has a very bad reputation. Several months ago, workers in a factory complained about their working conditions and rebelled. Díaz ordered his *federalist* troops in, and men, women, and also little children were shot to death. Their bodies were later dumped in the Gulf of Mexico to be eaten by the sharks."

"The terrible injustices in Mexico will not last long," ventured Juan, whose face had turned pallid at the news. He was not surprised at what he had just heard. "The anti-reelection group, of which I am a member, has already nominated Francisco Madero for the next president of the Republic of Mexico. With your help and others, we will succeed."

Mamá Maria walked out of the kitchen and yelled at Manuel to come and help her.

José Esquibel stood silent for a moment, and scratched his chin, trying to find words to respond to what Juan had just said. "I have heard about Francisco Madero, but the people in Mexico are afraid to speak or say anything. They talk only in rumors and in whispers. If an opposition comes from the government, no doubt there will be a revolution."

"Exactly," Juan snapped. "Mexico needs a change. We need a revolution to change the corrupt government. If Díaz dies while in the saddle, just think of what will become of Mexico and its people," Juan said with his face full of hate and his eyes as hard as emeralds.

Don Esquibel, who had been quiet through the conversation, spoke with much concern. "What is going to happen to us who live so close to the border, if war comes in Mexico?"

"It's going to be hell for all of the Mexican-Americans!" *Don* Federico replied gazing at the old *Don*. "How are the Mexicans any different here, than in Mexico?" he asked. "The white man looks at us as nobodies. The Mexicans are treated as dogs here in the Valley. You know that, *Don* Esquibel! And don't count on any sheriff or *los Rinches* to protect us! They are against us and have been since they first set foot in the Rio Grande Valley. We need to band together as ranchers and as Mexicans."

José was not surprised, for he heard, while he was away studying, of the terrible stories of the *Rinches* and what they were doing to the Mexican-American people in the Rio Grande Valley. He had experienced several hateful remarks in his younger years and worse, since his return while shopping in Harlingen and in McAllen. He was a handsome young man at the age of twenty-three, well-built, tall, thin, and had a studious face. His completion was fair, and his eyes and hair were a soft brown. His well-trimmed mustache enhanced his smile. For the moment, he was not interested in government problems. His reasoning was that his father had bragged several times of how he had saved Soledad. Several of the working *vaqueros* had told him how beautiful she was. José, curiosity piqued, wanted to view Soledad for himself. His eyes wandered toward the kitchen, and he tried to visualize what she might look like.

The conversation between the men and *vaqueros* continued for over an hour, going back and forth, joking among themselves and laughing. Occasionally, Juan would look towards Victoria's upstairs bedroom. Not necessarily knowing which one it was. He was not the only young man interested in the girls at Spanish Acres.

It did not take long before the busybody, *Don* Esquibel brought up the question of Soledad. "By the way," he interrupted. "How's the young girl Soledad doing?" He coughed and cleared his throat, caught in an embarrassing question. "It's been many weeks now. I hope she's getting along and feeling better." He was curious to a fault, nosey and meddlesome.

"As good as new," *Don* Federico said, smiling. "She's getting along just fine, and it's amazing how well she has adjusted to the hacienda and our household. We are all grateful to have her here."

ROOTS OF INDIFFERENCE

Roy, standing in the middle of the corral with a lariat in his hand, stopped his roping and eyed the *Don*, giving him a frown of disapproval.

"I want my son to meet her," mused the cankerous *Don* Esquibel, being very frank.

"Well! I don't know if she is up to seeing any company at this time," replied *Don* Federico, being apprehensive at the old man's demand. "She's normally in the kitchen helping Mamá Maria doing some light chores. She is still very fragile."

Don Esquibel exclaimed with authority, "My son and I took the time and effort to come here. I want José to meet her."

The rest of the *vaqueros* and Roy came to attention and waited for *Don* Federico to comment; all were aware of *el patrón's* dislike of *Señor* Esquibel. "She's inside the house and is very shy," he said. "Soledad is embarrassed to talk to anyone, except for the women members in the household. I'll see what I can do." Annoyed, he slid down from the fence. The *Don* glanced around the vicinity of the stables, trying to find Manuel, and began calling his name.

It was minutes before Manuel appeared, coming from the kitchen area.

"Manuel, please call Soledad! Go tell her to come here!" he commanded.

The sounds of Manuel's shout resonated throughout the yard and in the kitchen. "Soledad, Soledad! Ay! Ay" Manuel moving clumsily and as swiftly as his body would allow him. He was concerned, knowing that Roy was interested in Soledad. Roy had made them all aware by his actions and the way he talked and asked about her, almost claiming her. Now the neighbors' son was interested also. It seemed like the course of destiny was about to change, and there would be hell to pay.

"Soledad!" Maria spoke from inside the kitchen door. "*El patrón* is calling you, hurry!"

Roy stopped immediately what he was doing when he saw Soledad coming out from the house.

Dos Mío! José thought. Soledad was as pretty as the *vaqueros* had described her. "She is beautiful!" he said out loud in front of everyone. He felt as if the world were standing still. Her healing face still had blue and black marks but, she was a transcendent beauty. The dark *rebozo* on her head gave her the look of an angel and the light from the sun beamed around her hair like a halo. She stood looking timid with her eyes on the ground. Her hands fidgeted with the *rebozo* nervously.

"Soledad!" said *Don* Federico. "Do you remember *Señor* Esquibel? He was the one who helped you and is responsible for bringing you here." His voice was half rough, half affectionate and paternal.

"*Sí, Señor*," replied Soledad. Her voice was soft and low. She glanced up at *Señor* Esquibel. "*Gracias*," she said lowering her head and eyes. "I am very grateful to you for saving my life."

"Well, this is his son, José Esquibel. He wants to meet you," replied *Don* Federico.

Soledad's face flushed. She was now speechless, not knowing what to say. She looked up, past the young Esquibel, and saw Roy mounted and ready to ride the wild mustang, but eyeing her, watching her every move. "*Mucho gusto, Señor* Esquibel," she replied humbly.

"Call me José."

"Very well, José." She appeared quiet and gentle, a totally submissive creature.

"Can I please call on you?" José Esquibel replied, taking her hand and kissing it in front of everyone watching. The rest of the *vaqueros* cheered when he kissed her hand, finding it very romantic.

Soledad nodded. Her face was flushed, and she turned quickly. Adjusting her *rebozo*, she headed back to the house. She felt totally humiliated and disappointed, wondering why Roy, who had an interest in her, didn't say something.

The *vaqueros* laughed and made remarks to Roy. "*Compadre!*" shouted a *vaquero*. "Somebody's eating your lunch, *hombre!*"

The rest of the *vaqueros* roared. Roy's angry face turned pale. Still sitting on the wild mustang, he had become careless, letting the reins go slack. Suddenly, the horse exploded in a wild rage and bucked him off. He was flying through the air before he realized it. In seconds, Roy was lying face down on the ground. Scraping himself up from the dirt, muttering, "Dang blast, dam' it!"

Don Federico could not keep from laughing, even though he could see Roy's frustration at what was happening. It was like the writing on the wall, and he grasped the psychological impact of the situation on Roy.

Shortly after, *Don* Esquibel and José left to take care of business at their ranch. José Esquibel would be visiting later; he would be seen at Spanish Acres again.

As the days grew shorter, the roads were dry and clear to use the buggies and wagons. *Don* Federico, Fred, and Juan were anxious to begin planning their trip to San Antonio. The newspapers, the *Brownsville Herald* and the *Mercedes Tribune*, were printing stories of Díaz's election in Mexico, telling of the overwhelming election results. For Díaz, it would be his eighth time on the throne. The same corrupt government that he had allowed, and had moved the election to every six years, instead of four. But Díaz was now eighty years old. His blood was running cold and slow. As grand and impressive a man as he had been, he had run the country with an iron hand, and he was not wise enough to retire at the right time.

The border was now hearing of a new redeemer, and opposition to the administration's rule—Francisco Madero was righteous and a man of his people; he was destined to become president of Mexico. He was drawn to the truth, and his tongue flowed with much wisdom. His rallying cries came in three expressions: "Effectual suffrage; no re-election; redistribution of the land."

Along the border towns, it had become a time of anarchy, a time of great peril. There were truce breakers, false accusers and despisers of those things that were honest and good. All conceivable *roots of evil* were evident. Crimes went unpunished. There were many skirmishes that involved murder, the burning of property, and robberies that were being committed so atrociously *all* lawman looked the other way, especially if the victims were Mexican. No one was sure of anything, and the rumors of war kept the people in the Rio Grande Valley at a fever pitch. Many of the Mexican-Americans prayed to the Saints, some of whom had predicted years before that the end of time was coming.

All the dirt roads were now clear and dry. Very early on a morning in the month of October, Manuel drove *Don* Federico, Fred, and Juan Alvarez in their Cadillac coach to catch the train to the big city of San Antonio. They would meet the train on the land given to the railroad by his father.

The game of revenge was working powerfully on *Don* Federico's mind as they boarded the train. Memories of his father, especially his death, set the pulse of his emotions throbbing faster. He had found himself involved in a spider web of mischance that grew more dense and black. It was like playing a game of Russian roulette with one bullet in the chamber, not knowing when it was going to fire and who might end up dead. A plan had to be mapped out, especially in Monterrey.

"Back to what we were discussing last night," Juan said as the train traveled along, its wheels clacking rhythmically on the tracks. He was sitting in the coachman seat, facing *Don* Federico and Fred. "There is a way of getting rid of a certain *Rinche* in Mexico," said the revolutionist, lifting an eyebrow.

"Death will come to him, sooner or later. Live by the gun, you'll die by the gun. He will die like most unworthy men, and violently," retorted *Don* Federico.

"But, my friend, there are ways in which a man can talk!" answered Juan, leaning toward the *Don*. His words were very convincing. "For a few gold pieces, the Mexican *bandidos*, being so desperate, will do anything, *Señor* Juelson! And you want Hanson to admit that he killed your father!"

Don Federico pursed his lips and frowned. "Just what are you trying to tell me, Juan? Keep talking, the idea is starting to appeal to me," he answered, as he rubbed his chin in thought.

"Hire a couple of desperate men. When you go to the gold mine, make believe that they are going to kill all of you for your possessions. Teach Hanson a lesson, as they say here in Texas."

"I don't mind them working on Hanson a little, like kicking his ass. He damned deserves it, but suppose they decide to kill me, too! I just don't know. We'll have to talk some more on this idea."

Fred, listening intently, thought about his father's comments.

"Let me think about it," repeated the *Don*. "We'll be in San Antonio shortly and will have plenty of time to talk."

For several hours while on the train, *Don* Federico and Juan shared their frank, open thoughts to each other, planning and deciding what was best. *Don* Federico had begun to have a lot of respect for the young revolutionist who had sacrificed his profession in order to join the Madero cause.

From the western horizon a purple twilight was starting to form as the sun was beginning to set. The train had passed the Old Spanish Trail, a trail on which thousands of Mexicans and white men had died conquering Texas and making it a great republic. Straight north were the lights of the city of San Antonio, and in the distance was the mission of *San Antonio DeVallero*, the good ol' Alamo; it was the white man who had called it that, shouting for so many years, "Remember the Alamo!"

The streets were bustling with traffic, including several fancy coaches, and a few Model-T cars caused the public to stand in awe and amazement. Occasionally, an old Mexican man with his burro-cart, full of supplies and grain would be in traffic. Every business man was dressed in their best suits, tipping their hats to the passing ladies. Beautiful women dressed in fancy designed handbags, gloves and elaborate big colorful feathered hats, underneath their bouffant hairdos styles. Everyone was hurrying.

San Antonio was a city that had combined the old with the new. Ancient landmarks stood beside new modern buildings. It was a town that, in 1718, was founded in order to establish the Spanish ownership of Texas, where priests and soldiers alike, tamed a wild and dangerous wilderness. San Antonio was truly a city built upon Spanish culture, and it would never lose its famous traditions.

Arriving in the evening, *Don* Federico, Fred, and Juan decided to stay at the famous San Antonio Hotel in which many of the supporters of the Revolution were staying and where they would conduct their meeting. Most of the men were brilliant and well educated in Europe; all were fed up with Díaz's tyrannies, the terrible conditions, and the oppression of the poor. All of them were determined to put in the one man who was right for the job— Francisco Madero!

"Where is Madero?" *Don* Federico questioned. He was torn between doubt and enthusiasm to see his friend and colleague become the next president of Mexico.

"*Señor*, Madero is meditating at this moment," said Sanches Azcona, a journalist who had met them at the entrance of the hotel. "Pancho Madero became a spiritualist while he was in Paris, France." He kept talking while he led the three into a large waiting room suite.

"A spiritualist," *Don* Federico mused. "But—" He never completed his sentence, as his thoughts took him back many years. Come to think about it, it was the Madero family who always said that little *Panchito,* as he was called, was the "chosen one" in their family. Members of his family, and also a spiritualist, had told him that he was special and would do great and wonderful things, and that one day he would be President of Mexico.

Juan and *Don* Federico found themselves being introduced to other important men present, such as Aquiles Serdan, from the state of Puebla; Roque Estrada; Gilardo Magana; Francisco J. Mugica, another journalist from the state of Michoacan; and Venustiano Carranza, governor of Coahuila, under the Díaz regime. They also met several businessmen from San Antonio, Ernesto Arteaga, and José Vasconcelos, a lawyer. Many important Mexican-American *tejanos* with money like himself were there to help and support Madero. The whole hotel looked like a Mexican convention held in that city.

Coming out from one of the other rooms, *Señor* Madero appeared. He was small in stature but known for his big heartedness. His face was round and pleasant, with eyes alert, and an openness giving him the look of someone who had never known bitterness, much less hardship. Everyone stood up, and the animated talk and laughter that had gone on immediately prior changed to a deep silence.

"*Compadre,* Federico!" shouted Madero. Both men embraced in an *abrazo.* "It's been a long time. I'm glad you're here and that Juan convinced you to come to my cause."

ROOTS OF INDIFFERENCE

"I would not have missed it for the world! But! What happened to you, *compadre*?" replied *Don* Federico, trying to figure out what was so different about Madero. His face reflected a frown, but instantly turned into a pleasant smile.

"Oh! That's a long story, *amigo*. Come! Let's sit down and I'll explain. But who do you have with you?" Madero was looking at Fred.

"This is my oldest son, Fred. He's only ten years old but he was already anxious to meet you. One day he will tell the story of this great reunion. He is attending the military school in the spring and will continue his education later for higher things. Fred! Shake *Señor* Madero's hand!" demanded *Don* Federico.

Fred stood in awe, shaking the hand of the next President of Mexico, and felt honored and proud.

"You are only ten years old and already you're as tall as I am," retorted Madero, who was looking squarely into Fred's eyes. "You are going to be a very tall man." He laughed and patted Fred on the back.

Making their way through a mix of elaborate living room furniture, all sat down on an old Victorian velvet couch while Madero ordered one of the men to bring drinks for him and his guests.

Madero explained to *Don* Federico that he had disguised himself as a railroader, working as a brakeman, and had to shave his beard off. He said that his life had been in danger since his arrest in Monterrey, and that *Don* Porfirio Díaz had given the order to shoot to kill. His life wasn't worth a peso in Mexico while Díaz was running the country. He went into a lengthy discussion of the thousands of men and women who would risk their lives for the goodness of their country. Texas was the perfect place, and here in San Antonio they would all join together to plan the Revolution.

Don Federico could see that Madero had changed. Not only in his voice, which was soft but high-pitched, but also in his manners, which were eloquent and kind, sensitive to the needs of his people, as he would say. He spoke with his hands, a sign of extreme nervousness.

On the third day of the convention, Gustavo Madero joined his brother and the rest of the revolutionists. He had been to Washington, D.C., to take on the difficult assignment of raising more funds. Gustavo was the tallest of the Madero family, dashing and gregarious, fair-skinned, with light blue eyes, one of which was made of glass. As the days passed, the men became acquainted with each other and contributed their thoughts and feelings, taking on the difficult task of the coming struggle.

⌘ ⌘ ⌘

On the fourth day, and by *Señor* Madero's request, *Don* Federico addressed the men of the convention in the main ballroom, to say a few words of encouragement.

"My friends and colleagues of the Revolution," he began. "Being a Mexican-American, a *Tejano*, I stand before you with mixed emotions. I have feelings for all mankind. Most of my colleagues on both side of the border are suffering. By looking like a Mexican and saying you're a Mexican, it suggests that there is much endurance and anguish mixed with misery ahead. The majority of our people on both sides, in Mexico and in Texas, are not educated, so they live by what means of survival given to them. Normally only hard labor is allowed to them, by reasons of our *'roots of indifference.'* My blood boils to know that all the years *Don* Porfirio Díaz, has been in office, he has not educated the people, especially the children, in Mexico. Education is the most important thing in people's lives. I'm a firm believer that reading and writing open the door to understanding. It gives you knowledge, and knowledge gives you power. Education is not expensive, but ignorance is, and we have most of the Mexicans living in both counties in an ignorant state, having to live as slaves, despised, because they do not know any better. After hearing and listening to the terrible stories of what's become of our beloved land, we need a change. It's never too late to remedy an evil in a good country, and a change with an honorable President is needed in Mexico. One who knows its people and is willing to sacrifice with his sweat in the upcoming struggle to get rid of corrupt people in that government. I feel deep in my heart that it is just to oppose the current government of President Díaz that for so many years has made slaves of its people, instead of educating them so they can better themselves. I'm donating this money and hope that all of you dig deep into your pockets and in your hearts for the better change and for a brighter future. In our hands, we hold the future of our Mexico. It's my country, too, my mother's country."

Don Federico paused and scanned the crowd. "It is with humility that I was honored to speak to you this way. Mexico is being run by tyrants and being dominated by greedy foreigners on both sides of the river. And wherever there is greed, there is cruelty and injustice. As long as there's injustice, there will never be peace. Mexico is our foundation as our country—it's our roots. We must defend what is rightfully ours: our country, our families, and our property. If we all band together and perform our highest duty by making it possible for all, we can surely overthrow the tyranny of Porfirio Díaz. Francisco Madero is a man of great courage! A man that is willing to stand against all odds, especially the great evils that have oppressed the people of Mexico. Let us give him the strength to support this cause—for the future, for Mexico. For this reason, I ask of you, as great men and patriots, to join hands and support the honorable, the impeccable man of unstained honor— *Señor* Pancho Madero."

"Bravo! Bravo!" Juan yelled standing up and clapping. "Bravo!" yelled the rest of the comrades. There arose a great roar, and then all stood up and joined in with great respect for *El Señor Don* Federico.

"It's a brave man who speaks those words," said one of the attendees.

"All of us should be able to speak in that form," replied another revolutionist.

Madero embraced *Don* Federico, as uncontrollable tears tickled down his round face. "It is wonderful, *compadre*, that you feel that way. Now I truly know my struggle will not be in vain."

"I trust that none of the colleagues here will refuse their aid in forming a government of justice and honor," added Juan with exaltation. "We are willing to die for our heritage."

ROOTS OF INDIFFERENCE

Madero, who now had the floor, spoke to the men of when he was brought before Díaz and later had been put in prison. "It is honesty that Mexico needs," said Madero to his colleagues. "There has been little of it. The crimes that are being committed on both sides of the border have lowered the prestige of both countries. Yes, *mi amigos* and patriots, it is honesty that Mexico needs."

The following days were full of encouragement and patriotism. Madero, with the help of his brothers and suggestions from Juan, *Don* Federico, and other eloquent members, drew up the plan of San Luis Potosi. It was for the restitution to the peasants of the lands in Mexico.

They all began organizing a formal government. It was a good feeling, among honest and courageous men, as they all joined together making decisions with mutual sympathy and kindness. It was also during the convention that *Don* Federico had invited all the honored guests to attend his daughter's 16th birthday celebration. Many thanked him and said they would attend.

Among the talking and chatting, there were many important names mentioned, including one Doroteo Arango, later to be known as Pancho Villa, who was staying at the moment in the city of Chihuahua, capital of the State of Chihuahua. His wisdom was referred to as "superior," knowing all the roads and paths in the Sierra Mountains. "Pancho Villa is not afraid of the devil himself," the crowd would say. The governor of Chihuahua, Abraham Gonzales, who at one time had had dealings with Don Federico's father in buying cattle, had also joined the Madero cause. Already, rumors of Emilio Zapata in the south of Mexico were becoming widespread along with talk of Felipe Angeles, who at the moment was living in exile in Paris, France. A brilliant authority on artillery tactics, he was regarded as a man of high principles and knew the finer intricacies of modern warfare.

Don Federico, Fred, and Juan had been in San Antonio for nine days and had enjoyed the historical, important meeting. At this time, Juan bid his farewell, with an *abrazo*, heading for the state of Chihuahua to be with Pancho Villa, but promising to do his best to get back for Victoria's party.

It was the beginning of the rainy season, and a gentle drizzle had begun to fall. The atmosphere was threatening in the city, as news of plotting the Revolution had leaked out. United States agents were like hornets all around the hotel trying to get secret information about what was happening. The great *Don* had an urgent instinct to leave the city as soon as possible, not wanting his name or Fred's connected to the Revolution or to have any involvement with any political news. War hawks and some reporters wanting to get the news first were already printing pamphlets, recruiting volunteers, asking for money to fight for the Mexican cause, and mercenaries began to enter the country of Mexico for hire.

Don Federico felt the trip to San Antonio had been very successful, but there were activities awaiting him at Spanish Acres. The planning of Victoria's fiesta birthday party was in order with much work and preparations. Many important people were coming from Mexico, eminent people from both sides of the border, and many families from the surrounding *ranchitos.*

Taking advantage of their remaining time in San Antonio, *Don* Federico and Fred went to the large department stores on Commerce Street with a list a mile long to do their shopping: tailored suits; shoes and socks of all different sizes for every male member of the family and household; bolts of material that consisted of plain and different patterns and colors, lace, organdy, broadcloth, silk, Irish linen, and gabardine; ornaments for the ladies' hair; belts, ties and buckles for the men. Across the street was a small Sears and Roebuck mail-order store, in which the *Don* decided to buy the largest Acme Regal enameled steel range made, to surprise Mamá Maria and the rest of the ladies who worked in the kitchen. Seroco ready-mixed house paint in tinted white was bought in twenty-five and fifty gallon barrels. Everything would be loaded onto the train for shipping the following day.

On the other side of the cobblestone street, the two entered the Western Union Telegraph Office to send a message to the hacienda, advising his wife of the time of their arrival, and to be ready for Roy or Manuel with two mule wagons for the enormous amount of supplies that would be coming.

Several blocks from the mercantile building in an upstairs room was the office of the Pinkerton Detective Agency. *Don* Federico decided to visit Tom White and pay the rest of the money that he owed him. Surprisingly, he was met at the door by a short, elderly woman, with her white hair pinned on top of her head, and wrinkles displaying every one of her years. Holding papers in her hands, she greeted him very professionally. "May I help you?" she addressed him warmly.

"I'm looking for Tom White," said *Don* Federico, bringing out a swollen envelope from his dark vest and handing it to the lady. "He did some investigation for me down in South Texas, for the last sixteen months, with which I am very pleased. While I'm staying in San Antonio, I thought I would bring him the rest of the money I owe him."

"Tom White is one of our finest agents, but we have not heard from him in over three weeks now. He mailed us some information from Harlingen, which we turned over to the United States Marshal in Austin. That was the last message we have gotten from him. Some of the other agents have questioned his silence. Maybe he decided to stay down in the Rio Grande Valley and retire there, as he's of a retiring age, you know!" The elderly woman returned to her desk with the envelope.

"That's very odd!" the *Don* replied, mystified and rubbing his chin. "It's been several weeks since I last talked to him, and he gave me the information I needed from the investigation that he was doing. And as for retiring in the Valley—I don't think so! By the tone of his voice, he was planning to leave that same night, on the next train back to San Antonio. He said he was leaving. Well, anyway, tell him I said hello and that his services are paid."

"We will, sir! And your name is?" she cautiously asked.

"*Señor* Federico Juelson, at your service," he said proudly.

"Why, of course." She stood at her desk and looked inside the envelope and counted the money, handing him a written receipt for his payment. "We surely will. And thank you very much for the money. I will put a message in his locker drawer. Thanks again."

ROOTS OF INDIFFERENCE

Don Federico and Fred walked downstairs and headed for the hotel. Stunned by the information, he wondered what had happened to Tom White. Thinking back, Tom was planning to leave as soon as possible because he had felt his life was in danger in the Lower Valley. Perhaps he had decided to stay longer and finish more of his work. *That's it! That must be it. Why would he have stayed? Did something happen to him when he returned to Harlingen?* The *Don's* mind wandered. He was also surprised to see a woman running an office, and so efficiently. For the moment, he decided he would not let anything interfere with his vacation and especially, spending time with his son. He was going to enjoy every minute of it with Fred in the beautiful city of San Antonio.

Taking advantage of being in the big city, *Don* Federico went to visit his sister, Josie, whom he had not seen in several years. In the beginning, when she first had gotten married to Morris McCormach, her letters were prompt, full of joy and happiness. He had received one every week. As the years passed, the letters that were so regular were now non-existent. His sister had not responded to any of his correspondence in almost two years; not even when she received the news of her father's death. *Don* Federico had written her many letters, and even after the death telegram, she had never replied.

Renting a one-horse buggy with a driver from the San Antonio Hotel, he and Fred rode across the city of San Antonio, seeing the beautiful views and the quaint old Spanish hacienda-style houses. At Grayson Street and North Brounfels Avenue was the military post called Fort Sam Houston. There stood a ninety-foot clock tower, and Fred, being so young and impressionable, was in complete awe. He had never seen anything so tall and beautiful.

They approached an area that looked like barracks quarters—rows and rows, side by side, each against the other. They were all painted in a greenish-gray paint and unpleasant to the eye, as a matter of fact, depressing, in alphabetical rows. Looking at his notebook and checking the last address he had, *Don* Federico began tapping gently on the door at number L-125. Nobody answered, and the place looked like it was vacant. As *Don* Federico peeked in one of the open windows, a young couple was coming into the apartment next door, arms full of packages. They stopped and stared. "Are you looking for the people who lived there? They have moved five doors up to L-130. It's the one on the corner." The man said, "Are you related?"

"Why, yes!" *Don* Federico answered. "Josie is my sister. But, I have not heard from her in years. While we are visiting San Antonio, I wanted to see her."

"Well! I hope she's still alive!" stated the young man harshly. "The military police have been at their apartment many times. Some of the neighbors on both sides of the quarters have complained. Apparently her husband beats her up all the time."

Don Federico was shocked and at a complete loss. "Thank you very much for your information." He slowly put the address book in his pocket. "I will see if I can find her," he answered, walking away and getting into the buggy. His face was puckered, concealing his anger, as his blood was boiling.

"What it is? Papá," Fred replied, already looking tired and weary sitting in the buggy. "Is Aunt Josie gone?"

"No, son, she is just around the corner," he said, advising the driver to drive up several doors away. Tapping gently again on the number L-130's door, *Don* Federico knocked again. No one answered. He tapped again and stood for a moment, stupefied. Finally, he saw the door knob turn.

"Josie!"

From the inside darkness a woman appeared, then, "Lico!" she cried, using the name she called him when they were growing up. She hugged his neck and held him for a very long time. Letting go of his shoulders, she gently said, "What brings you to San Antonio?"

"I'm here on political business and to do some trading and some shopping. And because I haven't heard from you in so long, I was worried. You have never responded to my letters or messages, not even to Dad's death. I was expecting you at Dad's funeral! Did you get my telegram? What's wrong? What has happened to you?" he questioned. By looking at her, he could see that she was troubled. Her body was thin and fragile, she was hollow-eyed, and her hair, which had been intense black, was now disheveled and turning gray at her young age. Her face reflected joy at seeing him, but it was not hard to see a sad, spiritually depressed woman. Her appearance was of a woman who had lived through many hours of almost certain death.

In her younger years, she was perhaps the prettiest, next to Francisca, that he had ever seen in a woman. Her life, as well as her childhood would have been called "romantic." She was always falling in love with every stranger their father brought to the hacienda as a guest. His father's friends were people involved in military strategy. She was drawn to them, because they were important and related stories about battles and war. She was married at fifteen to Morris McCormach, the son of her father's friend, and moved away to San Antonio, where her life took a different turn. He could understand, because Josie was a baby when their mother died, and never received the bonding love of a mother.

"Tell me what's happening with you?" he repeated again, not wanting to reveal what the couple who lived next door had told him. He waited.

"I don't know!" she answered in dismay, but irritably. She moved inside the cluttered, dark living room, her hands over her face, and sat down on a couch and began to cry and shake. "I have not felt good in many months. I don't feel good about myself. Look at me!" she exclaimed, standing up and opening up her robe, displaying her distended stomach. "I've gotten fat and ugly."

It wasn't hard for *Don* Federico to recognize his sister was with child. "Why, I think it's beautiful! I think it's wonderful! And you have always been beautiful. Women are the prettiest when they are with child, and what a blessing it is to have children," he responded, smiling. "Josie! By the way and speaking of children," he said enthusiastically. "I have a surprise for you. I have Fred with me. He is out in the buggy, let me go and get him. He is now ten years old and is growing like a weed."

Closing her robe, wiping her face and blowing her nose into a handkerchief, Josie followed her brother to the door and pulled her hair back, where the light reflected on her face.

ROOTS OF INDIFFERENCE

Don Federico walked outdoors and called to Fred. Returning with his son, he noticed one of her eyes was blackened. "Look! Can you believe he's that tall?" he said as Josie hugged Fred.

She stood for a moment looking at the young lad. "I can't believe he's so tall. He's going to be a handsome and very tall man. All the women better watch out," she said jokingly, turning to face her brother. "Come in. Let me make you some coffee. Can I get you some cold water to drink?" she said nervously, as they entered the narrow hallway.

"I would like some water," Fred answered, surprised at the crammed and messy conditions in which his aunt was living. He had heard so many stories about her, and he thought she had many of the same characteristics as Victoria in looks and in actions.

"The kitchen is down the hall. I have a pitcher of water on the counter. There's a glass on top of the shelf," she said, pointing as Fred hurried down the hall.

"Where is McCormach?" *Don* Federico questioned, looking straight into Josie's eyes.

"He's gone. He's always gone and never tells me anything. Never tells me his official duties. He leaves for days, sometimes weeks, and I never know when he is supposed to come back. He always surprises me when he returns."

"What happened to your eye?" questioned the *Don* with great concern.

"It's nothing! It looks worse than it feels," she said, placing her hand over her right eye, trying to hide her abused face. "I lost my balance and stumbled against the corner of the door going into the kitchen," she responded nervously, with a little laugh.

"I don't believe you, Josie!" He could tell when his sister was not telling the truth by her actions and her giddy remarks.

"I did fall" she remarked sullenly.

"Yes! But at who's hands?"

"Lico!" She turned cautiously to face him. "What are you implying?"

"Face it, Josie! You married a man that's not worth your name and heritage. He's a military man that cares only about himself and the Army. In one of your old letters, you talked of your concern about his drinking all the time, making you unhappy. The situation is getting worse. Is that it? McCormach is drinking all the time and has become a drunk? And when he comes home, he takes it out on you. Beats you, and you make excuses for his actions. Am I correct? You better tell me now, since you're coming home with me. You'll need help when the baby comes." His voice got progressively louder.

"No! No!" cried Josie hysterically. "I can't go anywhere!" she begged. "I'll be all right. I need to stay here. I don't want to face anyone at Spanish Acres. I don't want anyone to see me like this, especially Mamá Maria who raised me. That's the reason I couldn't come home for Dad's funeral. I was with child then and had a miscarriage." She began sobbing uncontrollably.

"Spanish Acres is your home." *Don* Federico was overcome with a deep, profound, compassion for his sister. "And everyone in the hacienda would love to see you. Everyone would love to see a new baby in the household. Nobody is going to mistreat you there. Get your clothes ready!" he ordered. "You're coming home with me. I will not have my sister being mistreated and beaten up, especially in your condition. You don't need McCormach. All he needs you for is to clean up after him and have his meals ready, and someone to warm his bed. He's using you. Can't you see that?"

"It's not McCormach's fault," she retorted, blaming herself, trying hard to protect her husband's image. Her hands cuddled her face. She then looked up at her brother who was standing over her, and she sighed resignedly. "It's my fault. I was lonely. He's away all the time, and I needed some comfort and affection. I needed someone I could talk with. McCormach will not let me have or make friends. He does not want them to be influencing me. He's afraid that friends would give me ideas." She paused, and then came the final shock. "The baby does not belong to McCormach."

"What are you saying?" *Don* Federico stormed. "Well, whose is it?" He tried to curb his temper. "For hell's fire sakes! Tell me!" He blurted out the words, gasping in disbelief.

There was a long discreet pause. "It belongs to a man who has been good to me and would help me fix things inside the house. The windows always needed fixing and the hinges on the door. The pipes that the military installs for the kitchen sinks leak all the time and he would fix them, especially the pump. The nails on this floor needed pounding. I had no way of doing things. I have no tools. McCormach would not allow me to have any money. I was never taught anything when I was growing up, especially when it comes to doing a man's work. He works here at the base as a handyman, fixing things up. He's a very good man and occasionally he would bring me flowers, a box of chocolates, and listen to what I had to say. He is very patient with me, and I look forward to seeing him."

"A good fixer-upper, huh, and he fixed you up good!" said *Don* Federico. "And now what are you going to do? Does McCormach want the baby? Do you? These are things that you are going to be confronted with in the near future. Does the man you have been sleeping with know you're pregnant? And is he ready to take on the responsibility?"

"No!"

"No! To which question? What's all the mystery?"

Josie began sobbing again, making no comment to the questions. "No, I made a big mistake," she replied miserably. "And now I'll have to pay for it, by myself. I can't go home with you, Lico. I need to stay here and confront my mistake, regardless of the cost."

"When is the baby due, Josie?" *Don* Federico took a deep breath, trying to cool down and control his temper, while confronting her predicament. There had to be a solution to her problems.

"In April of next year," she said soberly, with a grim look. "I don't know if I'll keep the child or not. I will probably have to give the child away."

"Have you gone crazy? You are not making any sense!"

"If I stay with McCormach, I'll have to give the child away."

"You can come home with me, where you'll be taken care of. Be with Mamá Maria and Manuel who raised you and loved you. I'll see that greedy McCormach does not touch you and hurt you any more. If you decide to stay, I'll leave you some money, and please hide it in a safe place, for an emergency so that when you need to leave, you'll have it. My train leaves early in the morning if you want to come with us. It's full of items we bought for Victoria's fiesta, coming up in November. We want you to come and enjoy the festivities with us."

While she wiped her eyes and blew her nose, Josie asked. "How is Victoria? She must be getting real big, by now," she questioned in her strident voice, "and pretty, too!"

"Victoria is getting too big for her boots, if that's what you mean. She'll be leaving for Monterrey in January." His tone of voice became calmer and he became more patient. "She is going to get an education, attending the same school that Francisca attended when she was growing up."

Fred had remained quiet, listening, fascinated by the exciting news and problems.

"Oh! My! Before you know it, Victoria will be getting married." Josie's bloodshot eyes lowered while she talked, and there was a despairing sadness in them.

"Not for a while," remarked *Don* Federico, glancing at his pocket watch. "She needs schooling and a good education first. Josie!" he announced. "I'm afraid time is against us. We are going to have to go. Please! Promise me to take care of yourself." And while talking, he reached his right hand inside of his vest and brought out five one hundred dollar bills. "Take this and put it where McCormach will not see it. Use it when you think it is necessary. C'mon Fred! We had better go. It's getting late and we still have packing to do at the hotel. The driver must think we have forgotten him."

"Lico!" said Josie, getting up, holding onto the money, and hugging *Don* Federico's neck. "I hate to see you and Fred leave, but you must. I will write to you. I promise to let you know what I plan to do. I love you," she said, and kissed his cheek.

"Remember," he told her seriously. "Telegraph me if you find yourself in danger."

After climbing into the buggy he and Fred were silent. An empty feeling engulfed both of them. *What a pity*, thought *Don* Federico. Josie was a woman who had deserved the best. She had been as lovely as a picture and could have had any young man with education and money, but she chose otherwise. It was truly a shame, he kept thinking, for the glamour and splendor that once was hers had been taken away forever. She was now a thin, confused, grieving person, instead of the beauty that she had been. Marriage was a sacred thing, yet in some cases, when men abused their privileges, taking advantages of their rights, the holy sacrament had to be dissolved.

In the early hours of the morning, *Don* Federico and Fred departed San Antonio by train on the first route south to the Rio Grande Valley. Sprinkles of a light rain had developed, making it difficult to carry their baggage and load the two wagonloads of supplies.

The long drive home would give the great *Don* time to think. His new worries about his sister had complicated his life and plans. He had a disquieting feeling about her, and he hoped his sister would not do anything drastic to herself. Other things were on *Don* Federico's mind as well; he was concerned about Tom White and what had happened to him in not returning to his station in San Antonio; the planning of Victoria's birthday party and her future. Her schooling in Monterrey was more reassuring with the prospect that Madero would become president. And had they found the body of the *gringa*? The thoughts kept haunting him. He had not had time to think of his wife's illness, and ashamedly had enjoyed the break from the hacienda. He anxiously waited to see her and his young son, Carlos, and Victoria again. He was excited about the accomplishment and the contribution that he had given in the famous meeting in San Antonio. It would be an historical event. The light drizzle of rain had increased, making the weather uncomfortable and sticky as the train rolled south toward the Rio Grande Valley.

It was during this long ride home on the train, that *Don* Federico was able to talk to his son about the complications of marriage, profession, and life, giving Fred direction and advice that was best for him to take. "See why it's so important to become a lawyer?" he asked Fred. "You get to know the laws of the land. Know your rights. This way nobody can make a fool of you, because you have learned and studied and given advice to others. You can advance in your career later by becoming a politician and helping your community and country. Make a name for yourself!"

"But Papá, I want to become a doctor. Like Juan! I want to help people, too. I want Mamá to get better and to find out what her illness is. I can help people and heal them with medicine. I want to learn and study." He began yawning, turning his head to the window.

"All right, my son!" *Don* Federico smiled and sighed, pleased with his oldest son so full of dreams and so full of "I wants." He was still a child and had so much to learn about the cruelty of society, especially in the Rio Grande Valley, which was so full of bias and hatred toward the Mexican-American people. He would have to learn it the hard way, like everyone else did—the harsh reality and the terrible hurt that festers deep inside your soul from rejection.

"For the moment you can be whatever you want to be. We'll see! And we will talk later about what's best for you. You have many years to think about a good education and a wonderful career. My main point is that the Mexican-American people in the Valley could surely use you as an attorney."

Don Federico wanted to tell him how hard life really was. He wanted to tell him how life had been for him, and how difficult it had been for him growing up. He understood Fred's uneasiness. All of the harshness of life in the Rio Grande Valley would become more apparent as he got older.

Fred would have to confront the problems of his identify, his mixed-race among white people in a society that was biased, especially in Texas. The *Don* wanted to tell him so much, but could not come to terms with himself in explaining so many important things that matter in life. He kept studying Fred, who seemed so unaware and unconcerned, so gangling and awkward, and so damn mischievous.

The many hours on the train were spent together with food, soft drinks, humor, laughter, and the anticipation of getting home to all of their animals and loved ones. When the time came for *Don* Federico to say something, he glanced toward Fred, who had been busy at the window counting the poles along the railroad tracks.

But there was no answer. Fred was slumped down on the seat, sound asleep.

CHAPTER 9

"Next stop, coming up," announced the black porter with the Missouri and Southern Pacific Line. The stop was only a short pause, in desolate cacti and bush country, where several wooden cattle pens used to load *Don* Federico's and other ranchers' cattle, sat empty. The donated land made it convenient for the inhabitants who lived within the twenty-mile district to load or unload their animals.

Don Federico and Fred were tired and both had anxiously been awaiting their return home. It had been a long trip, and ten days had seemed like an eternity. San Antonio was very nice; however, coming home was wonderful.

They hoped Roy would be at the location to pick them up, since it was already getting late in the afternoon. *Don* Federico was excited to get home and see if there had been any new news. The train came to a screeching halt. Already from the window, Fred had caught a glimpse of Manuel sitting on one wagon and in another wagon was Manuel's friend Yo-Yo, from a little *ranchito* close to the border on the Mexico side. Yo-Yo wasn't his real name, but everyone had called him that ever since he could remember. He got his name simply because his answer to everything was, "Yo, yo, yo." In Spanish, it meant "me." He would visit Spanish Acres about six times a year, especially when he was low on money, and would help Roy and the rest of the *vaqueros* with the cattle and the horses. He was an expert on cattle, knowing everything there was to know about them. Yo-Yo was an older, graying man, about fifty-nine, tall and thin, the opposite of Manuel. His face was always jolly and swarthy, with an aquiline nose and Indian high-cheekbone features. He was a *vaquero* by profession and a fiddler by heart. Yo-Yo and Manuel had something special in common—they both liked to drink. "And you could bet your boots," mumbled *Don* Federico under his breath to Fred, "that the two of them have already had a real hummer of a fandango."

Fred laughed out loud as he picked up his packages and followed his father outside, where he felt the difference in the humid temperature.

"*Patrón, Don* Federico! Over here!" shouted Manuel, waving his hands frantically, as though *el patrón* might not have seen him. He weighed over two hundred pounds, and there was no way *Don* Federico could have failed to notice him. There were two wagons, with two mules hitched to them, and there was nothing else around except the desolate isolation surrounding the rampant undergrowth, the wilderness, and the abandoned cattle pens.

"Ay! *Don* Federico we have miss' jeu." He spoke Spanish in between his broken English. *Tanto gusto* to have jeu safe back," Manuel said, smiling. "And jeu been goon' for a very long *tiempo*."

Yo-Yo staggered towards *Don* Federico and gave him an *abrazo* and turned to Fred and gave him one, too. You could smell the spirits drenched in and out of his body. Both men were soaked with the besotting liquids. His breath would melt paint.

"Ah, ha, *qué pasa, Don* Federico." Yo-Yo's greeting came with a cheerful smile and few teeth.

"I am a little tired," answered the *Don*. "Looks like the area had some rain." He surveyed the vast landscape and could see puddles of water. In the late afternoon, the fog was thick and rising.

"Uh huh, it rained a little last night. That's why it's so sticky and stuffy," answered Yo-Yo. And then another, "Uh huh! We had a real hell of a *tiempo* gettin' here. Yes sir, a real *tiempo* gettin' here, uh huh. The dirt *caminos* got big *arroyos* of water, uh huh."

"Afraid we did not get here in good *tiempo*," interrupted Manuel. Both of their conversations were confused, and they went on and on and made all kinds of excuses, rambling on, with so many unnecessary explanations that it was a wonder they found their way.

Yo-Yo would reply, "Uh huh," to every sentence, beginning and ending, it did not matter. Sometimes he would speak and then answer himself.

It took close to an hour before all of the merchandise was unloaded from the train and stacked into the two mule wagons. Many of the Negroes working on the train helped load. *Don* Federico gave each one a tip.

"Ay! *Hijo!*" shouted Manuel, scratching his head and looking at the merchandise.

"Ay! *Caramba!* Uh huh," retorted Yo-Yo, looking surprised, "Uh huh!"

The people waiting in the coach compartments of the train were being inquisitive, for they were looking out the windows, and many appeared to be getting restless, for their destination was Harlingen and on down to Brownsville. Finally, the train continued its destination south, leaving a foggy trail of smoke behind.

"Well! Let's get things moving, Manuel!" snapped *Don* Federico. His voice was firm and sharp, as he was eager to get home. He knew that it wasn't the bad roads up ahead, but the liquor that had perhaps complicated their directions in getting to the railroad tracks.

"*Como no, patrón. Los vámos!*" Manuel said.

"Uh huh," was the word of the day.

The sun was slowly going down in the west. It made the vapors rise, and before long all four were soaked and drenching wet with sweat. The unproductive land immediately gave way to the hostile mesquite and chaparral mixed with cacti. It swelled away toward the horizon that separated land and sky. Steam rose from the soaked, muddy ground like a ghostly mist. They could smell the fog and mist infiltrating their nostrils. The fickle weather was slowly changing from one season to the next, and in the distance they could see the tall cottonwood trees trading their green leaves for gold. Up ahead a black vulture was circling above one of the mesquite trees. Occasionally, a mockingbird would call out. Moss hung on many of the gray branches of the tall mesquite trees, imparting a feeling of eerie awe.

Up the muddy road, *Don* Federico asked Manuel, "How are things back at the hacienda?" Manuel did not answer immediately but shrugged with nervousness, and chewed his gum faster to the point of grinding his teeth between rigid jaws. *Don* Federico turned his head back to view Yo-Yo, who was driving the second wagon and making a snoring noise. The *Don* had known Manuel since he was a young man, and he was familiar with the man's actions and mannerisms. He decided the two were keeping some secret news between them.

"We gut's company at the hacienda," replied Manuel, blurting out the words. "*Ay! Dios!*" His words sounded like his mouth was full of mush.

Behind came the sounds of "Uh huh!"

"Oh?" *Don* Federico replied.

"Ay, *Don* Federico, please forgive me. *La Señora* Francisca, she tells me not to say nothin' to jeu. She tells jeu, herself. But I *sabe!* How much jeu hates *la Señora* Emma. Well! She had been at the *casa* for seven days. We have counted the hours." The two rolled their eyes.

"That's all I need!" he answered in disgust, "Emma and her big mouth, giving orders to all."

"Yo-Yo and Manuel have been out with the *vaqueros*, because Yo-Yo and Manuel don't like her talk. Uh huh!" replied Yo-Yo from behind, followed by another, "Uh huh!"

"That fat woman would make a saint cuss," replied the *Don*, frowning. "Foul mouthed witch, trampling everyone who gets in her way." But Manuel and Yo-Yo, these two old buzzards, did not need an excuse to get away. As long as there was drinking to do, it was considered serious business.

"Uh huh!" chimed in Yo-Yo, "Uh huh."

"Everyone at the hacienda is upset with each other since Emma got here. Uh huh! But *mí compadre*, Manuel, and Yo-Yo do not want to get into the wee'men's skirts. So we leave them alone." He coughed and then repeated, "Uh huh."

"Also," said Manuel, "Martin, *el Toro*, called 'the bull,' the young boy from the *ranchito Trevino* southwest of Spanish Acres, came looking for Fred. He ran away from home because his Papá, *Señor* Trevino, beat him good. A *chinga* of a beating the boy got. He was bleeding so badly that Maria had to put salve on his back. He'll be staying at the *Rancho* and helping Roy with the cattle."

Fred's eyes lit up. "Oh, great!" he responded. "I haven't seen him in a long time, and I'll have someone to play with."

Don Federico remained silent. He was watching the road and the mules up front, his mind deep in thought. The fog was thickening as the last sun rays beamed through the top of the mesquite trees. Passing along some large rocks in the middle of the dirt road, the wagons slowed to a snail's pace because of the roughness of the unpaved path that disappeared into the grayish jungle of cacti and cottonwood trees that had sprawled out in every direction.

But it was not long before they could see the windmills standing erect in the distance. Out in the gathering dusk could be seen several of the *vaqueros* riding herd on the many cattle. As the land became flatter, the wagons rolled faster, and they soon passed under the tall arches and around to the back of the big house.

The thought of Emma made *Don* Federico's blood boil. But Emma was Francisca's cousin, blood cousin. She was the only daughter of Francisca's mother's sister, *Señora* Dolores Ochoa, from Monterrey, Mexico, who had died many years ago. Emma came from the era of the "bosoms and buttocks" style of fashion—a "Gibson Girl" image. She had perhaps thrown her corset away many years ago, because companies did not make them that large. She had been blessed with heavy legs—piano legs, holding the enormous weight of her body, since the Lord, thank heavens, knew all the time what he was doing with her from the very beginning.

Emma's first husband was an infantry soldier stationed at Fort Ringgold, the Army post in Rio Grande City, and he was killed when their daughter Felicia was only a year old. The couple had been married for only three years when he died.

Grieving and with a young child, Emma in her early twenties had been attractive and thin. She attracted a new, older husband, Howard Ale, who was a retired military judge, as well as a widower and a womanizer. But he had money.

Immediately after their marriage, Emma's character began changing, and nothing could stop her from trampling over everyone who got in her way. Because of Howard Ale's status and money, Emma developed a tremendous ego. Her feeling of importance went straight to her head. Still a bride, she convinced Howard Ale to move to Mercedes City, buying several acres from the *Fuste Rancho* called Saddletree, which was previously owned by the Cavazos family. There they built their three-story home. It didn't take long before Emma became a nosey, busybody socialite, interfering in everyone's lives, having parties and social dinners for the rich and important people with vast amounts of wealth and income. She was unaware of her eating disorder and after the twins were born, she found an opportunity to rectify that and began gaining weight.

In *Don* Federico's imagination, he could hear her talking in her high-pitched voice that sounded like a handsaw in high gear; but Emma was family and he had to be receptive to her needs for his wife's sake, in spite of his feelings of intolerance toward her.

Outside, many of his servants and his immediate family were waiting for them: Elena and Miguel with all their children, including Yolanda; Roy, with several of the *vaqueros* and Martin; Victoria, and Felicia, holding hands with little Carlos; Soledad, who stood next to Mamá Maria; behind them was Olivia and Ophelia; and in the far corner—Emma. *Doña* Francisca was strangely absent, which left *Don* Federico puzzled.

Sounds of joy erupted from all, with hugs and kisses all around, except for Emma, who stood with her arms folded across her enormous waist, or what was called a waist, because she had a body that was balanced in all directions: four by four, short and heavy. Felicia, the only daughter of Emma by her first husband, was considered shy, quiet and reserved, and no wonder, for the girl was completely dominated by her mother.

ROOTS OF INDIFFERENCE

"Roy," hollered *Don* Federico, "have the rest of the men help you unload the packages and bring them inside. The large covered box, unload it off the wagon and leave it outside. I want to surprise Mamá Maria." Heading through the entrance, he went past Emma and suddenly, in pretend surprise, stopped and looked her way. "Why, Emma! What brings you to Spanish Acres?" he said mockingly.

"I came to see about Francisca, who is terribly sick," she replied, getting her feathers all ruffled. "You need to start paying attention to her and her illness," she scolded. "The cattle, horses, and animals get more attention than the human beings in this place!"

"She has only a cough! And you know better, that's not true!"

"She's got more than a cough," replied Emma obstinately, in her high pitched voice. Her eyes were dead set on the *Don* and full of venom. "We took her to the doctor in Reynosa a couple of days ago, and he claims she has consumption, and what is worse, a rare case of the disease—tuberculosis. She needs medication and plenty of rest."

"Where is Francisca now?" answered *Don* Federico, stunned and shaken, feeling a sense of humiliation and guilt and for traveling and having left her, not knowing she was that sick. It was like drawing a bad hand in poker.

"Lying down where she needs to be!" Emma answered angrily. "She is sleeping now."

"To tell you the truth, Emma," *Don* Federico answered, looking at her squarely, "I have been insisting on taking her to the doctor, but she has refused. She takes the medicine that *Doña* Adela gives her. Furthermore, I am not a doctor!" The *Don's* voice became louder and more irritable. "And your cousin, as you well know, is very stubborn. I can only do so much!"

"Bah! Witch things! What a poor excuse! That medicine hasn't helped her. You should have known better! As educated as you are, you should have detected that she was worse than she's letting on. The day I arrived, Francisca fainted and began coughing up blood. It scared all of us in the household. Victoria, Manuel, and I took her to Reynosa. We had no other choice! We took her to see my doctor across the border."

Don Federico, visibly shaken, dropped everything and hurried upstairs. Fred had already run upstairs to see his mother, but found her sleeping. He put his finger to his lips and whispered to his father as he approached the entrance. "Mom's asleep. I'm going downstairs to see Martin, *el Toro.*"

"Fred, I have to talk to Martin and ask him what happened at his house." *Don* Federico spoke very softly while looking at Fred seriously. "I do not want any trouble with his father. I know his father is very abusive to him, his brother, and his wife. Martin can stay here as long as he wants. I have no objection to that."

"Thank you, Papá," answered Fred. Anxious to find his friend, he hurried on down the stairs.

Entering into his wife's bedroom, the *Don* saw *Doña* Francisca lying against the white cotton pillows. Her face had a grayish look as she rested peacefully, with her hair falling down against her pale-blue, lace gown, and in her hands was a crucifix.

"*Querida!*" Spoke *Don* Federico quietly. He sat on the edge of her bed and took her hand. "*Querida!*" he said again. *Doña* Francisca did not answer. She lay breathing very softly and peacefully. The medication that the doctor gave her made her sleep soundly. He finally stood up and kissed her forehead. He noticed all of the surrounding candles were lit, reminding him of his father's funeral. *Dear God!* He thought. *Here I have been having a good time in San Antonio, making my name known in the Revolution, dining, shopping, and enjoying myself, while my wife is at home dying.* Overwhelmed with sadness, he slowly went back downstairs. Already Mamá Maria was at the bottom of the stairs looking up, waiting for him. She lowered her head and grabbed her apron, bringing it up to her face and wiping her eyes.

Teary eyed, he took her hand. "Come! I have a surprise for you! It is outside in the courtyard."

CHAPTER 10

In the next two weeks, *Doña* Francisca was feeling better, and it seemed that her health was improving, which pleased everyone. In anticipation, all held their breath, since everyone was anxiously waiting for the big fiesta celebration for Victoria's sixteenth birthday. Occasionally, *Doña* Francisca's fever would recur in the middle of the night, and she would break out in cold sweats, but the older women in the hacienda rumored she was also going into an early stage of menopause. With the medication, her coughing had subsided, being not as conspicuous as it had been before; she was sleeping better and was more alert and relaxed. Unbeknownst to all, the medicine contained large dosage of cocaine.

Don Federico had talked to the young, brawny Martin, called *el Toro*, the bull, with bulging muscles throughout his chest, arms, and legs. He stood medium-size, looking like a brick outhouse. On a previous occasion, *Don* Federico had asked him about his problems at his home. The young boy was an abused child. This he knew for a fact, because Martin was a runaway from his violent father and had previously found shelter in the barn at Spanish Acres. The family had accepted him and knew the sadistic situation at his *ranchito*. Martin could stay as long as he wanted in *Don* Federico's hacienda. The conditions were for him to help Roy and the other *vaqueros* with the cattle and other chores for his meals and shelter.

Apparently, Fred had given Martin a pup early in the year, when one of the bitch dogs had four puppies. Martin was overtaken with joy when Fred had offered him a little dog on one of his visits. Martin wanted the black male and took it to his *ranchito* when the little dog was weaned. He hid the puppy in their barn for over a month, until his father eventually found out, when the pup started to yap continually. *Señor* Trevino, a mean, cold-hearted and unsociable man, took the pup and beat him with a board over his head until the pup died. Then he proceeded to take a horsewhip and beat young Martin until he was not able to stand up, and locked him in the barn for days. Martin escaped and decided then to run away, never to return to his *rancho* again.

A cooler arctic wind from the north, called *El Norte,* had developed, leaving the climate during the day breezy and comfortable, but at night a warm blanket was needed. The mosquito swarms had decreased, and as the weather turned colder, mosquito nets were not in demand.

The people of Spanish Acres were all in a joyous state of mind and began preparing for the coming event. The Singer foot-pedal sewing machines were in full use—two from Spanish Acres, and two that Emma had brought, along with her entourage of ten servants. All were busy making dresses and costumes for the great fiesta. Anxious and excited, they could hardly wait to wear their new clothes, shoes, and other attire. Invitations had been sent to important families from both sides of the border. The news that everyone was welcome spread from rancho to rancho like wildfire.

Ten fat calves and seven hogs were slaughtered and left to drain for fourteen days. Later, three of the hogs were smoked with dry mesquite briquettes in the smokehouse; the others were used for the preparation of *tamales*. Other provisions were made to get the hacienda painted, with all of the barrels of paint brought from San Antonio. There would be enough to paint the entrance walls of the hacienda. The *Don* put Manuel and Yo-Yo in charge of that project. Arrangements were being made for those who would be sleeping in the guest quarters. Windows, rugs, and the woodwork were being cleaned, and the polishing of silverware and dusting of the massive house was left to Yolanda and Soledad.

Emma was in charge of making and designing Victoria's gowns, including Felicia's and *Doña* Francisca's dresses, as well as the arrangement of the food and drink distribution. Large tables with white linens were placed in the patios and courtyards. Mamá Maria, Ophelia, Olivia, and Emma's ten servants were busy making the *nixtamal. Don* Federico, who had thought of everything, surprised the women by buying five hand grinders, making it easier. The *masa* was made from the cooked soft corn and was ground, forming the dough for plain corn tortillas, enchiladas, or later be used for the more complicated food like *tamales.*

The night preceding the big fiesta, wagons of men, women, and dozens of children began to infiltrate the grounds of Spanish Acres. The total estimate was about two hundred and perhaps more for the coming occasion. *Don* Federico had hired three different bands of musicians, who came on the night of November twenty-third. He had also invited a professional group of *mariachis* from Matamoros, Mexico, that would serenade Victoria at five o'clock in the morning with the beautiful song *Las Mañanitas, The Dawn Serenade.* This would automatically start the fiesta and would continue for the next two days. The musicians and their families were escorted to their quarters that had been arranged for them a week before.

The night before the fiesta, Victoria's heart beat faster from the excitement. It was becoming very difficult for her to close her eyes, for the downstairs was all in a state of commotion. *Tía* Emma was in authority, giving orders to everyone, keeping the household in a total and utter state of confusion.

"*Buena's noches, Niñas,*" said Mamá Maria, bringing a glass of warm milk to Victoria and Felicia, who were sharing the same bed. The warm milk would help them relax and sleep better. "Tomorrow will be here soon. I still have a lot of work to do," she said, sweating profusely and waving her hands and nodding her head. "The we'men will not be able to sleep tonight for we have to make the *arroz con pollo,* chicken with rice, the *enchiladas, chicharrones, carnitas de puerco* and those devils, the *tamales.* The *menudo* is already cooking."

ROOTS OF INDIFFERENCE

As the night fell, Victoria and Felicia talked and giggled into the wee hours of the morning. Victoria could not stop talking, especially about her feelings for Juan Alvarez.

It seemed that the girls had just closed their eyes, when, like a dream, out of the darkness, was the sweet song being sung to Victoria from the courtyard below her bedroom window.

The guitar music and the voices were sweet and very romantic:

Estás son las Mañanitas	These are the morning-songs
Qué cantaba el Rey David	that King David used to sing,
Y a las muchachas bonitas	and to the prettiest girls
Cantamos así	They were sung like this.
(Coro)	(Chorus)
Despierta, mi bien, despierta!	Awake, my love, awake!
Mira qué ya amaneció	Look, the dawn has already come!
Ya las pajaritos cantan,	Already the little birds are singing
Ya la Luna se oculto.	Already the moon has gone down.

Victoria instantly grabbed for her robe, stretching and yawning. She opened the French doors to the wide balcony of her bedroom and marveled at the beautiful courtyard filled with lanterns and the chill of the morning dawn. *What a surprise*, she thought. *My parents went to a lot of trouble and used their time and money to get this all arranged. But it's too early in the morning to begin any function!* In her exuberance and excitement, she had forgotten to put a ribbon around her hair, which was long and hanging down to her waistline. The lanterns throughout the hacienda were already lit, but the melody was sweet, romantic, and wonderful. Out in the jungle cacti, the singing was joined by the singing of the coyotes, as though even they were celebrating her Saint's day. She leaned over the balcony and smiled and waved to the men below. The singing continued:

Las Mañanitas:

Qué Linda esta la mañana,	How beautiful is the morning
En qué vengo a saludarte.	As we come and waken you.
Venimos todos con gusto...	With God's early morning blessing
Y placer a felicitarte.	With pleasure we sing to you.

Felicia, still in bed, opened her eyes, moaned, and covered her head with a pillow. She rolled over, away from the bright light coming from the window.

Taking Victoria by surprise, her parents, *Tía* Emma, Mamá Maria, and many of the servants entered her bedroom, and soon all were standing next to her on the balcony singing with the rest of the musicians below.

"What a beautiful day this is going to be," cried Emma. "What a lovely occasion! Every girl's parents should be able to afford their daughter's Saint's day. Felicia had hers two years ago. Those were wonderful moments." She then left the balcony, moved inside and began ordering Felicia to get out of bed. "I also need to get the twins up. They were sleeping in Fred's bedroom, and I will bet they didn't sleep a wink last night."

"*Hija*," said *Doña* Francisca, who was still in her long robe with a white scarf around her head. "You will wear the long blue dress which reflects your beautiful eyes." She coughed.

"Later on this evening, you'll wear the beautiful white gown that your *Tía* Emma made you." She began choking.

"*Sí*, Mamá," Victoria answered softly.

"*Querida*," *Don* Federico addressed his wife. "You need to get back to your bed and rest. Everything has been arranged. I don't want you to worry about anything. I want you rested and be beautiful for tonight." He turned to his daughter, "How lovely you'll be tonight. This evening you'll be the prettiest girl in the valley. You and Felicia get dressed, and we'll wait for you both downstairs. Breakfast is being fixed for the musicians. There are lots of surprises!"

"*Hija*, I'll have Yolanda bring you girls some coffee, and later we will get the hot water for your baths and get your hair fixed." Mamá Maria smiled, eying the two girls.

Don Federico and *Doña* Francisca departed the bedroom to take care of other guests. The *Don* was feeling better and glad to see the event coming to full fruition. But deep in his mind, he was still concerned about his sister, Josie. It would be a miracle if they could all be together at the fiesta. He realized it was difficult for her to leave her alcoholic, abusive husband, accepting the knowledge that at this time it was probably impossible. Still concerned about Tom White as well, he had sent word with one of his *vaqueros* to Harlingen, but their reply was that the old drunkard had left town. He was happy to see his wife slowly recovering and joyous to see Victoria bursting with happiness. Their last squabble had made him feel guilty, but with the fiesta, he was making it up to her.

While Felicia was washing her face in a white flowered, porcelain basin, Victoria addressed Felicia with concern. "Do you think that Juan will be at my fiesta? Do you think he will come?"

"I don't know," replied Felicia drying her face in her sweet timid, simple way. "I have never met him, but I'm dying to see if he is as good looking as you have described him. He sounds very romantic." Saying this, she fell on the bed with the towel on her face and continued talking under the towel. "I'd like to meet someone too, just to get away from home, away from my stepfather and my mother—especially, my stepfather. I would like to meet a handsome man with lots of money to support me, and someone who will be good to me and love me. I'm of age you know!"

"Don't be silly, Felicia!" retorted Victoria, feeling giddy. "I want you to meet Juan and see how wonderful he truly is. You'll meet someone too, just like you have described, and it will probably be real soon."

"Not in the convent, I won't! But, who knows! I'm glad I'm not promised in an arranged marriage, like you. I have a choice. I will marry the man I fall in love with," replied Felicia, hastily putting on her long pink dress that Emma had just made her.

"You're lucky," Victoria said. "You'll find someone real soon, I can sense it." Then there was a long silence in between the hassle of slips, lace panties, and shoes. Victoria, sitting in front of the mirror, had finished tying her hair back with a blue ribbon. She turned to face her cousin. "Felicia, I hate to ask you this. It's almost repulsive and a delicate question, but I've had it on my mind for a long time."

"What? You can ask me anything." Felicia glanced over from her position on the edge of the bed, as she struggled with her stockings. "You know that," said the timid young girl.

"Is your stepfather still—?"

There was a pause and a long silence, as Felicia sat up. Then the answer came, soft and almost inaudible. "Yes!" replied Felicia, making a face and breaking down in tears and uttering a stomach-wrenching cry, concealing her face in her hands with the towel that was left lying on the bed. "I can't get away from him. I just don't even want to think about my situation at home. That's the reason I want to get away, as far as I can and go to school."

"Is your stepfather coming to the fiesta?"

"Yes! As far as I know. I'm going to ignore him as much as I can," she replied, sobbing again.

"Does *Tía* Emma know about your situation? Does she have any idea?"

"If I told my mother, she wouldn't believe me and would call me a liar, saying I'm making up the story, just to spite my stepfather. She knows I hate him. It would ruin her secure marriage for the three of us. A year ago, she discharged one of the young cleaning servants, because she'd accused my stepfather of molesting her. There was a big commotion. My stepfather, of course, denied everything, calling her a liar and a troublemaker. I suspect what she claimed was true, because he wasn't hounding me within that period of time. I felt sorry for the young girl who was just trying to make a living with the little money my mother was giving her. Everything is being kept hush-hush. I'm so ashamed! It's so horrible! I can't explain it! My life is ruined forever! No decent man with any honor would have me," cried Felicia, feeling despicable, as uncontrollable tears ran down her face.

Victoria found herself in a pickle, feeling guilty for bringing up the issue. She quickly rushed to hug her cousin. "Don't cry! Please don't cry. You know I love you, Felicia, and the rest of our family loves you too, my cousin and my best friend. You can stay here with me, until we have to leave for school." Victoria sat on the bed, next to Felicia, consoling and reassuring her. "You don't need to go back to Mercedes City. We won't talk about it now, but we'll discuss it later. Just tell *Tía* Emma that you want to stay with me. It will give you an excuse to get away from that hungry sex-manic she's married to." She handed Felicia another clean towel to wipe her face. "I'm sorry I brought up this conversation. You know that I wouldn't say anything. It's our secret. Your stepfather knows what he has done and is doing and getting away with! I think that Mamá Maria suspects something of what is going on."

"Do you think she knows?" Her words were muffled as she wiped her face and blew her nose.

"Remember the first time he violated you? You must have been nine or ten years old. Your stepfather brought you to stay with me for the summer, and you had blood all over your white skirt. Remember that? Everyone thought you had started your monthly period. Later you told me what had happened, and not to tell anyone, how he stopped the buggy on the road while bringing you here and ordered you out into the undergrowth, followed you, and forced you to take your underclothes off. Of course, the rest is history, but remember, it was

Mamá Maria that cleaned you up and comforted you. I guess it hurts the first time!" Victoria said, being inquisitive. "I want to know."

"I guess if you love someone, it doesn't matter when you're making love, but when you are forced into it, it's worse. It hurts, and that's how a man knows that a woman is a virgin. You'll bleed!"

"So that's why you were bleeding when Mamá Maria cleaned you up?" Making an ugly face, Victoria thought for a moment. "Doesn't sound fun to me," she said, exhaling in disgust.

"It's been so long, I don't remember everything," replied Felicia, wiping her eyes.

"Yes! That's how Mamá Maria knows. She has never said a word to your mother."

"So she knows!" sobbed Felicia, clutching the towel between her fingers. "He hasn't stopped since then. He takes advantage of me, especially when Mother leaves the house," she whimpered.

"You need to get away from him. Why don't you go shopping with *Tía* Emma when she goes out?"

"I have sometimes, at the last moment, but mother doesn't tell me what her plans are. She is so undecided and sometimes leaves the house without my knowing."

"Well! What does he do? Where are the rest of the people in the household?" questioned Victoria, trying to find a solution to her cousin's problem.

"He sends the boys to go and play with their friends outdoors. He instructs the servants to do their chores and orders me to go upstairs, and then he locks the bedroom door. He commands me to undress and enjoys seeing me take my garments off, one at a time," she continued through her tears. "He takes delight in seeing me without any clothes on and he fondles me. It's horrible! What's worse, is that he doesn't seem to be satisfied with doing it just once, but several times. It's rape every time, because I'm not willing!" She stopped crying and looked up at Victoria and asked, "What makes you think Maria knows?" Her eyes were red and bloodshot.

"The servants and Mamá Maria were in the kitchen at that time. They did not know that I was listening outside the hall, but I heard them talking in a concerned manner about you. Monthly periods don't start until about twelve years of age. And Mamá Maria thought it was very strange the way you were acting so terrified and scared. Of course, she wasn't about to tell my mother or *Tía* Emma, knowing how she hates your mother and the way she acts at any hint of impropriety."

Victoria decided to change the disturbing subject. "Let's enjoy ourselves! Let's dress and look pretty. You look gorgeous in that new dress! Here, let me get some pink ribbons and put them around your hair. This is a happy occasion!" said Victoria. They heard someone coming up the stairs.

Yolanda walked in with a large tray of fresh coffee, cups, cream, and sugar, and laid it on the dresser. "Breakfast is almost ready for you ladies. The musicians have just finished eating. *Don* Federico and the rest of the family guests are downstairs waiting for you girls."

She said it snobbishly and with an attitude, then turned and headed for the door, as the two girls ignored her and kept on talking.

Pouring her coffee, Victoria changed the subject. "I'm glad that Ricardo and his stuck-up family are not joining us," she continued, wishing now that she had not brought up the dark secret about Felicia's stepfather. "We received a telegram two days ago that Ricardo was sick. My parents were disappointed. But I was happy! I really don't care to see Ricardo nor his stuffy family around my birthday."

"I just don't understand you, Victoria!" exclaimed Felicia, still sitting on the edge of the bed. "According to my mother, the Del Calderónes are very rich and very romantic people." She got up and began pouring coffee into a cup, with sugar and cream, and began drinking it, hoping that it would make her feel better. She continued, "They like to travel to Europe and South America, buying expensive furniture and beautiful gifts. Their lives are supposedly full of excitement with social gatherings all the time. To marry Ricardo sounds wonderful. I wish I had somebody to marry. Yes! He's older than you are, but he's more mature. Now that he's gotten his education in France, he'll be able to have a wonderful job, probably with the government, like his father. And who knows! One day he may be the next president of Mexico!"

"Horse feathers, I'm not interested in politics! And I wouldn't make a good wife to a man who wants to pursue that career. I like the outdoors, being free, and not wearing those fancy dresses and jewelry. If you like him so much, then why don't you marry Ricardo? You're older than me."

Felicia turned to catch Victoria's eyes. "I think you're crazy!" she said, and they began giggling.

Throughout the course of the celebration, Victoria had received many lavish gifts and presents from her family, but she was not completely satisfied, nothing seemed to matter. Even with all the money and gifts, she felt empty. Something was missing, and she wouldn't be happy until she saw Juan. She couldn't wait to see his beautiful green eyes, and feel his arms around her, dancing, spinning her around the *sala*, to those wonderful Spanish and Mexican songs.

The Revolution was becoming a bad nightmare; it was on everyone lips. For the moment, the only important thing now was her fiesta. And tonight, she would make the best of it.

The two girls hurried downstairs. They were taken by complete surprise to see Victoria's Grandfather and Grandmother Hinojosa coming halfway up the stairs to meet them. Squeals of excitement were heard throughout the stairway. "*Abuellito, Abuellita!* When did you get here? We weren't expecting you until tonight!" A series of hugs and kisses were exchanged.

"Late last night. You had already gone to bed, my dear. We didn't want to wake you," answered *Doña* Gloria Hinojosa, pretty as a painted picture, reminding Victoria of her mother, tall and gracious. Beautiful jewelry of dark Alexandrite with diamond earrings hung on her ears, while her graying hair was pinned up and fastened on the back of her head with a lovely stone brooch of marcasites.

"Look at you girls. How *hermosas!*" exclaimed *Don* José Hinojosa, rubbing his white mustache and admiring the two girls with his joyous, earnest smile. His round body wiggled when he laughed. He turned to face Victoria. "Why, you must have grown a foot since we were here over a year ago."

"I'm so glad to see you, glad you were able to make it to my celebration," replied Victoria.

"We almost didn't get here in time," *Don* Hinojosa said. "The roads from the border are dangerous. That's all we heard from Monterrey to Reynosa—about *bandidos* and the new Revolution."

"Now, come!" interrupted *Señora* Hinojosa. "Let's not talk about politics, not on this happy occasion. That's all I've heard on the train from other couples. We want to enjoy the grandchildren and visit with everyone and enjoy ourselves while we're here." She smiled pleasantly, as the couple took both girls by the arm and headed down to meet the musicians and guests.

"There's a surprise for you from us, and it's outside."

"What is it?" questioned Victoria with anticipation.

"It will wait until later," replied *Señor* Hinojosa, smiling at the crowd downstairs.

The mansion was full of chatting people, rich and poor. Servants were scurrying everywhere, seeing that no one was being neglected. From the corral, boisterous noises and shouts were coming from the *vaqueros* galloping their horses back and forth with wild whoops. Loud shots were fired in air, starting the celebration. This was an old Mexican custom, especially in fiestas and celebrations, indicating killing the old year and beginning the new. Victoria had now turned sixteen, the beginning of her adult life. She was no longer a child, but a woman. Her destiny was beckoning.

By the mid-afternoon, the hacienda was even more crowded with people. The day had progressed fast, developing into the late afternoon. There was a good indication that there would be more people than expected. Buggies, hacks, and mule wagons continued to accumulate from all the *ranchitos* throughout the countryside.

The people came to socialize, sing, eat, and dance. How they did eat, and how they did talk! The people who had crossed the border from Mexico talked about the man they called Madero, and how he was going to change their country with his ideas and help the poor people. The people from the Texas side talked about the terrible injustices and the economic status, the intolerable adverse conditions and political abuses. No one was sure of anything, and no one reasonably believed in the corrupt political shenanigans that were being used in the Lower Rio Grande Valley of Texas to supposedly help the Mexican-American people. Conversations were deep relating to the deaths of many individuals, especially so many Mexicans, killed by the abusive local sheriffs and the so-called *Rinches*. Many of the white men would say "Whodunit?" The Mexicans in turn would say "*Quién sabe?*" It was becoming a matter of courage and honor.

The older *vaqueros* gathered outside to drink, dance, and tell stories of the great Mexican heroes. One of these was a man they called "Chino," Juan Nepomucena Cortinos, the redheaded Mexican hero. He terrorized the border, getting revenge on the white men, especially over the disputed theft of his family land grants. All the Mexicans would cheer with glee when told of how many whites he had killed and how he had outsmarted the majority of them throughout the region. Fred, Martin, John, and Jamie, with other young boys as guests, listened with much amusement to the tales. They laughed and giggled, forming a friendship that would last them a lifetime.

Others played blind Mexican poker, betting on blind cards, turning them over, with cheers, while money was being stacked up for whoever held the strongest hand. Many of the *vaqueros* and gentlemen were wearing their best outfits, and also displaying bridles and saddles lavishly adorned with gold and silver studs. Many of the men wore large-brimmed hats of different colors. Their shirts, assembled by loving hands, were embroidered with different colored designs as well. Other *vaqueros* wore bright scarves of China crepe, and many had spurs of gold and silver.

As the day had progressed into the late afternoon, Victoria was ordered to rest before she had her bath and her hair fixed. Fat chance! Many of the young children were playing with firecrackers, and the noise made it impossible to relax, much less sleep. The main event was in the evening with the upcoming dance. Up to this time, Victoria had spent most of her time meeting people and being introduced to so many she had never known—young and old, rich and poor, all dressed in their best attire.

There were dignitaries still coming to the fiesta later that afternoon, but not spending the night. Many were coming to eat, drink, and dance, but leaving later to return to their nearby *ranchitos*.

Later, Yolanda, Soledad, and several maids walked into her bedroom with buckets of hot water for the tub. All had orders to help her with the bath, fix her hair, and help her with her gown.

After her bath, Victoria, found it all very amusing, and she was excited. She sat admiring herself in front of the mirror, while the two women began helping her with her hair and began remarking about the fiesta. Soledad, who was always pleasant and humble, was complimentary about Victoria's hair and her lovely white lace floor-length gown. Fred's music box sat playing and looked lovely on her dresser.

"*Señorita*," remarked Soledad "is your *novio* coming to the dance tonight? What a lucky man to have you for his bride," she commented shyly, while drying Victoria's back and powdering her with an expensive, gardenia perfumed powder given to Victoria as one of her gifts.

The normally silent Yolanda, hovering over Victoria's hair, replied, "Which one?"

Soledad was stumped for words. "The handsome one. The one that was just here! The one with those beautiful green eyes, of course, *el doctor*. The one that helped me and made me feel like a person again." Soledad stopped what she was doing and faced Yolanda.

"No!" Yolanda replied, hatefully. She almost yanked Victoria's hair from her head. "He is not her *novio!* Victoria is promised to marry another man. Ricardo is her intended *novio* and was just here a couple of years ago. A very handsome man, too."

"Never mind!" Victoria yelled at Yolanda angrily. Her eyes were dead set on the servant, but she made every effort to curb her temper. "I'll marry whomever I want! I don't care what you heard, Yolanda! And it is none of your business anyhow! Why have you not gotten married? You're old enough!"

Yolanda stood stupefied. She stopped fixing Victoria's hair, and let her hands down, still holding the hairbrush. Glaring at Victoria and narrowing her eyes, she thought, *how I hate her! The spoiled witch brat!* "The right man hasn't asked me," she answered. "Frankly, I don't have to marry anyone, if I don't want to. I'm not being forced to marry anyone," she hissed, showing her claws.

"Right," said Victoria, unscrambling her hair with her hands. "No man has asked you to get married! That's the reason why. Forget about my hair! And go on downstairs— maybe Mamá Maria will put you to good use. I'll have Soledad finish my hair!"

Yolanda pitched the hairbrush against the mirror and almost knocked Fred's music box off, rushing with pursed lips out of Victoria's bedroom. And it was a good thing, because she had come close to slapping Victoria's face. As she got older, she had acquired patience in curbing her temperament and mouth. Such an act would have been a terrible mistake, for her parents depended on *Don* Federico for shelter and income. But she would wait. *One day, Victoria was going to regret and eat every one of those humiliating words*, thought Yolanda, cooling her heels. She was patient enough, and could wait until Hell froze over.

"We will put your hair up and back, with many ringlets, many ringlets," said the soft-spoken Soledad. Her hands trembled, not knowing what to expect next.

"How I hate that Yolanda!" said Victoria. Her face was flushed with anger. "She's always getting everyone in trouble in Spanish Acres. Always telling everything and gossiping about things she heard, and making a mountain out of a molehill."

"Who's making a mountain out of a molehill?" It was the voice of smiling Felicia, coming in from the downstairs and getting ready herself for the big festivities.

"Oh! It's that stupid Yolanda! Making comments about who my *novio* is!" The three girls giggled, and they laughed even harder when Victoria tried to put on her corset to make her look slimmer.

People in the hallways were scurrying in every direction. *Don* Federico and *Doña* Francisca walked into Victoria's bedroom. Her mother was already dressed in a beautiful full-length gown and was wearing a tiara on her head with diamond earrings and a necklace to match. Her father was wearing a dark, navy blue, three-piece, Italian silk suit.

"Mother, you look very beautiful. And Father you are so handsome."

"Thank you, *querida!*" answered her father, kissing Victoria on her forehead. He opened a small, black velvet box. "This is from the Del Calderóne family, brought to you by your grandparents. They had heard from your *Tía* Emma by letter about the color of the dress she was making for you, so they wanted you to have this. They want you to wear it tonight, a family heirloom, I suppose. It is their gift to you, for not being able to be with you this special night."

ROOTS OF INDIFFERENCE

"Have Soledad put the necklace and the earrings on after you have finished dressing," suggested *Doña* Francisca. She began coughing, excused herself and left the room. *Don* Federico followed her.

Victoria heard her father telling her mother that he was getting concerned about her coughing and to take more of the medication the doctor had given her.

"All of us must hurry!" *Tía* Emma commanded. She was coming from the opposite direction down the hall, with both hands up in the air. "Where is Felicia? Are you dressed and ready? The orchestra has just arrived, and they are setting up their instruments in the grand *sala*. The *mariachis* will be playing outside on the patio."

The two women acknowledged *Tía* Emma's command and nodded their heads. "The twins are already dressed and have gone downstairs. I'd better check and see what else needs to be done." Saying this, she hurried out, with the sound of her taffeta dress swishing down the hallway.

"Are you ready, Soledad?" questioned Victoria with concern and empathy toward the poor peasant girl. "What are you going to wear tonight?"

"Ay, *Señorita*. You know I don't have any decent clothes to wear for this kind of fiesta," she said, while picking up the clothes on the floor. "I have already seen the beautiful dresses that some of the young girls are wearing. I feel ashamed of myself. I would prefer not to mix with the crowd as a guest. Instead, I'll help in the kitchen and help serve the food."

"You can wear any of my clothes," said Felicia, slipping into her new black patent leather shoes. "We have plenty of dresses, and I think we all wear the same size."

"No, you won't be helping out in the kitchen. You need to be out in the *sala*, dancing," replied Victoria. "We have clothes here. My *armario* is full of clothes. Pick any one you like."

"But, *Señorita*, I can't wear your clothes. They are too beautiful for me to wear."

"*Basta*, we will not take no for an answer. This is my fiesta, and I want you to look pretty, too," replied Victoria, getting up from her chair and picking up several of her dresses that were piled on top of other garments on a recliner next to her *armario*. "Come! Put on that one—the golden embroidered one. It will look lovely with your long black hair and your beautiful complexion. José Esquibel will go out of his mind when he sees you. Quickly, let's hurry!"

Soledad stood up for a moment and smiled, dazzled by Victoria's comment, as if a light of hope in her life had been given. She lifted the golden dress with sequins and held it up in front of her, then lowered her eyes in humility and looked down to the floor. "Do you think it will look pretty on me, *Señorita* Victoria? Do you think any man would dance with me?"

"Why yes, Soledad, it will look beautiful on you. Come on! You must hurry, too! Why would you ask me that silly question? Any man would love to dance with you. Ah! What certain man? Besides José, someone else, anyone special, we know around here?" she teased.

"Do you think that the *gringo*, the foreman, would dance with me tonight?"

"Why, Soledad! Do you mean, Roy?"

"Yes! *Señorita*, Roy."

"Soledad!" Victoria looked bewildered. "Do you mean to tell me that you have feelings toward Roy? What about José?" Things were starting to get complicated for everyone.

"You and I are in the same situation," she answered, and her eyes clouded with tears. "I have had to meet with José because he asked me to. I felt obligated because his father helped me and saved my life. I want to be grateful. I like José, but not like I like Roy. I should be ashamed and not have feelings for anyone. In my situation, after what happened to me, at this time, I should hate them all."

"Oops!" replied Felicia. "I think I had better go on downstairs—things are getting too steamy hot for me here." She snickered, then with a wide smile, glanced toward Victoria, acting silly.

"Soledad, you are right," commented Victoria, seriously studying the problem as she gazed into the mirror. "I do love Juan, but I'm promised to marry someone else." She quickly ignited her spirit, and getting up from her chair, announced, "I am not going to worry about this now. Between the two of us, we will see that Roy dances with you tonight. I think he has the same feelings for you."

"Oh, *Señorita* Victoria, thank you! Look at you!" responded Soledad with amazement, with her hands clasped together close to her face. "You look like a dream. Every man will want to dance with you. I'll hurry and dress. I guess I'll have some explaining to do to José tonight."

Victoria took one last look in the mirror and smiled with pride. Her white silk, full-length gown covered over with white lace accentuated her small waist. White homemade silk flowers with pearls and sequins were embedded in the gown clear to the floor. The low décolletage revealed her full rounded breasts, and an array of more handmade, white silk flowers embedded with Austrian crystals adorned the shoulders. Her hair was pulled up with ringlets falling down the back, and a crystal Spanish tiara comb nested on top of her head. The necklace and earrings were magnificent, set with opals and diamonds resembling flowers and shining like gleaming fires. The finishing touch was her white gloves.

"Gorgeous, lovely!" said Emma, peeking in from the entryway. "Everyone is ready and anxious to see you. Hurry! The orchestra is starting to play *La Princesita Quinceañera*."

As Victoria approached the top of the stairs, the musicians began playing. The chatter of the guests stopped. The majority were holding glasses of champagne or other drinks, and all stood gasping in amazement. Dozens of diplomats, representatives from both sides of the border, began clapping their hands as she came downstairs. Low waves of compliments and remarks traveled like a sharp electric jolt around the great *sala*. "Ay qué Chula! La Borrada, Qué Bonita!"

Her parents and grandparents stood at the base of the stairs and gazed up smiling, watching her with pride as she approached the bottom step. The four looked so distinguished, as she turned to her father, who was patiently waiting with his chest puffed up. Fred, the twins, and Martin, who were standing next to her parents, looked handsome in their new suits. The servants were also dressed in fine clothing for the occasion. In one corner was Manuel and Yo-Yo, holding onto one another, smiling and beaming at her.

ROOTS OF INDIFFERENCE

Dear old Manuel, she thought, dressed in a Mexican *charro* suit, looking like Sancho-Panza from the novel of Cervantes *Don Quixote*. Skinny Yo-Yo looked like Ichabod Crane in Washington Irving's *The Legend of Sleepy Hollow*, in a suit one size too small. *Tía* Emma, who had worked endlessly organizing the fiesta, stood with her long, light blue gown and feathered hat, looking preposterous with coils of fat, like a stuffed pig, commanding her spot. Next to her was Felicia looking exceptionally pretty. In another section was Mamá Maria in a new dark dress, holding onto little Carlito's hand, and next to her was the scandalous Yolanda, dressed in a bright red, low-cut dress, like a spider making her web, ready to catch her victim, and already making eyes at Roy.

The grand *sala* was filled with bright lights, as all of the chandeliers were lit. People of all walks of life, rich and poor, young and old, stood before her, watching her and admiring her. The *sala* was filled with women, with men, and with younger girls wearing lavish dresses, and adorned with every splendor of gold and silver jewelry, with gem combs and mantillas on their heads. They had come from all over the Valley, especially from the named *ranchitos*: *La Blanca*, southwest of Spanish Acres; *La Rucias* five miles west of Brownsville, the prominent family of Don Barredo; *Rancho Tule* north of Brownsville; *the Norias* and *Majadas* close to Raymondville; *Ojo de Agua* and *La Talpa* close to Mission; *San Juanita*, the *Olmito*, the *Santa Anita* and the *Santa Rosa*, all close to McAllen; *the Velas* from *Laguna Seca*, northwest of Chapin; *Las Casitas* in Starr County; the *Tolucca*, southeast of Mercedes City; the *Santa Gertrudis* south of Ciudad Camargo, and so many more.

The diplomats and representatives wore their best dark silk suits, white shirts, and expensive black shoes; others wore high-top boots of patent leather or animal skins. The Mexican *caballeros* stood erect, looking splendid in their *charro* suits. Many trousers were made of velvet, with black braid slashed at the calves. Around their waist was a bright red sash, and on their boots silver and gold spurs.

Many of the young ladies wore bright, hand-embroidered peasant blouses and skirts adorned with sequins and beads. They were always chaperoned by an older member of the family, a duty that usually fell to old aunties, who were dressed in dark attire from head to toe. The *tias* sat watching every move the young girls made.

Don Federico offered his arm to Victoria as she approached the bottom step. He proceeded to offer a toast. "Guests and friends, tonight is a special night and a momentous event. I'm glad to see everyone here to join us in celebrating Victoria's sixteenth birthday." He held his glass of champagne up and shouted, "*Salud!* Now let's all enjoy the rest of the evening and the next few days, as we eat, drink, dance, and celebrate this special moment in time. The night is young—please enjoy!" He turned to the musicians and ordered them to finish playing the song, as he whirled Victoria out into the middle of the *sala*. Everyone shouted and applauded. There were several photos taken by a photographer who came all the way from Brownsville.

"Tonight is your night, my dear," her father whispered with pride. "You'll be able to meet and dance with every man here. They have come to pay us their respects and—" He did not finish his conversation, as *Señor* José Hinojosa, her grandfather, was already tapping *Don* Federico on the shoulder to dance with Victoria.

"I wanted to be able to dance with my beautiful granddaughter while the night is still young, and before the rest of the young *caballeros* cut me out," he said, laughing as he took Victoria by the waist.

Don Federico nodded, smiled, and turned to find *Doña* Francisca, who had been mingling with the crowd. He finally found her talking with Emma and others who attended the Lady of Mercy Catholic Church in Mercedes City, and who were busy chatting about rumors of a coming revolution. Many were concerned about their families living in Mexico.

Moments later the *Don* and *La Señora* were out on the dance floor. "I'm so disappointed and sorry that Ricardo and his family were not able to attend the celebration," he whispered into *Doña* Francisca's ear. "Victoria and Ricardo would have looked lovely dancing together."

"They will have plenty of time together, after they get married, to enjoy dancing and socializing." *Doña* Francisca paused and began coughing.

"Juan promised me that he would attend our celebration," *Don* Federico mentioned. "Let me know right away when he arrives. I want to make sure I talk to that young man first. I know he has feelings for Victoria. I don't want any trouble with a love affair involving our daughter; especially tonight with so many dignitaries present."

Don Federico continued dancing with *La Señora*, and mused, "I wonder why he hasn't shown up yet." He stopped that line of thought and looked at his wife with pride. "*Querida*, you look beautiful tonight. I can smell the perfume I bought for you in San Antonio. It smells divine. But you better take care of your cough. You might want to go upstairs and rest. I don't want you to get too tired."

"I'm afraid Victoria is infatuated with Juan," she said softly. "I will admit he is very handsome, and any woman would love to be with him. However, Victoria is already promised." *Doña* Francisca looked down and almost fell as her shoe got tangled with the hem of her long grown, but her husband held her in a strong grip. They laughed together and were happy as they danced.

Out on the dance floor, everybody was dancing to one of the famous, fast-paced *corridos*, border ballads that incorporated their culture, image, feeling, and lifestyle, all stamping their feet and whistling. Even Felicia already was dancing with one of the young Gonzales men from *Las Piedra Rancho*.

One dance followed another as Victoria was whirled around and around in the different waltzes. Then the music of the *Jota* came on. It was often compared to the Viennese Waltz because it moved in three-quarter time, but it was more fiery and robust. With each tap on the shoulder, the man wanting to dance with her would pin paper money on her dress. This was an old Mexican tradition to pay to dance with the honored guest. It was also done to the brides at wedding receptions as a sign of respect.

The music prompted a Fandango, then later a Bolero, and even a wild Polka. The happy celebration went on, as minutes ticked into hours. Victoria would occasionally glance at the entryway, wondering why Juan Alvarez had not arrived.

ROOTS OF INDIFFERENCE

While dancing with one of the young Garzas from *Relámpago Ranch*, Victoria was tapped on the shoulder by Roy Dale, who looked especially charming with his new cowboy shirt, red tie, and new boots. His blond hair was slicked back, making his blue eyes shine. "Ya' hasn't missed a lick since the dance started. Tho' I bet'er take my chance," he said, like a coyote turned lose in the chicken coop.

"I saw you dancing to a *corrido* with a young girl earlier and you were doing a pretty good job."

"Ya' look lovely! Smell good, too! After sev'ral drinks of dat, dat tequilas, I kin swing ta 'bout anythin'." He took her in his arms and began whirling her around.

It's time to break the news—perfect timing, thought Victoria. "Roy, have you had a chance to dance with Soledad? She told me she wants to dance with you."

"By dang golly, ya' mean dat? Ya' mean she wants t' dance with me? Ya' thin' she'll dance with me, by dang? Ye're a-meanin' with me?" His large, blue eyes were sparkling like sequins. "She told you dat?" His heart was throbbing. "I'm 'fraid to ask her."

"Why, of course she did. She can't wait to dance with you."

"But, she got dat, dat there feller José all wrapped up," he said, looking surprised. "Damn gumit! I've been hankerin' to take a lick at dancin' with her. Git my arms 'round her. Boy! She looks awfull-ee pree-tee, doesn't she?"

"Yes, she does. Awfully pretty! She wants to see you and be with you," replied Victoria, teasing him and enticing him, trying to get a rise out of him.

"No shit!" Roy said needed no coaxing. He was already drunk and overconfident, and had enough determination to kill a bearcat with his bare hands. He abruptly let go of Victoria and swaggered over to where Soledad was dancing with José.

Victoria stood for a minute and watched Roy leave as he made a beeline for Soledad and José. She felt someone behind her and turned to face another dancer.

"Remember me?"

It was Juan! Victoria felt her heart stop, instantly overcome with excitement and exhilaration. He was like the coming of spring, standing there and looking extraordinarily handsome in a dark, three-piece suit. He looked like a man ready to have fun. Her face glowed with joy as he embraced her with strength and grace, swinging and whirling her out into the middle of the floor.

"Happy sixteenth birthday, my love," whispered Juan, kissing her on the cheek. "You look lovely in your gown, reminds me of a wedding dress. You look good enough to—"

"People are watching us," Victoria replied, looking into the depth of his green eyes.

The older women sat with watchful eyes next to their young ladies, and *tías* with sequined fans leaned over to one another, questioning who the young gentleman was. "Is that her *novio*?" one asked. "What a handsome individual." Murmurs and discreet conversations rolled like a progression of thunder across the great sala.

"Let them talk! They can see that we are the most handsome couple on the floor," answered Juan proudly, dancing to *España de mi Corazón*. "I have the most beautiful woman here in my arms."

"Juan! Oh! Juan! I thought you were never going to get here. What took you so long?"

"It's a dangerous business that I'm in, my love. I have been dodging the spies and agents all along the border. I rode all the way from *Presidio Del Norte,* and a family in a small village close to Mission exchanged my horse for theirs. Tensions are becoming worse as the Revolution is starting, and people are talking all along the border."

"Are you in any danger, Juan?" she questioned with concern, passing her eyes over his shoulder to glance at one of the corners where Roy and José were standing. She could see Roy waving his hands as if explaining something to José. He appeared angry.

"At this moment, I'm not. Not now. I'm safe in your arms, romantically speaking." He smiled, holding her closer. Victoria glanced about and could see her father and grandfather watching her. Her father nodded his head with approval, but her grandfather had a serious, somber look, obviously questioning her actions.

Juan stopped for a moment, viewed her at arm's length, and took a deep breath. She was indeed beautiful, in her lovely white dress, and the magnificent jewelry made her look like a bride. His eyes dropped to the rounded curve of her breasts.

"Victoria," he said, "let's head out onto the patio, where it's cooler. I have something for you." Pausing for a moment, he looked around the *sala* and continued. "Don't worry about your father. I have already gotten his permission to dance with you, and we will talk later in his library."

"A surprise, please tell me! Oh, please show me," she answered nervously, too full of excitement to pay any attention to Juan's last sentence.

"Not here, my sweet. You are too impatient," Juan said.

Suspecting that others were watching them, Victoria stopped for a moment, glancing to see where her father and grandfather might be, but they were not there. She also searched the room for her mother, knowing she would disapprove of her actions, going outdoors with a man at night, especially with Juan. Minutes later, she caught a glimpse of *Doña* Francisca dancing and talking with the Texas lawyer from Brownsville, *Señor* Canalo, the family attorney.

Mamá Maria had watched the couple dancing and intercepted them as they moved toward the door on their way out into the courtyard. "*Hija!*" she exclaimed. "I don't think it's a good idea going outside with Juan." Maria looked tired and exhausted. "People are already talking about your conduct. I don't think your grandfather is very happy about it. He disapproves of you dancing only with Juan." She continued talking and looking at Juan with concern on her face, and then said, "Your father took your grandfather into his library trying to explain that Juan was a special guest and a doctor here in our household."

Victoria got fired up, bit her lip, and stared at Mamá Maria. "This is my celebration, Mamá Maria. We were just going outside to get some fresh air." She didn't want to tell the servant that Juan had suggested it, with a gift for her.

Juan smiled and answered politely. "We'll only be out for a couple of minutes. I just wanted to show her something. We'll be right back. It won't take us very long."

ROOTS OF INDIFFERENCE

Mamá Maria snapped. "Let me take some of the money that's hanging on your clothes. You are going to lose some of it outside." She began unpinning the money with the help of Juan. "I'll put it in my apron where it will be safe. You can get it later, whenever you want it."

Out the side entrance stormed José Esquibel, with a flushed and angry face, heading for the stable where he had left his horse. He was provoked, and his irate expression looked harsh enough to kill somebody. No one else noticed the commotion but the three who stood outside watching. "*Ay Dios!*" came out of Mamá Maria's mouth, without even thinking. "I hope we don't have any trouble." She turned to Victoria and Juan. "Go, then! I'll be waiting. Don't take too long!"

The guests outside in the courtyards were enjoying the loud *mariachi* music. Many were whirling, dancing, and stomping their feet, while others were standing with plates in their hands, eating and talking happily. Many were drinking spirits while the rest clapped their hands to the popular *El Corrido de Jacinto Trevino*. The song, celebrated throughout the Lower Rio Grande Valley, was written after the killing of the hated white sheriff who had killed a Mexican-American.

Tables laden with different appetizing dishes stretched across the courtyard. On the high arches were hung Japanese lanterns displaying romantic rainbow-colored lights. The couple passed the lush greenery and went away from the crowd into an open area. Victoria reached out her arm and grabbed onto Juan to balance herself on the uneven path. The smell of tequila, pique, and cooked spicy food infiltrated the soft breezy air. In the distance, the sound of José Esquibel's horse could be heard as he galloped south into the *resaca*.

It was getting close to midnight as Juan and Victoria walked out into a clearing. Farther up the path, close to the pond surrounded by sabino trees and bushes, they could hear movement and heavy, hard breathing. Among the shadows, in front of them on the ground, was a young couple that had decided to leave the festivities and, unable to contain their lascivious desires, were in the act of passionate lovemaking.

"In times of celebration, with a magical night like this one, the music, good food and liquor, it happens," whispered Juan. "It's a *machismo* thing. Young gentlemen have to prove themselves, especially when there are young women around." He said it with his eyes dancing with delight, making Victoria blush.

They headed up the narrow path and stood under the big Montezuma bald cypress tree, with its branches hanging over the water's edge. There, the water was dark and clear, illuminated like a mirror under the bright, full, harvest moon. The open space was all around them and the fragrance of the coming winter was in the air. Occasionally, the wind would shift and the stench of cow manure would infiltrate their nostrils, making them both wave their hands beneath their noses, giggling. The full moon hung high in the firmament as they faced each other with tranquility and peace, giving out happy sighs. They were together. They had each other, and both could feel their hearts beating faster. Their spirits and emotions were as high as the romantic music from the courtyard that claimed the perfect night. The silence was periodically broken by a loud "Ya-hoo," or wild laughter and yells, coming from the guests and *vaqueros* out in the courtyards, who were now three sheets to the wind.

Juan reached inside his suit pocket and brought out a small velvet box. Victoria's fingers nervously opened it. It was a golden amulet necklace with the imprint of the *Virgen de Guadalupe.*

Dazed with delight, Victoria brought it to her chest. "Juan, I love it. It's the most beautiful and precious gift I've received. I'll treasure it forever."

"I want you to wear it always, my love. In a couple of weeks, I'll be going to Chihuahua and be with *General* Villa, fighting for the Mexican cause. The necklace, it will be a reminder of me."

"Juan, I will. I'll wear it forever."

In the distance they could hear the singing of the musicians. The couple made a remarkable silhouette against the shadow of the crystal water. The stars shone brightly like a myriad of diamonds, but none compared to the brightness of Juan's and Victoria's dancing eyes. For a long moment Juan stood beholding Victoria. She was beautiful and untouchable, and the long white gown with all the sequins and stones adorning her body made her look like a sparkling princess. His eyes were like two burning emerald stones filled with hunger and passion. Without hesitation he put his hands on her shoulders, bringing her closer to him. He kissed her tenderly. She returned it with passion.

"I have been waiting for this moment for a long time," he whispered. "You've been on my mind since the first time I laid eyes on you." He then gave out a loud sigh.

Victoria sighed and then smiled. "The same thing happens with me."

"You're like a poison in my blood, that can't be taken out. When I think about you, my mind goes crazy. I am a poor man now, Victoria, but one day I will have everything that a man wants. I promise you that. One day I will be rich and have a villa twice as big as Spanish Acres. After the Revolution, I want you to marry me and share my life with me." He then kissed her again. "Please wait for me." He said softly. His hands moved caressingly up her back, supporting her trembling body. The emotion was too powerful and her arms embraced Juan with passion. Another kiss followed.

Out of the night, came the sounds of horsemen riding from the south in the direction of the hacienda. Dogs began barking. The couple instantly hid themselves among the bushes next to the cypress tree. "Who are they?" questioned Victoria. "What do they want? Are they *bandidos*?"

Juan peered from behind the branches. "Riders with big Stetson hats, looking to have a good time, probably! Wait! They don't look like *bandidos!*" he said, his eyes straining.

"Riders, so late during the night," said Victoria. It doesn't make sense."

"Bandits don't wear Stetson hats," said Juan, his eyes keeping a steady vigilance in the darkness. "Wait!" he said softly. "I think they're leaving. They just got close enough, curious to see what was going on in your home. I wonder what the strangers want. Why don't they come in and enjoy the celebration, like everyone else? Everybody is invited. Wait, they're going off in the same direction that José went."

"We had better get back, quickly," said Victoria, now becoming very nervous. "My parents will be missing me." Both hurried down the path to where the *mariachis* were playing on the courtyard.

"Victoria! Victoria," a voice was calling from under the tall arches. "Niña, the orchestra is going to play for you *La Barcelona*, and everyone has been asking for you," said Mamá Maria, excitedly and with her hands clapped together over her face with worry. "Come! You must hurry! Go in and dance before your Papá notices you have been outside with Juan."

"Mamá Maria," said Victoria, shaken, out of breath, and with a flushed face. "We have just seen riders coming from the south toward the house. They were strangers."

"*Madre de Dios!*" she exclaimed, crossing herself. She was afraid of bandits. "What do they want?"

"They didn't get close enough," replied Juan "for us to ask them. They sat on their horses for a while, observing the house and discussing something. I couldn't hear anything. The music and noise outside was too loud, and the dogs kept barking and running toward the gates." He paused. "I only heard murmurs. The wind was against us."

"Go, Victoria! The musicians are waiting for you. I'll go and tell Roy. Your father is busy in the library with your grandfather and several other men discussing politics. He doesn't want to be bothered. Your Mamá became ill, bless her heart, and was taken upstairs to her bedroom. The celebration has been too much for her. Her coughing has gotten worse. She got dizzy, not knowing that she had doubled up on her medicine. Emma and *la Señora* Hinojosa are with her."

"Mamá sick, again!"

"Everything is going to be all right with your mother. *Hija!* Hurry! Go!" Mamá Maria stood watching, as Victoria and Juan, so delighted with each other and so obviously in love, hurried to the big house. She shook her head, thinking with much concern. If Victoria only knew that the busy body, Emma, had already thrown a tantrum and complained to the grandparents and also to *Don* Federico about the way Victoria was promiscuously conducting herself with the young revolutionist.

Already the crowd was gathering in a wide circle inside the grand *sala* as Victoria and Juan entered. Victoria glanced toward the corner and viewed Roy being enthralled with Soledad. They were both laughing and enjoying themselves. He was going to have to leave her as soon as he got the bad news about the riders outside the hacienda.

As they danced, Juan whirled her around with a great flourish, and then noticed Miguel approaching Roy and some of the other *vaqueros*. He was telling them something, but what? The loud noise, the wild cheers, and the clapping of hands from the guests made it impossible to hear.

As she spun around in the dance, Victoria noticed Fred running in from the other side of the *sala* with the group of boys his age, the two cousins Jamie and John, and Martin, *el Toro*. Fred was also talking loud and waving his arms explaining something to Roy. Apparently the boys had noticed something suspicious inside the Spanish Acres gates. The crowd was beginning to stir, and Juan noticed it, too. They had stopped dancing and were talking and arguing amongst themselves.

"Maybe, I'd better go and join the *vaqueros* and help Roy," he said, feeling a little *machismo* coming on. "Better check to see what's happening outside!"

"Juan, please don't leave me. Roy is in charge of the hacienda, and it's up to him to see that everything is safe and all right."

"No, Victoria. I'll be a fool, if I don't help them. I think there's some kind of trouble outside. I wonder if anything happened to your neighbor's son, José. Did you see how mad he was when he left? Something must have happened! He rode out like a flying bullet in the direction the riders came from."

"But it is getting late," pleaded Victoria. "You don't know the countryside, especially at night, like Roy and the rest of the *vaqueros* do."

"I'm going!" he said firmly. "I'm going to the stable and get my horse, and ride out with Roy. I'll stay close to him and be by his side at all times. He will need some help. And I will be back shortly." He kissed her on her check, turned around, and in a quick rush headed outdoors.

Soledad, standing by herself in the middle of the *sala* in a state of confusion, turned and viewed Victoria, who stood around looking sad. Soledad walked over to her side.

Victoria questioned Soledad about José. "What happened? Why was he so angry? Did you tell him about your feelings toward Roy?"

"José wanted me to elope with him tonight. He said he would marry me later. I didn't like the idea. I refused. I told him that I was still traumatized. It was going to take time on my part, and patience from him. He was going too fast, dancing with me only, refusing the others, telling them I was his *novia*. When Roy approached us, he got angry. Roy told him off and said in so many words that I didn't belong to him yet, and I was free to dance with whomever. I was pleased, but so embarrassed."

"Good for Roy! I guess he told him how the cow ate the cabbage, "said Victoria, grinning.

The music continued, and Victoria was asked to dance by a young *vaquero* from a *ranchito* nearby. Soledad excused herself to see about *La Señora* who had been taken ill upstairs.

The laughter, music, and loud chattering continued. An hour had passed, and the families with small children and the very old crowd were beginning to thin out. It was getting late, way past midnight. The musicians kept playing the songs the rest of the crowd wanted to hear. Victoria was surprised to see Roy, Miguel, and Juan coming in from the front entrance. She overheard Roy tell Miguel that they would start out early in the morning. Juan walked in without his tailored coat on and began scanning for Victoria among the crowded *sala*. He waved and headed in her direction.

"What happened?" asked Victoria, rushing over to his side.

"We didn't see anything, only wild animals scurrying through the bushes. The moon was covered by dark clouds, and we were not able to see a thing. There were no signs of José Esquibel."

Most of the men and *vaqueros* were inebriated, and by now Yo-Yo, who had done his share of the drinking, stirred through the crowd carrying his worn-out fiddle. He had been drinking hard since last week and today more heavily than ever, with good reason. He still felt that he hadn't done the drinking any justice, and he insisted he was going to play a tune for Victoria.

"This one is a special tune, uh huh. The song is *Over the Waves,*" stammered Yo-Yo. "This tune was written by Juentino Rosas, uh huh, a Mexican who sold his soul to the devil, uh huh." He was barely managing to stay erect. "This *hombre* Rosas, for seventeen dollars he sold it to a European man, uh huh. The song became popular throughout the world, making the white *gringo* famous, uh huh." The crowd laughed. "Poor Juentino never got the credit he deserved, uh huh!"

As he slid the bow of his violin, his body would slide with it. He would weave a little but kept himself in an upright position. He would straighten himself up, making sure his steps were firm as he tapped his right foot with each note. The notes were soft and beautiful, and the crowd roared with delight. Juan pulled Victoria out into the middle of the floor. They were the only ones dancing. "This is our waltz, *Querida.*" The next tune was one of Spain's famous melodies, *Romanza de Amor.*

Two old spinsters sitting in one of the corners observing the entertaining spectacle turned to each other. "I wonder what the Del Calderónes would say if they saw Victoria dancing so amorously with the young *caballero,*" one said. "Have you noticed, she has not danced with anyone else since he arrived?"

"Rumors are that he is a revolutionist! Fighting for the Mexican cause! War is starting across the border, imagine that!" she exclaimed and started to fan herself hard.

"Oh! My! A revolutionist! Why would *Don* Federico and *Doña* Francisca allow Victoria to dance with him? He is below her class. Very common, I would say."

"But *comadre*, notice how handsome he is!" the other said, holding her fan close to her mouth.

"*Comadre*, if you and I had found a man like that when we were young, well, we would not be just sitting here." Looking at each another, they giggled like schoolgirls.

"True. I would hate to think what I would be doing." They both chuckled amidst the music and the noise. "By the way, did you hear that *Doña* Francisca was taken upstairs very seriously ill? That her coughing has gotten worse?" The old *comadre* raised her eyebrow.

"Hope it's nothing serious!" replied the other one.

"The tales are that she coughs all the time. And now her coughing is getting worse. There is talk that she's got the worse kind of sickness."

"That terrible disease of the lungs, and everybody is being discreet about it."

"Surely not," answered the old *tía*, fanning herself very fast. "She is still so young and so beautiful, and her children are still so young."

"They say it runs in her family. Emma's mother died from it, many years ago."

"What happened to Victoria's *novio*, her intended? Did he not come from Monterrey?"

"Emma mentioned to me, that the Del Calderóne family could not travel because Ricardo was taken ill right after he returned from the city of Paris. He probably picked up a French disease."

"Ay *comadre*! Families from Reynosa and Matamoros are talking of the terrible changes coming to their country. Most of the talk is of the coming Revolution. It is going to affect all of us living on the border, *Dios los libre y los favoresca!* God protect us!"

"It is shameful! Look, *Comadre*. Look at the way he is holding her."

"What difference does it make? They are both lovely. Look, it is so romantic to watch!"

Outside where the buggies and wagons were stationed, Fred and two young friends from a nearby *ranchitos*, mischievous boys, had decided to have themselves some fun by pulling a prank on the visitors who had brought their young families in wagons. Martin had already gone to bed in the *vaqueros'* bunkhouse, and Jamie and John had already been commanded by their mother Emma that it was getting very late for the twins to be up.

Couples would leave their little children fast asleep in the comfort of blankets and pillowed wagons, going back to enjoy the celebration. The boys would shift the sleeping children around to other wagons, causing much confusion upon the couples' return. The boys would double over with laugher and then run and hide.

"No one has seen us. And no one suspects us, I hope!" whispered one of the three young boys.

"No one!" answered Fred in a low voice, halfway laughing. His eyes sparkled with mischief. "If my father finds out, he will surely kill me."

"You?" replied little Pepito. "My father will give me a thrashing like I have never had. I don't think this is a good idea."

All three giggled. "I can already feel the beating," mused little Raul, pretending to hold onto his behind. "If we try to put the kids back where they belong, we may not remember and do it right. I don't think I can remember who's who. Or from which wagon we exchanged each one of them."

"Hush! Here comes another couple with some more sleepy children. Get down!" The three young boys held their breath and squatted in between the dark, still wagons.

The rest of the night had been like a dream come true for Victoria. One music beat led to another as Juan's arms, and his attention, was only for her. The musician was now playing *Señora*, which was a favorite song in both countries.

At two o'clock in the morning, Victoria began yawning and decided to call it a night. She excused herself from Juan. Her feet were hurting, and her corset was starting to become uncomfortable. "It's getting late and I have been up since five this morning. I need to check on mother on my way to my sleeping quarters. Let's call it a day. I'll see you tomorrow."

"I'll see you later today, you mean." They both laughed. "I'll see you for breakfast and you do look tired, *Querida!* Better rest for tomorrow. You had a wonderful day. And tomorrow will be another great day for you. I still have to talk with your father. We talked a little, while I was washing and grooming, and he suggested to me not to say anything in front of your grandfather about the Revolution, since he was part of Díaz's cabinet. He's retired, but he still wants Díaz to be president."

"Why, yes. Grandfather was very successful in Díaz's cabinet."

"Let's not talk about politics now," he suggested politely, but was serious. "I want to enjoy myself, and be with you. I'll go and wait outside, go see Roy, the *vaqueros*, and the rest of the people celebrating in the courtyard. I guess I'm sleeping in Roy's bunk tonight." He laughed. "It's too bad that I'm sleeping by myself!" He then gazed at Victoria, and smiled an enticing smile. He paused, changing the subject, knowing that perhaps, it was not a wise choice of words. With a flushed face, he remarked, "Roy will probably want to ride out in the morning to find out what's happening. I need to go to the stables and get some clean clothes from my bags and check my horse. Sleep tight."

Juan remained in the middle of the *sala*, looking up watching Victoria disappear up the steps and noticed that Mamá Maria was already waiting in attendance for her in the middle of the stairway. He turned around and headed out to the courtyard. Young girls swooned and giggled, covered their mouths with fans as he passed by; others whispered. From the corner of his eye he caught a glimpse of Yolanda, leaning against the outside entrance, almost expecting him, appearing to have waited for him. There the light of the lanterns was dimmer, reflecting intoxicated people, not caring about anything, only thinking of the wondrous pleasures the night would bring.

Yolanda was angry, but did not show it. She was patient. She had not had her way with Roy, but had been stalking Juan. In between her explosive actions with other *vaqueros*, Juan seemed like the perfect catch. She had watched and waited, until he was freed from Victoria. Immediately, she rushed over to his side. Her eyes were wild and glazed. Juan's eyes widened with interest, as would any hot-blooded young man with strong passion and desires. Yolanda was wearing her enticing, low-cut dress, exposing her sizeable, rounded, firm breasts, looking sleazy, easy, and wanting any type of action.

The *mariachis* were playing a *corrido*, and Juan whispered to Yolanda to have a drink of tequila together and then dance the number. Tables with cases of tequila, whiskey, wine, champagne, and glasses were stacked on every corner of the courtyard. Then the *mariachis* decided to play a slow dance. Hot sweat poured down Juan's forehead, his legs, and down the back of his shirt. His body was throbbing for wanton action, wild and urgent. He grabbed her close, looking into her eyes that were clear with desire. Then he glanced down at her bosom, and his thoughts veered, wishing she were Victoria. He became aroused, on the edge of something unthinkable, and ugly. He whispered in her ear imploringly, "You promised! Remember?" He raised his eyebrows, questioningly and began tantalizing her, mesmerizing her. "Tonight, remember!"

"Tonight!" She gazed at him with a smile and answered with a slurring response, as her left hand slowly slithered up to the back of his neck. Her red lips were almost touching his, and her firm body pressed strongly in a stimulating clockwise motion on his lower parts, wanting him. Yolanda had also gotten some special, black magic potion from *Doña* Adela, pertaining to amorous love. "Tonight!" she repeated. Whispering in his ear, "For as long as you like it, any way, any position you want. I'm yours tonight. Whatever you want and desire. I'm yours."

The rest of the dancing couples formed a circle around the amorous Juan and Yolanda, clapping their hands and offering words of enticement, for the evening was not over, and there would be many passionate earthquakes tonight. "*Aye Caramba,*" was all he could say.

CHAPTER 11

Before sunup, Roy, Miguel, and Juan headed south on their horses toward the thickets, the dense jungle of the mesquite and bushes, the great *brasada*, the boundless land holding to its own principles and convictions of the wilderness. All three were wearing protective *tapaderos* on their stirrups, heavy duck jackets, leather leggings, and gauntlets, riding toward the *resaca*, close to *Doña* Adela's house. All three men were suffering from a sleepless night and a heavy dose of hangover.

The weather had turned cold and many varieties of bushes were shedding their leaves, allowing them greater visibility in the distance.

"Its gittin' colder than a witch's tit," slurred Roy in the morning silence.

Miguel laughed out loud and said, "It's getting cold, but you won't have to worry about it any longer, *compadre*. It looks like you got lucky last night. Eh!" the *vaquero* mused, chewing on a straw. "I never thought you were ever going to dance with the beautiful Soledad. 'Course all of the *vaqueros* had a bet on you, and poor José lost."

"She's a slicker all right, mighty pree-tee. I never slept a wink just thinkin' 'bout her. Thinkin' 'bout her, in be'ween all of the snorin' and fartin' in the bunk, the noise and the sinks." He laughed. "I finally had da move outdoors to git any sleep and some fresh air."

"I'll bet within a year, you two will be hitched," joked Miguel. "Yes, *hombre*, that's the way life is, and that's the way it goes when the love bug gets your ass."

"I remember what *la bruja Doña* Adela told you, not too long ago. You'll be married soon!"

"Ah, shit! I still git that there feller, José Esquibel, to squabble with. He was a plenty mad *hombre* last night, when I asked to dance with Soledad. Damn! She acted like she really wanted me to fight with 'em. I was in no gaw'd dang mood to fight. I just wanted to make love."

"Ay, *Caramba*! And he never did come back to the fiesta?"

"Nah, and I'm sure glad he didn't," remarked Roy, as he recalled the thought of what the old witch *Doña* Adela had said to him earlier. *"Your future wife is here. She is here now."* By dang! Could it be possible? He thought maybe that old hag, crazier than a shit-house rat, was right all along. By dang!

"Ah! Shit-ta-lee, *Qué Tal!*" How about that!

"And you, *compadre?* Where did you sleep last night?" Miguel addressed Juan in a jolly mood.

"I can't remember! I woke up in one of the servant's quarters. I drank too much. I slept like a rock." He went into a deep silence. His thoughts were wandering, about the embarrassment he would encounter if *Don* Federico and the rest of the household found out about him in his irresponsible behavior. But it was the liquor and the music and Victoria's presence. He didn't want Miguel to know that it was his daughter he had slept with part of the night. And what a night!

"When we get back," stated Miguel, "we all will need some good *menudo* and a good cup of black coffee to get our stomach and head all clear and get our systems working again."

"Yore awf'ly quiet, *amigo*," commented Roy, curiously turning his head to view Juan.

"I'm just thinking, just thinking," replied Juan, following Miguel, who had gotten several yards ahead. "Who were the riders from last night? What did they want? Why didn't they come in and join us in the fiesta?"

"Thar's been a lot of mysterious shittin' things happenin' around the hacienda, since the great Haley's *Cometa* came out in May of this year," replied Roy. "At first we were all 'fraid that dat cattle would stampede. Now we have all gott'n use to it. Now, we see and hear strange *hombres* ridin' in en out of dat *brasada* and in the middle o' the *noche*." He paused for a minute. "*Quien sabe?*"

The sun was beginning to break through the top of the mesquite trees, when Miguel hollered and pointed to several vultures flying low over in the direction of the Juelson family cemetery. All three hurried, digging in their spurs, and followed at a fast trot, dodging wagging limbs from side to side, avoiding the *visnaga*, devil's head and cat's claw spines.

"There's bin some horses ridin' here," said Roy, climbing off his horse, and bending down and inspecting the soil. He kept looking at the ground, eyeing it hard. "See! Tracks of horses! Thar' must've been at least two. Nah! Thar's 'nother track over dere," he said, pointing to some horse droppings.

Miguel, who was small in stature, but was *muy alerto* with sharp eyes, dismounted. He was an excellent scout and an expert with cattle and horses. He could spot trouble anywhere. He smelled the ground and studied it for a while, tracing the tracks of the horses and where they led. He looked up, adjusting his straw hat. "Look!" he said in alarm, pointing to the gates of the cemetery.

The three mounted quickly and hurried to the open gates of the sacred grounds. A moment of chilled panic caught hold of the men, for there laid the body of José Esquibel, sprawled like a rag doll. They dismounted quickly. Vultures that were on the cemetery grounds flapped their wings and landed on the surrounding mesquite trees, creating an eerie presence. José's body looked like it had been beaten, and there were signs of a tremendous struggle. He had also been shot. Blood was spattered everywhere; one of the headstones had been smashed and defaced—the elaborate, granite headstone of George Albert Juelson. Big green flies swarmed over the man's lifeless body. His brains were scattered on a headstone. His eyes were wide open and staring into space.

ROOTS OF INDIFFERENCE

"Who in God's name could have done this?" said Juan, gasping through a handkerchief, holding his breath.

Roy pulled out his colored scarf and did the same. The stench was sickening, and the scene was horrific. "Another pr'blem for *el patrón*, addin' fuel to the fire," he said. "Da murder is gonna stir more shitin' harsh feelin's. It's gonna create tro'ble between *Don* Esquibel and *el patrón.*"

"Holy Mother of God!" screamed Miguel, looking over the body. "His throat and tongue have been ripped out. This sobered me up! The poor Esquibel's family is going to be sick."

"*Compadre*, you don't have to worry about this dead Mexican any more," said Juan, looking at Roy. He straightened himself up after inspecting the body of José, taking some time in determining what had taken place. He finally came to a conclusion. "First, he was beaten, his head smashed against the headstones, then he was shot, his tongue ripped out and his throat cut. A fine way of keeping someone silent, especially if they weren't sure he was dead." He gasped again.

"It happened on *el campo santo*, sacred ground. Ay! *Dios!* I see terrible things coming from this," added Miguel, with a realization that went beyond his reach.

"I'll git his horse," answered Roy, in distress and obviously shaken. "I saw it hidin' in deem dar bushes and mesquite trees. I hate this! We're gonna hav' to take da body to his *casa*. O' man Esquibel is gonna wan' da start shootin' us, and blame *el patrón* for dis."

"Wait!" exclaimed Juan. "Look, *amigos!* Over here!" He was bending over close to a shrub next to a headstone. He picked up something and studied it for several minutes. "I wonder if this will help in solving this murder." In his hands was a crushed, half-smoked, cheap cigar that had been pushed into the dirt with a shoe or a boot.

"I'll bet ya', *el patrón* will know who it belongs to," replied Roy in amazement, heading toward Juan to examine the object. "Lemme see it."

Miguel was squatting down, looking in the direction of the dense thickets outside of the graveyard's iron fence. With puzzlement on his face, he kept eyeing one particular area. Roy instantly noticed. Miguel put one finger to his lips, motioning him to keep quite.

"Whut is it, *amigo?*" whispered Roy, squatting down and drawing his pistol.

"I thought I saw movement and heard someone hiding in those bushes."

"Prob'ly a wildcat," suggested Roy, trying to focus in the direction Miguel was looking.

Miguel wasted no time in hurrying outside of the gates toward the bushes, then rushed in to grab whatever was behind the area covered with mesquite and *nopales*.

Roy stood up, still with his pistol in his hand and said, "Be careful, Miguel! Ya' might git a hold of somethin' you can't handle." He guffawed.

There was a loud scuffle coming from the thickets with terrifying sounds of dry leaves, moans, and hard breathing. Roy and Juan stood watching in suspense. In seconds, Miguel came out of the dense jungle dragging a tiny man by his shirt collar. It was Roberto Eagle, the dwarf son of *Señora* Adela, the witch woman.

"Whut da shit? Whut in the world is he doin' here?" Roy questioned, removing his hat and rubbing his hair with his left hand in startled surprise. "Whut da hell is he doin' in this area, especially in the cemetery? He normally roams the *brasada*."

Juan began talking to Roberto, but he didn't answer, and instead made weird sounds with his mouth and movements with his hands.

"The man is mute. Has been like this since birth," replied Miguel, with great concern, trying to dust off the leaves and dirt from his clothing, explaining his condition to Juan. Roy nodded agreeing. Roberto's appearance was like those from the Dark Ages. He was humped over and looked like Quasimodo from the novel, *Hunchback of Notre Dame*. He had big brown eyes, and his face and fingers were deformed. His build was short and stocky, and his hair was matted, messed up, with the fetid smell of someone not cleaning himself properly. He was trying to tell the three men something, as he kept pointing to his eyes.

"Your eyes," suggested Juan. "What about your eyes?" he asked, frowning. "Something must be wrong with his eyes!"

"You saw something?" suggested Miguel, being in tune with Roberto's deformed condition and having known him and *Doña* Adela for many years. "That's it! He saw something last night!"

Roberto nodded, "Yes!" The grotesque little dwarf then pointed to his head, cupping his hands, indicating something on top. He uttered gasping, chilling sounds.

"On your head," Juan questioned, "something on top of your head? Got problems with your head?" he asked.

"I think it's something else," retorted Miguel.

"Hat, yo' dumb shits," Roy said, looking at Miguel and Juan. All three laughed.

"Yes," nodded Roberto, cupping his hands wider again on top of his head.

"Big, big hats," remarked Miguel, trying to determine what Roberto was saying. Roberto again shook his head with a yes.

"Big man with sombreros, that's it. Sombrero—hats!"

Roberto shook his head with a no.

"Nah! Waal! Whut other hats? Let's see." Roy rubbed his chin, trying to think. "Derby hats, Stetson hats?"

Roberto shook his head yes at Stetson hats and then pointed to Roy.

"Me?" puzzled Roy, "Whut 'bout me? I wasn't out in the mid 'le of the *brasada* last night! Nah! siree! I was dancin' with my sweetie."

Roberto pulled his sleeve up and touched his skin. Then touched Juan's skin, and preceded to touch Miguel's skin, indicating the same skin with a no. But when he touched Roy's skin, he nodded with a yes.

"Skin?" asked Roy quizzically.

"White skin?" prompted Miguel.

Roberto shook his head with a yes.

"*Caramba, híjole! It's los gringos!*" said Miguel.

Roberto shook his head up and down very rapidly.

"Well! At least they were not *bandidos* from across the border as everyone would have suspected. But, what does all this mean?"

"Waal tis comin' clear to me, *amigos*," said Roy.

"What are you thinkin', *compadre*?" asked Miguel.

"Whut does this tell ya'? White *hombres* with Stetson hats, and left half a crushed smoked cigar. Very careless! Don't you thin'?"

"*Hijole!*" yelled Miguel. "Satan, *el Rinche* himself, from Harlingen. Damn! Texas Rangers!"

"*Caramba!* Juan mumbled under his breath. "Ah! You see, the fiesta last night, the commotion coming from the hacienda with people coming in and out, attracted Roberto while he was hiding in the *brasada*. He must have been watching and observing everything. He probably watched José riding away and must have confronted the riders. Who knows? Roberto is the only witness, and he can't talk. Then, when the riders rode toward the house, by then they had probably already beaten José. Roberto witnessed it, saw the whole thing, scaring him as he hid among the cactus. He must have spent the night here. He saw the whole thing! Is that right, Roberto?"

The disfigured little man nodded his head very rapidly, indicating a yes.

"He saw the whole thing. Well, I'll be dang, and by the way, you haven't seen a woman's body around this area, have you?" asked Miguel, hovering over Roberto.

Roberto's eyes went blank and his body recoiled. He lowered his head, bringing his malformed hands to his chest. He never replied with a yes or a no.

"How many dead women's bodies are found every day out in the *brasada?*" said Juan.

"Haven't seen one?" asked Miguel. He made a wave with both of his hands, like an hourglass shape, indicating the figure of a woman. "People just don't disappear into thin air. There has to be some traces of her, even if an animal got a hold of her." Roberto turned his head quizzically and glanced at Miguel. He never answered.

"You are confusing this man," interrupted Juan. "He doesn't understand if you're asking him about a woman last night, or a year ago. This was months ago, and nobody is going to find the body now, especially if she was left out in this area. The atmospheric conditions will destroy a body very quickly, especially in this muggy climate." He spoke both from his medical knowledge and from common logic.

"Well, shit! Reckon we'd better git. Let's load the body of José on his horse and take him to Spanish Acres and den to *Don* Esquibel's house."

"There will be shit-ta-lee to pay, and a lot of explaining," remarked Miguel. "Victoria is celebrating her birthday and there's still a lot of drinking, eating, and dancing to do."

"Go home, go to your *casa*. Shoo! Git away from this spook area, Roberto," ordered Roy, waving his arm. "*El patrón* will prob'ly wanna talk to ya' and prob'ly come over and have a chat with ya' later and will prob'ly wanna have some mumbo-jumbo with *Doña* Adela."

Already frightened, Roberto turned and ran off into jungle of *nopales*, disappearing like a deer into the dense brush.

"What seems funny to me," replied Miguel, rubbing his head then putting his straw hat back on, "was that it was ol' man George's headstone that was the only one damaged. I wonder if that has any significance?"

"*Quien sabe?*" Juan replied. "Who knows?"

"To the hacienda, *muchachos*, let's go!"

⌘ ⌘ ⌘

Don Federico and *Don* José Hinojosa had not slept a wink throughout the night. It had been a night of celebration and joy, seeing old friends, talking politics and the up-coming Revolution. *Señor* Hinojosa was concerned about his granddaughter Victoria's behavior, but mainly worried about his daughter, for *Doña* Francisca was sick and not getting any better.

After the two *Dons* had eaten their breakfast, they found themselves walking in the middle of the dirt road leading towards the gate of the hacienda; both were getting away from all the commotion of people, music, and loud noise. *Don* Federico was angry and trying to cool his heels after giving Fred a good licking, learning about the prank that he had instigated with the other young boys the night before.

"I just don't understand boys at this age. How I hate to whip my children. But they have to learn to respect their elders and other people's possessions."

"It's kind of comical, Fred being so intelligent," replied *Don* Hinojosa, laughing. "Who would have thought of planning such a ruse? It took some clever thought and planning, with a high capacity for mischief. He was pulling a fast one, anything for a laugh. Fred is smart and will probably use his intelligence later in his life, hopefully for the betterment of humanity. Don't worry; he'll grow up sooner than you think."

"He's smart all right, but always trying to make people laugh. For Fred to pull a prank like this one on this occasion, and on my friends and guests! Why, it's unacceptable. What do people think? That I'm running a nuthouse in the hacienda with crazy, imbecile children? It's an embarrassment, to say the least!" *Don* Federico cleared his throat while gazing toward the brasada and admiring the view of his beautiful house and his land. He sighed and turned to address *Señor* Hinojosa. "I have taught my children to behave and respect everyone. I have given them the best there is in this world, especially around this deprived area. Fred sometimes worries me. He seems so unconcerned about everything. He takes life for what it is. Maybe I want him to grow up too fast and be like I was at his age. While I was growing up, all I thought about was getting an education. Of course, Dad was very strict with Josie and me. More disciplined with me, because I was a man. Fred disappoints me at times. He acts so intelligent on many things, but on other occasions, he doesn't use his head and acts very foolish."

"Children will grow up very fast," replied *Senor* Hinojosa. "In the coming years, you will laugh and tell stories about him and the childish things he did."

Their walk had reached the entrance to the hacienda, and both stood leaning against the stone walls. *Don* Federico continued talking. "Well, Fred isn't laughing now. After the beating

ROOTS OF INDIFFERENCE

I gave him, he'll think twice before he pulls another one. He won't be able to sit for a while. Francisca was unhappy with me for hitting him, especially with Victoria's celebration and the guests in the household."

"My daughter is not well!" answered Hinojosa in a firm voice. "Francisca is not going to get any better in this area." He then looked away and cleared his throat, pondering, not knowing how his son-in-law was going to take his next comment. "Gloria and I have been very upset about Francisca's illness. We wouldn't have known this, because she never wrote or told anyone about her condition. Emma is very concerned also. We have decided to take Francisca back with us to Monterrey, where the air is clearer. We'll be able to get her a good doctor and several nurses who will attend her and be with her twenty-four hours a day. She'll be getting the best of care, I promise you, in our home and the best of medicine."

"Francisca is very stubborn. I have repeatedly begged her to get medical care, but she refuses," replied *Don* Federico. "I will talk to her and convince her to go with you, for her health's sake. It's an excellent idea. At this point, we have no other choice since the medication is not helping her, and yes, she is getting worse. I have noticed that myself. We all want her to get well and be herself again. The children and I hate to see her go, but I also want her to get better. Monterrey would be a perfect place for her to recover."

From the distance, they could hear the music and gaiety that had lingered all through the night in Spanish Acres. Some had danced nonstop. In the background could be heard shouts of *vaqueros* racing their horses, betting who was the fastest, and raucous laughter at poker, while others were betting on rooster fights. Their conversation was cut short by the sound of hooves pounding up the dirt road. Both men gasped at the horrific sight that presented itself.

"Is he—?"

"Dead, why yes!" Foolish question—a man hanging sideways from the horse's saddle, blood all over him, with his head and feet dangling.

It didn't take long to convince *Don* Federico who killed José Esquibel, after Juan showed the burned cigar and left it with him. It was evident that the Texas Rangers were on the prowl last night. Hearing the celebration and all the commotion, they knew the area had been left unguarded.

"Roy, you and Miguel take the body over to the Esquibel's place. Try to be as discreet as possible. Keep the horse outside of the gates," commanded *Don* Federico, "to keep the incident away from the guests, since they are having such a good time. It's going to be hard to keep the guests from learning about this. Sooner or later, it's bound to get out and everybody will know. Damn it!" He let out a deep breath. "Tell *Señor* Esquibel what you told me. I will send my condolences later. Please excuse myself to him. He'll understand. We will send him some of our food, if that's any consolation. Ask him if there is anything I can do for him. Anything he wants!"

Roy, still on his horse, nodded; Miguel nodded his head. They went on their way, leading the horse with the body of José, while Juan stayed. The aging Hinojosa was in a state of shock, pale-faced, and looking stricken. He excused himself as he went to see the where-abouts of his wife.

"*Señor* Juelson! Now, do you see what I mean?" remarked Juan, walking toward the house with *Don* Federico. "This Texas Ranger is a dangerous one, a smart fox. In Monterrey, if he has plans, you will not stand a chance. I have the perfect men that will do the job you wanted at your gold mine," he said, very convincingly.

Don Federico's skin crawled with dread and he was deep in thought. He finally replied, "Yes, take your horse to the stables and come and join me in the library. We need to talk."

The fiesta continued through the second day. It wasn't long before the news of José Esquibel's death had spread like wildfire. Several of the families celebrating had left in fear and gone home early, not wishing to stay for the following day's festivities. Those who stayed, especially the men, drank more heavily than before, using the incident as an excuse. The day had become full of fears and overshadowed by the evil omen.

"*Madre mía!*" said Mamá Maria nervously from the kitchen. "I knew something terrible was going to happen," she said with a sigh. "The day before the fiesta, while we were all so busy getting things ready, and on top of the big cottonwood trees next to the barn were three big gray owls. *Lechuzas!* It's a terrible omen to see owls. To see one is bad enough, but three! It signifies death. It scared me clear out of my wits."

"Such stupid foolishness, Maria," answered Emma. "Calm yourself! Owls are noctur-nal birds," she snapped, in her raucous voice that rattled throughout the house. She was sitting in a rocker next to the kitchen door with her shoes off and her feet resting on a small embroidered ottoman, fanning herself. "They have to sit somewhere," she replied dryly.

"Sitting in the daytime? Where the people could view them? Bad omen, bad things are going to happen!" Mamá Maria kept repeating those words, shaking her head, sweating profusely and wiping her forehead with her apron, all the while preparing more food for the guests. "There'll be evil things come of this. I can feel it in my bones. I don't like this. I don't like it!"

"Superstition, that's all," answered Emma, making a face in annoyance. "That's what happens, when you people here at Spanish Acres allow the witch woman to tell you what to do all the time. Filling your heads with such garbage, telling your future, giving everyone here potions and remedies, making believe they are cures. All such nonsense! Scaring everyone with signs and objects! Bah!" She laughed sarcastically.

"It may be superstition," growled Mamá Maria, taking all the guff she had allowed her-self from Emma, "but on the day before *Señor* Albert Juelson died, we all heard the mournful hooting of the *lechuzas* in the middle of the night. Everyone working in the kitchen and some of the *vaqueros* the next morning saw the ugly creature sitting in the same tree. It wouldn't go away. We all tried to throw stones at it and shoo it away. Owls are bad omens, and hearing and seeing one is worse. I've known that ever since I was a young girl." The exhausted servant turned and thrust her way through the crowd, thumping her feet as if going to fight a war with a bowl full of Spanish rice.

ROOTS OF INDIFFERENCE

"Such stupidity!" yelled Emma to the retreating figure. People heard her rude remark, and laughter could be heard in every corner of the big house. Emma laughed, as her big fat stomach quivered, while her feet remained propped up on the stool. She had a habit of wearing shoes too small for her feet, because it was the custom. Men adored women with small feet, and hers were the tiniest, if not the fattest.

Victoria and Felicia had not joined the rest of the guests; they had slept late. They sat on the bed giggling and talking about the previous night.

"Do you like it?" questioned Victoria, showing her cousin the golden amulet around her neck.

"Oh! Victoria, it's absolutely lovely! Juan is so handsome, too. You were right about him, his manners and looks. But what are you going to do about marrying Ricardo?"

"Ah! I do not know! But I knew I loved Juan the first week he was here." She put her index finger to her lips and lowered her voice. "My parents don't believe in instant love, and they arranged my marriage to someone they knew and his family, someone wealthy, for my security." She glanced around and quietly got off the bed in her nightgown and headed toward the door with a look of distrust. "I don't want anyone to hear me, especially Yolanda. She is such a snoop. Last night, Juan proposed to me."

"Oh! Victoria," cried Felicia with glee. "He proposed to you! Honestly! How romantic! But what are you going to do when we come back from school?"

"Honestly, Felicia! You surprise me. In two years, many things can happen, and by then, I'll have it all worked out. Now! Let's fix our hair and get dressed. We have an exciting day coming up."

"Will you be seeing Juan in Monterrey?" Felicia asked, with shock written all over her face, while she unraveled her hair to be combed. "He could get himself in a lot of trouble with the powerful Del Calderóne family. Politically I mean."

"What can they do?" replied Victoria. "And yes, he'll be seeing me at the convent," she said, feeling confident and so sure of her future. "But promise not to tell, especially your mother. She seems to be fond of Ricardo and his family. I wish that Ricardo's brother would be of interest to you."

"Come on! Ricardo's brother Luis is an outcast, according to my mother. He has spoken out against the Del Calderóne family, and was ordered out of their home never to return. Rumors are that he has also joined some of the revolutionists against his own family."

"All that my parents could do is dispatch me back home. Now, Felicia, promise not to tell!"

"I promise!"

"What happened last night with your stepfather? I noticed while I was dancing with Juan that he was standing over you and grabbed your arm, and you walked away. What did he want?"

"What he always wants! But one thing leads to another with him. I can't stand him holding me. He has a filthy mind, and I knew what he was wanting. He whispered in my ear that I have been gone too long, and how he missed me. He said more, but I can't repeat it. I told him to go dance with my mother. I turned around, leaving him standing on the floor. As I left, Victor Salinas asked me to dance, and I did. I had a good time. He made me laugh, and he's a good dancer."

"Good for you. How do you like the Salinas boy? He comes from a wealthy family. His family owns thousands of cattle on a ranch close to Chapin."

"He is divine! He asked if I would dance with him tonight. He said he would be waiting for me. He wants to be my dancing partner. I can't wait!"

Soledad had been attending *Doña* Francisca through the night. When she went downstairs to get *La Señora* and herself some food, she overheard Yolanda talking with some of Emma's servants, putting the blame for all the trouble on Soledad's coming to Spanish Acres. "Soledad is the problem," said Yolanda, still acting boastfully, after her nighttime tryst with Juan. "We have not had any trouble in this area, but she brought with her evil forces, evil roots, evil omens. And now, José Esquibel's death! How is she going to explain his death? Now, she has nobody to help her, except the Juelson family, who feel sorry for her, because she was raped and beaten. We are all raped when we make love." She laughed mockingly.

The rest of the busy servants giggled, but stopped when Soledad entered the kitchen area.

Doña Francisca cried upon hearing the news of José Esquibel's death, but consoled herself with her rosary, votive candles, and her statues of Catholic saints standing next to her bed.

"It's my fault!" cried Soledad sitting on a chair next to *Doña* Francisca's bed, sobbing and feeling guilty for José Esquibel's death and her presence at Spanish Acres.

Between her coughing fits, *Doña* Francisca replied, "Don't pay any attention to gossip, my dear. People will say anything in times of hysteria. Everyone is afraid, so they will say things to console themselves, always blaming someone else, as if blaming others will bring José back. You had nothing to do with the young Esquibel's death. We all know that."

"Everything bad has happened since I came to your place. I'm so grateful to all of you here. You have been so kind. All of you saved my life. I have no family." Sobbing, she blew her nose and wiped her eyes with a handkerchief.

"Soledad, calm yourself. Good things are coming to you. In spite of everything that has happened, you're a good person. God has a way of handing us burdens in life, but consider them as a good experience and a blessing. We have all suffered in our own way. It is how we handle the situation that matters. This is what life is all about. In our lifetime, we are all going to laugh and cry and suffer heartaches because it teaches us to be strong. It gives us strength and the indomitable will to survive. Be grateful that you were sent to us and to live here in this area. And be happy that José took an interest in you."

At that moment, *Don* Federico walked into the bedroom and surprised them. He was pleased to see his wife eating and feeling better. He thanked Soledad for caring for his wife, while others in his household were enjoying themselves. "*Corazon*, you're looking wonderful," he said. He smiled at her and sat down on the edge of her bed, then took her hand and kissed it.

Not wanting to upset her, he chose his words very carefully. "*Querida*," he began. "Your father and mother have asked to take you to Monterrey, where you'll have excellent medical care. They have good doctors and the best facilities for getting you back to normal." He said it with confidence, displaying a bright smile and a spark in his eyes. "I agree with your father. I think it best for you to go with them and get well again with better care."

Doña Francisca became obstinate. "I can't leave now! I have too many things to do! Mother has already suggested it, but I disagree. Victoria is leaving for Monterrey and staying there for the next eighteen months, and I have to get her clothes ready. And now José's death—" She began coughing, and quickly grabbed her handkerchief.

"I'll see that everything will be taken care. You don't have to worry or do anything. Victoria turned sixteen. She is a big girl now! She is not the same little girl we remember. She can take care of herself. Mamá Maria will oversee everything before she goes to school."

"Too many things to do before we get ready and leave for any trip," snapped *Doña* Francisca. "I need to get up from this bed and visit the Esquibel's family and console them for their terrible loss."

"You're in no shape to go anywhere!" said *Don* Federico. "Your illness has been a constant worry for me for months." He got up from her bed, his voice displaying his anguish. "All I want is for you to get well and be yourself again. I have spent many sleepless nights worrying about your condition, and it's about time you get the medical help you deserve. I will not take 'no' for an answer."

"But—"

"No buts. It's time you start thinking about yourself and your health instead of everyone else's problems. If you continue this way, you will not make it past this year."

"All I have is a bad cough," commented *Doña* Francisca weakly.

"Don't give me any excuses. You have more than a cough!" he said, raising his voice. "You need medical help. That's final! I'll have Yolanda or Mamá Maria, or for that matter, Soledad, start getting your clothes and bags ready. That's final! I don't want to hear another word," he repeated.

Soledad nodded her head and said humbly, "Why, of course, I'll do anything, *Señora.*"

"For now, you need your rest!" He kissed *Doña* Francisca on her forehead and began walking outside into the long hall. On his way out he said, "I'll have your mother come up and join you. Everybody is having a good time, and the fiesta is not over yet. If anybody needs me, I'll be in the library."

The *sala* and patio were full of people eating and drinking, while many of the couples danced to the beat of the musician's rhythm. The festivities had produced an eventful experience: Many people had become ill with indigestion or diarrhea; one small boy had fallen from a citrus tree and broken his leg; a small child was bitten by a scorpion; another had been bitten by a rattler; and, worst of all, Jose Esquibel was dead.

But the music and gaiety continued. Victoria and Felicia had finished their breakfast and headed to the stables, where her grandparents presented her birthday present: a four-year-old, pure white filly, from their villa in Monterrey.

"What are you going to name her?" questioned Felicia.

"I don't know. Why don't you help pick a name?"

"Since we're both going to Monterrey. How about calling her Reyes?"

"That's a man's name! How about calling her La Reyna?" The girls laughed and agreed.

They both swooned as they caught sight of Juan returning from the stables and looking serious, even in his smooth, charming, raffish manner.

Victoria, in her effervescent and joyous mood, approached him close-up, as if wanting a hug or a kiss. Wearing the golden amulet prominently displayed around her neck, she was expecting Juan's comment.

But he was solemn and in no mood for any serious affection. He said, "Did you hear about José?" His face was full of concern and his green eyes widened, indicating a feeling of uneasiness.

"No! What happened?" the two girls asked at the same time. They turned to look at each other, shocked.

"We found him dead, early this morning, inside the cemetery. He was beaten, tortured, and shot to death. Apparently, *Los Rinches* had a part in the murder. We found a burned-out cigar that belongs to one of them. Your father recognized the cigar. Roy said that it was probably those corrupt Texas Rangers. He thinks that man Hanson had a part in it and was spying on the hacienda last night, with the rest of his thugs." He decided not to describe the gory details of how they had found the body.

"So what is Father going to do?" asked Victoria, disappointed and concerned that the incident would disrupt her celebration.

"I don't know. I just got word that your father wants to talk to me in the library. I'm on my way." Juan, drained and nervous, was trying to sort out the turmoil in his head, but he could not forget the image imprinted on his mind of José's mutilated body. "I'll see you later tonight, Victoria." He smiled faintly.

The girls shuddered.

In the late afternoon, the great *sala* was set for Victoria and Fred to perform for the guests, with Miss Bell accompanying them at the piano. Sitting at the piano and perusing the music sheets, Victoria presented a stunning vision in her new low-cut, pink organdy dress. She kept a vigil on all the entrances coming into the grand *sala*, and caught a glimpse of Soledad coming from the kitchen with a tray full of champagne glasses. But Juan was nowhere in sight.

"Soledad," Victoria said. "Has anyone see Juan? I haven't seen him since noon, when he said he would meet me later. Do you know where he is? Have you seen him?" She spoke, trying to appear nonchalant, not realizing that other ears were listening.

Emma was sitting next to *Señor* and *Señora* Hinojosa in the large *sala*. They were all facing the group and overheard Victoria's questioning. Emma raised her voice and said, "He left several hours ago!" she hissed in a viperous tone. "Manuel and Yo-Yo helped him with his clothes and saddled his horse. They sent him on his way."

She smiled with superiority, pleased as though she had been given permission to discipline Victoria. She began fanning herself from her hot flashes, then spoke again, lashing out. "That young man has no business whirling you around the dance floor like he did last night," she said. "You are making a complete fool of yourself and leading him on. You have no shame, and its unbecoming, not ladylike behavior, knowing you'll be married in a couple of years to Ricardo Del Calderóne." She twisted her mouth with a smug smile, looking condescending, as if Victoria's parents themselves were delivering the hateful admonition.

Embarrassed, Victoria's face turned beet-red, and anxiety and uneasiness overtook her. People sitting and standing around her began laughing. Another wave of whispering from waggling tongues rolled around the room. Her grandmother Gloria was appalled; however, not *Don* Hinojosa, since he had already protested to *Don* Federico about Victoria's behavior.

Felicia, ambling in from the courtyards, stood and held her breath. Soledad tuned pale, set the tray of glasses down, and quietly walked away. Fred, standing next to Victoria's side, was wiggling his hurting hind-end and fiddling with his suit. He glanced at Victoria and grabbed his violin. He was shocked at the intense atmosphere and overcome by *Tía* Emma's remarks, worried that at any moment his sister might explode into one of her tantrums and start throwing things.

Miss Bell, who was dumfounded at the present dialogue, rescued the situation by waving her hands in front of Victoria and Fred. She was wearing a black, full-length skirt, and a white, high-collared, lace blouse with a cameo brooch at her throat. "Now children," she said. "First we will play Beethoven's *Moonlight Sonata*, and then we'll do *Für Else*, followed by John Philip Sousa's *El Capitán*." She cleared her throat. "And if the people want another tune, we will play the difficult piece by Frederic Chopin that we have been practicing this past week."

Controlling her dismay, Victoria managed to play the piano, as the color from her face receded slightly, but the frown did not. If women were lesser creatures than men and were being dominated, were not supposed to be objective, then how come *Tía* Emma got by with her domineering ways? Her Amazonian proportions were enough to gag any man, much less her repulsive mouth. Where was *Doña* Adela's potion? Victoria's anger fomented a demonic urge to clobber *Tía* Emma. As the moment passed, she did not have time to think of what became of Juan.

Victoria's forehead was perspiring and her fingers were sweating, sticking to the piano keys. She could feel the sweat rolling down her back as she played each note flawlessly. Fred followed with his violin, and the combination of the two musical instruments became intoxicating, with an almost mystic precision. The crowd applauded and showed their approval as the musical piece was played. They had never heard such beautiful music! Miss Bell bowed and smiled, pleased with her accomplishment as a music teacher, and with Victoria and Fred, who heaved a collective sigh of relief. She then pointed to the two students, as they bowed and curtsied. The crowd stood cheering, and applauded again. Many hugged the two students and praised them for their skill and expertise. Many questions were asked of Victoria, who was in her height of glory over her performance, pretending to be charming and giddy. Many of the elite crowd congregated around Miss Bell, congratulating her on her knowledge of music.

Don Federico had appeared, standing and applauding with the group of dignitaries with whom he had been having a discussion in his library.

The twin Montoya girls, who lived on a large ranch northwest of Mercedes City, approached Victoria in a friendly manner, as they, too, would also be going to the convent school.

"It's surprising that we're all attending the same school," replied Rosa, the nosey, seventeen-year-old, who was full of curiosity and questions, and talking inches away from Victoria's face. "By the way, the man that you were dancing with last night, is he your *novio*? He is so handsome that he stands out in the crowd. I couldn't keep my eyes off of him! I didn't see him here tonight. Did he have an emergency? Does he live in one of the *ranchitos* here in the valley? What's his name? And your mother, someone said she was ill. Is she feeling better? I didn't see her tonight enjoying the celebration."

Victoria could feel her blood beginning to boil. "No! His name is Juan Alvarez. He is not my *novio*. He is a friend of my father, and we met several months ago here in the hacienda. And yes, he had to leave. He is on a special mission. Yes, he is single and looking for a good-looking wife who has money!" She said it hatefully, knowing that it wouldn't apply to either of the twins, since they were both ugly, with bad complexions and protruding teeth. She continued, "And no, he is not from this area. He comes from Monterrey, Mexico. And yes, Mother is resting and feeling better. Thank you for your concern."

"Oh!" replied the other boisterous twin, Rosalinda. She brought her hand up to her mouth, tossed her head flirtatiously, and eyed Victoria mockingly. "So you say! He is single! What a catch!" She giggled and nudged her sister. They both looked like two fat hens.

The other twin addressed Victoria with much enthusiasm. "What does he do?" she asked, rolling her eyes.

She would ask that, the ugly witch! Thought Victoria, still sweating. She had to think fast to find the right words to describe Juan's occupation. She couldn't say that he was out collecting money for the benefit of the Revolution, since everyone was afraid of the coming war. She dared not mention Madero, for at this moment his name was like poison in political circles. Instantly she blurted out, "A diplomat! Yes, that's what he is. A diplomat! With a very important mission!"

"A diplomat for President Díaz? How impressive, "said Rosa. "And he lives in Monterrey? Will he be coming to visit you at the school?" She kept asking nosey questions.

"Yes, for the government of Díaz," she lied. If Juan knew that she had said that remark, he would have a fit and fall in it. For it was against Díaz that he was fighting, for the poor people of Mexico, for their liberation and freedom. As for answering whether Juan was coming to see her at the convent, Victoria was not going to put her foot in her mouth on that question. She curbed her temper and ignored it.

ROOTS OF INDIFFERENCE

"He sounds like a very interesting man. And so good-looking," swooned Rosalinda, with her mouth slightly agape. "Maybe we will be seeing your friend in Monterrey. Maybe you'll introduce us. I can hardy wait to see him again." She giggled out loud, showing her enormous, bizarre teeth.

"Thank you so much for inviting us to this great fiesta," said Rosa. "Our family has all enjoyed it, especially the food and music. This place is so beautiful. Everything is so elegant and wonderful. And you are so beautiful. How exciting for you to have danced with such a handsome man." She obviously had an interest in Juan and persisted in bringing him into her conversation.

"Thank you. My cousin and I look forward to seeing you at the school in January. And thank you for coming—I'm glad you enjoyed the fiesta. Please enjoy the rest of evening."

For Victoria, the rest of evening was like an eternity. There was more food and dancing and meeting new people and making friends. But between each dance, she kept thinking, *What happened to Juan? Why did he leave without saying goodbye? What happened in the library with my father?*

The final song was the *La Golondrina*, the Mexican sad farewell song, indicating that the celebration was over and the fiesta had come to an end. Many of the guests had left the celebration early, mostly because of fear and the uncertainly of the turmoil that existed in the area, not knowing who could be next. The remaining guests now gathered up children and belongings and left in their carriages that same night, after sharing sad tales and so many joyous moments. All embraced with mutual blessings, saying their goodbyes and wondering what the future held in store for them.

CHAPTER 12

The fiesta was over. The families had seen many friendly faces and important people from both sides of the border. It had been both a joyous and a sad occasion. With a cloudy, dreary, chilly day that brought sporadic light sprinkles, the funeral of José Esquibel had been extremely sad, especially for the two families whose ranches adjoined. At José's wake, *Señor* Esquibel, in his rage, swore to get revenge for his murdered son. It was another sad moment to see *Doña* Francisca leave with her parents. Miss Belle was given her wages, and with it, an extra token gift for her contribution to the fiesta. She then departed, leaving by carriage the following morning for her home.

Tía Emma stayed for several days afterwards, giving her maids and servants orders to gather all of the material and accessories for their trip back to Mercedes City. She had been at Spanish Acres close to a month and needed to get back to her active social life. Howard Ale, who had come alone in his own coach, pleaded with Felicia to come home with him, but she refused. He returned with only the twins and a carriage full of supplies, disgruntled at the Juelsons for encouraging Felicia to stay on.

He left feeling uncomfortable about his time at Spanish Acres. He belonged to a special group of elite society people and had never liked *Don* Federico, always referring to him as a "greaser cow man" behind his back. His hatred toward the *Don* grew worse, especially after their confrontation the night before, regarding his involvement with *Don* Federico's father and the gold mine.

In his mind, he relived the heated conversation with *Don* Federico that had put him on the spot.

"How was it that you became so interested in my father's property and money?" *Don* Federico had asked him.

"It was your father's idea to begin with, since we played cards all the time," Howard Ale had replied seriously. "He bragged about all the money he had made in the mine and decided for the three of us to celebrate with his money."

"Out of the goodness of his heart," *Don* Federico had snapped at him with anger. "That wasn't what Hanson said. He said that it was *your* idea to begin with. Hanson said to me, when I went to visit him several months ago, that you put the seed in motion. And that you knew a way to get some of my father's money. Does the word 'blackmail' mean anything to you—and its consequences?"

"Hanson said that? Why, that bastard! He was clear up to his neck involved with this mess. It was Hanson who came up with the idea, not me!" His voice had risen in anger.

"Who killed my father?" *Don* Federico had blurted, banging his fist on his desk. "I don't know of any killing," Howard Ale had replied, startled. "It's a figment of your imagination."

⌘ ⌘ ⌘

"Ungrateful girl!" Emma snarled, as she prepared to leave, dressed in her big, fancy, peacock-feather hat, gloves, shoes, and matching parasol. "We've tried to give Felicia everything, but she's getting a mind of her own. She's getting too big for her britches. Maybe by attending the convent for the next couple of years, she'll miss her home, and she'll learn to appreciate and respect us." With the help of her servants, she was lifted into her carriage full of several cases of champagne, along with a quarter of pork and pounds of beef. "I know what it is—it's that Victoria getting back at me, for bringing out the truth about her," she ranted. "Giving Felicia crazy ideas! And from a spoiled girl who gets everything she wants! All she has to do is ask, and everyone runs to her service. Felicia's attitude has taken a different turn, especially when she spends time with that ungrateful Victoria, doing what she pleases, and one day it's going to backfire on the two of them."

Don Federico paid no attention to Emma's remarks. There was a cold-as-ice attitude between the families. The entire household was relieved that she was going, all giving a real sigh of relief as she departed. "A real pain in the ass," the *Don* summed her up. "If it weren't for her mouth, she could be tolerable." He stood with his hands in both pockets watching her depart with her maids, then turned and disappeared inside his home.

Getting ready for the big trip to Monterrey, the *Don* got busy giving orders to Roy and his *vaqueros* in caring for the hacienda, the cattle, and their needs. First was the clearing and cleaning up of the area around the hacienda, with all of the debris that had been left, with so many people attending the fiesta. There was much branding to do, milking, and blacksmithing, as well as the repair of one of the barn's roofs. On the east side of his land, the fences needed to be fixed and other buildings too. Inside, the women were busy cleaning and changing linens, with the pot-bellied stoves outside boiling tablecloths, bath towels, and everything that had been used during the festivities. North of the kitchen, lines were strung for drying all the material goods.

Don Federico was generous to his workers, especially during the Christmas holidays. However, this year, he was going to be away for two months, so he decided to be charitable early. He handed Roy a large envelope full of money, for his end of the year gift, and a dozen envelopes for Miguel to distribute to the others, since he was in charge of the working *vaqueros* out in the *brasada*.

ROOTS OF INDIFFERENCE

During the short, rainy, winter season, there would be less to do outside, except keeping the cattle in check and being watchful that they didn't get onto other ranchers' property. Another order was given to start vigilance again around the area of the hacienda, by having two *vaqueros* spend the night in the south *brasada*, taking turns watching. "Everyone knows I'm going to be gone for a while, and with all of the activities happening lately," he told Roy, "I sure don't want to return to find my hacienda burned, cattle stampeded and killed, or the women harmed in any way."

Don Federico took solitude in his library in his favorite swivel chair and occasionally drifted into a state of nostalgia about the past year. Hardly a day had gone by that it had not brought exciting surprises, along with some good and some bad memories. He was still haunted by the body of the woman, never found in the dense cacti jungle. His mind struggled with it. There were just too many unanswered questions. He was still worried about his sister. Josie's condition and her marital problems were so serious that she never seemed to find the time to answer his letters. He wondered if Tom White had ever made it back to San Antonio. He also had a deep longing for his wife, to see her again. He missed Francisca and was sincerely hoping she would recover and get better in Monterrey. He was concerned about the trip to the gold mine. He wondered about Soledad, who couldn't seem to remember anything about her ordeal. Was it because she was embarrassed that she pretended not to know anything about the incident, as if her mind were closed on the delicate issue?

It had been a year with new words being added to the vocabulary: airplane, automobile, gasoline, black gold. It was the coming of the genius age, where everyone believed the new conditions and technologies would change human life for the better. How would this affect the Mexican-American people along the Rio Grande Valley of Texas? Already, there were evil forces at work—greedy land investors, buying the land and promoting it to the hungry hoards wanting to settle in a place that was cheap to buy. The white natives were calling it "The Magic Valley," using the slogan for advertising promotions, enticing rich people from the northern states to invest their money and settle in a paradise. It was all about money, rich schemes— greed— *evilness!!*

The Mexicans, who were by nature superstitious, had seen the sign in the skies and were constantly repeating stories about evil omens, leaving them all apprehensive. They would whisper to one another: "Look at the difference in the weather! Look at the signs in the sky! Something bad is coming—it's in the wind!" These pronouncements were usually followed by a long, sad sigh.

Gory sagas being repeated along the border were starting to take their toll. Much brutality was perpetuated between the two groups of people. The Texas Rangers were given full authority in the South Texas counties to suppress any trouble along the border. They took advantage of their supremacy, blaming the Mexican people for any incident that occurred. "Goddamn Mexicans! Greasers!" they would shout. All they had to do was get suspicious of any Mexican individual. If they disliked him, he was taken outside and lynched in a tall mesquite tree, without any explanation to anyone.

The Mexican people from both sides of the border hated the Rangers. It was always the Ranger's word against the ignorant soul who, in the first place, had trouble understanding English. There was no justice! But this did not stop the stream of refugees wanting to leave the hungry conditions in Mexico and cross over onto Texas soil to better themselves in Anglo country. They could find work in Texas, even if they had to work in the fields or work in white men's homes; they would become servants and *vaqueros* and clear the *brasada*—whatever it took to survive.

Several problems began to arise. Not only was the influx coming into Texas, but Mexican bandits were continuing to infest the Rio Grande River area. Other problems began emerging regarding contraband, guns, ammunition, and corruption.

Before long, the whole American border, from the mouth of the Boca Chica to El Paso, flared up. The middle-class revolted, touching off strong sentiments, and this was not going to stop until a new government was set up in Mexico. The imminent liberator of Mexico, Francisco Madero, had tried to cross over into the Rio Grande, but communications within his own circle had gone wrong and thwarted his efforts.

The whole countryside was like a dry bush, and any spark would cause the situation to erupt into a flaming inferno. Everyone, Mexican or white, was now experiencing a constant state of the "jitters."

Already, the corrupt government of Díaz had affected his own army. Soldiers were supplied with inadequate guns and equipment, and inferior ammunition, leading to a breakdown in discipline. Yet Madero, with very few men and supplies, and faced with deplorable conditions, began showing astonishing results in the rapid triumph of the Revolution. All throughout the border, the common people were now joining the cause and saying, "*Viva Madero! Abajo Díaz!*"

Victoria had become full of anxiety over concern about what lay on her horizons. The more she thought about Juan, the worse it got, not knowing why he had left without saying a word. How she missed him! Only God knew how long it would be before she saw him again. There were nights she had not been able to sleep and walked the floor out onto her balcony, thinking of the amorous Juan. When she slept, she would dream about him, and her days were filled with daydreams.

⌘ ⌘ ⌘

Already in the second week of December, the weather had gotten cold and brisk. Waiting for their long journey to Monterrey to begin, Victoria and Felicia were enjoying a midday horseback ride that would take them deep into the jungle *brasada*. "I'll race you to the fork in the road," challenged Victoria.

"You think it will be all right? Remember what you father told us. Nobody is to ride out unescorted. Especially, with the terrible death of the Esquibel man. Everyone's nerves are showing."

ROOTS OF INDIFFERENCE

"Oh! For crying out loud, Felicia! Horse feathers! Come now. I have my rifle with me. Who in the world is going to bother us during the day? There are *vaqueros* all over the *brasada*. No one will get close to us. No one will touch us with a ten-foot pole." She laughed abruptly. "How silly you are! And we are not unescorted. We have each other, so stop being afraid of everything!" A sly look came over her face.

"I don't like the look on your face," remarked the spiritless, timid Felicia. "What's on your mind? You don't do anything without a reason."

"What do you say if you and I go visiting?" she said enthusiastically.

"Visiting? Who? For heaven sakes! Who would you want to visit in this desolate, remote area?"

"*Doña* Adela lives right down this path! Do you remember the mute? Roberto Eagle, the one who saw José Esquibel getting killed, the night of my birthday? *Doña* Adela is his mother. Come! I'll show you. You have never met *Doña* Adela have you? She tells fortunes, and I feel like having my fortune told. I need to know what is happening with Juan. Maybe she'll read for you, too!"

"We mustn't go any further," remarked Felicia apprehensively. "Remember what your father advised—not to go any further than the fork in the road."

"Well, it's only two miles straight from here. And I'm going. What is there to fear? It will only take us minutes to ride to her house. Are you coming with me?" retorted Victoria, becoming angry. Felicia really was testing the limits of her patience! "You can go home, if you want, or come with me! Stop being so frightened of everything!"

Felicia did not answer. She felt trapped and reluctant, undecided as to what she should do. She reined her horse in to slow its pace and sat patiently waiting for Victoria to make the next move.

A cold breeze flared up, warmed only momentarily by the occasional rays of the sun. Low clouds hung oppressively in the heavens. Felicia's horse followed Victoria's white filly at a slow trot through the soundless, dreary country. Shades of winter-gray cottonwood and mesquite trees were absorbed into the gray environment of the *brasada* and seemed to have eyes watching them pass. Branches of the grayish, tangled, twisted trees were like arms ready to reach out and snatch them.

They trekked on until Victoria reined her horse in and stopped momentarily. Straightening up in the saddle, she pointed up ahead to a weathered hut, called a *jacale*, adjoining a home-made *ramada* kitchen amid the dense thicket jungle. There was a barn next to an old *jacale*, and other little adobe buildings of plastered mud with thatched roofs of *tule*. A fence of upright dry mesquite surrounded the shabby little complex.

Felicia hesitated, not knowing what they were getting themselves into. She had heard stories of *la bruja* and what she had done for so many people. She felt a cold chill pass through her body, like a sense of insufferable gloom. She tightened her woolen cape around her arms while holding the reins with her gloved hands. Her eyes were wide and she looked scared as she surveyed the well-traveled dirt path.

Around the bend, as they got closer, they viewed a dark shadow standing amidst the undergrowth on the edge of the dirt path. It stood for a moment among the shadows and watched them. Then the animal spun around and immediately disappeared into the dense jungle thicket.

"What was that?" said Felicia, sucking in her breath. Pulling her horse to a stop, she did not let the animal step any further. She felt the hair on the back of her neck stand up, and she was gripped by a chilling fear. From out of nowhere there came a wild, spinning, whirlwind that made both horses whinny and snort at its eerie sound.

"It was probably a *javalina*, or a coyote. Could be a wolf. We have many black panthers in the area, too," answered Victoria with nerves of steel, trying to control her horse. "It looked like a dog from a distance," she said. Minutes later, the wind calmed and both horses settled down. "Come!"

Several yards from the *jacale*, they dismounted, leaving their horses tied to a nearby mesquite tree yards away from the entrance to the place. Dogs began barking from underneath *Doña* Adela's hut as they got closer. Felicia was nervous dragging her feet, taking one slow step at a time. She gazed around the area with caution and clutched her cape more closely about her chest and head. Her eyes were wide with fear, and she felt that she and Victoria were intruding into a forbidden, haunted area.

Suddenly and without warning, *Doña* Adela appeared behind them, as if she had come from the same area where the grayish chaparral bush stood and they had seen the strange beast disappear. Both girls screamed at the same time in a chilling paralyzed action, and turned around and confronted *la bruja*. The dogs' barking became louder and more insistent.

"Who goes there? And what do you want?" demanded *la bruja*. Holding onto her cane, she stood with a basketful of weeds and dry herbs, eerily eyeing the two frightened girls. A black *rebozo* was wrapped around her head that blended with her long, dark attire.

"It's me, *Doña* Adela, Victoria!" she answered, feeling the blood come back to her face.

"Bah," replied *la bruja*. "Victoria, I didn't recognize you with all that get-up you have on, your cape and all, and from a distance. My eyes are going bad. I need glasses to see far away. What a coincidence! I was just thinking about you. Maybe our minds are starting to communicate with one another on a subconscious level. How did the fiesta go? Did it go well? I'm sorry I couldn't attend—with my old age, getting around is very hard for me."

"It went very well," she responded, smiling. "It was wonderful. Thank you for asking."

"Heard you poor Mamá left for Mexico with her parents. Manuel was here a day ago and brought me some meat, fresh eggs and milk, and several pounds of butter, which I have enjoyed very much. I get tired of eating wild rabbits all the time." She continued mumbling about how she missed *La Señora Doña* Francisca and her generosity, as she walked toward her *jacale*. "That's enough!" she yelled at her dogs, hitting the side of the steps with her cane. "What brings you girls to visit me? Let me guess. You girls want your fortune told, a reading?" The old woman cackled.

"Yes!" Victoria, nodding her head almost too anxiously. "I want you to meet my cousin, Felicia. She lives in Mercedes City and she's going to study in Monterrey with me. My cousin wants a reading before she goes to school. I was just telling her about you and how good you are at predicting the future."

Felicia turned her head in shock and glared at Victoria for lying. For all along, it was Victoria who wanted to know about Juan and their future.

"I can't refuse the devil himself. Come on in," she said congenially, making her way past the screen door. She laid the basket on a wooden stool next to the entrance, took off her *rebozos*, and walked over to a table close to her adobe fireplace.

Inside the hut was a luminous glow. A strong smell of sage incense permeated the whole place, infiltrating the two young ladies' nostrils. Candles of all colors burned on top of a large table, along with framed pictures of the saints, and statues of the saints hovering over both. It gave the girls a weird feeling, like being in religious sanctuary, with dry bushes hanging upside down from the ceiling, and bottles full of vinegar with odd weeds and objects inside. They felt they were in a completely different world. Pictures of distinctive faces, with black candles burning beneath them, were stationed on a separate table on the other side of the room. Uncommon trinkets of all sorts, especially unique, handmade dolls with pins in them, were placed next to the candles. Boxes full of canned goods and paper sacks were stacked next to the fresh cut mesquite wood near the stove, and water gourds hung along the side.

Doña Adela laid her cane next to her chair and found a bright red tablecloth and placed it on top of the round wooden table. She filled a glass of water from a colorful green and red Mexican clay water jar and set it on the table. "Always put out a glass of water for a reading," she said in a low tone. "After each reading, you throw it out, and it takes the evil spirits with it!" She continued talking while taking a chair and picking up the reading cards. While she sat, she shuffled the cards. "All right, who wants to go first?" she said and eyed the two girls hovering over her.

"Me!" answered Victoria quickly.

"You," said *Doña* Adela, pointing to Felicia, "sit over there." She aimed her bony finger at a chair across the room. "This way, I will not get the other person's vibrations." Eyeing Victoria seriously, she said, "Think strongly on what you want to know. Take the cards and shuffle them fourteen times and think of your wish. The first round is considered the past, the second is the present, and the final one is the most important, because it reveals your future. All three are necessary to complete the reading."

Carefully, and with much excitement and anticipation, Victoria grabbed the cards and began shuffling them as the old woman had instructed her. She couldn't help but admire the brightly colored cards as she began examining them. It reminded her of pictures she had seen in books about the Dark Ages and the Renaissance with kings, queens, and knights in shining armor.

"These are special Mexican cards," replied *la bruja*, delighted with her cards, and Victoria's enthusiasm for them. "There are only forty of them. Each card represents a purpose, depending on how they fall." She asked Victoria to cut them, making a stack of three and laying them on the red tablecloth. *Doña* Adela crossed herself, took the deck from the middle and began spreading them from left to right to the count of ten. Then she started down again into the second line, again counting to ten, even with the first line. When the last card was gone from her hand, she took up the first deck and continued into the same pattern, filling the second row, then to the third, and finally the last deck of cards until all of the forty cards lay spread on the table.

"Ah!" she whispered to herself, viewing the deck. "They look very interesting! I will check for the information you want to know."

The old *bruja* took her time in describing the meaning of the colorful cards. "Each knight represents a different color of the person's skin tone, and the same for the woman. There were only four men and four women in the deck of forty." Pointing to a king with a large green club, she said, "He is a very dark man, and the same for the woman with a green club." She then pointed to a king holding a cup. "This man, and also the woman holding the cup, are olive-skinned people. The one holding the spear is a medium-white complexioned person, and those holding the gold coin, both the man and woman are very light-complexioned, blonde people, referred to as *gringos*."

When *la bruja* pointed a finger to each card, Victoria couldn't help but notice her wrinkled hands that were all twisted and deformed and full of arthritis. An odd feeling overtook Victoria's excitement, but she felt comfortable that *Doña* Adela was an expert, who made a living at this art and knew what she was doing.

Doña Adela began to speak. "Now! When I start the reading, you mustn't speak. I don't want you girls talking to each other. No matter how much you want to say something, wait until I'm finished. I will lose my concentration, and it will be no use in continuing. I will ask the questions. Understand?"

Victoria nodded.

"Fine!" said *Doña* Adela, and her eyes were like two burning torches, reflecting the light from her kerosene lamp. She continued. "You, my dear, come from a family with lots of money. See! Here!" She pointed to the card with the gold coin. "And there will be more money coming. Ah! I see lots of money, pointing to the medium-light man who represented her father. I see your Papá making hundreds. That's good," said *Doña* Adela. Then she pointed to the medium-light woman card. "This woman is ill. I think this is your Mamá. And it shows that she has gone on a long journey," she said, pointing to a large club card, which indicated foreign soil. "There will be complications on her part, maybe death. I don't want to say that, but there is a possibility." She cleared her throat, viewing Victoria's face, whose eyes had widened and her face had turned pale at this prospect.

"Now, I'm showing two important men in your life. One loves you more. One perhaps, is your future husband, handsome and rich, full of promises and ideas to become wealthier. He is the light-colored man here." She pointed to the man with the spear. "The other one is olive, and he is the one that loves you the most. He thinks of you all the time, but at this moment in time he is struggling, because he sees himself not getting ahead in what he wants. I see him wanting material things, riches, and possessions, but having problems with government personnel." She looked up briefly, then continued.

ROOTS OF INDIFFERENCE

"I also see you going on a long trip. This is probably the school you were talking about. I see you crossing water with other people and another lady. Must be this young lady, your cousin! The light-colored man is very pleased and happy to see you. I think he is the one you will eventually marry. I don't know at this time. He also comes from a family with land and money, living on foreign soil. But—" *La bruja* hesitated for a moment and stuttered, trying to find the proper words. She studied the cards again with a frown on her face. "I see him being deceitful and tricky. I think it must be his family. Through some terrible circumstances, he, or maybe his family, will lose something. I don't know what all of this means, but it is the result of bad dealing or planning that happens much later." *La bruja* continued:

"Your trip to Monterrey is going to be very favorable while you are there. You are going to enjoy happy occasions, but things are going to change. I see you being lonely, maybe while attending school. You will see the olive man, under different circumstances—not the way you think. He will want to marry you, to have you elope with him, or something to that effect. But—" she frowned again and looked at the cards with much concentration. "Ah! You are going to refuse him. Under unusual conditions, you'll refuse him. Seems very odd, if you love someone," said the old woman. She glanced up at Victoria's face to see how she was reacting. "You, for some strange reason, will change your mind. Very strange! I see unhappy conditions after that event. I see illness and sickness around you. People around you are going to lose things, like their property, wealth, money, and even perhaps their lives! I don't know how this is going to relate to you, but you are going to be involved, because this is your reading and your cards. All of this, of course, is after you come back to Texas. I see dissimilar changes coming into your life, some good, some not so good. I also see that many deaths will occur."

The old *bruja* then went into a long silence, still reviewing the cards. Minutes later, she spoke again. "This is all the cards have to say. Sometimes they say more, depending on the person and circumstances, but for now and today this is all they say. Now! You can talk and ask me questions. Is there anything you want to say?"

Victoria cleared her throat and took a couple of minutes to express herself, after the shock of what she had heard. "You mean, I will not marry this man?" pointing to the card representing the olive man. "He's the one I truly love."

"Ah! I suspected that! He is the one you brought with little Fred to have a reading several months ago. Handsome! *Chulo!* I couldn't get my eyes off him. He has the most beautiful green eyes I have ever seen. Intelligent and well mannered, too! And if I had been forty years younger, I would have made a potion on my behalf toward him. He is gorgeous."

The two girls laughed.

"But because you love someone, that doesn't mean you'll marry them. There are other people controlling your life. People with power and money will not permit this to occur. And you happen to love money, with all of the comforts money brings. You will have a relationship with this olive man. The cards are funny," she said, cackling. "They say what's in the future. Nothing can change that. Maybe you can! You are the only one who controls your own destiny. You are the captain of your own ship, the driving force in your life. Only you can change your destiny."

Victoria did not answer. She began perspiring and felt her heart throb. Her head dropped to her chest, and she stared at the floor in disappointment, as if pride, arrogance, and her self-centered ego had vanished. She then glanced at Felicia, who was white as a ghost.

"You see my dear," suggested the old woman, acknowledging Victoria's distress and the disappointing information that she had just delivered. "Money isn't everything, and you love money. The love of money is the *roots of evil*. Money in itself is not the evil one, but the love of it is. You carry it in your blood, the seed of evil that comes with the blood of the white man in your ancestry."

Doña Adela's eyes were wide and clear, and her conversation full of anger and vengeance, as she expressed her hate for the white man. Her face became twisted, looking like a dried up fig hanging down from a tree. She continued, "The white men are all greedy, wanting all the possessions and materials things in life. In the end, I may not live long enough to see it, but they will fight among themselves for the land and boundaries and will eventually, in the far future destroy themselves. Many sorrows will come from that greediness."

She became angrier and her voice rose in pitch. She tapped her cane on the side of the wooden table, making the two girls jump from their seats. "The white man took our land, because we were Indians and had no legal papers to claim anything. We could not read or write," she said. "Your grandfather George was perhaps the only kind white man I knew. He became owner of this land where we have lived and wandered for centuries. My father loved him and worked for him many years and showed him where he could find the water in this region and other secrets of the land. Your grandfather was kind enough to give me a place where Roberto and I could live until I die."

She paused and looked reflective. "When Texas became self-governing, the white men burned our shacks, and killed my two brothers, and raped me and my older sister. Your grandfather was gone at that time and couldn't do a thing about our situation. Luckily for my sister, she died weeks later from the shame of her mishap. Shortly after, my father died of grief. Now, in my old age, I'm happy as long as I can serve the Mexican people in this area. It gives me something to do. I have everything here, all I have to do is ask." *La bruja* went into a long silence, than got up from her chair, grabbed her cane that supported her, and took the glass of water with her. Walking to the back of her *jacale*, she threw the water out the window. Minutes later, she returned and asked Felicia if she wanted her cards read.

Felicia, who was frozen in her chair, didn't know what to say. Dubious in her meek manner, she hesitated, but shyly responded, "Yes," then added softly, "but I need to go to the outhouse first."

All three women laughed. *Doña* Adela pointed with her ebony cane to the outside of the *jacale* towards the old barn. "I will wait until you return. Meanwhile I will keep Victoria's company," she said.

Felicia hurried toward the old barn, watching her steps, for the path was covered with debris of fallen leaves and dry grass. Walking beside the old barn and having a keen sense of smell, she started smelling a strong, fetid scent. It was such a different, pungent odor that she brought her hand to her nose. *My God,* she thought, *it's a smell like death! It smells like something died here!* Without giving any more thought to the hideous odor, she kept walking and finally closed the door to the outhouse.

Minutes later she found her way back.

Felicia's reading was completely unlike Victoria's. *Doña* Adela was able to see the torture that Felicia had suffered in her young, troubled life. She was informed of her stepfather's activities and his devious, crafty dealings, and said he would finally get his punishment. The reading was similar to Victoria's reading when it came to their schooling. She emphasized emphatically that a white man from across the border—a tall, handsome *gringo* with blond hair and blue eyes—would change the course of her life. How could it be possible? A white *gringo* in Mexico would change her entire life for the better? Many things were going to change, but that was after they returned from foreign soil. The *gringo* would become a very successful businessman. Felicia would marry him years later and have his children and find happiness as his wife. A fairytale marriage!

As the two girls departed and stood outside the screen door, Victoria and Felicia thanked the old woman for taking her time and being so kind in giving them the information. Victoria seemed depressed, feeling like a doomed victim. She asked, "*Doña* Adela, will you teach me how to read the cards like you do?" She said humbly, "I want to learn and know everything you do. I want to know about herbs and how they cure people. I also want to know about the magic of candles, potions, and how they perform their miracles."

Doña Adela laughed. "Ah! *Hija!* It takes many years of knowledge and experience to know everything. But, yes. Any time you want to learn, just come over. I will teach you everything I know. You first better get your father's permission, when you visit me. He doesn't believe in card reading. He was here months ago, but only to ask questions. He *will* believe!

"You mentioned to my father about giving him a reading?"

"Ah! Yes!" she chuckled. "He laughed at me and refused me, of course. He thinks I'm crazy. A little bit maybe," she admitted, giggling. "But he will pay me a visit in the near future, just like I told him several months ago. He will become perturbed over some situation in his life, wanting to know some answers. He will want to know things, and I will gladly tell him everything."

"You're right! Father doesn't believe in those things. He thinks they are unnatural."

"Ah! That's because your Papá has white men's blood in him. They are very skeptical."

"Don't hold your breath. It will take a miracle for him to come for a reading."

"I'm surprised *you* wanted a reading. You are so beautiful and have the world at your feet. But I can see why you wanted to know about the green-eyed man. He's quite the *mango!*"

"We had better leave, it's getting late. I don't want Father to know that I brought my cousin here. We wanted an excuse to exercise our horses and were told not to ride too far from the hacienda."

"My lips are sealed. I never repeat anything people tell me. That's the reason they come to me for so many special reasons."

Felicia was pleased in meeting *Doña* Adela and thanked the old woman.

"Ride with the spirits," replied *la bruja*, chuckling as she disappeared within her old *jacale*.

The two girls were anxious to leave the somber place, for it was already getting late in the afternoon. The few rays of the sun between the gloomy clouds had started to slant west, and evening was coming on. Mamá Maria and the rest of the servants would become worried if they didn't show up soon. Riding home, Victoria was silent and looked serious. She said, "You mustn't say a word that we came to visit *Doña* Adela for a reading. Tell nothing to any of the servants, especially Yolanda. Not even to Mamá Maria. She tells Papá everything. If Father finds out, he'll have me strung up!"

Felicia nodded. All she wanted was to get back to Spanish Acres, where she felt safe.

The hurried ride home was continued in silent contemplation.

Later, Felicia informed Victoria of the awful smell just past the old barn at *Doña* Adela's place, thinking that Victoria should be cautious when she returned for future readings. Victoria in turn ignored the information, suggesting that *Doña* Adela boiled herbs and dried them, sometimes creating foul smells. All together, it ended the suspense of the fetid odor.

Within the following weeks, Victoria, unafraid, was able to sneak out after the evening meal in a clandestine manner and ride to *Doña* Adela's home. She would leave Felicia at Spanish Acres to cover for her while she went to visit with *La Señora* in the dusk and learn some of the magical mysteries of life and its elements—all considered witchcraft and a total abomination to the Catholic faith, which considered them voodoo and evil medicine.

Returning, Victoria would ride in quietly, take her horse to the stables, and unsaddle, then creep through the side entrance of the house and up the cement stairs to her bedroom. Luck was with her, and nobody suspected her clandestine, adventurous, escapade; not even the dogs gave out a whimper.

Doña Adela, who was an excellent and patient teacher, was very generous. She gave Victoria a deck of old cards she had stored from years past and was able to teach Victoria the principals of card reading. She also showed her oil herb potions and how to protect herself from enemies that would infringe on her nature. Victoria was smart and intelligent and picked up things quickly. *Doña* Adela also taught her how to use her "third eye," which was unknown at that time, to use her mental awareness spiritually for the betterment of mankind. With that teaching, came "visualization," a method of seeing things in the spirit form to manifest conditions, create movements, and objects.

The old *bruja* was captivating and full of knowledge and wonders. One of the things that stayed on Victoria's mind perhaps more than anything was the power of the moon. *Doña* Adela introduced Victoria to the Old Farmer's Almanac. From the flimsy booklet, she showed her the meaning of the signs. "The new moon is powerful," she would say. "It brings in the newness, and you can ask wishes that you want to come to you, pertaining to the placement of certain signs at the time. All you have is to ask out loud, or make a ritual. The full moon is meant to make wishes go away and you can burn your wishes then." The teaching and studying of the moon was very intriguing, and to Victoria it was like discovering a mysterious secret. Within the short period of time before they left for Monterrey, Victoria felt comfortable enough to do a reading. She would spend hours at a time in her bedroom, sometimes after midnight, fascinated and intrigued, studying the cards, without getting caught.

CHAPTER 13

In the wee hours of the morning on December the eighteenth, *Don* Federico, Fred, and little Carlos, with the help of Manuel, loaded up the six-passenger' Cadillac coach and set off with Victoria and Felicia for the depot at Mercedes City. There, they would meet *Tía* Emma, who would join them on the trip. The train would carry them as far as Mission, where they would spend the night, then travel south to the town of Madero, and finally to Reynosa, taking a Mexican train to the city of Monterrey, Mexico.

Already Emma was waiting impatiently for them at the train station, wearing a large feathered hat, matching pink parasol, and gloves that coordinated with her fancy full-length dress, with dozens of trunks and luggage sitting on the pavement. Her two maids stood by as Emma walked back and forth in her tight pink shoes, looking like overstuffed pork. "What took you so long?" she said to the group, stomping her foot and waving her hands and parasol. She never greeted *Don* Federico, and she never acknowledged Felicia's presence. "The train is leaving in an hour. And I thought nobody was going to show up in time!"

The mood changed dramatically, quickly becoming tense, as *Don* Federico confronted Emma. "No need getting your feathers all ruffled up! It takes longer to drive from my place, than yours. You can practically walk to the depot, living blocks away," he answered back. "What a way to start a trip," he mumbled to himself, his face flushed. He didn't care, since he had never liked her anyway, only tolerated her because of Francisca.

Manuel laughed, showing his uneven teeth, and helped unload the trunks and luggage. He was glad he was returning to Spanish Acres, knowing that the two-day trip was not going to be a pleasant one for *Don* Federico and Emma.

By mid-afternoon the train had arrived in the town of McAllen. It was evident that most of the surrounding land was being cleared for the construction of new homes, using lumber shipped from Fort Brownsville.

Traveling straight west and within several hours, they passed the old town of Mission. Citrus trees by the thousands stood erect in the sun, loaded with fruit. The old Franciscan fathers brought the seeds to the location of the small old Church of the Lady of Guadalupe. It was in this same church that *Don* Federico's three children were baptized.

The passengers on the train would glance at graves along the side of the railroad tracks, indicating that some poor soul had either been murdered or killed on the spot. Wreaths of dried flowers hung on the homemade crosses, faded by the burning heat of the sun. Emma, who sat in front of *Don* Federico with her maids, was always making comments. She would automatically cross herself saying, "Poor souls."

Don Federico, in a fit of frenzy, would shift his position in the uncomfortable seat, cross his legs and roll his eyes, not wanting to comment on Emma's hypocritical remarks.

It was late at night when they reached a *ranchito* on the other side of Mission, the location that had made news and stirred up much controversy among the Mexican natives who lived close to the border in the late 1870s. It was during the Cortina and Guevas War that many Mexicans had died under the leadership of Leander H. McNelly, head of the Texas Rangers at that time. The comment was that "many a chili-pepper" was killed, according to the saying of the white men, who laughed about it. A time of great turmoil, it was called the "Terrible Seventies."

This side of Fort Ringgold, the travelers stayed with the old, prestigious family of *Del la* Torres, Emma's friends, when she had first lived there and had married Judge Howard Ale. The family was anxiously waiting for them at the Mission train depot with their buggies, and received them joyously.

The following morning, they left early, thanking the family for their gracious hospitality and accommodations. Then two of their drivers drove them in two large buggies south into the old town of Madero and into Mexico. Crossing the Rio Grande River by a large ferry, people of both nationalities were passing back and forth. On the American side were Texas Rangers, watching the border for any arising problems. All of the Rangers were wearing Stetson hats, heavy boots and pistols on both hips.

On the Mexican side, the region instantly appeared depressed. They viewed a drab jumble of whitewashed, box-shaped houses, with flat roofs, and windows at rude right angles with no screens, but with heavy iron bars to prevent intruders. There were thousands of dilapidated *jacales* and other ramshackle living quarters; others were plain wooden huts built next to the cobblestone sidewalk, or clinging to the sides of narrow ravines, so close that any strong flood would wash them away.

Old people sat next to the dusty sidewalks and at the train depot, with faces that were lost in time, wearing wretched, ragged clothes, begging for alms. Busy vendors in the dirty streets were selling soft drinks made of fruits; others were selling cheeses and homemade foods. Young girls could be seen with babies in their arms, looking old before their time—hard, swarthy faces covered with black *rebojos*. Barefoot children in tattered clothes ran through the filthy puddles of stagnant water, begging and selling trinkets. Flies were everywhere. Mounted soldiers rode by looking weary with dull, dusty uniforms and armed to the teeth with ammunition.

These were people who for centuries had been asleep, caught in a socialistic world, and struggled now that their souls were awakening from their stupor. Comments among the travelers getting onto the train in Reynosa stirred in whispers. "Be careful of the *Federalists*. The Díaz regime is hard and cruel, if they become suspicious."

There was little doubt, in spite of the bad treatment the Mexican people got in Texas, they were lucky compared to the peasants living under these deplorable conditions. A sickening sensation overcame them as they surveyed the degraded region, even though nobody said a word.

Inside the train was packed with people of all ages sitting in the aisles, others with three or four children and babes in arms. Luckily, *Don* Federico found three empty seats, as the rest sat behind him and the two boys. The swaying of the train and the loud clatter of the wheels made it impossible to hear anything anyone was saying. Behind Victoria and Felicia were three men who had indulged too much or were being very patriotic—two sang heart-pulsing ballads, their lips flapping like clothes on the line during the windy March season. The other *hombre* looked like a worn-out old shoe. Many muttered and protested the conditions of the close quarters. There was a distasteful smell of moldy body sweat.

The very poor peasants sat to the back and carried everything they possessed, with chickens, birds in cages, or goats, and occasionally one could hear a small pig squeal.

Once in awhile, the train would screech its brakes and force everyone forward in their seats, as their hearts leapt into their throats. Victoria and Felicia would trade looks and giggle out loud, causing *Don* Federico to turn and check on them.

The train rolled and clattered in urgency. The landscape swelled away and softly touched from horizon to horizon—sandy, grayish ground with barren patches of mesquite and cactus in some dense areas. The land that always lacked water looked lonely and dry; only the mesquite, the sharp-thorned coma, the black chaparral, and the rat-tailed *tasajillo* could survive in this desolate region.

By mid-afternoon, they had reached Monterrey. It had been over a seven-hour ride. Monterrey was a beautiful, sleepy city that sat in rich mineral country, surrounded by the high mountainous Sierras. It was the Pittsburgh of Mexico, having the biggest steel plants south of the border. Most of the industries were run by rich investors from the United States. The huge smelters supplied steel, by train and by ship, to all parts of the world. High above loomed the mountain called Saddle Mountain, *El Sierro de la Silla*, a rugged peak whose hump resembled a gigantic camel. The weary travelers delighted in the breathtaking scenery and the lighter air.

The majority of the houses that they could see were made of adobe and stucco. It seemed like a different world altogether. Streets were narrow and crossed at right angles, with a huge plaza and a fountain in the middle of the city. They marveled at the large, gold-embellished cathedral, from which peasants were coming and going, making their yearly pilgrimage, as it was getting close to time for the *Posadas*.

Outside the train depot, servants patiently waited for them, one in a large black carriage, the other with a buggy to accommodate their trunks and luggage. It was already getting late in the afternoon, and they felt the rays of the pale, setting sun caress them. The carriage took them up the mountainous path to the mansion of the Hinojosa's estates, a long and wearisome trip, even though the leather seats were plush and comfortable.

Don Federico looked tired and, up to this point, had very little to say. He studied the countryside dotted with cypress and sabino trees common to the region. High in the mountains were the Aztec pinos, which were dominant in the Sierras. Fields of corn, the most important crop of Mexico, grew in small areas against the mountainside throughout the fertile land.

His thoughts were lost in a hellish nightmare. First and foremost, he and his children were anxious to see *Doña* Francisca. Where was the Federal Marshal who was supposed to get in touch with him before he left? What was Hanson's plan? And if Hanson was going to get rid of him, how was he going to do it? He knew that the old devil's malicious plan would involve something of a surprise. He also wondered about Juan. Had he gotten his act together? Did he get the individual who was supposed to do the job, and on time?

The carriage moved slowly through a landscape of beautifully trimmed pinos that curved past the iron gates and under a beautiful iron carved archway opening onto the magnificent grounds of what heaven must look like. Yards away peasants stood ready to greet them on the sidewalk under the stucco porch in their white pants and shirts. They all went diligently to work, unloading the trunks, packages and luggage, separating them to each room that each individual was going to occupy.

Doña Gloria Hinojosa greeted and kissed everyone. "Welcome, welcome," she kept repeating. "Juana! Please hurry and see that the tables are set out on the patio. We'll be eating very shortly. Make sure that *Don* Federico's bedroom is ready. I want him to stay in the family guest room with all of the windows looking over the acreage. He'll love it!"

The white-haired servant nodded formally and went on her way through long corridors of colorful Mexican tile. She clapped her hands and gave out instructions to the rest of the servants. The whole area came alive, with people giggling and chattering as they embraced each other.

Don Federico instantly asked about his wife. Fred and Carlos were right behind him. "Is she well? Is *Doña* Francisca feeling better? Where is she?"

"Ah! Yes," replied *Señora* Hinojosa, looking very happy. She turned around and, without finishing her statement, was surprised to see her daughter standing in the middle of the winding stairs, with her arms wide open. She was wearing a long white gown and sash. Her hair was down at her sides, and she looked like an angel, but very pale. "*Hija!*" cried *Doña* Hinojosa. "You shouldn't have gotten up out of bed."

Don Federico wasted no time. He rushed up the stairs and kissed her. She embraced him. "I have missed you terribly," he whispered to her, with tear-filled eyes.

"You have no idea how much I missed you and the family. Where is Victoria, the children?"

"Mamá!" cried all three as they rushed to her side and hugged her. "Mother, I have missed you," replied Fred.

ROOTS OF INDIFFERENCE

"Me, too!" answered little Carlos with his head cuddled against his mother's leg.

"When are you coming home, Mamá?" asked Victoria. "You are looking well, and pretty like always." All of the children asked her questions, but *Doña* Francisca did not answer, as they were interrupted by *La Señora* Hinojosa.

"Come!" she yelled, clapping her hands. "The food is getting cold. Lets us all go out into the patio. Dinner is being served, and I know that all of you are hungry. Come! Francisca, you can talk to your children out in the patio," said her mother, from below the stairway. "José has been gone all day, trading some bulls with the neighboring haciendas. He should return any minute now," she said. The two boys ran out into the patio, and Victoria and Felicia followed. Emma's maids went to their quarters.

Downstairs, Emma hugged *Doña* Francisca. "You are looking well!" she said. "Let's go out into the patio where we can talk and eat. I'm starving to death!"

Don Federico, who was walking on *Doña* Francisca's left side holding her hand, spoke out. "I'll bet you are!" he said, rolling his eyes and making a face.

"*Querido*, don't be that way," replied *Doña* Francisca, and she hugged him again.

Out in the patio, the scenery was open and beautiful. Here was peace and tranquility in the open countryside of Monterrey, overlooking the tall majestic mountains, a living paradise where the air was lighter and clearer. All rooms, long halls, and corridors of the mansion surrounded and opened onto the patio. Several stucco stairways from the outside led to the sleeping quarters upstairs. Many water fountains were situated around the courtyard, with cupid statues spurting water that flowed like a waterfall down into ponds with colorful Mexican tile set around the edge. The ponds were filled with goldfish swimming and yellow water lilies on the surface exploding into full bloom. Tall palm and bananas trees reached the ceiling of the large, arched doorways. Papaya plants were all round the corner arches. There were other plants and many flowers: jasmine vines and gardenia bushes that filled the halls with exotic fragrance; large colorful hibiscus; bougainvillea vines in bright maroon, pink, and white that reached the top of the upstairs corridors. Clay pots stood on the colorful Mexican tile at every entrance, containing different varieties of small, hanging flowers. Wooden and iron cages hung from the ceiling on the open archways, with talking parrots and other tropical birds chattering away among themselves.

At the end of the hallways and far back from the big house were the many living quarters of servants, *vaqueros* and the several *majordomos* who ran the hacienda. Next to the quarters were the open kitchens, with huge adobe ovens and earthen pots. The women were singing, and while some were busy grinding the soft corn *nixtamal* in their *metates*, others clapped it into dough. Beside the open kitchen were large *lavaderos*, laundry tubs that served the peasants for doing their washing, laundry, and bathing.

The land sloped down toward the distant horizon, with huge stables of horses, and corrals where the prized bull was kept. On both sides of the mansion were rows of citrus orchards, brightening the scenery with colorful orange and yellow mangoes, guava, and avocado trees in a forestry of green. Rows of grapevines full of luscious varieties of the fruit could be seen in the distance.

A large glass table had been set out under a pagoda erected on the cobblestones. Large kerosene lanterns and fire-poles were set around the luxurious setting, and the finest glass-ware shone in the burning lights. Twenty servants hovered around the tables, surrounding the family with an array of food: *arroz con pollo*; homemade corn tortillas piled in baskets and wrapped in white linen cloths; red chili; and *mole*. Black beans were fried and served in large cut-glass bowls with tortilla chips and sliced *jicama; chayotes*, Mexican squash, had been boiled and mixed with garlic and other spices and blended with fresh butter; salsa was made with fresh tomatoes and spicy red chilies; two-inch cuts of boiled red beef steaks; cuts of fresh cooked fish soaked in tangy sweet sauce; slices of fresh papaya was served like the cantaloupe in Texas and the mango fruit. Fruit juice of the guava tree was served cold and refreshing to the two girls. *Don* Federico and Emma were served red wine.

Doña Francisca ate very little, picking at some of the fish and a slice of fruit. She stayed as long as she was able, since the cold night was harmful to her frail lungs. The excitement of seeing her husband and children was overwhelming. She began coughing and held a hand-kerchief to her mouth. She then excused herself, feeling embarrassment, as servants helped her to the upstairs bedroom.

Later in the evening little children from the hacienda dressed in colorful costumes came and sang songs of the little Christ Jesus, for it was the *Posada* season. *Don* Federico, Emma, Gloria, and the two girls gave each child some money as a token of good will for the com-ing season and for prosperity to all. Several workers with guitars sang around the patio for entertainment.

⌘   ⌘   ⌘

On the last day of December, everyone was excited to celebrate the end of a long year. For two weeks both families had enjoyed each other's company.

One of *Don* Hinojosa's *majordomos*, called Augustin, met *Don* Federico out in the horse stable while he was checking on the readiness of the horses for the upcoming trip to the gold mine.

"I heard you're leaving tomorrow to go up in the high *Sierra Madre Mountains* to see about the gold mine," he said, somber and concerned, chewing on a straw.

"Yes." Don Federico nodded, appearing serious. "Pedro is checking on a wagon at this moment. We will leave early in the morning, if I can get everything ready. I don't know how long it will take us, but I want to make sure we have plenty of supplies in the wagon."

"*Ay caray!* I heard there has been trouble at the mine. Three months ago, there were several men killed while working in the cave. The story from those who fled has been that too many *bandidos* want to get the gold. All of the gold was taken by them to buy guns and ammunition, and many of the workers were shot. Times are hard, and people are hungry. I don't think anybody is working it now. People are afraid. The old man, a friend of your father, who was taking care of the mine, still lives in the village below the mountains. Everybody has left, and I don't blame them, for they are more concerned for their own life and their family."

ROOTS OF INDIFFERENCE

"I'm going to check on the mine while I'm here. I've lived so far away, and have left things for others to take care of," replied *Don* Federico. "Need to see if I can salvage anything. I do doubt it now! I also need to check how much gold went into the smelters and was deposited into *El Banco Nacional de Monterrey*. It's going to take me many days to clear things up."

"Things are changing, especially in the political arena, and there's talk about the Revolution coming. It will change things and many people's lives."

"Augustin, you've heard of Madero and the Revolution already?" *Don* Federico asked, surprised.

"*Aye, si*," he said. "Talk of Madero has already reached this hacienda. We are all in anticipation of what is going to happen. They say that a man called Zapata has already started a revolution south of Mexico City and Pancho Villa is fighting in Chihuahua. They are killing landowners and burning the rich haciendas, like this one." He said it with much enthusiasm, a big smile spread on his face, as he eyed the Hinojosa's land surrounding them. "I sure hope it doesn't travel this far—if it does, your father-in-law will be in trouble. He will lose everything."

"I don't think you have to worry too much, *amigo*! When Madero becomes President of Mexico, he will give all the peasants their own land to cultivate food," answered *Don* Federico very confidently.

"*Ay, qué bueno!* Did you want me to go with you? I know the land very well, like the palm of my hand. I have lived and traveled these parts for many years. I know the route to the mine very well."

"Good idea!" replied *Don* Federico. "I'll talk to my father-in-law about your going with us, so you can help me find the trail up to the mine. We're going to spend days up there, so put on warm clothes."

"Ah! *Chihuahua!*" he said. "I will talk to Pedro and Jorge—they are probably getting things ready. I will let my family know that I'm going with you."

Out in the main sala, *Don* José Hinojosa was resting and drinking some of his homemade wine. He had been out in the corrals, in the very early morning hours, struggling with his newborn calves, putting tags in their ears, indicating the year and brands, according to each calf. He saw *Don* Federico walking in from the side entrance and shouted to him. "Are you getting ready to go to the mine? Have you got everything you need? Take as many of the workers as you need with you. They are more than willing to go," replied the old *Don*. "Sit and have some wine with me."

"Thank you, I think I will, and smoke my pipe. I think I have everything pretty well lined up. Pedro and Jorge, and now one of your *majordomos*, Augustin, wants to go with me. He said he knows the area of the mine very well."

"Better take him with you! Augustin knows the land, and he's good with the rifle and guns. Just last month there were reports of *bandidos* up in the area. It's getting too dangerous to travel anymore. Are you going to meet that Texas Ranger, Hanson, up in the mountains? I'd be real careful with that Ranger. Somehow I just don't trust him! If the *bandidos* don't get you, he will! Or the bandits will get you both!"

"I'll have to take my chances," said *Don* Federico. "I don't trust him either, but he inherited half of the mine you sold my father years ago. I want to see what's left of it. I want to first make sure whether to keep it, or forget about it and give the damn thing to Hanson, and let him worry about it."

"I don't blame you," replied the old man. "The other two mines that belong to other investors have been left empty. I don't think there is any gold left in them. I sold those years ago—too much trouble and worries. You have to be right on top of things, or the workers will steal and lie, if you are not there to oversee them. I was getting too old to walk up those mountains. I made lots of money in the gold mines, bought and built this rancho, and made it very comfortable for my family and me. Your father became wealthy also. I later devoted myself to politics. It was an easy job to sit around the cabinet with Díaz."

"Díaz's days are about over," remarked *Don* Federico. He crossed his legs and glanced at *Don* Hinojosa, as he sat comfortably on the plush, white sofa and drank his wine.

"There's much talk now of Madero starting his conquest of the capital. It seems he has all of the bandits on his side," the old man replied sarcastically. He was not in favor of anyone taking over the Mexican government, apparently thinking that Díaz was going to live forever.

Outside of the villa it had started to rain, a little drizzle that made the temperature drop. The fireplace in the main *sala* was blazing.

"If Madero becomes president, *Don* Hinojosa, where will that put you?" asked *Don* Federico with concern for his father-in-law. "Will that affect you in any way, especially your land?"

"Ay! *Hijo*, I'm getting too old to worry about political things anymore. I leave those things for the young people who want to worry and concern themselves with so many problems in this country. I just want to enjoy my bulls and my land in my old age." He paused and took another sip of wine. "The only thing that worries me now is Francisca, needing good medical care. Just last week, Dr. Mendez moved to the border, in Reynosa, close to you. He thought it was safer for him and his family, with all of the talk of Revolution. I guess if it gets any worse, he'll move to Texas. You might have to move from Spanish Acres, closer to the border, where the doctor is. She's going to need medical attention and a doctor to look after her. Francisca worries me terribly. Your father had bought some land years ago where Emma lives, in Mercedes City. You might want to check on that piece of property."

"Yes, as a matter of fact I was going to Mercedes City to look over the acreage in the near future. I've been thinking about it lately. I could build Francisca a house where she could be closer to Emma. The estate is only a mile from Emma's property."

"Leave Spanish Acres and start clearing it and begin a new life in Mercedes City," he suggested. "Plant cotton, and hire laborers to work the fields. It's supposed to be very lucrative in Texas, and you can enjoy the profits. You can still have all the cattle you want by keeping the *vaqueros* and Roy to do the work at Spanish Acres, and you could check on it weekly. Build Francisca a large, beautiful home in Mercedes City, since lumber is so cheap." *Don* Hinojosa became more animate and kept giving out suggestions as if *Don* Federico had no common sense regarding his future or his children's. He seemed more concerned about his daughter and her illness.

Don Federico got the drift that Emma had been doing her humanitarian gossip behind his back with his in-laws and had convinced them Francisca should move away from Spanish Acres.

With greater insistence, he continued talking. "With a new home, the both of you can enjoy socializing. You were talking about oil on your property. Better have it checked! Oil is the upcoming thing. Ah! *Hombre!* If a revolution breaks out, you'll have all kinds of *peóns* at your front door, all wanting to go to Texas for work and safety. You will not have to worry about making an income. As a matter of fact, Gloria and I may be at your door if war breaks out. I'm getting too old for any trouble."

At that moment, Victoria and Felicia returned from riding. Their clothes and hair were damp from the light rainfall. "Grandfather, I love the horse I rode!" expressed Victoria in a happy mood, removing her hat, gloves, and leather jacket.

"The horse is yours to ride anytime you want," he said, bringing the glass of wine to his mouth. "You'll be coming to see us once a month from the convent and you can ride it then. Go! The both of you get yourselves dried off before you get pneumonia!"

"Thank you, Grandfather," answered Victoria, as she kissed him on his forehead. The two girls hurried upstairs, giggling.

That night, the family, wrapped together in a pulsation of comforting warmth, watched the last gleam of the setting sun between the light and darkness, aglow with all the hues of the dusk. The countryside echoed with the shooting of firecrackers, and many of the *vaqueros* brought out rifles and pistols, which they pointed to the sky, shooting several rounds, a common tradition that killed the year. Many sang songs out in the patio accompanied by Mexican guitars; yet, there was an overtone of sadness at the ending of the year, and the singing slowly faded away. Grapes were set in large glass bowls as a tradition to eat for prosperity in the coming year. It was a night to remember.

It had been two weeks since they had left Spanish Acres, and over a month since Victoria's fiesta. While sitting with Felicia on the patio and watching the display of the New Year's celebration, she kept thinking about Juan and wondered where he was. She reflected on the past year and how it had changed her life, the meeting of Juan, and how much she had fallen in love with him. Was he fighting with Madero? How soon would it be before she saw him again? She was torn between doubts and enthusiasm, but his memory lingered on as an enigma. She had brought the deck of cards that *Doña* Adela had given her, concealing them in her trunk while Mamá Maria, and Soledad were busy packing. She was going to read them and check if they would read correctly. Tonight!

The coming of the New Year—1911.

.

CHAPTER 14

The New Year came with a soft drizzle that had continued since midnight, making the morning dawn damp and cold. *Don* Federico gathered up numerous rifles belonging to *Don* Hinojosa, along with rounds of shells and his .45 Colt pistol. The wagon was loaded with an abundance of food consisting of beans, potatoes, coffee, bacon, and several pots of cookware and blankets. Pedro and Jorge rode their horses, fully rigged, headstall and bit, carrying plenty of ammunition, while Augustin held the reins of the four black mules that were pulling the wagon. The men all wore large sombreros, leather jackets, and gloves to protect them from the chilly, oncoming rain.

The two Mexicans followed behind as they slowly traversed the slippery, muddy road up the steep, rocky slope of the mountain. "The sun is not going to show today. It may not show for days now," stated Augustin. "Up the mountain we may come into snow. It's not unusual at this time of the year."

Don Federico looked back and yelled to the two men riding behind. "I hope you men brought plenty of bullets for your rifles. I think we are going to need them sooner or later," he said apprehensively. Already his heart pumped faster and his stomach churned. This was the moment in time that he had been dreading, but the business of the gold mine had to be settled once and for all.

"In this part of the country," shouted one of them, "we always carry enough ammunition. You never know who is going to jump you from behind." The three men laughed.

Don Federico nodded, flashed a brief smile, then turned back around, hanging onto the bouncing wagon seat, as well as his hat.

They rode for many hours, it seemed, until coming to a barren flat spot on the rugged mountainous trail; around it was a jungle of tall undergrowth. "We'll rest for a little while," *Don* Federico suggested. "And determine how long it will take us to get to the mines. Boys, make some coffee so we can warm up and decide what we are going to do next," he said, rubbing his hands and arms.

The men made camp surrounded by the lush green vegetation of semitropical plants: elephant ear, some bananas trees, several cypress trees, and jungles of pinos. There were many branches underneath the Aztec pinos that were dry enough for a small fire. Just below the trail on a ragged slope was a stream of water coming from the high Sierras. Pedro and Jorge walked carefully down the sharp rocks and gathered the water in two small buckets, some for the mules and horses, and the other one for drinking and making coffee.

The air was thinner here, making it harder to breathe, and the weather was getting cooler. The black coffee was a blessing, with the persistent light rain, which was not going to give up any time soon. While sitting around the fire, Augustin, inspecting the ground underneath his feet, spoke. "Horses have been in this area, probably *bandidos.* There's been horses up here all right, and the grass beneath has been mashed to the earth. Up along the very edge of the slope are horse droppings. They do not seem to be very old. However, with the rain coming, it makes it look like they are still fresh."

"It could be perhaps mountain lions or pumas?" questioned *Don* Federico, rubbing his hands and then spreading them over the warm fire and stamping his feet to get warm.

"No, the droppings are from horses. I've helped raise horses all of my life, especially at *Don* Hinojosa's hacienda, so I know what I'm taking about."

"No! Maybe wolves—the two-legged kind," *Don* Federico snapped, as he observed the fresh ground also. He felt his body go weak and his heart pump faster. No doubt Hanson had already been up here with several of his so-called henchmen. Fearing that the Texas Ranger would leap any minute from underneath one of the rocks, he touched his Colt .45 and glanced up toward the high slope. There was nothing but rocks and the silence of the slow drizzle.

"*Don* Federico, looks like you are getting the jitters," said Jorge, laughing and shaking the rain off his big sombrero. He was the youngest of the *vaqueros.* "Come! Have some more coffee. It will warm you up."

They camped for several hours, resting themselves and the animals, talking and deciding how many days it would take to get *Don* Federico's business taken care of at the mine. After packing the utensils into the wagon, the men continued up the rugged trail. The mules began to protest, for they kept sliding backwards, and the wagon with its heavy load kept sliding sideways. The rain was coming faster, mixed with small flakes of snow, and rockslides were inevitable. Large rocks were coming down on both sides of the steep trail. The mules began braying their discontent.

"Let's try and get to that slope up there!" shouted Augustin, looking worried and giving the mules a hard lash. "I think that we are close to the area, if I remember right!" The mules staggered but began pulling the wagon faster, and Augustin continued lashing them with hard blows, not giving up until the wagon had straightened itself. The pace began getting faster.

Don Federico's adrenalin was at its highest, giving him the mad impulse to get to the mine before dark. They had been on the steep trail all day, and the light was starting to fade. Trepidation, or terror of the unknown, he really did not know what was causing him to feel the way he did. It had rained on them all day long. They were hungry, and now the *Don* was feeling like an old piece of sodden driftwood that had stayed out in the rain too long. His thoughts and mind were beginning to play tricks on his vision and actions. A feeling of intense anticipation ran through his edgy nerves, as the mules carried them along the rocky ledge.

"*Ay, Chihuahua!*" exclaimed Augustin, ecstatic and proud that he had driven the mules on a dangerous trail and under tremendously bad conditions. "We made it! We are here! There's the mine over there."

A strange sensation of loneliness aroused mutual feelings in all four men as they stood overlooking the valley before them. "We need to hurry and make it before we lose the light of the sun," remarked Jorge, viewing the location shrewdly.

Don Federico was silent. He could not voice the feeling throbbing through his veins. For most of the time it took to get to the mine, his mind was blank, but now he regained his normal senses. It had become a dangerous and risky piece of business, coming here and not knowing what lay ahead. The coming days would be a mystery, especially if Hanson, second only to the great Genghis Khan himself, showed up full of lies and tricks.

They reached the mine at the last rays of a sinking sun. Visible in the wet soil at the entrance of the cave were wagon tracks and hoofprints. Huge steam pumps were left to rust in the elements and were scattered along with old picks, rusty tramcars, and tools. The long, wooden sluice boxes had given way to rot and decay.

Much of the bigger machinery had apparently been stolen. Penetrating deep inside the entrance of the cave with torches, *Don* Federico was met only by silence and rushing water. There was no one to tell him why the place had been abandoned. And yet he had mailed money to *Señor* Martinez for his contribution in keeping the mine running. He noticed that some of the timbers holding the walls of the tunnel had fallen, and many of the walls had caved in, leaving the tramcar tracks unusable. Water flooded in from different directions in the lower tunnels and offered proof of why the miners were not around.

"We need to make camp," remarked Augustin. "The entrance of the cave will be safest, a refuge from the cold and rain and the animals that roam the area." All four men agreed. "We can build a fire with all of the wood that has been left, if we can find some that's dry."

They made camp halfway inside the cave with a large fire, good protection from the cold drizzle. A pale, pearly Mexican dust shivered between the stormy clouds outside; gradually it grew darker to a pitch black. After an enjoyable meal of dry meat, canned beans, and fried potatoes with coffee, the flaming fire caressed all four men, who were sitting around smoking, sharing their bottles of spirits, singing and telling stories as they laughed. All three Mexicans had strong swigs of tequila hours before, and they soon slipped into a snoring siesta.

Don Federico smoked his pipe while wandering to the opening of the cave and leaned on the cold rocks, away from the drizzle. He gave thanks for the blessings of the day, concentrating on the moments that had brought him to this situation. His thoughts were on his family and his concern for his sister Josie, who was with child. What was going to become of her? The silence was deep and somber, broken only occasionally by the mournful howl of wolves somewhere in the distance.

⌘ ⌘ ⌘

When the first beam of sun shone upon the four men, sounds of thundering hooves rocked the area. Augustin, who had woken up earlier, had made the coffee and had been seeing about the mules and picking up pieces of dry wood for the campfire inside. He rushed into the cave shouting, "Horses, horses are coming!" He dropped the pieces of dry wood on the cave floor and grabbed for his rifle. The rest of the sleeping men ran for cover, grabbing ammunition and their guns. The rain had ceased and drifts of fog were starting to rise and thin out.

Pedro was the first one out of the cave. He ran behind an old piece of iron pump equipment and lay down on the ground in the wet grass, staring toward the mountainous trail, seeing the figures of men and horses between the thick, low fog. "Two *gringos!*" he yelled. "They have *Tejanos* hats." Augustin rushed out with his rifle and hid close to Pedro, next to a decaying wooden wagon. *Don* Federico with his gun, and Jorge trying to load his rifle, ran and hid behind a tramcar, still full of ore that had been left to rust in the environment.

From the clearing up ahead on the trail, without warning, a bullet zipped over Augustin's head. Several bullets began popping, one hitting the wagon and the other close to where *Don* Federico and Jorge were hiding. Another bullet hit the entrance of the cave.

"I'm going to confront these *hombres*," said *Don* Federico to his companions. "We won't get anywhere shooting and killing each other. I'm responsible for the mine, and I don't want any of you men killed."

"Don't be a fool, *Señor!*" cried Jorge, who was the closest to *Don* Federico, lying low on the ground and looking toward the two riders sitting on their horses. "These men aren't here to talk, they mean business. And there is going to be some killing."

"Hanson!" hollered *Don* Federico from his squatting position. "Is that you?"

"Yeah!" he replied. "Put your guns down." Hanson turned to face his companion, and raised his arm up in a false truce and began approaching the cave very slowly on his horse. "For a moment, I thought you fellers were *bandidos!*" He began laughing insanely, as if the joke was on him. "We've been hangin' around these mines for two days, dodging sonsabitchin' bandits."

Don Federico got up slowly, still holding onto his pistol, then put it in his holster. He began taking steps towards Hanson. He turned and spoke softly but in a commanding voice to his *vaqueros*. "Hold onto your triggers. I'll handle this," he said. He was not going to take any chances, especially with a known killer who respected no one.

There stood Hanson, as sure as God had created poisonous rattlers, with the young Ranger Smith holding onto another saddled horse. *Don* Federico kept eyeing the horse, a mare that looked strangely familiar, and he recognized what he was up against. His blood froze.

"Juelson," remarked Hanson, grinning and displaying his ugly brown teeth. He leaned forward on his horse. "I want you to see who's with me."

"Who?" answered *Don* Federico, approaching Hanson with shrewd confidence, standing at close range, as hate-filled memories began to be rekindled in his mind.

ROOTS OF INDIFFERENCE

"The meanest, the roughest, the best son-of-a-bitch this side of the Rio Grande," roared Hanson, with a loud guffaw. "And he wants to see you." He continued talking with much profanity.

A tall Texan, dressed in an old cowhide leather jacket, appeared from behind a large pinos tree, wearing a large, beige Stetson hat covering his white hair. He wore two cannons on his hips. A retired Texas Ranger, known to be a killer and a hero in the McNelly War, he was extremely prejudiced and hated the Mexican people as a whole.

Don Federico swallowed hard, but regained his composure. *These were the real Devil's people,* he thought. *In other words, a flock of vultures.* "Taking time out of your busy schedule to come to Mexico, Hobbs?" said *Don* Federico coldly.

"I was running out of greasers to kill in the Valley, so I decided to join in with Hanson's schemes, make a fortune, and look elsewhere," answered Hobbs in a feisty way, holding his gloved hands inches away from both of his pistols. He burst out laughing and Hanson joined in.

"So what brings you to the mines?" snapped *Don* Federico with contempt. "Are you planning to fix anything inside the gold mine? You're claiming it is all yours. So take care of it and fix it! It is full of water and no work can be done until it is drained. No gold and no profits!"

"Surprised, Juelson? Well, Hobbs and I made a deal several months ago, back when you told me you were going to ditch me out from my gold mine. Do you want to hear about it, Mister Big Shot?" sneered Hanson, as he began dismounting from his horse.

"From you, Hanson, nothing surprises me. Go ahead and speak. Tell me!" said *Don* Federico, as the climax of a pointless, contemptuous dispute was coming to a climax. Up to this point, he had never heard Hanson say what he planned to fix, how he would repair the mine, or how he expected any gain. The mine, as it stood, was irreparable for the time being until the water was drained, and it would take hundreds of dollars to fix it and get it into operation again in order to make any profits.

"I gave Hobbs half of my part in the mine, if he would get rid of you," said Hanson, grinning and coming closer to *Don* Federico as he puffed his cheap cigar. His cold, black, demon eyes were fixed on the great *Don.* "Now, how do you like those apples?"

"And just how do you plan to do that?" questioned *Don* Federico with a scornful frown. "First of all, you have no claims to the mine, and in Mexico you must have ownership, which you and Hobbs have none. These mines were first owned by *General* Del Calderóne, then sold to my father-in-law, and later, my father took over, and it belongs to our family. The two of you have no claims to anything in Mexico. You two have no money, and the mine needs fixing before it goes into operation."

"We have a sworn statement from your father, signed in Judge Parker's office, giving me ownership. I appointed Hobbs to be my partner," Hanson boasted.

"Sounds just like you, Hanson! Always getting someone involved in your cunning schemes, always getting someone else to do your dirty work. All for evil and the love of money! Well! How do you plan to get rid of me? The same way you killed my father?" *Don* Federico was trying to keep his temper under control, and not rise to the demon's bait.

"Right now, don't move!" The order came from behind a tree and behind the back of *Don* Federico. "Put your gun down! Quickly! Pronto!" demanded the stranger. The other rider with Hanson dismounted.

Don Federico dropped his gun and turned to face a tall, lanky, ragged stranger named Jones, a ruffian that Roy in years past had fought with over a tramp in a saloon in Harlingen, Texas. "How many did you bring to kill me?" questioned *Don* Federico. "What did you promise them, pure gold coins?"

"Several!" he said. "Why don't you shut up?" Hanson instantly pulled out his pistol and demanded that *Don* Federico raise his arms. He yelled to the rest of his *vaqueros* to come out from hiding.

Jorge, the youngest *vaquero*, dropped his rifle, throwing it out in front of Hanson, but he carried a pistol in his vest and made a sudden grab for it. A loud explosion erupted, and the ex-Texas Ranger pumped him full of bullets, faster than winking an eye. "We said, don't move, goddamn it! You dirty, cockroach Mexican!"

The older *vaqueros* surfaced from behind the wagon with their hands up in the air and began to shake. Augustin gazed down at his *compadre* bleeding to death on the ground. He replied nervously, "But we haven't done anything, *Señor!*"

"You have done plenty! You goddamn greasers! Just being a Mexican is a good excuse to pump you full of lead too," answered Jones.

"What do you plan to do with the rest of us?" questioned *Don* Federico. He kept waiting for Juan's plan to materialize. What had happened? What had gone wrong?

Hanson, Hobbs, and Smith laughed. The other rider sneered.

"You know too goddamn much, already, Juelson! If you made it back to good ol' Texas, do we think you'd blab about this? Well, you would!" Hanson grinned again, displaying his brown teeth. "Do we think for one minute you are not going to tell on us and what we are doing down here in Mexico? If Cameron County finds out about me and my deals with the gold mine and what I am doing, I'll be in hot shit. I'll be in a heap of trouble, especially with my job. I'll be fired and my reputation ruined, especially with the State of Texas."

"Your reputation is already in the shit house. You should have thought of that earlier," said *Don* Federico coldly, his nerves at raw ends. "You're gonna have to answer to the United States Marshal as soon as you get back to *good ol'Texas.*"

"Well, now! How's that?" snapped Hanson in a fit of bulldog rage.

"Does the name Tom White mean anything to you? Does the Pinkerton Agency sound familiar?" replied *Don* Federico. He kept eyeing the gray mare. It was Tom White's gray mare. He remembered seeing Tom riding the horse the last time he spoke with him at the fork in the road near La Villa. The initials T.W. were branded on the horse and saddle, and Tom White never went anywhere without his horse. Matter of fact, he had a special train car for his animal when he was on assignment. "Didn't even bother to take the saddle off or hide his initials on his saddle, did you, Hanson? You have the gall!"

ROOTS OF INDIFFERENCE

"He was a drunkard and a fool." Hanson laughed in *Don* Federico's face. The three others snickered nervously, but they could see that Hanson was twitching and beginning to sweat.

"What did you do with him?" asked *Don* Federico hotly, as he stood his ground. "Did you find out that White was an informer and had your number?" He said it with a good deal of animosity, tantalizing Hanson to blurt out the truth.

"What do you take me for, a fool?" spat Hanson in a state of frenzy. "White was pretending to be a drunk until I put him to the test with some real whiskey, and I realized that he couldn't take the stuff. When he really got drunk, he confessed what he was doing."

The younger Texas Ranger laughed and spoke out of turn. "Yeah! With a little help, 'cause you were suspecting him of something, and you tied him to a chair and forced him to drink the bottle of whiskey, with a gun to his head. Remember, I was there!"

Hanson's face turned red with anger. His brains already fried, he faced the young Ranger and yelled, "You shut your goddamn trap of a mouth! You may not have a job when you get back! You stupid, dumb bastard! Remember who gave you your job!"

Hobbs and Jones grinned. Smith's face flushed from embarrassment and humiliation, and he became quiet.

"So what did you do with him?" questioned *Don* Federico again, holding onto his courage. "I guess I know the answer. You killed him like you killed my father—for greed, and this gold mine, for money—and you're not getting away with it. You're not getting this mine either. And even if you kill me, everyone else knows the real truth. The United States Marshal has all of the important papers they need to convict you of my fathers' death, José Esquibel's killing, and now White. Your ass in Texas is naught; and your ass, too, Hobbs."

Hanson's anger sent him spiraling into a state of violent temper. "You hired him to spy on me, you sonsabitch. You have the money, the power, and influence, but it won't do you a bit of good now, since you're not going back to Texas, at least not alive. I should kill you right now!" He went into a state of insanity and raised his rifle, hitting *Don* Federico on the right temple with the butt of his gun, using all the force that a two-hundred-fifty-pound individual could.

Don Federico moaned and fell backward to the ground, holding his head. Blood was pouring from his temple, and he reached for his handkerchief to stop the bleeding. The kind young Ranger Smith stepped forward and handed him his bandana.

Hanson went into a wild rage. "What the hell are you doing?!" he screamed at the young Ranger. "Shit for brains! We're here to kill this son-of-a-bitch and you're helping him?" The two other men found it amusing and began laughing out loud, not realizing that they were being watched.

While *Don* Federico was trying to regain control of his emotions and trying to get up from the ground, the click of a hundred guns sounded behind them.

"Ah! *Buenos días*," commented a rugged looking individual sitting on his horse. It was the same leader of a group of *bandidos* that had stormed in, killed some miners, and raided the mines on previous occasions. "*Señor!*" he said. "Please put your guns down. *Pronto!* Throw them down to the ground right now, or we will kill all of you immediately. Put your hands up! I'm an impatient man. Pronto!" he hollered.

"Where in the hell did you come from?" commented Hanson, clearly confused. "I didn't hear any horses." He stood frozen and, in shock, dropped his gun. The other three did the same.

"I see that you are not laughing anymore, *Señor!*" the bandit answered. "We all have been observing you and your little circus, from the trees up there. See!" He pointed with his rifle to a group of trees above them. "But what difference does it make now? All of you are dead men anyway." He laughed, and his companions, sitting on their horses with large machetes at their sides and crisscrossed cartridge belts on their chests, began laughing also. The bandit's eyes were like two hot black coals. "Have you got any money? Have some silver or perhaps some gold?" he said. "No? It will be too bad, *hombres!* It's going to be very unfortunate for all of you if you don't!" The bandit then nodded his head and gave the order to the others to get off their horses and search the *gringos*.

The *bandidos* wasted no time, taking guns and ammunition, stripping the men of their money, belts, and knives, even ransacking the packs on the horses. Others went into the cave, taking what was left inside, including the rest of their food, pots and pans. Of course, they would take blankets, saddles, the wagon and the mules.

The bandit leader was Máximo Castillo, notorious for terrorizing the border towns. He was well known for his brutal and unreasonable actions, killing men of all nationalities, Mexicans and white, raping the women, and stealing everything in sight. He was of medium size, and thin, with black hair and a long black mustache that matched his hard, cold, carbon-black eyes. He was a commoner with no education, but he knew his business well. He was hated by the Texans, but mostly by the Díaz faction.

Regaining his feet, *Don* Federico was able to gather his thoughts and managed to find another handkerchief inside the pocket of his leather jacket. He placed it on top of the one that the young Ranger Smith had given him, because blood was still flowing from his temple. Was this the bandit that Juan had hired? If so, he was a brute of a man. *Surely not,* thought *Don* Federico. *If Juan had chosen Máximo Castillo for the hired bandido, everyone would be killed, including himself.* He wished now that he had never plotted the conspiracy. All of them would be killed. Both factions were killers by trade and he was caught in between. These men were all bloodthirsty, craving for action, and all desperate for some kind of a get-rich-quick plan. He could feel his mind going crazy with thoughts, but he was still conscious that the whole idea was senseless.

"Very little money," said a disgusted Castillo. "This is not enough for my time and effort!" Grinning, he showed several of his few and uneven brown teeth, which were big and ugly, like him. The rest of the soiled *bandidos* sported identical smiles, for among them was not even one full set of dentures. "Come! *Muchachos*," he commanded. "Bring these outlaws down to the valley below the mines. I want to teach these *gringos* a lesson." He bellowed a loud guffaw. The rest of the *bandidos* laughed aloud. He continued, "You *pinche, ponchos* from *Tejas, eh!* Coming to Mexico to rob us! You have already been in our country too long. You *bastardos!*

We will kill all of you and send your sorry asses back in a pine box!" He kept on talking, not making any sense with his uncouth language.

Still holding the handkerchief to his head, *Don* Federico was dumbfounded by the unfortunate turn of events. He could see the dead *vaquero*. How was he going to explain his death to his family? He had been responsible for bringing him home safely. He approached Castillo and explained, "*Señor*, these two men are Mexicans. They are from the Hinojosa Hacienda and are *Mestizos*, people like you, and are also very poor. They have families and children. They are only peasants. They have done nothing wrong, only helped me and guided me to this area. Do what you will with us, but please let them go."

"Silence! You fool! You *idiota*! No one tells me what to do! I'll decide who comes and goes!" He was raving mad and showed no sympathy, not even to his own people. "Here, I give the orders. What do I care what rich hacienda they are from?"

"You can't get away with this," yelled Hanson, taking verbal pot shots at the bandit. "The Texas Rangers will be coming to get your ugly, brown ass. You bastard! Who the hell do think you are anyway?"

"Silence! You *pendejo!* There is no law up here in these mountains. I'm the only law now. And if you think you can come to Mexico and tell us what to do, you're crazy." Castillo gave a nod with his head to the other twenty *bandidos*. He thought, then stared at Hanson and replied, "Since you are so smart, *Señor*, take off your clothes. We need your clothes to keep warm." He glared at the rest of the captured men. "All of you!" he ordered. "Take them off!"

"*Malditos gringos!*" shouted the other *bandidos*, who were now hot on the *gringos'* heels. All of them were ugly, dirty, smelly, and armed to the teeth with weapons and ammunition.

Hanson, reeling from the shock to his overblown ego, turned to face Castillo. "What did you say? Take our clothes off?"

"I'm not taking my clothes off!" Hobbs said. "It's too goddamn cold!"

"Silence! Do as I say, or be killed like dogs, like your friend here! Do you want the same?" He pointed to the dead *vaquero* lying like a rag doll on the ground in a puddle of blood. "Hurry," Castillo raged, still sitting on his fidgeting horse. "We haven't much time!" He began swinging his rifle like a baton. "We will take them down to the village so that everyone can see them, especially the old women. To remind them of what they are missing. So they can see the white *gringos* and how powerless they are, without their guns and money. They are just like we are." He turned and viewed Hanson. "*Now, how do you like these apples?*" Castillo mimicked Hanson and broke into a hilarious laugh.

"Take my clothes off?" Remarked Hanson again in absolute disbelief. "But it's too sonavabitching cold! I'm not going to! I'll get pneumonia!"

"Enough!" yelled Castillo, icily. Trying to control his restless horse, which was going around in circles, he blasted a bullet inches away from Hanson's feet. "What difference does it matter now? With your clothes on or off, you are all dead men. Hurry," he yelled again, pointing his rifle toward Hanson and blasting another closer bullet between his boots.

Hanson was dancing like he had hot coals in his ass and began gasping for air, madder than a hornet. He could have killed them all with his bare hands for his demon spirit was all raw nerve ends. He began slowly taking off his clothes, first his hat, then his boots, one fetid sock, and then the other. He began unbuttoning his shirt, and with each button he would say, "Sonavabitches! Sonavabitches! How in the hell did I get into this mess! Damn! Damn!" He was down to his red long johns when he turned around and saw Hobbs, shaking terribly and redder than hot coals, trying in slow motion to get his pants off. Hanson wanted to laugh at first, and then had the irresistible urge to cry, knowing that his life was over. No, perhaps he would escape into the dense jungle like a wild heathen. The *bandidos* were occupied, busy picking up their boots and clothes, and would never notice him missing. But the thought was cowardly, and Hanson had never been known for his cowardliness. They all knew they were dead men.

"You stupid asshole," Hobbs shouted wildly at Hanson. Every time he opened his mouth, steam rolled out of it. "This was all your brilliant idea, thinking of taking over the gold mine. You'll be rich, you said! Just think of all that gold and what it will buy you in Texas! Lawdy, it's like swimming in cow shit. You stupid fool! You never mentioned *bandidos*, and how you can get your ass killed. I should have known better! How in the hell did you sell me on this idea? The damn gold! We should have stayed with selling the guns, like you were and already making a profit on the side. We already made a ton of money, across the border with the Rio Rico trade. We still could have sold tons of rifles and guns to the revolutionists in Mexico and would have come out all right."

"Shut up!" Hanson snapped. "You're talking too gawddamn much!" He turned and glanced at *Don* Federico who was stripping down to his pants and was listening to Hobbs' delirious ramblings.

"So, the raid in Rio Rico was your men's idea!" said *Don* Federico with interest.

"Yeah," Hobbs replied mindlessly, shaking with cold, continuing his nervous blather. "Hanson also talked me into that idea, and it worked. The idea was brilliant, especially dressing up like *bandidos*, trading with the two revolutionists, and raiding the village, killing the old people because they witnessed the chaos. What was fun was raping the Mexican greaser girl—I wouldn't mind doing that again!" He went silent, knowing that his life was on the line, but then continued, "What did it get us? Not a goddamn thing. We are all going to die, and the Mexican government doesn't give a rat's ass about us."

"You've said too goddamn much!" interrupted Hanson, infuriated at Hobbs' admission of their guilt.

"Raping women, stealing, killing, sounds very interesting," *Don* Federico interrupted. He had put two and two together and had gotten his memory working on the incident with Soledad. He turned and glared at Hanson, who was naked as a jaybird. "Good job, Hanson," he said hatefully. "It's funny how things come full circle. Here you were blaming the *bandidos* for killing those people, and now it's the *bandidos* who are going to kill you. Excellent justice! You and Hobbs are now going to get yours. You had everyone convinced in the Valley of how terrible the Mexicans *bandidos* were, killing and ransacking the border towns, when all along it was you and your henchmen who were doing all the murdering, and making it look like the Mexicans did it. The whole story is coming to a full conclusion. So tell me, Hanson, about Howard Ale—what part did he have in this plot?"

"He gave us the idea, all along convincing us how to get the money from your father."

"And who killed José Esquibel, during our fiesta? And who gave you permission to trespass onto my property during the night?" *Don* Federico was utterly convinced of Hobbs' story. By putting two and two together, all the pieces were being joined in the puzzle. What happened with the redheaded woman who was never found on his property? And what part did she have?

Hanson never answered, because he was startled by a hard blow to his back, hit by one of the *bandidos* and shoved with the end of a rifle. They were all being rounded up like cattle. They huddled there, stark naked to the world, as the bandits all fought among themselves, trying to measure up to the clothes. "What fine boots," one said. "But, they are too big," answered another one. "Fine, fine!" said another one. "Put old rags in them." Others were trying on the pants. *"Hijole,* how big," one commented. "I'll put a rope around them."

"Fine leather jackets," another added, "this one will keep me warm during the winter."

"Bring the shovels from the mine," shouted Castillo from his horse. "These *hombres* are going to dig their own graves. One at a time, and we have all the time in the world." He laughed again.

Don Federico seemed to have neither mind nor tongue. Every time he breathed, he exhaled white vapor. He was terrified by the bombshell announcement, and his legs wobbled dangerously. He knew at a gut level that something had gone terribly wrong. Surely Juan had not hired Castillo, for he was notorious for his brutality on both sides of the border. He was known for not sparing anyone. The silence of the countryside gripped *Don* Federico, as all of the men were being rounded up and forced down into a ravine.

Everyone was thinking of death. Hanson and Hobbs, who were in front, kept arguing between themselves as to who did what and vice-versa. Occasionally, Castillo would insist, "That's enough!" and, "No more talking, you stupid *gringos!*" as bullets carved themselves into the dirt close to the men's bare feet. Hanson and *Don* Federico had been playing a game with death, and now it was all coming into reality. His heart fluttered. *It could be possible,* thought *Don* Federico. *But it was so damn cruel to die this way and never have a chance to write anything or to tell anyone what happened.* He kept holding his temple with one hand, with the other cupped between his legs, as he trailed behind the other men. He noticed that his thighs and legs were starting to turn purple.

The bandits knew where they were going, and the prisoners were being driven like cattle down into a rocky area where small, sharp-edged stones cut the bottoms of their feet. They came upon a dry field of corn that cut their arms and legs, then into a field of maguey, the century plant. Everyone had grown strangely silent. Each was feeling like a damn fool, trying to cover his body with his hands, but they found no comfort from the freezing cold. White clouds of vapor spewed into the cold air with every panting breath. The naked men kept walking hunched over, huddling together, and occasionally rubbing their arms and shoulders to keep warm.

They came to an ancient, rundown ruin of a church in a small village with several un-painted adobe huts. At one time the church had been a beautiful place where people prayed to the one God everyone worshipped. *Where was God now? Don* Federico was thinking. All his riches, money, and high education would not get him out of this situation. And if there were a God, would he help him? Was there anything that would get him out of this ridiculous mess?

Standing at the rear of the group, *Don* Federico heard Hobbs trying to compromise with Castillo. As Hobbs looked up, Castillo, mounted on his horse, kicked him with his boot. "You *estúpido!*" he screamed. "You are going to die, you *gringo!*" Hobbs fell to the ground, while the rest of the naked men stood shivering, waiting for their executioner to give the orders. Hanson began cussing. The rest of the bandits, who couldn't have cared less, laughed and squatted down to smoke, wearing the clothes, hats, and boots that were way too big for them, giving them the comical appearance of swashbuckling pirates.

Among the group of rugged bandits was one who looked like a refugee from the funny farm and cross-eyed to boot. He had one wayward eye that consistently refused to position itself with the other one, and he could have easily directed traffic both ways standing in the middle of the crossway. He kept pinching the naked men's behinds and was enjoying what he saw and would calmly rub his hand over the men's bodies and testicles, while Castillo was yelling to the villagers to come out of their huts. Hanson, already spooked, cold and irritable, doubled up his fist and hit the cross-eyed one on the side of his jaw. "Don't touch me, you asshole!" he shouted. The bandit fell to the ground, and then slowly got up, shocked and angry.

"*Maldito gringo,*" he said, glaring at Hanson with hatred in his eyes. The other bandits laughed between their smoking siestas. It was almost becoming comical to the rest of the naked men, in spite of their tense, terrifying situation.

"Did you knock him on his ass?" commented Hobbs, snickering and quivering while holding onto his privates. "You probably straightened his other eye out so they will focus right."

"Ah, hell," remarked Hanson, holding onto his testicles and shaking with cold, teeth chattering. "My peter is frozen and about to fall off. I was planning to use it later."

"Later, hell, you wouldn't be worth a damn after today!" said Hobbs dubiously cocky and cold.

Dark-complexioned old women with black *rebozos* covering their heads and old men with white beards and white clothes with serapes wrapped around their shoulders began coming out of their adobe huts. Younger women holding babies, and small children clinging to the mothers' skirts, looked on with shock and terrified dismay, crossing themselves. "*Hijole,*" they would remark. Another spoke, "*Dios mío!*" One of the younger women with an infant in her arms put her hand over her face, than spread her fingers, as if hiding from embarrassment.

ROOTS OF INDIFFERENCE

"Take them out into those bushes and have them dig their own graves over by those other fresh ones," Castillo yelled, giving out the orders showing his furious, mindless strength backed up by his rifle. This was a demonstration of bitterness generated by the terrible years of oppression that had fomented resentment among the commoners of the Mexican countryside.

Mangy, starving dogs came to the digging scene, slouching and sniffing the fresh earth, while the men began furiously using the shovels.

Don Federico began shoveling the ground and was busy praying, praying to a God who seemingly did not listen, struggling to restrain his emotions. He hesitated for a few minutes and thought of his education, his class as a human being, and all of his studies in dealing with people. He decided to use his diplomacy, which had always won in the past. Appalled by Castillo's audacity and onerous demands, he put his shovel down and began walking toward one of the bandits who was in charge of the digging assignment.

"I want to speak to your high excellency, *Señor* Castillo," the *Don* demanded.

"Ah, you sound like a man with much class." The bandit laughed rudely.

Castillo, observing the conversation, rode over to where the two were talking. "Why is this man not digging?" he demanded angrily.

"Máximo, this man with much class wants to talk to you," replied the soiled, smelly, ragged bandit nervously, saying the words in mockery. "Your high excellency, I present *Señor* Castillo!"

"Silence, you fool!"

Don Federico grimaced. Standing proud and fearless, he looked straight into the cold, dark eyes of Castillo. The other men were busy digging many yards away, so he was able to speak to the vile, ruthless leader in private.

"Well?"

"Does the name Juan Alvarez sound familiar to you? Is this the way you treat gentlemen that want to help your people?" *Don* Federico felt a new strength that had overtaken him, as his voice became loud and strong, for fear had now become his greatest friend.

"Ah! Juanito! Why, of course. How do you know Alvarez?"

"I paid him for this mission. I paid Juan for you to do your job. I do not want the Mexican *vaqueros* killed," *Don* Federico demanded with much authority.

"Ah! Telling me what do? Giving me orders? When have you *Hijos de la Chingada* ever helped our people here in Mexico?" Agitated, Castillo's eyes became as dark as the peak of night; he grumpily curled his lips. "You come into our country, with all of your high superiority, demanding everything for yourselves. Taking our women, taking our land with gold and silver, and this is what you call help?" he retorted, with fury like a wild animal knowing no keeper. No doubt, the mescal had fried what little brains he had. "Because you stupid foreigners come from the bully of the United States, you think you can tell us what to do. Look at us, we are hungry. We have become *bandidos* to be able to survive in this country. With the little that we have, you men come and take everything."

Don Federico nearly swallowed his tongue in anguish, not knowing if he was making any sense to the *bandido* Castillo. He tried not to rise to the monster's bait. "I suppose you have never heard of the new liberator of Mexico?"

"New liberator, who in the hell is he? What do we all care?" he raged.

"Francisco Madero, my friend, will be the next President of Mexico. With your help, that of Juan Alvarez, and mine, we can nominate him for the office."

"Madero," answered Castillo, calming himself and rubbing his chin. "But I have heard of other great *hombres* who want to help the poor, but when they get on the throne in Mexico City, they forget about the little people like me and my *compadres.*"

Several of the *bandidos* had formed a circle around *Don* Federico, intrigued at the conversation, nodding their heads and smiling at Castillo's remarks, and fascinated by the *Don's* courage. Castillo continued, "Look at Díaz, sitting on his great throne of gold, with all the fancy ladies and men coming from all over the world, having parties and good times. No, no, *Señor!* The only way to do things is our way and by ourselves. My law is the only law here, do as I say or get killed! We are the only ones who know the land. We live here, and you do not."

"Why don't you join Madero and help him? He will help the people when he gets elected. There is going to be a new election, with Madero leading the party in the future. Men with power and money like me are helping and trying to overthrow the government for the same reasons you just mentioned. Look at Pancho Villa from the North and Zapata from the South. They are considered bandits but have joined Madero with his troops, helping with the new Revolution for the betterment of Mexico."

"But, what do you have to do with all of this? You come from rich Texas and shouldn't care what happens here in Mexico."

"Madero and I have been friends for a long time, we went to school together. He sent Juan to me for help. I'm one of the supporters of Madero. I have been helping him with money for guns and ammunition to overthrow Díaz's corrupt government." *Don* Federico was talking as fast as he could, grasping for words, and nervously trying to save his skin and that of the other two workers, hoping that Castillo understood his predicament. He realized that Castillo was a bandit, and a thief, and even worse, he was ignorant, uneducated, not understanding political issues. His talk had gone over his head. The only world that Castillo knew was killing and stealing. He was a tyrant, ignorant in his own land.

"I have heard enough of this foolishness," snapped Castillo, now very angry. "Nothing is going to save your skins, or the others. Get back to digging!" He glanced toward the sky as angry clouds had started to surround them. "You have wasted too much of my time! Hurry and go on and dig!" He turned his horse around and galloped toward the villagers who stood in awe watching the exhibition of naked men busy digging. He began showing his ego and pride, displaying what could be done with guns and power, especially in controlling the rich foreigners from the North.

A thin, ragged old man dressed in dingy, white cotton pants and shirt, and wearing a straw hat, approached *Don* Federico, bravely making his way though the group of bandits.

ROOTS OF INDIFFERENCE

He had lived in this village all his life and had been the foreman of the gold mine for many years, first for *Señor* Hinojosa, then a faithful worker for his father. "*Don* Federico, *Don* Federico!" repeated the old man. He was shocked to see the son of George Juelson, naked, cold and hurt, at first not knowing if he should hug him or shake his hand. "I was so sorry to hear about your father's death." He said it with much sorrow. "Things have not been the same here, as you can see." The old man looked shaken and aghast; his face was thin, gaunt and drawn, covered by wrinkles, stricken by the condition in which he found *Don* Federico.

"*Señor* Martinez," replied *Don* Federico, pleased to see the old man and a familiar face. "We didn't find you at the mine. We rode in last night and found it abandoned and in terrible disrepair." He said it very fast, ignoring Castillo's orders, holding onto his temple and for the moment forgetting that he was cold, naked, and the hellish awkward condition he was in. Time and death were moving fast for him.

"I got your letter many months ago with the money," answered the old man. "It has helped me and the people of the village. We have not been able to work at the mine, as you are aware of the flooding. Those who stayed, wanting to find more gold, all ended up being killed. See all those crosses? Those were the husbands and fathers of these poor little orphan children. Most of the women here are widowed." He pointed to where the rest of the men were digging. "We have also been raided several times and have seen many deaths. We have no horses and no guns. We are all afraid, as you can see." Saying it, he mouthed his words cautiously.

Don Federico, weary, sickened, and still shaken, felt his heart palpitate, and in the distance he could hear Hanson and Hobbs cussing. "Plans have changed and there is nothing that I can do now, as you are very well aware of the situation I'm in—" He never finished, because Castillo was on his heels.

"What is this?" shouted Castillo in raging anger from the back of his restless horse. "A family reunion?"

"No, *Señor*," answered *Señor* Martinez, terror-stricken. His voice became meek and humble. Removing his worn-out straw hat, he replied, "I have known *Don* Federico since he was a young man, and he comes from a fine family in Texas. His father was very patriotic to this country. If it wasn't for his family, we at this village wouldn't have survived—"

"Patriotic to this country," yelled Castillo, repeating like a parrot. "What the hell do I care about the word patriotic? Those are just stupid words that someone thought up. Enough! It doesn't matter now!" railed Castillo, who had no sympathy and very little patience. His nerves were out of control. He began kicking the old man with his boot and blasted several shots into the ground at his feet. "You, old man get back to your people or be shot," he shouted. "You, mister big wheel from Texas, start digging." He turned his horse around and announced to the other bandits, "Before the sun comes to this peak," pointing to an old wooden cross that was decaying with age, "I will start the execution." The threat was not a figment of his imagination, but the unvarnished truth.

The young Texas Ranger Smith had other ideas. Hearing *Don* Federico talking to Castillo, and seeing the bandits being distracted with their backs to them, he decided to make a desperate escape through the dense, hostile fields of maguey. Not knowing where he was going or where he was heading, naked, barefooted, no guns, no horse, only to run and get away, he ran as fast as his feet would carry him over the rough ground. They were all going to be killed sooner or later. He was too young to die. He knew too much. He knew the truth about Hanson and Hobbs marauding in the little village of Rio Rico, raiding, killing, and raping, selling the United States' guns and rifles for their own profit. He knew about Tom White and how he and Hanson had killed him, because he also knew too much. He wanted no part of this, only to escape and get back to Texas, where he would get back and find his wife and inform the Texas government about Hanson and Hobbs.

There was a loud shout and commotion before *Don Federico* got back to digging his own grave. One of the *bandidos* was screaming, "The *gringo* has escaped!"

"*Estúpidos!* You fools, *imbéciles!*" Castillo shouted, madder than a hornet. "What are you waiting for? Go get him! We mustn't let him escape. They must all be killed!" He went into a wild rage, pointing his rifle and shooting bullets at the feet of the naked, shivering men.

Mass confusion erupted as the *bandidos* carrying large machetes, looked like cockroaches running through the fields of maguey. Two had mounted their horses and headed in the opposite direction, trying to block the runaway *gringo* Ranger. Loud screams were coming from the dense field. After several minutes had passed, suddenly the commotion and the shouting stopped. Time felt like eternity. Everyone's heart was beating fast. Everyone had stopped digging and stood still, standing, waiting. Moments later the *bandidos* returned with the body of Smith. His head had been severed. One of the bandits was holding his head by its hair, with bright red blood still pouring from his neck. The others were dragging his body with their horses as a prize for Castillo.

Hanson and Hobbs were infuriated. "You will hear from the Texas government for this you bastard!" said Hanson, brazenly.

Castillo fired several bullets into the ground again where Hanson was standing. "Silence, *gringo!*" he yelled. "Your turn will come very soon. *Hijos de la Chingada!*" he said, along with more foul words in Spanish. "The government up north doesn't owe me a shittin' thing!" he stormed. "Keep digging, you *bastardos*, or you will get the same thing with the machetes."

Don Federico was now grasping at straws. His knees jerked. He could not escape. He did not want to die. He had too much to live for. His entire life was unraveling before his very eyes. He kept thinking about all of his years of education and success, all of his money, cattle, and influence—for what? And those poor village people could not help him. They were afraid, hungry, uneducated, powerless, and without guns or horses. *Why?* He kept asking himself. *What about Juan? Did he plan it this way, so that if I died, it would be easy for him to have his way with my daughter? Surely not,* he thought. His mind was starting to play games with him. It was all becoming a nightmare, far beyond what he had expected. The beasts of the Revolution were starting to stalk the land. It was amazing what men would do and say in times of desperation.

ROOTS OF INDIFFERENCE

Dreadful hours passed, with the sun periodically peeking out of the clouds. Castillo then gave a motion with his rifle, "Bring the tall one here," indicating Jones. "Put him against the church wall!"

"But, I have only dug two feet!" replied Jones with hostility and rebellion, stalling for time.

"Three feet," corrected Castillo.

"Yeah, maybe three feet," he replied argumentatively with Texas pride. "Look shit-face! This is not deep enough! In Texas we bury people six feet deep."

"Three feet, four feet," fumed Castillo. "What differences does it make?" He averted his eyes to the other *bandidos*, who stood dumbly waiting for his orders. "He says six feet." They all went into loud guffaws and Castillo cackled. "When you are dead, you are dead, *hombre*. Understand? And this country is not Texas. What difference does it make when you are dead? You're dead!" saying it in a sarcastic manner and halfway laughing at himself. "Believe me you will not feel a thing, *gringo*."

"Like hell!" Jones resisted in a confrontational attitude, provoking Castillo. "I have not dug six feet yet, and I refuse to be killed and buried in only three feet," he challenged, and with a fierce glare, stood his ground.

"You have big balls, *hombre*, speaking to me that way, when in several minutes you are going to die," said Castillo. He motioned with his eyes and head to his men.

Still resisting, Jones tried to fight off the *bandidos* holding onto his arms. Several bandits dragged him, putting him in position against the whitewashed church.

The rest of the *bandidos* nudged the other prisoners with their rifles. Everyone stood at attention. The village women in meekness fell quiet and knelt down on the damp earth with their handmade rosaries. The village men took off their straw hats and sombreros, slowly crossing themselves. They had witnessed the same scene many times. There was a nervous whisper as a baby cried in the background. Then the afternoon went silent at the click of rifles pointed toward the church wall.

"It's your fault and your crazy ideas," screamed Hobbs at Hanson. "You bastard! We are all going to get killed with your shit-brain idea about the gold! Who in the hell is going to save our skins?"

The cross-eyed bandit hit Hobbs on the head, cold-conking him with his rifle, forcing him to quiet down. Hobbs fell to the cold ground holding his head.

Then Castillo gave the orders. There was a crash of several rifles firing simultaneously, and at the first shot, Jones fell down the wall broadside and collapsed like a rag puppet in a heap. There were loud cries coming from the women kneeling. The wall of the whitewashed church was spattered with blood, rippling down, as the waiting naked prisoners all gasped in horror, speechless. Who was next?

The *bandidos* uttered profanities and reloaded their rifles.

The terror grew in intensity, driving them all into uncontrollable hysterics. Any minute, thought *Don* Federico, he would become insane. But he managed to keep his composure, trying to never let go of his senses. He was losing all sight of rationality and could feel the sweat breaking out on his entire body. How ridiculous, since it was so bitterly cold.

Castillo laughed crazily, then pointed to *Don* Federico. "Take him! He's next!" He laughed insanely, again looking directly at the *Don*. "See if the Great Madero will come and help you!"

There was a great stir, and much whispered protest among the villagers. "No, please, not *Don* Federico," begged *Señor* Martinez, making himself known, as he stepped out from the wailing crowd, pleading with his hands. "He is a good, honest man and has been my friend!"

"Silence, old man! Get back to your stupid crying woman, or you will be next!"

Don Federico felt his blood go cold and his face turned pallid. He took a deep breath and bravely walked slowly to where the body of Jones lay sprawled on the ground. He calmly turned and faced the horror of the firing squad while his hands covered his privates. His feet felt rooted in the rocky ground. His stomach lurched, feeling as if he were going to vomit. His fingers trembled, his knees shook. *My God!* He kept saying to himself. *My God!* His heart raced. He thought in that anguished, desperate moments. *Is this what was in store for me throughout all of my years? God, please have mercy on my soul.* He swallowed hard.

Castillo then gave the orders. Now, seven rifles pointed in *Don* Federico's direction like canons ready to go off at any minute. He could see the people from the village crying. Several yards away stood the aging *Señor* Martinez, grieving, helpless. He turned to view Hanson and Hobbs looking shocked and desperate, with gray, hollow faces, awestruck, trying to cover themselves with their hands. Too bad they could not have been first. Somewhere in the deep cavern of his mind, his mother's words seemed to come flooding back from the first book of Psalms:

"*Blessed is the man that walks not in the counsel of the ungodly, nor stands in the way of sinners and scornful. For the Lord knows the way of the good; and the way of the ungodly shall perish.*"

Don Federico then blinked. Those were the memories and the words that his mother used to preach to him from the Holy Book. How ironic, since he had never believed in anything, especially in any religion. He had been a good man, and yet he now stood condemned like a criminal, among thieves and vile people. This was the conclusion, his *coup de grâce* moment, and soon he would be with his parents in the great unknown. His thoughts wandered to his family. What would become of them? He wanted so much for his children. He wanted so much for his sons, especially Fred, who showed much promise in the near future. Soon he would stand in judgment before the Almighty.

All stood at attention, when someone from the villagers announced to Castillo, "Look! Look!" A *peón* pointed to the clouds that had gathered in the sky. Castillo looked befuddled, gazing at the vision in the sky.

"It's a sign, Castillo! It's a sign," cried one of the ladies who was kneeling with her hand pointing toward the sky. "*Hijole, Dios Mío,*" she replied. "This is a godly man and needs to be spared," replied the villagers, who were now standing with their heads tilted up and hands pointing toward the heavens. The commotion grew as they began stirring and speaking, voicing their opposition, believing *Don* Federico to be a saintly man. "*Piedad, piedad,* mercy," they chanted.

The configuration of the clouds had formed a huge cross, creating a spectacular panorama, with gleaming pink, yellow, and gold glowing streaks penetrating through the heaviness of the clouds and illuminating the full-figured cross from all sides.

"It's a miracle! A miracle!" cried the excited villagers, and they began chanting again, "*Aucellio,* mercy, mercy for that man!"

Castillo glanced up and stood for a minute, not knowing if he was on foot or horseback, and shuddered, horrified. "*Madre de Dios!*" he exclaimed out loud. "I have never in my life seen anything like this!" Removing his sombrero, he began scratching his head. The other *bandidos* removed their hats also, copying Castillo and doing the same. All stood gazing toward the sky in total amazement.

From the dirt road leading to the mine, could be heard the sound of thundering hooves. "Castillo!" yelled one of the bandits, "I think I hear horses coming!" The cross-eyed *bandido* knelt and dropped his head, putting his ear to the ground. "I hear horses coming from the gold mine," he said. "Someone is coming!" cried another. The *bandidos* scattered like mad ants—everyone gathering up their stolen goods, guns, and ammunition. Then someone cried in alarm, "*Los Federalists!*" The scene erupted into chaos. Everyone became distracted, and in the mass confusion, the *bandidos* forgot about the prisoners. The villagers were all smiling and standing in the middle of the dirt road.

Don Federico struggled to curb his emotions, feeling that angels from the heavens had given him another chance in life. His mind scrambled to make sense of the supernatural event. He had tears flowing down his cheeks, and used the dead Smith's bloodstained handkerchief to wipe his eyes. He had forgotten that he was holding onto it so tightly. His hands still trembled, and perspiration ran down his sides. He gasped in utter disbelief, realizing he had been saved. How good it was to be alive and to breathe again. He had never experienced anything so spiritual. It had truly been a miracle!

"*Los Federalists! Ay, Chihuahua!* Hurry! We must leave, quickly!" They all rushed to load the wagon and their horses with their stolen goods. Everything was in a mad state of confusion. With wild shouts to the mules, they took off in a cloud of dust down the opposite slope and out of the village.

The prisoners stood in awe, staring at each other in amazement; they were in a total state of shock. They all looked like fools, speechless and immoveable, standing naked and bewildered. The villagers quickly went into their humble adobe huts, children, dogs, and all, and closed their doors. If the *Federalists* were coming, they were no different than the *bandidos,* for they were just as ruthless.

The *Federalists* rode in with twenty-five soldiers in full uniform, looking weary and cold. The *Capitán* Emiliano Nafarrate, was startled, seeing a group of naked men standing around in the cold temperature with purple bodies and trying to cover their private parts. It was hard not to laugh!

"*Caray!* What do we have here?" He said, snickering and slightly embarrassed. The rest of the soldiers grinned, and one laughed out loud. "Quiet!" He commanded. The *Capitán's* conversation was sprinkled with soldierly curses. "We have just come from José Hinojosa's hacienda and were ordered to come this way and see if we could help. *Señor* Hinojosa was worried about his *vaqueros* and sent word to come and help a *Señor* Juelson. Who is *Señor* Juelson?" He said in a loud voice.

Don Federico stepped up from behind the other naked men, trying to get his cold lips to form the words. "I'm *Señor* Juelson," he replied, feeling weary and fatigued. His pale face was stricken and drawn, his body cold, purple, and quivering with goosebumps. He felt as though he was on the fringes of insanity. "I am José Hinojosa's son-in-law." His voice was trembling as he talked to the *Capitán*, and explaining what had taken place, and the main reason he was up at the mines. "Our family has owned the mine with the approval of Díaz —"

"Say no more, *hombre*," interrupted *Capitán* Nafarrate by raising his hand. "Don't waste any more of your energy. You are tired, cold, and hungry. *Señor* Hinojosa has already explained everything to me."

The young and ambitious *Capitán* Nafarrate adjusted his cap and looked around, grasping the situation at a glance. He could clearly see what had taken place, given the bloodstains on the church wall. "How many are dead?" he asked *Don* Federico somberly.

"Three," answered the *Don*, as his voice rose to an impressive gravity, forgetting that he was cold and hungry, feeling his hatred rekindling for Hanson and Hobbs. "The two over there," he pointed out, "were killed by the *bandido*, Castillo, and his highwaymen. The Mexican *vaquero*, Jorge, from the Hinojosa's hacienda, whose body is up by the mine, was killed by these *gringos*," he said, indicating Hanson and Hobbs.

The determined and impressive captain then gave the orders and motioned to his soldiers. "Take them! Take the *gringos* and put them under arrest. Better find some clothes for them, and for the other two *vaqueros*, and for *Señor* Juelson." He also gave orders to ten of his men to follow the tracks of the *bandidos* and round them up. The *bandidos*, if caught, would be killed.

"No clothes are going to fit your big ass, Hanson. You're too goddamn big," said Hobbs, quivering and stammering.

"Shut up, you shit-face. What is it to you, what the hell fits me? You've said enough already. Our asses are in big trouble now," roared Hanson, pugnacious as ever. "We get out of one shit-hole and now we are going into another. I'm not too crazy about those goddamn Mexican jails, feeding you shit, with rats and cockroaches all over. I'll take any clothing wrapped around me for now. I'm too damn cold, but a swig of undiluted White Mule would sure calm my nerves."

"Well, we're alive," replied Hobbs. "And we can figure some way of getting out of this rat shit-hole sooner or later. It will require more planning," he said cynically.

"And go where?" Hanson shouted. "Frankly I don't give a rats-ass what happens to you, but the U.S. Marshals will be waiting for me up there, and I'll have to justify to the Commander of the Texas Rangers why the hell I left my post. You should have kept your trap shut all along. It would have worked out all right, but now we have a bunch of explaining to do." Hanson and Hobbs continued their squabble, blaming each other for who did what. For Hanson it was like a bad draw to an inside straight, coming full circle.

The *Capitán* addressed *Don* Federico once again. "*Señor!* These *gringos* will go to jail in Monterrey, until we and the Mexican government decide what to do with them. My soldiers will help carry the body of the dead Mexican back to the hacienda. The rest of the men will have to ride together on the horses with some of my soldiers." He then ordered his men to bury the two dead *gringos*.

"My father-in-law and I will pay you well for this service, *Capitán*. And we will see that your commander hears about your goodwill service rendered."

"It's not necessary. We are on duty and in the service of *General* Antonio Garcia in Monterrey. He will be happy that you were pleased with our service to you and to *Señor* Hinojosa. And my soldiers and I will be rewarded with other commendation. Very well, it will be done! *Adelante.*"

CHAPTER 15

For the first three weeks, Victoria and Felicia had enjoyed their stay in the Hinojosa's hacienda, with all the traditional comforts. The days had passed in a whirl of meeting many high-class, educated, influential people, all dressed with a European flair. Up to now Victoria felt lucky, for she hadn't had to confront the Calderóne family.

While *Don* Federico was gone, an unpleasant incident had occurred. One of the *peón* men had grabbed and fondled Felicia's leg while helping her onto her horse. Emma had made a fuss and had demanded punishment for his having touched Felicia. It was horrible the way in which the foreman had strung the peasant over a wagon wheel and whipped him, giving him over thirty lashes. The two girls still shivered and talked for days following the incident, after witnessing the episode from their upstairs window, and seeing the bloody stripes across the servant's back. "But he deserved it," said Victoria, trying to make Felicia feel better. "It wasn't your fault. It seems that all of the Mexicans are love-starved crazies. Look at the comments when we go to the stables. Remember how they eyed us and made remarks among themselves in whispers, of what they would do because we are from Texas? They think that the *Tejanas*, are free and easy!"

"The servants have no rights, no freedom," cried Felicia. "I've heard them talk about a revolution. The poor Indian and Mexican people with no education, nobody can read or write. I feel sorry for the women with small children. They all smell of hard work, sweat, horses, and cattle," she lamented.

"It's their way of life here. What can they do if there is a revolution? The peasants are never satisfied with Grandfather, no matter what he does for them! They have food and shelter. Grandfather even built them a small chapel where they could pray, and he gave them Sundays off."

Another small incident had occurred while *Don* Federico was absent. Fred, Carlos, and other young boys from *Don* Hinojosa's estate had wandered into the mango groves and had discovered a large brown and grayish honeycomb made by wild bees and hanging from one of the trees. The curiosity had been too great for the young, inquisitive, Fred, who adored the outdoors and nature.

"Honey!" remarked one of the servant boys, pointing up at the tree.

"We have seen it grow for quite a while," said one of the other boys, "and the honey is dripping on the ground. It's delicious!"

Lo and behold, with those words, Fred's ears perked up. It must have taken several hours for the boys to figure out how to take the honeycomb away from the angry bees, Fred being the instigator. Hours later, they returned to the hacienda, all stung and swelling up, and with little Carlos crying. But they had retrieved pounds of honey. The women were alarmed and stripped off all of the boys' clothes in mid-afternoon out in the open, putting papaya and juice from the *nopales* mixed with other herbs on their skin. For several hours, the commotion stirred, but in the end, the boys got well, with no fever, and no complications.

Barking dogs soon announced the arrival of *Don* Federico and some of the soldiers coming down from the mountains and through the front gates of the Hinojosa's hacienda. The *peóns*, including women and children, and the working *vaqueros*, rushed out to meet the troupe.

The noisy activity caught the ear of Victoria's great-grandmother. Down the long corridors of the hacienda came *Señora* Maria Alvarado, who had lived with the Hinojosa's family for over twenty-five years. *Doña* Francisca's grandmother was in her late eighties and always dressed in her gloomy, black lace gown. She had her rosary hanging by her side at all times, a white handkerchief in her right hand, and a walking cane in her left. She was a petite woman, with silver-white hair piled on her head and clasped in a golden brooch. *La Señora* Alvarado was a true Spaniard and within her coursed the best blood, combined with preferential old-fashioned manners and formalities. She was a *Gachupin*, born in old Spain, God's mother country. Her life would have made a gripping, romantic novel of hushed secrets and love affairs of the once attractive Spanish woman. Her willowy face was the color of a pale rose and she had marvelous, expressive blue eyes that mirrored a fictitious innocence of naiveté, which translated as charm and old age. She was quiet and reserved, but when stirred up, had a spiky tongue like a weathered bullwhip. The old woman frowned upon the conduct of Victoria and Felicia, laughing and making a spectacle of themselves, taking the liberty of coming and going, and riding without a chaperone into the countryside alone.

"Such ways in which young girls are being taught nowadays is blasphemous," she said, meeting *Doña* Francisca and *Señora* Hinojosa in the hall, and hitting her cane hard on the tile on their way outside to meet *Don* Federico and the soldiers.

"Why, *Abuelita!* The girls are here visiting for only a short period of time. They are happy and ready to attend school at the convent," *Doña* Francisca answered gently.

"Good thing!" she said. "The girls need discipline, especially Victoria. It's a good thing she is attending the convent. She will need it when she marries the son of *General* Del Calderóne."

"*Sí, Mamá,*" *Señora* Hinojosa replied awkwardly, not wanting to be disrespectful.

"It's no wonder girls are so willful, getting bad ideas from the people up North. They dress too loosely, and too colorfully—it's disgraceful! Bah!" She spoke with a razor-sharp tongue. "Shame on the two of you for allowing them to do whatever they please around the hacienda grounds," remarked the old woman, with quivering lips. "The time is getting closer to the destruction, the war that the Holy Catholic Church has been telling us about—when *La Virgen de Guadalupe* appeared to the Indian servant and revealed to him the coming struggle."

"*Sí, Mamá!*" Answered *Señora* Hinojosa and was thinking that *La Virgen de Guadalupe* had appeared to the Indian servant over four hundred years ago.

"*Sí, Abuelita,*" replied *Doña* Francisca.

Mother and daughter looked at each other with a resigned sigh, and then turned to the old woman, being respectful and treating her with kid gloves. "We are just stepping outside to meet Federico after his long journey from the mountains. He was seeing about the gold mine."

"*Vaya, Sera por Dios*, that everything is well with him. I had a terrible dream last night about Federico. I got up and prayed to the saints for his safety. They have answered my prayers. We must give of our alms, light a candle, and give our thanks."

"*Sí, Mamá*, whatever you say," Señora Hinojosa replied respectfully, as they hurried outdoors, leaving *La Señora* Alvarado talking to herself in the long marble corridor. The old woman stood for a moment in a daze, then walked back to her bedroom, which was at the far end of the hacienda.

Horses were being unsaddled outside, and the atmosphere had become full of activity, like a humming beehive. Somewhere in the crowd a woman with a small child in her arms cried out in anguish. Another child gripped his mother's leg and wept.

Don Federico's face sagged with a haunted look, a soul from which all the grand spirit of nobility had fled. His eyes were dull and lifeless, and on his forehead, the swollen purple bruise was still visible. He wore borrowed khaki clothes one size too small and was barefooted. He refused to answer any of the questions coming from *Señor* Hinojosa, who wanted an explanation. He glanced toward *Señora* Hinojosa and *Doña* Francisca, who were in shock upon seeing the dead *vaquero* being taken from the horse.

"Have Juana and the rest of the servants prepare my bath and fresh clothes. I need to get clean," he said weakly. "I'm too cold and shaken right now, but I will answer all your questions later tonight." He walked inside, down the long tile corridors, and up the stairs. *Doña* Francisca followed him.

It was late that night before the *Don* was able to talk about his horrible experience. They had consumed a splendid dinner and the women were all dressed in their best evening gowns and finest jewels. *Don* Federico, Fred, Carlos and *Señor* Hinojosa, dressed in their expensive silk suits, had gathered in the large *sala* where the warmth of the enormous, elegant fireplace warmed them.

Don Federico leaned back in his chair and slowly related the details of his horrific ordeal at the hands of the bandit Castillo and his men. "*Los malditos bandidos!*" He spoke the words with vehemence. "Of all the people to disappoint me, the least expected was—Juan!" he said sadly. "Castillo was the worse bandit to hire. I do not know what Juan was thinking. I was a fool thinking that Juan could solve my problems with Hanson. It was an expensive lesson. Those *bandidos* were not going to spare anyone. They were going to kill all of us. It's a good thing that you sent *Capitán* Nafarrate, or nobody would be left alive to tell the story of what happened."

"I was concerned," replied *Señor* Hinojosa. "I sent a message to *General* Garcia earlier and I will thank him later."

"Good thinking on your part. *General* Garcia must be paid well."

"He will be well compensated. I will see to that."

"I was surprised to see Hanson's corrupt partner, Hobbs. The two of them have been doing unspeakable, illegal things across the border. The good news is, I found out the truth about my father's killer. Hanson and Hobbs have been taken to jail here in Monterrey and will probably be extradited later to the courts in Texas. As for Juan, I shall deal with him later. I can't believe he set me up with that *bandido*, Castillo!"

"There's been a mistake, a misunderstanding, perhaps," countered Victoria, in Juan's defense. "He's too nice of a man to do anything like this to you, Papá," she sputtered, trying to protect Juan's name that had been repeatedly brought up during the evening's conversation by the Hinojosa clan.

"He's a revolutionist!" retorted *Don* Hinojosa. "Trying to uproot the Mexican government and going against Díaz's regime. I don't think that Madero knows what he's doing, and frankly, he is not going to come up with anything. Madero doesn't know a thing about military politics," he muttered, nursing his pipe. "If he is not careful, he will eventually be shot."

Victoria interrupted again. "You trusted Juan and went with him to San Antonio. So many times I heard you say how much you admire him for his courage in what he is trying to accomplish. You invited him to my fiesta and shared our home. It's a misunderstanding, it has to be," she said, turning to stare at Felicia who was rapidly fanning herself, wishing to stay out of it.

Emma, in an elegant black gown, was sitting next to *Doña* Francisca and Gloria Hinojosa, all the while watching the family and listening closely to their conversation. She was glad that *Don* Federico had returned safely, for the sake of *Doña* Francisca. "I've learned not to trust low class people," Emma finally said, "especially revolutionists!" She cleared her throat and continued, "Nobody is sure of their political motives, and what they expect to gain." It was obvious she was working her way into the good graces of *Don* Federico and the Hinojosa family.

"Well, we will never know. For we will never see *Señor* Alvarez again, and I will forbid anyone in my household to see or talk to him again," *Don* Federico remarked, casting a quick glance at Victoria. Relaxing for the first time in days, he held a cigar in one hand and a glass of wine in the other. "This case with Alvarez is over!"

"Bah! Those Alvarez are all liars," commented *La Señora* Alvarado, who had remained quite throughout the evening. Although she looked like an old corpse, her lips still quivered. She wore black lace from ankle to throat, providing the perfect setting to display her diamond jewelry. Everyone pivoted and listened to what the crotchety old woman had to say.

Señora Gloria raised her eyebrows and repeated, "Liars?"

ROOTS OF INDIFFERENCE

"Yes, liars!" repeated *Señora* Alvarado in an angry tone, as her hand clutched the cane.

"But, Mamá, I remember you used to talk about Juan's grandfather, *Señor* Diego Alvarez, very fondly, especially when I was very young. He would often come and visit you shortly after father passed away. Through the years, I always thought you were in love with him. I was surprised to see the handsome, young Alvarez at Victoria's birthday celebration, knowing who he was, and coming from Monterrey," she said calmly, looking at her mother directly.

"*Basta!* Enough!" thundered the old woman, banging her cane at the floor and almost choking. She began instantly fanning herself, feeling cornered about her past romantic encounter.

Victoria's eyes met Felicia's, and both flickered with amusement. They sensed the hint of a love secret, a hot romance that had turned cold. Fred and Carlos, sitting at *Doña* Francisca's side with swollen cheeks, listened with the utmost intensity. They, too, were amused.

"That whole family is trash!" hissed *Señora* Alvarado. "The Alvarez men have a terrible reputation of womanizing, starting with old Diego himself. His own wife caught him in bed with a fifteen-year-old girl who lived in the back of their hacienda, years ago. Of course, Diego denied it. Horrible scandals were being rumored. They lost everything from his estate and all of his property. It was said that he would disgrace young girls and sell them to men with money in the border towns. Of course those were rumors among the elite in Monterrey—anything for a story! Juan's father was killed many years ago by the *Federalists,* and now his mother and sister live in the poorest part of town." She turned to *Don* Federico with quivering lips. "When you deal with those kinds of people, you will get the worst results."

"When Juan first came to see me at Spanish Acres, he was very sincere," said *Don* Federico, groping for the right words, since the Hinojosas were confirmed Díaz loyalists. "He was helping Madero with the upcoming Revolution, which was the main reason Juan visited our home. I was very impressed with him, especially for leaving medical school to help with the struggling conditions here in Mexico."

"For heaven sakes!" said Victoria, jumping to her feet and contradicting her great-grandmother in Juan's defense. "That happened many years ago. Juan is different! He is not like his grandfather, or his father. Those are rumors and stories—people make them up and gossip. Is he responsible for his father's actions? Haven't you thought of that, Great Grandmamma Alvarado?"

"I suppose so," remarked the old woman, who glared at Victoria intensely. "But reputation is hard to live down, my dear, especially your name and who you are. The young Alvarez man has to prove otherwise to the rest of Monterrey. There are too many families that still remember and do not forget. Does a good tree bear evil fruit?" She shuddered.

"Why does he have to prove anything?" cried Victoria. "Here in Monterrey, people live by the old customs and traditions, many years behind the times. Everything is so ridiculous, dumb, and stupid!"

There was an audible sound as everyone in the *sala* sucked in their breath in a collective action. Victoria was being disrespectful. The rest of the ladies brought their hands to their mouths, aghast, including Felicia and all of the female servants.

"There is nothing wrong with the old ways, young lady!" *Señora* Alvarado shouted. She got strangled in her wording and held her handkerchief to her mouth. "The girls nowadays think they can do anything without any respect to their elders. They think they know all the answers and can get themselves into trouble, without any consequences, hurting the family's name." She hesitated and sat there scowling for a moment. "It's getting late, and I must say my prayers and rest."

The old woman gave a commanding motion with her hands and stood up with the help of two servants, who then followed along behind her as she prepared to leave the room. She stopped, turned and addressed *Don* Federico and *Doña* Francisca, still angry and being spiteful. "I have sent a message to the Del Calderóne family earlier, informing them that Victoria is here and will be spending the rest of the week with them before she goes to the convent. They want to get to know her better," she said, struggling with her steps.

"Thank you, Grandmother, for reminding them. It was good of you to be thinking of Victoria," answered *Doña* Francisca, who had been very quiet and coughed sporadically during the evening's conversations.

"Yes," answered *Don* Federico, who looked haggard and exhausted. "Next week we will get the girls in school." In an effort to lighten up the conversation and make *Doña* Francisca happy, he turned his attention to his wife and said, "In Texas, I will see about the land in Mercedes City and build you a house there so you and Emma will be close. I want you to be happy, my dear. Your doctor has moved to Reynosa, and living in Mercedes City will make it easier for you to see him. But it's getting late now, and I think you need your rest."

"Well, it's about time!" hissed Emma. "My prayers to Saint Michael have been heard."

Doña Francisca got up and kissed *Don* Federico on his forehead, then went upstairs to her quarters. Emma followed shortly and, with the help of Felicia, waddled to her bedroom.

Victoria was in deep thought. *Why, I can't believe that old woman!* To spend the rest of week with the Del Calderónes was going to be uncomfortable. All of the grandmothers, including her mother, were in conspiracy! They all had gotten the hint of the way she felt about Juan and were trying anything to keep them apart. She knew that Emma had a big part in this plot.

Don Federico turned to finish talking with *Señor* Hinojosa, who had been quiet throughout the long discussion in his large chair, for he had been asleep in spite of the hot topic the family had discussed. His head had dropped to his chest, and he was snoring peacefully.

CHAPTER 16

Soon, Victoria found herself sitting nervously with her father in the large elegant, *sala* of the Del Calderóne estate mansion, called "Castle Del Calderóne." Her mother was unable to accompany them, due to her illness and embarrassing cough.

Through the French gothic stained-glass windows, she could view the outside acreage of the mansion. The estate covered many miles in every direction, with wineries, horse stables, fields of sugar cane, hothouses for the orchids they grew, groves of various tropical fruits, and orchards of many varieties of citrus. The landscaped gardens were vibrant with color and neatly manicured, with waterfalls and ponds and hundreds of different walkways with flowers growing at the edges, and flowering vines hanging along driveways that led to the many courtyards between the main house and guest cottages. Set at the far back of the mansion grounds were ten dozen small huts in which the *peóns* lived.

Inside the enormous castle were paintings by European painters such as Goya, Degas, and Velázquez. The lavish marquetry fixtures were antique and imported from different parts of Europe. Many extravagant mahogany pieces of furniture with lion legs were gifts of the Emperor Maximilian and Empress Carlotta. The furniture had been brought overseas from his castle in Miramar and was later given to *Señor* Del Calderóne's grandfather from the castle at Chapultepec. Wide mezzanines joined rooms furnished with rich, dark furniture and sparkling silver tea services. Patina sets of wineglasses in silver and gold with matching decanters were arranged tastefully throughout the great ballrooms, as well as long-stemmed, fresh-cut orchids in crystal glasses. Enormous vases featuring colorful dragons and flower designs were stationed in every corner. Hundreds of marvelous Venetian mirrors reflected throughout. In the great *sala* were hanging crystal chandeliers, and Persian rugs covered the tile floors.

Victoria's Grandmother Hinojosa, her mother *Doña* Francisca, and the servant, Juana, had made sure that every detail of her clothing and hair had been arranged perfectly for her debut with the Del Calderónes. Victoria had asked Felicia to accompany her to the Del Calderóne estate, but Aunt Emma had intervened, saying that Felicia was going to be busy being fitted for several dresses she wanted made from the new patterns and materials, and that it was no business of Felicia's anyway. Victoria felt that Emma was almost jealous of her staying with the Del Calderóne family, and she wished that Felicia could be so lucky.

On the opposite side of the enormous sitting room sat *Señora* Del Calderóne with *El General* beside her, and on the other end of the white sofa sat Ricardo, striking in his dark Italian silk suit and white shirt. Although he appeared very handsomely aristocratic, he was nervously fumbling with his short-brimmed derby hat. His dark, piercing eyes would light up every time he exchanged glances with Victoria. They had all greeted each other formally, elegantly, and gracefully, and had been given some of the estate's famous wine, while they all relaxed and talked about the old days.

La Señora Del Calderóne sat stiff-laced in a dark printed dress up to her neck and a gemstone brooch at her throat. Her salt-and-pepper hair was piled on her head and held in place with a fan-shaped gold comb. Layers of jewelry hung from her neck, and on each finger were several rings with precious stones. *Señora* Del Calderóne stared at Victoria over her dark glasses, surveying her from head to toe, making sure that she would be acceptable as the perfect daughter-in-law.

"Did you like the opal necklace and earrings I sent you for your birthday, Victoria?" she asked, displaying no emotion. Behind her dark glasses was a person who had suffered greatly by being controlled and manipulated throughout her married life as *La Señora*, for she had been a victim of great deception, being totally submissive to her corrupt, womanizing husband. Her disposition was reserved, yet she showed some charm, with a fierce protective instinct about her children. She seemed wiser than her years, and could display a cherubic smile at will.

"Why, yes," responded Victoria very cheerfully. "They matched my dress perfectly. As a matter of fact, I brought them with me, along with my birthday dress. I will wear them tonight for the evening meal so you can see them. Thank you very much."

"How nice, I'm so glad you liked them," *Señora Del* Calderóne replied. "They are very expensive stones. I had the jewelry made from the finest gold from my own jeweler, who does only special requests, one of its kind and custom made."

"With your beautiful eyes, the opals must have been exquisite," said Ricardo, now speaking up. "I can't wait to see you wearing them this evening. I am sorry I couldn't attend your birthday. We heard from your Aunt Emma that it was an outstanding fiesta. I hope you had a good time."

"It was wonderful," answered Victoria, unsure of just how much they knew about her coquettish actions with Juan. Aunt Emma, the self-proclaimed newscaster, had probably written to them relating every detail of what had occurred.

"You turned sixteen already and are going to the convent," commented Ricardo, turning on the charm. "I can't believe my eyes! You have changed so much since I last saw you. It must have been over two years since I visited Spanish Acres with the hunting party of my friends."

"Yes," Victoria answered softly. She felt like a piece of merchandise being inspected before purchase. Or like a precious gem under a microscopic, revealing that one of her facets was cracked. Her father and *El General* Calderóne had disappeared out into the courtyard, discussing Mexico's current political crisis. As they strolled outside, she overheard *El General* laughing at Madero and how foolish he was, trying to control the government of the powerful Díaz.

"Victoria," said Ricardo, getting up from the white sofa, extending his hand to her, hoping to break the icy atmosphere. "Would you like to stroll outside into our lovely courtyards? After much rain, the sun is out, and it has become a lovely day."

Victoria reached out her hand, and together they moved outdoors among the white gardenia bushes that were in full bloom. She felt more comfortable outside, leaving behind the piercing, haunting eyes of *Señora* Del Calderóne. Feeling romantic, Ricardo picked one of the large gardenias and placed it on the left side of her hair. "Have I told you how beautiful you look this afternoon? How lovely the color of green accents your hazel eyes, and how much you have changed? You have grown into an exquisite *Chérie*," commented Ricardo sincerely. "I can't get over how grown up you look with your hair partly up and shining in the light. I have thought of you ever since I came back from Paris. I have counted the minutes. The women in Paris do not hold a candle to you—you would make them all green with envy."

"How kind of you to say that!" replied Victoria, who was overtaken by his flowery charm and polished manners. His handsome smile was edged by a thin, manicured, dark mustache. "Tell me about your education in Paris," she asked, duly impressed.

"Paris! Ah! *Merci*, Paris is wonderful. We must go there for our honeymoon," he said, sounding so full of promises, so excited, and so sure of himself. "I swear, you will enjoy seeing all of its beautiful sites. It's so different from Mexico. They have magnificent palaces, especially King Louis XIV, the Versailles, and the Louvre, their art museum. It has many lovely churches of historical interest, including the Madeleine, the St. Vincent de Paul, and other beautiful buildings. The educational institutions of Paris rank very high among those in modern Europe. The *Cathedral* of Notre Dame contains the burial place of Napoleon. I was very interested in Napoleon while growing up. I admired him in the way he controlled his armies. He was a very clever man indeed."

He talked as if he was there, with so much enthusiasm and intense feeling, wanting to go back, and his conversation was mixed with half Spanish and half French words. He suddenly realized he was relating too much of his adventures, and said abruptly, "Ah! *Perdón*. Here I am talking about myself, and I have forgotten to take you to your quarters. You'll be staying in one of the guest cottages. It's charming and you'll like it, it's very comfortable. The servants have already taken your luggage there. It's only a few yards away, and I'll escort you there." Holding her left arm, he walked her down a cobblestone path embraced by flowering vines. "We'll have plenty to talk about, since you're spending the rest of the week with us. Maybe we'll ride out into the surrounding fields, out into the countryside, so I can show you how delightful our place is."

"It's exquisite," she said. "Everything here is beautiful. Everything seems so perfect and in place. It's a dream come true, a colorful picture of Van Gogh's delight." She whirled around with her hands in the air, then smiled at Ricardo and gave him a quick hug.

They stopped at the entrance to the guest cottage, which was made of stucco with black, wrought-iron designs on the windows and the doorway. Colorful tiles lined the steps, and flowering clay pots sat on each side of the entrance. The sun was starting to go down behind an array of cirrus clouds that were transformed into a soft mauve as they caught the last splendor of the heavenly rays.

"I'll see you tonight for the evening meal," said Ricardo, smiling and letting go of her arm.

She hugged him again before he disappeared into the courtyards. She was let inside the cottage to find an enchanting place. Servant men in their white cotton shirts and trousers were already waiting for her as they scurried in and out with plates of bananas and oranges. A crystal pitcher of fresh, cold water was placed on the colored tile counter next to the fruit platters. A sizeable porcelain vase was full of fresh-cut flowers. Fresh linens and colored towels were at her disposal next to an oversized porcelain bathtub, which sat two steps down, next to a large, open window. A huge walnut, four-poster bed with hand-embroidered quilts of white satin and lace embraced the enormous featherbed. At the foot of the bed was a plush oriental rug. Two Indian-looking ladies, with long, black braids down to their waist, had already taken command of the situation and had removed Victoria's clothes from her trunks. Other Indian servants were busy bringing in large wooden tubs of boiling water, preparing her for a hot, relaxing bath before the evening gala.

⌘　⌘　⌘

That evening was full of surprises. In Mexico, people had their siestas from twelve to four, followed by a light snack. The evening meal was always served late and was the heaviest.

Victoria's father had proudly escorted her to the eighteen-seat dining room with arched windows at every corner. A huge fireplace burned intensely, while the servants, dressed in white cotton, scurried around the room at full attention. Lit candelabras and chandeliers brightened the room, displaying the China plates with gold edging next to a variety of gold silverware, European cut-crystal goblets, and embroidered napkins. A bouquet of fresh-cut flowers sat on top of the enormous dining table. Wines of different flavors and colors were waiting for them as they stepped into the room. A large corsage of lavender orchids was pinned on Victoria's dress by a *peón* girl, before she sat down, with Ricardo on her right and her father on the left. Audible murmurs and whispers circled the room, as people stared at Victoria with admiration.

El General Del Calderóne was wearing a handsome white uniform embroidered with gold edging, and stiff with a plethora of medals. He was of medium build, but stocky, with salt and pepper hair, dark eyes, and a mustache that was always waxed. Occasionally he would glance at his shiny black boots that one of his guests had brought to him as a gift from Germany. "Fine quality!" he would say.

He was seated at the head of the largest dining room table Victoria had ever seen. All eyes, ears, bodies, and souls were directed to *El General*, who spoke loudly and boastfully. His eyes were always watchful and sharp, like a hawk. He was a man who studied each individual carefully, with much keenness, discerning their strongest and weakest points. He knew the intricacies of war and was a brilliant authority on military games. His was always the last word.

Two Doberman pinschers lay at the side of *El General*, guarding him like a demigod. "They will not hurt you unless you try to strike them," *El General* remarked to *Don* Federico, who was startled by the dogs' presence in the dining area. "We keep them around for protection against the Indian workers that work the sugar cane fields. We simply cannot trust them. Never know what they will try next! Those that try to run away don't get very far," *El General* said, feeling proud of himself and his accomplishments. "Where would they have it any better? And if they do run away, the dogs will hunt them down." He took a slip of wine and continued, "This one is the mother of one of the dogs I gave you." He took another slip and said, "I'll bet that dog must be getting big. They are good hunting dogs, and you could sure use him at your hacienda."

"Yes," remarked *Don* Federico. "He's become a wonderful dog. Thank you!"

The general had business guests who had been staying at the castle for several days. Seated next to the general was a German by the name of Von Schmidt. He was tall, with blond hair, blue eyes, and dressed in an impressive navy-blue uniform. His white captain's cap was lying on top of the table next to his silverware. On the opposite side of Von Schmidt was a tall, thin, dark-skinned Frenchman introduced by the name of Bruno Pue, also wearing a dark navy, Italian silk suit. All the men stood up with a glass of wine when Victoria was introduced by Ricardo as his *novia*, his wife-to-be.

"Where did you find such an extraordinary beauty?" exclaimed Von Schmidt to Ricardo, holding up his wine glass as though in a toast. "My goodness," he said, in his broken English, "all of the ladies here are so beautiful!" He turned his attention to Ricardo's sister, Magdalena, who was petite, fair-skinned, and an exquisite beauty. She sat next to her mother, *Señora* Del Calderóne, on the opposite side of the table from Von Schmidt. Magdalena was three years younger than Ricardo and had just returned from attending the *Colegio de San Blas*, where she had received a formal education and catechism from the nuns there.

Victoria raised her wine glass with boldness and said, "Thank you for your compliment," to Von Schmidt, who was stealing curious glances at Ricardo's sister. Magdalena, in her sequined, low-cut, black lace gown, turned crimson as she looked down at her plate.

"Lucky, my dear man, I'm just plain lucky," Ricardo addressed Von Schmidt with his wine glass held high. He was taunting the German across the table, flaunting his fiancée in his face. There was loud laughter and the conversation continued with the men only, because the women rarely said a word, only whispered among themselves as the first course of dinner was served.

At one point, *La Señora* Del Calderóne studied Victoria and commented on her beautiful dress, and how appropriate the diamond and opal earrings and necklace were. She then fell silent and nothing more was heard from her during the rest of the meal. Magdalena would cautiously glance at Victoria, but acted cold and indifferent. Perhaps the gloom and doom atmosphere from the women was because of Luis, Ricardo's brother, who had joined the revolt against his father's regime and was considered an outcast to the prideful and egoistical *El General*. His name was never mentioned and everyone acted as if he had never existed. Instructed by *El General* never to say the name of *Luis* in his presence, *La Señora* was heartbroken. Luis was her youngest and the most beloved by her.

The conversation was sprinkled with jokes about the unsightly blue and purple bruise on *Don* Federico's head, until he explained to the group about the events that had happened at the gold mine, and how close he had come to dying. The conversation switched to lighter topics, and there were many comments and laughter as the evening progressed and dinner was served.

First on the menu was shrimp cocktail, which was placed in a beautiful cut glass dish and accentuated with a delicate tomato sauce. Each of the guests had his or her own waiter, who kept filling their cut-crystal glasses with water, and had towels draped over their arms. The shrimp was followed by a delightful soup of mixed vegetables and rice, and then a large salad. The main entrée was lobster, crab, squid, and snails—called *escargot*.

"My friend Bruno Pue was kind enough to bring us this delicacy from the wonderful country of France," exclaimed *El General* boisterously, happy about his gallant military career and the prosperity that had brought him such good friends. He motioned with his wine glass toward his French visitor, who was smiling at him. "Enjoy!" he exclaimed, standing up and turning to acknowledge everyone at the table. *El General* was the type of individual who had acquired so much wealth, one couldn't help but bask in his glow.

Don Federico took one look at the food they were being served and whispered into Victoria's ear, "How am I supposed to eat these hard-shelled critters? Especially the lobster, with its hard shell? I didn't bring a hammer with me! And I don't know if I can stomach the snails!"

Victoria began laughing. Ricardo overheard him. "You use these," he remarked, pointing to the instrument looking like a surgical tool lying on the table in front of him. He picked it up and began showing *Don* Federico how to crack open the shell. "Yes, you can use your hands, pull the meat out, and dip it in the rich butter. You'll love it! But, first of all, you better put your napkin on your lap and the other one on your chest, because it will be messy, and you wouldn't want to get it all over your suit." They all laughed. The conversation quieted down as they all began eating, and the servants brought in large plates of sliced papaya and mango on ice.

The scrumptious meal was followed by serenading musicians entertaining around the dining table with a guitar and a violin. The guests drank hot coffee and ate their dessert pastries made by a French chef that Ricardo had hired and brought back to teach the Calderóne kitchen staff French and European cuisine. He wanted to impress his family, creating a wider range of menu items utilizing French and Italian dishes—different foods, besides the *masa* for *tortillas, black beans, and arroz*.

Victoria noticed that from time to time, *El General* would cautiously glance at a young peasant girl serving the food. Her hair was in braids, and she had a red hibiscus flower in her hair. When she noticed *El General* staring at her, she would blush and cast her eyes to the floor in embarrassment.

"Mexico," said the arrogant Bruno Pue, "is my kind of country. Here, with money, you can buy anything. Look at our friend, *El General*. Here, he has everything. This is a paradise, with all the food and all the women you could want—all the pleasures!" He then toasted with his glass of wine and made a salute to the *General*.

Von Schmidt laughed loudly, saying, "That's why we must proceed with our plans. The *General* is very generous with his gifts and our stay at his villa. We will have to provide more guns and ammunition from Germany to help him in his cause."

"I'll be leaving in a couple of days." commented *El General*, and he smiled, then took a sip from his wine glass. "Díaz is getting a little concerned about the border incidents, but nothing is too big for me to handle. Huerta will go with me to the border. It seems that several bandits have risen against our government. We will take care of those who want to start a revolution. We have had peace for over thirty years in this country with Díaz, and now Francisco Madero, with the help of other bandits, has started to stir ideas in the peasants' heads. I hear he is a real weirdo." The rest of the guests and Ricardo laughed, while *Don* Federico flinched at those remarks.

As they retired to the grand *sala*, the musicians followed. *Don* Federico smoked his cigar and took a seat with the rest of the foreign guests, while Victoria and Ricardo sat together on a white loveseat, holding hands. Champagne was served after each became comfortably seated.

Then, the finale: a beautiful young lady with long, black hair wearing a white mantilla draped over a high tortoise comb, with a red rose in her hair, appeared and began singing songs from Spain. She was dressed in the Spanish traditional peasant fiesta costume of colorful embroideries, laces, and jewelry, with a bright red, fringed shawl, and she was playing castanets. Victoria noticed that *La Señora* Del Calderóne had not joined them but had retired to her quarters. Victoria found it very strange. She found it even stranger that the singer had not joined them at dinner. She also noticed that Magdalena had also disappeared and was not with the guests.

"Who is she?" Victoria questioned Ricardo.

"Her name is Maria Conesa," whispered Ricardo, "a professional singer from Spain. She has been performing and visiting the capital city. When my father was getting his orders from President Díaz, and Huerta, the head commander of the Mexican military, he was so impressed with her that he invited her to stay with us for a month."

"Is she staying in one of the guest cottages?" she asked innocently.

Ricardo remained still, as if avoiding the question, and squeezed her hand hard.

"Is she staying at the cottages?" she whispered again.

Annoyed, Ricardo turned and whispered in her ear. "It's best not to talk while Maria is singing. It's impolite and not proper. I will tell you later."

Maria Conesa was very attractive and extremely talented. Her voice echoed throughout the grand *sala* like a sweet violin singing *Cielito Lindo*. Using her fan, and the language of love, her sparkling eyes were directed toward *El General*. And when she finished her performance of *Granada*, *El General* stormed up to the singer, clapping boisterously, and displaying her with pride to Von Schmidt and Bruno Pue, both of whom also stood and clapped. *El General* hugged her and then presented her with a black velvet box.

"That reminds me," said Ricardo seriously addressing Victoria, his face flushed from the embarrassing situation. "Let's go outside in the moonlight. I also have a present for you. I have been waiting for the right moment, and this seems to be the right time." He stretched his hand out, and Victoria took it and followed him through the high French doors out into the night, where the flames of twenty torches reflected in the mirroring ponds in the courtyards. He handed her a small velvet box. And when she opened it, she could not believe her eyes. It was a diamond bracelet.

"Let me put it on for you," Ricardo said, with his flamboyant charm and grace. "It has a certain clamp that is difficult to put on. And guarantee not to come off!"

"Ricardo!" said Victoria, ecstatic with delight. "It so beautiful!" She kissed his cheek.

"There will be many more gifts once we are married," he said. "I want my wife to be the prettiest and most elegant in all of Monterrey. I want everyone to be envious of my fortune, being the *General's* son and having a beautiful wife."

"Is this what your father gave Maria Conesa also," she said without thinking, admiring her bracelet and being impressed with the singer's performance and her beautiful voice.

Ricardo's eyes narrowed and, in the light of the flaming torches, his brown eyes turned to blazing topaz. "The women in this country never ask questions, especially of their husbands. Women are supposed to keep quiet and keep to themselves. They have no rights and do what their husband tells them. Whatever my father gave Maria Conesa is his business, and in this household we never question, much less ask him, what his activities are. My father is a good provider and very generous with his guests. Did you not have a good time tonight?" He said it in a disappointing tone. Her asking questions at the Castle of Del Calderóne were not the genteel thing to do.

Victoria stood somber and shocked, not knowing whether to cry or apologize. She felt mortified by her innocent remarks. "I was just curious," she answered lamely, knowing she had hit a nerve. "I'm not used to the customs in Mexico!" But she was too rebellious and was not going to back off. Instead of being glad with the diamond bracelet, she was more concerned about a woman's status in the household. "If they're married, women have every right to speak and ask questions of their husbands about what he does!" Her speech became louder, and her eyes narrowed, becoming like cold steel.

Ricardo felt the tension building. He could see that Victoria was like an explosive ready to blow, and he realized she was unfamiliar with the Mexican customs, especially the rich landowners, *hacendados* like his father, who could afford to have several mistresses, any kind, and any age. "Now, now," he said soothingly, then grinned, trying to stem the tide of her anger. "Here we are, my love, just getting acquainted, and already we are fighting about unimportant things. Calm yourself!" he said, then added, "Let's change the subject to more pleasant things. Did I tell how extraordinarily stunning you look tonight? Your Aunt Emma did a beautiful job on your dress. She must have spent many hours and days completing it. And the earrings and necklace do fit your costume perfectly. I know Mother was very pleased."

He looked away for a moment. "Tomorrow is another day, and maybe we can go riding. You'll love the horse I picked for you to ride, an Arabian, bought from an owner in Cuba. My father paid a ransom price, but he was well worth it."

"You're right," Victoria said, calming down. "Tomorrow is another day, and I have a lot to think about, especially in our relationship!" She said it very seriously, giving him something to contemplate also. "We will go riding." Her instincts were calculating and difficult to control, and she was not going to be disciplined. "I must tell my father goodbye, for he is leaving very early in the morning to see about my mother, who is not feeling well."

Ricardo changed expressions, displaying his facade of congeniality, and replied, "Come, you're right. You've had a long day and need your rest. I will escort you back to the grand ballroom to see your father and then bring you back to your cottage, where you can retire for the evening. I think your father and the other men are engaged in a game of poker in father's private library. The gambling will be high stakes tonight, especially with Von Schmidt and *Señor* Pue."

⌘　⌘　⌘

Many hours had passed. Although in her sleeping chambers, Victoria was restless and unable to sleep. She tossed and turned in her bed, thinking about her marriage to Ricardo and trying to analyze her situation. Things were happening too fast. Her feelings were caught in a whirlpool of emotions that was dragging her under. Her parents wanted her to spend time with Ricardo so she could get to know him better. They knew how easily her temper could be sparked. She was a rebel by nature and would fight anything that stood in her way. She thought of the ridiculous customs of the old days, when rich families promised to marry their sons to other rich couples' daughters. *Dim-witted ways*, she thought, feeling uncomfortable with the manners in the Castle del Calderóne. *What if you weren't compatible with the other individual? Life would undoubtedly be hell, and you couldn't divorce them, being Catholic. So the woman suffers, regardless of the conditions or situation. Women were only used for the convenience of the men. This was truly a man's world. But times are changing*, she thought. *Things are going to be different.* She wondered about her father, who had little to say to her since he returned from his trip. Perhaps he was still in a state of shock after his terrible ordeal in the Sierras. And there was still the mystery about Juan. What in God's name had happened to him?

Little by little, Victoria had tried to understand her father's and Juan's ideals in liberating the poor, giving them their freedom and land, giving the poor Indian people an education, so they could read and write. She was wild with thoughts as the brilliant light of the moon shone its luminous beam upon her face.

Suddenly, she thought she heard sounds of shuffling feet outside her cottage. She lay motionless, holding her breath, as she heard several voices coming from behind the cottage. Victoria grabbed her robe and opened the door quietly. She walked outdoors barefooted and peeked through the trees and flowering bushes into the darkness. She caught sight of a couple talking; one of them was the attractive Indian girl she had seen earlier serving in the dining room. Her hair was no longer in braids, but combed out, flowing loose. She was wearing a white transparent gown and through the dim light, Victoria could see there was nothing underneath. With her was a young Indian boy she had seen working in the kitchen. They stood taking softly in the dark in a conflicting conversation. Victoria listened carefully, for the wind was in her favor.

"Go, Amparo!" the young Indian boy said desperately. "Go! You must go to the guest's bedroom. You have been ordered to go! You must obey *El General's* orders. If not, you and I will be punished. You know what will happen! Remember the last time?" the Indian boy spoke in anguish, pushing Amparo toward the guest cottage.

"It happens every time *El General* brings guests into his castle," cried Amparo, suffering in a state of sorrow. "I hate to sleep with his guests!" she sobbed. "It's not normal, but what can I do?" She put her head on the young boy's shoulder and cried bitterly. Minutes passed before Amparo straightened herself and looked into the Indian boy's eyes. "And you?" she said. "What are you going to do? Please don't do anything foolish!"

"I can take care of myself. I'll be all right. Don't worry about me, Amparo, it's you I worry about. You have to please the guests, or tomorrow we'll have hell to pay. You must go! Go, quickly!"

Victoria saw Amparo put her *rebozo* around her head and hurry toward the guest cottage. The Indian boy stood watching until she disappeared around the corner. He then sat quietly on a stone step and put his head in his hands, clearly worried sick about his sister.

Slowly, and with much interest, Victoria stepped forward. The night had become darker, with a heavy chill, for the moon was behind a cloud.

"Psst!" whispered Victoria softly, as she gently walked to where the Indian boy sat.

Startled by her presence, he immediately jumped up, and with much respect bowed to her, saying nothing. His eyes were big and in shock, and he was taking in deep breaths.

"Did you say her name was Amparo? Where is she going?" questioned Victoria to the boy.

The Indian boy could not look Victoria straight in the eye. He was nervous and fidgety. He kept looking down toward the stone steps and would not speak.

"Tell me!" demanded Victoria again. "I heard most of your conversation already."

"To one of the guest bedrooms," the boy struggled to answer, obviously feeling much shame.

"Amparo has been *El General's* mistress, since we were brought here to live. When he brings guests, she is supposed to please them, too. She is supposed to do what he tells her to do."

"What happens if she doesn't?"

"I'm her brother, *Señorita*, and *El General* will have me killed if she doesn't do what he tells her. *El General* uses me to persuade Amparo not to resist his commands. She will be sent away to other haciendas, and we will be separated. I don't want that for her, we are the only ones left in our family. *El General* and his soldiers came, killed our parents, and took us from our village and brought us here to live. We will do anything to stay alive. I must go, too. I'm supposed to go to the German man's quarters." After telling his story, he looked up at Victoria with misty eyes.

"You're—you're sleeping with the German man—Von Schmidt?" gasped Victoria.

"Yes, *Señorita*, but I will survive. It's Amparo that I'm worried about. If she becomes pregnant, it will be too bad for her. I must go!"

Victoria stood in shock, not believing her ears, as the young Indian boy quickly disappeared. Was this what power and money brought? What kinds of things were going on in Castle Del Calderóne? People with money are forcefully using these poor Indian people as slaves. *El General* sleeps with whomever he desires, since his wife has no say. Here in Mexico, the husband who has money, has a wife and several mistresses. What happened to their Catholic religious vows?

At sixteen she was starting to realize that life was more complicated than she thought. She stood outside for how long, she didn't remember. She pulled her robe about her more snugly, feeling a chill that had overtaken her, forgetting that she was barefooted. Ricardo knew all these things and was keeping it from her. She wondered if that was the main reason he didn't want her to ask questions. *Women are supposed to keep their mouth shut and not question anything!* The words crowded everything else out of her mind. She slowly walked inside her cottage, removed her robe, and fell into bed.

⌘ ⌘ ⌘

The following day, Victoria rode with Ricardo out into the countryside on the handsome Arabian horse, all the while admiring the beautiful morning and the view of the high Sierras. She was partial to the twilight colors that overlaid the purple mountains surrounding the spectacular Castle Del Calderóne.

For riding, Ricardo wore light brown riding pants, a beautiful white shirt with lace on the cuffs, high alligator boots, and his Yancey Derringer hat, looking very French and very charming. He wanted to show her the sugar cane fields, in which hundreds of *peóns*, in their loose white cotton shirts and trousers and large sombreros, were cutting the cane with razor-sharp machetes and loading the long stalks into flat-bed mule wagons.

Ricardo pointed out the process. "The cane is taken to the grinding mill, where hundreds of gallons of syrup are put into silver cases, set into hot ovens, then put out into the hot sun, with light cotton tarps over them, and dried for days, turning the white sugar into *piloncillo*. Father has taken pounds of it to President Díaz, General Huerta, and the rest of the cabinet members who requested it, and they loved it. We have taken many pounds during *Las Posadas* to your grandfather and grandmother as our gift to them. We use it quite frequently for making many of the Mexican pastries and to dip fruit into the boiling syrup. Come, I'll show you how to eat one of the purple stalks. The clear white meat is coarse but delicious," he said, sitting proudly on his horse. "*Señor* Mendoza!" Ricardo yelled and ordered the fore-man of the crew to cut a cane stalk and bring it over to him.

Victoria impatiently decided to get off her horse to view the workers from the ground. After handing a large stalk to Ricardo, *Señor* Mendoza kindly began helping Victoria off her horse. Being in a hurry, she slipped, and the hem of her long skirt got caught and snagged on the edge of her saddle. She fell, landing on top of *Señor* Mendoza, and ripping part of her skirt into a long shred.

Ricardo became furious and blamed *Señor* Mendoza. He jumped from his horse and lashed him with his horsewhip without stopping while the old man lay on the ground. The whip slashed his cotton shirt and cut his skin, as blood spattered from his back, shoulders, and arms. The old man yelled in terror and begged for mercy. The rest of the *peóns* stopped working and watched the torturing with intense fear. They stood with fists clenched, sweat on their foreheads, and hatred in their eyes, glaring at Ricardo with all the stoic patience of their race, but unable to do anything.

Victoria, mortified, began shouting in the midst of the chaos. "Stop!" she shrieked, and held her hands up in the air, getting in between the old man and Ricardo. "You can't do this, Ricardo! It was my fault, not the old man's!" Her face reflected her despair and horror. She squatted over the old man, seeing to his wounds. "This is cruel and unkind! People shouldn't be treated this way! This is worse than the Negro people were being treated before the Civil War in the United States. And it took a horrible war to stop this kind of torture." She was incensed at the treatment of poor *peóns*, who were treated worse than slaves, more like animals. She began to realize that they had no rights or any status of any kind and were completely ruled by landowner rules and laws. Freedom was a dream for them, and she started to understand more of what Juan had told her about the Mexican *peóns* and their sufferings.

"Victoria!" commanded Ricardo, infuriated. "Get on your horse!"

"I'm going to see about this poor old man!" she replied indignantly. She stood up and looked at Ricardo with hate in her eyes, her hands clenched in anger. "You can't leave him like this! He needs treatment!" With supreme self-control and confidence, she maintained her courage and disregarded Ricardo's orders. She knelt over the wounded man. Ricardo stormed toward her, grabbing her by the arm. She pulled away and stood there glaring at him with all the hate she possessed. "Don't touch me," she said angrily. "Leave me alone!"

Ricardo grabbed Victoria's hands. "What's come over you? Get on your horse, before trouble starts." He glanced toward the sugar cane workers and said: "Get back to work! Immediately! Do what I tell you!" he shouted, striking his whip hard against his open palm. There was a strong murmur among the workers, as they took several steps forward, and then stopped, as if wanting to help Victoria. Ricardo aggressively reached for Victoria's arm and insisted she get on her horse immediately. He felt an uneasy sense of danger here among the *peóns*. They were too many, and with sharp machetes, they could overpower him with no trouble. He grabbed Victoria's wrist roughly, and as he stepped back, the clasp on the diamond bracelet broke, and it flew into the grass.

ROOTS OF INDIFFERENCE

⌘ ⌘ ⌘

An hour later, they reached the Castle Del Calderóne's stables. Neither had said a word the entire way back. They dismounted, as several *peóns* took the reins of their horses. They began walking back to the guest cottage, when Ricardo spoke. "I'll get the diamond bracelet fixed and bring it to you at the convent. I'm sorry for that unfortunate scene. But with the Indian workers, you have to tell them what to do, or nothing ever gets done. They all need discipline. The majority of them are all worked up about rumors of an upcoming revolution. They are dangerous, and ready to fight at any provocation. It's a good thing they don't have guns and ammunition, or they would have killed us both. It was very foolish of you to disobey my orders, making me look like a fool. Don't ever do that again!" He ordered.

"The *peóns* don't look like they are dangerous to me. They are just poor laborers wanting to survive," said Victoria harshly, taking off her gloves, and dragging her torn skirt on the ground as she turned her back on Ricardo and walked away. Her pace was fast and furious and the tone of her voice was escalating. "They are just illiterate! They just need to be educated! If they knew how to read and write, it would be so much better for everyone, and much better for Mexico!"

"That goes to show you how little you know about Mexico and its people, my love," Ricardo countered, trying to match her pace. He caught up to Victoria as she reached her cottage door. "This is your last day here in our home, and we'll have a special dinner tonight for you, my love," he said, in a sarcastic dominating manner, almost as though she had been an imposition to his family. "We have a band of *mariachis* that are going to entertain this evening. We'll see if you enjoy it! We will probably have dinner out in the patio. Try to wear something warm. Wear something beautiful, but cover yourself," he ordered. "We'll get your skirt fixed."

Victoria stood by the door, angered by the orders given, and replied, "I'll try to make myself presentable as best I can, especially to your family."

Ricardo smiled, then gave her a kiss on the cheek and disappeared down the corridors.

Victoria stood numb inside her cottage thinking, *what terrible injustices are occurring here in Mexico! I feel so sorry for the old Indian worker and his struggling people! Why did Ricardo beat him the way he did?* She was more convinced about what Juan had told her, time and time again about the difference in the two classes of people. The rich got richer, and the poor were damned. She had been with Ricardo and his family for three days and was already getting nostalgic for the Hinojosa's hacienda. She felt a strong commitment to her parents and grandparents, and she was already homesick to see Felicia and to tell her everything that had happened.

CHAPTER 17

Victoria had spent three days with the Del Calderóne family, and while on her way back to her grandparent's hacienda, she was recalling the long memorable days. Her head was resting comfortably on the cushioned window of the horse-drawn coach, viewing the passing countryside. She was aware of an increasing anxiety to see her parents, grandparents, and Felicia. She had been wined and dined and entertained like a European queen enjoying all the luxuries and comforts that any human being would cherish, and yet all the money in the world could not take away her empty feeling. She still felt uncomfortable with the Del Calderónes, and wondered how much of his nature Ricardo had inherited from *El General.* She felt she could get to like Ricardo, if he weren't so arrogant and dependent upon the luxuries, which were so important to him, as if those things made him a real man; however, he had been raised in that style of living and could not be changed.

She remembered early this morning, *El General* laughing derisively while departing for the bordering state of Chihuahua, saying that he had received word that many of the *Federalist* troops had been killed, including many of the *Guerrilleros* who had started the Revolution. She must tell her father this news. He would be interested, since he was empathetic with Madero and his cohorts. *El General* had laughed out loud, telling his guests at breakfast how the *bandido*, Pascual Orozco, had stripped the dead *Federalist* soldiers' clothes and mailed them to President Díaz. The President replied that the uniforms were only the wrappers, and for Orozco to send him more tamales. Everyone in the dining room roared with laughter, including Ricardo, who had also made a sarcastic remark.

From the news dispensed by *El General* and the comments he made, it seemed the northern border states were already aflame with war. The poor *Mestizos*, with their vast knowledge of the land, were also taking up arms, willing to strap on cartridge belts, and become an unnamed army without uniforms. The name of Francisco Madero was becoming a thorn in the side of the *Federalist* troops and President Díaz.

The driver of the coach slowed down guiding the horses to the right of the dirt road out of respect. Several Indian men passed by carrying a small pink coffin, while all the women were dressed in black, crying and fingering their rosaries. As they shuffled by, Victoria overheard one of the women remarking that the little girl was so much better off now, what with the predictions of impending disaster in Mexico.

An hour had passed when the driver came to a stop again to let another group of several Indians in white muslin clothing file by on the narrow road. They were carrying large, heavy loads of hay and wood on their backs. With them were ten goats, one with a loud bell hung around its neck, which reminded Victoria of Blanca, back in Spanish Acres. This procession was followed by many burros loaded with barrels of water. Several women walked along the road hauling water jugs on top of their rebozo-covered heads. Below the road in a small creek, she viewed Indian women pounding their laundry on the surface of the rocks.

⌘   ⌘   ⌘

It was getting close to the noon hour when they finally reached the Hinojosa's hacienda. The sun was high, but in the shadows there was a cold and bitter chill. This was still January, but soon the green leaves would sprout again from every direction, continuing the cycle of life.

Like wine to Victoria's spirit, the whole family was outside to warmly greet her. Victoria thanked the driver and began hugging everyone, while her baggage was being taken upstairs by the servants.

Wide-eyed with glee, Felicia joined Victoria, and they both hurried upstairs hugging and giggling. Felicia kept looking both ways, talking louder and asking questions, which was very uncommon to her personality. Occasionally she would look behind her, checking if anyone was listening. "Ricardo is so handsome. Do you like him, Victoria? Did you have a good time? What do you think of him?" In all the excitement, her questions were like rapid firing bullets, which made Victoria wonder.

When they turned the corner, toward the long halls, Victoria noticed on Felicia's face a tension that could not be missed. They reached their room, and Victoria fell backward on the bed, with her hair sprawling on the pink satin bedspread. She was so happy to see Felicia. "I have so much to tell you—so much has happened!"

"You have no idea what has happened since you left," interrupted Felicia, out of breath as she closed the door and stood eying Victoria like an intellectual force keeping a secret.

"What could have possibly happened?" replied Victoria, turning to face Felicia, and sighing with exhaustion. She was not interested in small talk.

"Ricardo is handsome—but so is Juan!" she whispered. "He was here, yesterday afternoon!"

"Who was here?" questioned Victoria, shocked.

"Juan!" Felicia put one finger to her lips. "I'm telling you, he was here yesterday."

"Juan! Here!" Victoria uttered, almost speechless. Like a mechanical doll, she quickly straightened herself up on the bed. Her hazel eyes were like two candles that had been lit. "No way," she said, doubting. "What happened? Tell me, quickly! My God! Juan? Here?"

"I had decided to go riding yesterday afternoon—"

"And—"

"—out into the orchards, and I had stopped and gotten off my horse to let him drink from the creek, when I noticed someone was behind me. I was scared, of course, because of the incident when the *peón* grabbed my leg—"

"Tell me!" pleaded Victoria, impatient with Felicia's detailed account.

"I turned around when two arms took hold of me from behind. I almost screamed, but he put his hand over my mouth. I struggled, but, as I turned quickly around, of all people— and speaking of the devil—it was Juan! He was looking right into my eyes. My heart was pounding, and I almost melted as I stared back at him. He must have thought that I was you." Felicia could not speak without her hands and had them flying in every direction. "Anyway, he wanted to know where you were staying at this time. I told him you were visiting a family several miles away at another hacienda and were coming back tomorrow. But anyway, he also wanted to talk with your father, about the gold mine, and explain what happened, and anyway—"

"Oh, stop with the anyways and get on with the story!" retorted Victoria, thinking that her cousin had the sense God gave a goose.

"I felt so sorry for Juan. As we walked towards the hacienda, he told me that hours after he had given the money to the *bandido* Castillo, he had been ambushed. He received a big gash on the side of his face, with black and blue marks on his forehead, and had been left for dead. Peasants found him lying on the road and took care of him. It took several weeks, almost a month, before he recovered."

"I knew something like that had happened!" Victoria smiled triumphantly. "I knew something terrible had happened to him. I knew Juan wouldn't have put Papá in harm's way. I knew he'd have some kind of an explanation."

"Yes, yes, but that's not all of it," Felicia nervously continued. "When your father and grandfather saw Juan approaching the hacienda, your grandfather demanded that he get off his property. Your father told him to leave as well. Your grandfather called Juan trash and that he was also a *bandido*, just like the rest that had been hired to kill your father. I've never seen your grandfather so angry! He pulled out a revolver and told him to get out or he would shoot him like a dog."

She paused and looked at Victoria sympathetically. "Poor Juan! He tried to explain to your father what had happened, but your father told him to leave, and that he didn't want to talk about the mine anymore. Your father said he was finished with the gold mine, and that he didn't believe a word Juan said. Juan kept backing off, while trying to speak with your father, and all the time your grandfather was pointing the gun at him. Juan spoke about you, about how much he loved you, and how he wanted to marry you. Your father and grandfather both laughed in his face. Your father told him about Ricardo Del Calderóne, your future marriage to him, and how special you were, you being his only daughter, and that he wanted the very best for you. He said you were marrying the best, with money and power, and he, Juan, did not have a pot to pee in."

"Father said that!" gasped Victoria. She held her right hand to her forehead and went silent for a few moments. "Dear God! I can't believe this is happening!" Then both hands covered her face and she murmured between her fingers, falling to pieces emotionally. "Juan will not want to see me anymore. It's all ruined! It's all over! It's finished! I can't believe this! Oh! Dear God!" She began crying hysterically.

"No, no!" insisted Felicia. "You have it all wrong. Juan does love you and told your father that he was going to have you regardless of what anyone said. That was when your father pointed his own gun at Juan's chest and told him to leave immediately or he would shoot him like a common thief."

After saying those words, Felicia checked the long halls to see if anyone was around or was listening and came back and closed the door again. "I'm telling you that Juan will be here, tonight! He told me to tell you. He wants to see you and talk with you. He wants you to meet him at the entrance of the hacienda. This is so romantic!" she said. "Tonight," she said, excitement dancing in her eyes, "this very night!"

"Tonight!" answered Victoria.

"Tonight, at the entrance of the gates, Juan will be there. He will be waiting for you!"

"How are we going to work it? How are we going to see Juan?"

"We?" answered Felicia, puzzled. "We, it's always 'we.' 'We' are going to get into trouble, especially if the family finds out. Trouble, that's what you mean, if 'we' get caught."

"Felicia, you have got to help me! I have got to see him!" Victoria pouted, with misty eyes and directed her gaze to the floor. Her mind was working overtime. She wanted sympathy from her cousin as she poured out her thoughts. "I have always helped you, when you needed it, and you have got to help me tonight! If I don't see him, I probably will never see him again!"

"All right, what do you want me to do?" uttered Felicia, helpless.

"You can go with me and keep guard," replied Victoria, feeling the tide turning her way. "If we wear our black capes and in the dark, no one will see us."

"Remember, you talked me into it. Remember!"

⌘ ⌘ ⌘

As the nighttime drew near, purple shadows slowly fell across the breathless hush of the enormous hacienda. They waited until the household retired to their quarters for the night. The two girls crept quietly down the side steps of the mansion and glanced both ways. Victoria took the lead as they made their way toward the front gate path to the edge of the flowering bushes and pinos orchards. A cold night breeze had risen, and in the distance they could see the heavy, thick fog on the slopes of the dark purple mountains. They stood together, like they always had since childhood, not knowing what would happen or what steps to follow next. The moon kept peeking from behind dark, stormy clouds as the wind became chilly, unpredictable, and uncomfortable.

ROOTS OF INDIFFERENCE

From behind one of the working quarters, the same *peón* who had been whipped for grabbing Felicia's leg, noticed a movement among the bushes and pinos trees. Eyeing the figures with keen intensity, he realized it was the two *Tejanas* girls—*el patrón*, Señor Hinojosa's relatives—and his hatred flared. His wounds were not completely healed, and his anger overtook all emotions. He decided it was time to get even. He stalked the two girls, glaring at them with unbridled vengeance. He had been drinking hard Mexican mescal and had been ordered, early during the evening, to take his turn keeping guard on the hacienda's grounds. He huddled patiently beneath the bushes, watching to see where the two girls were going in the late hours of the night. His lustful passion was enhanced with liquor, developing into a magnitude of bravery, and he was determined to get his revenge.

Victoria motioned to Felicia and pointed toward the sky to wait until the moon had gone behind the hovering, black clouds, making it easier to move forward without causing suspicion. The outdoors at night, inside the Hinojosa's estate was perilous, since there were many guards who stayed awake into the late night and were not to be trusted. In the distance they could see the lights of the city far below, glowing and glittering, becoming shrouded in the oncoming fog.

The two girls followed the path through the edge of the pinos taking them closer to the iron-gated fence. The wind numbed their senses, and they tucked their heads inside their dark, woolen capes. They could hear the crisp sounds of their footsteps gently stepping on the dry leaves in the chilled air. Watching cautiously in all directions, the two girls hurried toward the entrance. When they finally reached the high, stone walls and approached the heavy iron gates, Victoria said in a low whisper to Felicia, "Stay here while I open the gates and see if Juan is out there—somewhere." As she unfastened the iron latch and pulled it upward, the old gate creaked and clanged as she slowly opened it, complaining with a screeching sound that could be heard several yards away.

"I'm afraid," said Felicia, "and I'm cold." She said it in a soft whisper to herself as her voice was lost in the strong wind and the jamming of the iron gates. She saw her impatient cousin's silhouette disappear onto the dark road outside of the stone walls. She pulled her cape and her hood closely around her body and head, and then sat quietly alone near the gates. She wished now that she hadn't mentioned "Juan," for his name had become notoriously dangerous. She was nervous and scared out of her wits. And worse, if her mother found out about this escapade, she would never hear the end of it! Oh, the punishment!

Victoria, with nerves of steel, nudged her cape around her as the night-chilled air was becoming very cold, cutting deep into her bones. She walked out into the middle of the dark, dirt road, taking a risky chance. If anyone was out there in the dark, they would see her.

There were only sounds of the current of air among the trees and the strong, cold breeze that hovered around Victoria's head. The wind suddenly flipped her cape as it blew past her on its way through the jungle of wild bushes and wild pinos along the lonely road. Suddenly, she heard footsteps.

From behind her, a hand reached toward her mouth and one arm grabbed her in an instant, pulling her toward the edge of the road and into the bushes. Victoria shuddered from the shock and numbness, wanting to fight. Everything was happening very fast, as she was being lifted and dragged into the wilderness, her shoes not touching the ground. She felt the warm breath on the back of her neck, as the individual was holding on to her with a strong grip and then laying her down on the cold surface of dry leaves.

"Victoria, it's Juan!"

He was disguised in a *peón* outfit, a dark serape and a large straw sombrero. Underneath he wore the loose, white cotton muslins like the *peóns* wore. His eyes glowed in the dark with joy as he pinned her to the earth and kissed her until her breath was almost gone. His body thrilled with desire. Their love was so strong that in this sacred emotional moment, Victoria felt like there was no winter, no frigid wind, no sorrows, no worries, only warmth and joy.

"You frightened me for a moment," gasped Victoria, trying to recover from the abrupt surprise, her hands held to her chest. "I should have known that you would pull a trick like this." Panting for air, and with her heart pounding in her chest, she tried to straighten herself from the cold ground.

"I didn't want you to scream, *Querida*," he whispered, "and cause an alarm in your grandfather's household. I've been here waiting for you for hours, not knowing whether you'd show up and meet me. Your father will have me shot and killed, if he knew I was out here waiting for you."

"I know! I've heard all about it from Felicia," replied Victoria, still shaken up. She clutched her cape, which had come away loose from her body. She sat up and let her hood down from her head.

"You have no idea how much I have waited for this moment." Juan, sitting beside her, moved closer and kissed her again very passionately. His magnetism was so powerful that no one would be able to resist. His arms tightened around her and drew her closer to him and down to the ground in a breathless kiss. He whispered in her ear. "Victoria, will you come with me?"

Victoria's admiration for Juan had become boundless. She sat up and pulled herself away, looking into his eyes, as if viewing the surface of the apple-green sea. She remained quiet and then spoke softly, "And where would we go?"

"Go with me! I'm going to the state of Chihuahua and fight with Pancho Villa. This is what I wanted to tell you so that you would know. Come with me! We can make a good life together."

"This is not the time to elope," suggested Victoria rationally. "I start school next week and will be there for the next two years, getting an education, which will please my family very much. I don't think this is the right time to discuss our future. I need that education, especially after what I have seen and heard here in Mexico and in Texas."

"More than me?" he said indignantly, and then softened his voice. "I understand," he said, almost apologetic. "I see, I understand. I'm sorry I'm imposing myself on you. I should have known better," he continued. "Is it because I'm not wealthy, as your future husband is, or is it because my family doesn't have power or prestige? Your father and grandfather made sure I knew that—they made me feel like a common *peón*." His head hung down in shame.

ROOTS OF INDIFFERENCE

"Someday, I promise you, I'll be rich and wealthy, coming with prestige. It seems that without money, a person is nobody. Someday I'll have everything in the world I want—"

"No, Juan!" cried Victoria, as she hugged him even more tightly. "I didn't mean it that way. I love you, only you, regardless of the plans my family made a long time ago. I can't help that, but Grandfather Hinojosa's influence and power will destroy you. He will find you and have you killed. Having worked for Díaz, his word here in Monterrey is like a god's; with all of the control he has in politics."

"What do you think I'm doing here? I'm taking the risk of getting killed, right? I even took time to come and talk to your father and explain to him what had happened. It was also an opportunity to see you and love you. My nights have been very lonely without you. This is all I think about, day and night." He cleaved to her tightly and changed the subject. He began playing with her hair. "Your hair is like the ray of sunlight that beams." He took a deep breath and blurted, "I can't live without you!"

"Juan, I do love you, you know that, but I just can't leave with you now. I just can't see myself out on the battlefields, like a *soldadera*, dirty, without shelter, like a commoner. Our love will vanish very quickly under those conditions. You're asking for the impossible at this time."

Juan's looked at the ground in desperation. "It's because you are used to the best things in life," he said sadly. "At this moment, I can only give you my love, nothing else. Perhaps you are right. I'm letting my passions run away with my mind. Just let me know when the right time comes, and I will come from the end of the world for you." He then immediately changed the subject again. "Do you remember Aquiles Serdan from Puebla?"

"I've heard Papá talk about him occasionally."

"Serdan and his whole family were killed by the damn *Federalists* because they were fighting for our cause. Your father will remember him from San Antonio. I was heartbroken. What a shame!"

A chill wind arose, and Victoria covered herself with her cape. Juan noticed that she had started shaking. He hugged her and said, "Victoria, your hands are so cold and you're freezing. You'll have pneumonia. Let's get away from the wind, and hide near the stone walls."

Juan took Victoria's hand, and both stepped out onto the dark road. Making sure the road was clear, they ran to the other side to the warm shelter of the high walls.

"It's better here, no draft," Juan said, as he stretched himself out on the grassy ground.

The moon had appeared once again from behind the dark, stormy clouds, allowing Victoria to view Juan's face. He had a large gash on the side of his face and on his forehead was a black and blue mark. She leaned over to touch his face, caressing it. "How did this happen?" she whispered.

"On the road to the gold mines," Juan answered. "After dealing with the cursed *bandido* Castillo, and giving him the money and the plans for your father. When I was coming down from the mountain, his group of *bandidos* ambushed me on the road to Monterrey. I was left for dead. They beat me and took the rest of the money I had in my pockets. A poor Indian family rescued me, took me in, fed me, and gave me herbs to heal my wounds. For two weeks,

I lay on the floor under straw blankets, trying to recover my senses. I wanted to hurry back to the gold mines to help your father, but—you know the rest."

"That doesn't change my love for you, Juan! What happened at my fiesta that made you leave in such a hurry without saying a word?"

"It's your damn Aunt Emma. Pardon my words against her, but she gossiped to your grandparents about me—how I was paying too much attention to you, and that I was becoming very dangerous, especially if something happened to you."

"Aunt Emma was the cause of all that! You are right, she is a damn witch!"

"I promised your father that nothing had happened when we were out at the pond getting some fresh air. It was your grandfather that informed me to leave you alone. He said plans were being made for your future wedding with Ricardo Del Calderóne, and that it was best for me to leave. I felt like I was intruding. Your father had given me the money to take care of Castillo in the mountains, so I had no reason to stay any longer. My horse and belongings were brought for me to leave. It pleased your *Tía* Emma and your grandfather."

Victoria was embarrassed and lowered her head, "I'm sorry, Juan," she said sincerely.

He smiled. "Speaking of your fiesta, and the trouble I got into, giving you my gift. Was my gift at your fiesta not good enough for you?" he asked. "I don't see you wearing it."

Victoria's hand went to her chest. Her cape fell underneath her to the ground. She was wearing a high collared blouse. "I do have it. I'm wearing it now. I never take it off."

"I don't see it. However, your neck deserves much better jewelry than a plain golden amulet. Your neck is made for fine stones, like rubies, emeralds, and diamonds fit for a royal queen. Your future husband will probably be giving you all of that. He has the money to be able to support your special rich needs." Juan rolled his eyes, and then repressed a smile, teasingly.

His rebuke annoyed her. "I do wear it!" She said, teasing him as she gently unbuttoned her blouse to prove him wrong, not realizing that she was exposing more than she had meant to. Her uncovered chest lured him enticingly. The moon beamed down on her high, firm breasts with the amulet nestled between them.

Touching the charm, and without warning, Juan was overcome by a pang of excitement. He reached for her, his hands on her breasts, feeling and caressing her.

"Juan!" Victoria gasped, not wanting to let her passion overrule her. "I must go! I must leave!" She was trying hard to control her emotions, trying to think of letting go. "If father finds me out here, I'll be in trouble. I must go! No! Not now!"

Juan's mouth stopped her from saying anymore; his sensual lips covered her mouth passionately and then moved to her breasts, kissed them, leaving her with an uncontrollable desire and emotion she had never felt before. His hands were on her legs, feeling and caressing.

"I have waited for this moment for a long time," he uttered, breathless, and kissed her again on her lips and then her breasts. Juan was a master artist in the game of love.

Victoria's soul felt like it had left her body. Thrilled with a forbidden desire as the hour had become a feverish one, her heart was like a butterfly's wing. She was not fighting back anymore, and her body had gone limp, responding to his touch, letting go and welcoming him. Her own body sought him, arched fiercely toward him, without caring. It was hard to believe that within those moments the only thing existing was their own animal desire. She felt no cold, only his warm body. For almost an hour they lay on the ground, but it seemed like hours had passed. The world had come to a complete halt, spinning overhead above them. For the first time in Victoria's life, she had known what it was to be with a man, knowing that love was the most important thing.

The time came when Juan had to leave, and he decided that Victoria needed to get back inside the hacienda. If the family found her and her cousin missing, there would be hell to pay. He reminded her that he would visit her at the convent, when he wasn't fighting for Madero's cause. They savored one final, lingering kiss, and Juan left her with loving memories.

For a moment, she had forgotten all about Felicia. *Oh God, I must go and see about Felicia. Lord! May the saints pardon me! I must say a prayer to the Lady of Guadalupe, and many Ave Marias!*

It took all the strength Victoria could muster to slowly pick herself up, almost in a daze. Frazzled, she walked back to the hacienda's gates. She flung them open, then walked inside and closed them. Her whole body surged with strange sensations and emotions, as she began to fumble with her buttons and cover herself with the cape. Her breasts were aching with pain. *Funny!* She thought. *The night that had been so cold now seemed warm.* Perspiration dotted her forehead, and the chilly wind felt good against it. She did not realize that the adventurous night was not yet over.

Approaching the pinos trees, Victoria heard a commotion coming from underneath the flowering bushes. She could hear voices, but was not able to distinguish them from that distance. *Felicia!* She kept thinking. *What is Felicia doing? Has father found her?*

The moon was partly shining as Victoria came upon the scene. The same worker who had been whipped several weeks ago had Felicia on the ground, trying to rape her. The *peón* had her pinned down with his elbows and was between her legs on top of her. Felicia struggled and tried to scream, but one of his hands was covering her mouth.

A cold hatred and ferociousness overcame Victoria. Looking around, she searched for something solid to cold-cock him with. She hurried toward the irrigation ditch and found piles of rocks. She could hear the peasant talking in raspy whispers and cursing Felicia. "You are a *puta*! Whore! The two of you are *putas*! Whores! Giving your bodies to the *gringos* and everyone else, why not me?" The smell of liquor was strong.

Disoriented among the shadows of the trees, Victoria searched the rock pile and found the biggest rock that she could hold in her hand. Rushing to the scene, she hit the *peón* on the back of the head as hard as she could. He gave out a loud screech. He hollered profanities and staggered up from his position, holding the back of his head, and rushed toward Victoria, forgetting Felicia. Victoria wasted no time with her attacker. She plunged toward him and began throwing blows with the rock in her hand. She was not contented with one fierce blow, but gave him another one, as hard as the force of her will. She hit him again on his head and then again on his temple, hitting him again and again. Blood splattered all over his shirt, until his body went limp and fell to the ground.

"Stop it!" Felicia shouted from the ground, and got up from her compromising position. "You've killed him!" she said, and began crying hysterically in anguish. "Now what are we going to do?" They exchanged quick, horrifying glances.

"God damn it, Felicia. Stop your crying now! This is horse feathers, bullshit! This man was going to rape you, and perhaps kill you later. What was I to do?" she said angrily, trying to catch her breath. "He deserves what he got! I have always protected you, haven't I?" Victoria's jaw was set and there was a cold savagery in her eyes, as she breathed hard.

"This man is dead, and we have his soul to worry about. What are we going to do? How are we going to explain this?" said Felicia, feeling a sickening dread.

"Bullshit feathers! Why cry now! He is stone cold, graveyard dead! This *peón* knew all about us and knew what we were up to from the very beginning. Don't you think for one moment he wasn't going to blab about us to Grandfather and Papá? How ungrateful can you get?"

"I don't know!" cried Felicia, as she wiped her tears with her cape. "I don't want to know!" She turned away, shaking. "All I know is that we have to get back quickly. Someone has surely missed us! We have been gone for a long time. What are we going to do? What are we going to do with the body? He's dead, I know he's dead, and we are responsible!" She bent over and began vomiting, then wiped her mouth with her cape.

"Shut up and stop your damn crying for a minute! Someone will surely hear us and find out we've been gone, and we will have to explain what happened here," Victoria said harshly. "You can help me drag the body out into the road. Outside the gates, anything can happen out there. Who knows, *bandidos* could have attacked him, after all, he was such a good fellow, and got what he deserved! He was just doing his duty, guarding the hacienda."

Felicia, terrified, felt her blood grow cold. Still nauseated, she realized that Victoria's dark side would cause her to go to any length to get her way, even as far as killing a human being and not feeling any remorse. She was grateful that Victoria had protected her from devastating results, but killing someone was different. They would both pay for his soul and regret it later. Victoria seemed to have no compassion, and she was just sixteen years of age. Felicia hated the thought of what Victoria would become as she got older, with her nerves of steel, unafraid of the devil himself. It was true what the old *bruja*, *Dona* Adela had foretold. She had the *roots of evil* in her blood. How cruel life was! And now, she hoped that no one had missed them. They would have a lot of explaining to do if they got caught. They must hurry!

CHAPTER 18

El Colegio de Santa Maria was founded by the Spanish Franciscan monks in the seventeenth century and was situated in the high *Sierra Madre Mountains*, many *kilómetros* southwest of Monterrey. In charge was Mother Superior Maria Angelina. She greeted them dressed in a white, stiffly-starched wimple, looking like a giant penguin ready to put the students' noses to the grindstone.

She addressed the crowd. "Here at this convent we exemplify discipline, and we require it!" She spoke between stained teeth, and her eyes peered over her bifocals. "Everyone, including the girls who are going to be educated, has to be up by six o'clock in the morning. There will be no exception, as they need to be at Mass by six-thirty. Later, the girls will all line up to be inspected for cleanliness, their fingernails, their hair, and so on. Each will be given special assignments to follow during the week. Nobody does the work of another, as each has her own responsibilities. The girls will be kept so busy that they will not have time to think of their families or loved ones. We specialize in etiquette and all fields of art, sewing, needlework from Europe, Central and South American hand embroidery."

Mother Superior eyed the crowd and continued. "We have been very blessed with donations given to us from the very rich and wealthy landowners from the State of Nuevo León and were able to obtain several typewriters that will automatically be put to good use. All of our textbooks, especially *Español*, come from Spain, and we have the best training in all of Mexico. Each girl will be required to attend the medical ward in helping the sick, especially the very young and very old, when they are not studying. We have many women and young girls, from the very poor, who come from far away to have their babies here. For those young girls that leave their little babies, the girls studying here are required to take care of them with the help of the attending nuns."

She paused a moment before continuing. "Outside activity is only permitted on Saturdays and Sundays. If parents want the student to come home with them, they can, but their rooms have to be clean and in order. Permission to leave the premises is only by a signed order. By the time your daughter leaves this *Colegio*," snapped the pure figure of a virgin, "they will be perfect ladies of poise and refinement, ready to enter the social world and become women of grace and charm for their future husbands. I'm so very pleased that you chose our school for your daughter's training."

Don Federico and Emma, sitting in the chapel audience, stood up, clapped and nodded. They seemed very pleased. *Victoria will be well trained, and the Del Calderónes will be pleased and proud. She will become the very example of what a wife should be,* thought *Don* Federico. *All of the gracefulness that comes in the social world will be hers.* He turned toward Victoria and noticed how lovely she looked this morning, with her navy gloves and matching hat—so appropriate with her light gray suit.

Mother Superior rose from the back of her ancient, dark desk and came forward to shake *Don* Federico's and Emma's hands. "I'm so pleased to meet you, *Senor* Juelson, and thank you for the great contribution given to the convent. I promise you that it will be put to good use. We are so glad to have your daughter attend the school. I hear she will be marrying the son of the great *General* Del Calderóne after she finishes with her studies. How wonderful! The *General* occasionally visits our school and is very generous with his money."

"My pleasure," answered *Don* Federico, very pleased. "Please write to me if there is anything I can do to make the school more productive, or if you have any questions regarding my daughter. Thank you for having us. We will be going back to Texas next week."

For the next twenty-four months, Victoria and Felicia would learn reading and writing in *Español*, with the highest degree of all formal learning, which included: discipline in all formal manners of etiquette; formal writing of correspondence; code of behavior in proper speaking; formal dining and table-setting for guests; wearing proper clothing for the occasion; and so much more in protocol. The needlework and embroidery were not to her liking, but were part of the curriculum. She would have preferred riding horses and being outdoors.

To Victoria, Mother Superior resembled a tortoise hiding her body beneath its hard, horny shell. She stood frozen and listened to all the commotion, as the many parents kissed their daughters goodbye, expecting the best achievement from each of them. All were dressed in the newest fashion. From the far side of the room, she viewed the Montoya twins, Rosalinda and Rosa, who had come to her fiesta, kissing their mother and hugging their father. They waved and smiled, showing their large teeth to her from the distance. The word "discipline" kept ringing in Victoria's head. She was not used to that word, and it would be difficult to follow. The nuns running the convent meant business and would see that each girl did their chores and got an education.

Victoria and Felicia were led into a long corridor of Mexican tile floors. Branches of dry bougainvillea vines hung tightly intertwined around the whitewashed, cement arches. Next to their dormitory, which both girls would share, was a small courtyard patio with a small statue of an angel pouring water from a fountain. In the middle of the landscape was a large statue of the Virgin Mary, surrounded by flowering bushes waiting to sprout at the first breath of spring. Toward the large chapel were many trees of *alamos, sausos,* and *jacaranda.* In the spring they would bear violet-colored flowers. Other trees nearby were *árboles de cedro,* a few *ahuehuete,* and an abundance of castor-oil trees. All around the high arches on the grounds were bright red poinsettias stranding a foot high and in full bloom. Out and beyond, were several small huts intermixed along the jungle of trees and bushes where the *peóns* lived and helped with the upkeep of the convent grounds and *El Colegio.* This was a village called *cuadrillas,* meaning small groups of buildings enclosed for their protection by six-foot limestone walls.

There was an excitement in Victoria's memory; like a metaphor, the thrilling moment of seeing new things, thinking of Juan and the events of several nights before. How could she forget the early morning, as they were leaving for the *Colegio*? She heard a commotion from the servants upon finding a body outside the Hinojosa's stone walls. Victoria turned to Felicia, who had been very quiet as she was removing her lingerie from a drawer on her side of the room.

"Did you hear the workers when they found the body this morning as we were leaving?"

"Yes, Victoria, and your grandfather sent for the *Federalists* to investigate the incident. They are suspecting Juan Alvarez of the murder. I couldn't say anything to you because Mother kept hanging on to me until now, and I was afraid and acted surprised, pretending to be shocked. Mother was appalled."

"Who told you that they were suspecting Juan?"

"Mother did! Your grandfather has put two and two together. That young, green-eyed *bandido,* as your grandfather called him. Your grandfather claims he must have wanted some kind of revenge, since there is very little crime committed in this part of the country, especially among the large haciendas."

"In that case, Juan is going to be in grave danger. I hope he leaves the area before anything gets investigated." Victoria frowned and began to worry, chewing on her nails.

⌘　⌘　⌘

Within the two months stay in Monterrey, *Don* Federico took care of the legal implications that came with the gold mine and closed the bank account. The money that was left in the account was given to Jorge's wife and her two children. The moment in time came to return to Texas.

Early in the month of March, *Don* Federico, *Doña* Francisca, Emma and her maids, Fred and young Carlos, began their long trip home. At the border, they reached the town of Reynosa, where Emma and her servants left them and headed back to Mercedes City. *Don* Federico and *Doña* Francisca spent several days with their good friends the Solis, distant cousins by marriage of *La Señora.*

In the town of Reynosa, *Doña* Francisca consulted with her old physician, Dr. Cantu, since they had been informed that Dr. Mendez had left and moved to El Paso. Dr. Cantu saw that her illness was becoming extremely critical and ordered her to see him twice a week. Several sanitariums were recommended for treatment. He gave her some red liquid medicine and several glass bottles of pills, including herbs to boil with tea. This situation automatically complicated the possibility of where they would be staying on the Texas side before arriving at Spanish Acres. Francisca needed her rest and could not travel very far, for her health was fast deteriorating and the coughing exhausted her to the point of fainting.

After spending three days with the Solis family, *Don* Federico decided to leave, and thanked the family for their generous hospitality. The Solis's driver drove the Juelson family in their six-passenger carriage onto a ferryboat crossing the Rio Grande River into Hidalgo, Texas, which several years back had been the county seat. Here they visited with *Don* Florencio Saenz and his family on the *Toluca Rancho* a half-mile into the interior of Texas. *Señor* Saenz owned a grocery store and did his business under a barter system with the surrounding *ranchitos*. As an act of gratefulness for finding sweet well water, he had built St. Joseph's Church, now one of the oldest in the area.

After resting for several hours, they discussed the Mexican conditions across the border and how serious the situation was getting. *Don* Federico warned *Señor* Saenz to move up to Mercedes City. Being so close to the border was dangerous. The bandit raids had become frequent and dangerous.

Finally, after several hours of visiting, the family got on the road and continued on to the home of Emma and Howard Ale in Mercedes City, where Francisca could rest for the night, until they drove north to their hacienda. The thought of having to face Howard Ale irritated *Don* Federico, since Ale was the main plotter of the gold mine conspiracy. However, he had no choice, since Francisca was ill, and he needed to find the best hospital for *La Señora*.

Emma received them with a joyous reception; however, Howard Ale, in a striking suit and smoking his pipe, only nodded to them, displeased, and went into his library and closed the door. "Don't pay any attention to him," Emma remarked, "Howard hasn't been feeling very well. He's had a touch of *resfrío* and is just recovering. So! Pay no mind."

⌘ ⌘ ⌘

After a late supper, all, including Howard Ale, retired to the big *sala* where the women continued to talk about the two girls entering the convent and how proud they were going to be when they graduated. John and Jamie, Fred and Carlos went outside to play. Emma's inferiority complex over her enormous weight and compulsive, habitual eating made her a garrulous conversationalist; she would talk forever, leaving out commas, pauses, and periods in her long, stretched sentences. Her maids in the kitchen had made fresh pumpkin *empanadas*, which they were serving with a hot cup of Mexican coffee for dessert.

Emma launched into another running commentary. "Mercedes City is developing into a very nice place to live, becoming the darling of the small towns around us. Some of the land is already going for only a dollar an acre and many of the *gringos* from up north are buying it like it was going out of style. With the coming of the American Rio Grande Irrigation Company, many lots have been cleared for the newcomers."

Emma's behind wobbled like cold *menudo* as she got up and lumbered toward the large picture window and opened her beautiful scarlet velvet drapes, then the white lace curtains underneath. Pointing across the dirt road, she proudly exclaimed, "Look at the new two-story independent school being built for the white children. A superintendent was just hired. It will be a beautiful school teaching many children." She stopped and sat down in her rocking chair, putting her feet up on her ottoman, in time to eat a dozen of her warm *empanadas* and coffee, and then continued, "They need another teacher for the Mexican children across the tracks, to help *Señora* Agapita Tijerina."

Don Federico and Howard Ale had been quiet throughout the entire evening, listening to the promotion that Emma gave the Juelson's about the town of Mercedes City. The *Don* looked straight into Emma's eyes and commented, "Can't this town find a teacher who can teach those poor Mexican children proper English in reading and writing?"

Howard Ale finally spoke up. "Well, I suppose there are plenty of whites that have an education in this community and can speak Spanish, but they do not want to teach the cockroach, greaser, Mexican children. They don't want to deal with those dirty people."

"Howard!" Emma twisted around, as her face became beet-red from embarrassment and shock. "Stop being so hateful and so disrespectful, speaking that way in front of my family!" She lifted her enormous body from her comfortable position and stomped toward Howard in a nervous dither, as the china and crystal on all the shelves rattled. She stood in front of him, pointing her finger. "You know they need a good teacher with good morals and a high education."

Don Federico interrupted her, "Where is the school?" he asked, his face flushing with anger.

"Why, across the tracks! Next to our Lady of Mercy Church being helped and run by the nuns," exclaimed Emma in her high-pitched voice. "They have added three more rooms to the one room shack, and Father Joseph Couturier has been pleading with us at church, asking if we know of someone to help teach the Mexican children. He needs someone that speaks bilingual that would help and make it easier for the children to better understand— someone with a high education. That's what's wrong with the Mexican children—few know how to read and write. And you, Federico, are the right person."

Howard Ale took a puff from his pipe, made a disgusting face, and got up from his chair. He walked over and stared out his picture window, turning his back on *Don* Federico and the rest of the family. "They don't need to be educated!" His voice rose, laced with hatred and egotism. "All the Mexican fathers do is have more children so they can be put out to work in the fields and farms to support them so they can get drunk on Saturdays and Sundays. They beat their wives when they come home. That's what they are good for, living in dirty and greasy shacks. They don't want to educate themselves."

"Howard!" bellowed a flush-faced Emma.

Don Federico wanted to get up from his chair and punch Howard Ale in the face, but he was a man of much honor and this was not the right time to confront Ale's bigotry. He wasn't about to take advantage of Emma's gracious hospitality. Humiliating her and his family in front of everyone in the grand *sala* was out of the question.

Emma continued, "I don't know of any other person in this part of the country who has the ability to teach the Mexican children both languages. A man with your education should put it to good use, instead of being out in Spanish Acres fooling around with a bunch of cattle. You are wasting your talents."

"Emma is right!" agreed *Doña* Francisca, while resting with her feet on a stool and a warm blanket wrapped around her. She spoke out for the first time. "The Mexican children should have a chance to be educated. Victoria and I taught the children at Spanish Acres and were very successful. With Victoria gone and my illness—" She coughed and grabbed her handkerchief.

Emma shook her head, "See, Francisca is very sick and needs the doctor's attention twice a week. She has no more business out in the boondocks with all that work and cattle, than the man in the moon. She needs to be here, close to the doctor. Use the land that your father got several years ago and build her a house. The land needs clearing, and with so many people moving into this area, you can find many Mexicans to hire, and they would gladly help you. Many of the poor people are without jobs, and with many hungry children to feed."

Don Federico nodded and went silent, rubbing his chin. Here in Mercedes City, the Ales seemed to live very comfortably. Already the small town had elected a new mayor. The *Don* liked the small palms that had been planted along the main street and the many trees and vines that landscaped the newly constructed homes. There were two hotels, the Mercedes Hotel and the American Hotel, that were separated by several lots. A small newspaper, *The Mercedes Tribune* had been started by a man named Isador Mority and already had over two hundred subscribers in the surrounding area. There were several churches: a new First Baptist church, the Seventh - Day Adventist Congregation, Methodist, and The Lady of Mercy Mexican Catholic church across the tracks. On the white side, there was a large feed store, a livery stable, a barbershop, a small bakery café, several mercantile stores, a lumber company, and the Hidalgo county bank. The irrigation company hired the Mexicans coming from across the border by the thousands practically every day. Many tents were provided for the working Mexican laborer. For the first time in his life, the *Don* had to admit to himself that even with the thought of living close to Emma, with her loquacious mouth and overbearing attitude, she was right and made sense. But he would have to confront Howard Ale before he made any more commitments.

"I will have to make the arrangements, but my first concern is Francisca and getting her well. I'm taking Fred to military school next month, and from there I will make plans and see about my father's property that he owned years ago. I'm sure the land is not worth much, but it will need cultivating. Plans have to be made for Spanish Acres, too." *Don* Federico turned to his wife. "We could build us a real nice home here, *querida*, if that's what you want."

Doña Francisca nodded with joy and went into a coughing spell.

Emma was ecstatic. "Just think, Francisca being close to me where we can visit every day and raise our children and be a family again."

"Howard!" said *Don* Federico. "I wonder if you want to step outside with me. I have several things I need to discuss with you that I would rather not say in front of the family."

The two men walked past the kitchen, and onto the adjacent screened porch. *Don* Federico lit his pipe, found a comfortable white wicker chair and sat. He crossed his legs and stared out into the horizon of thick undergrowth, not looking toward Howard Ale, and began talking. "You know that Bernard Hanson and his butcher buddy were arrested in Monterrey. The Mexican *Federalists* have them in jail and have named you as the main conspirator in the plot to have me killed. I knew all along that you had a part in my father's death," *Don* Federico said, without sparing any words.

"That's a damn lie!" shouted Ale.

"Oh?" *Don* Federico turned and glared at a man caught in his own trap. He resembled a frightened, shaking jackrabbit when caught. "It's funny what a dying man will say, especially when they are ready to face a firing squad. Well, that's what your two friends did. They talked."

"Not true! I had nothing to do with anything!"

"But all along, you knew about everything. You even got paid from my father's gold mine. Didn't you? And all along, you knew what Hanson and Hobbs were planning. They were getting the information from you, since you were getting it from your wife. Yet you never bothered to tell me. Was the old fart Judge Parker convinced how rich he was going to be in his old age? I call that blackmail and bribery, and it comes with a high price."

"I've been a retired judge for years," roared Ale, "and I'm much respected in this community, and you had better Goddamn prove your accusations!"

"I don't have to. But you'll have your chance to do all the talking in the world and prove how respectful and decent in this community you really are, when the Texas U.S. Marshal pays you a visit. He's got all of the information that was mailed to him in Austin with your name included in it."

"Goddamn, Juelson!" Ale stared in anger from behind his thick bifocals. "Your father did a lot of bragging about his money and cattle. He would tell us about his gold mine and how it made his life very comfortable. This started as a joke among us, when your father wasn't playing cards. Do you want me to tell you what he was doing, when he wasn't with us?"

"Go ahead and tell me, as if I didn't already know."

"He was sleeping with one of the young Texas Ranger's wives, the redheaded one." Howard Ale went silent for a moment and adjusted his glasses. "Matter of fact, she's been missing for over seven to eight months. No one has seen her. Her husband received money under the table from Hanson. It seems they were not getting enough money for being Texas Rangers, so the idea occurred to him."

"Whose idea?"

"Hanson's, of course!" He answered and went on. "He convinced young Smith of how easy it was to get more money, buy more land since it was so cheap—more cattle—so on and so forth. He used his wife to sleep with your father so they could blackmail him."

"In case you don't know, Smith was killed by *bandidos* close to the village near the gold mines in Monterrey. He tried to escape, and his head was severed."

"Smith killed? What a shame!" He went silent for a moment and began shaking. "Well, I guess nobody will be looking for her now. In an hour, she was gone. Nobody seems to know what happened to her. The incident has never been reported to any newspaper or authority because she had no family—she was an orphan from Mississippi when Smith found her in some whorehouse. The only family she had was young Smith. Hanson convinced Smith to keep quiet, and he would eventually find out her whereabouts."

"No doubt, Hanson would say that." *Don* Federico retorted angrily, looking into Ale's eyes. "You know how my father was killed and how it was done?"

"Hanson!" stuttered Ale. "He waited until we left the Mercedes Hotel that night and then killed him with a sharp knife to the back of the neck, made it looked like a heart attack. This I know for a fact, because Hanson bragged about it to us later. I wanted to stay out of it, because your father had given me some money from his gold mine and because I knew about his romantic encounters. Yes, I kept quiet, and I took the money. Hell! He gave it to me, and I took it!"

"Well! Hanson and Hobbs are going to rot in the Monterrey jails, because I am going to see that the Mexican Federal Courts do not release them to the Texas authorities until I'm good and ready. When Hobbs thought he was going to be killed by the *bandidos*, he admitted Hanson also murdered Tom White, the Pinkerton detective. Tom was on his trail of his deceitfulness and treacherous conduct in killing my father and how he treated the Mexican-American people. Hanson was after their property, including mine. Everything is coming to light, everything that has been evil is coming to its full circle, and everyone who had a part in it is going to pay."

"Juelson," said Ale, shaken. "I did suggest it to Hanson, but in a joking manner. It was a game for us. We all laughed about it, when your father was not with us at the hotel. The three of us found the situation amusing, but Hanson went too far and killed your father, thinking he then owned the gold mine. Now you know the full story. And as for convicting Judge Parker, my friend, he died from a heart attack one month ago, and all of his records were destroyed."

"Well, that makes it three down and you're the last," mocked the cattle baron angrily. "My suggestion to you, Howard, is that you had better talk to Emma and tell her the truth about what's happened. You better be straight with her, because you are going to have to do a lot of explaining, testifying to the Federal Courts in Brownsville. You'll be spending a lot of time away, explaining how your little joke got out of control. I was almost killed, but by the grace of some miraculous event was given another chance. Your little threesome's joke will not bring my father back to life. I don't give a rat's ass how long you've been a judge or how decent you've been. You are going to have to prove everything you just said, not to me, but in front of the Federal Brownsville's Courts." *Don* Federico got up and walked back through the kitchen, where the Mexicans maids were cleaning the floor and drying dishes.

Emma, who was coming into the kitchen, heard her name mentioned in *Don* Federico's loud conversation. Apprehensive, she asked, "What am I supposed to know? Tell me, Howard! What about the Federal Courts in Brownsville? What do you have to do with that?" She could see by *Don* Federico's face that he was very angry as he walked past her into the *sala*.

ROOTS OF INDIFFERENCE

Don Federico walked over to *Doña* Francisca and told her that he was going to round up the children. They were spending the night at the American Hotel and traveling early, back to Spanish Acres.

Emma, perplexed, returned to the *sala* and asked, "Federico what is going on?" Why are you leaving? We have plenty of room and no need to move Francisca away. You can rest the night and leave for Spanish Acres in the morning. Tell me what has happened? I know Howard has been acting very strange since I returned home."

"Better ask your husband, since he has a lot of explaining to do. He needs to be frank and truthful, especially to you, Emma, since he may be spending many hours away, explaining to the Federal Courts about his conduct. We thank you for your generous hospitality. You have been very gracious and kind. Your food is wonderful and your home is very comfortable. Thank you again. Please come and visit with us with the twins at Spanish Acres when you can. For the time being, we must leave."

⌘ ⌘ ⌘

In the following weeks, *Don* Federico spent many hours going over the condition of his land, his cattle and *vaqueros*, as well as some of the property claims and deeds for Spanish Acres. The family was shocked to learn that their favorite dog, J.D., had died mysteriously. Fred and Carlos were inconsolable.

Don Federico returned to the town of Mercedes City investigating the property his father had bought years ago. The area consisted of over twenty-five acres, which needed clearing of the rough mesquite and cacti. He hired fifty Mexican laborers to begin the arduous work, and talked to a builder with plans for a beautiful Victorian house featuring Gothic style decorations on the outside. The residence would be three-stories, with a brick foundation, with the rest built of fine wood to be shipped in by train.

While the house was being built, *Don* Federico and *Doña* Francisca stayed at the Mercedes City Hotel, built in 1907 by the American Rio Grande Land and Irrigation Company for their guests and for many engineers' families, who later bought property and made the region their home. The hotel provided a pleasant stay with its tall ceilings, large windows, open French doors, and very fashionable verandas, with beautiful surroundings of greenery. Emma taught Spanish classes to the Women's Study Club, making her quite the center of both societies and social life.

While *Doña* Francisca rested, either at the hotel or with Emma, *Don* Federico met with an elderly man named H. A. Marsh, who was head of the Hidalgo County school system. Marsh was distinguished looking, tall, with white hair and beard, and had an exceptional education, for he knew several languages. *Don* Federico was able to get the lowdown on the school system, the Jim Crow laws, and made known his concern about the many children who couldn't read or write. Marsh took a liking to *Don* Federico and begged him to consider becoming a schoolteacher for the North Ward School. The Texas school board, still in its infancy, was not yet forcing parents to send their children to school. That would not come until several years later.

Don Federico and *Doña* Francisca would frequently travel to and from Spanish Acres to Mercedes City, then across the border onto the ferryboat to the town of Reynosa. There they visited Dr. Cantu, who advised them of *Doña* Francisca's diagnosis, which did not sound good. Dr. Cantu recommended a new medicine just available on the market, containing much stronger cocaine and thought to be more powerful.

A month later, *Don* Federico left *Doña* Francisca in the care of Emma. He took Fred by train to the Military Academy run by the Baptist Church in Temple, Texas. He spent a day on the school grounds with his son, getting to know all of their rules and regulations and what was expected of Fred. From there, *Don* Federico took the train to San Antonio to check on his sister Josie, who appeared to be happy. Perhaps she was putting on a front, for she seemed content with her husband; however, she had not delivered her child. For the time being, the pressure of responsibility came off his shoulders, and he decided not to worry about Josie's problems. He returned the following week and found *Doña* Francisca happy, with rosy cheeks, and he was very pleased to read several letters from Victoria that sounded very positive regarding her studies. They had also received a note from Fred, writing that he was adjusting and starting to enjoy his schooling.

The Mexican newspapers throughout the Rio Grande Valley announced that Madero's troops had entered into Mexico for the second time and had led an attack on Casas Grandes. The government of Texas became disturbed by the activities in Mexico and feared for the people living so close to the border. High officials stood mute and tense and wondered whether or not to call on the National Guard. Any violence so close to the border would automatically affect the majority of the people on both sides of the river.

Shortly after, the city of Ciudad Juarez was under attack, and thousands of residents in El Paso climbed to their rooftops to watch the battle on the opposite side of the Rio Grande. Many cities and towns in Mexico fell into revolutionary hands. The press became increasingly critical of the Díaz regime, and many of the *Federalist* troops who had been loyal to the Mexican President started deserting and crossed over onto Texas soil. All were suffering from malnutrition and had various horror stories to tell.

The immediate result was easily foreseen. *Don* Porfirio Díaz, once grand and impressive, had withered like a dry leaf. It became the time for the people, and the movement surged like a great tidal wave throughout the whole country of Mexico. The little man, Madero, began winning as he had predicted, and before long, Díaz, the powerful and indifferent, was talking of leaving his comfortable throne.

A treaty was eventually signed. Forcing Díaz and Vice President Corral resign. Fransico Leon de la Barra assumed the interim presidential post until new elections could be held.

The Revolution had been successful, and Francisco Madero was taking over Mexico. The majority of the Madero supporters were pleased, especially *Don* Federico, who had fought for the victory with his money, and also for the protection of his daughter in Mexican territory.

ROOTS OF INDIFFERENCE

Time flew rapidly by, and with so much help from Mexican laborers, the new house in Mercedes City was completed by late fall. Behind the big mansion was a huge barn built for the horses and buggies, for the automobile were still in its infancy, and few in the Valley had one. Next to the barn was a tall windmill that piped fresh water into the residence.

At Spanish Acres, Roy had already informed *Don* Federico that he was going to marry Soledad. This was upsetting to some of the women at Spanish Acres and a surprise to the Juelsons; nevertheless, *Don* Federico gave them his blessing. Roy's marriage would not interfere with his taking care of Spanish Acres, and he would continue in his position as foreman.

The surprising news had automatically created a big stir with Yolanda's parents, Miguel and Elena. Yolanda, in early September, had delivered a healthy baby boy and believed it had been Roy's child. Roy denied it to *Don* Federico, and claimed that he had not slept with her since long before Victoria's celebration. Questions swirled as to who had fathered the child. Yolanda played dumb and would not confess to her parents who the father was. Miguel, finding out about her pregnancy, had given her a beating so severe that Elena would not let him get close to her again. It created such a ruckus that both of the parents had stopped talking to one another.

Don Federico decided if Roy wanted to get married and settle down into a serious relationship, he would offer him some of the Spanish Acres land. Roy could pick the part he wanted and cultivate it. The *Don* would also donate several prime cattle with which to start his ranch. As for Yolanda's escapade, *Don* Federico decided that he would not get involved, for it was none of his business. He had too much to think about, especially his wife, children, moving, and his status. Within two weeks, Roy and Soledad were married in a small ceremony in Harlingen before the Justice of the Peace.

Dona Adela's prophecy had come true.

⌘   ⌘   ⌘

In Mercedes City, several mule wagons from Spanish Acres came to unload some of the furniture and fill the newly built, opulent home. New furniture was on order from the San Antonio Sears and Roebuck store for new mattresses, a cooking stove, and other commodities for the spacious bedrooms that featured large, tinted, cut-glass windows for the delight and comfort of their many guests. An enormous, circular porch surrounded the lower level, and upstairs there were screened-in verandas. *Doña* Francisca had always wanted a place where she could sit and rock, doing her quilting outdoors, especially during the hot summer months. Plants were imported from Brownsville, including several palm trees and varieties of flowering bushes for the front yard, as well as varieties of citrus trees from Mission, Texas.

On the north side of the house, *Don* Federico insisted on planting several black walnut, pecan, and mulberry trees. Fig trees were planted on the south side, and aromatic magnolia trees and gardenia bushes were planted in front of the house on both sides of the driveway to perfume the air on hot days. The Mexican-American friends living on the north side of town would come and visit, bringing food and gifts, commenting on how lovely the house was and how lucky they were to be living on the *gringo* side.

Within a month of moving into their new home, Emma threw a large party welcoming the Juelsons into their community. Many of the guests were the engineers and wives of the Rio Grande Irrigation Land Company and included the mayor of the town, the banker, and several prominent families with high social standing who had moved into the area from the northern states and from the Deep South.

⌘　⌘　⌘

Don Federico started volunteering his services in a four-room wooden schoolhouse across the tracks. In later years, it would be known as Hidalgo Street and Indiana Avenue, North Ward School. He became acquainted with the Catholic nuns from Our Lady of Mercy School and with the other teacher, *Señora* Agapita.

When not teaching during the week, he would take Francisca to see her doctor, and on Saturdays and Sundays, he would spend most of his days at Spanish Acres, attending to his cattle with Roy, and seeing about his people. Manuel was getting disoriented, drinking all the time, and Mamá Maria was getting older and was suffering from a severe case of arthritis in her hands, elbows, knees, and back.

In Mexico, never did peace seem so close at hand. Madero, the great redeemer, won his first free election, an event that had not occurred in over thirty years. But, when he entered Mexico City, a severe earthquake had shaken the city and had caused destructive consequences to many buildings, killing over two hundred, and injuring thousands. "This was an omen of terrible things to come," the populace would say.

There was still a vast disparity of indifference between the Mexican-American people and the whites, who had traveled from the northern states and had settled in the lovely town of Mercedes City. On Sundays, families would go to their own church services and spend their afternoon at *Campacuas* Lake to socialize and seek relief from the humid summer heat. The Mexican men would bring their rifles and shoot birds on one side of the bank, while the whites socialized on the other side. Small children, innocent of prejudice, were told not to mix with the other race, even though both enjoyed swimming together. The topics of conversation would inevitably turn to the terrible injustices being committed upon the Mexican-American people, and yet there was nothing anyone could do about it. On the south side of Mercedes City, past the railroad tracks were the *gringo* merchant places of business with posters nailed to the newly planted palm trees: "No Mexicans Allowed." Ironically, it was the Mexican people who did all the work for the white men and made them rich.

⌘　⌘　⌘

Late in the month of November, after the Mexican people had celebrated the *Días de los Muertos*, the day of the dead, early one morning, before the chickens were up, a tall, thin man, mostly all legs, wearing a silver badge on his dark jacket, knocked on *Don* Federico's front door. There was a stir of commotion in the household, waking *Don* Federico up. The gentleman introduced himself as Captain Marshall Bishop, a United States Deputy Marshal. He had come to get straight all the information that *Don* Federico had mailed to the office in Austin earlier. On his hips he wore two, big, long pistols. He seemed serious, but cordial. *Don* Federico found him to be the spitting image of Wyatt Earp, even to his stiff, dark mustache and Stetson hat. The *Don* ordered his servants to bring a pot of coffee with two cups out to the porch.

Captain Bishop's first words were, "What a nice home."

"It's not even a year old," remarked the *Don*. "I had it built for my sick wife."

Bishop wasted no time getting down to business. "Got your letter, and it brought up some perplexing questions."

"It's been over two years," commented *Don* Federico, still half asleep, but thinking, *Could it be that something is finally going to be done about the injustices in the Valley?* It did not take long to tell Captain Bishop the full story about his father's death, Tom White's murder, about the Rio Rico incident, about Soledad, about José Esquibel's death, and the story of the gold mine in Monterrey. He continued explaining how it was all linked to the Texas Rangers' activities and their cruelty, especially to the Mexican people in the surrounding region.

Captain Bishop's face was stoic and without expression as he listened. He seemed to know more than he was letting on. "I am not surprised," he retorted wryly. "I have been sent also by the Department of Justice to investigate several rumors of a conspiracy going on here in the Rio Grande Valley and across the river, getting wind of this information in San Antonio. From the correspondence you sent us, we surmised you know more about the people who live here, and I was asked to talk to you personally."

"Conspiracy? Here in this town?" quizzed *Don* Federico, almost choking on his coffee.

"Well, we don't know for sure, if it's in this town, but it's all over here in the Valley. Several Germans, with the help of some Mexicans, would like to take this country over," he said. He rolled his tobacco from one side of his mouth to the other and spit among the bushes next to the porch. "The word is, two or three of these conspirators supposedly live here in this town. They have been under suspicion and we have some names."

"Germans," said *Don* Federico. He shook his head. "There are many German people in this town, but they are considered good, upstanding citizens, many with wives and children, only wanting the best for this community."

The Captain looked at the *Don*, then glanced around the porch, left and right—a habit of his suspicious nature. "Ah, bullshit!" He spit again and took several sips of black coffee. "The clever Germans I'm talking about want to take the State of Texas and Mexico together! There are those that are Madero-haters and want him out of office. An assassination plot has already begun. A man by the name of Reyes was stopped and questioned near San Antonio with documents concerning the plot. He said he was going to Mexico City to get things organized with high Mexican officials. One of our special agents lost him between the town of Laredo and the border. The Germans have spies living here with families, and they are infiltrating various groups, and reporting back to who knows who? Reports on Morse code are going out to German ships in Boca Chica Bay close to Ft. Brown. The Germans are starting a war with other countries in Europe, and we think they are including Mexico."

"Killing Madero!" answered *Don* Federico, aghast, thinking of Victoria and Felicia in Monterrey. "Has the State Department notified Madero and his cabinet about this?"

"Several times," he remarked, "but it doesn't seem to bother Madero or his staff." He shrugged, turned his head, and then spit. "Madero has been warned, and it's up to him to do something about it. We have been sending him telegrams, but he doesn't seem to be concerned. Madero seems to be reveling in his victory, having won the election, and not concentrating on his future. That's all we can do for now. We are just glad that peace is being restored in Mexico, at least for the time being. I don't think it's the end. I still think we are going to hear a helluva lot more in the coming year."

Captain Bishop took another sip of his coffee and started on the subject of Hanson. "Regarding Hanson, I don't think we have to worry too much about him right now. The Mexican government is going to keep him for a long time. Those Mexican jails are tough. The Justice Department wants him extradited in the next couple of months to the Brownsville Federal jails, but it takes time and so much paperwork that it may take years to get him indicted. The Mexican government normally, does not comply with our laws. I don't know what is going to happen with Hobbs, since he was retired from the Texas Rangers, and with honors, believe it or not! We are still debating his case."

Marshall Bishop paused, cleared his throat, and then continued. "The Pinkerton agency has put a bulletin out on Tom White. Without a body, things are hard to prove. Another thing, we got a tip that several of the officers are involved with the Ku Klux Klan. How many, we are not sure, but an investigation is on in the matter. I used to think that the Klan was only in the Deep South, but to my surprise, we have it here in this valley—Mexican-haters. We also learned that many of the business merchants are also involved with this dangerous operation, mainly to protect themselves, pat each other on the back, and keep quiet on any bad activities in relation to the Mexican-Americans."

Don Federico was speechless for a moment, but finally found his voice. "The Ku Klux Klan! Heaven helps us! They hate the Mexican-Americans, Negroes or for that matter, any minority. Heaven help the Mexican-American families in this area!"

"Yeah, can you believe that? There is more than meets the eye here in the small border towns, especially so close to the river." Marshall Bishop grabbed for his hat. "I must leave for now. I'll be in touch as soon as my Special Agent David McLean goes down to Brownsville and talks to Federal Judge Barnes. I don't suppose he'll believe a damn thing we tell him, but I'll show him the documents and our orders from the State Department." He said it with a slow drawl, concerned though not overly optimistic.

"I suppose not," remarked *Don* Federico. "The Mexican-Americans are silent, they don't complain—they just go on about their own business. Nobody is going to believe that the Mexican people in the Valley are suffering from injustice. But, how can they not? Mexicans are found every day strung up from tall cottonwood trees, having been tortured all night long, horsewhipped, or shot in the back with the excuse that they were escaping! Nobody here can help them, or answer for them, nobody here speaks out! Every Mexican-American family is afraid."

"Maybe you should take a good look at yourself and run for office and become a politician. You're the perfect man with an education to get things started. You are the main man bringing all of this together, simply by asking questions. You have already questioned the injustice in this area and have gotten the State of Texas and the Federal Government interested and started with this investigation."

"I'm still new in this community," replied *Don* Federico, "but the thought has run through my mind. Someone has to stand up to all of these injustices."

Bishop rose to leave. "I plan to spend however many years it takes getting to the bottom of all this goin' on with the conspiracy and with hundreds of documents, investigating what the people of the Valley have to say and trying to prove it." He spit to his side. "I'm gonna have to hire people in Austin to help me with all the paperwork. I don't trust anyone here dealing with classified documents. Thanks for your help. I'll be in touch."

"Let's have dinner sometime. Just send me word when you're coming to Mercedes City, and we'll have a feast for you. My family and I would be honored having you as our guest. We have plenty of room."

Don Federico was still unnerved by the disturbing information imparted by the Captain. He watched as he mounted his horse. "By the way," he commented, "you didn't tell me the names of the suspected Germans in this town."

"Didn't say, but if it would help you with some of the information, one of the names in the classified documents is Foster. The other one, I think, was a retired judge. Both are friends who are involved in this conspiracy. The other person—we're not sure yet if he's providing the money for these destructive doings, which will be dangerous to the production of cotton in the Valley. The three men under suspicion are being paid by Germans living in Mexico, who are trying to disrupt the production of cotton, which is like gold, as you know. Foster is a German chemist. Rumors are that he is trying to amass a huge accumulation of boll-weevil beetles and release them into this community, destroying the production of cotton. But we can't prove it at this time."

"I'm new to this community and don't know the names of many that live here. I don't know a Foster. The only person that I know that's a retired judge is Judge Howard Ale."

"I think that was the name mentioned. He's under investigation already, thanks to your written documents that you mailed us. He's in tough shit, clear up to his neck!"

"Not Howard Ale!"

"Yep, I think that's the name! Sounds familiar."

Don Federico stood with his mouth open, staring at the impressive gentleman riding away on his fine horse.

CHAPTER 19

The universe was always busy throwing another mind-boggling curve, so did the evil omens begin to stir with evil forces; all seemed to be living in the lawless, turbulent conditions that prevailed around the Rio Grande Valley. There was much talk among the Mexican-Americans and it was starting to take its toll, as everyone was beginning to live in constant fear. It was anarchic and dangerous to cross over the border at night from either side; a killing here; a lynching there; someone found dead, shot through the head; someone with his head severed; bloated bodies floating in the river; robberies; hundreds of cattle missing; and many horses stolen. The natives with cash in hand started to hide their money, especially gold and silver dollars, in strongboxes. They hoarded and buried the coins in secret places in the ground, and many in their chimneys.

The feelings of hatred from both races caused them to blame each other for the crimes; however, the majority of deaths were those of the Mexican-American people. All this brought emotional hostility, which boiled and seethed underneath the surface. The face-slapping terms, "greaser," or *gabacho*, or *gringo* occasionally would create a scuffle and a fight would break out, with someone knifed or killed by stray bullets. Rumors of another revolutionary threat became the main topic throughout the Rio Grande Valley.

Don Federico continued diligently with his volunteering and taught the small children from across the tracks, in spite of the rumors of war and problems in the Lower Rio Grande Valley. He was proud of his achievements. In the fall, he had started with five boys and nine girls, and by the spring of 1912, he had over twenty-two Mexican-American children in his classroom. When he was not seeing about his cattle at Spanish Acres, he would roam out into the *barrios* where the poor Mexicans lived in their one-room shacks and hovels, and hand out baskets of food. He would stop and talk to the parents about the importance of an education for their children. So many of their children, especially the boys, would start school, but, come spring, when the fields had to be planted and later harvested, they would not return.

"They must be taught," was *Don* Federico's urgent request and his anxious concern. "The children must be trained to think for themselves. We are living in a new democracy, and with a good education they can become important in our new society. They need to learn—they need to be able to read and write."

"We are very poor," the fathers of growing boys in the Mexicans *barrios* would say. "We need our boys to help us in the fields. Look at my wife breastfeeding, with another one on the way. We need the money to provide us with food on the table." Most of the barefoot Mexican children would come to school with sad, haunted eyes, hungry bellies, and ragged clothes, the same ones that they would wear all during the school week. So pathetic and pitiful, they did not have enough food in their bodies to keep a fly alive.

"The children need to get an education," cried *Don* Federico. "Send them to school to learn and be educated. You want to be slaves forever? Is that what you want for your children? With knowledge, they can buy all the shoes and clothes they want later. Their education will never go away, now is the right time to learn. Let me teach them, and I will furnish the children with food." This he graciously did.

Don Federico was quickly becoming a great man in the eyes of the poor Mexican people, but a harsh thorn in the side of many of the white farmers who made a living working the young Mexicans out in the fields. Most whites did not want the Mexicans to be educated. It would put thoughts in their minds—next they will be demanding more rights, they would say. If they go to school, who is going to work the fields and farms in the coming years?

Discontent began to develop among many of the white farmers, saying that the *Don* was stirring up trouble, giving the Mexican-Americans all kinds of ideas. Rumors began spreading to discredit *Don* Federico's background as being black, that old man George had come from up north and had changed his name to conceal his identity. Others were disputing his last name of Juelson. "What kind of name is that? Sounds Jewish to me!" they would say. The Jews were hated and those who dared come to Texas, especially the southern part, changed their names. Few Jews were residents of the Rio Grande Valley.

Don Federico's thirst for educating the small children was like seething lava ready to erupt within him. He would keep silent, continue to study and teach, and help the Mexican-Americans with anything he could, even with food. When it came time for him to be in the classroom, he would tell each child that they were the most important person in the world, that each child could make a difference in the community. The children would stare at him in wonder. He would never punish his students, but would praise them highly. Little by little, the *Don* would tell them the story of the great Aztecs and Mayans, their great civilization, and the one great race, the *Mestizos*, which had developed from the Mexican melting pot.

Don Federico would teach them of Father Hidalgo's words:

Don't ever forget who you are. There is pride in your Mexican heritage. Don't be ashamed of your nationality. Stand straight, with your head held high, walk side-by-side, fearless in the sun. Keep our customs and traditions, for they must never die. Shake the burden of servitude and meet everyone with an equal eye; seek peace and pursue it; spurn all that is evil. Defend what is right, and you will never go wrong. Educate yourself, for without it, you will not be a light unto the world. Learn about life, for so many things are not written in books.

He felt the children needed to know that someone did care, for they were all part of the great social cause. So many Mexican-American families had already lost their self-esteem and did not care who they were—they were only trying to survive in a cruel, prejudiced, and discriminating world.

The Mexicans coming from Mexico feared the trouble in their land; in turn, they would look north toward the United States, with many children and not enough jobs to fill each need. *Don* Federico took his father-in-law's advice. He appointed Miguel Garcia at Spanish Acres to hire the Mexican workers with five or more children, who were willing to do a day's work to clear five hundred acres for the development of cotton. They began putting up tents around Spanish Acres, giving them places to live.

Another project that had triggered *Don* Federico's interest was the coming of oil. He had to thank Bernard Hanson for that, since the Ranger was so adamant in taking over some of his land, and even took the liberty of probing his property with the strangers that wandered into the *resaca*. If there was black gold on his land, he wanted to get to the bottom of the issue. He hired a man by the name of John Shaw, to inspect his land and find out for sure if there was any possibility of oil. Shaw was a retired engineer who had worked in Houston's refinery and had come to the Rio Grande Valley, buying land west of Mercedes City called "Jackass Prairie."

Within a week Shaw responded back and told *Don* Federico that the possibility was there. *Don* Federico gave orders to Roy Dale and his *vaqueros* to give Shaw full authority in bringing in the equipment needed to begin the operation of drilling for oil. The *vaqueros* would see that the cattle did not interfere with the operation. It would take months to begin this costly procedure, since many of the pipes and machinery were being imported from Houston by ship to Brownsville and then hauled with mule wagons to the *resaca*.

The farmers and merchants in the Valley were becoming very prosperous; however, in Mexico, things did not seem to be going well for Madero. Those who had cherished the hope of peace, like *Don* Federico and his father-in-law, *Don* José Hinojosa, were all due for a rude awakening.

In Mexico, Madero had failed to use stern measures against the counter-revolutionaries who were increasingly becoming the subject of unpopular criticism. Madero had appointed various members of his family to cabinet offices, thus exposing them to charges of nepotism. The Madero's women were also the target of critical newspaper gossip, many reporting that they were all indifferent, looking like European queens rather than Mexican women. And jealousy arose within the Madero's families.

There had been separate messages being transmitted through Mexico's Washington Embassy by Henry Lane Wilson saying that Madero was corrupt, dishonest, and very insincere. Ambassador Wilson, who had many rich interests in Mexico and favored Huerta, disliked Madero from the beginning of his taking office. Madero complained to the United States that the American Ambassador was meddling in the internal affairs of Mexico, knowing he had liked Díaz but had preferred for Huerta to become president.

When the time came for Madero to give the people "forty acres and a mule," it seemed that only those who were already rich got more. Madero had lost interest in the cause that had put him in the office, and he failed to carry out his agrarian promise. He did not work fast enough to satisfy the poor in his county, like the mango tree that took years before it yields fruit. Madero had fallen from grace.

⌘ ⌘ ⌘

In the spring of 1912, newspapers throughout the valley were reporting the spectacular news of the fateful sinking of the "unsinkable" ship, the Titanic, making its maiden voyage and colliding with an iceberg. Headlines never spoke of the hundreds of poor Irish, Scottish, and other European immigrants coming to the United States to make a better life for themselves who lost their lives trapped in the bottom of the ship by drowning and freezing in the Arctic waters. During the same year, *Don* Federico got word that his friend *Don* Yturria, his banker and a rancher friend from Brownsville, had died. The two had shared the breeding of *Santa Gertrudis*, the Angus, and other varieties of cattle.

During that same year, there were serious outbreaks in Mexico against the administration. Zapata, the gentle Indian *campesino*, with the help of other Indians in the state of Morelos, held the state against the *Federalist* troops to subdue them. Zapata was demanding the redistribution of the great land estates that were never distributed. Other similar outbreaks occurred in the state of Yucatan. Former *Maderistas* renounced allegiance to their great chief. The "Apostle of Democracy," the great redeemer, Madero, had begun like so many of his previous predecessors, making promises that were never kept. His presidency ended as a terrible disaster, fulfilling the prophecy.

⌘ ⌘ ⌘

As the year of 1912 came to a close, *Don* Federico's estate had flourished with many cattle, several hundred bales of cotton, and the oil being pumped in the *resaca*. By the end of the year, they had shipped several hundred barrels from Brownsville to an oil company in Houston.

In the early part of January, 1913, as the skies were clearing from an overcast, cloudy month, *Doña* Francisca received a letter from her mother in Monterrey telling her that her father, *Señor* Hinojosa, had gone to Mexico City on business, to sell some of his bulls, and had not returned home. *Don* Federico found *Doña* Francisca on the front porch, despairing and in tears.

"It's my father!" she cried desperately, holding the letter in her hands. "Father has been gone for over three weeks, and Mother had not heard a word. She thinks something happened and fears the worst!"

Don Federico read the letter, frowned and replied, "I think your mother is overreacting. Your father knows Mexico City like the palm of his hand. He knows what he's doing. Surely *General* Del Calderóne, with whom he is staying in the Capital, knows where he is. The last time we heard from him, he was staying in his villa close to La Reforma with *El General*." Saying this, he kissed her on her forehead and found a wicker chair and sat next to her, trying to console her. "Before long, we will all be together again like it was two years ago. You are already feeling better. Victoria will be here, getting married, and Fred should be home from his academic studies."

Doña Francisca began crying again.

"Francisca!" Yelled Emma, coming up the road in her one horse-buggy. Her voice that was always high pitched now sounded dull and flat. In her hand was a telegram. Triumphantly, in her high-heeled shoes and feather hat, she approached the porch. "It's your father, Francisca! Grandmother Alvarado said that he was put in prison on suspicion of supporting Madero's policies and accused of being a spy!"

Doña Francisca stood up. "In prison!" she cried. "Spy! What's going on? What's with Madero's policies? He is the President of Mexico. Father only wants eternal peace for Mexico."

"According to the telegram, *General* Huerta has arrested your father and several others, including Madero's brother, Gustavo, and put them all in prison. Huerta has seized the National Palace with the help of the *Federalist* troops and the military cadets," answered Emma, hugging *Doña* Francisca.

"*Dios mío!*" she said. "My family, what will happen to them—and the girls in the convent?"

"Grandmother Alvarado said there is trouble in Mexico City and that the newspapers are not giving out much information. She heard this from a message sent to your mother from a family friend in Mexico City, who is trying to help get your father out of prison. I'm starting to worry about the girls."

Doña Francisca sat back in her rocking chair. Startled and horrified, she stared for a moment and brought her hands to her face. She sobbed and gasped for air in between her coughing, as tears rolled down her face. Mamá Maria, who was staying with them in Mercedes City, opened the screen door and looked shocked, having overheard the conversation. *Don* Federico motioned for Mamá Maria to take Carlos inside.

"I'm sending a telegram to *General* Del Calderóne in Mexico City immediately," murmured *Don* Federico in shock. "He should know what is going on with Madero." He looked puzzled, as the frown lines on his forehead became heavy. What was he to expect, remembering what the United States Marshal Bishop had told him about Madero? And the girls in the convent, what was going to happen to them? "I'm beginning to think that I should go to Monterrey and get Victoria and Felicia out of the convent," he declared.

⌘ ⌘ ⌘

As the days passed, time seemed like an eternity. There was no message back from Mexico City. The *Brownville Herald* kept reporting trouble in Mexico, that Huerta had overthrown Madero. The *San Antonio Weekly Express* was coming with eyewitness accounts and dispatches from consular officials in the capitol saying that Gustavo had been killed and that Madero, with his vice president, had been arrested. Everyone in the Rio Grande Valley became frantic.

War hawks and reporters kept coming from the frontier, telling of gory sagas that were happening in the interior of Mexico.

Finally, on February 24, came the final blow. The newspapers were reporting that Madero and José Maria Piño Suarez, his vice president, had been brutally killed. U.S. President Woodrow Wilson had just taken office, and the whole border was in chaos. Men were lined up, five deep in the *cantinas* in Reynosa and all over the border towns, talking of taking up arms.

The area from the mouth of the Rio Grande River to Baja California was aflame with panic. War had broken out in Mexico. The atmosphere was tense. It split Mexico wide open, since Ambassador Wilson was being blamed for his meddling in foreign affairs between Mexico and the United States, bringing discontent and hatred toward all Americans.

The winds of evil had stirred. It was as if the devil with his demon angels had been cast out of the bottomless pit to devour anything and everything, making a furious and futile effort to regain possession of the earth. The oceans roared and the roll of distant thunder sounded—the devil was marshalling his hosts from within.

Looting and killing became widespread in southern Texas, causing Governor O.B. Colquitt to send five companies of state militia and several groups of Texas Rangers under the command of Captain Sanders to the Rio Grande Valley. All of the newspapers were busy with headlines of a Mexican War.

After reading the news, panic-filled *Don* Federico wasted no time in riding toward Spanish Acres, ordering Roy with several of his best gunmen to travel with him to Monterrey to get Victoria and Felicia. The train from Monterrey to the frontier had been derailed, and the only way to travel now was by horse. While the men were getting their gear and horses ready, *Don* Federico decided to pay a visit to *La Señora Doña* Adela, remembering what the old witch woman had said to him twenty-two months back. *You will need my advice and real soon. You will come and pay me a visit, for you will need some answers that only I can tell you.*

Don Federico was amazed at her accurate information, even though he had once laughed and made fun of her prophecies. What the old *bruja* had predicted for him had all come to pass, especially about guns and ammunition. All of the information was revealed after he had put two and two together on Hanson and Hobbs after returning from the gold mine trip. Soledad had been raped by Hanson and Hobbs. Hanson was a friend of his father. She did have a connection. It was all making sense.

CHAPTER 20

The innocent blue skies of spring were coming as the days were getting longer, and after the serenity of the long, dull winter, the convent's landscape brought forth a peaceful blanket of colorful wild flowers into their midst. The buttercups and flowering vines burst with delicate blooms that scented the air and showed their faces throughout the tranquil region. The brooks ran proud with soft rainwater, and the nights were cold and breezy. The season was rapidly changing into one of excitement, and so was the region of Monterrey, Mexico.

Late in the evening, the peaceful convent had hunched its shoulders after the quiet evening meal. The nuns had settled into their prayer, and students were preparing for tomorrow's lessons.

The evening had settled softly down for the day, except for Victoria and Felicia and another group of girls washing dishes, pot, and pans furiously in an ancient, iron washtub *lavadero* that drained its water out into the gardens and acreage. It was a job for disorderly slaves.

Rosalinda, the ugly Montoya twin, wanting to find favor with Mother Superior, had reported to the head of housecleaning that Victoria had been seen reading *devil* cards. In a Catholic convent, this did not set too well. Consequently, the head of housecleaning reported it to the head nun, who reported to Mother Superior. All were flabbergasted. The Holy Mother became furious with Victoria and demanded for her to turn over the cards. Victoria refused, saying they were hers and nobody else's. To refuse the orders of Mother Superior was like giving two thumbs down to God. It was going to be a painful punishment: one hundred Hail Marys in consistent order, and walking on her knees from the chapel entrance to the altar without stopping, and praying for forgiveness. This was not exactly Victoria's favorite pastime!

And finally, the nastiest demoralizing discipline that every decent girl hated while staying at the convent was: doing double kitchen-duty of the worse kind, and in the evening, which was the heaviest. Felicia threw herself into Victoria's defense and was ordered to join the rest of the "liars' club" in the kitchen. They had to stay until all the pot and pans were completely clean and the kitchen spotless.

Victoria washed and Felicia and two other girls were drying, putting the pans and dishes in their cupboards. At each doorway, duty nuns hunched like penguins and sat in their chairs, their hands tucked inside their habits, as they observed and guarded the girls at their duties. While scrubbing, Victoria kept thinking of the Catholic nun's life. *They are always going around looking bland, in silence and never allowed to express their true feelings. Their lives never had tragic events or joyous occasions and they never shared any occurrence about their childhood, family or talked directly to the girls. They were like puppets. No excitement. What a boring life!*

Outside, an old peasant man with a cart pulled by a burro, who brought milk, cheese, fresh fruits, and vegetables for the convent, came in hysterical and out of breath. His cry was: "Revolution! The Revolution has broken out! Madero, our savior has been killed!" Instantly, the girls stopped their work and stood immobile, staring at each other, in shock at the old man's announcement. Several of the sisters stood up, and regular workers in the kitchen listened with the utmost surprised interest. "Most all of the haciendas in Saltillo have already been ransacked! Men are taking up guns and rifles to fight for Mexico's cause! Our liberator Madero has been assassinated, and Father Herrera in Monterrey was shot to death, and the nuns were raped and murdered. The world is coming to an end!"

"Dear God!" said Victoria out loud, strands of damp, matted hair hanging in her face. She turned to Felicia. "With Madero dead, what's going to happen?" Her memory wandered as she stood in a daze, finding time to brush her hair back. Whatever happened to Juan? It was going on two years since she had seen or heard from him, and her heart ached for his presence. Surely he didn't have anything to do with any killing. "I wonder if there has been any word in Mexico City on Grandfather."

"Maybe he got caught up in a political mess in the capital. He probably got involved in something," said Felicia, shrugging her shoulders.

There was a frightened commotion in the kitchen as everyone began talking about their loved ones and their families, forgetting their duties. There was another tornado-wind coming down the long hallways. It was Mother Superior, the matriarch herself, who had heard from a tattletale nun of the worldly politics occurring outside. Perhaps Mother Superior had been disturbed in her weekly agonizing flagellation that the nuns performed as a penance and a constant reminder that sins had to be punished, even evil thoughts.

Regardless of the reason, she was incensed. Her eyes glared like two burning torches, and her white-starched habit cracked like ice when she turned and faced Victoria. She did not approve of Victoria because, on previous occasions, Victoria had interrupted her and spoken out bravely on her worldly views. "Never mind the talk of war!" she declared now. "That doesn't pertain to this convent. This is a house of God, and war should never enter these doors. We do not live outside these convent walls. All of you get back to cleaning this kitchen," she ordered. "And as for you—Victoria, you still have to finish your punishments, and after cleaning this kitchen, you still have homework for tomorrow's lessons." Mother Superior's face was stern with discipline. She turned to address the other girls, her eyes boring into them. "Talk of war is no concern to any of you girls. You are here to be educated." Her words hung in the air and echoed throughout the kitchen. "Now get back to work!"

ROOTS OF INDIFFERENCE

The words kept ringing in Victoria's ears. *Victoria, you still have to finish your punishments.* This did not surprise Victoria, for during the past nine months, she had developed a repressed hate for Mother Superior, who kept finding fault with her actions, degrading her to do servant's work. She had no palpable evidence, nor could she pinpoint the reason. She only knew that she could not do anything to please her. Perhaps Mother Superior had a dislike for her, since she was always speaking out in class on so many injustices on women's issues and giving the other girls bright ideas. This did not set well with the Holy Mother who was in favor of "a man's world." Women were supposed to keep quiet and obey their husbands, regardless of the circumstances. Victoria kept thinking, *Go and beat yourself some more!* Her hateful thoughts led her to visualizing like *Doña* Adela had taught her, using some of the white witchcraft methods of wishing that something terrible would happen to the Reverend Mother.

Hesitating for an instant, the Holy Mother turned to Felicia saying, "Please, would you go down to the basement and get me three bottles of fine wine for the morning Mass?"

Felicia nodded obediently and slowly walked down the passageway to the downstairs winery.

There were more noises coming from outside the walls of the convent, as the thunder of horses, soldiers, and peasants with rifles began descending upon the quiet, serene house of God. Carts and wagons pulled by horses and burros and loaded with pillaged goods started to close in on the area. Loud sounds of guns being fired into the air began frightening and awakening the convent.

The sounds of boots with heavy silver spurs rang on the marble floors. A tall, dark-haired, bearded man with dark eyes appeared at the doorway and entered the kitchen. "Who's in charge here?" He spoke roughly, removing his large sombrero, dusting off his woolen trousers, and leggings that came to his knees.

The kitchen area became like a still night. No one said a word. Each kitchen worker and the attending girls stood frozen and immobile, staring at each other. The nuns stood frightened and began touching their rosaries; some crossed themselves trying to find comfort and solace.

"Who's running this place?" he repeated. Propping one of his boots on a wooden stool, he began to unfasten the double cartridge belts across his chest.

From outside the corridor halls, Mother Superior appeared with prideful confidence and stepped into the kitchen. She looked surprised that anyone would dare disturb the peaceful convent. She approached the dusty, rugged character and replied, "I'm in charge of this convent. What can we help you with?" She flinched visibly and touched the rosary that hung at her waist.

"I'm Luis Del Calderóne, *Capitán* of this platoon. We are heading for the border. We are all hungry and one of the men has been shot in the chest and needs doctoring, *pronto!*"

"Very well, we will see what we can do." Mother Superior hesitated and fumbled for words, then eyed one of the kitchen servants and gestured with her hands. "Have these men fed. I'll send two of the nuns to fetch the village doctor." She turned to Luis in her pride and said, "You may stay here tonight, but in the morning all of you will have to leave and find another place of shelter. This is a convent, a house of God, and we only take care of emergencies. We are not a hospital. We only take care of unfortunate girls who are having babies. And I have a school to run."

Luis's eyes became like two icebergs filled with hate. He drew his pistol and clicked the hammer back, approaching Mother Superior and pointing it at her chest. There was a long hush and some whispers of "Mother of God!" as the room was now filled with suspense. Everyone was caught in a moment of fright. Several of the revolutionists had started to fill the kitchen, their hands full of guns and rifles, lust in their thoughts, eyeing each girl.

"We will stay here as long as we want, *Señora!*" he snapped. "We are at war. And we will take anything we want. Do you understand what I am saying? If my orders are not carried out or complied with quickly, you and your so-called nuns will be put against the wall and shot. Now, do we understand each other?"

"This is the house of God," she said bravely. "You cannot come in here and order us around. We know nothing about your worldly wars. I should have known who you are. I didn't recognize you with all of the evil ammunition across your chest. I didn't remember you being so disrespectful. You should be ashamed, being the son of *El General* Del Calderóne, and your mother a great supporter of this convent."

Luis laughed. "My father and I have not spoken in years. I was able to see through his deception and knew all along what he was doing, especially to this country. He was the main cause of Madero's death, with the help of his friend Huerta, who wants to take over this country for himself. And I will fight until my death for the good and the justice of the poor *peóns*."

"You will not get away with this—the *Federalists* will be coming to get you and your killers."

"Fernando!" shouted Luis. "Take this *Señora* and lock her up. I will deal with her tomorrow. Now, I need a full meal and a good rest. And maybe a nice, soft, warm body that will cuddle up with me." He laughed. "I will give the orders from now on!" He grabbed the stool from underneath his boot and sat. "And where is the food? Bring us some food! We are all hungry and haven't eaten since we left the prison in Mexico City four days ago."

Two of the revolutionists grabbed Mother Superior by her arms and gave her a hard shove. She kept her balance as she was led into the long tile corridors inside of the convent. There were gunshots and screams coming from other parts of the convent. "*Pronto, pronto!*" they said.

The sudden cries of anguish were coming from the bedrooms where the nuns and students were being raped, their possessions looted and ransacked, the ruffians taking everything they owned of any value. The crash of axes and crowbars was heard against the wooden doors, along with the thud of furniture being flung out into the halls and patio, and the constant smashing of glass.

Victoria's blood ran cold. She wanted to run and hide, but where? She turned her head to try and find Felicia, but Felicia was downstairs in the cellar getting some wine for Mother

Superior, as she had been ordered. Was this what came with the Revolution? The two of them were caught in the middle of this nightmare with no way of escape.

The enraged men burst into the kitchen in a reckless fury, grabbing and eating everything that was put in front of them. One of the bandits, with crossed cartridge belts on his chest, grabbed one of the kitchen helpers, an Indian girl about fifteen years old. With his long knife he slit the front of her white peasant blouse, exposing her breasts. She tried to scream, but was too paralyzed. She stood helpless. Like an animal obeying primitive urges, the man advanced toward the terrified girl, then dragged her by her hair across the floor, tearing her clothes, pulling her toward the cellar, where the supplies and wines were kept. He bent her over a barrel and spread her legs. His animal lust could not be held back, and he let his pants down and began mounting her from behind, like the bulls do to the cows in the spring.

Another revolutionist grabbed Victoria by the left shoulder. With her closed right fist, she hit the man in the face as hard as she could, dropped him against the wall. Everything was happening so fast and all the girls were terrified.

"Luis!" cried Victoria, frightened out of her wits. She hurried past some tables and chairs, as the revolutionist got up and tried to chase her. "Luis!" she yelled.

"I have found my little turtle dove." The revolutionist laughed, still groggy from the hard blow to his face. He rubbed his cheeks and headed toward Victoria again. "I will not be cold tonight!"

"Luis!" shouted Victoria, leaning over the table toward him, her face showing terror. "Don't you remember me, Luis? I'm Victoria, your future sister-in-law! You must stop this raping and killing!" she begged. With an unyielding glare she stared into Luis's cold, angry eyes. "We have nothing to do with the war in Mexico. We are only students, trying to get educated."

"Victoria?" He paused for a minute, trying to focus on who she was. "Wait a minute!" he said, as he proceeded to stand up, wiping his mouth on his sleeves. "Ricardo's future wife?" He gave out a hearty laugh. "I knew your face looked familiar. I knew I had seen you somewhere, but I have seen so many faces in the last three years that everyone looks the same. Well, well, it's a small world!" He smiled and turned around to get the attention of the other revolutionists. "My future *cuñada*, sister-in-law, getting educated to please my brother. And I might say a good looking one." He eyed her up and down.

The dirty, amorous revolutionist approached Luis, hissing and out of breath, shaking his head. "You mean that I can't have this little dove, *Capitán?*" The others at the table eating, roared with laughter.

"This one is special," commented Luis making a gesture with his hand. "Find yourself another one. There are plenty in this convent. Get yourself a nun. They have never had sex. Show them how it works."

The rest of the starving men laughed, and Luis continued talking to Victoria. "Ricardo will be a very lucky man. But tell me, when is this great day coming? You can bet your boots that I will not be invited!" He laughed again. "Come, sit with me. You'll be unharmed with me."

"This coming June," answered Victoria nervously, still shaking with fear and making a disgusted face.

"You're not happy about your coming wedding? Or am I detecting that my brother and my father don't have you fooled. Ricardo and my father are always scheming, full of deceit and treacherous doings, always thinking of ways of getting more money."

There were sounds of more shooting, coming from the outside of the patio, and the building where the nuns stayed and worshipped was being burned. Cavalry and horse-drawn cannons were being placed in the middle of the entry way. The peasants living in the nearby village below the convent were being rounded up to join in with the rest of the men for Mexico's cause. The few that refused were shot. There were other men racing up and down the courtyard yelling, "*Viva Mexico!*"

"Luis!" Victoria pleaded, trembling. "You have got to stop all of this killing and looting. These girls and nuns are innocent of any wrongdoing."

"This is war. Blood and suffering comes with war. Some have to die so that others may live—brothers against brothers and fathers against their own sons. You can blame my father and the rest of the Díaz regime for what's happening. The peasants are hungry for the land and food. Madero tried, but failed, not being quick enough, so they conspired against him and they killed him. It's left up to us to fight for our freedom," he said with a sarcastic tone, narrowing his eyes.

Luis stood up and addressed the revolutionists. "I know you men have almost forgotten what a woman looks like. Leave the women alone for now. There are plenty of them in Mexico and very willing if I may say, more plentiful in Monterrey. We will take the food and what is needed for the coming battle. All of you men had better get some rest. See that your guns and rifles are in good working order. We are going to use them very soon!"

Luis sat down and, with a sad face, turned to Victoria. "My mother," he said, with sadness in his eyes. "Have you seen her lately? I haven't seen her in several years, ever since my father found out that I was against his corrupt ways and ordered me out of the house, never to return. I went against his orders, and he sent me out into the cold world. Maybe it was for the best. I have learned a lot about life."

"Your mother is doing fine. She was here two weeks ago with Ricardo."

"So, you've heard about the killing."

"About the killing of Madero, yes!" she said, lowering her head.

"No! About your grandfather in Mexico City and what happened to him."

"What happened to Grandfather?" asked Victoria, panicked. "You know what happened to him? Please tell me! He's been gone for some time and everyone in the Hinojosa hacienda is worried."

Felicia had managed to get out of the cellar and began helping the Indian girl whose clothes were torn to ribbons. Her face was pallid and full of fear, as she had witnessed the incident from her hiding place among the cellar wines. An elderly Indian servant whisked the crying young girl away, as Felicia found Victoria and sat down beside her.

"Felicia! Are you all right?" questioned Victoria, already distressed. Felicia's face was strained and without color. She did not answer. "Luis do you remember Felicia, my cousin, Aunt Emma's daughter?"

"You have grown up, too. I remember seeing you as a little girl."

"What about Grandfather?" Victoria prodded.

"*Señor* Hinojosa was in the capital. When Huerta found out he was in the city, he accused him of being a traitor to the Díaz regime. It was an excuse, of course, since your grandfather has always remained neutral even after his retirement. When Madero took office, the conspiracy began pointing the finger at those who had not supported Díaz. Bernardo Reyes was shot down at the foot of the steps of the palace by the cadets of the military school being led by the Minister of War, Huerta. Two days after Madero and Suarez were assassinated, your grandfather was hung from a large *ahuehuete* tree."

Victoria felt as if her heart were being pulled from her chest, as tears filled her eyes. "Grandfather is dead? I can't believe that!" she cried, bringing her hands up to her face.

"The prison walls were opened and many of us prisoners joined together fighting for the cause of Mexico. We left the capitol and joined with some of Zapata's men. We are on our way to join Venustiano Carranza up north. He has chartered the Plan of Guadalupe for the constitutionalist movement. I'm sorry about your grandfather, but being in politics comes with a high price."

Felicia hugged Victoria and tried to console her. "It's going to be all right, Victoria. There is nothing we can do."

Between her uncontrollable sobs and wiping her eyes, Victoria stammered, "What's going to happen now?"

"Do not cry, *Chiquita!*" said Luis. "The best suggestion I can give you two girls is to go back to Texas and leave Mexico forever. This is only the beginning, and it's going to get worse."

"Going back to Texas is going to be an ordeal. We are going to have to wait until Father comes to get us," said Victoria.

"You can ride with us. We are going as far as Camargo, then to the state of Coahulila, waiting for orders from Carranza and the other regiment under the command of Juan Alvarez to join us."

"Juan Alvarez, did you say?" This news shook Victoria, who looked up at Luis, her eyes widening.

"You know him?" answered Luis, puzzled and scratching his head.

"Why, yes, where is he now?" queried Victoria.

"Several miles south of here. He should be arriving soon. Our plans were to take the southeastern part of Monterrey, then head up north, where we will gain more recruits and more forces." Luis could not help noticing that the look in Victoria's eyes had turned from tears to joy. "I understand now," he said, smiling. "You must have been the *Tejana* girl he talked about all the time while in prison. Small world! He had all of us prisoners dreaming, keeping our hopes up. How do you know Juan?"

"He was a guest at my birthday party and gave me this golden amulet as a surprise." Victoria pulled her golden necklace from inside her blouse, embracing it like the priceless possession it was. "Ricardo had just returned from Paris and was sick and not able to attend my fiesta."

"Oh! I see! While the cat is away, the mouse will play!" Luis grinned and winked at her. "Juan should be here by now!" he said, viewing Victoria as a young, foolish girl, infatuated with the revolutionist Juan, and never having known want or hunger.

Then he spoke with sadness in his voice, staring down at the empty plate on the table. "Those were bad times for me," he said softly. "Ricardo was away in France, and my father ordered me out of our hacienda, leaving me penniless. He never gave me one single peso, and I had to defend myself, finding food wherever I could get it. I learned my lesson the hard way. I was hungry and got put in prison for stealing a few morsels of food. My father knew about it and never tried to help me." He looked up. "Now about Juan—he's quite the *hombre*, Victoria! Be real careful! He's not the marrying type!"

Victoria's heart pumped faster at hearing those shocking words. She felt disappointed and her mind was spinning. *Juan promised to marry me. He wanted to elope with me. Has he changed his mind?*

There was more noise and commotion coming from the courtyard. Entering from the archway into the kitchen was a ragged young man, barefooted, with an old faded serape wrapped around him, holding onto a woman. The woman's face was covered by a dark *rebozo* and she was draped in a colorful blanket, as the night air was chilly. As they approached, Victoria's eyes grew wider with recognition as she viewed the woman's face. "Amparo! It's Amparo and her brother!" shouted Victoria, looking at Luis. "Don't you recognize them, Luis? They come from your father's villa."

Luis frowned and looked puzzled. "They must have come to my father's hacienda after I left. No, I don't know them. But she is very beautiful."

The two individuals picked their way through the crowd of revolutionists scattered around the kitchen, which looked like a battlefield inside the convent. Amparo and her brother appeared weak from exhaustion. A soldier still eating and chewing his food smiled at Luis and then winked, remarking, "A fine woman for you, Luis! You will not be cold tonight, *compadre*, eh!"

Victoria and Felicia rushed to help Amparo, who looked faint.

Amparo's brother spoke in words barely audible, for he was out of breath. "We escaped with only the clothes on our backs. I managed to kill one of the dogs, but the other dogs got away and killed two *peóns* who were running and risked their lives for us to leave. It's been five days since we left. Last night was spent in the shelter of some rocks, cold and in fear, knowing that we could find refuge in the convent. We have been running all day, never stopped or dared to look back. Please, can we have some water to drink?"

"Bring them some water. What is your name, *amigo*?" asked Luis, getting up from the table.

ROOTS OF INDIFFERENCE

"My name, *Señor*, is Mario. I want to help with the Revolution. My sister and I have been used as slaves at *El General* Del Calderóne's hacienda. We waited for the chance to leave and did when the *campesinos* from the hills came down with pitch forks and plows to destroy the Del Calderóne's villa. Many buildings were burned and, with the distractions, my sister and I decided to run or be killed."

"We need all who will join us," said Luis to Mario and then to the beautiful Amparo.

"*Si, Señor!* My sister and I will do anything. We both want our freedom. We will go with you," he said, breathing very rapidly.

"But tell me, what about the family that lived in the villa? What happened to them?" questioned Luis with much concern. "Were the members of the family killed?" How were they to know that the family that Luis was referring to was his own blood?

"*La Señora* and *El General* left with their son Ricardo several days ago to *El Distrito Federal*. They probably do not know what has happened to their villa. It was the *Mayordomos* and several of the hatred *patrónes* who were killed. The granaries and fields were all destroyed and the hacienda was burned down. It was still burning when we left. The peasants took most of the furniture and ransacked the storehouse, taking all the food. The *peóns* are heading to destroy the other villas and do the same."

The revolutionist who had grabbed Victoria earlier, rushed over and whispered in Luis's ear.

Felicia shook with fear and became panic-stricken, turning to Victoria. "What are we going to do now? The *peóns* are going to destroy the Hinojosa's hacienda."

"We mustn't stay here for very long," explained Luis. "We just got word that all the telegraph lines have been cut. Several trains have also been derailed. We need to stay and get some sleep tonight and then leave this area early tomorrow as soon as possible."

"But—"

"Nothing doing! After we leave, the *Federalists* will come and devour everything. You think my men are terrible—wait until the *Federalists* show up! I know! My father and the rest of the animals are experts in torturing and making people talk."

In the midst of his conversation, Luis was interrupted. "*Capitán* Luis!" shouted a revolutionist, rushing in from the courtyard. "Two nuns have escaped!"

"Fool!" Luis expressed angrily. "Go and get several men and get them. Find them, quickly! If you men hadn't been fooling around with the young girls, you would have paid more attention to the nuns. They are yours to keep. Don't come back until you find them. They are going directly to get help from the *Federalists*. We have come a long way, and the horses need rest."

"*Sí, mi Capitán!*" Said the soldier.

After saying that, Luis ordered another soldier to go and check on Mother Superior. "I don't trust her," he declared flatly. "Most of the money that comes from a place like this," he said, "comes from the corrupt government." His eyes wandered up to the convent's high ceilings and the elegant long corridors.

After an hour had passed, a shaken Mexican doctor arrived at the convent with his black bag, looking for the dying man for whom Mother Superior had ordered medical care. He was taken down the hall to the wounded man.

Thousands of thoughts were running through both girls' minds. Felicia nervously got up from the table and went outside. Victoria followed her. The sky had become a mirage of stars, with a soft wind that had stirred and become chilled. Most of the skirmish had ceased, and out in the courtyard the peasants had built a huge fire to keep warm. The two girls sat on a low cement wall where they could feel some of the heat.

Victoria felt Felicia shake and helped her wipe her tears. "We cannot stay here, Felicia! We will have to go with Luis as far as Carmago. There, he will give us some good horses so we can get back across the border into Texas."

"We'll never make it!" cried Felicia in between her whimpers. "I have a horrible fear that something terrible is going to happen to us. You heard about your grandfather Hinojosa and what happened to him. He was an important man, and we are nothing."

"We will make it, Felicia! Stop your bawling! You heard Luis tell us that Juan will be coming, and he will see that we are safe. Stop crying! You are going to attract the other crazy men," Victoria whispered between clenched teeth, trying to convince Felicia that things were going to be all right.

Felicia trembled and wailed loudly and more bitterly. "Going back to Texas is going to be worse. If I go back home, I'll have to put up with my stepfather again. I'm fighting two evils. I like it here, where nobody bothers me. If I go back home, I'll have to confront my stepfather and tell my mother what has happened. Things are going to be worse. I was thinking of joining the nuns."

"Horse feathers, Felicia! Becoming a nun? You're out of your mind! There is nothing worse. We will get back to Texas, and things are going to be all right, you'll see."

Suddenly, from the iron gates came the sounds of horses and a group of riders, then a haunting silhouette; the familiar figure ambled toward the kitchen. Victoria's heart began beating wildly.

It was Juan. The others with him were three Americans, and all were weighted down with rifles and double-crossed cartridge belts full of bullets. They made a brilliant display throughout the shadows of the filtering light.

Juan did not see Victoria. His handsome face looked burned by the sun; only his eyes were like two reflections that guided him inside the convent, where Luis and the rest of the revolutionaries were carousing drunk. He had dismounted in a quick bounce, and two of the Americans had followed, while one delayed getting off his horse. There was loud laughter and joking when Juan and the *Americanos* entered the kitchen. The one *Americano*, who remained outside heard Felicia's sniffles and, after hesitating for a few seconds, dismounted and strolled toward the two girls.

"Felicia," whispered Victoria. "I wish you would stop crying. It's not going to help us. You have attracted the attention of the *gringo*, and he's coming this way."

In the dim light of the kitchen and the campfire outside, they could see that he was a tall, blond young man. Taking off his hat, he apologized for the way he looked.

"We've been traveling for a several days," he said. "I normally don't look like this, and I need a bath real bad. You ladies speak any English?" His eyes wandered to Felicia.

Both girls eyed him and remained silent.

"What's the matter with this good-looking girl?" he asked. "I couldn't help hearing her crying," he said sympathetically. His concern for them was puzzling. He continued talking as he squatted down near Felicia. "Well, now! Things couldn't be too bad. What seems to have happened here?" His eyes sparkled in the firelight.

Victoria got up and snapped, "What does it look like has happened? We are like the rest, caught in the middle of a revolution and trying to find a way to get back to Texas!"

"You're from ol' Texas! Which part?" He grinned with delight.

"I'm from Spanish Acres north of Mercedes City, and Felicia," she said, pointing to Felicia, "she's my cousin from Mercedes City."

"Well, I'll be a monkey's uncle. I'll swan," he said in his Texas brogue. "I'm from McAllen and have been away from the Valley for almost nine months. Felicia, eh? That's a right pretty name." He pulled out a bandanna and tried to wipe Felicia's eyes. "Pardon me. My name is Dan—Dan Land. And your name is Felicia? Now there is no reason why a pretty girl like you should be sitting on the cold cement crying. I'm headed to the border myself and will gladly travel with both of you misses. That's if it's all right, and you'll let me. Pardon me for coming on so strong, missy, but I've been away for so long and haven't seen such pretty girls."

"Where are you men coming from?" questioned Victoria.

"Well, I'll tell you miss. Ten months ago, I was doing some investments for my father. Well, I had several tequilas in an ol' *cantina* close to Mexico City. I questioned the charges. There were words and a dispute. The *cantina* owner ended up calling the *Federalists,* and I ended up in a real hellhole. Those confounded men accused me of causing trouble in a foreign country and locked me up, and I thought I was never going to see daylight again. Several days ago, this revolutionist, Juan, and his friends opened the prison door and let all of us out of the dungeon."

He paused and shook his head. "There were several other Americans from up north who kept me company in there, or I would have gone completely insane. There were two from Harlingen, Texas. One was a retired Texas Ranger, and the other one was a big brute of a man, a Ranger also. Anyway, all they talked about was if they got out alive, they were going to kill a bigwig across the border because of a gold mine. They left quickly and did not want to come with us." He then turned his full attention to Felicia.

Coincidence or fate, did *Doña* Adela not predict this?

Mother of God, sighed Victoria. Any minute she would join Felicia and start her own bawling fit. *Juan actually let the demons out of the dungeon—the two devils that my father was sure he was safe from, and now they are free! They were turned loose to come back into Texas and haunt my father!* Victoria felt her body go limp and leaned against the whitewashed wall, not knowing if it was anger, love, or fear that she felt inside. She closed her eyes. The world was coming to an end for her entire family.

"Olga, mister *gringo!*" roared a revolutionist, who staggered out of the kitchen half drunk. They had broken into the cellar and had emptied the wine storehouse. "How goes it? Are you going to fight with us?"

Dan Land did not respond. He seemed to be taken with Felicia. The peasant stumbled, tried to keep his balance, and went back inside holding onto the wall with one hand and grasping a bottle of wine in the other.

From the flaming courtyard, a lone Mexican had procured a guitar. Several joined in the singing of a new song, *Estrellita*. The words were beautiful and so much like the symbol of Mexico, with its struggles, bitterness, love, and death.

Victoria leaned against the stone wall and closed her eyes again, listening to the sweet music that filtered throughout the still night. It was pleasant memories that would keep her strong on a night like this. The music reminded her of her birthday, Spanish Acres, her family, Juan, and all of the people she loved.

Then, from out of nowhere, the spirit of *La bruja* seemed to envelope her mind. What *Doña* Adela had told them in the reading of the cards was all coming to pass: guns, arms and ammunition; the killing; the destruction of the big haciendas. She began to wonder if the two of them would be able to get back to Texas safely. She thought about her father. He was probably going out of his mind with worry.

Felicia seemed more relaxed as she stood up and walked out into the courtyard, talking with the *gringo*, Dan Land, leaving Victoria alone against the arched walls.

A shadow slipped out from the noisy lit kitchen, sauntered forward, and stood still in front of her. With her eyes closed, the figure blocked the flickering light, surprising her. When she opened her eyes, there was the familiar face she had dreamed about for so many countless, sleepless nights.

Victoria smiled an uneasy smile, and slipped away into that certain weakness that came with love, but at the same time, she hated him for not corresponding with her within the last two years.

Juan's breath had the smell of liquor and cigarettes, and he stood close enough that he could kiss her, but he only glared at her with malice. His olive skin reflected against the shadow of the night, as he stood with his dirty, white shirt loose and open. He leaned his hand against the stone wall over her head and began talking with haste.

"I'm surprised to find you here, still hanging around this convent. Haven't you gotten enough religion already? I thought that by now your high-priced family had taken you away to Texas and married you off to the fancy Del Calderóne general's son." His voice was full of sarcasm and contempt, his eyes glaring at her as if knives were slashing into her body. He stood looking down at her with scorn, uncertain of what to do with her next.

Victoria wanted to fall into his arms and love him, and began to speak. As her mouth opened to reply, he stopped her with a long, cruel kiss. Her body stiffened. His fingers gripped her hair, and he pushed his body full against her, crushing her against the rough wall. *Was this the same man she had known and made love with two years before? Why was he treating her like a two-bit whore? How dare him!* When he gave her hair a hard tug, she lashed out in sheer agony. "Damn you!" she hissed in a breathless sound, trying to fight against his hard, cruel grip. "Aren't you glad to see me? What has gotten into you?"

Juan was angry, tired, and hungry for ardor. Seeing her again had only brought out the hellish passion he once had for her. She had been in his mind all the time he had spent in prison. He had been left to rot, accused of killing a man in the Hinojosa's hacienda, a person he didn't even know, all because her damned family had pointed their finger at him and used him as a scapegoat. He was going to forget he was once a gentleman—he would spend the night with her and show her what real love meant.

"Juan!" Victoria pleaded with him. "What in the world has gotten into you?" Puzzled by his roughness, she demanded, "What has happened to you since I last saw you? All this time you never wrote me a letter or came to see me."

"Come to see you?" he said. "How could I have come to see you? All this time I've been rotting in prison because your damn grandfather accused me of killing one of his *peóns!*"

"Dear God!" Victoria whispered to herself in shock. Her body went weak with fear, knowing that her grandfather, the accuser, was already dead.

Juan's hand went around her body roughly and with a quick, swift whirl he picked her up and dragged her into one of the tile corridors in the dark. Finding an empty room, he kicked the door open and let Victoria down, giving her a hard shove. Landing on the floor, she tried to balance herself. Everything was happening so fast, and her puzzled mind was starting to spin; she was at a loss for words, panting, out of breath. Through the filtering light from the window, she could tell that he was furious as he came toward her, talking in a cruel voice.

"You hypocrite!" he roared. "In the last two years I have cursed you for ever setting eyes on you. You are a serpent—a snake in the grass and the type of woman that gets a man into trouble. What happened two years ago, Victoria? You tell me? It was a week after we made love—remember? Or have you conveniently forgotten it! I was arrested in my home, put in jail for killing a man, a man that I did not know. The *Federalists* beat and tortured me until I had to confess that I had been at your grandfather's hacienda, the Lord and Master *Don* Hinojosa. I don't know who killed his worker, God only knows, but I was dumped in a cell and given only bread and water to survive. Later I was transported to a jail in Mexico City, because I was considered dangerous to the *Federalists*—a threat to the *Federalist* regime. A degrading experience, don't you agree? One week ago, I finally managed to escape from prison, letting the rest of the men out, along with the lice on my body. I ate with rats and cockroaches, nothing but filth. I swore that if I ever got out alive, I would get my revenge. Your grandfather found it convenient to blame me. It's the way political games are played."

"Felicia! I'll have to check on Felicia and see if she is safe," Victoria said, stalling for time.

Juan grabbed her and said, "No, you don't! Felicia is very safe with the *Americano*." He then commanded harshly, "Now—take your clothes off! Or I will take them off myself!"

Panic stricken, Victoria stood in shock for a moment and then moved swiftly. She could feel herself shudder as he came toward her and removed his shirt and unfastened his trousers.

Juan made his movements deliberately and quickly against her as he savagely ripped her blouse from one shoulder. His eyes were glazed with animal lust. His hands were like burning branding irons over her skin and breast, his mouth like a wild man thirsty for pleasure over her petrified lips. He began kissing her on the throat and then further down, groping her tingling breasts and enticing the desire from her, as her knees went weak. He continued to tear every stitch from her body, even tearing the chain of the golden amulet he had given her from around her neck. They were both caught in a feverish whirlwind of love and hate, as her body went limp to his wanton needs.

Victoria had dreamed of making love to Juan so many nights, but not in this savage way. She quickly responded with nonresistance to his actions, but in fear. She could hear his breath becoming harder as Juan took his time in his pleasure, their bodies melding into one.

CHAPTER 21

The moonlight coming from the iron barred window reflecting on her face made Victoria blink. How long she lay on the cold floor with a woolen blanket, she did not know. All she could remember was the thrill of excitement she had finally reached by pure passion, a new and unknown experience. She realized now why adultery was so common; she knew now what it was to be a woman and the pleasure of satisfying a man's wants. A moment of guilt seemed to engulf her and possess her.

"*Virgen de Guadalupe,*" she said softly to herself, and then she began to cry. She was tortured with so many unanswered questions and now doubted if there was any future for her. Life's reality faced her squarely: how could she admit to Juan that it was she alone who killed the worker at her grandfather's hacienda, for which he had been blamed? Juan had already suffered too much in prison. Everyone had paid for their mistakes, including her. Grandfather was dead, and the two demons, Hanson and Hobbs, had been turned loose on her father. She had no other choice but to leave with Luis and Juan and return to her grandfather's hacienda and hope it had not been destroyed. All she wanted was to be back in the safe arms of her mother and Mamá Maria back in Texas, where she belonged. She would learn to accept the ridiculous situation they were in. Her father would be coming to get them out of this conflagration. She felt hopeless and without strength. Only degradation and despair seemed left. She was embarrassed having to explain to Felicia what took place, but Felicia knew all about feeling hopeless and embarrassed.

Heavy footsteps were coming down the corridor. Victoria sat up and grabbed the blanket to hide her bare chest. She held her breath.

With a sudden jerk, Juan opened the door. In his hands was a bundle of clothes, including men's trousers, a white muslin shirt, and a straw hat. He threw them down on the floor beside her. "Put them on!" he ordered coldly. "You will need them to keep you warm, especially up in the mountains where we are heading. There has been a change in plans. These clothes will disguise you from being a woman, and you are aware of how amorous we Mexicans are. We don't want to attract attention on the road up ahead. There are too many *Federalists* and *bandidos* on the road nowadays. We don't want any men to get any ideas, do we, *Querida?*"

Victoria felt trapped, and there was nothing she could do but to go along with his orders and suggestions. She tried to protest in silence, but her eyes and the look on her face gave her away. She managed to find her fortune reading cards on the floor among the shredded clothes, in the pocket of her apron, and slipped them inside the pants that she was supposed to wear. She retrieved the broken amulet from the floor and, still in a daze, sat there and began to cry.

Juan stood over her, suddenly feeling guilty for his conduct of last night. "Victoria," he said gently, his tone changing to one more endearing. "I want to apologize for last night. That is not normally like me. I will get your golden amulet fixed and send it to you." He took the amulet out of her hands and put it in his pocket. "I don't know what came over me. I saw you and—anger overcame me. Thinking of the long hours and nights I suffered in that damn rotten prison, thinking only of you, thinking of all the things I could have been doing to help Madero. I am sorry for what I said I. I truly love you. Every time I think of you being married to that pompous Ricardo, it completely destroys me." He squatted down and wiped Victoria's eyes. "Please forgive me. All I want to do is to help you get out of this country and get you safely back home."

From outside the courtyard there were several loud explosions of rifles. Victoria quickly sprang to her feet and exclaimed, "Shots! Who is being shot?" She was worried about Felicia, since she had not seen her in several hours.

"Traitors, my dear, by Luis's orders," he answered. "The stupid nuns who got away were caught and are getting what they deserve. And now there is the Queen of Traitors— Mother Superior, who couldn't wait to sell us out to the damn *Federalists* and tell them everything. She's been supporting their cause for many years. Selling little babies to high-priced families all over this area and getting money to support her needs. This is all part of the dirty little game of war—the concession of good and evil."

While bent over and putting her hair under the straw hat, Victoria straightened herself up and said, "Dear God! Not Mother Superior, too! You are all sick!" she hissed. "I'll be glad to get back to Texas where I belong, where people are civilized!"

"Really *Corazón*, you don't think that Mother Superior did not hurt the poor Indian girls that would come to the clinic to have their babies? And then later she would tell them goodbye and send them off empty-handed, without their infants? The young girls were impregnated by the rich *hacendados*, like the Del Calderónes, and brought here to keep silent for big bucks. Where do you think the babies go? They were sold to wealthy couples around the region and throughout Mexico. She was collecting quite a bundle of money."

"I can't believe that! Those are lies! All of you are making up these ungodly stories. All of the nuns were very kind to the Indians girls. All I want is to leave Mexico forever!"

"Believe it, it's the truth. Everybody in this region has known about her little game and how she was piling up money for her cause. Real convenient, making her a hero for helping the poor peasant girls, while putting money in her pocket and laughing all the way to her deposit box."

"I don't know anything about how Mother Superior operated the convent. All I want is to leave and go back to Texas, where I belong."

"And leave my undying love? How else would you have learned to make love with so much ecstasy to a real *hombre* like myself?" His sea-green eyes were glowing through his sarcastic grin. "You didn't seem to mind us making love again so early this morning. You seemed to be ready to really enjoy it. Ricardo has taught you well."

"Oh!" Victoria hissed. Wearily, she walked out into the long corridor, wrapping the serape around her. "A real *hombre*!" she snarled. "Real *hombres* don't treat women like this! And as for your information, how would I know of another man? You are the only one I've ever made love to."

"Honestly, *Querida!* You are not trying to tell me that, in the last two years, dear Ricardo hasn't gotten into your bloomers?"

Indignant and burning with anger, Victoria turned to Juan and gave him a vicious look. She could not believe what came out of his mouth. One minute he was kind, and the next, horrid.

Juan mocked her and pinched her buttock, wanting to get more of a response. "*Querida,* from this angle no one would recognize that you are a woman. And what a woman!" He then laughed out loud, mockingly. "You are so beautiful when you're angry."

"Oh! The nerve," she said. "How quickly you have forgotten that you were in prison!"

⌘ ⌘ ⌘

It was a long time afterwards, while riding double on horseback with Juan, that Victoria came to her senses. She couldn't erase from her mind the bloody scene as they exited the convent courtyard: the nuns shot in the head; Mother Superior sprawled on the cold ground with blood all over her white habit; the poor *peón* women praying; nuns crying; blood everywhere; and the shallow graves.

But Victoria could not escape the fact that she had wished *evil* on Mother Superior and had witnessed it coming to pass. She recalled seeing Felicia, her face red and swollen from crying, while holding on tightly to the *Americano*, Dan Land. Everything had happened so fast. There was Luis Del Calderóne, Amparo, and her brother Mario telling them to go with God. They would be leaving later, but along a different, rougher route.

"*Vaya con Dios.*" Luis had tears in his eyes, and his words were like echoes in her ears. "When you see my mother, tell her to pray for me. I have blood on my hands for trying to do what's right. One day when this war is over, maybe I'll be able to see her. She is the only one who has understood me."

⌘ ⌘ ⌘

Juan pulled the reins tight against the bit of the horse to keep it from whinnying, while Victoria sat square in the middle in front of him. They had taken a path off the main road. The country was at war, and they did not want to look suspicious to any *Federalists* army.

Dan and Felicia kept pace in front of them, with the two other *Americanos* several yards ahead. With the light of the setting moon, they could see the fog rising from the impenetrable jungle of tropical trees, ferns and wild vegetation. They could hear the trickling of water coming from a stream below that had melted from the snow-covered *Sierra Madre Mountains*. They rested for a little while and then continued following the path up toward the towering mountains.

The dawn of day was coming, and dew on the foliage glittered from the rays of the morning light. Soon the mountainside became steep and dangerous. Huge rocks jutted from the slopes. They slowed their pace, keeping a close watch on the enormous boulders on both sides of the path. Hours later, the trail sloped down into a green valley with fields of buttercups and purple and white verbena flowers, mixed with tall yellow hedges of wild sunflowers. It was breathtaking, and the first signs of spring.

Juan, always suspicious, would occasionally stop his horse and look backwards and in every direction, making sure that nobody was following them. The *Federalists* and bandits were everywhere and easily could shoot them from yards away. He made sure to stay away from any clearing. The sun was already at high noon when Juan yelled to the others in front of him, suggesting that the horses needed water and rest. They came upon tall trees where they could be sheltered from any intruders, and a stream where the horses could drink and be relieved of their heavy load. They built a small fire and made coffee, sharing strips of dry beef.

They rested for an hour or more, and then began riding on the elevated, rocky path again. The vegetation became less green, looking more like a desert environment with a variety of cacti, mixed chaparrals, sage, and other rugged bushes, an undulation of dreary landscape on which only the tough maguey and cactus could grow. The heat gradually became unbearable. Juan suggested that they plaster mud on their arms and face to keep the burning sun from infiltrating their skin. On both sides of the low, dry valley they could see the magnificence purple of the Sierra Madres covered with snow. The wind began blowing strongly, forcing the riders to slow their pace.

The ride had become a long, exhausting trip up the rocky, winding trail. Finally, the sun began going down over the mountain range, and it glowed like a supreme god, ruling both the heavens and dry earth. At last, the sun's rays kissed the foreheads of the two lovers, who dared not disturb the silence of the lonely path.

It was not long before the glittering sky finally took possession of the coming night. The surrounding land looked empty and lonely, and the darkness became cold with sprinkles of millions of brilliant stars overhead.

Through the darkness, Dan Land, riding double with Felicia, backtracked toward Juan and Victoria. "Felicia is sick. She has been ill since we left the convent, but she didn't want to say anything, not wanting to delay our journey to Monterrey. It got dark so fast. We're gonna have to stop. She is exhausted and has a fever."

"We'll stop and find shelter among those caves. It will keep us from the cold wind during the night," replied Juan. The wind had gotten stronger, and bitter cold, coming off the snowfields of the rugged Sierras.

Dismounting, Dan carried Felicia over to a large cave. Inside, he took his jacket off and laid her head on it. He unfastened his horse's saddle and brought it over to Felicia, propped her head up on it and laid his jacket over her shoulders. Felicia's face was drawn by the mud on her face and fatigued by the long weary trip; already she made gasping noises, trying to catch her breath.

"I just don't know if this poor gal will be able to travel any longer," declared Dan with a frown. "She needs rest, food, and a doctor to look after her. She's got a fever."

"We'll find food," commented Juan dismounting, as Victoria hurried over to comfort Felicia. "I'll see if I can catch some rabbits that are plentiful in this region." He informed the other *Americanos*, "We must not use our guns or rifles in any way. The noise will attract bandits who roam the countryside. We must be real careful. We will take turns watching during the night."

Inside the hollow cave, the rest of the men built a fire to keep warm, and then made strong, black coffee. One of the *Americano* poured water from his canteen on his bandana and placed it on Felicia's forehead. Victoria used the bandana to wipe the mud off Felicia's face.

Juan had disappeared among the rocky, snowy ground and, within an hour, had brought back five rabbits, hanging by their ears. After being cleaned, they were put on a stout twig to roast.

After eating, Juan showed the men how to make small trenches for their beds by pouring hot embers into them, filling them with dirt then branches, and using their blankets. This would keep them warm though the cold night. More branches of dry *mogotes* and tough pinos trees were put on the fire to keep it burning all night within the cave.

While the men began digging their trenches, Juan mentioned that they could not slow down their traveling. "Not now!" he said emphatically. "*Bandidos* use this road for their hide-outs, and it's too dangerous being on this road without an army. I have an appointment in Monterrey that has to be kept. I promised Luis. Even if we ride very hard, we still have more days of rough riding."

The air had become crisp, and the night wind blew sharply around the rocks surrounding the cave. From the empty, infinitely lonely distance came the howling of wolves.

Victoria sat down in silence close to the fire to keep herself warm, and Juan joined her. She was trying to keep to herself, her thoughts becoming distant. She was weary to the point of exhaustion. She was cold and shivering. She needed a warm bath. She was afraid of the dangerous country they were confronting. What lay ahead? Felicia was sick. Her memory wandered. It had been almost two years ago that the two had visited *Doña* Adela. It became vivid in her mind what the old *bruja* had told them: *You will have a wonderful trip while you are away and will enjoy dining and dancing, seeing your family, but on the return trip I see many deaths, many, many deaths!* It had already begun: the killing of nuns; the brutal killing of Mother Superior; her grandfather now dead. What else would she encounter when they reached the Hinojosa's hacienda?

Juan put his arm around her. He could tell that she was worried and concerned about Felicia's illness. He brought several blankets that had been stolen from the convent and gently put them over Victoria's shoulders, kissing her on the cheek. "We've got a rough day coming, and don't worry too much about Felicia. It looks like Dan has taken a liking to her and is taking care of her. Unfortunately, without the proper medicine, there is nothing I can do to help. We are headed up the mountain where there's a village, near the gold mine your family owns, where some friends of mine will take care of you and your cousin. I don't know how long I can stay, but I'll see if I can help Felicia get over her fever. I fear she has some kind of infection. Normally that's what brings fevers."

Victoria noticed how tender his voice was, so kind and full of compassion—so different from the night before. She never spoke a word. She was hungry, cold, and exhausted. As she curved her neck on the saddle and cuddled cozily in a fetal position, she pulled the blanket up and over her. Juan crawled next to her and rolled into his blanket and went to sleep. One of the *Americanos* had volunteered to stay up all night and count the brilliant, endless stars.

CHAPTER 22

By the time the first rays of the morning sun shone over the mountain peaks, the group was already traveling through high, mountainous and hostile country. It had been a short, restless night for all of them.

Felicia's condition had worsened; she was weak and limp and unable to hold her head up. Dan carried her in his arms while riding. Everyone had become concerned, even Juan, who was so anxious to get to Monterrey.

Juan yelled to the other riders, "The village is several miles down this path and will probably take us most of the day to get there. They will assist us and help Felicia. Most of the peasants work in the gold and silver mines up in the high Sierras." Juan pressed his arms against Victoria's legs as she rode in front of him, and whispered. "See! I'm not such a bad *hombre*, after all."

Victoria kept her silence. They were traveling in the direction of the gold mines. *Those were my father's and grandfather's mines, where he almost got killed,* she thought.

Ignoring Juan's remark, all she could think of at the moment was visions of the wonderful *desayunos*, breakfasts; she used to have at Spanish Acres. The delicious beefsteaks, fried eggs, warm tortillas with melted butter, and hot chocolate moved deliriously through her mind. Her body ached from the stony, solid ground on which she had laid, a poor excuse for a bed. She was not used to this kind of existence and probably could never get accustomed to these conditions. She felt dirty, and her peasant shirt and trousers carried the smell of ashes; her face and arms were covered with a white, chalky powder from the dried mud; her hair was like straw. Occasionally, her stomach would growl.

"*Querida*," remarked Juan. "I'll have to get some food for you. Don't want you to get too skinny. I prefer my *muchachas* on the plump side."

Horse feathers! Men are as fickle as weather vanes, she thought. Even so, it was amazing how Juan took care of her and protected all of them from danger. Two nights ago he could have killed her. He seemed to have inner strength, courage, and fortitude and had forgotten the time he spent in prison by the way he treated and teased her. Juan was like an Indian and knew where every waterhole and shelter was located. He had lived in the mountains too long. He was more like a renegade than a revolutionist.

Juan's hands would now and then rub against her thighs and would travel slowly under her long peasant pants. Her legs spread apart on the saddle made it easy for him to reach her with his incessant movements. Victoria shuddered, bringing on the desire and passion. With a half-mocking laugh, he would whisper to her from behind. "Try to contain yourself, *Querida*." His strong arms would tighten around her waist, drawing her closer.

"Juan! Please stop it," she pleaded, blushing. "The others will turn around and see us!"

"Let them see us! What do I care?" he answered sharply. "Love is a natural thing. They all know that we are not just friends. If God hadn't made love, just think how dull life would be for all of us, and the world would die. All the time that I was in prison, if it hadn't been for dreaming of making passionate love with you, I would have died a thousand deaths." He kissed her on the back of her neck, his whiskers rubbing sharply on her skin. He bit her ears playfully. He let his tongue roll on the back of her neck, mocking her and teasing her until she squirmed.

"The Mexican man has an enormous sexual appetite that has to be satisfied. It's part of our *macho* image and heritage, and I wouldn't be considered a man if I didn't have those desires, *Querida*."

"Let's not display it out here in this desolate wilderness in front of everyone," she said irritably.

They had traveled for hours, following one another like a small caravan, when one of the *Americanos* in the front of the pack yelled out. "I see an old church and some huts down below," he said. "It looks like a village!"

Juan rode his horse faster and moved in front of the other riders, leading them down the ravine. They followed in a slow trot through huge boulders on both sides of the mountainous trail and into green vegetation. They had traveled all day, and the sun was going down between the high ranges. Small huts made of mud and straw were whitewashed and built together in single file on both sides of the dirt road; an old whitewashed church stood in the town square, empty, faded, and desolate. Several small boys playing downstream eyed them and ran to meet them but acted apprehensive and leery, not knowing what to expect.

"Is *Señor* Martinez here at the village?" Juan questioned the boys, who stood by the dirt trail, hiding behind some of the trees, immobile, and acting frightened and nervous.

"*Sí, Señor*," timidly answered one of the boys. "I'll go and find him!"

Within minutes, several women in dark, drab clothes, with *rebozos* around their heads came out of their huts with their children and stood with anticipation, watching the group come closer. *Señor* Martinez showed up from behind one of the buildings wearing faded muslin clothes. He humbly removed his worn-out straw hat, exposing his white head of hair.

"Juan!" said *Señor* Martinez. "You are not safe here. The *Federalists* are looking for you. They were here several days ago and took everything we had. They searched the huts to see if you were hiding here. They caught us off guard. *Los desgraciados* even raped some of our young girls. We did not have time to hide them. It will be very dangerous for all of us. If they find you, we will all be shot!"

"I've had that suspicion," said Juan, "but, *Señor* Martinez, we need your help and that of the rest of your people. Not for me, but for this young *Señorita* who is really sick. I'm on my way to Monterrey to gather more forces for the Revolution and help free the people from the *Federalists.*"

"Headed for Monterrey? Surely not! It's crawling with *Federalists*—it's their main headquarters. It will not be safe there."

"I'll take my chances," replied Juan, getting off his horse. "The moment is urgent, and we need your help. I will repay you some day, but for now please help us with the *Tejana* girl who is very ill." Juan motioned to Dan to bring Felicia down from the horse.

Señor Martinez took one look at Felicia and said, "*Dios mío!* The girl is burning with fever." Being humble and not forgetting his Mexican manners and hospitality, he requested Felicia be brought into one of the huts. For the moment, he forgot how dangerous it was to shelter any revolutionists.

Felicia was placed inside on a blanket covering the dirt floor. Victoria followed. Several women knowledgeable about herbs and medicine entered the hut and studied Felicia. "She's got the *Evil Eye*," commented one, "better get a fresh egg."

"Bah!" rebutted Juan. Squatting down, he felt Felicia's pulse. "What I think she has is pneumonia. We have to break the fever first." He took off his jacket and ammunition and rolled up his sleeves. Addressing the older woman, he asked if they had any alcohol in the village. She shook her head and said no. "Dan!" he ordered, "Have the others unload their horses behind the huts so it won't seem so obvious that we are here, and bring the tequila bottle from my saddle. He turned to Victoria. "Help me undress Felicia!"

"Undress Felicia?" Victoria questioned, visibly shaken.

"*Sí, mujer,* I've seen plenty of naked women and women giving birth, especially studying pre-med in Puebla. We have to break the fever first or—"

"What will happen?"

"She'll die. That's what will happen."

"Oh, no, Felicia, Felicia, Felicia," cried Victoria, as she hunkered down next to her cousin.

"Don't go to pieces on me now, Victoria!" pleaded Juan. "I need you to help me. Come on!"

"She can't die! I won't let her! She is my one and only cousin whom I love, and the only one I can trust." Victoria shook while sobbing, yet a powerful courage seemed to overcome her, causing her to forget how tired she really was from their long journey. She began helping Juan remove Felicia's clothes.

Dan Land entered the room and put one hand over his eyes, while holding the bottle. "I didn't see anything. What else can I do for you?" His voice was full of concern.

"She needs to drink lots of water or tea; as much as she can hold. Have the old women make some *manzanilla* tea, if they have some. If not, go help them find the bush. We'll have to bring some heat into the hut and steam the area so that her breathing can come easier."

Big Dan Land took his hat off and rubbed his blond head, then nodded and hurried outside. Within minutes, he returned with a pan full of hot embers and placed them close to where Felicia lay. "One of the old woman said that there is no *manzanilla* available, but she has some medicine, a root used as a medication that is even better. She knows exactly what she needs." After saying that, he squatted down close to Juan and watched him and Victoria furiously rubbing the tequila all over Felicia's body.

The old woman brought in the tea called *Oshá* and *Sauco*, mixed with *piloncillo*, to reduce the fever.

"We'll have to take turns giving Felicia this tea. She needs to drink as much as possible."

"I'll stay with her," replied the kindly Dan.

Hours passed before they got anything to eat, then it was corn tortillas with black beans and black coffee. Victoria preferred the fresh goat milk. They all stood outside the hut waiting for some signs of improvement from Felicia.

"When will you leave?" inquired *Señor* Martinez to Juan.

"As soon as I see some stable vital signs from the *Tejana* girl," he said. "She may not make it. I don't know how long that's going to take. I will wait until her fever breaks, probably spend the night here, and then leave as soon as it happens."

"Go and get your rest." *Señor* Martinez replied. "The older women will look after the young girl tonight." Having noticed Victoria's disheveled condition, he commented, "If you need a bath, we have natural hot water that comes from the mountains. You can take a bath there and sleep close to the rocks and be safe. Next to it are large caves. Or you can stay at the stall where the donkeys were, until the *bandidos* stole them. I will put the young boys to watch and see if anyone is coming from the road up ahead. Take your *Señora* and go and rest. There is a new moon tonight."

Victoria tried to speak, but Juan wrapped his arm around her waist, pulling her toward him and guiding her toward the hot baths.

"Come, *Señora!*" he said with a smirk. "We mustn't keep the bath and donkey stall waiting."

"You're not going to leave me out in this wilderness with Felicia sick," Victoria said, coming to her senses. She realized that Juan would be leaving with the other two *Americanos*.

"I didn't plan it this way. If Felicia hadn't gotten sick, we would have already been on the outskirts of Monterrey. The only reason we came to this village was to help your cousin—be grateful for that. I'm already late for my appointment with Luis." Juan removed the blankets from his horse and his saddle and took it with him. "This has always come in handy for a pillow," he said, laughing.

They climbed a winding ravine among the rocks that was verdant with vegetation. When they reached the top they were amazed to see a small waterfall cascading into a pool of clear water, with warm vapors coming from the rocks. It was a hidden paradise among the mountains, with the light of the new moon reflecting on the steamy surface. There were large rock formations around the water and entrances to caves where people could hide. Juan was surprised. In all of the time he had roamed this area, he had never known about this great secret. The Indian people were superstitious and prone to silence, but they could be trusted if shown justice, kindness, and respect.

It didn't take long before the two naked lovers were in the pool splashing and enjoying the delicious, exotic, warm water. As they swam and got closer to the waterfall, the water seemed to get much hotter, so they swam back to a comfortable temperature, closer to the edge by one of the large smooth rocks. There in the enjoyment of the water, Juan grabbed Victoria and turned her toward him, kissed her and pinned her against the rocks. He probed with his tongue deep into her mouth and caressed his hands down her back to her buttocks and pressed them against his body, arousing the longing and passion he had for her. Spreading her legs, he pulled them up around his waist. He stroked her breasts with his mouth as Victoria, limp from the hot water, moaned. Juan's hands moved between her legs, felt and touched, implanting his hard maleness, and then began thrusting with vigorous unbroken movements inside of her. He was now driven to a passion beyond his control, making her groan and pant. He reached the final climax. Their bodies merge into one, forgetting who they were, and for the moment, there were no *mañanas*. They had desired each other for so long. The earth stood still. They remembered only this priceless moment, as they basked in the joy of their union.

Victoria felt wrung out from their passionate lovemaking and from the hot water, which had drained her last ounce of strength. Her body steamed as she climbed out into the chilled air and covered herself with a woolen blanket. She lay on the ground of the cave, her hair splayed out and wet. Juan joined her and began drying her with a cloth. The moon reflected on the two naked lovers' silhouettes on the solid rock floor.

"I'm going to show you how a real man makes love to you, Victoria," Juan whispered in her ear. He kissed her throat gently, his mouth brushing on down to her breasts. Her nipples became erect as he caressed them tenderly with his tongue and hands. He was again driven to a passion beyond his control. She moaned. His kisses lowered down to her waist and navel, and then between her legs, as his tongue went searching, reaching areas in her being she had never imagined before, bringing out intense emotions in her very soul.

Yards away, a goat herder had watched the two lovers intensely from a hole among the rocks where he made camp and became aroused. From the shadows of the bright moon, he observed their performance again. He began rubbing the front of his pants, to the point of ejaculation.

The couple lay on the ground with their arms wrapped around each other for several hours. By the time the dawn of day began shining its light through the trees, Juan had made love to her many times, and the two had not slept. It was their honeymoon in paradise. Juan splashed into the warm water pool for the last time and cleaned himself, then began dressing, knowing that this was perhaps the last time he would ever see Victoria. He was concerned about meeting Luis in Monterrey and afraid of missing him and the rest of the other revolutionists.

While Juan was putting his last garment on, he heard the rustling of feet through the rocks. "Who goes there," said Juan, as he grabbed for his gun belt.

"The fever has already broken," answered the voice. "The *Tejana* woman is going to get better."

"Very well, I will be right down. Have the boys see that my horse is ready. I'll bring the saddle and be right down. I must leave as soon as possible."

Victoria scurried to dress herself in the borrowed *peón* clothes. She was overjoyed to hear that Felicia was better and hastened down to see her cousin and Dan Land. The man was a priceless treasure. *Wait a minute*, she caught herself thinking. *Didn't Doña Adela mention something about a tall, blond man, a foreigner in Mexico? "You will meet your husband in Mexico," she had told Felicia.*

In the village, Juan had already strapped the saddle on his horse, after checking on Victoria's cousin, and was pleased to see Felicia smiling, but still weak.

The other two *Americanos* were waiting on their horses for Juan at the edge of the dirt road.

Victoria glanced at Dan. "You're not leaving us?" she said to the tall, blond man, since fear had begun to grip her, and reality was starting to stare her in the face.

"I'm not about to leave you two out here," Dan replied. "I'm in no hurry to go nowhere, Missy. I'll get to the Valley in my own good time. All I want is for Felicia to get well again," he said, pleased that he had played a part in her recovery.

With tears in her eyes, Victoria ran and hugged Dan, the gentle giant. "You are wonderful!" she said.

Juan, mounted on his horse, approached the two. He bent down and kissed Victoria. "Are you sure you don't want to come with me?"

"And leave Felicia here?"

"Felicia will be all right. Dan is going to take her safely back to Texas. If you truly love me, then you'll come with me. Make up your mind now."

Caught between love and fear, Victoria stood speechless. She loved Juan, but not enough to go with him under the conditions they would all be in. The timing was off.

Juan understood her predicament. "If you ever need to get in touch with me, write to my mother in Monterrey. She will see that I get my messages." He handed her his pistol. "You will need this," he said.

"Juan, I—"Victoria could not speak anymore and burst into tears. She laid the gun down on the ground and covered her face in her hands, trying to hide her uncontrollable grief and fear. "Please don't leave us here! We need you more than ever!" She continued to weep.

"Take good care of Felicia. She is a good person." Juan said. Then he glanced toward Dan and said, "*Adiós, amigo!* God be with you. Some day, I'll see you in Texas." Looking toward *Señor* Martinez, he said, "*Gracias, Señor,* for everything you have done for us, the *Americanos,* and the girls. One day I will replay you—you can mark my words! *Gracias!*"

After speaking those words, Juan rode off toward the gold mines and disappeared over the high Sierras road, catching up with the two *Americanos,* heading to his important meeting with Luis.

⌘ ⌘ ⌘

For the next six days in the high mountainous village, Victoria and Dan watched over Felicia until she was strong enough to make the final trip back to the hacienda in Monterrey. They had only one horse among the three of them. Felicia would have to do most of the riding, while the other two would have to walk; the trip would be slow and treacherous. They were fortunate that Dan had a canteen to carry water. The area was desolate after they passed the gold mines and dangerously full of bandits. They had to be cautious and always on their guard as they traveled the mountains path.

While they hiked the unfamiliar trail, Dan occasionally held the reins to the horse, all the while keeping an eye on Felicia. He tried to console Victoria. "Don't worry, Missy," he said. "You'll see Juan again. I'll promise you that. I'll see that we all get back to ol' Monterrey and back to the border. Everything is going to be just fine, you'll see."

"One thing I have to tell you, Dan, is that when we reach the hacienda, my father will be waiting for us. Please don't say anything about Juan. Please don't mention his name around my father. There is a long story behind this, and I will tell you the whole sordid affair while we walk."

Dan Land promised Victoria never to repeat Juan's name, as he listened to her relate the details of the story.

Victoria felt empty inside and her thoughts swirled and eddied. She went for hours without saying a word, while watching her step on the harsh terrain. Felicia was still weak, but kept a good grip on the reins of the weary horse. The first day they traveled most of the day and during the night, through the thickest part of the country. But the second day, they traveled during the night and rested during the day. Water was getting hard to find, and their faces and lips were starting to burn and chap.

Once in a while, they would hear horses galloping in their direction, either *Federalist* soldiers or *bandidos*. They did not know for sure, for they would always hide in the dense mountainous forest. On one occasion, they had to hide in a dry ditch among the parched branches, holding onto the horse's nose to keep him quiet, while soldiers hurried by several yards away. The three were haggard, weary, and hungry, but before long, they eventually found themselves at the Hinojosa hacienda.

CHAPTER 23

It had been a long journey, and a strange haunting loneliness possessed Victoria, Felicia, and Dan Land, when they finally reached their destination at the Hinojosa's hacienda.

As they approached the iron gates, they saw that one was torn off; the other one hung in midair by its hinges as a soft wind from the east made it squeak. They looked at each other, baffled, and then saw the devastating destruction. The evidence of war was all around them; the three stood and faced the bare facts of evil.

From the driveway leading to the hacienda, they could see that some of the orchards were destroyed and uprooted, and others were lean but remained in bloom. There was no hacienda. Smoke swirled upward from the remains of the big house and the peasants' quarters. Only the whitewashed walls and archery range remained. Much of the greenery of the vines and bushes lingered. Time and time again, the revolutionists had proved themselves skilled at destruction.

"Where are Grandmother and Great-grandmother? Where are they?" cried Victoria, out of despair and frustration.

They kept walking toward the smoking hacienda. Dan and Victoria staggered abreast, leading the skeletal horse that Felicia barely hung onto, and continued their slow trek towards the burning rubble. The three appeared skeletal themselves, looking drawn and ghostly.

"How this poor horse made it this far, beats me! He hasn't had any water except for the little juice of maguey cactus several hours ago," remarked Dan, gaunt and wearier than ever. "I don't have the heart to kill him."

Hours before, they had stopped to rest and check on Felicia's condition. Out of the dense jungle cacti, an old man appeared with a burro loaded with all of his worldly goods, heading out of the city. He reported that the revolutionists had taken over all of the rich haciendas. There was no food to be found anywhere. The water was unsafe to drink, he told them, except for the mountain creeks. In the big city of Monterrey, the people were dying like flies from the "Black Plague." The *Federalists* had driven *General* Garcia out of town, and now *General* Nafarrate was going to take over Matamoros. The majority of the radicals that were caught had been shot.

"I don't think I can take another step," gasped Victoria faintly. She had walked most of the way with Dan at her side, occasionally riding with Felicia to rest her bleeding feet.

"Yes, you can!" Dan encouraged her. He was kinder than any man they had ever met.

All three travelers were emaciated. Their eyes had retreated deep into their sockets. Their garments were tattered and threadbare. Food had been so scarce that they had eaten only roots and berries that twisted and pained their growling, empty stomachs. They looked more like hunted coyotes, with doom dangling over them like the angel of death.

Getting closer to the ruins, they caught a glimpse of a woman with a black shawl covering her head, trying to find the remains of any food or valuable trinkets. A crying baby clung to her breasts. Seeing the trio approach, she became startled and ran and hid among the fallen walls and smoking debris.

"Wait, *Señora*," yelled Victoria. "What happened to this hacienda? Where are the people who used to live in this place? Where is *La Señora* Hinojosa? Where is everybody?"

Hearing the name Hinojosa, the peasant woman peeked through fallen stone and lumber, and eyed them intently before she said anything. "Who goes there?"

"We belong to this hacienda. What happened to the people who lived here?"

"A war has started," replied the woman, surprised. "Where have you been? Weeks ago, the news of Madero's death brought chaos and destruction to all of the big landowners. All of the peasants in this hacienda, along with the revolutionists, destroyed and burned this place down and killed many. My husband was killed trying to defend our children and me. Many of my relatives were killed and many of the young girls were raped and dragged away by the revolutionaries to become *soldadera* and do their cooking. Most of the young men joined and were taken into the war. The *Federalists* came after, but it was already too late. We heard that there was a shoot-out between them in Monterrey. I stayed here because of my children. Everyone who has stayed is frightened. Most of the men are now fighting for Pancho Villa or have joined Carranza to take over the Republic."

At a loss for words, Victoria desperately responded, "And the people who lived here were all killed?"

"*La Señora* Alvarado was killed from a hard blow to her head. Juana died with a bullet through her heart, trying to help the old *Señora*. It was a miracle that *La Señora* Hinojosa had left several days before to go to Mexico City to recover the body of her dead husband."

"All dead, all killed!" cried Victoria, now terrified. "What are we going to do now?"

The young infant started to cry, and the woman began rocking it in her arms. She continued, "Yesterday, several men with guns and riding horses mentioned they were from Texas and were looking for two young girls. They were wondering if you had returned from school."

"Father was already here? Where did they go?" Victoria asked hopefully.

"They were asking a lot of questions. The older man with white hair, I think it was your father, since I had seen him visiting the hacienda many times, said they were going to the Del Calderóne hacienda to see what they could find. Everything is lost! Everything is gone!" She kept saying that with much sorrow and departed with her baby in her arms still crying.

She disappeared behind the burning, fallen wreckage to where the rest of her children were hiding.

All dead! All killed! Dead! The words rang through Victoria's mind. Any minute she was going to lose control and faint. Dan grabbed her just in time and supported her. He had already taken Felicia off the horse, laid her on the ground, and had found water in the nearby running creek for all of them to drink. He had taken the blanket off the horse and had led the dying horse into the creek to drink and recover from the grueling trip.

"Hold on," remarked Dan. "We will stay here and find shelter until your father returns. We'll find food and rest. You'll see. Everything is going to be all right."

Victoria, finally succumbing to the horror, fell limply into Dan's arms.

⌘ ⌘ ⌘

Many hours had passed when Victoria came to her senses. She opened her eyes to find her father *Don* Federico, Roy Dale, Ricardo, and several *vaqueros* from Spanish Acres hovered over her, waiting for her to regain consciousness. Ricardo had hold of her hand and spoke. "*Querida*, you are going to be all right. I'm so glad we found you in one piece."

Don Federico's face was burnt and hardened by the sun. His hair had now turned white, and he had aged considerably since she had last seen him. Thinking it was perhaps a vision or a dream, Victoria opened her chapped lips and tried to speak. "Papá!"

Later, she vaguely remembered being lifted into a wagon and, for the first time, feeling warm again, with blankets covering her chilled body. She could hear the whinnying of horses and the crunch of wagon wheels rolling. She could feel Felicia's body next to her as the bumpy and uncomfortable trip progressed. Time passed, but how much, she did not know. Occasionally, she would feel the pull from the wagon as it turned, and the hard bumps from the rocky road causing the wagon to lurch and sway.

She could hear voices of different people talking in the distance, but she couldn't catch their words. Her mind kept spinning. A vision of *Doña* Adela appeared. She could see her old and wrinkled face, with her fingers all twisted, pointing to the Mexican fortune cards. *The trip back will be many deaths. You will not marry Juan. He will marry another woman. You have the evil seeds in your blood; that's the seed of the white man in your veins. It will destroy all of you.*"

Victoria sank into a deep whirlpool, which took her under, deeper and deeper into an abyss of unconsciousness. She remembered screaming, "Juan!" In the recesses of her mind, she could hear someone trying to talk to her. It was Ricardo, and he was saying, "You are safe in my arms. There is nothing for you to worry about. Everything is going to be all right. We'll be married as soon as you get well."

There were other women's voices. It was her mother talking in between her coughing spells.

"Mother—"

"Victoria, you are home, in your new home here in Mercedes City, and you are safe. Your father, and Roy, and Ricardo brought you and Felicia safely home to us. Look, Mamá Maria and Soledad are here to take care of you. We are all happy to see you. *Por Dios, Hija!*" Doña Francisca took her lace handkerchief up to her face and wiped her eyes. "This ordeal has been too much for her! For the love of God, someone go and get the priest!" She went into a coughing spell sitting next to the bed and began wailing uncontrollably.

There were men's voices talking in the background. "What happened at the convent? It must have been horrible. Look how thin she is, and her feet are all bloody and swollen."

Aunt Emma, wiping her eyes with a handkerchief, appeared from nowhere and spoke from the entrance of the doorway. "Look at Felicia and how horrible she looks. The two girls are so thin—they must have not eaten anything. It's a wonder they are both alive!"

Victoria heard another voice of a woman she did not recognize. When she opened her eyes, she saw the woman had a pretty face and was dressed in black with a black lace mantilla covering her head. The woman sat next to the bed patting Victoria's hand, while she lay incoherent. Then she addressed the other worried ladies. "It took Mamá Maria and Soledad forever to clean her up. Victoria mustn't have had a bath in months, and her hair was like straw." She turned to face Victoria once again. "Everything is going to be all right now. You are safe with your mother and father. Ricardo is here, and the marriage will take place right away." Victoria discovered that it was her Grandmother Hinojosa, who had escaped the trauma in Mexico and had found her way back to Texas. She had been rescued and was now staying at the Juelson home in Mercedes City.

Victoria was cognizant enough to respond, "Felicia. Where is Felicia? Is Felicia all right? And Dan Land, is he still here and staying with us? He is so wonderful, the way he took care of us."

"Felicia is here. She is in the next bedroom and is feeling better, already eating. Dan Land is also staying here and will not leave without Felicia. I think we are going to have twin marriages," answered Mamá Maria, hovering over Victoria, patting her forehead with a cold wet cloth with her right hand and holding a cup of hot *manzanilla* tea in her left. "Your father doesn't want Dan to leave. He wants to reward him for taking care of you and Felicia. He has offered him some money, but the brave young man has refused. He is going to stay until Felicia gets better, and he wants you to get better also. Please drink this tea, *Hija.*" The kindly servant put the cup on a stand next to the bed. Mamá Maria turned away, not wanting Victoria to see her tormented face. Pulling out her handkerchief, she blew her nose and went out the door, crossed herself, and whispered, "*Dios mío!*"

CHAPTER 24

For the next two weeks, while recovering from her hellish nightmare, Victoria tossed and turned in her elaborate, four-poster French bed. She was content to stay in her bedroom with large windows that looked out on the horizon of mesquite and cacti. She had vivid recollections of the Mexican Revolution. Francisco Madero, the President of Mexico had been killed, and now Victoriano Huerta, called "The Jackal," was ruling the country. Still, Mexico was in a state of turmoil, and different factions like Carranza, Pancho Villa, and Emiliano Zapata, the pure Indian Revolutionist, who said that it was better to die on your feet than to live on your knees, were trying to take control of the country for the rights of the Indians who had been left landless under the thirty-year regime of Díaz.

Relatives living on both sides of the Rio Grande were being tremendously affected. On the Texas side of the river, the Mexican-American descendants were being stirred to rise against the injustices that were being committed against their families. Many sons and blood relatives were taking up arms and fighting against the white authorities: *Los Rinches.* The dreaded Texas Rangers had complete power over the Mexican-American people in the Valley and would shoot the Mexicans in the back, with the old excuse, *they were trying to escape.* The Mexican Revolution forcing the enormous influx of immigrants coming into Texas only exacerbated the problem.

Victoria wondered what had happened to Juan since she had last laid eyes on him in the village halfway between the convent and the outskirts of Monterrey. She had heard disturbing rumors from her father and other men talking outside the halls of the new home that he had been captured and perhaps been killed. What would have happened if she had eloped with him? Juan had given her a choice to be poor like him or come home to Texas and marry Ricardo. She remembered Juan telling her that God must have loved the poor, the innocents, the simple-minded people, because he made so many of them. If things had been different, if times were changed, she would have clung to Juan forever, since she loved him so much. But she had preferred comfort, and now there was talk of moving the wedding up as soon as possible. Ricardo had proved himself to be faithful to her throughout her unfortunate ordeal. He had not left her side, admirably, and constantly talked of marriage.

Days had passed and Victoria had still not been able to eat solid food, only teas and soups. The thought of food was revolting and nothing seemed edible; even the smell would make her ill. She lost more weight, making the household frown with concern. She had never felt this way before, and every time she tried to get out of bed to explore the new house, she would feel faint.

Whenever anyone in the household tried to question her about what had happened in the convent, she could go to pieces and weep. How could she explain it? Recalling her evil curse on the Mother Superior, she felt flames biting at her heels, and guilt dangled over her head like a Mexican machete. She spent many waking hours staring at the contemporary, high arched-glass ceiling, trying to put the pieces back together. Thoughts of Juan's torrid passion would replay over and over again during her waking hours, and he would appear so many times in her dreams. There would never be another man who could take Juan's place, and he would remain in the silence of her heart for as long as she lived.

On an early Monday morning, Manuel came, as he did every other day, in a horse wagon from Spanish Acres, bringing fresh milk, cheese, eggs, and sometimes other supplies for the family. Concerned, Mamá Maria took Victoria back to Spanish Acres. They felt that being in the hacienda would help Victoria recover faster, hoping that fresh dairy products, vegetables, and fruits would start restoring her health. And having her horse, *La Reyna*, would encourage Victoria to ride like she used to before she went to the convent. Felicia had recuperated very fast with the help of Dan Land, and they both decided to join Victoria in Spanish Acres, taking a separate buggy and following Manuel to the hacienda. Dan had heard of the hacienda so much that he was enthusiastic to see the cattle and the vast Juelson empire.

Ricardo stayed in Mercedes City as a guest of *Don* Federico, who was making plans for his new son-in-law in running the production of the oil wells. It would be a new venture for Ricardo, since his family had lost everything in Mexico, and returning to his home in Monterrey was pointless. The thought of making money in oil motivated and challenged Ricardo, and by marrying Victoria, he would automatically take control of her land and possessions. He was seeing dollar signs and thinking of becoming wealthy again. He also hoped to find a way of getting his mother and sister to Texas, but that would take a great deal of money.

As the time slipped away, nothing seemed to please Victoria's taste. She would get out of bed and stroll only to the edge of the balcony to view the courtyard below. She would wave to Dan and Felicia as they rode their horses down to the pastures or out into the *brasada*. However, she seemed happier being in Spanish Acres with Ophelia, Olivia, and Soledad, who constantly consoled her. Felicia, with rosy cheeks, had her health restored. She seemed happy, laughed, and was more talkative than she had ever been. She would check on Victoria every day, and now talked about her future wedding with Dan Land.

Yolanda, looking heavier than before, pursed her lips and rolled her eyes with a hateful attitude, when she appeared occasionally in Victoria's bedroom. She would bring Victoria trays of soups and hot chocolate, but would never speak a word to her. Mamá Maria had told Victoria that Yolanda had a handsome baby boy, now over a year old, and was still not married. Elena and Miguel adored the child and took care of him as their own. Mamá Maria, who watched Victoria like a hawk, even took refuge, sleeping on a cot next to her bed. Aging and in failing health, she would still bring her remedies of teas, homemade foods, different pastries, and many chicken soups fixed with herbs in different ways, suggesting that if Victoria did not eat, she would surely die.

A future wedding was being prepared for Victoria, and it was something she should be looking forward to with happiness. A wedding was considered a holy sacrament and a special day for any young *Señorita.* The white dress symbolized that the new bride was a virgin, pure and untouched.

On the fourth week of Victoria's homecoming in Spanish Acres, *Don* Federico and *Doña* Francisca, followed by Emma and her servants, all arrived at the hacienda by carriage. Emma, always the overseer, was already starting to help *Doña* Francisca make plans for the upcoming wedding.

Earlier in the morning Mamá Maria, still worried about Victoria's condition, had sent Manuel and Yo-yo to fetch *Doña* Adela. Yo-yo had returned to Spanish Acres from the chaotic Revolution in Mexico several weeks before, and with him had brought his two sons, José and Memo, who were now working as skilled *vaqueros* with Roy, Miguel, and Martin at the hacienda.

The whole household waited patiently outside in the corridors for *Doña* Adela's verdict. *Don* Federico, with more and more anxiety lines etched across his forehead, paced up and down with Roy. Emma fumed, fussed, and sighed, saying that Victoria should be taken to see a regular doctor, instead of a common witch healer. Mamá Maria said nothing, but glared and bore her black eyes into Emma.

An hour had passed when the stooped old *Doña* Adela painfully opened the bedroom door and stepped outside with her cane, quietly closing the door behind her. From the inside they could hear Victoria sobbing. The suspense was too much for Roy, and he decided to join Dan Land downstairs.

Doña Francisca, Mamá Maria, Soledad, Emma, Felicia, and Elena rushed to console the distraught Victoria. Yolanda entered the bedroom with curiosity, tagging along behind the other ladies. A bewildered array of questions followed, with all the women talking at the same time.

"Well?" *Don* Federico said impatiently, questioning *la bruja.* "Is she going to live?"

"Very much so, *hombre*," replied *Doña* Adela, cackling. "I think you had better sit down. What I have to say may not be so pleasant for you people at this time, since you're preparing a wedding, and it better be real soon." The old witch woman found a chair out in the hall, and her joints cracked when she sat down. She slipped off her bifocals and, with her white cloth handkerchief, began cleaning them. "I'm getting too old for this type of commotion." She cleared her throat, as anxiety mounted and doom hung in every corner.

"Well," *Don* Federico went on, "my main concern is Victoria! Is she going to get over her illness? Is she going to be all right?"

"*Ah, sí*, she is going to be all right in about eight months." *Doña* Adela's eyes bored into *Don* Federico's. "Your daughter is with child. She'll feel better in another month or two. I estimate the arrival of the baby will be around the middle of December."

The *Don* stiffened and his eyes widened, as though someone had sprayed skunk urine in his face. "With child? Not possible!" He felt his legs buckle. His heart pounded. His worst nightmare was unfolding. "How can this be? How could she possibly get pregnant in the convent? That's beyond me!" He was furious with rage, and his face registered fear as his heart raced. "But she is marrying Ricardo!"

"*Cómo sí, no hombre, Don* Federico." The old woman laughed. "There is only one way she could get pregnant. After all, Victoria is not the immaculate conception." She put her glasses on, peering over them, looking like an old gorilla and addressed the great *Don* Federico. "Just be glad that there is nothing seriously wrong with her. By the way poor ol' Manuel described her illness, I was beginning to worry."

Unable to control his anger, *Don* Federico walked into Victoria's bedroom and demanded an explanation. *Doña* Adela's crackling bones and cane followed, repeating under her breath, "*Aye qué estúpido*—typical man!"

"Who's the father, Victoria?" *Don* Federico roared.

"*Dios mío!*" wailed *Doña* Francisca, kissing her rosary. She began to faint.

"Holy Mother of God!" cursed Mamá Maria, while Elena, Soledad, and Yolanda all reached out to catch *Doña* Francisca. Emma and Felicia were holding Victoria's hands. The tension in the room was charged like thunderbolts; such a thing was scandalous and absurd!

Someone suggested the fainting salts. Excited voices were mingled with lamentations. *Don* Federico's face was contorted with anger, and he became carried away by his own voice. "I'm asking you a question, Victoria! Now, who's the father?"

Victoria's countenance was that of a martyr. Every minute had become an eternity. She wasn't about to divulge any information regarding Juan. Mamá Maria and Elena got down on their knees and gasped the prayer: "Our Father, *Padre Nuestro qué está. . .*" Both moaned with grief, not because Victoria was with child, but by the simple fact that *Don* Federico was so distressed. This was just too scandalous, and perhaps the *Don* was going to send her away.

"Silence!" snapped Don Federico to the two praying women on the floor. "Quiet."

Victoria felt embarrassed and full of guilt. The wrath that had come upon her was making her feel hopeless. Her fate was signed and sealed. Her father would send her away.

"I don't know," she replied, sobbing. Her brain scrambled to make some sense and use the right words. What else could she say? The name of Juan could not be mentioned, as she was keeping it as her life's great secret.

Felicia's face was numb. Her color went from pink to white.

"You don't know? What happened at the convent? What happened in this great mystery that has twisted and puzzled all of us?"

"I was raped!" wailed Victoria, with tears streaming down her face.

"You were what?" Sackcloth and ashes fell, not a pin drop was heard, as the problem took a different twist. "Who raped you?"

"The revolutionists who invaded the convent raped most of the girls, including the nuns. They killed the majority of them, including Mother Superior. That was the main reason we left with Ricardo's brother, Luis, and Dan Land, who saved our lives."

"*Virgen de Guadalupe!*" was the chorus from the other women and *Doña* Francisca, who began sobbing in between her coughing spells.

"Did Felicia get raped in the convent?" yelled Emma hysterically, looking at Felicia, while trying to hold onto *Doña* Francisca, who was now completely overcome.

"No, Mamá," Felicia answered her mother. "I was in the cellar and was rescued by Dan Land. It doesn't matter anyway. We were there, it was horrible, and we were all victims."

"As a matter of fact," said Emma, calming down. "One of the Montoya twins was brought back to Texas very traumatized. Apparently, something happened to her also. The parents are devastated. The other girl will not say anything, just like Victoria, because it's much too scandalous!"

Doña Adela's eyes glistened over her spectacles in amazement—it was a scene from a Greek tragedy. Everybody was in a yelling match, and the situation was becoming a three-ring circus.

Soledad, with tears in her eyes, quietly walked out and downstairs. Halfway down, she met Roy and Dan; both had been concerned and awaiting the final truth.

"Who died?" questioned Roy. "Or who's gonna die?" he asked. The chatter coming from the adjoining rooms downstairs indicated other *vaqueros* who were also concerned.

"Nobody," whispered Soledad. With her head hanging in shame, she wiped her nose with her apron. The mention of the word "rape" had come crashing in her ears like a dagger. It had brought too many painful memories. "Victoria is pregnant. I'm going to the kitchen and take something for my headache."

"Waal, whut's the big deal?" Roy snickered. "Wummin have babies all the time! But, this 'un is diff'ernt. She's *patrón's* daughter and—oh, Gee Golly!" Roy's eyes widened. "Thar's gonna be some helluva, crock-a-shittin' e'plainin' to do, 'specia 'ly to the anxious, waiting novio—*El Señor* Ricardo!"

Dan Land stood around and frowned, acting innocent, not saying a word. He was not surprised. He was not about to repeat what Victoria had told him on their trip back, and now he understood why.

Doña Francisca, with her handkerchief cupped in her hand and up to her mouth, immediately came to her daughter's defense. Her gracious patience and rare talent of blending words with an air of humility always conveyed good thoughts for every human being. This was her beloved daughter and her heart ached for her. Her gentle words were full of compassion, her face lined from years of caring. She sat on the bed where Victoria lay sobbing and touched her hand. "*Hija.* That was a terrible ordeal. It wasn't your fault that this happened. I'm just glad you are safe and home with us. That's what is most important, that you are back in Texas. So often the devil is in the mist of everything. Having a baby is wonderful, and you'll have it. You will marry Ricardo, for he loves you so, and it will probably not make any difference to him, one way or another."

"Have you gone mad?" responded *Don* Federico, frantically pacing up and down the bedroom floor. "It will make a difference, and this is out of the question!" he ranted. "Absurd! It's absolutely ridiculous on our part, wouldn't you say? We'll be liars to ourselves and Ricardo's family. We will have to tell the Del Calderónes of what happened. After all, it was their own son, Luis, who was the head of the takeover in the convent. How will we explain the child being born a month too early?"

"Ricardo doesn't have to know," suggested *Doña* Francisca, pleading. "It wasn't Victoria's fault. He does not have to know about this terrible incident. He will never know about what happened. Things do happen and life must go on."

Doña Adela interjected: "Children have been known to be born months early and have lived. No reason why the couple can't get married now. This sort of thing happens in this part of the country all the time, *hombre*." She cackled again, knowing the real truth from Victoria.

"Not to my daughter! It does matter! This child will not resemble our family or the Del Calderóne blood. How are we going to explain that the child will not look like either of the couple?" Grieved, *Don* Federico scratched his head and searched his mind to salvage his prestigious name, pride and honor, trying to find a solution to the complex problem now facing them. Turning to *Doña* Adela, he said without thinking, "Is there anything that Victoria can take to get rid of this child?"

There was a collective gasp, coming from every woman in the bedroom, "*Dios mío!*"

"Oh, no!" cried *Doña* Adela, raising her twisted fingers. She shook her head in disgust. "I don't kill children. It's murder, if you ask me. It's even worse for the mothers, especially how it affects them later. I'm a healer, not a murderer." She shook her head again pityingly, and picked up her cane and bag. "I must go. I have stayed here too long. I have more important things to do, other people to help. Have Manuel take me back to my house."

"Kill the baby?" cried *Doña* Francisca, and she began coughing, regaining her words. "Impossible! The devil has gotten a hold of your brains and tongue. Think of all the stray people we have helped. Think of how they have made our lives so much richer by their souls. You have never turned anyone away. This is your daughter, our only daughter, who needs our help now. This was not her fault and she couldn't help it. What was she supposed to do? I will hear no more of this! The Holy Catholic Church will cast our souls into Hell. We would burn in Hell forever for doing such a terrible thing!"

Victoria, Elena, Mamá Maria, Emma and Felicia felt waves of comfort move over them. It had become the climax of a pointless dispute, regardless of all the screaming. They were all facing a difficult problem, except Yolanda, who was actually treasuring the upheaval.

Humiliated, and with much shame for having thought and said such a terrible thing, *Don* Federico felt like a criminal. After all, it was he who had encouraged Victoria to go to Monterrey for a good education. It was he who had condoned her marriage into the Del Calderóne family. He lowered his head and struggled to restrain his emotions. He started to walk out into the hall, then turned back and faced his wife and the rest of the weeping ladies. "Francisca!" He addressed her with much authority. "You will have to answer for this child.

The family's punishment will be great, and we will suffer the consequences in the years to come. Count me out! I'm washing my hands of this whole ordeal. Better have Emma start the wedding dress and procedures. Let us begin the lies, the sooner the better," he said. "Lies!" He closed the bedroom door behind him and walked out into the long hall, entered his own bedroom, and slammed the door.

"The marriage will go on," announced the shaken *Doña* Francisca, to all of the ladies in the bedroom. They smiled through their tears, and nodded. "As soon as Victoria feels better, we will fit her into a wedding dress. There will be a wedding as soon as possible. Nobody has to know anything. The Del Calderónes must never find out about this child." *Doña* Francisca felt more at ease with the situation, and her shoulders sagged with relief. "We will all pray, for the salvation of our souls." Saying this, *La Señora* departed for her bedroom, the ever-present cough tickling her throat, and held her handkerchief up to her face. The committee of Emma, Mamá Maria, and Felicia followed her out. Elena went downstairs.

Yolanda repressed a spiteful grin as she remained at the foot of the bed, her hands gripping the wrought iron rails with intensity. Her eyes danced with delight as she glowered at Victoria in her grief and despair. She treasured the spectacle, watching the young bride-to-be present a pitiful sight, and she stood there thinking: *People with money can do anything, buy anything and anyone, and can get away with almost anything, Making a mockery, almost a joke of the situation, trying to hide the truth of what really happened, like trying to hide the sun with one finger. Getting Victoria to marry Ricardo and have the dumb, loving groom not knowing anything about what took place in Monterrey is laughable. How does the Juelson family think they can get away with this?*

Yolanda was haunted by the fact that Roy Dale had been given a section of the land promised to her by George Juelson, before he died. Spanish Acres was the land that her father had worked for so many years and now, it had been given to the foreman. Yolanda hated Victoria for her spoiled, selfish attitude, her sassy, outspokenness and blunt ways. She always got what she wanted, always having the best of things in life. Well, this time was going to be different. She would cook Victoria's goose for good. She would create a wonderful scandal!

CHAPTER 25

In the weeks that followed, Victoria was quickly fitted into a simple, white satin wedding dress that Emma and her servants sewed. Emma was a wizard seamstress and had an eye for effortlessly inventing clothes like she saw in the new fashion magazines. Dresses in the new fashions were made simpler without all the adornments, and the hems were shorter. Hurried arrangements were secretly and quietly made for a ceremony with only the family members in attendance. It was customary for the Mexican groom to pay for all of the wedding attire, but since Ricardo and his family had lost everything, it posed a problem. *Don* Federico, reluctantly but with the help of *Doña* Francisca, paid the tab and was glad to get the simple wedding over and done with, as soon as possible.

In his own selfish-interest, Ricardo saw the opportunity for making money, acquiring wealth from the oil wells, and becoming rich again. He was pleased to marry Victoria, as quickly as possible, before Victoria changed her mind. The family had agreed with Ricardo's suggestions to have the wedding in Reynosa, on the Mexican side, so that his mother and sister, who were now destitute and staying with a family member in Monterrey, could attend.

The Del Calderóne family had not heard from *El General* since the Revolution had broken out, and did not know if he were dead of alive. They would occasionally see stories in the newspapers that the *Federalist* troops were busy trying to catch Venustiano Carranza, the former Governor of the State of Coahuila. His headquarters were now at Piedra Negras, and he had sponsored another revolt against the *Jackal*, Huerta, who had taken control as President of Mexico. Carranza issued his Plan de Guadalupe, the charter that became the Constitutionalist Movement and a declaration of civil war to disavow Huerta. He sent telegrams to all the governors asking for them to "unfurl the flag of legality and sustain the constitutional government chosen in the last election." Carranza had also named himself as the First Chief of the Constitutionalist Movement. The partisan Felix Díaz, nephew of former President Díaz, had taken command over the garrison in Matamoros.

Gory tales were being told by the residents living close to the Rio Grande River, of Mexican bodies riddled with bullets washing up on the riverbanks, but they did not know who was doing the killing.

The newly elected idealist U.S. President Woodrow Wilson adopted a policy of "watch-ful waiting," and decided not to intervene, but to keep a close eye on the border, and he kept the military stationed close at hand. President Wilson refused to recognize Huerta as the leader of Mexico, blaming him for the murder of Madero. He recommended and warned that all American citizens should leave Mexico immediately.

Henry Lane Wilson, the United States Ambassador to Mexico, was drawn to Huerta. Both alcoholics, they played a sinister role in Madero's overthrow conspiracy, and the am-bassador was later fired by President Wilson. Later, in the fall of the year, Wilson made his policy more clear, declaring that the United States was staying out of Mexico's problems—words that he would recant later.

Looting became so widespread throughout the border towns, that the county judges and sheriffs requested aid in the form of an immediate backup from Texas Governor O.B. Colquitt. The governor ordered five companies of State Militia and Texas Rangers to the border under the command of Captain Sanders.

The contentious wedding took place between the feisty, Victoria and Ricardo at the *Catedral de Guadalupe*, in Reynosa. It was a hushed affair, with only her parents, Ricardo's mother, Grandmother Gloria, Aunt Emma, Felicia, and Dan Land to witness the ceremony. Ricardo's sister did not come, as she was too poor to attend a wedding in the custom that she was raised. The majority of the people living in Spanish Acres did not attend. Mamá Maria was too ill; Manuel, Roy, and Soledad did not care to attend, saying it was too much of a fuss, and that it was too long a trip, and they did not have good enough clothes to wear. The rest of the Spanish Acres household were not told of the importance of the wedding. The only *Padrinos*, Godparents, were the family of the wealthy Solis, who lived several miles south of Reynosa. Grandmother Gloria produced a small diamond ring for Victoria, a ring which had belonged to her dead mother, *Señora* Alvarado. The golden wedding band for Ricardo was one of the many rings of José Hinojosa. To wear dead people's rings was a bad omen, for both of the previous owners had been killed violently.

A dinner reception with plenty of food had been prepared in the gracious hacienda of the Solis family, with plenty of hard liquor served, including champagne imported from Brownsville. As the fiesta ended and evening came, the couple took off in a carriage toward Brownville. There they would board a ship headed for the city of New Orleans. *Don* Federico, who paid for the wedding, had asked Ricardo earlier about his preference for a month-long honeymoon. Ricardo, feeling humiliated in not being able to pay for the ceremony, had mentioned New Orleans, so accustomed was he to the French language and cuisine, after his many years studying in Paris.

While the newlyweds were away on their honeymoon trip, Lucio Blanco, one of Carranza's generals, captured the town of Reynosa in May of 1913. Many of the defenders were killed. Some he took as prisoners, and those who refused to join his army were executed. This created panic on both sides of the river. Blanco was smart and had a military educa-tion. He cleverly devised a plan to accumulate huge tax revenues on cattle, and on exports and imports that crossed the river both ways. He began forcing the U.S. military, cattlemen, and business owners to pay high tariffs. The military commanders at Fort Brown refused Blanco's demands and sent a wire to Governor Colquitt, informing him of the trumped-up charges at the border. The governor of Texas requested federal troops from President Wilson. When this was refused, Governor Colquitt sent more Texas state troops to the area.

⌘ ⌘ ⌘

One month later, Fred, now twelve, returned home by train from his military academy to the new house in Mercedes City, where a big celebration was given by *Doña* Francisca and Emma. The twins were ecstatic seeing Fred again, wanting to hear about his education and what he had learned at the academy. Fred was taller than ever, close to six feet, more disciplined, with muscular arms and shoulders, and had gained weight. As a child, Fred had never known sorrow or hardship. He had been aloof and undisciplined, but he had come home with a different attitude. He was overjoyed with the new modern house, and very talkative, telling stories of the different people who attended the school, and the contrast between different groups, who were mostly Irish and German. Fred had shared a dormitory with another boy from a ranch close to Corpus Christi, Texas, named Jim Gray, who was Apache Indian and Irish. The two boys had become friends, with each enriching the other's knowledge and character. By the end of the season, both had become champions in football, causing the rest of the boys to be jealous.

Fred described the attitudes of the generals who ran the academy. They were pleased with Fred's intelligence, but had not given Jim any encouragement in his future education, often flogging him because of his background and race. This had left Jim Gray discouraged and disheartened, and he had left five months earlier without finishing his courses. Fred found himself lonely and unsure of himself, as the two had formed a close pact. The rest of the boys attending were uncaring after Jim left.

He remarked about the cruel harshness of what it was like to be of mixed-race, and how he had learned in two years just how much the different nationalities disliked each other. There was a strong feeling of resentment, and each group was keenly aware of the '*roots of indifferences*' that divided them. The majority of the Germans and Irish boys' animosity came from what they had been taught at home; they would not associate with Fred or Jim, only tolerated them and laughed at their ethnic background, with cruel remarks and jokes. The two boys were not able to "tell," because it was against an unwritten law of the school to "tattle" on one another. For Fred, it had been a humiliating experience, being in a special school and not being wanted. But it had taught him discipline, fortitude, good manners, and even how to keep his room clean and tidy.

"A good lesson in life," commented *Don* Federico, proudly. He was very impressed with Fred's attitude, manner, and looks. *Don* Federico was disturbed by Fred's story, but was not surprised— discrimination was everywhere, especially in the white-run schools. "They must have done something right, because you look great!" he said. "Now you know why I want you to be an attorney. So you can get to know the laws and fight for justice, equality, and for what's right, especially here in the Valley."

"I spent many nights thinking, Dad, and I still would like to attend a good college, maybe up North, and become a doctor."

"Nonsense," remarked *Don* Federico. "For now, you will go to school here in Mercedes City and we will have plenty of time to talk about your future profession." Saying this, he disappeared from the kitchen and joined the ladies in the *sala,* where he overheard the remarks of Emma's twin boys.

"I will become an attorney," announced Jamie, who was pleased to see Fred again.

"I don't know what I will be," replied John.

⌘　⌘　⌘

Heroic stories were being told in the press on the Texas side, stories of victory from Pancho Villa, the Centaur of the North, as he was called by the Mexican-American citizens living in Texas. Tales of the Mexican war were being put to music: *La Valentina, Adelita, Tres Piedras, Esperanza, El Pagare, Los Higos Dela Noche, Historia Triste De Amor,* and *Recuerdos de Durango* were being sung from the coast of California to the mouth of the Rio Grande. Most of the songs were sad ballads that told how the Mexicans felt about their lonely life, their women, and the loved ones who were left behind to fight for justice.

Within a month Victoria and Ricardo returned from their honeymoon trip. Already, Victoria showed signs of unhappiness with Ricardo, as outbursts of loud, angry disputes, and the breaking of glass had been heard from their upstairs bedroom several times. The servants, busy in their duties, would trade glances and whisper among themselves. Victoria's face was etched with frown lines, and she seemed angry all the time. In her unhappiness, she would occasionally erupt angrily at the servants for no apparent reason.

The evening meal provided the center of communication for the family, but exchanges between the newlywed couple were always subtle. Of course, there would be a difference of opinion at times, with animated discussion and disagreement, making everyone uneasy.

Feisty as ever, Victoria detested the egotistical Ricardo. He was controlling and had the habit of correcting her speech every time she opened her mouth. Her heart was hostile toward him, especially knowing she loved someone else. She felt cheated, and resented her parents for forcing her into an arranged marriage. With jaws clenched, she watched him from across the dining room table, glowering at him as he inspected and picked at his food so meticulously, cutting his steak and chewing it with so much gusto. Or, on many occasions, if displeased with the food, Ricardo would push his plate away as though he found it inedible and not fit for his expensive taste. Victoria had the urge to walk into the kitchen and pick up the heaviest frying pan and smash his smug face.

She often noticed her father watching her, knowing what she was thinking. Her demeanor clearly showed that they were incompatible. The truth of the ill-fated marriage showed in the young, dishearten bride's face; she cried repeatedly, and her eyes were always red and swollen. She railed against everyone, and the only time she was seen to smile was when she embraced Fred upon his return. Her life had become a nightmare.

Victoria had decided to make Mercedes City her home, since *Doña* Francisca had relapsed from her long illness. Tension mounted from the Mexican war, and everywhere along the border, even inside Texas, life was becoming dangerous.

Ricardo wasted no time in returning to Spanish Acres, where he found interest and excitement working in the oil fields. And there, inevitably, he discovered the insatiable Yolanda.

⌘ ⌘ ⌘

Within six months, Shaw, the engineer in charge of the operation of the oil fields, wrote a letter to *Don* Federico stating that he was quitting the operation immediately. The unhappy engineer said that Ricardo was never at his job and spent too much time with a gal at Spanish Acres, who, from Shaw's description, was none other than the notorious Yolanda. Furthermore, Ricardo, who was in charge of shipping the barrels of oil, and collecting the checks from Houston, was neglecting to make any deposits into *Don* Federico's bank in Brownsville, and the workers were not being paid. All Shaw was getting was complaints, for everyone in the field was discontented.

Don Federico went into angry frenzy. Ricardo had taken advantage of his position, was stealing money from the company, and had no responsibility to his marriage, only seeing Victoria when he felt like it, in Mercedes City. The news put *Don* Federico in a very peculiar, almost bizarre situation. The couple had already announced the coming of the newborn several months ago. He wondered if Ricardo was suspicious about Victoria's pregnancy. Mexican men expected their brides to be pure and untouched, especially on their wedding night. The groom, under the traditional *machismo* Mexican custom, could return the bride to her parents, leaving the family and her shamed. However, months had now passed, and Ricardo up to this point, had remained silent. To question him on his amorous adventures was going to create a problem.

The other problem was Yolanda, knowing her loose morals. Her father, Miguel, had worked for the family for years, first with the cattle, and now overseeing the three hundred laborers working the land and cotton fields. The introduction of cotton had been very profitable, and the laborers were being paid good wages.

Immediately *Don* Federico went into a state of rage. He donned his Stetson hat and gun belt and ordered his carriage to be hitched up without delay. In his rush to leave, he had left the open letter and the rest of his mail on top of the small mahogany desk, next to his chair in the *sala*. The ride to Spanish Acres would give him time to think over his words when confronting Ricardo about his absences at work and his negligence. *What could Ricardo be doing with the bank checks, if he was not depositing them at the Brownsville bank? He was cashing them!*

Curious, Victoria rushed downstairs wanting to question her father on his urgency. Her first thought was that something had happened to Fred or Carlos at school. Victoria went to the window and looked out as her father stormed out from the barn, whipping the team of horses in haste. She was wearing a loose-fitting top, for already her pregnancy was showing, and her long skirt whirled as she turned to go back upstairs. As she brushed past the desk, the letter her father had been reading fluttered to the floor. She picked it up and read it. Language gave no utterance to what went through her mind. The household heard a terrifyingly loud voice screech, followed by the word "*Puta!*" It rang throughout the house, rattling china, dishes, and servants. "Bastard!" she screamed again, trembling with anger, unable to contain her rage and fury.

Servants scurried in from the kitchen, and the two gardeners ran into the house bewildered, one with a rake still in his hands. *Doña* Francisca, who lay dying in the upstairs bedroom, woke up and managed to stagger to the edge of the staircase and, holding onto the rails of the steps, looked down.

"*Ah, Señora,*" said Panchita to Victoria. She was a heavy-set, widow woman, whom the household had hired as their main cook. "*Señora,*" she said, "Is something wrong?" She questioned the state of emotion of *La Señora* Del Calderóne, as she wiped her hands clean on her apron and began holding onto Victoria to console her. "What could possibly be wrong?"

"It's my husband! He's cheating on me!" cried Victoria, embracing Panchita.

"*Ah, Sera por Dios,*" said the other helpers, showing sympathy for the young bride. The helper whispered, "*Ah, Dios!*" as they stood in a state of mortification, feeling sorry for Victoria, who was already over six months along.

The two gardeners, who felt like they were intruding in this delicate, women's conversation, slowly and cautiously walked out, and made their way outdoors, puzzled.

Startled and concerned at Victoria's loud scream, *Doña* Francisca had gotten out of bed and now lay in a heap at the top of the stairs, coughing uncontrollably and with blood pouring from her mouth.

Victoria wiped her eyes and looked up in shock. "Mother," she screamed, "you shouldn't have gotten up!"

Victoria hurried to her mother's side. She left the letter on her father's desk and called out that her mother needed help. With the assistance of the three women, she was able to put *Doña* Francisca back in bed, and then they cleaned the area. Victoria, exhausted and drained, and needing rest herself, staggered to her bedroom and closed the door.

Doña Francisca died that afternoon. Fred and Carlos, returning from school, were horrified to learn of their mother's death, and were taken to a different section of the mansion. The household was already full of people dressed in black, including Emma, who was unable to speak from crying. *Doña* Gloria Hinojosa was inconsolable. Felicia, Dan Land, and many other friends and neighbors, hearing of the news, brought trays of food and flowers, all with heartfelt condolences. The members of the Catholic prayer committee began making preparations for the three-day wake.

Arriving back from the oil fields late that night, *Don* Federico was stunned to learn of the death of his beloved wife. He knew it was coming, but *Lord, not this soon*, he kept telling himself. *Doña* Francisca was already dressed in one of the gowns she wore for Victoria's fiesta and lay on a table resting in the main *sala* of their new home. In a state of shock, teary-eyed, not sleeping or eating, the *Don* began making the funeral arrangements. He wanted Fred to be one of the pallbearers.

Doña Francisca's bed and mattress were destroyed and her bedroom was cleaned with lye-water.

The funeral Mass was said in the Lady of Mercy Church, with the burial in the family plot at Spanish Acres. Hundreds of horse-drawn wagons, carriages and buggies traveled to the burial amidst the wind and on-coming rain. The masses of people dressed in black were in anguish, not believing that the great lady had died, including Mamá Maria and Manuel, both in ill health.

The weather had turned into a light drizzle, then began pouring steadily, with lighting bolts striking across the horizon, making a petrifying exhibition across the heavens. At the far end of the cemetery could be seen a gruesome silhouette: *Doña* Adela and her son Roberto standing on a small hill overlooking the cemetery. *La bruja* had previously predicted *Doña* Francisca's death. She hovered at a distance now, like a spiritual demon evil force, watching and holding onto her cane, with her long, black cape flapping in the wind, and Roberto at her side. Grieving people in attendance caught the specter of the two figures and stood in awe of *Doña* Adela and the image she presented. They whispered among themselves and wiped their eyes in between their mourning, shocked by the weirdness of *la bruja* coming to the funeral. For a long time afterwards, people told stories of how terrified they had felt in her company on that day.

⌘   ⌘   ⌘

It took many weeks of tortuous moments before *Don* Federico came to the grim reality that his beloved companion was gone. The thought of living by himself, without his beautiful wife, left him inconsolable. For many days after the funeral, he had walked around like a zombie, not wanting to face the real truth. In the following weeks he spent most of his days at Spanish Acres, being close to his wife's final resting place. He would sit on a cement block staring at his wife's grave all day—whether sunny, cloudy or rainy, it did not matter.

Finally, in the third week, Roy and several of the *vaqueros*, including Martin and Miguel Garcia, concerned about *Don* Federico's state of mind, went to visit him at the gravesite. The great *Don* was barely sleeping or eating, and Roy and the rest of the *vaqueros* needed instructions pertaining to the shipment of over five hundred head of cattle.

Don Federico finally came to his senses. He came to terms with his lonely life, and realized he had to think of his two boys, their education, and their future. Victoria was already married and with a child coming. She could take care of herself, even though she had a poor excuse of a husband. The incident with Ricardo's cashing the oil checks had been put on the back burner because of the funeral, but it had not been forgotten.

He finally met with Ricardo at Spanish Acres and had asked him point blank what he was doing with the money coming in from the oil wells. Ricardo told him that he had used it for his mother and sister who needed help from him in Mexico, as they were now considered destitute and needed money from him to survive. They were not receiving any income from *El General,* and had not heard from him in months. With the money, they could move to Mercedes City, where Ricardo told them he would build them a house.

Don Federico informed Ricardo that he was not responsible for the support of other families, and that arrangements were being made to appoint another man to be in charge of the finances of his oil company. He told Ricardo that he was not to be trusted with other people's money, and also brought up his lack of responsibility toward Victoria. Ricardo got angry and accused *Don* Federico and *Doña* Francisca of concealing the fact that Victoria was already with child and not a virgin when he took on the responsibility of marrying her. The fact that Victoria was not a virgin was a dark matter in their relationship, and he felt he had been taken for a fool. He knew now, why the urgency in their marriage had been so imperative. He wanted no bastard child. If it weren't for the fact of the Mexican Revolution, he would leave and return to Monterrey, where he preferred to live. Ironically, he would have never known the truth about Victoria's heartbreaking story if Yolanda had not told him.

Don Federico then asked him sharply, "Nobody pointed a gun to your head to marry Victoria. You were very willing and in a hurry also to join her in marriage. How much money will it take for you to leave and never return?"

Ricardo bristled up and responded in his cocky attitude, "Don't be silly, *hombre!* Why should I leave? Do you take me for a fool? I have already married your daughter. I will not leave this area, at least not for a while. This area is not to my liking, but it's convenient for me to stay. I will not be forced to leave, and I will shout it out to the world. I will tell everyone how you and your wife conned me for the main purpose of naming the child. I don't think you want me repeating Victoria's little secret of the upcoming bastard child and embarrassing your whole family."

Don Federico, being an honest and fair man, was caught between a rock and a hard place. He decided to make a compromise with Ricardo and changed his attitude. He did not want his name or Victoria's name tarnished among the so-called wagging-tongue socialites of Mercedes City or the praying ladies of the Lady of Mercy Church. It would be a family disgrace and shameful for his two sons later to explain. Victoria was already unhappy with their marriage and hated his presence. "All right," he replied. "I'll make a compromise with you. The profits coming from the yearly cotton sale will be divided half and half with you. I want no trouble between the families, and I do not want our family name trashed in this community. Leave Victoria alone, we will take care of her. It's too late for an annulment and we cannot think of a divorce. That would be too scandalous, and trying to explain to all who knows my family—that's too shameful."

Ricardo glared at him with guilt, knowing what he had done—stolen the money, a common thief.

The *Don* fumbled for the right words, but soon continued, "I know now that we made a mistake in having you marry our daughter. Victoria is unhappy and it shows. We have accepted Victoria's tragedy and have tried to make things right." The *Don* paused and then went on, his voice steely. "I will ask that you leave Yolanda alone, too. She is just an infatuated girl helping in the kitchen and becomes enamored with every man who comes to the hacienda." He noticed Ricardo raise an eyebrow in doubt and surprise, acting like he didn't know what Federico was saying. "Yes, I know all about you and Yolanda," stated the *Don*. "I will confront Yolanda, and also have a talk with her father."

"She's a grown woman, and she does as she pleases," countered Ricardo. "Yolanda has been more than kind to me in taking care of me. She washes and even irons my clothes, things that Victoria was never taught!"

"No, Yolanda does not do as she pleases. She takes orders just like the rest of the workers in my hacienda. She has taken advantage of the circumstances, while we're gone. Victoria has never been taught because she doesn't have to. We have paid servants who are willing to do any household job."

"Yolanda, a servant? When she has valid legal documents to prove that she's entitled to part of Spanish Acres?" Ricardo replied arrogantly.

"What documents?" *Don* Federico questioned, in total amazement.

"Your father apparently had papers made up that were legally recorded at the Cameron County Courts several years before he died, leaving Yolanda part of the land in Spanish Acres. Those papers were transferred to the new Edinburg County Court House, now Hidalgo County, where she went and got the evidence. She went to see an attorney on the matter," said Ricardo.

"That's the first I've heard of my father giving anything away, especially the land, and to a woman, who doesn't have any legal rights in owing any land. I'll have to talk to Yolanda and with her father Miguel about this. I'll have to see the documents for myself. If Yolanda and her family want part of the land, I will give them a small portion where they live now. Miguel has been very reliable and has been on the payroll for many years, and probably deserves a section. Lord knows, he worked hard enough for it. I do not want to lose Miguel as a worker. When did you get wind of this, if I may ask?"

"Yolanda showed me the documents."

"When?" *Don* Federico questioned, adding testily, "Why did she feel that she had to show you the documents?"

"Yolanda wanted my opinion. She wanted to know what I thought of the documents. And *when*, you ask? When I started to work on the oil wells. Apparently, she had done all the research when you began building your new home in Mercedes City."

"How convenient for the two of you," replied the *Don*, holding Ricardo in a rigid stare. "The two of you, it seems, have been plotting this together. You saw the opportunity that if Yolanda gets part of the land, she would share it with you—that's real convenient!"

"I had nothing to do with the documents, and if you're suggesting that I'm plotting anything with Yolanda, sir, you are wrong."

"And as for you, I will not say it again. It would be wise, to stay away from Yolanda, or there will be serious consequences to follow. This is not a threat, but a promise. You need to be responsible. You need to be a husband or leave this area. Victoria will probably shoot you, if she gets a wind of your infidelities. As for the upcoming baby, it will be taken care of.

We will not need any of your suggestions or consultations. You are welcome to stay at Spanish Acres and work, if you like. You'll be paid just like the rest of workers."

⌘ ⌘ ⌘

It was one of the days that *Don* Federico had spent quietly soul-searching on *Doña* Francisca's peaceful grave, as he had done so many days after her death. He found it comforting, as he tried to find answers to her passing into another world. She had left him devastated; he had gone mad, not wanting to come to the realization of her dying. His mind descended into Hell. He would call out *Doña* Francisca's name in vain, something so uncharacteristic of his personality. He felt guilt-ridden for not having taken her to a tuberculosis hospital, as had been suggested. Perhaps it would have given her several more years to live. His mind had gone void and he had forgotten about his Spanish Acres responsibilities, his children, his home in Mercedes City, or any of the many projects he had going. He did not care to live anymore. He wanted to die and be with his wife. He was a man who did not believe in spirits, but found comfort in speaking her name out loud while he cried. He had worn out many handkerchiefs as he sat in the quiet environment of the grave, immersed in deep thought about the brevity of life, and listening to the chatter of the mischievous mockingbirds in the nearby mesquites.

A loud voice from out of nowhere called to him from behind, "Ah, *hombre* why do you punish yourself, spending such a waste of time in this cold graveyard!"

Don Federico, rudely startled, jumped several inches into the air! Swiftly, he yanked his pistol and spun around. He was confronted by the shriveled, hunched *Doña* Adela, who had been picking fresh *quelite*, chickweed, which she used as a blood cleaner. "*Doña* Francisca's spirit appeared before me early this morning," she grumbled. "She told me to tell you not to be worrying about her. She is at peace, but was concerned about you and the children and your wasting of your time. You have neglected the responsibilities of taking care of your sons by spending your time in a senseless graveyard. They need your love and guidance." She clucked her tongue, pointing her twisted finger at him, as her depthless, light-colored eyes held his gaze.

Don Federico's neck hairs bristled. With furrowed brow he stood immobile, and then took a deep breath in a soul-stirring moan. "You have talked to my wife?" he replied. He gulped as his body shook and his eyes widened with astonishment as he faced the old *bruja*.

"Ay, *hombre*, I speak to many spirits of the families that need my help. The spirits come to me from the other side and tell me things of importance to relay and tell their families what to do." The old woman persisted in telling him several stories from the past, and the final conclusion that had transpired with the assistance of the spirits. What the old *bruja* was not telling the *Don*, was that Mamá Maria had become so concerned with *Don* Federico's actions, especially not eating, that she made Manuel take her to visit the witch and ask for her help. Everyone in Spanish Acres knew where they could find the *Don*, spending most of his time at the gravesite. The two women plotted the confrontation, so that *Doña* Adela would pretend to be picking up herbs at the cemetery, and would snap the *Don* out of his misery and bring him back to reality.

After several hours of animated conversation about dead spirits and ghosts, *Don* Federico brought up the subject of the body of the murdered redheaded woman, who had never been found, and to this day was still a mystery to all of the residents of Spanish Acres. He asked the old witch if she had seen anything or knew anything about her, since she roamed the *brasada* for her herbs.

La bruja disclaimed any knowledge.

They were surprised to see the figure of Martin approach the cemetery. He was riding his horse fast, looking for *Don* Federico to tell him about an accident involving Roy. His face was drained.

"Roy is hurt!" exclaimed Martin. "One of the barbed wires cut loose while he was stretching it and hammering the posts, and it cut Roy's stomach in half—his intestines are hanging out! They are taking him over to your house, *Doña* Adela." He addressed the old woman nervously. "The *vaqueros* went and got the flat-wagon, loaded Roy, and are on their way to your *jacale*, right now."

It seemed that something snapped in *Don* Federico's mind; a surge of energy and fear overwhelmed him. "I'll get my horse and meet all of you at *Doña* Adela's house," he said. He turned stern-faced to the bent old *bruja*. "If you want to ride with me, *Doña* Adela, I'll take you back to your house. It will be faster on the horse, than in your wagon. We will all be thankful for your help." The *Don* suggested to Martin to tie his horse behind *Doña* Adela's wagon and return it to her house.

They rode fast and furious, through the rough *brasada*, with *Doña* Adela behind him, holding on to his waist, hoping they would get there in time. The horror of losing Roy overwhelmed *Don* Federico; never once did he complain of the hunched old woman's fetid smell, or that something might jump on his body. He never thought of it, for his priority at the time was Roy's health, for it was Roy who truly ran his cattle kingdom. Losing his foreman would be the final blow.

The wagon with Roy was already waiting at *Doña* Adela's hut for her expertise in healing. Immediately, several *vaqueros* took the moaning Roy inside, while one held onto his bleeding stomach that had been wrapped in some of the men's cotton shirts. Bright red blood seeped through the cloth.

There was another surprise waiting for *Doña* Adela at her domain. Martin's younger brother, José Trevino, needed her help as soon as possible. He too was panicky, beaten and hurt. Outside the hut, the *vaqueros* and José waited around for half an hour, when Martin finally rode up with *Doña* Adela's wagon.

"Martin," said the young José, "you need to come home! Something terrible has happened at our house. Our thirteen-year-old sister, Juana, is pregnant! She finally confessed to mother who the father is—our own father! Mother is in agony. She was severely beaten when she confronted father about Juana's condition. I tried to stop him from hitting mother, but he is too strong for me. He whipped me while mother was trying to explain how, shamelessly, he was taking Juana out into the barn, with the excuse of showing her how to milk the cow and goats. I broke away from him, ran out of the house, and saddled my horse in haste, while he was whipping her. Mother has several broken ribs and she has been beaten around her face. She may not make it. I had no choice and decided to seek the help of *Doña* Adela. I cannot go home without getting help and telling on him." The young José kept repeating the words, "He will kill me!" over and over again.

"I'll kill him!" yelled Martin, out of control, adjusting his gunbelt. "*El desgraciado!*" he kept muttering. "He forced me out of the house after the last thrashing he gave me, and he knew what he was doing all the time. Juana was his favorite, and he showed it."

Don Federico, who had heard everything, stood stunned like the rest of the men; the atmosphere frothed with tension while waiting for Roy, who had been given whiskey to drink, had his intestines washed with warm water and placed back into his stomach. It was as simple as that. He was being sewed up with a common needle and thread. His hollering could be heard for miles around the vast *brasada*, as the waiting *vaquero's* sipped mescal from a bottle to calm each other's nerves. All were waiting to return him back to the hacienda and have him rest, restoring his health.

"Any of you men want to come with me over to Martin's house and take care of this little problem?" commanded *Don* Federico in anger, adjusting his gunbelt. "We will wait until *Doña* Adela is finished with her operation and take her with us."

The majority of the men agreed and strapped on their gunbelts. They pulled out double-barreled shotguns that were in the wagon, and began loading their ammunition, as if going to the border and joining in fighting the Mexican War.

Don Federico ordered Martin and José to stay at *Doña* Adela's place until the *bruja* had finished sewing Roy up. Then they were to put the foreman in the wagon and take him back to Spanish Acres. It was safer and better for the two of them to stay at the hacienda at the moment and not to do anything foolish. The rest of them would escort *Doña* Adela to see about *Señora* Trevino.

One of the *vaqueros* commented, "Old man Trevino is a tough son-of-a-bitch. It's terrible how a father would abuse his own daughter—a terrible sin. It's going to be interesting how this is going to turn out, especially for poor Martin, who is getting the short stick of this." Another replied, "It's going to be sad walking and sad singing, after *Don* Federico gets through with him." These were the comments from the *vaqueros*, as they traveled through the hostile *brasada* toward the Trevino home.

Old man Trevino lived southwest of Spanish Acres, close to *Don* Federico's land and several miles west of La Villa. There was a strip of land between them that no one had claimed and nobody wanted, since it was full of alkali and salt. It was a true fact that Trevino was a cruel man, not only to his own family, but also to his animals. He was surly and disliked by his neighbors for being aloof, ungracious, and not having anything to do with the rest of the families living close by. He lived by his own rules, regardless of any other laws. He used his own children like pawns, especially his boys. He used them like slaves, and threatened and whipped them to do his will, and denied them nourishment as punishment.

ROOTS OF INDIFFERENCE

It was getting toward evening, and shadows were getting long. During the winter season the days were shorter, and the sun was vermillion in color and setting toward the west. There was an eerie feeling as *Don* Federico, *la bruja*, and his *vaqueros* approached the Trevino's property, not knowing what to expect. Few entered onto Trevino's unwelcoming territory; he was known to be a man of few words and considered to be unreasonable and vindictive. All were nervous, even *Doña* Adela, who rode next to the *Don*, all bundled up. Who knew when a wild animal might jump them at any moment, or when gunshots would come from any direction from either side of the harsh *brasada?*

The trail ahead disappeared between the dark walls of hanging branches. Brambles cracked and shattered as they rode the lonely route, avoiding the prickly cactus, *tasajillo,* and the *agarita* on the side of the rutted road. A flock of birds erupted from the silence of the trees and fled and circled and broke the utter stillness, making the men all jumpy. One of the *vaqueros* passed gas in his excitement; others chuckled in their nervousness and offered him some whiskey. Dogs barked loudly in the distance, howling as if the angel of death crept among them sweeping around over and through the *huisache,* cactus, and mesquite. As they approached the open gate made of mesquite and wires, they rode close together, watching each step the horses took, expecting the unexpected to happen. The air became full of awe and mystery, almost threatening, in their invasion of another man's property. They entered the muddy road leading toward the small hut, seeing white wood smoke curl from the chimney of the adobe *jacale.* The quiet was broken by the spinning of the old, rusty windmill, and yapping dogs that ran out to meet them, surrounding the nervous horses' legs.

Jumping off his horse and holding onto his reins, *Don* Federico used the animal as a shield as he eased his way closer to the door of the Trevino's house. The other men did the same. He called out. "*Don* Trevino, I need to talk to you!" He shouted again. "*Don* Trevino, we have *Doña* Adela with us. We hear that *Señora* Trevino is sick and needs help."

A bullet came from one of the side windows of the hut, hurtling toward the men hunched behind their horses with *Doña* Adela. They all scrambled with their animals toward the windmill's watertank, including *la bruja* with her large herb bag. Squatting down with rifles and guns in their hands, they watched the front door of the *jacale* for several minutes to see if there was any movement. The door of the hut opened slightly to reveal a small, thin figure of a very pregnant girl. It was Juana.

"Did you say that *Señora* Adela is with you? Where is José?" she inquired, her voice frantic. She stood in the doorway holding a rifle, which she let drop to the ground in complete defeat. "Mother was beaten and needs her help," she cried, and then began sobbing. Another child, a boy about eleven, ran to his sister and buried his head into her, crying.

"*Sí, Hija,*" cried out *Doña* Adela, approaching the entrance, holding her herbs and potion bundle. "I'm here to help your mother. Where is she?"

Juana pointed to the interior of the house.

Doña Adela walked up and embraced the crying Juana. "Everything is going to be all right, *Hija.*" The men hurried to the door, picked up the rifle, and helped *Doña* Adela toward the back of the *jacale,* where *Señora* Trevino was being kept hidden.

"Where is *Don* Trevino?" *Don* Federico inquired of the skinny, young girl, who was wiping tears from her eyes with her apron. Her swelled stomach looked like a ripe watermelon. He figured she was about seven months into her pregnancy. "I need to talk to him!"

"He's out in the pasture. He went to get the cows with young calves back into the barn. They will need milking later. He should be back any minute now," replied the frightened girl.

One of the *vaqueros* who assisted *Doña* Adela to the rear of the *jacale* returned shaking his head. "*Señora* Trevino needs to be in a place where she can be taken care of. She is in serious trouble. She is bleeding from her mouth, with broken ribs, and she's moaning, in so much pain she doesn't want to be moved. But she will die if she stays here."

"We can always take her back to Spanish Acres, but the ride would be rough in the back of a wagon. Seems like the hacienda is becoming a refuge for the ill and wounded," *Don* Federico mused. "We will have to wait until *Don* Trevino returns. I'm not leaving until this is settled."

The sun had finally gone down and only the dusk remained. It was not long before the dogs began barking. There was the lowing of cattle being driven. Soon a booming voice yelled, "*Quien son?* Who are you?"

Don Federico and of his *vaqueros* walked outside and faced an angry *Don* Trevino.

"What the hell do you want here?" *Señor* Trevino growled. "What the hell are all of you doing on my property?" His rifle swung in all directions toward the *Don* and his *vaqueros*. "All of you get the hell out of my house and off my land!"

"Wait a minute!" *Don* Federico said, raising his left hand, then adjusting his gunbelt with his right, he sauntered toward the frenzied madman. "*Señor* Trevino you have some explaining to do," he stated flatly, "especially about your children, the beating of your wife, and the condition of your daughter."

"Says who?" *Don* Trevino raged. "Who gives you the right to come to my house and tell me what to do?" His double-barrel shotgun swept them all again, causing the alarmed *vaqueros* to duck.

"Apparently your own children," suggested the *Don*. "Your son Martin has been living at Spanish Acres for over two years now, after the beating you gave him, and your starving him, in case you have forgotten. Your other son just informed us that you had beaten him also, and your wife. By the looks of her, she may not live. José told all of us that he cannot return home because you're going to kill him. Now, that causes us all to become concerned, especially since we're your neighbors. What are we supposed to do?"

Before *Señor* Trevino could answer, a loud blast came from the direction of the front gate. Tension had been building up to this point, and any kind of noise was nerve-racking. Everyone was caught off-guard and fell to the ground. Figures in the dark scrambled in all directions—then silence. Out of the commotion one said, "*Ay Chin!*" Another yelled, "*qué paso?*" As the moments passed, everyone checked themselves in the darkness to see if they had taken a bullet. Who had fired? What had happened? Then, they saw it. *Don* Trevino lay sprawled on the ground, a bullet to the side of his head. His shotgun lay by his side.

With lantern in hand, Juana and her little brother ran to their father and shrieked. The gutsy *Doña* Adela, who had heard the confrontation from behind the screen door, walked toward the downed man to check on his condition, never fearing, for as old as she was, she thought she would live forever. Whether another bullet would be heading in her direction, she did not care.

"Ay, it's all over," replied the *bruja*, bent over and checking things out. "*Señor* Trevino is dead, but who did this?" The old witch woman straightened herself up as she heard the sound of a horse's hooves coming from the gate. She reached out for the distraught Juana and hugged her. A horse soon appeared out of darkness carrying Martin, with rifle in hand, and his brother José riding behind.

The *vaqueros* and *Don* Federico began straightening up and dusting themselves off, looking horror-stricken and perplexed; everything had happened so fast.

"Martin!" said *Don* Federico, finding his way close to the horse and looking up at the young *vaquero*. "I thought I told you to stay at Spanish Acres until we returned! Did Roy make it back all right?" He watched Martin climb off his horse still holding the rifle and not saying a word, his eyes in a wild trance. He walked over to his dead father, like the great hunter checking and reassuring himself of his kill. His brother José followed behind him inspecting the lifeless body lying like an animal in a pool of blood. Martin stood for over a second, hovering over the body of his father, then, raising his gun, he blasted him with another bullet, and another, without remorse.

Don Federico and the *vaqueros* who watched were horrified and scrambled to hold Martin down trying to avoid his rifle, forgetting the terror. "Hold him down, men. Take the rifle away. It's going to be all right now, Martin." *Don* Federico kept reassuring him, speaking in a low, commanding tone. He felt empathy for the young, struggling Martin. The rest of *vaqueros* kept talking to Martin, consoling him, but they continued holding him down by his shoulders and arms. They were in agreement with what he did; they were siding with him. They would have done the same thing—they would have killed any member of their family, if they had known the truth in the same situation.

Juana and José rushed to Martin's side crying, but this time with happiness. The younger one hung on to Martin's legs. He and Juana had not seen Martin in over two years; the presence of their oldest brother brought overwhelming joy. They were now free from their tormenting life of hell.

"Martin, it's all over," said the *Don*. "Your father will not be hurting you or any member of your family. He will not be beating your mother, or you, or anyone else. You are the man of the house now. You can take care of your family, and later have a family of your own." He kept talking, trying to get Martin to come to his senses. Finally, he gave him a strong slap across his face, shocking everyone.

Instantly, Martin snapped out of his despondency and spoke. "Is my mother is going to live?" He lowered his head in shame and brought his hands to his face covering his eyes. He burst into tears and began bawling like a child, knowing the murderous act he had committed. He was ashamed of himself and for his family.

They all knew how much his father had hurt him and his family, and that the young man was emotionally disturbed by his father's actions over the years. Martin was a hard worker, basically quiet and reserved, and had never mentioned much about his father's cruelty. But the *vaqueros* knew his life had been in total despair for a young boy turning fifteen.

"*Ay, si,*" answered *Doña* Adela. "In a couple of weeks, your mother will be fine," she reassured him. "It's going to take some time before your family will be back to normal. But things will get better, for you, and your family. You and your mother will be free!"

"It's over! Let's get the body inside the barn," commanded *Don* Federico. "It's getting dark, and it's gonna be a long night. I have to get back to Spanish Acres and see about Roy. We'll see what Martin and his family want to do with the body. We can bury him out in the family's graveyard if they want."

Martin, weighed down by his actions, stood like a young, innocent boy with tears in his eyes looked toward the great *Don*. He felt his tormented life being lifted. They were all free. He stretched out his arms to explain and said, "You're not calling *Los Rinches* on me? You're not having me arrested for this killing?" It was evident that he had come to his senses; he wanted to take responsibility for his actions, especially killing his own father, whom he had hated for so many years. It was a strange spectacle. Everyone had the same feeling about the killing of *Señor* Trevino. Martin's father was a menace to society and had deserved to die— exterminated, execution style! The shocking part was that nobody expected his own son to kill him.

"I did not see anything, Martin. All standing here hate *Los Rinches*," *Don* Federico replied. Turning, he faced the rest of the *vaqueros*, *la bruja*, and Martin's brother and sister. "Did any of you see anything?" He waved his hands. "Did anyone here see who fired the shots in the dark?"

There was a long pause as the night closed in on them. The only light glowing came from the children's lantern, shadowing the individual presence, while dancing upon each of their thoughts. Each searched his mind for what they would have done, if they were in the young Martin's shoes. They marveled at the braveness of the young lad. The dogs did not even bark. All replied, "No."

"Well, there's your answer. Better see about your mother and sister." The *Don* then addressed his *vaqueros*. "*Muchachos*, let's go home! We have lots of work to do back at the ranch!"

The death of one individual had brought sadness to some, and joy to others. The *vaqueros* smiled, realizing that perhaps everything would start getting back to normal, for it seemed that *Don* Federico had regained his senses, again being the impartial, generous, noble man getting on with his responsibility after the death of his wife. He spoke to *la bruja*. "*Señora* Adela, do you want to stay with Martin and *La Señora* Trevino tonight? You might want to stay with her this night, and keep an eye on her condition until she gets better. I will have one of my *muchachos* come tomorrow and check on the situation, and bring over some food and supplies. I will see that you get back home safely."

La bruja rose to the bait and chuckled. "*Ay, Sí Hombre, Señora* Trevino and her children will need me to help them. I will stay the night with *La Señora.*" The witch was pleased and delighted. There was a dead body, and she was like a vulture that smelled blood. *Señor* Trevino was dead, and dead bodies were what she used for many of her remedies and potions. *La bruja* would have her hands full. She had work to do; she would work all night as she performed her spiritual ritual.

And finally, Martin, *el Toro*, the desperate runaway boy, became the household hero.

CHAPTER 26

Don Federico was true to his word. Within the following weeks, he ordered his workers of Spanish Acres to check on *Señora* Trevino's health and to take food to the family. Martin had buried his father under a tree, in a homemade casket that one of the family's carpenter cousins had made.

It had been a long, weary year for everyone and especially for the Juelson family, losing *Doña* Francisca to the dread disease of tuberculosis. There had also been many beloved friends and neighbors that had died during the year. They placed their hope in the Mexican superstitious saying: "One soul dies, and leaves, but two other souls enter into this world."

Roy continued to fight an infection. He had been delirious and not getting any better, his condition deteriorating, with a temperature of 105. *Doña* Adela had tried all of her herbs, but the swelling in his stomach kept getting worse. Greatly concerned, *Don* Federico was forced to take Manuel and two other *vaqueros* to travel with him across the border into Reynosa and, hopefully, convince Dr. Cantu to travel with them to Spanish Acres and check on Roy personally. He would be well paid.

They took four mules pulling the wide wagon, for they planned while there to get supplies that they were unable to get on the Texas side of the border, and also bring back the doctor. *Don* Federico suggested that Fred tag along with him and Manuel, riding in the wagon, while the other two *vaqueros* rode their horses.

The conditions in Mexico had gotten worse. Díaz had fled the country and was now living in exile in France. The United States government did not recognize Huerta as president, and the bickering between Pancho Villa and Carranza, who were both fighting for political control of the government, made it dangerous to travel into the interior of Mexico. It had become "a free for all," without any firm government rule. Earlier in the month of June, Blanco had taken the law in his own hands and was trying to take control of the city of Matamoros. He was now commanding over 1,500 soldiers along the border.

Soldiers immediately stopped *Don* Federico and his entourage and interrogated them as soon as they crossed the Rio Grande, and asked what business they had in Mexico. Mexico was at war, and everyone was eyed with suspicion.

While in Reynosa, the men were in total shock to find out that Dr. Cantu had been shot and killed. The closest real practicing doctor to be found was in Monterrey, over two hundreds miles into the interior of Mexico. They had another choice, and that was driving sixty miles east to Matamoros.

"No doctors anywhere!" *Don* Federico lamented. "Nobody here knows anything about medicine. What happened to his practice?" he inquired of one of the soldiers who seemed to be more intelligent then the rest and seemed to be more aware of the situation in Reynosa and on the border.

"Dr. Cantu's practice is being occupied by *El Capitán* Alvarez, who knows a little bit of medicine. He was appointed by *General* Lucio Blanco after Dr. Cantu was killed, to help the wounded soldiers." He pointed to a whitewashed, stucco building riddled with bullets, a block down from the plaza. Apparently they had had several skirmishes with the *Villistas* and the Carranza forces known as the Constitutionalists, or better known as the *Carranzistas*, who were in control.

"Does this Alvarez man know anything about medicine?" the *Don* questioned.

"*Ay, si,*" the polite soldier replied, so willing to be of assistance. "He has helped many wounded people, has delivered several babies, and has operated on many soldiers."

"Where is Blanco?" asked the *Don* inquisitively, knowing that Blanco was charging taxes on foreign imports being brought into Mexico, as well as outgoing exports including cattle and goods.

"He is gone to a village fifty miles down on the Gulf Coast, getting guns and more supplies from the Germans. The German boat landed a couple of days ago. He will not be back until the end of the week. Everything here has been peaceful, since the *Villistas* left several months ago."

Don Federico found it convenient that Blanco was gone, for he might be able to buy all of his supplies without being charged the exporting tariff. Perhaps he could also take the new doctor back home to aid Roy.

They drove the wagon up past the plaza and around the corner close to the rundown stucco building. *Don* Federico's thoughts were running wild: *Mexicans buying German guns from the Germans?* His thoughts wandered from the visit earlier in the year that he had from the U.S. Marshal Bishop, and the conversation concerning the Germans trying to take over the Mexican government. *Don* Federico found it puzzling. He mind kept turning over the name Alvarez. *Alvarez! Why does that name sound so familiar? Don* Federico gave orders to Manuel and the rest of men to take the wagon with his long list of needed supplies down to *el mercado* and get as much as possible, while he made arrangements with the doctor to bring him back to Spanish Acres. The bells atop the *Virgen de Guadalupe Catedral* rang out, announcing that it was noon.

Fred did not wait for his father to halt the wagon. He jumped down while it was still moving and walked into the open hospital building and began wandering around. There were four cots on both sides of the dirty, discolored walls, with wounded men in each of the beds.

Flies were everywhere. The place smelled of rot, alcohol, chloroform, whiskey, and jalapeño peppers.

A thin man with a white coat and a stethoscope around his neck approached him, coming from the back of the building, asking what he wanted. At first, Fred did not recognize him, but as the person got closer, he shouted, "Juan!" Fred dashed towards him, and both embraced into an *abrazo*. "I knew you'd stick to being a doctor!" replied Fred with joy.

Don Federico stood in the doorway aghast, not knowing what to say. Then, everything made sense; of all the people to encounter, it was Juan Alvarez! With so many things in the past to forget, so many bridges that had been burned—at this urgent moment everything needed to be erased. He had no other choice but to confront Juan, eat his own words, and ask him for the biggest favor of his life.

Juan was surprised. He walked toward the *Don*, and in his gracious nature, stretched out his hand. "*Don* Federico, it's so nice to see you! Small world! What brings you to this side of the border and to this poor, humble place?" He smiled, displaying his pleasant attitude, acting like nothing had ever come between them. "How can I help you? How may I be of service to you?" He was kind, charming, and interested in knowing what was troubling this great man whom he so much admired.

"Juan!" said *Don* Federico. He was almost afraid to ask him for help. "I have come to ask you for the biggest favor of my life. But I don't know if you are able to help me at this time." He was pleading like a miserable peasant, with his hat in his hands, and for the first time stood humble. "Frankly, I'm short on words," he said. His hands were shaking. "I'm shocked to find you here on the border, especially in this rat hole. I was flabbergasted to hear that Dr. Cantu was killed, and I wasn't expecting this big surprise of finding you here. But, you remember my foreman, Roy? Well, he is going to die on me, if I don't get some medical help for him quickly. I need a doctor!" his voice quivered and his eyes misted. "I'll pay any price you ask, if you'll come with me."

Juan, delighted to see the two Juelson men, interrupted by waving his hands. He pointed to the rear of the dilapidated building and suggested that the two have a cold drink and sit down and rest. There they could talk and get a clear picture of what had taken place at his hacienda.

Within an hour *Don* Federico had explained about Roy's accident. Juan, hearing about *Doña* Francisca's death, was sincerely heartbroken and expressed his deepest sympathy. He learned, too, about Victoria's marriage and her soon-to-be-delivered baby. He felt his heart faintly stir, but swallowed his disappointing hurt and smiled graciously.

So many things had happened in Juan's own life during the last eight months. He told *Don* Federico that his mother had died, and his sister had married a nice, respectable businessman from a town close to Monterrey.

But he didn't tell him that he had envisioned himself wanting wealth, fame, and a nice mansion with the girl of his dreams—Victoria. And Victoria had wanted the same: money, property, and more important, a name. The Del Calderóne's name in itself was famous and known throughout the entire country of Mexico. He hoped she was happy with the man of her dreams. He wished that someday he would find a woman he could love, have many children, and live a contented life. Yes, there were other women, beautiful women in Mexico, and he had had plenty of them, but nothing approached the depth of the love he had for Victoria. From the moment he met her out in the *brasada*, she had captured his heart and soul, and he thought he had captured hers.

Now, he told *Don* Federico, all he wanted was to help mankind and help the least fortunate in healing them and make them well, contented with being ranked only *El Doctor Capitán.*

Fred sat and listened while both men talked of years past and brought up their trip to San Antonio and what a good time they had had. Madero's name came up and brought sad memories. Juan remarked that the situation in Mexico was becoming more alarming every day. "After Madero's death, the only leader we have now is Carranza," he said, "but I have chosen the medical field and play it safe. I want to accomplish my lifetime dream, and I'm making it possible a little at a time helping the poor and helpless. I have decided to help the wounded and get out of the battlefield. It's a political mess. I'll use my head and my brains for healing, instead of my physical body with guns and killing."

"A worthy cause, well taken." said *Don* Federico.

It wasn't long before the two talked like years before. Juan began making the arrangements to leave with *Don* Federico. Two of his women helpers, dressed in white uniforms, would stay and help until his assistant returned in a couple of hours. Juan would come with *Don* Federico, as soon as the supply wagon returned from *el mercado.* He began packing his large, black bag with medicine and instruments.

⌘ ⌘ ⌘

It was late in the evening when the weary group finally reached Spanish Acres. They had not stopped in Mercedes City, going right past the town, because of the immediate urgency. On the trip, Juan learned that *Don* Federico had built a new house in Mercedes City and that Fred had returned from military school but still wanting to become a doctor. Juan was thrilled.

The majority of the workers at Spanish Acres had been taking turns, through many sleepless nights, taking care of Roy. They had nearly given up hope for an intervention, although candles and prayers and many *novenas* had been said to save the foreman. Still, they were pacing the floor, patiently waiting for the arrival of any miracle.

After seeing Roy's condition, Juan immediately began to give orders. He had been up since five o'clock that same day, had not stopped, not even to rest, but he was used to this daily life and accustomed to this routine. He asked for some black coffee and ordered as many buckets of hot water as could be provided, along with soap to scrub the area. He requested a flat bed, or a board with fresh linens to lay Roy on. He also requested as many oil lanterns as possible, needing as much light as possible to see what he was doing. Finally, he would need help with the operation itself. Fred, Miguel, Soledad, and Yolanda all volunteered. It was important especially to Fred, who realized this could be the experience of a lifetime.

In a flash, the women diligently went to work, scattering in all directions, trying to get the supplies and do whatever they could do to save the dying *gringo*.

The operation began, with Juan and his helpers working on the elegant dining room table, under the twenty oil lamp chandeliers. Nobody slept. The natives stood around into the wee hours of the night, waiting. Tension and suspense were part of the daily life here.

There was blood everywhere. Fred stood at Roy's head, dropping chloroform from an eyedropper on a soft, white cloth over his nose. Each time Roy groaned, he placed another drop. Soledad experienced so much anxiety that she became sick and was whisked away. Yolanda, who could not take her eyes from Juan at first, had fainted at the sight of blood and was dragged onto a couch. Fred's face would occasionally turn different colors, and he would excuse himself from the scene at intervals. The only one still standing was Miguel, his face contorted by what his eyes were viewing, as if he were experiencing the pain himself. Several times he became concerned about Juan and would pat his sweaty forehead with a clean cloth.

After three hours, Juan finished the last stitch and almost collapsed. He managed to clean his hands and dispose of the once white smock, now drenched in blood, that he had put on over his own clothes. Black coffee was brought to him as he sat in one of the dining room chairs and began wiping his face with a warm cloth. Hot chicken soup and a bottle of whiskey were placed on the table for him. "It will be a matter of time," he said. "Only time will tell. After the chloroform wears off, Roy will be in a lot of pain. Give him all the whiskey he wants. It will be morning soon."

⌘ ⌘ ⌘

The following morning, *Don* Federico received a message from Victoria, by way of the daily milk-wagon going back and forth between Spanish Acres and Mercedes City. The letter informed *Don* Federico that Ricardo's mother and his sister had arrived in Texas and were staying at the Ale's house. They would remain there until Ricardo found them a place to stay or built them a new house. Victoria's grandmother Gloria had been living with Victoria and was watching and waiting for signs of labor. Word came that Emma had been in bed for over a week, not feeling very well, and had been having fainting spells. Some suspected, strictly speculated that, with her weight, she could be having heart problems. Felicia and Dan had also been staying at the Juleson house, and had been traveling back and forth to Emma's. On a daily basis, they were all taking turns and keeping a watchful eye on Victoria's upcoming delivery and watching for any changes in Emma's condition.

Things did not look good for the Ale family. Victoria also suggested in her note that since Dr. Cantu was taking care of Roy, perhaps he could drop by Emma's home and make a diagnosis.

Don Federico laughed after reading the message. *She needs to stop eating and stop putting food in her mouth. Poor Emma*, he thought.

It was close to noon before *Don* Federico, Fred, and Juan drove back to Mercedes City in their Cadillac carriage. Fred was dropped off in front of the Juelson's new home, to wash and change clothes, while the two men drove several blocks to Emma's home. Within an hour Fred walked back to *Tía* Emma's to visit with Juan before he returned to Reynosa.

At Emma's home, they found Felicia and Dan, who greeted the two men at the door. Dan especially was excited and surprised to see Juan, of all people. Felicia, too, was speechless and surprised to see Juan, but was grateful since he knew about medicine. *Don* Federico found it puzzling that the two men knew each other.

As Dan hugged Juan and called him *compadre*, the *Don* questioned, "How is it that you know each other?"

"Small world!" exclaimed Dan. "It's a long story." He paused, still holding on to Juan's shoulder. "We were both in prison in Mexico City and got to be good friends. We traveled together when we got out of jail and met Luis Del Calderóne, Ricardo's brother, on the road to Monterrey and joined his band of fighters." Dan paused, watching his words. Somehow he had to omit Juan's name and not connect him with the convent in Monterrey. *Don* Federico was wise and would pick up on what really happened on their trip back when they fled Mexico. He must not reveal Victoria's and Juan's secret love affair.

Don Federico was amused and pleased, but was still mystified. Then, still wondering, he asked Dan, "Where did you meet the two girls?"

Juan stood silent, holding his medical bag, and glancing around, studying the Ale's house, avoiding the conversation and pretending the discussion did not pertain to him.

Dan had to think fast! He rolled his eyes. "Why, it was Luis Del Calderóne who convinced me and my other two buddies to get food and shelter at the convent." He spoke with a slight laugh, and he stammered his words, trying to be convincing. "We must have left Juan many miles behind." He wanted to say as little as possible and not let the cat out of the bag. He was already getting himself into trouble, as his face turned beet red, feeling he was caught in a damn lie, when *Señora* Del Calderóne and Magdalena showed up in the living room. Dan gave a relieved sigh. Felicia was white as a sheet and stood frozen, her hands cupping her mouth, knowing that if Dan kept talking, *Don* Federico would have gotten the drift, and would have put two and two together, figuring everything out about Victoria and how she had gotten pregnant.

They performed the normal social formalities with each other. There was the introducing of Juan to *Señora* Del Calderóne and her daughter. There was a spark between the two young people, a faint smile, and a formal kiss for her hand. Magdalena stood breathless and enchanted by the handsome doctor.

Juan was taken upstairs to Emma's room where her enormous four-poster bed stood. It was over an hour before he came down and informed Felicia that her mother was suffering from the disease called diabetes, and perhaps, with her weight, would have heart problems later. Emma needed to stop eating heavy foods, stop eating pastries, and breads, and eliminate sugary desserts. She needed to lose weight and start exercising. She needed to be put on a diet that included plenty of vegetables, because eventually the disease could cause serious complications.

Within an hour Juan was traveling back across the border to Reynosa, back to his patients.

CHAPTER 27

"Juan was here?" Victoria stormed. "What happened to Dr. Cantu?" she questioned.

"He was killed!" Fred answered. He gave her the full story of what happened in Reynosa and at Spanish Acres within the last two days, and how Juan had saved Roy's life. "He's gonna come back, he told Father, when he left. He gave *Tía* Emma a new diet and is coming back to check on her next week. And he is going to start courting Magdalena. The whole family of *Señora* Calderóne and Emma were excited to see Magdalena so happy."

"He is going to do what?" she said. "I cannot believe this is happening!" Victoria paced the floor with her fists closed, her face flushed with anger. "What about Felicia?" she questioned. "What about Dan? What did they have to say?"

"They did not say anything! What are they supposed to say? They were happy to see Juan. They were worried about *Tía* Emma's condition. I thought you liked Juan?" Fred asked. "You sound like you do not like what he did. I mean he saved Roy's life and is looking after Aunt Emma and is going to teach me medicine and all—" Fred in his naiveté and innocence went on talking.

Of all people, the beautiful Magdalena! *Well, of course,* thought Victoria. No wonder she was so friendly, as if coming to Texas had transformed her into a new person. She was happy, like a breath of fresh air, and even hugged her. Magdalena had even asked to borrow one of Victoria's evening dresses, which she graciously loaned her. As a matter of fact, she had borrowed more than one, some that Aunt Emma had made for her, some very colorful. Her friendliness was a real surprise, since in the past, she hardly spoke to her. Victoria could not believe that if Juan fell in love with Magdalena and decided to marry her, he would be her—brother-in-law. *God! That cannot be possible. What is he trying to do? Is he trying to get back at me?* And yet, there was nothing that she could do. Her hands were tied. There was nothing, she could only wait.

⌘   ⌘   ⌘

Within the following three weeks, everyone within the Juelson clan and other important social circles were invited to Emma and Howard Ale's home for a banquet dinner honoring Juan and thanking him for his heroic service in saving Emma's and Roy's life.

As the time approached to go to the party, Ricardo and Victoria were alone in their upstairs bedroom. Except for the few servants in the downstairs kitchen and in the laundry room, the rest had gone to be with their families. Her father would be joining them later at Emma's home. He had gone to Spanish Acres to check on Roy's condition and on the shipment of crude oil being shipped out to the port of Brownsville. Her grandmother Gloria, Fred, and Carlos were already at Emma's house along with Felicia and Dan. Everyone was helping Emma with the banquet and with the preparations for the coming festivities of *las Posadas* and with decorations for the Christmas holidays.

"Well, I'm not going," replied Victoria. "The baby is due very soon, and I'm exhausted. I do not feel very well." She rolled over on her side on the edge of the bed.

"Well, you're going," Ricardo answered. "Get up from that bed, get dressed, and fix your hair," he said arrogantly, ordering her dismissively. "I'm going there and be with people, with my family. You don't want to insult my mother and your Aunt Emma by not showing up. Get dressed! They are expecting us to be at their dinner!" he said, controlling as always.

"And if I refuse?" she argued. "Everyone knows that I'm due any minute now. I look so terrible and do not feel like getting dressed. My hands and feet are swollen, and I barely have any energy." In the past months, she had been depressed over losing her mother and the humiliation of her pregnancy.

Ricardo was finishing buttoning his white, stiff cotton shirt, wanting to look his best, especially with his mother and his sister present. His face was flushed and twisted into a wild rage toward her. He grabbed her by her arm and began forcing her to sit up, being abusive, demeaning her with profanities.

Trying to defend herself, Victoria pushed him away from her. She grabbed his shirt, began pulling, and jerked so hard that one of the bottom buttons came off. This enraged him more, and he grabbed her hair and began pulling it. Victoria struggled to get up. From the Juelson's fire that burned in her soul, she managed to make a fist and throw a furious blow to his face, walloped him, striking so hard that he fell across the floor. With all of his arrogance and abusiveness, she hated him and wished him dead. Victoria did not know how long she was going to tolerate him, with his narcissistic, egocentric ways. She did not love him, nor would she ever.

Within minutes there was a knock and the door to their bedroom door flew open. *Don* Federico had returned early, and unexpectedly, walked in with one of the household servants.

"What's going on here?" He looked perplexed, as he scratched his head and eyed the condition of the bedroom, which resembled a Mexican train derailment. "From downstairs," he said, "it sounded like a boxing match was going on up here. Well! Who won?" He stifled a laugh at Ricardo who was still stunned and in a daze, trying to catch his breath and straighten himself up. He had a big shiner on his left eye, and Victoria's hair was a disheveled mess, standing partly up, looked like an orangutan.

"*Hija*," he said, "it'll take me forty-five minutes to take a warm shower, to clean up and dress and be at your Aunt Emma's house. Get ready! It will give you enough time to dress. I think you'll feel better. I will drive you." He winked at her, and then addressed Ricardo, "You can come with us, or I'll order a driver for you." He walked out of their bedroom and downstairs into his bedroom. His instincts told him what had happened; he found it almost comical, for he knew Victoria's temper.

⌘   ⌘   ⌘

It had already turned twilight dusk and the weather was chilled. The wind had started blowing, and coming with it was a light drizzling rain. Humidity and coldness cut right through to everyone's bones.

Within an hour, the gaiety at Aunt Emma's was at hand. Lanterns made with homemade candles planted in sand-filled paper bags lit the sidewalk up to the entrance of the home. Giant wreaths of fresh pine, with colorful red ribbons, were attached to the front door. They were greeted by Felicia dressed in a beautiful, golden brocade gown with golden chandelier earrings and necklace to match. Grandma Gloria kissed Victoria's cheeks and took her cape. Inside, people were dressed in their finest evening clothes of silk, lace, red and black velvet and their preeminent jewels. The family had hired a five-piece orchestra from Brownsville to play cocktail music for their entertainment. Homemade eggnog had been introduced by one of the families attending from the northern states and set on an elaborate side table with a large cut-crystal bowl and cups; several large doses of vodka had already been conspicuously poured and mixed.

The table was set for sixteen people and already was being filled up by the guests. *Don* Federico took a seat next to his two boys on his left. Directly in front of him was Mildred McCray, a plump, newly bereaved widow, her peppered hair up in a bun. Her grating, high-pitched voice echoed throughout the dining room. Between her and Emma, their voices would have made a fine croon. She kept eying *Don* Federico with a big smile, putting her white lace handkerchief up to her mouth and blinking her eyelashes, trying to catch his attention. She laughed at everything that was said and was becoming an annoyance to those seated next to her. *Her husband must have died from a chronic ear infection*, thought *Don* Federico. Fred and Carlos found her comical and would glance at her and laugh to each other. *Don* Federico, being a wealthy widower, had become a prize to win for any available woman. Emma had been talking to all of her Spanish Club friends, telling them how lonely and how rich he was, and had conspicuously invited Mildred on the pretence of meeting the great *Don*.

"*Señor* Juelson, it's so nice that I finally got the chance to meet you. Emma has been so charming in telling the women at our club about you and your great accomplishments."

"Its nice meeting you, too, Mrs. McCray, and I'm glad you were able to attend Emma's social affair. She is known for her great parties. How welcome you are." *Don* Federico turned and snapped his fingers at the two boys next to him who were covering their mouths, giggling.

Emma, hampered by over a hundred and fifty pounds of fat, was at the head of the table looking radiant with bright trinkets and feathers on her head, intimating the Christmas tree with all of its ornaments. The sarcastic, bigoted, Howard Ale wore a black suit and red tie at the opposite end of the table, looking gloomy and eyeing the young girls, from behind his heavy spectacles, and grabbing their behinds, unexpectedly, if he got the chance. Dan Land and Felicia sat next to Emma. Victoria was seated next to Ricardo and in front of them, across the table was Juan and at his side was Magdalena, wearing Victoria's elegant gown. The gown was beautiful, but being too big in the bust, it hung awkwardly on her body. *Señora* Del Calderóne, in a handsome, dark brocade dress, was on Ricardo's left, and kept stretching her neck, trying to spy on Victoria. She was always complaining and disapproved of Victoria's behavior, and she was trying to find some reason to find fault with her.

After the champagne glasses were filled, Emma stood up, with her enormous weight eclipsing the view of the Christmas tree behind her. The dining room had become a chattering room. She brought her glass up in the air to make a toast, waiting for the others to join her and do the same. Everyone was talking, engrossed in their own conversation with their table partners, so she tapped the glass of water in front of her with a spoon to catch the guests' attention.

"I have invited all of you, who have an important part in this community, first to contribute to charity and donate money, if you wish, to the families who have very little for their children during the coming holidays. All the women members of the Catholic ladies club are busy cooking and making cakes and food to take to some of the families, who are in terrible need at this time. All of this takes time and money. I also need to introduce you to, *El Doctor* Juan," Emma said. "He has been totally wonderful, finding out what my medical problem was, and he is going to heal me. Juan is courting Magdalena, and we need to celebrate that blessing; also Felicia and Dan have gotten engaged and will be announcing their marriage in the coming year." There were cheers and laughter, and the majority clapped their hands with joy, except Howard Ale, who had been sipping heavily all afternoon did not find any of this expensive, joyous occasion necessary. He was still searching for ways to get even with Felicia.

Victoria looked beautiful with her hair piled up on her head, a diamond hair comb, a diamond broach, and dangling diamond earrings to compliment her black velvet, loose-fitting top. On her shoulders was a brightly colored embroidered shawl that fell to her side. She was already feeling the tension among the guests, tension that could be cut with a knife. She was amazed that Aunt Emma, of all people, who had complained and criticized Juan at her birthday party, was actually praising him and throwing this grand party for him.

Victoria tried to remain aloof from everybody and was avoiding eye contact with Juan, but she was feeling the pressure from across the table. She took a sip of eggnog and instinctively her eyes raised and lingered toward the other side of the table. Juan honored her with a warm, congenial, loving smile. How could she forget his radiant smile, so pleasant, accentuated by his trimmed, dark mustache. It lit up her spirit. Their eyes locked for a fleeting moment. Heaven knows what each one was thinking. Perhaps they were remembering their last encounter in the little mining village at the hot springs cave high in the mountains above Monterrey, where they had made passionate love. Did he know she was carrying his child? He averted his gaze. However, he had been casually watching her actions and expressions, not letting others become suspicious of his interest, and yet, his attention had never left her.

In the background the musicians were playing *Over the Waves*, and it brought back memories of Juan dancing with her at Spanish Acres. So many weeks and months had flown by since that happy time, with so many memories and tears of grief.

Ricardo, even in his arrogance, felt out of place, and was livid, since all the attention was being lavished on "the great doctor." He was embarrassed over the shiner on his left eye, which created an uncharacteristic sense of inadequacy, causing him to feel comfortable only with his mother. He felt a pang of jealousy and immediately stopped his conversation and pivoting, viewed Juan, who at the moment was obviously enthralled with Victoria.

"It's so nice to see you again, *Señora* Del Calderóne." Juan nodded his head and spoke politely, but his eyes narrowed, becoming magnetic, boring right though to her soul. "It's been a long time," he said, smiling warmly.

Victoria blushed and her heart was pounding. She nodded her head. "Yes," she answered, "it's nice seeing you again—and yes, it's been a while."

The conversation was interrupted by Ricardo's belligerent personality. He had lost complete control. *How dare Juan be speaking so dotingly to my wife!* With all the sarcasm he could muster, he leaned forward, confronting Juan. "How long has that been?" he said, tapping the table with his fingers, making a point. "Yes, tell me how long?" His question was taunting; he was unmistakably begging for a fight, ignoring basic social etiquette.

Victoria turned to Ricardo angrily, lips pursed, face flushed, and glared at him, as he was completely out of line. She glanced up and viewed her father's reddened face. Ricardo had gotten the attention he craved, as the guests were now captivated by the scene unfolding before them.

Don Federico heard the conversation, stood up instantly with a glass full of hard liquor in his hand. "Ricardo! Juan's our guest and a friend of the family." He spoke with authority and with direct command. "We've been friends for some time now. We are all very thankful that he came all the way from his post in Reynosa to help us with all of our medical emergencies. This joyous, grand dinner is for Juan, and let's all enjoy the evening!"

Juan was obviously embarrassed by the accolade, but smiled at Victoria with a charming smile. Ricardo glared at Juan and remained annoyed.

There was loud applauding and cheers, since the guests at the table had not yet eaten and were already feeling the effects of the strong liquor.

"What I want to know—" the calculating Howard Ale spoke loudly, holding himself halfway up on the table, his speech slurred, already his body limp, feeling the whiskey he had earlier and a large glass of the newly flavored eggnog, "—is where in the hell did you get that goddamn black eye?"

Everyone laughed. Ricardo's face turned pink. From the far end of the table, the enormous figure of Emma called out, "Howard, mind your manners!" She sighed with embarrassment.

"Have the doctor give you something for that, will ya'? Where's the food? I'm hungry," her husband yelled.

There was another roar and applause as the servants began circling the guests. A huge pig with an apple in its mouth was brought on a gigantic platter; large slices of ham had already been cut and arranged on the side of the plate along with a large silver fork. The food served was amazing: big saucers of mashed potatoes; a bowl containing dark gravy; cut glass crystal bowls of buttered corn, broccoli, and cauliflower; fresh green beans mixed with almonds and onions; and candied sweet potatoes covered with dark *piloncillo* and cinnamon. The finest imported wine from France was offered. The servants brought in an enormous crystal platter with different fruits, including white and red grapes, which in this region and at this time of year were hard to find. These were placed in between the two tall, lit candelabras in the middle of the massive table.

As the servants passed the platters of food around, the conversation naturally turned to the conditions in Mexico and of the instability of the Mexican government. Many had relatives who sons who had died earlier in June in Matamoros; now the city was being controlled by the *Carranzistas*. Everyone was asking about the newly elected President Huerta and about the horror stories they were hearing of how dangerous it was to travel to Mexico. Venustiano Carranza was opposing Huerta, the President of Mexico and so was the United States. Carranza's right-hand man was General Alvaro Obregón, who with Pancho Villa's other allies, were fighting in both the northern states and Zapata down south. Much of the news was propaganda, some guests were saying. "They'll write anything to get a story."

After dinner, the guests stepped out into the large *sala* with a drink in hand to enjoy the music. All of the distinguished men were given Cuban cigars. Some couples danced. All were talking and mingling with each other.

Felicia's glance met Victoria's, and she motioned with her head, raising her eyebrows, for the two to go upstairs. Felicia noticed that Ricardo was hovering directly over his mother, apparently in a deep discussion about a business venture. Juan and Magdalena had their heads together, each with a drink in their hand. Howard was arguing with a guest. Emma was busy in the kitchen with the servants. *Don* Federico was talking to a circle of businessmen. Next to him was *La Señora* McCray, who was visiting with another guest, with an ear turned to *Don* Federico's conversation. *La Señora* Hinojosa talked to several of the woman, as they were asking her questions about the death of her husband in Mexico City and the situation in Mexico. The older children, Fred, Carlos, and the twins, played hide and seek and chased and caught each other, running around the house, going up and down the stairs, making a racket. Dan Land had gone outdoors checking on one of horses that was causing some disturbance. Perhaps a hungry coyote nearby had smelled food.

ROOTS OF INDIFFERENCE

Felicia's eyes wandered toward the end of the *sala* as if counting each individual in a great game of chess, making sure where each person fitted in the move and where everyone was stationed.

Victoria quietly passed through the noisy crowd and slowly made her way upstairs to meet with Felicia. There, in one of bedrooms, Felicia quietly informed her in a low whisper that *Don* Federico was questioning Dan about their trip coming home from school in Monterrey. "I think your father knows about Juan and the mystery of your baby. He was asking too many questions. Dan had gotten real nervous and had twisted the story to make it sound right, but by looking at your father's puzzled face, he wasn't buying it. I don't think he was convinced by Dan's story."

"What surprises me is how my father and your mother have taken such a great liking toward Juan," Victoria replied. "We are grateful, of course, that he was able to save Roy's life and get him well, and help with *Tía* Emma's health. Do you remember how mad my dad was with Juan in Monterrey? My father has changed since mother's death. He's made a complete turnaround in his attitude towards me. I get the impression that something happened between Ricardo and Dad. It changed his feeling toward the Del Calderóne family. Father knows that I do not love Ricardo and knows how unhappy I have been. I think that Father knows something, and I think he has an idea who the baby's father is. I think Dad and my mother both knew that it was a mistake in having me marry Ricardo."

"Victoria, you are with child, and be grateful that he married you. If not, imagine what the church people and the community would have said. How would you have explained about your baby?"

"Well, at this point all Ricardo thinks about is his mother and sister. He is not concerned about me and my condition."

"Why?" answered Felicia, looking right into Victoria's eyes and sounding serious. "What makes you think that he is only looking out for his family?"

"Because of the money he stole from the oil company instead of paying the workers. He used it to bring his mother and sister from across the border into the Valley. He wanted to protect his mother and make sure that his sister is well taken care of. He is not only selfish, but a liar, too. Father doesn't trust him and keeps a constant eye on him."

"That must have been when he appointed Dan to handle the company's money. However, things are working better for everyone in the oil fields and everyone is getting good money. Ricardo seems to be happy living most of the time in Spanish Acres and working there."

"Sure!" snapped Victoria. "Because Yolanda is there and pleasing Ricardo all the time."

"Oh! Yolanda is a stupid, uneducated girl. She has no class, no dowry. She sleeps with anybody, just to get attention. I wouldn't let her bother me." Felicia paused, "Getting back to your story about your Father and Juan—"

Victoria interrupted. "I don't know what Juan has told Dad. It would be stupid if he did admit to anything. I still cannot believe that Juan is pretending that he's so in love with Magdalena. I think he's putting on a theatrical show to get back at me. A person just can't forget what happened in the past so lightly. And I still love him!"

"Maybe," answered Felicia, "but, remember, you are now married." She said it as if that were the final word on the subject. "You are Catholic and married and there's no divorce."

"And I hate it!" Victoria spoke with her head down, regretfully, feeling tricked, cheated and trapped. Tears rolled down her face.

"I'm sorry," answered Felicia. "Don't try to do anything foolish. It's your baby that needs attention." Her eyes blinked rapidly, betraying her anxiety. "We must hurry down to our guests."

Victoria hugged her cousin and wished her the best with Dan. She was so happy for them and knew that the coming year was going to be a real challenge. "We will talk later when we are alone and have more time."

Felicia hurried downstairs, as Victoria stood in the bedroom collecting her thoughts, trying to compose herself. She brought her shawl over her head, and blew her runny nose with her laced handkerchief. She heard a noise coming from the back of one of the tall dressers. She peeked over the side, and there was Fred looking up at her, blinking nervously, crouched down and holding his knees.

"How long have you been here?" she said angrily, and felt her blood drain down to her feet.

"Long enough to hear everything!"

"You heard everything?" Victoria wanted to scream, but managed to compose herself. "Well, now you know! Keep it to yourself and don't repeat any of this, especially to Father or Ricardo!" she commanded nervously. "Absolutely no one else must know— only you and Felicia."

"I knew that you have always loved Juan," answered Fred, who seemed to understand her dilemma. "But I didn't know that you were going to have his baby. That's going to create family problems."

"Not if nobody knows! Keep this to yourself, and there will not be any problems. You and I will talk later, when we are alone. Promise?"

"Promise," Fred said.

⌘ ⌘ ⌘

The evening ended with *Don* Federico's suggestion that Juan spend the night with them at their new home. Juan had not seen the modern house and Emma already had too many other guests staying with her. Juan would be leaving early in the morning back to his post in Reynosa. As each guest departed the evening's festivities, they were given a basket full of apples, with packages of homemade fudge, candies, and cookies from Mexico and a large package of peanuts, which were not in season and were hard to find.

Ricardo had informed *Don* Federico that he was staying a while longer at Emma's, wanting to have a word with his mother and his sister about their future plans. He would have one of Emma's drivers take him home later.

ROOTS OF INDIFFERENCE

Upon entering the big Juelson mansion, Juan stood amazed as he viewed the beautiful, large, contemporary house with its Gothic structure, with its wide stained-glass windows, its winding staircase, and the spectacular glass chandeliers.

The servants helped Juan with his baggage and took him to a studio bedroom on the first floor next to *Don* Federico's expansive library. He and *Don* Federico talked into the night, with the *Don* making arrangements to reward the young doctor for his service and his willingness to come to Texas.

Ricardo returned in the middle of the night, drunk and disorderly, wanting to pick a fight with the household. *Don* Federico, already disgusted with his behavior, ordered him to leave the premises. Perhaps Spanish Acres would have a bed for him, since he was still working on the oilrigs.

By the crack of dawn, Juan was gone, but on the little ornate mirror table near the front entrance, he had left a handwritten envelope inscribed with Victoria's name on the outside. One of the servants had found it early in the morning as she was cleaning and dusting the furniture. She gave it to Victoria the following day with her breakfast tray. Inside was the repaired golden amulet with the chain that had been torn from her neck at the convent in Monterrey. On the back was the etched inscription: "All my love forever."

Juan had included a beautiful poem that he had dedicated to Victoria:

Your Marvelous Face
In order for God to find two superlative foreign stones, rare of its kind,
And to form two precious ideal eyes, God searched in the carunculous of the porous minerals; created the tears more divine and pure. Overlooked the mother-of-pearl colored coral, seabed blue. Disregarded the luxurious, opulence of the oriental stones; by-passed the magnificent brilliant fire of the Aurora-Borealis domes; Unheeded the particular facets of the sumptuous, sparking diamonds. And not being able to find luminous material to adorn and be fair, for your marvelous face, and for that matter, expressive and rare. God bit his red lips in anger and gazed with love… took his own eyes…and carefully placed them in your face.

The poem had been written in Spanish by Señor Miguel Cervantes, but Juan had translated it into English.

Victoria stayed in her bedroom and cried for two days; perhaps this was the cause and the beginning of her labor pains. How she loved him!

CHAPTER 28

Days before *Las Posadas,* the holidays leading up to Christmas, Victoria delivered a seven-pound boy. The baby was named Luis Martin Del Calderóne after Ricardo's brother Luis, who had been injured in a battle fighting with Carranza close to the port of Tampico, Mexico. The newborn's name had pleased *La Señora* Del Calderóne, since she had not seen or heard from Luis in many years, and her heart yearned to see him again. It was a joyous occasion. Mamá Maria and Yolanda had been brought from Spanish Acres to assist Victoria. Soledad had wished to come, but stayed at Spanish Acres to nurse the ailing Roy. The house became crowded, with Grandmother Gloria, Emma, *Señora* Del Calderóne, and the servants, all trying to assist by giving orders regarding the newborn.

Immediately, the women from the community, the wagging-tongue social clubs and the ladies from the Lady of Mercy prayer group began counting on their fingers from the time Victoria was married to the day the child was born. "Is the child full-term? It does not add up then. Something is fishy!"

No one knew if Ricardo had been contacted about the birth. Since the majority of Victoria's family was aware of the incident in Monterrey, many believed that it was not an important event in his life. Ricardo was spending most of his time at Spanish Acres with many others, including Dan Land, who worked many hours on the oilrigs and pumps. Not informing Ricardo about the birth of his baby boy was another hint to *La Señora* Del Calderóne that there was definitely something dubious concerning their marriage and the pregnancy.

Don Federico, Fred, and Carlos steered clear of all of the women's commotion. They were spending time at Spanish Acres, checking on Roy's health, cleaning the cemetery, sending food to *la bruja,* and helping with the development and improvements to the farmland. When inquiring about the family of Martin *el Toro,* they learned that his sister, Juana, gave birth to a stillborn child. Perhaps it was for the best, they all agreed. Furthermore, *Doña* Trevino's health had greatly improved.

During this time *Don* Federico checked his property documents in regard to what Ricardo had told him about his father leaving Yolanda some land in Spanish Acres. He knew that his father had some dealings with Yolanda, and of her reputation, and he did not want to venture further in learning what may have transpired between them. He gathered Miguel, Elena, and Yolanda in his library and handed Miguel the deed to Spanish Quarters, telling them all how sincerely grateful he was to have them as employees all these years. Spanish Quarters consisted of just over ten acres, which became their property to do with as they pleased; however, it had one stipulation: The water rights at Spanish Acres would still be controlled by *Don* Federico and his estate. Miguel and Elena were in tears, being so grateful, but Yolanda had protested, saying they deserved more land.

Victoria, upon hearing of the land transaction at Spanish Acres, was unable to sleep or breastfeed the baby. She was so upset; she was not able to produce any milk. The thought of giving Yolanda part of the land was driving her insane. The word went out among the community, and within a day, two wet nurses were hired, taking turns feeding the little boy. Victoria's breasts were wrapped tightly with linen cloth to keep her milk from being produced.

⌘ ⌘ ⌘

The year 1914 came as rumors of war were brewing in Europe, and the fighting across the border continued. Pancho Villa, Emiliano Zapata, and Carranza all were fighting against President Huerta's forces that were steadily driven back toward the capital. Families and relatives in south Texas crossed the border with caution, since President Wilson, who was staying neutral in the Mexican affairs, had asked for all Americans to steer clear of any involvement in the Mexican territories.

North of the railroad tracks in Mercedes City, Antonio Garcia and his sons had started a little grocery store, which offered limited quantities of staples at the time, providing canned goods for the Mexican families in the *barrios*. His specialty was fresh-picked coffee beans that were imported from Orizaba, Mexico. However, most Mexican families drove across the border into Mexico with mule wagons to buy their supplies and merchandise, since it was cheaper. Many of the specialty bridal shops were run by the whites in the Valley, and the Mexican families were not allowed to shop in their stores, a fact reinforced by signs posted on their front windows. Consequently, the Mexican-Americans would also drive across the border to the larger cities of Reynosa or Matamoros to buy wedding supplies.

⌘ ⌘ ⌘

When the population of Mercedes City topped 1,800, a new city charter was adopted, designating it now as "Mercedes," leaving out the "City." The south school for whites had been fully completed, with the acquisition of a wood-burning heating stove used during the cold days of December through March. Janitors were kept busy cleaning the building and cutting wood. Children went to school from 9:00 a.m. to 3:30 p.m. As always, there were problems that stemmed from not having enough money to operate the school. Many borrowed from the bank and from the citizens, who would sign notes to cover their expenses during the school months. New laws and regulations were added also, stating that a teacher had to have a college diploma to be able to teach.

H.A. Marsh, the county superintendent, was still hounding *Don* Federico to come back to teach at the school, which the *Don* had refused, telling Marsh that he had too many things boiling on the stove, and after his wife died, all of his yearning to teach had dissipated. At this moment, he felt he needed to find himself. His biggest priority, for now, was his growing family.

The same year, the children developed pink eye and were all sent home from school and told not to return until they had gotten over the infection. Fred and Carlos did not contract it, but they played it safe and stayed home for over a month, spending time with Victoria and her newborn baby.

Don Federico hired over a hundred workers to clear more of the land around Spanish Acres to begin planting cotton, which had become a very profitable commodity along with the coming of oil. He realized that some of the other farmers were having trouble in the last couple of years with the pink bollworm, which affected the growing of cotton. He decided to try to find ways to correct that destruction.

The community was growing, and no doubt, with indecisive winds of change was coming. Over half of Mexico's populace were displaced and were moving in by the droves. Rich white people were still arriving from the northern states, buying up land as if it were going out of style, in spite of the rumors of war so close at hand. Mexican-Americans who had been landowners for a long time were selling for ten cents an acre to speculators paying them with gold and silver coins. The development began with clearing the land and groundbreaking, putting up new brick buildings and churches, according to the new city charter. With all of the cheap help supplied by the Mexican immigrant workers, massive irrigation systems were also being established.

Ricardo had saved hundreds of dollars and bought several acres between Emma's and *Don* Federico's house for a home for his mother and sister. It took two months to clear the land. Builders began building a small, two-story stucco house, with a large patio and a high stucco fence for protection. With the Revolution in Mexico being so close, his mother said, "I need all of the high fences in the world for safety." Mexican tile was imported from Monterrey by train, and workers had to drive to Reynosa to pick up the load. On one occasion, the workers almost did not make it back across the border, as they did not have enough money to pay the export taxes.

⌘ ⌘ ⌘

In early April, *The Mercedes Enterprise* newspaper printed a shocking announcement that rocked the border: Nine American soldiers had been arrested by Huerta's army for entering a restricted area in the port of Veracruz. President Wilson sent the U.S.S. Dolphin to invade the port. The Mexicans responded with riots, and the Latin American and European presses denounced the United States' intervention. As much as President Wilson did not want to get involved with the Mexican affairs, it became necessary and inevitable for him to respond. Two American Marines had been arrested earlier by Mexican officials in Tampico. Huerta had refused to comply with the act of giving a twenty-one-gun salute to the American flag. Wilson saw these as unfriendly acts and asked Congress for intervention. A German ship attempted to unload guns and munitions at the Gulf port of Veracruz on April 21 and was bombarded. Nineteen United States Marines and 300 Mexicans were killed and many wounded. Loud clamors within the U.S. demanded war with Mexico.

Already along the border with Mexico, relations were unstable, and the incident caused the Rio Grande Valley residents great suffering between the two epic groups—the beginning of '*roots of indifferences.*'

The governor of Texas had given the Texas Rangers the power of full authority to terrorize and kill without explanation any suspicious Mexicans regardless if they were American citizens or not. Any person without an excuse for traveling, especially at night, into Texas from across the border would be shot—no explanations, and all individuals would be considered with suspicion, since there was much gun-running contraband across the border.

Two months later, at the end of June, the newspapers announced another bombshell. Archduke Franz Ferdinand and his wife Sophie were killed, shot to death in their motorcade while in Sarajevo, capital of the Austro-Hungarian province of Bosnia. This incident ignited war between Austria and Serbia, and eventually escalated into World War I. Urgent prayer meetings and *novenas* were conducted by the women from the Catholic Society in Mercedes, who took turns lighting candles in their homes, and other churches and social clubs elsewhere were also busy praying. Everyone was hoping that the United States would not get involved in the upcoming war, for many were afraid of their sons or husbands being drafted.

In Mexico during the month of July, steady insurgent military pressures from Villa, Carranza, and Zapata forced Huerta to resign his presidency and flee to Europe in exile. This left the country without a government, so Fransico Carvajal became interim president. With this taking place, it left the country of Mexico wide open, without any rule of government to keep order along the border. *General* Alvaro Obregón took military control of Mexico City, and Carranza assumed the title of the First Chief in charge of executive powers.

⌘ ⌘ ⌘

Juan would travel to Mercedes once a week, checking on Roy and Emma's condition, and at the same time, would romance Magdalena. He would stay sometimes with the Ale family, or spend the night at *Don* Federico's home. Juan enjoyed his stay in Mercedes, especially when he was able to take a peek at Victoria, who had grown more beautiful each day, even after her baby was born. He tried to find opportunities to speak with her; however, their precarious situation would not permit it. He treaded carefully and avoided any confrontation with the extremely jealous, hotheaded Ricardo.

When Juan was not with Magdalena, there were many other people around with ears like antennas that heard everything and loved to gossip. Juan wondered if the wise old owl, *Don*

Federico, who had a fatherly fondness for him, had read their gestures and knew more than he was letting on. Little Luis was now eight months old and weighed twenty-five pounds, already crawling. He had dark, shining hair, and his eyes were big and green—a handsome child who did not look anything like Ricardo.

One unbearably hot afternoon in the month of August, Juan and *Don* Federico were pleasantly enjoying the red-orange sunset on *Don* Federico's beautiful circular porch, both with their feet up on short rattan stools. Juan was puffing a Cuban cigar, while *Don* Federico was calmly smoking his pipe.

It was then that Juan cautiously brought up the subject of military papers that were circulating around the medical and military headquarters in Reynosa and wondered if *Don* Federico had heard anything about it. "They are calling it 'The Secret Plan,' which involved Carranza, alleged to be heading the plot, and it includes many important Mexican people in high office, several wealthy Mexican-American landowners in Texas, the Germans, and I'm not sure how deeply the Japanese are involved."

"How do you know this?" replied *Don* Federico, obviously shocked to hear this information from Juan. He recalled Captain Marshall Bishop telling him, a couple of years ago, of the secret agents and Germans spies who could be creating trouble between Mexico and the United States.

Juan continued, "Carranza has ordered General Emilio Nafarrate from Matamoros, with the help of the Germans, to start trouble along the border by initiating raids into Texas, creating havoc among the citizens this side of the Rio Grande. This will keep the United States Army occupied sending troops to the border and away from the great European war. Creating problems inside of Texas will also force the United States to notice and accept Carranza as the President of Mexico. The Germans want to establish their own haven in Mexico. They see all of the natural resources, gold and silver mines, and now the oil that's so valuable for them to use. *General* Blanco is being demoted. He got his orders yesterday to serve under *General* Obregón in Sonora. Blanco's regiment is being replaced by *General* Pablo Gonzalez. I saw the alarming orders myself and have heard of some of the maneuvers that are going to take place on the Texas side of the border."

"What secret plan and maneuvers?" *Don* Federico asked, distressed over the growing tension among the Mexican-Americans and the whites.

Juan became even more serious. "Going back to the Treaty of Guadalupe Hidalgo, the Mexican land that Santa Anna sold to the United States—Arizona, New Mexico, and the State of Texas—are being questioned by Carranza. But, surprisingly, not California."

"Well, yes, that has always been a sore spot in the Mexican-American controversy, since Santa Anna, in his greed, betrayed his own country for money. It was the beginning of our *'roots of indifference.'* We all know he was a traitor and is now hated by the Mexican people." *Don* Federico chewed on his pipe nervously.

"Well, with the help of the Germans and German warfare, they plan to take back from the United States all the 'stolen land' that Santa Anna so graciously gave away."

"Sounds like somebody's illogical, wild pipe dream," retorted *Don* Federico. "Sounds impossible! Sounds like a big lie! How are they planning to do this?" He scratched his head and took another puff on his pipe. "If Mexico can't handle their problems now, how in God's name will they be able to take care of more land?" He shook his head in total disbelief.

"The Germans are convincing the Mexican government that they will stand behind them on this takeover. They are furnishing hundreds of shiploads of guns, bombs, ammunition, and warfare gasses, hoping to kill every white male over sixteen years old this side of the border."

"For God sakes, man! Kill the white people?" *Don* Federico sounded off, not believing what he was hearing.

"Every one of them over sixteen years of age," repeated Juan somberly. "Serious business!"

"With this takeover, how are the Germans gonna know who's white, who's Mexican-American? Hell! The majority of the people here are mixed with Spanish blood, looking like white people, so that means nobody is going to be spared."

"That's it! Doesn't make any sense! Everyone wants more, more power, more money, wanting control of more land. An evil thought…an evil seed," Juan said dismally.

Getting up from his chair, *Don* Federico took a deep breath and expelled it in alarm. "Someone needs to be informed of this situation." His haggard face was somber and pale as he began to pace the porch. "This can't happen! This is total madness!" His voice was ragged. "I'll need to get in touch with Marshall Bishop and my friend Canalo in Brownsville as soon as possible, to see if they already know of this. This is conspiracy!"

Juan continued. "The Germans have already organized groups inside the Texas border and have had several secret meetings. Two of them have already been conducted in McAllen. I personally met a German by the name of Von Schmidt, who was sick and needed some bromide for his stomach."

"What are you going to do?" The *Don's* voice was strained with anxiety, causing him almost to choke. He stopped his pacing, stood, and stared at Juan astounded, waving his hand. "Since you're still in the military and have to take orders, surely you are not going to take part in this?"

"No! I want no part of this situation!"

"The name Von Schmidt sounds familiar," said *Don* Federico, rubbing his chin, "but the man I met at the Del Calderóne home in Monterrey years ago couldn't be the same person, could he?"

"I had never met him before. He's a very strange man, with a thick accent, but he did mention that he has been staying with high authoritative military people in Mexico for several years, studying the activities and conditions of the country."

"So what are you going to do now?"

"As for me, I have been kicking my situation around for awhile and have decided to leave the military and finish my medical education." Juan's tone of voice became dour. "Frankly, I want no part of this. I am completely shocked and in no way can I see how this is going to end. There will be many deaths. Doctors heal people regardless of color, not kill them."

"What's going to happen to Magdalena? You're not getting married?"

"I'm a confirmed bachelor. I like Magdalena very much, but only as a friend."

"That's a shame," answered *Don* Federico gravely. "I think her family had big plans for you."

"Yes, but back to our original conversation," said Juan guardedly. "I'd kindly ask you not to repeat my name to any high authority here in Texas or mention that I'm in the Mexican military. In the future, I plan to live in Mexico, and I will be in danger of being murdered."

Don Federico, now intensely concerned, answered, "Why of course not! You can rest assured that your name will not be mentioned in any way." He was in total disbelief of what he was hearing. The thought of losing Juan as a doctor in this area left him devastated and disheartened. "I'll get in touch with Bishop in Brownsville as soon as possible and tell him what you have confided to me. They may already know." He turned to Juan and spoke with sincerity. "I'm disappointed, because I'll miss you, and so will Emma who has a special fondness for you. It's going to completely upset Fred when he finds out that you are leaving us. I know that I'm truly grateful to you for saving Roy's life." He continued pacing the wooden floor back and forth remaining silent and brooded for a short time and then sat back down in his chair. He was pondering all that Juan had told him, and it left him heartsick, feeling like he was losing a son.

"Juan, why not study medicine here in the state of Texas? We have excellent medical schools."

Juan hesitated, trying to get his mind around what *Don* Federico was saying.

"Houston has a special medical school, a very fine one. How about Baylor School of Medicine up north? Any of the medical schools here in Texas are great."

Juan's eyes illuminated with surprise. "What are you suggesting?" he questioned.

"Come and make your home here in Mercedes—be part of the family. I'll see that all of your expenses are taken care of. You will never have to worry about a thing. It will please all of us, and all of the Mexican-American community will have open arms for you." *Don* Federico's face lit up. "We need a Mexican doctor in this area. Just think what a blessing it would be for everyone. What do you say?"

For the first time, in the dusk of evening, there was a positive excitement in the air.

It took Juan several minutes to put his thoughts together and for *Don* Federico's suggestions to sink in. His mind spun in a whirlpool of troubled emotions. He felt conflicted, knowing his situation was critical. His life was now coming to a fork in the road—decisions had to be made. No doubt, the eloquent *Don* understood the necessity of medicine among the Mexican-American people, especially in this isolated area where no doctors existed.

He also understood that the *Don* was no fool and probably knew more than he was expressing, understanding the love he had for Victoria, and the feeling Victoria had for him. Love was stronger than any other force. Juan's instincts told him that *Don* Federico had read their gestures—their body language had betrayed them. Their electricity was so strong that even an illiterate person could understand and feel it, and yet it had become a self-inflicting torture for him each time they had an encounter.

He was willing to do anything for the *Don*. And this was his chance to be close to Victoria, knowing that little Luis was actually his child—his son. He curbed his impatience, only for the opportunity to see Victoria and his boy. And no, he was not going to marry Magdalena, at least not now. She was only a front. She was only a puppet, a convenient replacement. And yet, what the *Don* had said was right, he was only trying to help him to better himself. Perhaps the *Don* had a vision of the future with them all together. Living here in Mercedes! But what about Ricardo, where did he fit into the picture?

Juan amiably replied, "I'll give you my answer next week."

CHAPTER 29

Within the next several weeks, telegrams flooded the law enforcement offices, bombarding the major border towns of Brownsville, Harlingen, and McAllen, and as far north as Rio Grande City and El Paso, with the threatening news of an invasion. All law enforcement offices in small towns, as well as the Texas Rangers, became aware of possible raids. All of the United States senators and state representatives of the bordering states and the governor of Texas had been informed. U.S. Marshal Bishop responded with messages to thank *Don* Federico for his concern. Bishop informed him that officials on the Texas side were aware of mysterious activities, and that all secret agents were on the lookout for any possible suspects on both sides of the Rio Grande. Bishop also notified *Don* Federico that the information about the Germans was correct, and many of them were already living among the Mexican-American citizens on the Texas side. *Don* Federico had candidly asked Captain Marshall Bishop in his last message: "Any word on Hanson? Does anyone know where he is?" Bishop had replied back that his two United States Deputy Marshals were having trouble locating him in Mexico and were unsure where he was.

Meanwhile, Juan had decided to abandon his military career in Mexico. He took *Don* Federico's safe suggestion and seized the opportunity to gain a wonderful career at the *Don's* expense. This was his opening to learn new medical research that was needed in Mexico, where so many deadly diseases ran rampant. He began taking classes at a small university in Houston and would come to the Rio Grande Valley on different occasions as a guest of Emma or *Don* Federico.

This action made Ricardo furious. He realized that *Don* Federico was playing favoritism by paying Juan's expenses, and it was also beginning to confirm his suspicions about Juan and Victoria. Both he and his mother had noticed how Victoria acted when she was in Juan's presence, and they had picked up on how spontaneously jovial and witty she would be, trying to impress the young doctor. Magdalena was hurt and felt out of place, as Juan never mentioned marriage. This left both families wondering just what Juan's real intentions were.

According to Victoria, *Doña* Adela's magic had worked, and her prediction was being fulfilled. The year 1914 had seen World War I break out in Europe; Henry Ford was offering his workers in Detroit five dollars a day for labor; the Panama Canal finally opened to shipping traffic, leaving over 30,000 casualties; Mahatma Gandhi returned home to India after living in South Africa and began a non-violent campaign against the hated British. In eleven states, it saw the start of the women's rights movement, and women had finally won full voting rights, prompting Congress to declare the second Sunday in May as "Mother's Day."

Well into 1915, most of the talk among the communities and newspapers was about the growing intensity of the war in Europe. The British navy had attacked a German U-boat hauling supplies to Russia on the Black Sea. The Mexican war along the border had escalated. Suspicions of spies were everywhere, as German U-boats were seen along the Gulf of Mexico on the Texas side. The average person expected a full invasion.

Perhaps 1915 was the climactic year in the battle against the injustice that had been showing its ugly face to the Mexican-American citizens living along the Rio Grande. It was the beginning of a reign of terror and turbulent conditions for every person living on both sides of the river.

In the middle of January, an arrest was made in McAllen, Texas, of one Basilio Ramos, who was carrying suspicious classified documents. Charges were made by the Department of Justice against Ramos for being a conspirator. *Don* Federico's friend, Marshall Bishop, with his special agent, took Ramos to Brownsville Federal Jail to await his trial. Ramos did not have money to make bail. A telegram was sent to Fort Sam Houston in San Antonio to Major General Frederick Funston, who had been keeping a watchful eye on the conditions at the border. Ramos's documents indicated organized meetings among the Mexican-American people pertaining to a Mexican uprising. Panic ensued, especially among the Mexican-American people, the majority of whom were innocent of any wrongdoing. The relatives and friends of Ramos spread the news of his arrest like wildfire among the Mexican-American families throughout the border.

"The Plan of San Diego," as it was called, since the document originated in San Diego, Texas, created confusion on the border, for nothing was revealed to the public regarding its contents and gruesome details. *Don* Federico, knowing of the secret plan, kept his eye on the newspaper to find out more of what was taking place, but little information was given out. Within two weeks, the *Don* received a telegram from Captain Marshall Bishop, telling him that other meetings were interrupted; one especially in Laredo, Texas, but Bishop also suggested that the judges were looking at the documents as a joke, saying that it was only a visionary scheme among lunatics. They discarded them as insignificant. Bishop wrote that he wanted to have a word with *Don* Federico, and asked if he would be willing to have dinner with him and Judge Barnes in Brownsville. The *Don's* reply was "yes." He would let him know of his arrival ahead of time, since he would be traveling by train.

The exiled ex-president of Mexico, Huerta, had stayed in Spain and England and wished to return to Mexico with a plan to overthrow his enemies and set up a pro-German government. Huerta was deeply involved with the spy, Franz von Schmidt, who had been a close friend of *El General* Del Calderóne. Huerta wanted the Kaiser to finance his return to Mexico to become president. Unknown to anyone, Del Calderóne had also been in hiding, staying in Matamoros. He wanted to take control of his military career, but he needed the backup of strong allies. Del Calderóne had been secretly corresponding with Huerta through telegrams, informing him through assumed names, of the appropriate time to sail back home. Together they could form a conspiracy against Carranza and Villa and regain their power.

In another clandestine scheme, Carranza ordered *General* Nafarrate to advance his career by organizing raids into the Texas side of the border, keeping the military of the *Americanos* occupied, and eventually acknowledging Carranza for the presidency. Nafarrate, who was ambitious by nature, went along, since his dream was to make Matamoros the capitol of Tamaulipas, of which he would be governor. The plot had thickened, becoming a triangle, an intriguing conspiracy, with many actors taking part in the "devil's schemes." With Villa and Zapata fighting against Carranza and Obregón, Huerta thought he could step in and take control of the Mexican presidency.

The following week, *Don* Federico and Fred took the train to Brownsville. The meeting with Captain Marshall Bishop and several federal court judges took place in a lavish Elizabeth Street restaurant. A heavy, balding, white-haired federal judge by the name of Thomas Barnes, wearing thick bifocals, had joined them and did most of the talking. His idea was to name the *Don* as an "Ambassador of Goodwill." His job would be to calm and appease the turbulent situation between Mexico and the United States. Judge Barnes already had the approval of the governor of Texas. The Judge mentioned that the *Don* had all of the qualifications they needed: a man of integrity who was well educated and bilingual. *Don* Federico would have an office in Mercedes and Brownville, and would do some long-distance traveling to Mexico, when the occasion arose, with all expenses paid. The *Don* had to document and record his work and could have his own secretary if it were necessary. It took some time before *Don* Federico was able to concentrate on the idea. He finally replied, "I am not looking for a job, but if it will help relations with both our countries, I'll give it serious thought and consideration. I'll give you my answer as soon as possible."

While in Brownsville, he decided to visit his lawyer friend, Tomas Canalo, whose family name went way back to the first arrival of affluent Spanish blood. Canalo was a refined Texas-Mexican *vaquero*, with the charm of a sociable South Texas intellect. He called himself a refined *Tejano* and a rebel. He had studied law in Dallas and was well liked by the local citizenry, especially the Mexican-Americans who were discriminated against most all the time. He was disliked by the local white judges, who ruled and controlled the city, and he was often in and out of courts trying to defend Mexican landowner rights. Canalo was of medium size, stout in stature, and perhaps around the same age as the *Don*, in his mid-fifties, with a light complexion and salt and pepper hair. He always wore stylish clothes, with a Stetson hat and alligator boots. He could out-talk anyone on any subject regardless of place and time, and he loved to argue, always having the last word. When he spoke, it was always with an accent, mixed with both Spanish and English phrases, and he waved his hands and made facial expressions to convey his thoughts.

"*Hola! Don* Federico, what a surprise! How are you, *mí amigo?*" He said, extending his hand. "I haven't seen you since your daughter's birthday party!" He moved his hand to *Don*

Federico's shoulder. "Sorry to hear about your wife—she was a lovely person." Then, eyeing Fred up and down, he asked, "Who is this with you, your oldest *hijo*? I remember seeing him when he was a young boy. He has really gotten big!"

"Yes, you remember my son, Fred," said the *Don*. Canalo and Fred shook hands.

"You're going to be a tall man," Canalo said. "Going to be an attorney, I'll bet!"

"Well, we sure can use good lawyers. We need smart Mexican men to handle the Mexican-American relations across the border and with *los gringos* situation. *Es una chinga*, how they mistreat the Mexican people here."

Fred giggled, trying to control his genuine laughter. His face flushed, but he managed to respond with confidence. "I'm going to study medicine and be a doctor."

"Ah! *Un doctor! Muy bien*, a great profession!" Canalo waved his hand, inviting the two visitors into his small cramped office. Taking a seat at his desk piled high with papers, Canalo leaned back in his black leather chair and turned to address *Don* Federico.

"What brings you to Brownsville?"

"I'm here on business with U.S. Marshal Bishop and Judge Barnes," replied the *Don*.

Canalo's demeanor changed and he became more professional. "Talked with Judge Barnes, did you? Does it have to do with the Ramos case? There are eight poor Mexicans locked up in the federal jail here, awaiting a federal grand jury coming up in the near future. Judge Barnes *es un Viejo* that I do not trust—he is a confirmed Mexican-hater. He doesn't like me, because I stand up for the poor Mexicans."

"No! Not the Ramos case. I'm here for other reasons. Captain Bishop and Judge Barnes offered me a job to help out with the Mexican-American relations on both sides of the river. Another issue is the Texas Ranger, Hanson. The other reason is, questioning the disturbing rumors about Mexico invading Texas with the help of the Germans."

"The Mexicans and Germans invading Texas?" inquired Canalo, obviously shocked. "Well! They can have it, if they can put up with all the problems the Mexican-American people have here with the *gringos!*" He laughed, and then stopped for a moment considering the situation. "Now that I think of it, there has been talk of seeing U-boats out in the Gulf. I don't think anybody is paying much attention. I do not see what the problem is with the Germans, but they are crawling all over in Mexico. And what did you say about a job offer?"

"They want me to be an ambassador to Mexico to help our strained relations," replied *Don* Federico.

"Excellent!" responded Canalo. "And how did you meet Marshall Bishop?" he questioned, becoming a little envious because he had not been offered the position. "He's a Northerner and is making his authority known quite strongly with the other authorities in the federal courts."

Don Federico summarized the charges he had filed with the state legislators in Austin naming Ranger Hanson in the death of his father, and explaining the hiring of the Pinkerton detective a couple of years prior. He continued, "Several months later, Captain Bishop showed up at my door asking me questions."

ROOTS OF INDIFFERENCE

Canalo listened intently. "Did they find the body of the Pinkerton man? Anybody witness his death?"

"No!" *Don* Federico said, shaking his head.

"I'll tell you, my friend, nothing is going to be done. Without a body, nobody can prove anything—it's all speculation." Canalo frowned as he straightened in his chair and folded his arms on his desk, looking serious. "The Pinkerton Agency is the one who needs to file charges and force the issue and begin pressing hard for an investigation against Hanson if they have any evidence. But without evidence, nothing is going to get done. The Pinkerton Agency knows that."

"The Pinkerton Agency has all of the information they need. They also have sworn statements of what took place. Even Howard Ale confessed that Hanson killed my father. What about José Esquibel's death? What about my father's death? Can nothing be done?"

"I'm afraid not, *mí amigo!* Not unless Hanson readily admits in writing that he did all the killing, but you know he's not going to. And nobody respects the testimony of any Mexican. They believe we all think alike, and that we are bound together against the white people. What we are dealing with is that most of the Mexican people are illiterate. We are dealing with a superstitious culture, and traditions, and a race of people who do not want to change to better themselves, and the white men know that, too. At the risk of repeating myself, nobody is going to go against the word of a law enforcement officer. Remember that!"

"Hanson is a murderer and a thief, and the Mexican-American people have no rights in this state," the *Don* answered, disheartened at the injustice to his father and the other victims.

"Very little to no laws represent them," Canalo replied. "We have few Mexican attorneys in the Valley. We also have Mexican-*Tejanos,* here in Brownsville, stirring the waves, by the name of Aniceto Pizaña, and two more by the name of Augustin Garza and Luis *De la* Rosa, trying to fight the injustices perpetrated against the Mexican-American people. They distribute copies of their party's platform, the Army of the Liberation Party, but the authorities, especially the Texas Rangers, are watching them like a hawk. The Mexican-American citizen gets blamed for anything that happens. I have several cases of property unfairly taken by white men, and several cases of Mexican-American families being killed. The Liberation Party has asked me to join, but I have so much to do and will stick to dealing with legalities."

"Perhaps I should have run for office," the *Don* said with a sigh. "But maybe I can make a difference with the Ambassadorship, as U.S. Marshal Bishop and Judge Barnes have suggested."

"Ah! Good idea, good for our *raza,*" praised Canalo. "We need Mexican-American representatives in Texas state politics. You'd be an excellent person to represent them. Remember, by taking on the position the judge promised you, it could be your chance. You could make a difference. I've been fighting for years to become a judge, but I've been unsuccessful. The *gringos* have too much control over us, because of our '*roots of Indifference.*' I've tried to win cases for the Mexicans. I win a few but most of the time, I lose. You have to remember that the people on the jury are mostly white. *Es una chinga!* It's always a losing battle, but I'm not backing off. This is our land, too, and I'm fighting for our traditions and our dignity. I'm learning and keeping up with the new laws all the time."

"Good for you! We can't have our wonderful traditions and culture taken away, and we can't give up on our citizens' rights," repeated the *Don*. "But, we do need to fight for justice through negotiations and through education, not by waging war."

"So tell me, what is Bishop going to do with Hanson?" asked Canalo, with some apprehension. "I heard that Hobbs was killed in Mexico. How true that is, I do not know for sure, but if Hobbs is dead, he cannot testify against Hanson. Nobody can do anything with Hanson until he is caught. And even if they find him, they cannot prove anything without a body. He can deny everything. All they have on Hanson is leaving his official post as a Texas Ranger. Rumors are that he's become a renegade, running contraband liquor and guns across the border, in cahoots with other Rangers. I hear all of his possessions were confiscated by the Mexican government—a large estate was taken. He deserved what he got. He was a real *bastardo* to the Mexican people."

"I'll let Bishop handled that situation. He's receiving good wages in his investigations against the murderer," *Don* Federico answered bitterly. "I need to take a hard look at the job they offered me. If I accept the office, I'll give it my best."

"Hell, yes! Let Bishop do his job! I think he's hesitating to go get Hanson across the border because it could become a problem for him, since President Wilson has forbidden traveling into Mexico. However, he's a U.S. Marshal and has the jurisdiction. What the hell is he waiting for? He could take a couple of his tough Rangers with him. He's being paid regardless."

"You can believe he'll take his sweet time, knowing he'll be paid whether he captures Hanson or not." Seeing Canalo getting restless and rising from his chair, *Don* Federico did the same.

"Well, good luck!" Canalo laughed and reached for his Stetson that was hanging on a hat rack. "I've been trying to do all I can, but haven't gotten anywhere except getting a bad name among the *gringos* in court. The idea of running for office is very appealing. I'm going to concentrate on that myself for the 49 Judicial District of Texas." He put his hat on and looked out his window, seeing that it had begun to rain. He turned around and said, "*Don* Federico, I have some documents I have to run down to the court house. If you like, be my guest at my ranch for dinner tonight. Come and see my livestock. I have a new breed of cattle. Come and meet my wife and daughter. We'll be more than happy to have you as our guests this evening."

"Not on this trip, but thank you, anyway," acknowledged the *Don*. "I'm going to take Fred across the border over to Matamoros, so he can get a good education regarding the conditions over there, and we'll probably have supper in one of the restaurants. We will be taking the train back later on this evening. I have several things to concentrate on. Good luck running for office. You know that I'll be supporting you. Let me know if you need any money for your campaign."

ROOTS OF INDIFFERENCE

"The same here, *compadre*. And good luck on your newly appointed job! Better accept it! Sounds terrific! Let me know if there is any way I can help you, and keep me posted on what Bishop is doing with his investigation of Hanson."

"I will let you know my decision. Come and see me in Mercedes and be my guest," said the *Don*, as they parted ways.

⌘ ⌘ ⌘

The color of the sky was solid pewter-gray and it had started to rain harder and steady in the middle of the afternoon. *Don* Federico and Fred got into a buggy he had rented earlier and started toward the border. The horses trotted toward the river, leaving behind the trolley and the cobblestone streets, and headed down the muddy road. The odor of the damp earth and the smell of the ocean and the rushing waters of the Rio Grande hit them simultaneously, a powerful extrasensory experience. There was traffic coming and going from both sides of the river, a few Model-T cars, and many hand-driven mule wagons on the soggy road.

As they got closer to the wooden bridge, they could not help spotting hundreds of scraggly shacks built from waste materials such as cardboard boxes, and put together with tarps and blankets—slum encampments. Rows and rows of uneven, crowded shanties nestled together, very close to the river and interspersed among the ragged mesquite and shrubs on the waterfront. Strings of washed clothes were suspended along ropes tied from one tree to the other. Black iron pots hung over hot, sizzling coals, and smoke circled from cooking fires, mingling with the fog that entwined and engulfed the area.

Don Federico and Fred were distraught at the horrible, intolerable conditions of human suffering before their eyes! It was the result of an enormous exodus of Mexican people escaping and settling into a safer environment on the American side of the river. Women stood with shawls covering their heads, holding hungry, crying children with hollow eyes, as they stared at them from a distance. Several women on their knees were on the riverbank, pounding, scrubbing and washing clothes over crude rocks. In spite of the coming rain, children played in the murky, raging waters of the Rio Grande.

They reached the long, narrow, wooden bridge separating both countries and crossed over into the rich, cultured town of Matamoros, Mexico. The few Model-T cars going into the town were noisy, with loud horns and screeching brakes. Uniformed soldiers with rifles stood watching them, the majority in their early teens, young boys, still wet behind the ears. The other soldiers wandered around with their horses, munitions, and guns; others stood talking with each other and getting wet. Some were squatting on their haunches, smoking cigarettes under a homemade wooden shed. There was the thundering clatter of horses, as caissons rolled down the main thoroughfare.

The streets were crowded with inquisitive visitors, peddlers with pushcarts selling fruits and vegetables, and beggars in rags, with dirty, crying children hanging onto their mothers. The sidewalks and the narrow, uneven cobblestone streets were glutted with foul-smelling garbage, while the countless potholes filled with rainwater.

Immediately, an older soldier approached the buggy and asked them where they were heading. *Don* Federico replied that they were going to a good restaurant if there was one nearby. The soldier pointed up the hill at the enormous *Catedral Del Nuestra Señora del Refugio* that stood as the tallest building around. "For the best one, go up the hill and turn to your right, on the corner of *Calle Hidalgo Y Morelos*, next to the plaza. You cannot miss it. It's a large, white, brick building on the corner, called *Garcia's*. Most of the officers eat there with their families."

"*Gracias, Señor*," replied *Don* Federico, politely tipping his hat.

The restaurant was indeed a delight. *Mariachis* entertained them on the spacious patios, which were decorated with open flames and borders of palms trees and other tropical plants and flowers. The restaurant was circular, and in the middle stood a gigantic seven-layer water fountain. Its water trickled softly, flowing down to the white water lilies blooming, and with goldfish enjoying the oncoming rain. Gardenias and red and yellow hibiscus bloomed around the side of the fountain. The Juelsons dined on chicken-rice soup as their first entree, then a stuffed crab appetizer, and guacamole with a hot salsa, and a small green salad—all this while their meal of fresh fish and shrimp was being prepared.

Fred, at the age of fifteen, could easily appreciate the desperate conditions they had just witnessed in the streets of Matamoros, leaving an empathetic imprint on his young mind. "I don't understand why people are living like this. The children! I feel guilty eating all of this wonderful food, Father!" He felt overcome with guilt, eating at this expensive place, while just across the street, there were people starving. He was already mimicking his father's actions in using his hands to talk. He was going through puberty and his voice was changing; fuzzy hair was growing on his cheeks and chin.

"I'm glad you were able to come with me, son," acknowledged *Don* Federico. "I wanted you to see firsthand the atrocities that Mexicans are experiencing. There is a revolution going on here in Mexico. Revolution means that the poor people want a change, for the betterment of mankind—change in government politics, and be fair and impartial justice for all." He went on explaining. "Think of all of the hungry people in this world who go without eating day after day. Most of those people are uneducated and have no skills, except to work as a laborer. I think being a laborer is fine, we need them, but the people need to understand the importance of an education. It was the most important subject for my students and the significant reason for studying and learning. There is a change coming for the Mexican-American—especially the men—in Texas. The Mexican-American individual without an education remains simple-minded and ignorant, fighting with themselves and against the world with their '*roots of indifference*.'"

"Father, I understand what you are saying, but I still do not understand how people get into those situations. Why do they have to live close to the river and suffer so, especially the children?"

"The word is called poverty! And most of them were born in poverty, and still do not know any better." The *Don* looked sharply at Fred, then took a sip of his drink and continued. "They have no place to go, they are poor and unschooled. Some have relatives across the border in Texas, but none have developed a skill through education. However, we are all a melting pot of Mexican-Americans in Texas and the people from Mexico. And it will take a long time before you'll be able to understand the history. You are lucky. You have never known hunger, and I hope you never will." A poignant and thoughtful silence passed. *Don* Federico touched his son's hand lovingly, knowing that Fred's future would be completely different.

Fred glanced at his father, who looked happy and as distinguished as a diplomat in his dark gray, three-piece suit. For the first time in years, his dad was starting to enjoy his life and seem happy. After the death of his mother, he had deprived himself of living. Perhaps now, he would fulfill his passion in political justice and justify his ambition to help the Mexican-American people in the Rio Grande Valley. Fred kept asking questions, and the *Don* kept answering, imparting to him a veritable library of history.

Across the room were several inebriated soldiers, distracting those that dined, disputing and making a loud disturbance over a bet among themselves. The *Don* overheard one of the men talking about *General* Nafarrate, just as the *mariachis* began playing Mexican ballads telling the story of recent events: *No Dacia, Pancho Villa,* followed by *La Persecución de Villa.* There were loud shouts of applause and bravos of approval, since the majority of soldiers were *Carranzistas* fighting against the *Villistas. Don* Federico stopped eating and listened motionless, concentrating on the other table's conversation. He wiped his mouth, stood up, and walked toward the soldiers. Fred watched his father calmly approach the nearby table.

"Is *General* Nafarrate staying here in Matamoros?" the *Don* asked.

Caught off guard and startled, one soldier replied, "*Ah, sí!*"

"Why do you ask?" questioned another. Their conversation came to a complete halt, as they all looked up at the *Don.*

"What do you want with the *General?*" questioned a soldier who been drinking most of the afternoon, his speech slurred. "He'll be here any minute now." They all started laughing.

Don Federico stood bemused, observing the soldiers folded over in their seats, laughing so hysterically that it attracted the attention of other diners in the restaurant. The waiters carrying large trays of food slowed down to stare in their direction. The *Don* felt like a fool for not understanding their joke.

From behind him, he heard Fred call out, "Papá!"

The *Don* turned and was awestruck. *General* Nafarrate stood directly behind him in his stiff, khaki uniform displaying honored medals across his chest, noticeably annoyed. *Don* Federico's manners were instinctive as he stuck out his hand. "*General* Nafarrate, you probably do not remember me, but I'm the one you saved at the gold mines on the road outside the mountains of Monterrey. Do you remember the incident? It's been several years ago. I want to thank you again for your service. To this day, I have never repaid you for saving my life."

"Ah!" the *General* exclaimed. "You were the one with those dirty, foul-mouthed *gringo* fools up in the cold mountains, naked. How could I forget? You are the son-in-law of the late José Hinojosa." The handsome, polished *General* finished his sentence as the roar of the disorderly soldiers' laughter became obnoxious. "Quiet!" he addressed them indignantly. "Can't you see that this is a gentleman of esteemed honor in our presence?"

"What a good memory, *General*, and if you permit me, I would like to buy you your dinner tonight. My son and I are at this table." He pointed to where Fred was sitting. "We are still eating. I would very much like to talk with you about Carranza." He politely ushered Nafarrate to their table, since the *General* showed no resistance to his invitation. The soldiers behind them were still laughing in their drunken stupor.

"You have an interest in Carranza?" inquired the ambitious young *General*, wondering what was on *Don* Federico's mind. "What is it that you want to know? He's fighting the government of the United States for his right to become President of Mexico." He sat down, putting his cap on his lap, and tried to become more comfortable. *General* Nafarrate was a bachelor in his late thirties, and although years younger than the *Don*, was already showing signs of aging. His black hair was parted on one side and slicked down, and he sported a waxed mustache that stuck out on both sides. Nafarrate, with his fair complexion, was notably a mixture of Spanish and French blood. His dark eyes never rested, darting around from side to side, as if he were on constant guard and had been trained to be suspicious of everyone.

"Yes," answered the *Don*. "That's what I want to talk to you about." He stopped his conversation and signaled for a waiter to come to their table. "What kind of wine would you prefer?"

"Wine," the *General* replied in amazement. "Well, it's been a while since I've had any good wine. We haven't been able to afford it. Whatever you order will be satisfactory." The *General* smiled, becoming more at ease with being the honored guest of *Don* Federico.

Three waiters, wearing white shirts and black trousers with white cloths over their arms, displayed the choice selections, which included four kinds of Spanish, Italian, and French wine. Other waiters brought in three glasses to serve the fine liquor. It seemed that the restaurant staff was paying full attention, observing and watching as if dignitaries were being entertained.

The evening went smoothly and was very enjoyable. The *mariachis'* music was delightful, as they introduced the newest songs brought in by the *Villistas: Jesusita en Chihuahua* and *La Cucaracha*, which were being sung all along the border. The *General* and *Don* Federico conversed about the problems of Mexico and the chaos along the border. *Don* Federico had met Carranza in San Antonio with Juan, but never did get acquainted with him. He wanted to meet with Carranza and talk with him and wanted to know if a meeting could be arranged for the three to get together, in order to become more acquainted with *General* Nafarrate and his ideas as well. He thought that taking the initiative through diplomatic channels would be more rewarding. The *Don* was becoming more assured, convincing himself that he would start his new position.

He was on his way to becoming the "Texas Ambassador of Goodwill."

CHAPTER 30

Don Federico soon confirmed his appointed position with Judge Barnes, Captain Marshall Bishop, and the governor of Texas. He began his job by hiring a secretary, a man named James Johnson, a Northerner from Illinois. Johnson was an unmarried gent who had bought a small ranch south of Harlingen after seeing the Valley's advertising promotions. He was twenty-seven years old, tall, with brown hair and hazel eyes, quite distinguished looking, and with impeccable manners. He had longed to live in Mexico; however, with the conflicting problems there, the borderland was as close as he could get. He was fluent in Spanish and English and could write longhand and shorthand in both languages. While working with *Don* Federico, he would live in Mercedes during the weekdays and return to his ranch on weekends.

No sooner had James Johnson moved into his quarters at the *Don's* place, with his manual typewriter and pads of paper, than the gossip began. Tongues wagged in the white community. *Don* Federico's name was in all the newspapers confirming his appointed job and creating envy among the white merchants, who were afraid he would become superior to them. Within the Catholic prayer groups, those with unmarried daughters were gossiping endlessly and speculating about the new gentleman in town.

"Have you seen the handsome young man living at the Juelson's home?" inquired Mrs. McCray, more curious than most.

"*Don* Federico Juelson has just been appointed Ambassador of Goodwill between the two countries," answered Emma proudly, who was back to her feathered hats, gloves and small shoes. She had lost almost twenty pounds by following Juan's advice and was feeling better.

It was at Felicia's suggestion that a fiesta was given at the Juelson's home celebrating the coming of James Johnson and the appointment of *Don* Federico to the ambassadorship. A band of Mexican musicians from across the border was hired to play outdoors since the weather had become more pleasant. *Don* Federico provided the fresh steaks from Spanish Acres. Each family attending brought a dish of their favorite specialty and also their unmarried daughters to peruse the handsome new arrival.

Ricardo and his mother protested and were uncooperative in helping with the festivities. Only Magdalena agreed and helped Victoria and the servants. With Emma's enthusiasm and encouragement, and Felicia's excitement, they brought white linens, extra silverware, plates, and glasses. Long tables were set outside on the patio in back of the house. Large fires and torches were lit around the premises to keep the mosquitoes away. Close to a hundred prominent people attended, and close to twenty families had single daughters, who gushed and giggled and batted their eyes at James. Even the widow McCray had joined them and kept hanging annoyingly close to *Don* Federico's side. Everyone had a wonderful time and was in total anticipation of wanting to know what James had thought of the young women and which one he might pick.

"Well, James! What do you think of our little fiesta?" *Don* Federico smiled at the young man, pleased with his choice of secretary. Together they wandered outdoors and rested on his circular porch.

"Splendid!" James replied. "I have never met such wonderful people, and their daughters are all lovely. Everyone is so friendly and kind. Oh, and I love my new traveling attaché case. Thank you very much. I can sure use it now."

But he was not interested in their daughters. As handsome as James was, he remained single and confined himself to his specialty—secretarial work. He was shrouded by a mysterious secret that was never to be mentioned. It dictated that he remain a loner who needed his privacy, for James was a homosexual, which was taboo. But, as a member of the household, James quickly became known by his nickname, *"El Guapo,"* meaning "the handsome one."

In early March, the *Villistas* captured Reynosa and quickly following, *General* José Rodriguez, one of *Villistas* commanders, attacked Matamoros, which was defended by *General* Nafarrate, who triumphantly prevailed, killing over 700 *Villistas* soldiers and saving the town. The stench of dead bodies was so bad that they had to be soaked in fuel oil and burned, with the remaining ashes thrown into the Gulf of Mexico.

Later that same month, *Don* Federico and *El Guapo* James were summoned to attend a dinner held by Obregón from the *Carranzistas,* to try to reach an agreement between the two fighting groups. From the *Villistas, General* José Rodriguez was in attendance. It took place at the new Pharr Hotel in Pharr, Texas, but the fiesta to celebrate a compromise became a tense meeting, where each minute was carefully scrutinized. The *Don* helped translate from the slanted and indignant words being used, trying to keep the language civil.

The building was filled with *Villistas* and *Carranzistas* fighters, each wearing ammo belts across their chests and pistols inside their jackets. The arsenal of ammunition hanging from their bodies could have blown the building to kingdom come. From outside, the opposing forces were being carefully watched. Several spies, sheriffs, and federal government men could be seen hanging around the building. Afterwards, the telegraph lines were humming fast and furious, as reports were sent to Brownsville.

This was James's first assignment, and his eagerness and sense of humor had turned to nervousness. He commented later as they drove back to Mercedes, "Man! I'm glad that's over! I felt like the whole place was going to blow up at any minute!"

Don Federico laughed. "And that's living here in Texas! Just wait 'til we travel into Mexico. Then, we really have to watch out for ourselves. We'll have to carry our *pistolas*."

A skirmish between the *Carranzistas* and Villa's men took place at the small town of Las Rucias, west of Brownsville. Several wounded *Villistas* soldiers crossed the border. Many of the alarmed American citizens at Fort Brown cared for the sick men, who were later turned over to the *Villistas* at Laredo. One of the dead was *General* Navarro, one of Pancho Villa's favorite commanders and a faithful friend.

April 1915 brought more rumors of conspiracy. Huerta had returned from Europe and landed in New York City, traveled to Dallas, and disappeared. He ended up secretly staying in Matamoros and had been seen with several Germans, possibly making plans. He had also been sighted with *General* Nafarrate and another mysterious man known for his military tactics. It was also in April that Pancho Villa was defeated in two decisive battles, leaving him a desperate marauder in the Chihuahua Sierra Mountains.

As for Ricardo, he had been spending most of his time in Brownsville seeing about the shipments of crude oil being delivered to the large ships headed for Houston. Everyone agreed he seemed to be acting strange when he returned to Mercedes.

A series of raids began to occur along the Rio Grande River, with ranchers claiming that horses, cattle, and goats were being stolen. They were suggesting that something terrible was pending and became very frightened. Strange happenings were underway as mysterious riders rode through the *brasada* at night. There were no explanations as to what their activities were. The natives locked their doors, and at dusk, they would not turn their lanterns on, or light their fires. Those who had money, silver, and gold coins began burying it in trunks and tin cans in certain areas around their property, with favorite places being the fireplace or under a loose board in the floor.

People were afraid and built houses with high, brick and cement fences for protection. Some incorporated barbed wire or broken pieces of glass bottles atop their fences, as a defensive device.

In early May, off the coast of Ireland, the passenger liner *Lusitania* was torpedoed by the Germans. Many prominent Americans were killed, and still President Wilson would not commit the country to war. The incident created increasing nervousness among the people living along the coastline.

The local newspapers criticized the federal courts in Brownsville by relating that the scary and menacing Basilio Ramos had been released from jail after his bond was reduced to only a hundred dollars. Judge Barnes stated he should have been tried for lunacy, claiming the so-called "classified documents," was a made-up story, and the whole incident had no validity. The Mexican-American people, who had been waiting patiently for the trial, were elated to hear of Ramos's release. Ramos immediately crossed into Matamoros, where the *Carranzistas* welcomed him, honoring him with a big banquet; all were laughing and talking about how he had outsmarted the dim-witted *gringos*.

During the spring and summer months, the raiding became so common that Texas Governor Ferguson desperately pleaded and demanded that the United States Army head for the border. The army did not feel that it was a priority, for no man's life had been taken. The activities were considered "local rustling" and problematic to Texas only. But in early July, outside the town of Sebastian, a young American was killed, supposedly by a band of marauders. The raids kept coming, with a band of well-armed intruders killing two Americans near a ranch in Lyford, Texas, followed by the robbing of stores and post offices, the burning of bridges, and more killings of Americans in a shootout. The citizens of South Texas became ever more panic-stricken.

White vigilante groups sprang up, and rumors were spreading about a "secret society" called the Ku Klux Klan, which promoted the evil ideology of White Supremacy and had worked its way into the lives of many Rio Grande Valley merchants. Many newcomers arriving from Mississippi, Louisiana, Georgia, and Alabama firmly believed that the only way the Negroes and Mexicans could be restrained was by fear, through flogging, lynching, or outright shooting without any explanation.

⌘ ⌘ ⌘

Victoria traveled twice a week from Mercedes to Spanish Acres to return the empty glass milk bottles that Manuel delivered to the house in Mercedes. Little Luis was left with his wet nurses and the four servants of the house, giving Victoria the freedom that she craved. When she wasn't spending time with Mamá Maria, who felt poorly most of the time from old age and arthritis, she would take Soledad with her in her carriage and spend the majority of her time with *Doña* Adela, learning the uses of herbs. Victoria was becoming a master in reading the fortune-telling cards, and she also learned special spells, potions, and the use of liniments.

While at *Doña* Adela's place, Soledad occupied herself by sewing, cooking, crocheting or knitting, and helped the old *bruja* with her household duties. One hot afternoon Soledad went outside to keep from being smothered by the humid heat, while the other two women were engrossed in lessons and conversation. She carried a small woven basket among the tall grasses and bushes where *Doña* Adela had some of her greens planted and began picking the tender leaves of the abundant spearmint bush for a cup of tea. She frowned, wondering why *la bruja's* dogs were making such a clamor.

As she picked the therapeutic herbs, she thought she saw something moving in the undergrowth. She straightened up, startled to see two men on horseback wandering among the *brasada's* bushes and mesquite trees. They did not see her, as she wrapped her shawl around her head, and concealed her presence behind a thick, overhanging mesquite tree. She observed them for a short time between the limbs and leaves of the trees, as the dogs' barks became more frantic.

A gray horse came closer and instantly she recognized the rider's face, even though it was covered with a salt-and-pepper beard—the face that had given her nightmares for so many years—the man who had so brutally raped her. It was Hanson! Numb with horror, she dropped her basket. She covered her mouth and swallowed the lump in her throat for fear she would begin to scream hysterically. The other man she did not recognize, but eventually the two disappeared into the cactus and undergrowth. Her heart fluttered and pounded uncontrollably. Her stomach was in knots, and her feet felt paralyzed. Almost in slow motion, she eased herself down on the ground and into a fetal position, her hands covering her face.

Doña Adela, slow in her actions, appeared at the door of her hut. She peeked out the screen door and finally ventured out of her *jacale*, followed by Victoria. *La bruja* began banging the porch floor with her cane to stop the dogs from further barking. Victoria looked around in all directions, then stepped down from the wooden porch and walked toward the herb garden, calling out for Soledad.

⌘　⌘　⌘

Back at Mercedes, and late in the evening, Victoria waited anxiously for her father to return from his trip to advise him of the news that Hanson was on the loose, in the area of Spanish Acres. It made sense in explaining the several mysterious happenings in the *brasada*. For one, several cattle had been missing, then, one of the worker's dogs had been found dead with several bullets lodged in the head and stomach of the animal. Another found a dead goat hanging on *Don* Federico's gate. Only the insides had been removed, and it had been skinned, letting the blood drain down along the side of a tall cactus. Was this an omen? What did it mean? There were several complaints from the workers at the oil field of sabotage to the wells—dynamite was missing, tools were gone. Strange riders, strange happenings were occurring all over the area.

A family of three had crossed the border from Mexico on a ferry at the Santa Maria Crossing with their wagon full of supplies. Later that evening the bodies of a man and a woman were found, riddled with shots in their backs. Their ten-year-old son had run and hidden among the undergrowth and later told the story of how the Texas Rangers bullied his parents and decided to help themselves to their goods, killing them both when they resisted. This incident was ignored and never reported. This enraged many of the relatives and put fear in families.

By the end of July, two Mexicans living south of Harlingen were shot in the back by the Texas Rangers without any explanation, only because they looked suspicious. Then, on the old military road near San Benito, masked vigilantes seized a Mexican prisoner from a deputy sheriff and hung him in broad daylight from an old cottonwood tree.

Early in August, reportedly twenty Mexican bandits crossed the river west of Brownsville. They stole horses and disappeared into the bushes. Texas Rangers, a cavalry officer, and several customs inspectors, along with groups of angry citizens, took off in pursuit to catch the bandits.

Aniceto Pizaña, who lived at *los Tulitos Rancho* near Brownsville, was already being fingered with suspicion, since he and Augustin Garza and *De la* Rosa had been involved in remedying injustices. They were putting out leaflets and mouthing off about the atrocities being committed against the Mexican people in the Valley. Aniceto Pizaña's ranch became the target of retribution. There was no warning of their approach, only when gunshots rang out, and white officers bellowed for Aniceto to come out of the house and give himself up. A volley of rifle shots was fired and a gunfight ensued.

When the dust settled, several of the Texas Rangers and several in the angry mob were wounded, and a United States soldier was killed. Aniceto managed to escape through the back of his house; however, his wife was shot in the shoulder and his son was shot in the leg, which later had to be amputated. His brother was roughly mistreated and tortured, then taken to a federal jail. In the house, many pamphlets were found containing words condemning the United States. Pizaña swore revenge and began the "Pizaña raids," shocking the entire lower Rio Grande Valley. He organized Mexican nationals already pro-German and anti-American to attack the Los Fresno pumps, which were burned down and its staff killed. One of the witnesses stated he was German, so his life was spared, which led folks to believe that the Germans were as involved in instigating the raids as any of the Mexican *Carranzistas*.

By the end of the long, muggy summer, *Don* Federico and James had worked back and forth between Brownsville courts and the Mexican Consul in Matamoros and had returned by train late at night. The *Don* found his whole household up in arms. Apparently several men in white hoods had placed a large burning cross in front of their home. The *Don*, exhausted from his long journey, went outside and began asking questions of his workers. "Did anybody see who these men were? Did anyone recognize any of them?"

One of the alarmed workers came forward. "The wagon is from a downtown *gringo* merchant—the one that has the fancy gingerbread inscribed on the side of the wagon," said one of the gardeners who witnessed the scene from his small hut next to the barn. He and several of the others worked the landscape, took care of the horses, and lived behind the great house. They saw the riders coming toward the house with torches, looking like spirits in the dark. It had scared them to death, being superstitious, and they wondered if ghosts were roaming the area. They stood frightened and astounded behind the barn, peeking around the corner in total shock, watching and waiting to see what was going to happen.

"How do you know which merchant?" queried *Don* Federico.

Chico, who knew little of the English alphabet, made an inscription in the dirt, indicating the letter "M" that was inscribed on the wagon. "My brother and I deliver hundred pounds of grain to his business on Saturdays. We have made comments on the wagon, which sits in the back of the granary. We dream of how we would like to have one just like it."

"You mean ol' man Milton? Who was riding in the wagon, or did you see his face? *Don* Federico was mystified.

"No, I did not see his face, but that was the same wagon, the only wagon like that around here."

"Did you recognize anybody else? Did anyone else look familiar?"

"No," Chico answered, stifling a yawn.

Don Federico thanked the men and told them to go back to bed. He apologized for having disturbed them and told them he would talk to them in the morning.

James had already gone to bed, but the *Don* went into his private library and lit his pipe. He studied the situation realistically, as he always did in any emergency. He chewed his inner cheeks; it made him think better. Old man Milton, a widower, was in his late sixties, and had migrated to South Texas from Mississippi several years ago when the explosive economic boom was beginning. He came with his two children—two boys who were older than Fred. His business merchandising farm equipment and grains had become quite successful. Milton had always been polite and very attentive to the *Don's* needs, especially in selling him supplies and grain for his horses and mules. What did Milton have against him? Could it be that the merchants were jealous of his appointed position? Why? Why did they care? Why attack his home?

The next morning *Don* Federico learned from Fred that the oldest Milton boy was bullying him after school and making fun of him, calling him names like "Greaser" and "dirty Mexican." Fred's easy-going attitude and his grandfather's hot, temper had intermixed into a tremendous impulse and instant temptation. He had slugged the boy in the face, whacked him hard, and left him crying on the school grounds. The other boys who watched laughed and made fun of the Milton boy, as the tide turned. No doubt ol' man Milton had gotten wind of the incident and was going to get even. Could it be possible that the oldest boy had been driving Milton's wagon?

Fred told his father when he returned home from the military academy he had wandered into the Milton Mercantile out of curiosity and to shop. He had run into the oldest boy, a redheaded, freckle-faced kid who hollered at him as soon as Fred entered the store. "We do not allow Mexicans to buy in this place." Fred had left the store feeling embarrassed and humiliated, not knowing what to say when white people in the store wrinkled up their noses at him. That was the first encounter he had had with the oldest Milton boy, and later, in school, he kept "messing" with him, as Fred called it.

"If ol' man Milton is so upset about you putting his boy in his place, why did he not come and talk to me? That's no reason to have burning crosses on my lawn. But I'll handle this with ol' man Milton when I see him," *Don* Federico replied adamantly.

He was also disturbed upon learning that Hanson was riding onto his property. The devious, murderous Hanson would never forget what happened in Monterrey—losing all of his possessions; losing his creditability with the Texas Rangers; and rotting in the jails of Mexico City. *No doubt he's out to get me*, thought *Don* Federico.

By the end of August, many of the national newspapers, including *The New York Times* and *The Corpus Christi Caller*, were reporting men being arrested in Brownsville for shouting, "Time to kill the *gringos!*" *El Progreso*, the Laredo Mexican paper, was reporting that anti-American sentiment and anger had reached a climax. It was rumored that over five thousand raiders were ready to attack the Texas border.

Stories also proliferated about the vigilantes, enforcement agents, and the Texas Rangers taking the law into their own hands, killing purely to instill fear in the innocent Mexican-American people.

The horror stories and evil forces kept getting worse, and by the end of the summer, the tense citizens went to sleep with their guns next to their beds. While Pizaña escaped across the river, *De la* Rosa, accompanied by Luis Vasquez and several marauders, split their forces into several raids and rode into Sebastian, Texas, and robbed several stores. They killed a man and his son, burned the building, and led away the livestock. United States soldiers were notified and began trailing them and exchanged gunfire in a battle that lasted for over two hours, killing five of the raiders. Pictures were featured in the newspapers showing the Rangers proudly dragging the bodies of the *bandidos* with lassoes tied to their saddles. The Mexican-Americans were appalled, while the Anglos began pressuring the federal government to send in more help.

In Mercedes, tents sprang up among the palm trees on the south end of Main Street, where soldiers from the United States Army 12th Cavalry set up their outpost. Young men from all parts of the United States were being recruited for the Border Patrol to fight the border raiders. The white citizens of Mercedes, especially the young ladies, began helping out and accommodating the soldiers in whatever way they could.

In August, amid the oppressive, humid heat, the cavalry patrol stationed in Mercedes got word that around thirty bandits were riding near the town. At the river, several of the Mexican riders fired at the soldiers, and one American was killed and several wounded. Later in the same month, the Sheriff of Hidalgo County was informed that soldiers from the Carranza army were crossing into Texas. There was a great pursuit and nine of the raiders were killed, with several crossing the river back to safety. The conflict continued as the U.S. Cavalry fired toward the river, and bandits fired back, killing two horses. The following morning a group of heavily armed men burned a bridge north of Brownsville.

In the early fall, fourteen Mexicans were killed, shot down close to the new town of Donna with no explanation. Their bodies were displayed along the road as an example of white supremacy and law enforcement power. This created a worse fear among the two races and especially the Mexican people living on the Texas side. Many of the Mexican workers began leaving their jobs for fear of being killed by their Anglo bosses.

In the first week of September, a band of twenty-five Mexicans showed up at the pumping plant of the Los Fresno Canal Company and burned the building down. The employees were taken prisoners, and on their way met another man who was also taken prisoner. Up the road, two employees were killed. The prisoner who was left was released, because he was a member of one of the families that had helped the wounded *Villistas* bandits during their crossing into Las Rucias; in gratitude, his life was spared.

Angry civilians with detachments of the U.S. Cavalry galloped to the scene. As they caught up with the raiders, a fierce skirmish followed. Several of the Mexican raiders were killed; the others escaped into the thick *brasada*.

All throughout the month of September, looting, shooting, burning bridges, killing, and robbing stores bore testimony to the vengeance of Pizaña, Garza, and *De la* Rosa. The citizens had almost forgotten that a war was taking place in Europe; they were fighting their own war here—a racist war.

ROOTS OF INDIFFERENCE

As *Don* Federico had predicted years ago, by the end of September, *Señor* Saenz and his wife Sostenes showed up with their wagon at one of their friend's home, escaping the raiders. Apparently, a band of eighty raiders had attacked their store in Progreso, Texas, and demanded grain and apparel. Lieutenant King of the Twenty-Sixth Infantry arrived at the Progreso store, and soon one of his soldiers was dead and another was wounded. One of his soldiers was missing and had been captured and taken across the river. King and his men rushed to the river and encountered the raiders; a two-hour battle ensued. The captured soldier had his ears cut off first and was later decapitated. His head was being displayed on a pole across the river. Horror and outrage erupted.

The turbulent conditions along the border were already wearing thin between the Mexican-American, the *gringos* and the incidents with the Mexican raiders. After Madero's death, the two countries were on the verge of diplomatic quandary.

Early one morning, close to Ebenezer, several Mexicans from the *Carranzistas* army were found shot to death by a vigilante group of businessmen and were later buried at the same spot. Very little was said about this incident in the newspapers. Many of the Mexicans who were living in the area declared later that the victims were deserters who wanted to give up the fighting but were killed by *gringo* ranchers. News traveled fast, and it infuriated *De la* Rosa. He went into a rage and wrecked a train six miles north of Brownsville, killed the engineer, and injured innocent passengers. *De la* Rosa and his marauders entered the train and began shooting at the civilians and robbing them. One of the passengers, who claimed he was German, was spared. When Captain Ransom arrived at the scene, the raiders were gone. They found four Mexicans working on a nearby ranch, which were taken and executed by the Captain, confirming his hatred toward the Mexican people. Innocent Mexican field workers were rounded-up and tortured for information and then lynched; others were shot. This enraged the Mexican-American citizens, who began complaining to Texas Senators and State Representatives.

Throughout the fall and early winter, General Funston became convinced that the *Carranzistas* were coming into the United States in a full-scale invasion. By the end of the year almost half of the available forces were stationed on the borders. The rural economy was devastated. Many of the scared Anglo families left their farms and relocated north for safety. Many Mexican-American families fled to San Antonio and far up in the Dallas-Fort Worth area, while other families with relatives in Mexico fled back across the border with their children for fear of being killed by vigilantes or the Texas Rangers.

Don Federico and James were ordered to attend a meeting in Brownsville under a priority command, and the *Don* was to make arrangements for a bilateral meeting with Carranza. President Wilson was applying diplomatic pressure to the U.S. Army and Houston's generals, wanting to pacify Mexico. Wilson wanted his troops out of the border area. After several correspondences back and forth with Nafarrate and Carranza initiated an agreement, arrangements were made in Matamoros. *Don* Federico had become friendly with *General* Nafarrate, but he cautioned the *Don* to be careful with Carranza and to watch his words. Carranza's intentions were not what they seemed; too many undercurrents were coursing below the surface.

In the middle of October, *Don* Federico met with Carranza in Matamoros. There the two faced one another at a large banquet held by Nafarrate and several other Mexican commanders.

President Carranza presented himself with dignity, resembling a grand nobleman from the Spanish courts, with his light complexion, white hair and beard, and his uniform covered with silver and gold medals. Surprisingly, he greeted *Don* Federico as if they were childhood chums. The banquet room was full of uniformed soldiers standing on both sides, fully armed. There were several generals attending: *General* Alfredo Ricaut, *General* Pablo Gonzalez, *General* Juan Antonio Acosta, and *General* Maurillo Rodriguez, along with several Germans from the German Consul, and *General* Nafarrate, who was graciously greeting the guests at the door.

It was also at this meeting that the *Don* came face to face with Franz Von Schmidt and the elder *Señor* Del Calderóne. Von Schmidt remembered meeting *Don* Federico at the Castle Del Calderóne. The father of the *Don's* son-in-law Ricardo seemed surprised at first to see *Don* Federico. At the meeting, *Don* Federico realized Von Schmidt had convinced Carranza of the German undertaking toward the United States, and Del Calderóne was back to his old self again. If he had his way with Carranza, he would be in charge once again and head of the Mexican military. They were all stroking each others' egos, not realizing the consequences of war with the United States.

Earlier, newspapers had reported that Huerta had fled Matamoros, realizing that several American spies had spotted him and gotten wind of his activities. He had been captured in the state of New Mexico, arrested, and taken to jail at Fort Bliss near El Paso.

Jittery *El Guapo* James was very attentive and took down every word that was being said, but he jumped nervously at every loud outburst. In the meeting, the stoic Carranza expressed to *Don* Federico that the U.S. was ignoring the Mexican government and had forgotten their neighbors to the south. Not until this changed, upon his orders, would the raids into Texas completely cease. *Don* Federico found it interesting that in previous meetings and conversations with the *Carranzistas*, both Nafarrate and Carranza had denied any responsibility for the raids across the border.

The *Don* realized that the "Plan of San Diego" was being conducted by Augustin Leon Garza, Basilio Ramos, Abel Sandoval, Aniceto Pizaña, Maurillo Rodriguez, Chino Garcia, A. Saenz, and Luis *De la* Rosa and several more. They were being paid by the Germans to put pressure on the United States to recognize Carranza for President. It was a carefully constructed plan, and well carried out at the expense of poor innocent Mexicans-American civilians in Texas who were being fingered, tortured, and killed.

At the meeting *Don* Federico took Del Calderóne aside and asked if he was aware that his family was now living in Mercedes. The pompous ex-Huerta general remarked, "Ricardo has known where I've lived for three years now, and has fully supported me in all activities. I now have a young, sixteen-year-old mistress living with me in Matamoros and do not care to see my old wife."

Infuriated, *Don* Federico, who was completely repulsed, answered as civilly as he could. "It's none of my business what you do with your life, but Ricardo has never mentioned to any of us where you were. My only concern is my daughter, and as a gentleman, I do not care for your actions and do not care if we ever speak again, sir!" Del Calderóne stiffened his shoulders in rebuttal and acted as if he did not care; he was as narcissistic as Ricardo. *Don* Federico decided to keep this shocking information to himself until the proper time to confront his egotistical son-in-law.

Within a week, Washington recognized Carranza as supreme chief of Mexico and opened the doors wide for the *Carranzistas* armies to travel though Texas via Sonora and get rid of Pancho Villa.

Shortly after the Carranza meeting, there was an attack on the St. Louis, Brownsville and Mexico Railway northwest of Brownsville, in which a bridge was also burned. Raiders, unaware of the agreement and still out of control, killed several businessmen and wounded others, seizing all of their valuables. Angry posses pursuing the raiders hanged four and shot six. American soldiers were attacked north of Harlingen in a battle that lasted for over an hour, with three killed and others wounded. General Funston was enraged and asked for bloodhounds and as many Apache Indians as he could get to help track the raiders. The War Department began questioning General Funston's ideas, as they were completely taken aback by his request; consequently, no new regiment of infantrymen was furnished. The harsh press was fed up and lambasted the impotent tactics of the U.S. Army.

It was in 1915, too, that the region suffered from a smallpox epidemic. All schools were closed and many children died. The turbulent times had brought different movements in the Lower Rio Grande Valley of Texas, from financial and economic changes, to educational changes that made sure every child attended school, but in segregated classes, since the "Jim Crow Laws" were still very evident in the Valley. Without the Mexican laborers, the South Texas economy had come to a halt; it was the Mexicans who performed the arduous labor in the fields. Half of the population had been evicted and moved elsewhere, and the merchants were scrounging for help.

In Brownsville, the Federal District Courts were busy with Mexican suspects being jailed for participating in the raids with the marauders from across the border. Over fifty individuals were indicted for murderous acts, and several were hanged. Mexican-American families stood for days outside the courts waiting for justice.

In December, Felicia and Dan were married at the Lady of Mercy Church in Mercedes. Close family members attended, along with many of the workers who worked the ranch and the oil field. A small reception followed, since Emma had been experiencing the flu with a persistent cough and was not up to making a big fuss. It was also very dangerous for people to travel in and out of the Rio Grande Valley, and especially to cross the border.

It was later learned that, after the wedding reception dance, a group of seven young, single Mexican farm workers, who had attended and had stayed late, were riding north on a rural road. They were stopped by two mounted Texas Rangers, who bullied them and trotted their horses in circles around them. They were interrogated and asked if they were carrying any guns. *Los Rinches* shouted at them, called them dirty names and displayed their rifles menacingly. Several shots were fired into the ground as the Rangers attempted to arrest the young men. When they started to round up the frightened young men, two escaped, running into the bushes, three were shot in the back, and the two who were caught were hung from a cottonwood tree by the side of the road.

The news traveled like a wildfire in dry grass among the dead Mexicans' families. Sorrow mixed with terror and panic sent tremors of fear through the town. Ironically, nothing was ever said of this incident in the newspapers, and according to the local sheriffs, the Rangers who patrolled the area had an alibi; consequently, the news was insignificant. Mexican-American families were alarmed and wanted justice, they wanted revenge. Many started their own vigilante groups, especially the men, who wanted to join the *Carranzistas* to get back at the "white pigs."

One of the young boys shot in the shoulder while escaping was the youngest son of *Señor* Esquibel. *Los Rinches* in the area would have hell to pay, dealing with him. *Señor* Esquibel went as far as to consult *Doña* Adela, getting her to perform black witchcraft rituals condemning the Rangers and cursing them. Indian drums were heard, unsettling the serenading cicadas on the Esquibel's property and stampeding cattle. Interrupting the cockroaches and scorpions skittered away from the throbbing vibrations.

The new year of 1916 rolled in fast. The raids along the border ceased for the moment in South Texas, but the hatred between the Mexican-American families and the Anglos remained, especially for the disliked *Rinches,* who enforced the law as it suited them and thought they were above reproach. All Mexicans were still looked upon with suspicion.

Huerta's alcoholic abuse finally caught up with him, and news of his death was all over the newspapers. He died of cirrhosis of the liver at Fort Bliss near El Paso. Carranza was true to his word; however, Pizaña, and *De la* Rosa remained at large, so the governor of Texas offered a large reward for the capture of both men. For the first three months of the New Year, activities on both sides of the river remained peaceful. For a while, normal activities resumed; Mexican-American citizens were traveling back and forth, buying merchandise again.

In Chihuahua, Pancho Villa went berserk when the United States openly supported Carranza for the Mexican presidency. In retaliation, he rode into the mining town of Santa Isabel and murdered seventeen American miners. Early in the month of March, Villa marched with over a thousand of his soldiers into the town of Columbus, New Mexico, and disregarded the agreement that Carranza had made with the United States. He burned part of the town, robbed and killed seventeen civilians and sent waves of terror throughout the border towns once again. This action enraged Carranza, having to answer to the United States for Villa going against his orders. Another raid took place around the Big Bend town of Glenn Springs, Texas. The U.S. militia was called out to mobilize the National Guard along the border. Several other depredations took place in Laredo, Texas, with killings and hangings, and the burning of bridges, with many Mexicans shot to death.

ROOTS OF INDIFFERENCE

Washington began imposing an arms embargo on Carranza and sent General John Pershing with 6,000 troops into Mexico to chase Villa in the mountains of Chihuahua, but the troops were eventually recalled later to fight in Europe.

Carranza, who was secretly sponsoring the whole charade that was the Plan of San Diego went crazy, and in retaliation he ordered his generals to begin raiding again along the Texas border. Carranza had replaced *General* Nafarrate and his entire command at Matamoros with the gloomy *General* Eugenio López. He authorized López to organize a backdoor series of raids, cutting telegraph lines, destroying railroad trestles, and killing people in the U.S.

An unexpected turn of events happened. *General* Nafarrate supposedly went into military retirement and was going into politics. He remained friendly with *Don* Federico and requested in a telegram that the *Don* meet him covertly in Reynosa. *Don* Federico responded immediately, finding Nafarrate's dismissal as a general in Carranza army suspicious and questionable.

This time, *Don* Federico traveled by himself and left James behind. He feared that he was going to find out sooner or later the secrecy of the Carranza movement. At dusk, in a clandestine meeting in a local *cantina* in downtown Reynosa, the *Don* met with *General* Nafarrate. The *General* was alone, in civilian clothes, and unrecognizable. There he discussed major problems, as the *Don* listened. He discovered that the Kaiser in Germany was paying large amounts of money to Carranza—something the *Don* had already suspected. The Japanese were also paying Carranza, in return for the valuable oil along the Gulf that was fueling their submarines and other machinery. German agents and spies were controlling the country, teaching Mexican army officers military science and setting up a powerful wireless station in Mexico City. The Germans, uniting with Japan, were going to support Carranza in the war with the United States, ostensibly so Mexicans could take back their land.

There were spies throughout Mexico and also in the United States, especially in the Valley, ready to take up arms when the time came. Carranza had ordered several of his soldiers involved in the San Diego Plan to travel to the border towns of Texas and kill the informants who were betraying his cause by revealing the Plan to the *Americanos*. Nafarrate also mentioned that the main reason he was relieved of his duties was because he knew too much about Carranza's secrecy and was too friendly with the people of the United States. He was perhaps being spied on at that very moment by Carranza's henchmen. He feared for his life.

"Well, I hope you stay safe," remarked the *Don*, visibly upset. He tried to change the subject. "I do hope we can remain friends," he suggested. "Now that you're out of the military service and have more time on your hands, we can visit one another." The *Don's* reply was spoken in gracious sincerity toward Nafarrate, for he liked him as a friend.

"*Cómo no*," replied Nafarrate. "I'm going to run for governor of Tamaulipas, making Matamoros the capital. The people of Matamoros truly love me. You can come and be my guest in the city with my new *novia*." I'm marrying the most beautiful woman in the world, Maria Luisa." The retired general was sad at leaving the military, but happy with his new civilian future. After those words, and much more, the *Don* returned home without divulging a word of it to James.

In June, Abel Sandoval with twenty raiders crossed the river into Brownsville, wrecked a train, and assassinated several Mexican-Americans who had informed on and pointed the finger at the insurgents. General James Parker, who at the time was patrolling the area, called the 26th Infantry to reinforce him, and chased the raiders across the bridge into the city of Matamoros.

General Alfredo Ricaut, who was now commander of the Mexican forces in Matamoros, challenged General Parker by evacuating the town. General Parker stood his ground and refused to take orders from the Mexican general. General Parker's bravery alarmed Ricaut and so worried Carranza that the Americans would overtake the town of Matamoros, that he promised to stop the raids. Parker and his troops returned to Fort Brown. In Laredo, the *Laredo Daily Times* reported that several violent melees with insurgents and the Texas Rangers had occurred. By this time, Carranza, involved with the German diplomats, had lost his hold on the San Diego Plan, since many of his followers in Texas were being caught and killed. Many of the raiders were paid off in large amounts, and many of them vanished into Mexico, perhaps changing their names. Meanwhile, *Del la* Rosa was dying from consumption.

In the Rio Grande Valley, the tension and hatred between the two nationalities still existed as a backlash from the Rangers, vigilantes, and Anglo law enforcement brutality taking revenge against the local Mexican-American natives. Other vigilante groups were evolving within the business merchants of the white population. It was easy for any group to take advantage of the despicable, horrendous conditions occurring, to commit a crime, and then blame it on the Mexican raiders.

CHAPTER 31

Amidst the suffering, chaos, and confusion in the fall of 1916, a traveling ministry of so-called "movers and shakers" promoting their beliefs came to Mercedes and set up their huge white tent north of the town for a three-day revival. The majority of the population was loyal Mexican-American Catholics and had never heard of other religions. They never knew anything like that even existed.

But the tension with the Mexican Revolution, the invading raiders, and *Los Rinches* with their lynching mobs, had been so intense that any encouragement and inspiration was deemed welcome. By the second day of bringing forth light, saving souls, and promising miracles, all the excitement had gotten everyone's attention. People were wondering what the "moving and shaking" was all about. The majority was skeptical, but curiosity overcame hesitation, and many found the event too hard to resist.

Many of the workers from Spanish Acres decided to see what the hullabaloo was all about. Roy was recovering from his surgery. Manuel could not stop drinking and suffered from a bad case of hemorrhoids. Yo-Yo, with arthritis in his joints, agreed to attend.

Others who attended were members of the white Presbyterian and Methodist churches and the Catholic praying party, including Emma and Mrs. McCray, members of the wagging-tongue society. All tried to hide themselves under feathered hats, and mantillas wrapped around their faces, embarrassed and in fear of being recognized. Most of the white folks sat in the front rows, and as usual, the Mexican people sat to the back.

The tension mounted as a group of six white singers in long black robes stood four feet above the ground on a wooden platform singing and clapping their hands. To the side of the podium was a large woman playing the piano and accompanying the choir. The spectators below were sitting in rows and rows of wooden chairs, and they joined in and began clapping also.

From behind the curtains appeared a balding Anglo man in his late sixties, weighing over three hundred pounds. He wore a black suit and white shirt and carried a Bible in his hand. He approached the pulpit and shouted, "Amen, folks!" The rest of the fanatic fundamentalists repeated "Amen!"

Everyone stood up as he asked. "Do we want to be saved and go to heaven?" His reverberating tenor voice was deep and loud. He gave a commanding impression of a high authority sent from above.

"Yes!" the audience answered, reverberating throughout the close-quartered tent.

"Do you want Jesus in your heart and be saved?" he hollered.

"Yes! Yes!" was the answer from his congregation.

"Before we get started and forget in our excitement, we're going to pass the donation plate." His voice was strong and vibrant. "It cost us money to travel and set up the tent, and to pay our fellow traveling Christians. And as soon as we pass the money plate, we'll go into a prayer. There will be testimonies of miracles, and we'll continue with our wonderful visit with Jesus."

The passing of the contribution plates was done at the beginning of the service, since the sermons were sometimes harsh and severe, and many times the preaching got out of hand. They were afraid that if people got frightened, they would leave without giving any contribution to their work.

"There's da catch," said Roy, addressing Manuel. "It's always da gawddamn money!"

Manuel, full of excitement, grinned.

Yo-Yo glanced at Manuel and said, "Uh huh."

Several of the Anglos sitting in front of them, mostly women with enormous fancy hats, turned around and stared at Roy. If looks could kill, well, this was the moment. A loud "shush" was voiced and repeated. Manuel smiled, displayed his few teeth and Yo-Yo repeated, "Uh huh."

The choir began singing. There were several "Hallelujahs," coming from the audience. Four large water buckets—not ordinary plates, but buckets—were passed around and were soon full of loose gold and silver dollars.

Roy noticed several individuals standing against the walls on both sides, looking pallid. He found it curious, since there were chairs to sit in. All seemed old and looked weak, crippled, and sick, with wooden crutches, or in wheelchairs. Did these folks come with the tent show as a testimony to save their sorry souls? Or was this all a circus to make money and entertain the crowd?

After many minutes of exhorting the congregation to seek Jesus and be saved, the preacher shouted at the top of his lungs. "Jesus! Jesus! Our only savior!"

The congregation responded with shouts of "Jesus! Jesus!" in a wave of chanting awe in fear of going to Hell. "Hallelujah!" responded others, their waving hands held high.

The preacher then went into a trance and began speaking in tongues.

The audience went wild again. "Hallelujah!" they shouted. Rumbling followed, as feet began hitting the floor in rhythmical, reverberating, pounding waves; the noise got louder and made people want to get up and shout in a spellbinding ecstasy. Several ladies sitting in the front row fainted. They were calmly picked up by others, as if nothing had taken place, and without missing a beat.

A young girl about twenty fell to the ground, close to where Roy and the *vaqueros* were sitting. As she began twitching, with contractions of her muscles racking her whole body, her dress crawled up around her hips, revealing her underpants. The *vaqueros* all leaned forward and looked down at the scene with interest.

"Don't look or you'll go blind," said someone in the audience.

"I'll risk one eye," said one of the Mexican *vaqueros*, as he put his hand over his left eye. Another said, "Me too." Others snickered with embarrassment.

The excitement became so great that it was like a bolt of electricity hitting the earth in a hard rain shower with lightning and thunder. From the aisle, a cripple dropped his crutches, hit the floor and began shaking, like the young girl. Startled, Roy and the *vaqueros* jumped when his crutches hit the floor beside them. Another person claimed he was free from pain and ailments; he raised his hands into the air calling out "Jesus! Jesus!" *Ah! Qué, bueno!*

The music stopped. There was a long silence, with no one quite knowing what was coming. Emma and several of the other ladies were all frantically fanning themselves.

The preacher stopped and looked out into the crowd. He was in a soporific trance with his eyes closed, his arms stretched out. He began prophesying: "A heavy Mexican woman in our midst suffers from sugar sickness. She will be healed— healed!"

Emma drew back, knowing that he was talking about her.

"I see a widow woman who will find her sweetheart and will marry in the next five years and will be very happy."

Mrs. McCray smiled, while Emma nodded her approval.

"I feel someone with heart problems will be healed by the power of the Lord— healed!"

The preacher continued: "I feel that a white man who has been paralyzed will be healed tonight— healed! He will walk again!" He shouted and his voice pulsated against the tent walls. One of the feeble old men dropped his crutches and started to walk down the aisle, raising his hands. "Hallelujah, praise Jesus!" he said. Two others in their wheelchairs got up and began walking, lifting their hands in the air and shouting loudly, "Jesus! Lord Jesus!" The crowd went wild again and shouted, "Hallelujah!"

The crowd was now in a hypnotic trance, waiting to see what surprising new miracles were coming their way. The preacher put his hand out to silence them so he could read from the Bible: "They shall take up serpents; they shall lay hands on the sick, and they shall recover." He closed the Bible and shouted, "Bring in the box!"

A large wooden box with small holes on each side was placed on a table in front of the platform. Everyone had their eyes on the wooden box. What was inside? Everyone became silent. The preacher stood over the box and spoke. "Who sits in the audience that is without faith?" he shouted, pointing his index finger and waving his arm across the room. "Who out there is thinking that they are brave enough and need faith?" There was a soft murmur from the audience. The two box-handlers opened the box, and the preacher started to put his hand inside. Everyone was quiet, everything still.

"Friends," he said, "you need faith to hold this beautiful creature of God in your hands." What creature? All eyes widened as the preacher took his suit coat off, rolled up his sleeves, and reached into the box. In slow motion, he brought out the biggest, the ugliest, rattlesnake ever seen in South Texas.

Roy's eyes almost popped out of his head, and he leaned forward. "Gawddamn and holy shit!" he exclaimed, not realizing he was speaking out loud. Manuel shrank back in his seat. Yo-Yo's eyes were as big as they could get, and he swallowed hard. Several of the *vaqueros* appeared jittery. Others chuckled to themselves, thinking this was the funniest thing they had ever seen—playing with the deadly *culebra*. The subdued churchwomen began fanning faster and breathing harder. Emma almost fainted. She wanted to get up and leave, remarking she was not in love with any species of vermin, and she especially hated snakes.

The preacher put the heavy snake around his neck and cuddled it, soothing it like a pet.

Laws me! Thought Roy, entranced at what he was seeing. *If that snake bites him, he'll be dead in minutes.* All of the *vaqueros* were stunned at the scene before them, and they looked around to find an exit. They had seen rattlers, but not this whopping ass big!

"You!" the preacher said, coming down the aisle with the beast around his neck. His eyes were wide and wild. He caught the attention of Roy, who was looking guilty, and eyed him up and down.

Roy straightened himself up, perplexed. His body went so weak he almost fell from his chair. "Me?" He almost wet his pants when he looked up at the venomous snake with its forked tongue darting in and out.

"Are you a man of faith?" the preacher said, hovering over him with the devil snake. "I feel that not too long ago, you encountered death, almost died, but you have been saved to become a soldier in the army of Jesus." His smoldering eyes were piercing and fervent.

"Yes," answered Roy. *How the hell did he know?* He felt his body shaking and sinking lower in his seat. At this very moment he did not know whether he was afoot or on horseback and wanted to run out of the tent as fast as his feet would carry him.

"That's what I thought!" roared the preacher. He closed his eyes and went into a trance. "I'm being told that all of you sitting in this section need to be healed and saved in the name of Jesus." He was apparently being told something again, as his body began shaking in a tremor, but the snake clung to him like a faithful partner.

The congregations went wild and began screaming, "Jesus, sweet Jesus!"

The preacher turned to Manuel, and shouted, "You, sir, are infested with the devil's liquid desire, and if you do not repent, you shall burn in Hell with all of the demonic angels, and you shall be punished by God!"

Manuel squirmed nervously and nodded yes. Everyone had turned and was staring at him, even Emma and Mrs. McCray, who were shaking their heads in disgust.

The preacher bent over Yo-Yo and snarled, "Do you drink? Do you like tobacco? How about the women? Adulterous ways! You are traveling with the devil's desires and nothing pleases him more than burning you eternally in Hell. You'll be damned forever!" He bellowed fire and damnation, his face was red, and he was sweating on his forehead and under his armpits. The people sitting close by felt a spray of sweat and spit sprinkle over them. "Folks," he said, glaring out into the audience, "we have three men here who need praying and saving."

"Hallelujah!" shouted the congregation, as they stood with their arms extended, shouting and pounding their feet and clapping their hands. The vibration throbbed in everyone's body, and all were caught up in rapture.

"These men need the Holy Spirit to come into their hearts, and they need faith. Now, here is what we are going to do!" shouted the preacher.

Well, hell, thought Roy. *Here it comes. The big surprise!*

The preacher stood before them, head up, as if receiving a special message from above. He closed his eyes, mumbled some words, and then opened his eyes. He uncoiled the rattler from his shoulders and, in an instant, wrapped the snake around Roy's neck. People sitting close by scrambled away in panic. Roy jumped up. He flipped the snake off in a tangled mass toward Manuel. Manuel jerked backwards and almost had a heart attack. The huge rattler fell to the floor and slithered toward Yo-Yo, who jumped and hollered. Fear replaced the miracle Manuel was expecting, and he began running outside. The other *vaqueros* followed, including Yo-Yo, whose belt had come undone, causing him to almost lose his pants! If it was faith they needed, they had come to the wrong place. It was not going to be given by a fat rattler! The choir kept singing and clapping their hands, and the clamor continued as if nothing had happened.

Other startled people began leaving the premises, including Emma and Mrs. McCray and other members of the wagging-tongue society who had had the living daylights scared out of them.

Outside the tent, one of the *vaqueros* found a bottle of whiskey inside his jacket and shared it with his nervous and frightened *compadres*. Some began rolling cigarettes to calm their nerves. All were men who drank and smoked; they were going to Hell anyway.

Roy, still flabbergasted, began laughing. It was an amazing and unexplainable feeling. Whether they were saved or not, he was feeling better and breathing better; however, his nerves were traumatized. "Dat git rid of yore hem'hoids?" Roy asked Manuel, laughing so hard, holding his stomach that tears came to his eyes. Manuel's few white hairs stood straight up and Yo-Yo unsure where he was. Both looked like the victims of an explosion.

"No, not my hemorrhoids," answered Manuel, who had come out of his shock and was laughing with them. "But maybe something else," he muttered, as they all took notice of a foul smell that hung in the damp foggy air. The men looked at one another, trying to determine where the fetid smell was coming from. At the same time, Manuel discovered the reason for the warmth in his lower regions. He had crapped his pants.

Yo-Yo giggled and grabbed for the buttons on the front of his trousers, which felt wet and warm. He had soaked his drawers. He looked up, grinned, and said, "Uh huh!"

CHAPTER 32

In February of 1917, Brigadier General Blackjack Pershing withdrew his troops from Mexico. His army had suffered enormous casualties south of the border, at the hands of the Mexican fighters and also from the harsh *Sierra Madre's* mountainous environment. The last United States Army unit rode out defeated and unable to capture Pancho Villa in the mountains of Chihuahua.

It was also in that month that Major General Frederick Funston died in San Antonio from a heart attack. This left the United States Army in limbo and in total chaos, especially when dealing with the disturbing border problems.

The following month, Carranza was elected president of Mexico. He had already ordered a convention for the writing of a new constitution, modifying it for labor rights, rights over territory, and restricting the power of the Catholic Church.

Carranza started making remarks against the U.S. regarding the violation of Mexico's rights, and in retaliation and to prove his point; he sent several troops to the border. With the U.S. National Guard patrolling the Rio Grande River, war with Mexico seemed imminent. Around this time, the so-called Zimmermann Note wired to Carranza was intercepted and decoded by British Naval Intelligence. President Wilson was notified. In it, the German ambassador reassured Mexico of being their ally and seemed to indicate that Mexico was going to war with the United States, and Mexico would be rewarded by getting back the states sold by Santa Anna. The Zimmermann Note was being kept from the public, for fear of causing panic, while the Germans were using highly convincing propaganda in Mexico, tying to distract the United States from the European war.

The German submarines that roamed the seas began sinking American ships on sight, and in April of 1917, the United States declared war on Germany. Newspapers went ballistic in reporting the news on the front page. Gross caricatures of political figures appeared in the editorial pages. Young men eighteen and over were being recruited into the service. Many Mexican-American boys enlisted, but many others in the Mexican-American families, who were already hostile and full of resentment against American injustice and *los Rinches'* brutality, refused to join the service. Many falsified their birth certificates, claiming they were baptized in Mexico and were Mexican citizens.

Shortly after the United States declared war on Germany, it was business as usual for the Texas Rangers, who began their own little war by sending callous, ruthless Rangers to Mexican homes, demanding that they surrender their firearms. Many Mexican men refused to give up their arms, and consequently, they were taken outside in front of their families and lynched or shot while "resisting arrest." The vigilante posses, which were made up of mostly white Anglo men and the Texas Rangers, simply got out of control, making up their own laws. The raids occurred during the night when families were asleep, surprising them. On several occasions Rangers used the horrific methods of the K.K.K., burning homes with torches and leaving burning crosses, a form of intimidation no different from what occurred in the Deep South. The Rangers were also busy questioning the birth certificates of the Mexican-American citizens, trying to prove they were evading registration. They also invaded any meeting or organization that the Mexican people conducted, and an indication of their disregard for the border laws.

In early spring, upon Manuel's delivery to Mercedes, he had informed Victoria of his concern for Mama Maria, whose illness had gotten worse. Victoria began spending most of her time at Spanish Acres, giving out orders to Soledad, Ophelia, and Olivia, who were now running the kitchen and overseeing the household duties. She had heard the mournful sounds of the *lechuzas* several times, warning of death as the owls circled Spanish Acres during the night hours, and it had worried Victoria.

Don Federico and James spent most of their time in Brownsville's federal courts and at the Mexican Consulate in Matamoros, keeping them away for days at a time. *Don* Federico had advised Victoria earlier, while at Spanish Acres, to pick up the bookkeeping ledger books from the oil wells, and Victoria had spent part of this morning traveling to retrieve the books. One of the oil wells had stopped producing, and fewer workmen remained. A geologist had been hired to prospect for another drill. Dan Land was now in charge and ran the company as best he could. Those who were not working on the oil wells were put to work in the fields and helped with the weeding and irrigating of the land. Hundreds of acres had been cleared in preparation for planting cotton, but the majority of the land in Spanish Acres was still the domain of hundreds of cattle.

Returning to Spanish Acres after retrieving the bookkeeping ledgers, Victoria's instincts drove her toward *Doña* Adela's home. She wanted to see the old *bruja* for her advice and had not seen her in several weeks. About a mile out, on the dirt path to *Doña* Adela's place, Victoria was startled by a loud explosion but was unable to tell where it came from. Up ahead and above the mesquite and undergrowth, she soon saw smoke rising high up into the sky. She rushed in fear as fast as her one-horse buggy would take her to approach *la bruja's* place, but it still took over thirty minutes before she came close to the *jacale*. She could see black smoke circling up from beyond the trees. When she got close enough to tie her horse on the side of the road, she stood watching the unbelievable scene. There was nobody around, only silence. *Doña* Adela's hut had been blown to pieces. The explosion had killed her three dogs that lived under the porch and protected her shack—gruesome body parts were scattered about—but *Doña* Adela was nowhere to be found.

Victoria shouted for her several times, knowing she often roamed the woods gathering special weeds. Who could have done this terrible thing? She stood there, unbelieving, then began inspecting pieces of the smoldering debris. The burnt smell was unbearable. Apparently, dynamite had been thrown into *Doña* Adela's wooden heating stove. Where was her son Roberto? He was always hiding; he was always shy.

She walked toward the barn, which was still standing and opened the door. It was dark, except for the light coming through the cracks between the boards. Thick cobwebs clung to boards and rafters, and thick smoke from the explosion tainted the muggy atmosphere. There were harness and ropes hanging along the walls, and *Doña* Adela's dry weeds hanging from the rafters. Victoria yelled, "*Doña* Adela!" and then, "Roberto!" She stood for several minutes assessing the situation, caught her breath, and glanced toward a small room on the other side of the barn. It looked like sleeping quarters—perhaps it was Roberto's room.

She moved closer and opened the door. The tiny alcove was dark and smelly. There was a small window, but little light shone through the murky glass. Next to the wall was a spring cot, and on top of the cot was—what looked like a person—a dead body! Victoria jumped and wanted to scream. Was it a dead person whose body had dehydrated and perhaps lay on this cot for several years and had deteriorated into that condition? She was confused and horrified, but thinking back, she recollected Felicia saying something about an unexplainable odor around the barn, even before they left for school in Monterrey.

She hesitated, then cautiously leaned over and viewed the desiccated corpse in the dim light. She could see that it was that of a woman, wearing a dress with ruffles and lace that was discolored and rotted with age. Her body fluids had drained around the old cot, dried, and decayed. Her skin was mummified, like dry parchment over bone. There was a decomposed mildew smell—the familiar smell of death. Long, tangled, red hair framed the skull on the pillow. *Red hair! Oh, my God!* Victoria was horror-stricken. Her skin crawled. *Could this be the missing red-haired woman that was murdered in the brasada, and her body lost for all these years? It's no wonder she was never found—no one would have thought to look here! The vaqueros could have looked out in the bushes until kingdom come and would never have found her. But what is the body doing here? And why hadn't Doña Adela said anything about her?* Suddenly, Victoria remembered. *She uses dead bodies for her rituals!*

She stood petrified, as a cold chill crept over her body. The barn door squeaked. She spun around and glanced toward the shaft of sunlight coming through the open door. In the light there appeared the figure of a wolf! An illusion! Victoria squinted and called out, "*Doña* Adela! Is that you? Roberto?" She was confused and awestruck and thought her fears must be playing games with her emotions. She looked again and there was nothing, only the bright sunlight and the door squeaking in the wind. She felt nauseated and lightheaded and fled for the door before she fainted.

Outside, she took in a deep breath and stood for a time to compose herself. She heard galloping horses coming her way from the direction of Spanish Acres. Unsure who the riders might be, she hurried back inside the barn and looked through the cracks. With great relief, she recognized Roy, Miguel, and the other *vaqueros* from Spanish Acres.

"Whut da Hell? Whut da shit happen here?" exclaimed Roy, looking around in amazement. "Boy, oh man!" He removed his hat and scratched his head, viewing the destruction. "Wunder where dat ol' *bruja* is at?"

"Did she blow herself to pieces?" answered Miguel, who was just as baffled. Just as they spied the horse and buggy hitched out on the road, Victoria approached them from the direction of the barn.

"Roy! Miguel!" Victoria shouted, her right hand against her forehead. She was almost in a state of collapse. "There's a body in there!" she said, pointing toward the barn.

"Is it *la bruja*?" questioned Miguel, concerned. He got off his horse and rushed to help Victoria, who was obviously in distress.

"No," answered Victoria, looking pale and feeling faint.

Miguel grabbed her by the waist and helped her over to the waiting horse and buggy.

Roy and the *vaqueros* dismounted and cautiously stepped inside the old barn. One was already holding his bandana up to his nose, for fear of what they were going to find.

Victoria rushed back to Spanish Acres, all the while feeling dizzy and nauseated. Perhaps it had been the smoke, or maybe she needed something to eat. Mystified, she kept thinking of *Doña* Adela and wondering what could have happened to her. Where was she? Where was Roberto?

It took two days before *Doña* Adela was found, deep in the *brasada*. Several *vaqueros* discovered her by following the mournful call of *lechuzas* roosting overhead in a tall cottonwood tree. Owls and large ravens guarded the tree where she was hanging. It presented a chilling scene, causing every hair on the backs of their necks to stand straight up. The blackbirds had eaten her eyes out. The *vaqueros* who took her down reported that her tongue and ears were cut off, and her arthritic hands had been crushed. It appeared she had been tortured while trying to get information out of her. To console her grieving followers, they pointed out that she had probably died before she was hung.

Several families in the area, who had been watching for any strange activities on their property, remarked they had seen two *gringos* on horseback riding toward *Doña* Adela's home. One of the men said he had recognized the ex-Texas Ranger, Hanson. He was older, uglier, and heavier, but it was him. He recognized him from years back when the family's older boy had a run-in with the *los Rinches* in Harlingen.

Victoria was inconsolable over *la bruja's* death, and so were hundreds of people around the area. The old woman was her friend since childhood, and she had taught her so much. What were they going to do without her healings and consultations?

For many days after the death of *Doña* Adela, Victoria felt ill, and not knowing why, until the discovery that she was actually pregnant—a child from Ricardo. How could she forget the time he had come home from one of his escapades in the bordellos of Reynosa? He had stormed into her bedroom, drunk and angry, and torn her nightgown off, then forced her to have sex. She was married; she had no other choice but to comply, for fear of waking the whole household in the middle of the night.

ROOTS OF INDIFFERENCE

The body of the red-haired *gringa* found in *Doña* Adela's barn was quickly buried in the Juelson's family cemetery in a handmade wooden casket. Only those who remembered that certain day and the many months that had followed the mysterious event attended. All the wondering and searching had finally come to an end. They considered the case closed, although the mystery remained—how had she ended up at *Doña* Adela's place?

Doña Adela's funeral was held in the small chapel at Spanish Acres. Hundreds of humble Mexican people attended from all over the region. She was buried in the Juelson family cemetery exactly a week after the *gringa* was found in her barn. She had lived in Spanish Acres all her life and was considered part of the family. Roberto still had not been located. The land where *Doña* Adela lived was cleared of debris, leaving only part of the dilapidated barn and the old chimney. The area was considered sacred ground for so many of the natives.

Months later, several robbers who were discovered looking for the "pot of gold coins" she was thought to have hidden, were frightened away with shotguns. The *vaqueros* from Spanish Acres started to patrol the land with guns and rifles. Roy had hired twenty more *vaqueros* to work the cattle and protect the area. Many swore they had seen a black wolf and heard *la bruja* cackle as they followed a burning flame they saw on her land, thinking that it was *Doña* Adela's spirit.

As the circling *lechuzas* were still being heard, and since the superstitious natives said death came in threes, everyone held their breath in anticipation. No less than six months later, Mamá Maria died, apparently from a heart attack, while sitting in a rocking chair crocheting a baby garment for Victoria's child. She was also buried in the Juelson's family plot. Victoria, distressed and with child, going into her seventh month, was grief-stricken and swore if she had a girl, she would name her Maria. Manuel was inconsolable, and with his failing health, felt poorly and drank more heavily than usual. He had not long to live, and he did not care. Yo-Yo's sons, Memo and José, were given the morning duties of delivering milk, cheese, and butter to Lozano's in Harlingen, Garcia's in La Feria and to *Don* Antonio's local grocery store in Mercedes.

Victoria was delighted when Felicia informed her that she was also expecting a child in the following year. No word was heard from Juan, except for several letters mailed to *Don* Federico and Magdalena, telling them that he had finished his studies, but was now doing residency work in nearby hospitals and would soon return to Mercedes.

Life in the Rio Grande Valley continued.

Over a thousand U.S. Army soldiers were quartered and stationed in Mercedes Park, called Camp Mercedes. Other soldiers were camped on the west end of town close to a small lake where soldiers built footbridges over a canal. Tents pitched among the mesquite and undergrowth included a small hospital for the sick soldiers.

There were several activities to keep the soldiers occupied; however, the dances that took place at the Mercedes Hotel were segregated. Written signs inside stated "Whites Only" and "Mexicans Only," for people to use the toilets and their services. Social activities for the Army were also being conducted in the white school, including dancing, but it would stop at midnight, as the electric plant turned the electricity off at twelve o'clock and back on the following morning at six. Mixed-racial couples on picnics, especially at the *Campacuas* Lake, would cause an ethnic uproar. Many of the Mexican-American girls fell in love with the handsome blond, blue-eyed *gringo* soldiers, in spite of protests from their Mexican-American parents. Those young girls often found out they were pregnant, months later after the solders left. Luckily, some did get married, but most had hell to pay and raised their children without a father. Many soldiers left the area before becoming committed because of the national tensions, and many Mexican-American children grew up having an English last name but no father.

Many changes were coming about between the two ethnic groups. The Mexican-American citizens were integrating into the Texas-American culture and laws and slowly adapting to the *gringo* ways.

During this time *Don* Federico received news of varying degrees—some good, some bad. He was heartbroken to learn that the old educator, H. Marsh, whom he considered a wonderful mentor and a good friend, had died and was buried in Edinburg.

The most shocking and disturbing news came when he heard that the Esquibel family had found *Don* Esquibel swinging from a tall cottonwood tree several miles south of their property. There was evidence of several horses' tracks in the soft earth, and Mexican families living nearby had seen Rangers riding around earlier. The Esquibel family was devastated.

The only good news was a wedding invitation from *General* Nafarrate. He was marrying an aristocrat from Ciudad Victoria, *La Señorita* Maria Luisa.

Fred and the twins would hurry home from school and then walk over to the depot, five blocks away, where the train came whistling in at four o'clock. They would stand close to the tracks and wave, watching the people getting on and off the train. The big attraction, though, was next to the depot, where the boys would spend time watching the military soldiers at their encampment, where the echoing resonance of bugles would startle the residents of the town in the early morning dawn like a habitual sounding alarm clock.

The Mexican raids had caused the coming of the North Dakota Infantry and later the First Illinois Cavalry to Mercedes. This created excitement in the youth, especially for young boys who had once played with tin soldiers and dreamed of one day being in the military. Fascination was the word; seeing the soldiers in their sharp uniforms doing their afternoon maneuvers or traveling with caissons down the main street was stimulating. Since both schools let out at the same time in the afternoon, Mexican-American boys from the North School would also join in the excitement. Poor, scrawny boys with bare, dirty feet and torn and faded threadbare clothes would watch the soldiers and dream, hoping that someday they could perhaps live that life.

From outside the wire fence, the two racial groups stood separated and nudged each other, mimicked the soldiers, and all joined in their ceremony with their salutes, especially when raising the flag. The marching of the soldiers was spellbinding, with every boy stomping their feet, cheering and pantomiming each step.

But when the reverberating sound of the cannon boomed, everyone trembled, and then cheered.

After the soldiers finished their maneuvers, the Mexican-American boys would leave with sad faces, heads down, and walk back across the tracks. The isolated Mexican-American children learned early in life the feeling of banishment and castigation and always were aware of the ill feeling against them. They never had their dreams fulfilled, always had to tolerate the dislike, the hatred, and the intimidation from the white world. Bigotry was so prevalent that even small children, not knowing much of life, felt ostracized. The facts of life were this: growing up was going to be hard and cruel.

⌘ ⌘ ⌘

Those were exciting times, in the warmth of the sultry nights, when mischievous young boys found the darkness of the shadows intriguing. Fred and the twins would sneak out when nobody was looking and hide among the bushes behind Stoler's warehouse, which sold caskets, and observe the corpses of dead soldiers. Soldiers were dying away from their homes, torn from their families and loved ones, to protect the American citizens from foreign invaders in this strange land of summer's tormenting heat. Sometimes the boys would get close enough to inspect the bodies, without the proprietor knowing, giving them chills and a frightening kind of excitement.

John, who had a weaker stomach than the other twin, decided that viewing dead soldiers was not for him and was keeping him from sleeping at night. He was also experiencing terrible nightmares that would make him wet the bed, so he refused to join the daredevils on their thrill-seeking adventure. Besides, if mother Emma found out, he would have a nightmare of a different kind. John's hormones were beginning to stir, and he was more interested in girls—and what was underneath their clothing.

On a dark night in the middle of summer, while hiding among the palms at the Mercedes Park, the boys heard horses. Fred and the twins watched a band of thirty desperadoes heading in their direction, speaking in rough Spanish. The three glanced at each other and all of them froze. The riders were obviously drunk and cussed and bellowed loudly, proclaiming their loyalty to Mexico. Several began to urinate on the street while still on their horses, and they all guffawed at this. One of the riders had an extra horse, which had a blanket wrapped around its middle with words emblazoned upon it. Leaving the animal in the park, the marauders took off across the railroads tracks, traveling north. The boys stood quietly, and after a while, they went over to the horse and read the inscription: "Liberator Army of the Mexico-Texans." The scared boys ran home and vowed to each other not to say a word to any of their parents. The horse was found the following day, turned over to the Army, and pictures were taken.

Jamie and John, who were in their last year of school that only went to the eleventh grade, and Fred, who was a year behind, began socializing with the military camp soldiers after school. One of the young officers, a Dr. David Hedrick, would take the boys aside and show them how to use the microscope. Fred, who was the most curious, spent many hours observing the different bacteria that caused the different illnesses in the human body. His mentor, Juan Alvarez, and now Dr. Hedrick, had increased his desire to become a doctor more than ever.

Wounded soldiers, who were suffering from fevers, gunshot wounds, malaria, insect and snakebites, pneumonia, and some with consumption, lay on cots, attended by nurses who had come from all parts of the nation. Fred had become very popular with the nurses and with the wounded soldiers, and they would expect him on a daily basis. He would spend hours at their side, observing and listening to every word the doctor and nurses would say. He learned to take blood pressure and temperature readings, and was already being called the "young doctor."

One rainy day during the fall, Memo drove the delivery wagon to Mercedes bringing the news that a family of four, with a sickly mother ready to deliver a child, was found in an ox-cart several miles east of Spanish Acres, having traveled clear from Arkansas. The father was looking for work in the Valley and had gotten lost. The *vaqueros* had found them distressed and starving, and had brought them to Spanish Acres.

Victoria immediately rushed to Spanish Acres and found a family by the name of Anderson, with the mother close to delivering her baby. Very shortly, the mother, with the help of Soledad, Ophelia, Elena, and Olivia gave birth to a little boy. The following day, the woman died and left the husband devastated and having to care for his remaining children. The baby boy was named Aaron Anderson.

Don Federico and James had returned from Mexico City, having been with the ostensibly gracious and charming President Carranza, who had given *Don* Federico a commemorative plaque denoting goodwill relations. They had been his guests for several days, and had even been taken on a two-seater bi-plane ride around the high *Sierra Madre Mountains* surrounding Mexico City, viewing two active volcanoes—a truly fascinating excursion.

But Carranza's conversation was not exactly telling the whole truth, for he avoided mentioning his relations with the Germans and Japanese. Carranza's plans revolved around crushing the United States, but he needed the support of more powerful allies—the Germans and Japanese, who already controlled the seas. Carranza was cynically manipulating the weaker groups, the ignorant and the illiterate, controlling the border with hatred and propaganda. His orders were to kill, derail trains, rob stores, and steal horses and cattle, causing confusion and disorder inside the Texas border.

Carranza's greed was causing the Mexican-Americans to suffer in Texas, by carrying on his international policies with the Germans and Japanese. Farms close to the border on the Mexican side were being used by the Japanese to make bombs from bolts and other bits of metal, all being wrapped in wet cowhide.

Don Federico rode with James to Spanish Acres after hearing the news of the mysterious stranded couple and their newborn child. He was introduced to Mr. Clovis Anderson, a small, thin, man with reddish-brown hair. Anderson, in his grief, spoke very little of his wife or where he was going to bury her. He was incoherent, unsure of what to do with his children, thinking maybe he should return to Arkansas, where his relatives lived.

"The baby needs nourishment and will need a wet nurse, which we can furnish for you," *Don* Federico reassured him. "We have women here with children all the time delivering babies. I don't know if we can take care of the two little girls, but they are welcome to stay, until you have made plans for them."

Clovis Anderson was poor as any person could be. Homeless and destitute, except for the ox-cart he possessed, and with another mouth to feed, he had a problem. The soles of his shoes had holes, and his pants were patched and re-patched. Both he and his clothes were dirty; he stank; he had few teeth in his upper gums, and the lower were a rotten brown. He spoke with a drawl, similar to Roy's language. Up to this time he had never said, "Thank you, for helping us." In spite of his deplorable condition, his background was that of hating any nationality different from his. He was biased and hated foreigners.

"I don't believe in having any Mes'kins nursing my boy. I don't want any greaser feeding my child," he said flatly.

"Well, all right! Everything is not all fine, but—" retorted *Don* Federico, clearing his throat and trying to control his temper, for he was ready to send this rude, uneducated person away after his bigoted remarks. "What do you suggest? The problem is, your baby needs nourishment, and how are you going to provide that?"

They could hear the newborn crying inside. One of the women had made a nipple out of cotton cloth, attached it to a small, glass bottle gave the child *manzanilla* tea with sugar, to relax and settled the baby's stomach, but the baby's bawling continued for lack of milk.

After hours of listening to the agonized crying of the newborn, and with the women in the household ready to pull their hair, Clovis Anderson decided that perhaps the *Don* had sense in what he was saying. Whether it was a white or brown woman feeding him, the newborn only wanted to nurse and bond with the woman. Hunger was a terrible thing. Anderson had once seen a mother dog nursing a baby cat, which was not surprising. Within an hour, they found a woman living in the encampment of the cotton pickers. She worked out in the fields and was nursing a month-old child. *Señora* Guadalupe volunteered, since she had more milk than her child required. Instantly the baby became content, and the ladies from Spanish Acres were relieved.

After a month of continuous griping and not being able to do any work except blacksmithing at Spanish Acres, the ungrateful, warped-minded Clovis Anderson decided to return to his hometown in the Ozarks with his two young daughters, having no choice but to leave young Aaron at Spanish Acres in the care of the resident women. Anderson had been given clean clothes to wear and shoes that fit. *Don* Federico had even given him money to take care of the two little girls. While the *Don* was gone to Mexico for a governmental meeting, Anderson told Roy that he would return several months later and claim little Aaron and visit his wife's grave in the Juelson's cemetery.

⌘ ⌘ ⌘

Because of the war with Germany and the raids coming from the border, several laws were being enforced among the border towns. The German population in Mercedes was getting out of control and becoming what was considered a serious threat. Secret agents were not only investigating Mexican-American families, but citizens of German descent living near the border.

Many times after school, when not playing football, Fred would walk over to Howard and Emma's house and visit with John and Jamie. The twin's father Howard always seemed to have an excuse to visit with his friend, a German by the name of Otto Foster, a strange man who lived several miles northwest of Mercedes. Foster by trade was a horticulturist and entomologist, and lived on a forty-acre secluded farm encircled by mesquite, cactus, and chaparral. Two huge greenhouses were attached to his barn, one full of plants, and the other full of insects.

Once a month, Uncle Howard would drive Fred, John, and Jaime to Otto Foster's place, where they would spend time riding Foster's special breed of horses, which were Peruvians imported from South America. To Fred, this was always a special occasion, to be invited and to be with Howard and the twins, and especially to ride the magnificent horses, which he loved. Mexican workers helped train the Peruvians, which were beautiful animals that trotted and galloped gracefully, and were known for their sideways movements.

Foster had bought the land several years ago while it was cheap. He was a widower and spoke with a thick accent, small in build and balding, and he wore thick lens eyeglasses. He had two married daughters, Heidi Coffman, who lived in Mercedes and had children going to Fred's school, and the other married daughter, Mary Ferguson, who lived on a ranch close to La Feria.

While the boys were riding, Howard and Foster would automatically disappear into a dugout that had been used for a cellar. Inside was radio equipment and instruments for sending Morse code messages. Foster's last name was an alias; his real last name was *Füeir*. For years, he had been exchanging information received from foreign intelligence across Mexico. He was being highly paid by the Germans to research the use of different insects to sabotage the cotton crops, which were the largest moneymaking industry, next to cattle, in the Rio Grande Valley. Howard Ale became aware of Otto's intentions and illegal activities, and with his greedy mind, befriended Otto, wanting to get part of the ill-gotten money that Otto had been secretly receiving since early 1911.

On one occasion, Fred's horse lost a shoe, and he returned to Foster's so one of the blacksmiths could attend to the animal. There was no one outside the residence as he unsaddled the horse and called out for the two older men. The Mexican workers were all either working in the barn or in the greenhouses. He went inside the house and called for his Uncle Howard, but no one answered. He stood in the messy, cluttered kitchen and looked around. On top of a counter, the inquisitive young man found several busy insects inside a glass container. Fred looked closely. Curious, he picked one up and looked at it, then put it inside his shirt pocket. He wanted to show his Army friend Dr. Hedrick, and ask him if he could inspect it under the microscope, since he had never seen this type of insect and found it interesting and unusual.

Immediately, from out of the cellar, Howard and Otto appeared behind him. One cleared his throat, startling Fred. Otto stood numb, staring through his thick spectacles with suspicion. His Uncle Howard looked shaken and nervous, as if being caught doing something he shouldn't. "Back from your ride so soon?" he grumbled.

Fred felt as if draggers had attacked his body. "My horse lost a shoe, so I had to bring him back," he replied innocently.

Howard and Otto glanced at each other and both sighed with relief.

That evening, Fred walked toward the military grounds and found Dr. Hedrick, who was busy attending two wounded soldiers. As always, the doctor smiled and the nurses and other soldiers who were already acquainted with Fred greeted him. Fred headed for the microscope area. He brought the already dead grayish insect and placed it on the dry glass plate. Dr. Hedrick joined him. "What kind of insect is that?" he said, examining it more closely. He called out to one of his assistants, "Max, take a look at this. What do you think?"

Max, a husky, dark-bearded assistant, had studied agriculture before going into the medical profession. He put an eye to the microscope and studied the creature for a little while. "Hmm," he mused. "I believe you're either looking at *anthonomus grandis,* or the pink boll weevil—it's one or the other. Both are pests and dangerous as hell."

"Anth—what?" asked Dr. Hedrick.

"What you're looking at is the dangerous boll weevil," replied Max, "and I'm sure glad it's dead."

"Where did you get this?" questioned Dr. Hedrick, looking seriously at Fred.

"There are millions in a greenhouse north of here, being used for experimental research."

"Good heavens, boy! How in the world did you get a hold of one of these?" Dr. Hedrick said in alarm. He quickly put the insect in alcohol in a glass container with a lid.

"A man by the name of Otto Foster has a greenhouse where he does scientific research," answered Fred feeling the pressure of having done something wrong. He was always getting himself into trouble because of his curiosity.

Dr. Hedrick glanced at Max. "Better contact the head of agriculture and tell them the story. I don't believe they are aware of what's happening or know of the experiments being conducted out there." He slapped Fred on the back and said, "Good work, son!"

⌘ ⌘ ⌘

By the end of the long hot summer, the natives were anxious for a cool fall. *Don* Federico and James had returned from Mexico via Brownsville and spent time in Mercedes, taking some time for leisure. The newspapers were full of news concerning Governor James Ferguson being indicted on nine charges of misappropriation of public funds, and suspicious income and financial ties. He was being impeached and removed from office, to be succeeded by William Pettus Hobby, who became the youngest governor of the State of Texas.

The plague of the *roots of evil* showed its face everywhere, and corruption flourished in every department of the Texas state government, where greed and the love of money thrived. By taking advantage of a bad situation and chaotic circumstances, judges, sheriffs, deputies, law officers, and Texas Rangers were all on the take and often being paid under the table, giving them the opportunity to enrich themselves.

Meanwhile, the killing of innocent Mexicans-American continued. "Shot to death while resisting arrest," was a common phrase and was becoming routine as lynching. Most of the reports were falsely written by the law enforcement officers. Each patted the other on the back for any incident blaming the Mexican-American individual. Many stories were kept hush-hush among themselves, honoring their own code of silence. The *Corpus Christi Caller* and the *San Antonio Express* had a few reporters that felt sympathy for the Mexican-American families and put in writing the truth of what was really happening. The finding of dead Mexicans created no interest; however, if a white American was killed, the people immediately wanted revenge.

CHAPTER 33

In the late fall, a tall, muscular man in his forties, wearing a khaki uniform, approached the Juelson residence and knocked on the door. Victoria, who was expecting her second child, greeted him at the door and led him into the parlor. It was Major Morris McCormach from San Antonio, Josie's husband, who had been sent to the Valley to help the battalion of the First Illinois Cavalry. He stood looking around the house almost in a daze but not saying a word. Victoria found him strange acting and asked if she could get him something to drink. He asked for a glass of water and asked if he could talk to *Don* Federico. He needed to discuss something with him regarding his wife.

"Is Aunt Josie all right? How is she feeling?" Victoria frowned while questioning him. She ordered one of the servants to bring in some lemonade and sat down heavily in one of the sofa chairs. She turned to face her uncle and said, "Father is not here, but will return by train later this afternoon. He spends most of his time in Brownsville and in Matamoros with the Mexican and German consuls."

"I see!" McCormach said. He lowered his head, looking serious, while his fingers nervously folded his military cap. His eyes were concentrated on the floor, as if he were afraid to look up at Victoria.

In the long, tense silence, Victoria asked, "Is something wrong with Aunt Josie? We have not heard from her in several years, not even after she had her child."

"That's what I have to speak with your father about," he said, rather rudely, as though it were none of her business.

"Is something wrong with Aunt Josie or your child?" asked Victoria, becoming concerned with her uncle's strangely reticent attitude.

"Very much so," he said bluntly. "That's the reason I have to discuss your Aunt Josie's problem with your father. Josie was committed to an insane asylum about a year ago. I have been kept so busy with the troops, and the German war, that I have not had time to write anyone."

"A nut house!" retorted Victoria. "Impossible!" She stood up and watched his facial expressions.

Morris McCormach swallowed his lemonade in haste, put the glass down on the table and stood up. "I'll return tonight and speak with your father on this subject. It is best that I speak to him and explain what has been happening with his sister." Putting his cap on, he walked out of the house and disappeared in the direction of the military camp.

That evening, Morris McCormach met with *Don* Federico in his private library. Victoria and the servants could feel that something was seriously wrong by the major's attitude and actions. From outside the library, loud voices could be heard.

James was reading a book, became uneasy, and excused himself to exercise in the nearby park.

Victoria paced nervously up and down the corridors of the big house, knowing that something unusual was going to take place. She was getting proficient in card reading and foretelling events that came about as she had predicted. Before her father had returned home that evening, she had read cards indicating that her father was going on a long trip; however, it was concerning a relative, not politics. In the cards, she saw her father upset concerning additional responsibilities. What more responsibilities could *Don* Federico have?

It wasn't long before the door to the library opened, and Morris McCormach stormed out the entrance door without saying goodbye. The servants and Victoria had waited for an eternity, glancing at each other nervously, wondering what eventful thing was coming. Before long *Don* Federico walked out of his library scowling and informed the servants to get his clothes ready, for he would be leaving on the first train to San Antonio.

Victoria's predictions were coming to pass.

After he arrived in San Antonio, *Don* Federico went directly to the San Antonio Mental Hospital, which was a nice name for an insane asylum. The place was located in an isolated area among the undulating hills of the city and looked more like a brick prison surrounded by a high cement fence. He requested to talk to the doctor in charge of administration and was escorted into a small, sparsely furnished office. After a while, a thin, balding man wearing glasses and a white coat entered the room and introduced himself as Dr. Adkins. He had brought with him a large envelope of what looked like confidential patient information.

The *Don* stood up, holding his hat in his left hand, and shook hands with the doctor. "I'm Federico Juelson. I'm here to see about my sister, Josie McCormach."

The doctor sat down at the table and glanced over the papers for several minutes. "We are talking about a very serious condition that Mrs. McCormach has," he said finally.

"Which is what?" *Don* Federico interrupted. "Josie has never been sick, and there has never been any kind of craziness in our family."

"Perhaps not," Dr. Adkins answered, clearing his throat, while thinking what to say next, and being put on the spot. "But the mind is difficult, and it is hard to detect what goes on inside our brains. Few know. Many times, generations go by before anything is evident."

"Why was my sister put in this place, anyway? She has no business being in a place like this!" *Don* Federico questioned him, his voice rising in frustration.

Dr. Adkins detected this and frowned, eying him. He spoke calmly and in low tones, a habit formed through long years of dealing with his patients. He continued reading the notes. "According to this report, your sister was brought in sedated about a year ago. She had apparently been given several pills to calm her down. Awakened, Mrs. McCormach became violent, hitting some of the assistants and nurses. They were unable to restrain her, so we were forced to give her several electrical shock treatments to calm her down. She is diagnosed as a psychoneurotic person, called psychotic, with a defective nervous system, and her condition, of course, is incurable. Her condition may become dangerous. She has to be kept in a restraint area and watched around the clock."

It was unfamiliar medical language using big words, completely unrelated to *Don* Federico's educational knowledge and beyond his comprehension. While going over the notes and concentrating on what to say, Dr. Adkins felt the tension mounting, never looking toward *Don* Federico, whose face was now flushed with anger, but kept looking at the reports, slipping pieces of paper on top of each other, and adjusting his glasses.

"Is she violent now?" *Don* Federico asked.

"Not after she had the shock treatment. She seems to be happy and calm now and seems to like it here."

Why, of course! He thought. *People are dying to come here to stay—it's so wonderful being given electric shocks!* Before he had a chance to answer there was a scuffle down the hall and bells began clanging. There were loud screams, a scraping of feet on the marble floor, and people running. An assistant poked his head in the door, requesting the doctor's assistance as quickly as possible.

"Is Henry, the big German brute, out again?" Dr. Adkins inquired of the assistant.

"Two of us are not able to handle him. We need an injection, quickly!" The assistant, who was a big man himself, was breathing heavily, and sweat was running down his forehead. He stepped back into the hall.

Dr. Adkins excused himself and hurried out, forgetting about the confidential papers on the table.

Don Federico stood up and waited for several moments and looked toward the door. Everybody was busy elsewhere. Curious, he stepped toward the table and eyed the written material, occasionally sneaking a quick look toward the door. Nobody seemed to be too concerned about his presence. He stood for many minutes reading the notes. He was shocked and felt the blood drain from his body. The papers told in writing how Morris McCormach had paid a great deal of money to the insane asylum to commit his wife. In a military correspondence letter was an explanation of how he wanted her, in time, to be put away. *Don* Federico grabbed the letter and confidential papers and slipped them inside his coat pocket, leaving the folder and other information.

He walked to the receptionist area where a young lady was attending the desk, and requested by name to see his sister. Everybody from doctors, nurses, and assistants were being distracted by the commotion down the hallway. The assistant never spoke, being preoccupied with paperwork, but she took her keys and found the one for Josie's room. She walked with *Don* Federico down a long corridor. The assistant opened the door, they both stepped in, and then she walked away, leaving the *Don* by himself with the patient.

In a small, dark room with a tiny caged window allowing little light, the *Don* found his sister sitting in a rocking chair swaying back and forth in rhythm, hugging herself and staring at the empty wall.

"Josie! Josie!" whispered *Don* Federico, crouching down by her side. "Get your things. You're coming with me!"

Josie recognized *Don* Federico in the dim light and began speaking his nickname. "Lico, you have come to take me home?" Josie stood up and, in an emotional embrace, the two cried. They were the only two left alive from the older generation.

Full of emotion and grief, *Don* Federico had to use his handkerchief. "Come! We do not have much time," he said. "You're getting out of here! You're coming home with me!"

Josie was in a daze, her hands cupping her mouth. "And you have forgiven me! You have forgiven me, haven't you Lico?" One minute her mind made sense in what she was saying, and then, it would switch into a defiant, belligerent attitude. "If you haven't forgiven me, I will not go anywhere!"

"Come, Josie! Be quiet! Be still! Why, yes, I love you. You are my sister, and I have forgiven you." He spoke directly to her only inches from her face. He would say anything at this moment to calm her. He had to hurry. He had to drag her out of this insane place. He figured if you weren't insane when you went in, you were when you left. She wore a long pink flannel nightgown, but that would not matter. He would buy her some clothes later, much later, after he took her out of this place.

He found a white shawl and held it around her shoulders as the two walked down the long, dark, passageway. He warned her not to say a word. He hesitated at the end of the hall, peeked around the corner and saw that the reception desk was empty, as were the hallways. *Don* Federico hurried Josie out of the building and into freedom, into a waiting new, shiny, black Packard automobile he had just bought in San Antonio.

⌘ ⌘ ⌘

Victoria, Grandmother Gloria, and the rest of the Juelson household, along with Emma and her household, Ricardo's mother and sister, and friends and neighbors were in complete awe of *Don* Federico's heroic escapade. Everyone was also admiring the new shining, black car that was sitting under the breezeway next to the veranda. Victoria and Fred were especially thrilled, and both wanted to learn to drive it.

Victoria was uneasy, but she had to respect her father's wishes. She was not sure if Mercedes was the right choice to place her aunt, with little Luis Martin still so young and another child on the way. After all, Josie did not act completely normal. How crazy was she? Victoria would have to hire a nurse or two around the clock to watch over her aunt for the protection of the family.

Josie's appearance was also pitiful; her hair was completely snow white, tangled and unkempt. A person needed to catch her in just the right moment when asking her a question, for she did not speak in logical sentences. Most of the time, she babbled incoherently, with no comprehension of what anyone was saying to her.

During dinner, *Don* Federico told the household the true story of what had happened to his sister while being married to McCormach. He had abused her for years. He would habitually beat her and yell at her, using abusive language. That, perhaps, and too many beatings about her head had caused a broken blood vessel in her brain. Josie had also suffered several broken ribs and fractures, according to the report he had read. What was really tragic was that she had delivered a black child. According to the story, because of her loneliness, she had an affair with a Negro handyman working in the Army barracks.

As *Don* Federico continued with his story, his voice would often crack. What had become of the Negro baby was a mystery. Nobody knew if the child was dead or alive. Nobody would discuss it. Not even Josie knew what had happened to her baby. The doctors in the mental facility were aware of the delivery of the Negro child, but no other information was available.

As if the beatings and abuse were not bad enough, McCormach used this indiscretion against her and began bringing prostitutes home. He suspended her by the feet, naked, in the closet and had her watch while he made love to the trollops. Then, more beatings would occur. With all of the battering and abuse and not having family to help her, her mind snapped. She was put on tranquillizers and was shoved into the mental hospital to end her life of desperation.

"Does McCormach know that Aunt Josie is now staying here in Mercedes?" inquired Victoria, feeling threatened and horrified after hearing about her Uncle Morris's abusiveness toward women.

"Absolutely not, and nobody better repeat any of what I have just said," he demanded. He emphasized his words by hitting his hand on the table, rattling the china and dishes, as tears misted his eyes.

Overwhelmed with grief, *Don* Federico excused himself from the table. The rest of the family glanced at one another in total shock. Without saying a word, they continued eating. The servants, after hearing the story, traded glances and continued serving. James looked down at his plate and ate in silence. The household was uncertain how to act or to speak about the strange, crazy aunt who was now hidden in the furthest back room of the house. Fred looked at Carlos. Carlos glanced at Fred. Mischievous thoughts about their nutty old aunt whirled in their heads; the boys found it amusing, and the two couldn't help giggling.

During the following months, there were reports of several Mexicans with cattle, camped out near the Mercedes pumps. Without any explanation, Morris McCormach and several of his cavalry shot and killed five of them, two were caught and hung, and the rest escaped across the river. The dead bodies were brought to Mercedes and displayed outside at one of the grain warehouses, so that all the citizens of the city would see the punishment and be forewarned of what would happen to Mexicans not complying with the laws and regulations of the town. McCormach, who lived by his own high expectations, was given words of praise and recognition by the newspapers for his heroism. The white citizens even threw a banquet in his honor. Everyone was singing, *You're in the Army Now*, and the most popular song of the war, *Over There*. Later, a bottle of expensive wine was delivered to Morris McCormach's headquarters with a note from an anonymous person congratulating him on his bravery.

Don Federico read the local headlines and fumed. What was not being reported was the fact that the so-called bandits were a group of Mexican *vaqueros* delivering cattle from Mexico to one of the Mexican ranchers in the Valley. The Mexican *vaqueros*, not being familiar with their location, got lost. Most of them did not speak English; they were innocent, working Mexicans with families and several children to feed. The Mexican-American citizens were appalled at this abuse and the bigotry displayed and complained to *Don* Federico, legislators, senators, and higher-ups.

The day following his celebration party, Morris McCormach was found dead.

⌘   ⌘   ⌘

In November, Victoria gave birth to a nine-pound baby girl that she named Maria Theresa Del Calderóne. The baby was too large, and she was in hard labor for over twenty-six hours, which completely exhausted her. She spent several weeks in her bedroom, while two wet nurses were brought in to help feed the baby.

In his Brownsville office, *Don* Federico was able to talk to his attorney friend Tomas Canalo, now a State Representative, who was receiving threats from several of the Texas Rangers. One of the threats came from a Ranger named Frank Horner, a friend and buddy of ex-Ranger Hanson, who was considered a renegade and was still running from the law. Horner was a reincarnated roughneck from the last century of the Austin-Taylor regime, a tall brute of a man with mean, cold eyes. He hated Mexicans and anyone that was involved with them. Stories were told that he had shot a Mexican prisoner in his jail cell because he snored. It was no wonder that Hanson still ran loose in Mexico with the aid of fearless Frank Horner and other corrupt Rangers. It was rumored that guns and rifles were being transported across the border by the Texas Rangers during the night for favors of Mexican tequila, mescal, and women.

Canalo had put a campaign together and had won the Democratic State Representative for his district in Brownsville. One of Canalo's last cases had been a run-in with Frank Horner, who tried to finagle twenty acres away from a simple-minded Mexican-American rancher. Canalo won, and the jubilant farmer rewarded Canalo with money and also with several milk cows. Frank Horner's hatred fomented an outburst of wrath and the desire to get rid of Canalo. The Rangers had immunity and power of pardon from the governor and the freedom to terrorize and kill the Mexican people; but Canalo had the power to file charges on the Texas Rangers for their unfit conduct and the disregarding of civil rights. With *Don* Federico and his secretary James agreeing that it was time, Canalo had enough confidence and plenty of evidence. He wrote up all of the horror stories, filed charges against the Texas Rangers, and presented the list to the joint House-Senate Committee.

ROOTS OF INDIFFERENCE

Returning home to Mercedes, *Don* Federico was confronted by Clovis Anderson, who had returned to Spanish Acres from Arkansas, wanting to know if the *Don* wanted to adopt his baby son, Aaron. Anderson conceded that he was not capable of taking care of his son, as he was unable to work and needed money. *Don* Federico made it clear to Anderson that if he were going to raise his boy, it had to be legal. Anderson agreed, and within a week, papers were drawn up that designated Aaron was legally a Juelson child. Before Anderson left, *Don* Federico handed him a thick white envelope of money.

Within a period of a week, Victoria had more than her hands full. She had now inherited Aaron, who was two months old, had her own baby girl, and little Luis, who would be four years old in December.

The Posadas and Christmas came and went, and before long, the new year of 1918. The Ale's twins were going to graduate in the spring and, as customary, leave home to take up studies in college. Jamie was going to Austin to study law, and John engineering. It would be Fred's last year in the local school, as it only went to the eleventh grade. The following year, Fred would be heading for Houston Medical School.

The violence on the border grew worse; the newly elected Governor William Hobby continued the policy initiated by Governor Ferguson, giving even more authority to the Texas Rangers, called "Loyalty Rangers," to continue policing the border. It was once again business as usual. Stories began to intensify regarding the heavy-handed bullying of the local Mexican population: the confiscating of their firearms; the entering of private homes without warrants; making improper arrests without explanation.

In one instance, the sheriff of a small town close to Brownsville refused to hand over his Mexican prisoners to the Loyalty Rangers. One of the Rangers was Frank Horner. The Rangers ransacked the jail, took the prisoners, and hanged all of them, most of whom were American citizens. Relatives in mourning complained. The Cameron County Sheriff filed charges against the Rangers and threatened to jail the next law enforcement officer who threatened him. Within two weeks, the sheriff was found shot to death execution style, riddled with bullets in his back. Reports heard later were that all charges had been dismissed. Within the year, new legislation required immigrants to pass literacy tests and severely restricted immigration into the United States.

In January of 1918, newspapers all over the Rio Grande Valley were filled with the shocking news from the tiny community of Porvenir, Texas, where fifteen Mexican-American boys and old men ranging from sixteen to seventy years of age were shot to death by heavily armed Texas Rangers, ranchmen, and several members of U.S. Cavalry, who descended on the village during the night, lined up the fifteen prisoners, and shot them to death, execution-style. Newsmen and reporters from all parts of the country swarmed into the area wanting to get a better picture of the scandalous news of what would soon become known as the Porvenir Massacre, especially when it included the involvement of the U. S. Cavalry.

The few Mexican lawyers in the Rio Grande Valley protested, including Tomas Canalo, all wanting justice for these cruel actions. Governors, Senators, and State Representatives from other states questioned the government of Texas, and how it was being run—by hoodlums? Many of the white citizens who learned of the horror were completely appalled, declaring that perhaps they were as safe living in Mexico as living in Texas. With this war going on, what else could happen?

Don Federico and James were ordered to help out with the investigation, since many of the people spoke only Spanish. It took a long grueling day and a half by train getting to the town of Presidio, Texas. The hotel accommodations were slim to none, so they stayed with friendly families who knew what had happened and offered them living quarters until the investigation was done.

In the rural community of Porvenir, several of the older, sickly Mexican men had been spared and the *Don* and *El Guapo* were able to talk to them and get their version of what took place. Many of the Mexican-American women were left widows, and over fifty children were orphaned, not counting those women who were pregnant. The widow ladies were anxious to give their accounts as well. Dozens of newspaper reporters were on the scene, making it convenient for the *Don* and James to use their skills as interpreters to clarify the facts.

Many told the same story: the Texas Rangers and several other masked *gringos* searched their little huts. Already the accused were "white-washing" the story and blaming each other for the killing. There were conflicting stories, saying that they were killing bandits. The story did not fly, for it contained too many contradictions. The newspapers referred to it as the worst Texas Ranger misconduct in history; however, the United States Cavalry supposedly had nothing to do with the killings. Several of the Mexican-American widows filed claims with the Mexican authorities and with the Mexican Ambassador, Ygnacio Bonilla, newly appointed by Carranza. The city of Presidio, Texas, took no action and claimed no responsibility for any of the killings.

Don Federico and James returned exhausted and troubled after a week of notes and sending letters to their Congressmen and State Senators. They filed the reports and filed charges blaming the Texas Rangers for the shocking atrocities. A special separate letter was mailed to Representative Tomas Canalo in Brownville with a clear statement describing the crimes perpetrated against the Mexican-American people.

Shortly after the reports, *Don* Federico and James were ordered to travel to the city of Ciudad Victoria and visit with *General* Nafarrate. He had proclaimed himself provisional governor of the state of Tamaulipas, and they needed to get his statement. The United States did not want any more trouble with Mexico. The two men were met with a friendly embrace, and introduced to Nafarrate's newlywed wife, Maria. The couple sent them home with dozens of gifts, including sweet chocolate and cases of Mexican liquors.

After their return, *Don* Federico had messages from Canalo telling him that they had made good progress. Governor Hobby had been under so much pressure that he ordered the disbandment of Company B of the Texas Rangers and had dismissed five of the accused killers, as if that were any consolation for the innocent deaths. It became front page news in all of the big newspapers.

In early April, newspapers confirmed the death of *General* Nafarrate, who was murdered near the city of Tampico, Mexico. James was terrified. *Don* Federico was heartbroken over the death, and it took several weeks before his nerves settled. *General* Nafarrate had been his friend. In confidence, *General* Nafarrate had confirmed that Carranza was playing the strategy game regarding the United States and using the German money for his own use. Making a threat against the President of Mexico in public was risky, and it had cost Nafarrate his life.

On a dreary, rainy day in early April, Otto Foster was arrested escaping into Mexico in a horse-drawn wagon, with several trunks full of his possessions. Special agents from the Agriculture Department, secret agents, and some Texas Rangers searched Foster's residence and found radio transmissions with letters and coding, all in the German language. Many papers indicated several plots and contracts with German spies across the river, and coding to U-boats out in the Gulf of Mexico. Otto Foster's bug greenhouse, which had been left wide open, was subsequently destroyed, but it appeared that all of the insects had been turned loose to destroy the cotton crops in the Valley. Otto's prized horses were gone, his workers had disappeared, and his place was left vacant.

The news became sensational and threatening to the citizens of Mercedes. Having marauding bandits, lynchings, and killings was bad enough, but having German spies in their own backyard was dangerous and even more unspeakable. The newspaper had gotten word that information had been leaked to authorities regarding Otto's insect experiments. Everyone in town wanted to know who the individual was who had discovered the plot, and Otto's two daughters began asking questions about the informer. Fred never confessed.

Three days later, secret agents arrested three German-Americans in Mercedes on the basis that they were collaborating with the Germans and charged them with treason, one of whom was Howard Ale. The Ale's household was searched and ransacked. Emma was so beside herself with shame that she became physically ill; she took to her bedroom, locked the door, and would not eat. The twins were in total shock and refused to go to school. Felicia, seven months pregnant and living with her parents, turned to *Don* Federico and James for advice. She hated Howard Ale, but hated even worse the shame her mother was enduring, especially with all of the wagging tongues in the community.

The concerned Mercedes Chamber of Commerce passed an ordinance that no German language was to be spoken in the town or schools, including public or private places, and that it was also illegal to trade or lecture in the language used by the enemy. The Lutheran Church services that were conducted in German now had to be spoken in English. Anyone caught speaking the German language was arrested and suspected of being a spy; everyone was walking on eggshells.

Don Federico and James intervened with the federal courts on behalf of Howard Ale. They spoke to Captain Bishop, and Judge Barnes in Brownville, but were told the processing took time and there was nothing they could do but wait. Ale was charged with treason, and it could mean death. Meanwhile, he was in a federal cell, nervously chewing his fingernails and claiming chest pains.

Within months, Howard Ale died of a supposed heart attack, but the reports were left unclear as to the actual cause of his death. While going through the torment and shame of her husband's accusation of being disloyal to his country, Emma had lost fifty pounds. But the community opened their arms to her and the twins, bringing food, and cards and letters of condolence, for she was well thought of, having been involved in all kinds of community services, helping people however she could, teaching the Anglo women Spanish, and donating to charities.

Within the next two months, Felicia, so distressed, gave birth to a six-pound baby boy and named him Steven Allen Land; Emma was beside herself with joy.

In the month of June, several horrible incidents took place. A group of American Army soldiers were swimming with their horses near La Feria pumps. One of the soldiers slipped and drowned, and while making the search for the drowned soldier, a lieutenant in charge of the group crossed the river. The lieutenant was murdered and two of the soldiers, who went looking for their commander across the border, were taken prisoners by the *Carranzistas*.

Telegram reports were sent to Brownsville immediately by *El Guapo* James, and he and *Don* Federico were called to intercede. Many hours were spent with the *Carranzista* officials, and finally they obtained and returned the body of the young lieutenant. The other two soldiers, who had been roughed up by the *Carranzistas*, were grateful to be back at Camp Llano Grande.

Carranza soldiers and revolutionists battled on the Texas side of the river close to Progresso later that same month, and over fifty men were reported killed. Apparently there had been a train robbery in which over sixty thousand dollars in gold had been taken. The gold was never recovered.

The headlines again brought a shocker: Czar Nicholas II and the rest of Russia's royal family had been executed by the Bolsheviks.

As the year progressed, the plight of the Mexican-Americans grew considerably worse. They called this period in time, *Hora de Sangre*, the Bloody Hour, because the Texas Rangers would shoot and kill innocent Mexican-American men who were supposedly mistaken for Mexican bandits. There was a tremendous wall of fear between the two nationalities, such that the white Anglo citizen was advised to stay away from the Mexican-American *barrios*.

Eventually, after several quiet months of no killing, lynching, or shooting incidents, it appeared that peace was finally coming to the Valley. People were hopeful the war with the Germans was ending as well, for there was talk of negotiations.

John and Jamie graduated from high school and began making preparations for the University of Texas in Austin.

Ricardo returned from Mexico, making his presence known, and claimed his percentage of the cotton sales. With his pockets full of money, he would splurge in the red light district with wild women and liquor across the river. He was living in Matamoros part of the time and returned to Monterrey trying to reclaim his property, hoping to resume the lifestyle in which he was raised. He would visit his mother and sister in Mercedes but only stayed for a week. He saw Yolanda and then departed again, knowing with confidence that *Don* Federico would take care of his family.

Ricardo did not assume any responsibility of spending time with his newborn daughter. Victoria's spine would stiffen when he was around, and she continually wished him dead. On his last visit he ordered Victoria to get his dinner ready, and Victoria asked the kitchen servants to fix it for him. He then became hateful and insulted the servants on their cooking. He spat his food out, accusing them of trying to poison him, and threw his plate clear across the room.

Poison! Victoria's thoughts began taking an evil turn. *Not a bad idea!*

At the same time, *la Señora* Del Calderóne and Ricardo's sister walked in to see the new granddaughter, the baby Aaron, and little Luis Martin. They stood in awe seeing Ricardo angry, brushing himself off with the table napkin, and food and broken china scattered all over the dining room. Servants were busy picking up the debris, and others were on their knees with damp cloths, wiping up the tile floor. "Ricardo!" his mother said, in exasperation.

Don Federico, who heard the commotion from his office, walked into the kitchen and viewed the disastrous atmosphere. "What happened here?" he asked. "What's going on?"

It was Ricardo who spoke. "This food is terrible!" he scoffed. "Pigs might enjoy this food, but I don't!" He continued belittling and insulting the Juelson clan.

It did not set well with *Don* Federico, who was already fed up with *la Señora* Del Calderóne, who complained all the time and had become a pain in his side. He also resented her comments ridiculing Victoria's children, as if his daughter had the children all by herself. And Ricardo was never home, never a father, and to this day had never considered supporting them.

"Are you saying that the food is not to your liking?" said the *Don*, irritated. He crossed his arms over his chest, and addressed the egotistical ass that was his son-in-law. He was completely disgusted with both Ricardo and his father, *El General.*

Ricardo stood up and demanded a better quality of food. Victoria stood there holding her baby, with Fred, Carlos, *El Guapo*, all of the kitchen servants, and *Señora* Hinojosa now observing the skirmish.

"We all had the same meal earlier. And nobody is dead—nobody got sick. If you expect a better meal, then why don't you go buy the food fresh and have the servants fix it for you?" The *Don's* voice was rising in anger.

Ricardo gasped. His mother was dumbstruck and put little Luis down. His sister was stunned.

"No need to be shocked!" *Don* Federico answered hotly, staring at Ricardo and the rest of the Del Calderóne clan. "Don't you think it's about time you started being a father to your children and started supporting them like a real man supports his family? You find the time to be away and have all of your financial business across the border. Sounds strange, don't you think? You seem to enjoy your marriage as a regular bachelor! Demanding and giving out orders as if you owned this home and the world. Your attitude stinks! Who do you think you are? You act like you have a corncob up your ass. Your time of being single—being a playboy—is over!"

"Why support bastards!" Ricardo's nasty remark cut like a knife into flesh.

"Ricardo!" *Señora* Del Calderóne's voice rang out. "How can you say such a thing?"

"Why sure, Mother!" he snapped. "Haven't the Juelsons told you the real story?" He turned his attention to his mother and sister who stood stunned. "Don't you remember how they were in such a hurry for us to get married? Well! It was because Victoria was already pregnant! Long time family friends—huh! They were using us! I was set up! It was real convenient for their cover-up."

Señora Del Calderóne found a chair and sat down next to the table. Her forehead rested on her left hand and with her right, she held a handkerchief to her face. Magdalena's countenance was drained of color. She went toward her mother and began comforting her by patting her back. *Señora* Hinojosa picked up little Luis and walked out of the dining room to her upstairs bedroom. *El Guapo* excused himself and went to his quarters. Fred and Carlos stood wide-eyed, mouths open, feeling the explosion from the military cannon was coming any minute now. Fire and brimstone—the truth was coming out!

"So, little Luis Martin is not our grandson," cried *Señora* Del Calderóne. "What about little Maria Theresa?"

Victoria screamed at Ricardo. "You know darn well that little Maria Theresa is your daughter! What an excuse to keep away and not be responsible. Who do you think you are?"

"As for little Maria Theresa being my daughter, I do not know that!" he said, thus excusing himself and leaving him without any responsibilities.

Señora Del Calderóne started to cry. "I cannot believe this! I cannot believe that my *comadre, Doña* Francisca, would lie to me. I knew there was something wrong with this marriage all along, but I could not put my finger on what was happening. I wish that my husband was here to witness all of this."

"Wait a minute!" *Don* Federico interjected. "Who is using who? Let's get the story straight, before we go any further. Ricardo has known all along the true story. We have discussed the situation and both agreed." The *Don* proceeded to detail their previous agreement and described the final resolution of Ricardo receiving half of the cotton money. Ricardo had accepted it to stay in the marriage. But Ricardo had overstepped his bounds and had taken advantage of the situation.

Don Federico also revealed to *la Señora* Del Calderóne: "As for your husband, *Señora*, he is very much alive and well, living very comfortably dealing covertly with the Germans in Matamoros and getting rich. Why, hasn't Ricardo told you?"

Señora Del Calderóne walked over to Ricardo. "You have known? You have always known where your father was hiding? You have kept it away from me? For shame! Why?"

Ricardo never moved. They all knew the *Don* was telling the truth. *La Señora* slapped her son across the face several times, her anger raging. "You've been with your father all this time and have never said anything to me, while your sister and I have struggled? What kind of a son are you?"

Victoria's face lit up with an exultant feeling of triumph; perhaps now her mother-in-law would realize what kind of a son she really had. He had never been a husband or a father. However, the Calderónes had never liked Victoria, regardless of the outcome of the marriage relationship. She was glad her father had finally exposed Ricardo's true character.

La Señora Del Calderóne cursed, saying hateful words. She cursed the ground in Mercedes, the entire area, the people, and their unsophisticated customs, and said she wished she were back living in Monterrey. The two women walked out of the house, Magdalena's arm around the shoulders of her terribly distraught mother, leaving Ricardo embarrassed and red-faced.

In spite of all of the commotion, the selfish Ricardo, without saying a word, rubbed his cheeks and picked up his hat and left. Victoria assumed he probably went to visit the insatiable Yolanda at Spanish Acres, since they were both alike, and she was more likely to feed him. He had money in his pocket, a hatred of not getting his way, and a ruthless ambition to get rich.

No sooner said than done in cursing the peaceful area, in the fall of that year soldiers throughout the military posts started dying from a germ the Anglos called the "flu." Since the majority of the people were of Mexican ancestry, they called it "Spanish influenza." Families with children became victims of the deadly virus; it was already interwoven with the spread of a deadly whooping cough epidemic. The children and the old were particularly vulnerable, regardless of race or color. According to the rumors, it came from the many soldiers returning home from the war in Europe and ended up in a military post in Kansas. The soldiers were then being reassigned to the post in the Valley where emergency guards on the border were needed.

It became a worldwide epidemic. Hundreds and thousands of families became sick. People were afraid to touch each other or embrace, and heaven forbid, kiss, for fear of catching the virus. Schools, churches, and businesses were closed, social events cancelled; people could not work and the economy suffered a drastic loss. The traffic crossing the river between the two counties became less, and business began to suffer.

People from the churches began saying that it was a curse from God. With the Great War raging in Europe and so many dying now with the flu, the world was surely coming to an end. The community began praying. Perhaps this was what God intended all along, and in the end a blessing, many would say. Nevertheless, millions died throughout the world, and in the Valley many hundreds passed away. The influenza epidemic was unlike anything seen in world history since the Black Plague. The only profitable commodity was caskets—they couldn't make them fast enough.

There was no Christmas celebration that year. Communities did not make social contact with each other for fear of contracting the disease. Multiple caskets were shipped by train carrying the bodies of dead soldiers to their home destinations. Hundreds of caskets became a problem in the crowded cemeteries, for even in death, there was discrimination—where to bury the bodies? The Mexicans were buried in their own section, and the whites in theirs.

Fred had been warned; he was forbidden to visit any of the military camps or the medical soldiers. Emma and Felicia stayed away from everyone as long as possible, not socializing at all. Word was sent to *Don* Federico that one of the flu victims had been Miss Bell, the piano teacher.

Fortunately, by the coming of the new year, the scare was over.

CHAPTER 34

The year of 1919 rolled in with newspaper headlines proclaiming "Prohibition," banning the manufacturing, sale, and transportation of alcohol with the ratification of the Eighteenth Amendment to the U.S. Constitution, to take effect in 1920. This, of course, was a joke. No levelheaded, *macho* individual close to the border was going to stop drinking alcohol! And no one did. Contraband liquor from Mexico became profitable. Drinking was done privately. Jazz was born, and up north there was a new generation of unconventional, daring women called "flappers," with changing hairstyles, and dresses that were looser and shorter.

Just when everyone thought the racial hostilities were dying down, there came another scandal of nineteen charges of misconduct and indictments against the Loyalty Texas Rangers. It was estimated that over 5,000 Mexican-Americans were killed by the Rangers between 1914 and 1919, but there were many more deaths that were not recorded. Millions of dollars in property and merchandise were destroyed in the unrest during this time. The Texas legislature formed a joint House-Senate Committee to look into the charges, headed by *Don* Federico's friend, Tomas Canalo, who had compelling evidence of atrocities against the Mexican-American people. Canalo received death threats from several Texas Rangers, especially Ranger Frank Horner. His hatred toward Canalo became so abhorrent that Texas Governor Hobby had to intervene with legal restraint.

Many ranchers and business owners of Mexican-American descent throughout the Valley were called to testify against the Loyalty Rangers, with testimonies that lasted over two weeks. Each told his own story of the injustices toward their families and neighbors and of the many sordid acts of brutality by the Texas Rangers that they had witnessed.

One of them was *Don* Federico, who accused the Rangers of taking advantage of the governor's pardon and of abusing their oath. He told the committee that the Rangers took advantage of their appointed authority and acted more like vigilante squads. Because of their '*roots of indifference*,' thousands of innocent Mexican families suffered, and many of them fled the area for fear of being killed. The city of Brownsville already saw growing opposition to the Texas Rangers, which reached a climax in this sweeping legislative investigation, although it raised an uproar among some Anglo citizens who had forgotten the true meaning of democracy.

In the end, and as a result of so many eyewitness testimonies, the State of Texas found it necessary to abolish the Loyalty Texas Rangers, thus closing for the moment a "black era" in history for its Mexican-American citizens. The Texas legislature reduced their forces and recruited individuals of higher standards, increasing their pay and establishing a new force with new orders of enforcement. All so-called special Ranger groups were disbanded, and the force was reduced to a group of fifteen high quality officers. Citizens would have the right to articulate complaints against the Rangers regarding any further abuses or misdeeds. However, mistrust of the Rangers never left the Mexican-American community.

New changes began with the new reforms of the Texas Rangers, but it did not change the uneasiness between the two groups. There had been too many deaths of young Mexican-Americans in the long reign of terror, and many of the old core Mexican-American families resented the white *gringos*. The many justifiable changes in Texas laws would not bring back their sons from the grave.

Changes were also being made in the Mercedes educational system. So many children were coming in from the rural ranch areas that the public schools were at full capacity. The curriculum was expanded, and the city had to deal with buying land to build another school.

Money was donated by many of the Mexican-American families who had small businesses and wanted a new Lady of Mercy Church, with a parochial school. Lots south of the railroad tracks in the Anglo section were given to the Catholic Church by the American Rio Grande Land and Irrigation Company. This raised eyebrows of the Anglo city fathers, but, since it was a church and not yet built, the matter was laid to rest.

In the headlines, the Allied troops in Europe were winning the war, and a peace conference met in Paris to sign the Treaty of Versailles. In Hollywood, the three actors called the "flying Barrymores" were making movie headlines. And in New York, the escape artist Harry Houdini, who freed himself from strait jackets and chains, was considered the best stunt performer in history.

Across the border in Mexico news of the killing of Emiliano Zapata sent chills up the spine of many of the Mexican people, who had dreams of Zapata one day being their leader. Zapata was slain, having been led into a trap by one of Carranza's officers, who set up the ambush and was greatly rewarded by the President. Obregón, who had retired, returned to live in his native state of Sonora but later declared his candidacy for the presidential election. This concerned Carranza. Another candidate in the presidential race was Pablo Gonzalez, and Mexico was on fire again as to who had the strongest military forces to win. The country was rampant with rumors of war, and sporadic gunfire.

The Presidential race worried Carranza, and he organized a train convoy loaded with all the money and valuables he could get, taking it all to Veracruz. During the trip, there was an attack, which caused Carranza to abandon the train and escape on foot. He found a hut near a village, and while he slept, one Rodolfo Herrera treacherously fired several fatal bullets into the President of Mexico.

Obregón had Herrera put on trial, but in the end, he was acquitted. Governor Adolfo de la Huerta of Sonora was installed as interim President. During this period, all of the revolutionary factions decided on reconciliation, and peace finally came to Mexico. Pancho Villa, who had lost his influence as a conqueror, accepted amnesty and retired to his home in Canutillo, Chihuahua.

⌘ ⌘ ⌘

Fred's graduation came sooner than anticipated, and it was followed by an elaborate celebration party that evening. All the people who were privileged to know the Juelsons were invited to celebrate the prodigy child who was going to medical school. As a graduation gift from his father, Fred received a Smith and Wesson .38 revolver with his name engraved on the grip.

The weather had been hot and sultry, but a gentle wind made it perfect for the outside evening entertainment. A *mariachi* band from Brownsville with ten musicians was hired. Tables covered with white linens and filled with different foods and fruits filled the patio. On the menu were several huge roast beefs and several *cabritos* roasting on skewers over a blazing fire; servants occasionally twisted the iron rods and put hot sauce on the meats, as dripping grease flared and ignited. Cases of beverages, including hard liquor imported from Mexico, had been smuggled, sitting in barrels of ice. Twenty lighted torches surrounded the patio area, and glowing Chinese lanterns hung from the gutters of the house and within the greenery of oleanders, bougainvilleas, gardenias, hibiscus, elephant vines, and small palm trees.

Victoria, who was in charge of the arrangements, hired twenty more helpers and servants to accommodate the large gathering. Extra chairs were added around the patio for people to sit, converse, and mingle, and extra china and silverware were brought by Emma and her household. Victoria hired two ladies, said to be nurses, to watch and care for Aunt Josie, who lived at the rear of the house.

Imparting an impression of authority, *Don* Federico stood on the patio, proud and erect, grateful for his patriarchal life. He concealed a feeling of weariness, not fully satisfied with his accomplishments so far, but one thing was certain, his son was going to be great and successful in the medical field. How proud he was of Fred. He had watched him grow like a tall, healthy tree, and too, his admiration for Carlos held no bounds. He was going to see that they had the best in life, regardless of cost.

Many prominent families had been invited. The owner of the bank, his wife, and many teachers had joined in the celebration. Several families from Brownsville related to his mother were staying as guests in the large mansion. James and U.S. Marshal Bishop also decided to join the festivities. Martin Trevino, now grown and married, showed up with his wife, Maria, Yolanda's sister, to greet Fred. Elena and Miguel looked older, Roy had gained weight and was balding, but Soledad looked cheerful and as beautiful as ever.

Roy cautioned *Don* Federico while traveling to Spanish Acres to be aware of a wild boar that had attacked some of his *vaqueros* out in the *brasada*, seriously injuring one of them. Wild boars were always dangerous, but this one was especially so.

By the middle of the evening, hundreds of people were enjoying the gaiety. It had been a long hard struggle with the incessant raids, so many murders, the deaths of so many people from the Spanish influenza, and the residual hatred on both sides of the border. Changes were coming and presidential political rallies touting Warren G. Harding and his opponent were going on throughout the country.

Times were changing: dresses were made of soft, colorful, chiffon, silk, and cotton material; styles were looser, and hems were getting shorter, exposing the legs. Customs were also changing, with those of Mexican descent becoming more Americanized. And there were more automobiles instead of buggies or wagons pulled by horses.

Victoria looked charming and magnificent as she greeted the crowd and embraced the majority of them. Her hair was down loose around her shoulders making her look like a young girl instead of a married woman having birthed two children and in her mid-twenties. But in spite of her pleasant facade, Victoria's attitude had also changed; her ugly side was like a viper, coiled and ready to strike out. Driven by the dissatisfaction of her matrimonial situation, she was becoming obstinate and ruthless, often having to curb her words and her temper.

The wagging-tongue society was also busy talking about the Juelsons: the widower *Don* Federico; rumors of his crazy sister; the so-called married Victoria, whose husband was never around; and the money they had acquired through cattle, oil and cotton. People envied them and talked behind their backs, in spite of enjoying all the food and comforts the Juelsons had to offer them. The Mexican-American people were proud and stubborn, almost pretentious about their heritage, and yet begrudged the Juelsons, especially Fred, so young, so tall, and so handsome, going into medical school, saying he had the money, the guts, and the brains to be a great success.

Late that evening, the demented Aunt Josie managed to unlock the door after discovering the two drunken nurses had fallen asleep. She was anxious to see what all the noise and laughter were about, and she dreamed of her youth when *mariachis* entertained her with sweet music and dozens of red roses, admiring her beauty. Moving along the long corridors, she gazed into the mirrors on the walls, envisioning herself as she was before she had gotten married and victimized. Wearing only a white, light cotton nightgown, she stood before a large, full-length mirror at the end of the gallery.

Josie studied the reflection of her full figure amidst the shadows of the candlelight glow. Within her deranged mind, she was only eighteen, with an hourglass figure, full, round breasts, and beautiful curved hips, and her dark hair was long and hanging to her waist. With her hazel eyes sparking, she thought that any man would want her.

A table next to the mirror held fresh red roses in a vase, and she took one. She found a hairpin stuck in her fuzzy white hair and put the rose on top of her head and gazed in the mirror. Wiggling out of the nightgown, her thoughts went back to her early marriage to McCormach and how it used to please him, watching her take her clothes off.

She remembered how she stood naked in full daylight, and he would throw dry beans on the floor, having her bend over to pick them up while he watched her. He would utter a screeching noise, holding himself. Each time, it would trigger an electrical charge of energy for him, and he raped her time and time again until he was satisfied.

Looking at the full-sized mirror, she straightened her back and fondled her full breasts as she reveled in her thoughts. He used to love them. The memories rolled in, and she was young again. Within her crazy mind, she decided she would stroll outside into the evening, without any clothes on, with her one red rose, amidst the loud music. She would find her lover.

It was already getting past ten o'clock, and many of the older folks had started to pick up their shawls, canes, and belongings, calling it a day. Fred, Jamie and John had invited schoolgirls to enjoy the celebration and were out in the patio dancing. Victoria had gone upstairs to check on her sleeping children. The drinking had come to a peak as the majority of the male guests had already too much to drink and their legs were like soft noodles out on the dancing floor.

One tired guest, *Señor* Diego Saldaña, was slumped over on a bench facing the entrance to the patio. He had had his fill of liquor; he had eaten to his heart's content; he had danced with his wife and other *comadres*. Now he had decided to take a nap before he continued with the rest of the night's follies. He opened one eye and saw Josie without any clothes on, standing in the doorway, swaying her hips, and cuddling her rose in both hands. *This must be the finale*, he thought. *Damn! These people with money have the nerve! I must be dreaming. Or, I'm in the red-light district in Reynosa. I must've had too much to drink.* He rubbed his eyes, trying to focus. "*Dios!*" he exclaimed. "*Ay, Dios!*"

Those who were still conscious and able to stand— did. The band stopped playing. The young boys began laughing and others giggled. The young girls stood still, paralyzed, with their hands clasped over their mouths. Emma, in her tight shoes and feathered hat, sitting with the fuzzy old hen, Mrs. McCray, looked up and froze at the scene. Felicia, Dan, and *la Señora* Del Calderóne stared in shock. Magdalena's eyeballs became transfixed. The female servants waiting on the tables stood bemused and immobile, not knowing which path to take back to the kitchen with their empty trays. The male servants who had been drinking and slicing the meats, just smiled. Several young men standing and talking began chuckling. One of the older ladies from the wagging- tongue society fainted, and someone among the rest of the church ladies said, "*Dios mío!*"

Marshall Bishop had joined *El Guapo* James, and *Don* Federico in conversation. They were huddled in a political debate about the peace and harmony and the inconsistency of Mexico's problems. Bishop and James had been indulging quite heavily in the spirits. They all heard the commotion coming from the back entrance of the house. All three hurried to see what the fuss was about, whereupon they encountered the smiling, prancing Josie with only one rose, entertaining the crowd.

"Oh, wow!" said James.

"Lordy me!" replied Bishop, thinking the whiskey had worked its way throughout his body and was now frying his brains.

Stunned and embarrassed, *Don* Federico immediately took off his suit coat and wrapped it around the struggling Josie, dragging his sister inside the house. He was angry and scowled at her, telling her that her actions were not acceptable.

Victoria, coming down the stairs, heard her father's voice loud and urgent, and she was surprised to find him struggling with her aunt, who was completely nude!

"Please take her to her room," suggested the frustrated *Don*, and he turned Josie over to Victoria. "I have to apologize to our guests for her behavior. Better find out how she got out of her room!" The *Don*, upset and perspiring, put his coat on, brushed it off, and returned to the patio.

Victoria grabbed Josie by both arms and guided her back to her bedroom, while Josie yelled and fought, wanting to get loose. In the bedroom she found the two nurses sound asleep. She snatched the oldest one up and slapped her hard across the face. The woman landed against the wall, alarmed and now fully awake. The other one awoke and began to run into the hall. Mad as a hornet, Victoria caught her by her hair and slapped her several times across the face. "Here's your money!" She threw the money on the floor for the two women to pick up. "Don't ever come back to this house again, and don't ever ask for any kind of work here! The two of you cannot be trusted," she said angrily and began soothing her hands that now stung from the blows she had delivered.

It took several days before the *Don* stopped apologizing to everyone. It took weeks and months before the members of the wagging-tongue society stopped gossiping at their quilting sessions, and months before the ladies from the Catholic Church Praying Society stopped talking about what happened, and how scandalous it was, and oh, how it had been so very shameful! Many white candles burned brightly on the altar at the Lady of Mercy Catholic Church on behalf of the Juelsons.

While enjoying a stay at Spanish Acres, Marshall Bishop announced to *Don* Federico that he was resigning his post, leaving Brownsville, and returning back to Austin. He explained that he was disappointed in the final conclusion on his documents, since the majority of the federal judges had discredited most of his reports as being biased and discriminating. They felt that Bishop was working against them and was too sympathetic toward the Mexican-American people. Accordingly, he had not been satisfied with the justices regarding the Mexican natives in the Valley, and he was going to document all of his findings and turn them over to the archives.

There was little he could do about the renegade Hanson, who was still not apprehended. Bishop also told the *Don* there was so much work to be done in achieving a common peace among the Mexican-American citizens in the Valley, and he felt *Don* Federico had a very positive objective as far as his profession was concerned. But the *Don's* main goal was to see that Fred and his younger son Carlos got an education.

ROOTS OF INDIFFERENCE

⌘　⌘　⌘

Fred had now turned nineteen and was very excited to start his medical studies. He arrived in Houston with his father to meet with Juan Alvarez, who had already completed his residency and was heading back to the Valley. Juan would travel back with *Don* Federico and make plans for his future.

In Mercedes, Emma and the rest of the family, including *Señora* Del Calderóne and Magdalena, anxiously awaited his return into their midst. Victoria, like a spider on her prey, was also nervously anticipating his arrival, wanting to know his future plans and if fate included her in his destiny.

The Great War was over and the German Empire was dismantled. Riots began breaking out in many of the states and American cities as African-American soldiers returned from the war and were demanding civil rights and were being opposed by the KKK mobs. Many African-American soldiers, who had escaped dying in the war overseas, had returned only to be lynched by mobs incited by pure ignorant hatred.

Juan's announcement that he would not be setting up his practice in Mercedes came as a disappointment to *Don* Federico, who wanted him to stay, but he understood his desires. Juan had changed considerably. He was more discrete in his actions and thoughts, and his manners had become more polished. But his discretion did not apply to his lovemaking—he had been gone too long. Since his arrival, he and Victoria had spent dozens of passionate, pleasurable moments in Victoria's upstairs bedroom, while *Don* Federico was away on business and all the servants were downstairs working. The two lovers made up for lost time. He was having his cake and eating it, too, and Victoria was enjoying every minute of it and never wanting it to end. Juan promised her that he loved her and that she was the only one in his life. He convinced her that he could not marry her, at least not now, since she was already too committed.

The worst blow came as a total shock to Victoria when Juan announced to the family that he had decided to marry Magdalena and return to Monterrey to practice medicine.

Victoria threw a whopping temper tantrum and cried for days.

It became apparent to Victoria that in Magdalena's letters to Juan; she had totally convinced the young doctor of the peace coming to Mexico. They would be happy back in Monterrey, where there was less confusion and less danger from the raids experienced by those living close to the border. And medical doctors were in great demand in Mexico.

Likewise, several of the Army doctors had decided to make the Valley their home, including Dr. Hedrick, who preferred to make Mercedes his residence.

Days after Juan and Magdalena left for Monterrey, Felicia came to visit with a secret, handwritten note from Juan to explain his decision. In his note, Juan declared his love for Victoria, but his conclusion had been urgent because of his professionalism, and also because Magdalena had gotten pregnant. He wrote in the note that Magdalena wanted it that way, not wanting *Señora* Calderóne to get upset and find out this soon. His actions were a complete puzzle to Victoria, and she wondered where Juan had gotten all of his sexual energy. When did he get Magdalena pregnant? He had spent more of his amorous time with her. Juan's note indicated that he would write to her and send her his private address when he got settled. This seemed to appease Victoria's feelings, and she understood; she would contact him as soon as she got his new address.

The following year, Alvaro Obregón became president of Mexico and was known as a pragmatic reformer favoring land for the peasant farmers. Property being taken over by greedy foreign investors ceased, and this edict affected *Don* Federico's gold mine. Obregón was also determined to curtail the Catholic Church's power in controlling the poor peasants and keeping them oppressed.

In 1920, Warren G. Harding became the twenty-ninth president of the United States but did not live to complete his term. Harding's cabinet members brought upon themselves scandalous criticism, especially with the Teapot Dome Affair, which implicated Albert B. Fall, previously in charge of the investigation into the Mexican affairs during the Mexican raids along the border. Fall spent several years in federal prison for taking bribes, leading to his political demise. Edwin Denby resigned, as did Attorney General Daugherty, who conspired with Albert Fall in receiving prohibition payments.

The year also brought in the women's vote, ratifying the Nineteenth Amendment granting suffrage to American women. Women could now participate in politics, and the world would never be the same. The American Civil Liberties Union (ACLU) began as social reformers.

For several months *Don* Federico had not felt well, experiencing dizzy spells and shortness of breath. This happened when he got up from his bed or from his reading chair. He decided to see Dr. Hedrick, who had opened his practice in Mercedes after the Army had left the area and was using his home to receive patients. After a complete examination, Dr. Hedrick suspected heart problems.

"There could be a possibility of having too much fat in your arteries, causing a blockage of oxygen to the brain. Better start exercising and eating less red meat," suggested the doctor. "You have probably gained weight sitting and writing classified documents. Eat small portions several times during the day. Start eating more fruits and vegetables, which is best for your body, and begin walking more. Take a long stroll around the park during the evening hours. It would do you a world of good. Take a spoonful of cider vinegar with honey in water every morning. Vinegar thins the blood."

It was hard to believe that he was having heart problems, but yes, he had gained considerably over twenty pounds since he started his job as Ambassador of Goodwill. The *Don* was often eating on the run, sitting for long periods, and writing documents for hours, not being as active as when he was living full-time at Spanish Acres, riding horses and roping calves.

Perhaps the doctor was right in having him curb his eating habits, but that was like dying, too. He would have to give up the golden, rich butter, cold glasses of milk, and those thick steaks, not to mention the delicious Mexican meals, full of rich sauces and thick cheeses. Eating fruits and vegetables would turn him into a rabbit.

ROOTS OF INDIFFERENCE

In the early part of 1921, the *Don* decided to resign his appointed ambassadorship. The raids had ended, and Mexico's new president was restoring peace along the border; there was little paperwork that needed to be documented.

For the time being, he would rest and take care of his health and his property. James returned to the federal courts in Brownsville and informed Canalo of *Don* Federico's decision. Tomas Canalo, upon learning of Don Federico's resignation, immediately wired him, asking him to consider the senatorial position in his district coming up in the fall. Canalo had retired from public office and was spending his time on his ranch. He had been threatened by several Texas Rangers, especially one Frank Horner. "It's the only way you can help the Mexican-American people and voice your opinion," he suggested.

With the support and encouragement of the Mexican-American citizens around the county, the *Don* could not resist the temptation. He decided to place his name into the hat in the race for State Senator that was coming up in the fall. It took long and arduous hours of planning speeches and talking to people in the small towns of Hidalgo County. Many prosperous Mexican-American citizens contributed money and valuable time, including members of his extended family and many people from the Catholic Church. All the children began helping him with posters and arranging meetings with new Mexican-American social clubs that were beginning to form.

Thanks to his standing in the community, *Don* Federico won by a landslide and began his elected job by traveling to Austin and meeting with many of the other newly elected Senators. He would spend many days and weeks at the state capital developing new laws that were beneficial for the Mexican citizens throughout the state of Texas. He was even more interested in the educational process and in improving the quality of learning in the schools. His proposal was opposed by the other Senators, who thought the idea was not relevant at that particular time, since the Jim Crow Laws were still strong. He offered many other ideas for reducing property taxes, and for removal of poll taxes, and for allowing Mexican-American citizens to vote who did not own property. Traveling home, he would take the train to Houston first and spend some time with Fred.

Coming home to Mercedes was always a comfortable feeling, after staying in hotels and boarding houses. Seeing his boy Carlos growing into a man and watching the grandchildren playing and growing around him provided him with much satisfaction. He would spend weeks at Spanish Acres, supervising the clearing of ever more land, seeing the cotton growing and the two oil wells producing crude oil, and his cattle, which had become large herds. His *vaqueros* were growing older and their families were leaving the nest. His life was comfortable and good.

A year had come and was almost gone. Another hot summer had passed and in late fall, the *Don* decided to drive to Spanish Acres in his one-horse buggy. He was excited to check on the special breed of Brahma cattle he had gotten the previous year. He had bought five cows and a bull from a German breeder north of Austin. The cattle's color was different from his reddish-brown Santa Gertrudis and Hereford breeds. The Brahmas were gray, humped, heat-resistant and tick-resistant cattle imported from the east, and they were showing good results so far. He had decided to interbreed and see what kind of results it would bring in the coming years.

It was a cool morning, and he decided to wear his white, poplin hat and a dark wool jacket that was the style in Austin and Houston. After leaving La Villa, the *Don* made a turn onto the road that once led to *Doña* Adela's property. The area had been cleared, except for some mesquite and jangled scrubs, the broken bricks of the chimney, and part of the old barn. Weeds and grass had taken over. As he drove by the old place, he wondered why the kindly old woman had been killed. He was saddened by her loss, since *Doña* Adela had always meant well to all of the people who patronized her. He slowed down, gazing at the area, remembering all the good memories he had of being a little boy, and his mother bringing him to visit *Doña* Adela.

He expelled a deep breath and turned his buggy north and headed for Spanish Acres. The seldom-used path had become thick with impenetrable underbrush on both sides of the road, interspersed with towering cottonwood trees and mesquite, sage, Mexican pine, and chaparral. Many dry bushes had died and had piled up from year to year, falling into a bulky thick tangle of vines and brambles.

As the horse pushed forward, *Don* Federico kept wondering about Hanson. He knew he was still alive and was sneaking across the border occasionally. He also knew that he was probably working on a scheme of some kind, trying to find some way of getting back at him. It had been several years now, since the gold mine incident, but a man like Hanson would never give up.

Don Federico did not remember what happened next. When he woke up, he was on a cot at Spanish Acres with a terrible headache, a large gash on the side of his head, his legs were on fire, and his back hurt terribly. He was being taken care of by the two kindly old ladies, Ophelia and Olivia. Soledad, with a concerned look on her face, kept putting a cold towel on his forehead. Memo was sent to Mercedes to inform Victoria of the accident.

"What happened?" The moaning *Don* questioned.

"Ya' tell us!" Roy answered, with a puzzled look. "All we know is dat we found ya' dis mornin' fainted an' sittin' in yore buggy inside o' the gate entrance. It was pretty damn queer, ya' sittin' thar, all slumped over. The *vaqueros* brought ya' inside."

"What day is it?"

"Da day is Wednesda', why? When did ya' leave Mercedes?"

"Monday!" he said with a bewildered concern. "Monday morning," He repeated himself like a drunken parrot. "Wednesday, you said. And it took me two days to get here, when it's only a half day's drive?" He frowned, obviously shaken. "The horse and the buggy—are they all right?"

"Git sev'al scrat'hes on his right, back leg and a big pur'pull bump up high'r on the same side. W'en we git him, he was preettee spooked. He's gonna be all right after some bag balm is put on 'em. It'll take a couple o' days, but he'll be okay."

"Something hit us!" The *Don* narrowed his eyes and wrinkled his brow, trying to remember, trying to grasp reality. "It threw me out of the buggy, and my head landed against a tree. I remember the sounds of the horse, snorting, rearing, and his hooves pounding. I can vaguely remember a bad smell, a stink. And someone picked me up and put me in the buggy, but I must have been there for a long time—it was later—hours later. I can't remember any more."

"Bet'er rest!" commented Roy interrupting his *patrón*. He shook his head, and then signaled to Soledad to meet him in the kitchen.

"Somethin' strange, somethin' odd's goin' on," Roy told Soledad. "Whut ya' think, *Querida*?" They both looked at each other, at a loss to explain it. "He mentioned a smell. What kinda smell? Thar's all kinds o' stinks 'round here."

Soledad agreed and felt the strangeness all around her, causing her to become more worried. "There is something strange. Having someone pick up *Don* Federico and just leave him hurt at the entrance of the gate is odd. Was someone afraid to bring him inside the grounds of Spanish Acres?"

"Yon have a point, but... who?"

Like a wild wind, Victoria entered from the kitchen side and interrupted the two. "What happened to Papá?" she asked nervously, dropping her shawl, a package, and her pocketbook on the dining room table. "Is he going to be all right?"

"We do not know yet," answered Soledad. "He's hurt and must have broken some bones the way he's moaning. He must have been out for a whole day and a half. He's in the bedroom by the kitchen."

Frantically, she hurried to find her father lying in bed groaning, with a white linen cloth over his forehead.

"We had no choice but to put him close to the kitchen, where we could attend to him," said Soledad, who trailed behind Victoria, with Roy behind Soledad. "We were afraid to move him."

"I s'pect it could have been dat giant javelina boar dat's been roamin' 'round the *brasada*," Roy suggested, not finding any other explanation for what had happened to *Don* Federico. "Dat beast musta hit 'em straight on!" Roy said, but in the confusion of everyone talking, no one paid any attention.

It was two days before Dr. Hedrick was able to travel to Spanish Acres and attend *Don* Federico; he had been notified the day before, but got busy with his clientele. After his diagnosis, he informed Victoria that *Don* Federico was going to have trouble walking, for he was paralyzed from his waist down. He suspected that a disc had pinched his spine, and though surgery might bring his feeling back, for the moment there was nothing he could do but give him syrup containing the drug cocaine to relieve the pain. Dr. Hedrick informed Victoria that he was only a family doctor and did not have the skill to operate, that her father needed a specialist that performed delicate spinal operations. The Mercedes Surgical and Obstetrical Hospital was the only hospital around, and it was only used for emergencies, mostly white women having babies.

The dire news sent waves of helplessness through everyone who knew *Don* Federico. Victoria was beside herself. She was going to need help figuring out what to do now with the hired help, and with the huge herd of cattle that needed to be shipped north.

With the new women's rights, she was able to take control of her father's business and run it her own way. First she would have to change the banking deposits, especially the oil company account, from Brownsville's Yturria Bank into the bank in Mercedes. It was simple, for instead of viewing the ledgers every month, she would be able to review them and pay the workers weekly. In her empowerment, Victoria began using her head to become a business-woman, regardless of what others thought.

What hit her father in the buggy and left him so distressed and helpless? And who had picked him up and put him back in the buggy? Who? Someone must have brought the horse and him to the entrance gate of Spanish Acres. Someone must have known who he was. Victoria began using her fortune-telling expertise and went into a trance like *Doña* Adela had taught her. What she visualized was—*Roberto! Well, yes! It has to be Roberto,* she thought. *Roberto is alive? He has to be. Who else knew her father and knew where to bring him? He is still roaming the brasada like he always did. But what hit her father and the buggy?* She began visualizing again, seeing a dark, blunt figure, only a blur, and she could not bring into focus the exact cause.

"Roy!" she said out loud. "Has anyone seen any sign of Roberto around? His body was never found, remember? He must still be living in the *brasada* and pretended he was an animal. I believe he is still alive and found my father and put him in the buggy. Dad recalled a stink! Who else would stink that bad—only someone who hadn't had a bath in years!"

"Waal, Lardy al bee gawddamn!" Roy sputtered, knowing that Victoria was right in her deduction of what had happened. "Waal, yo're gettin' as good as *la bruja* was in predictin' thangs. Yes sirree, jus' as good!"

Don Federico was convinced after hearing what Victoria had said, and it seemed correct and obvious. In a gesture of kindness, he ordered the household to put food outside the gate every day, no matter what day it was. He was grateful to Roberto for saving his life and wanted to repay him. Roberto and *Don* Federico had a secret they shared in common, and Roberto was aware of it. Putting out food for him every single day would symbolize the *Don's* kindness and appreciation toward him. He knew he was still alive and lived among the wild animals in the *brasada*.

Victoria's estimations were correct. On an early morning one of the *vaqueros* who took a large plate of food to the entrance gate brought back the missing white poplin hat which he found sitting on the empty plate.

Victoria also got the impression that a large wild animal had hit the buggy. Roy agreed and was positive that a razorback *javalina* had hit it, by the holes punched in the side. The following morning, he ordered two of the *vaqueros* to hunt down the wild boar. Over a year ago, one of his hired hands had been bucked down and was sliced by a wild *javalina's* tucks. On another occasion, an oilrig worker had encountered several of the wild pigs and, though hurt, climbed a mesquite tree, which was the only thing that saved his life.

ROOTS OF INDIFFERENCE

Victoria sent a telegram to Fred in Houston and advised him of their father's ill-fated accident and indicated in the telegram that *Don* Federico needed special attention on his back and for him to check on doctors who specialized in back surgeries as soon as possible.

Within two weeks, Fred arrived by train, surprising everyone, with two different doctors who were willing to check *Don* Federico and give a diagnosis on what could be done for him to walk again. They were Dr. Benjamin Burr from Galveston, who was teaching at the University in Houston, and his assistant, a young Indian by the name of White Eagle, who came from Oklahoma to study medicine; the two had taken time off to examine Fred's father.

Dr. Burr was Italian, a burly, heavyset man in his sixties with dark brown hair mixed with white, including his beard. He wore spectacles and was meticulous about everything, and he talked with his hands. White Eagle was from the Cherokee tribe in Oklahoma and was tall and athletic looking, with golden-olive skin, and black hair in a single braid down his back. His family had inherited several oil wells and had sent him to study medicine to help save his people from so many infectious diseases. Fred and White Eagle had hit it off from the very start of their studies. Both had come from the same background, except from different nationalities, and had the same sentiments on people wanting to help heal their own kind. White Eagle was quite and reserved and would merely nod or frown when answering a direct question.

Fred and the two doctors were welcomed like gods in the household, with banquets of food and wine and servants to assist them with everything. Dr. Burr, a widower, fell in love with the Rio Grande Valley and its people. He ended up being smitten by Emma and her wonderful cooking and stated to her that his retirement was coming soon, and he would come to Mercedes to live. Emma was beside herself.

After visiting *Don* Federico at Spanish Acres with all the gracious formalities, it was agreed that the delicate operation would have to be done in Houston where they had the facilities to operate on his spine. Arrangements were made to bring *Don* Federico on a flat wagon to the train station east of his hacienda. The train would take him to the town of Alice, and he would then be transported to Houston. All of this would take some maneuvering and the assistance of everyone at Spanish Acres.

Victoria began making the arrangements with Fred, Dan Land, and Roy to accompany her father to Houston. The busybody but goodhearted Mrs. McCray decided to volunteer her services by going with them, and would take care of *Don* Federico during his recovery. She was a retired nurse, and nobody took care of people like a woman, she kept repeating.

At their departure, Victoria whispered to Fred as they embraced, "Let me know as soon as the operation is over and how it went. As soon as father begins recovering from the surgery, please send me a telegram as quickly as possible, so I won't be worrying so much. I'll be praying! I have to stay and take care of things, my children, Aunt Josie, our grandmother Gloria, the books, and payroll." In other words, Victoria would be doing some hot voodooing, just like *Doña* Adela had taught her was needed in time of trouble, especially burning candles, going into trance, and reading the cards.

"Don't worry, *Manita*," he said, using the endearing word for sister. "In the hands of these doctors, Father will be fine. And as soon as he is better, I'll bring him back home."

CHAPTER 35

The operation was successful. The return trip by train was slow and painful as Fred and the rest brought *Don* Federico back to Mercedes to be greeted by his family and many loyal friends. It took many months of recovery, and Mrs. McCray, so willing and so congenial and so busy talking, moved into the house and was there to please his every whim to the point of annoyance. When the *Don* began walking again, he had to use a cane, a special silver cane ordered from the finest retail store in Dallas. At other times, he would sit for hours in a wheelchair at his desk writing documents and corresponding with the Texas State Senate and Representatives.

For the town of Mercedes, the year 1922 was one of the worst ever, with a hurricane hitting in the fall and bringing devastation, typhoid, and dysentery. Doctors were in great demand. Stagnate water stood for many days and weeks breeding mosquitoes and other insects. Water had to be boiled for drinking. The saturated ground produced a build-up of green slime and moss on the sides of trees and buildings, and the air smelled of moldy compost. Life came to a standstill. Schools and businesses were closed, and ranchers and farmers with cattle and cotton and other agricultural products all suffered huge losses.

Months after the flood, the town began renovation by building the new South Graham High School for whites, and a two-story City Hall. Downtown on the white side of town, new lamplights were erected with large lampposts on each corner, and palm trees were planted all along Main Street, enhancing that area.

The Catholic citizens were busy completing the new Lady of Mercy Church on Vermont Street. *Don* Florencio Saenz and *Don* Federico were contributors of money for that project, along with many other citizens. Many Mexican-American families became anxious to send their children to the new private parochial school, which would be built in the coming years. Victoria was looking forward to sending her son Luis Martin, who was growing up very fast and learned so quickly. By being educated in the Catholic schools, the Mexican-American children had a better chance of learning, being given close attention by the nuns who ran the schools.

To the west of Mercedes, the newly reconstructed town of Weslaco had been formed with a new Chamber of Commerce, a newspaper, a bank, community housing where children were attending elementary school classes, and a new station for the Texas Rangers.

The segregation and discrimination within the new town was the same as Mercedes: *El Pueblo Americano* to the south, and to the north, *El Pueblo Mexicano*, which was also the industrial area. The hypothesis was the same, pretty homes for the whites, with paved streets and sewer systems. To the north were unpainted ramshackle homes, no civic services, and Mexican schools that were second-rate in education.

Intimidation of the Mexican-American people was still prevalent, especially in *El Pueblo Americano*. Mexican workers had to be home before dark. "No Mexican was to be found in Anglo town after dark," was still the edict among the Anglos ruling South Texas with their new laws. The hatred continued, in spite of the ending of the Mexican raids. Evil forces were alive and well. The Mexican-American citizen living in Texas was still blamed for any and all mishaps and was punished with death through lynching or shooting, saving the expense of a trial.

It was the same old established pattern. In November of the same year a young Mexican-American by the name of Elias Zarate, living in the tin shacks north of Weslaco, got in trouble with a smart-ass Anglo because the white man had insulted his beautiful sister by calling her a whore. Zarate, who believed in *machismo*, got into a fistfight protecting his sister's honor. Zarate was arrested by the Texas Rangers, without any investigation of who was actually to blame. The young Anglo was looked upon as a victim and patted on the back as "doing good." Zarate was ruffed up and later lynched without explanation.

This sent the Mexican residents of Weslaco, and families related to Zarate, into a rage, demanding justice. Many associates of the Zarate family lived in surrounding ranching areas of Mercedes. The Mexican-American families stormed over to *Don* Federico's home demanding that he, as an official State Representative, order the Texas legislature to help fight the injustice. *Don* Federico paid for the poor family to hire an attorney from McAllen, and filed charges against the Texas Rangers for disregarding civil rights in not giving Zarate justice in court. He received anonymous death threat letters from white Mexican-haters. The courts took many months as they dragged their feet, never coming to any conclusion, and finally it was taken out of court. This did not set well with many of the Mexican people who had elected *Don* Federico and wanted immediate justice. His term was coming up and he would have a hard time convincing the Mexican citizens of his power to enact justice.

That same year in June, the country heard about the great discovery by British Egyptologist George Carnarvon and Howard Carter, who unearthed King Tutankhamen's tomb in the Valley of the Kings in Egypt.

The arrogant, egotistical Ricardo had unexpectedly returned, but only to receive his income from the cotton profits. He was becoming more obstinate and controlling to the point of being ruthless. Victoria preoccupied herself and avoided his presence as much as possible. He had stayed for only two weeks, visiting Yolanda in Spanish Acres, and his mother, who was so willing to return to Monterrey. Ricardo had started an engineering business in

Monterrey and was preparing to build his mother a home. He was trying to organize and rebuild their property that had been completely demolished by the Revolutionists; however, this time there would be no slaves or workers he could whip and order around. This time, if he wanted any work done, he would have to pay for the labor, and material, too, was not cheap. There was no conversation about his sister Magdalena or their young baby, and nothing was said about how Juan's practice was going.

Complaints from the servants circulated within the household about Mrs. McCray giving orders and taking over *Don* Federico's care. It did not sit well with Victoria that Mrs. McCray was insinuating to anyone who would listen, that *Don* Federico was her "soul-mate" and she intended to marry him. In her garrulous conversation with Emma and Grandmother Gloria, she raved about how lucky the *Don* was to have her around. It sent a jealous rage through Victoria, knowing that Emma was behind this entire charade! Victoria told Mrs. McCray, kindly, that it was time to leave.

With the coming elections, *Don* Federico, who was still walking with a cane and was weak and felt ill, decided not to take any part in politics. He had grown older and was dealing with the problems of the two nationalities and the hassles of traveling as well. He retired to stay close to his home in Mercedes and spend most of his time at Spanish Acres. Mrs. McCray would occasionally join him when he traveled back and forth on these visits. Carlos had graduated, but had decided not to attend college; he wanted to be with his father and stay close to the cattle and help out with the oil wells and cotton. He became Victoria's right hand man with the family business and helped her with the bookkeeping.

Fred finished his residency and returned home to Mercedes to a fully furnished, spacious building with all of the modern medical equipment he would need to run his practice. Dr. Hedrick had helped *Don* Federico in the purchase of the instruments. The edifice for his medical practice was several yards away on the north side of the family mansion. The Juelson's name was still controversial among the white business citizens in the town. *Don* Federico had made these preparations, since the Mercedes Hospital had objected to having Fred, being half-Mexican with Mexican clients, join the staff. There was no room for them in that hospital, especially in pediatrics and obstetrics. The Mexican-American women were having children by the dozens but were not accepted there. They were anxious to have a Mexican doctor to take care of them in the area.

Dr. Hedrick was not biased and had stayed in Mercedes after the Mexican raids and was pleased to accommodate Fred in helping him get established.

The year 1923 delivered perhaps the most shocking news for the Mexican people, who were stunned to learn that Pancho Villa had been assassinated. He was considered the "Robin Hood of Mexico" and was respected by many people.

It was also in this year that a Mexican, Ramon Delgado, was shot and killed by an Anglo near Hondo, Texas. News traveled fast among the Mexican-American natives and fomented hatred and anger throughout the Valley. In protest, the *Cinco de Mayo* festivities were cancelled that year.

President Warren Harding suddenly died in office. Charges of corruption involving his cabinet members became a big scandal. The Union of Soviet Socialist Republics was headed by Vladimir Lenin, who began building forced-labor camps in Russia.

In the following years, Fred's medical practice prospered, mostly from word of mouth. He had more patients than the regular white doctors. Sick people showed up from Weslaco, La Villa, and from as far away as Edinburg, as well as people living on *ranchitos* around the area. Three large rooms were added for patients who needed extra care in their recovery, and for women in labor. With so many people who needed help and care after minor surgery, a total of six Mexican women nurses were hired to assist Dr. Fred around the clock.

Many of the Mexican-American people who were being treated were very poor and brought baskets of fresh fruits and vegetables as payment for their treatment. Fred never asked for money and never kept track of his patients' debts. He was happy that his wishes and desires had come true, for he was doing what he had dreamed of many years ago—taking care of the Mexican-American people. His father and Victoria were very proud. He only wished his mother had lived long enough so that he could have taken care of her. Medicine had become modern, with new drugs and instruments, and pills were becoming more effective. Victoria took on the responsibilities of keeping Fred's books and deposited his money in the Hidalgo Bank once a week.

In the winter year of 1925, the gods played a joke on the residents of the Rio Grande Valley and had a hearty laugh. The unthinkable happened—snow! Nobody had ever seen snow. It was a historical event. The residents were asking if the world had turned on its axis!

Within the next several years, the government of Texas was being run by the only woman governor in the history of the state up to that time. Miriam Amanda Ferguson, called "Ma" because of her initials, was the wife of impeached governor James Ferguson, who was in office when the raids were at their worst in the lower Rio Grande Valley. Ma Ferguson became famous for pardoning fugitives, murderers, and people who had been in prior trouble with the law. On her list of priorities was one name that was pardoned: Bernard Edward Hanson. His Ranger friends had sent numerous telegrams urging her to pardon him, and now the monster Hanson, full of hatred and revenge, had been pardoned and was welcomed back into Texas with open arms.

There were rumors of bribes and kickbacks as Ma Ferguson took a firm stand against the Ku Klux Klan groups that were made up of state government workers controlling the state of Texas. The KKK included many members of the Texas Rangers, sheriffs, judges, attorneys, and city merchants. Their underhanded secret activities kept the Mexican-American citizens from their civil rights and economic advancement, and kept their public schools inferior.

The new parochial school had been built so the Mexican-American children could be educated and motivated and encouraged to go forward into college. Victoria's children, starting with Luis Martin, now fourteen years old, Aaron, now going on eight, and little Maria Theresa, were all attending the Catholic school.

ROOTS OF INDIFFERENCE

⌘ ⌘ ⌘

In 1927, Calvin Coolidge was president of the United States. The theory of evolution was being whispered and talked about in secret meetings, and being discussed among intellectuals, while being hush-hushed in the public schools. Charles A. Lindbergh had flown a nonstop flight from New York to Paris. The Latin lover and movie star Rudolph Valentino died. The Hollywood revolution had started by bringing "talkies" to the scene, and Al Jolson was singing melodies in a black painted face. Douglas Fairbanks and Mary Pickford were big names. Charlie Chaplin could make everyone laugh in one movie; in another, he would make people cry. The radio had brought the American people closer by bringing instant news. The telephone brought communication to those who could afford one, and folks would take turns answering when the Bell phone rang. The white people danced to the Charleston, and the Mexican-American people listened to the sounds of the newly invented radio. The first radio station in the Valley was KRGV in Harlingen. A Spanish-owned radio station was started in Brownsville for Mexican citizens, who would have their ears close to the instrument listening to the beautiful Latin songs: *Los Boleros*, *Las Sambas*, *Los Corridos* and the *Tangos*.

The rainy season started near the beginning of the fall, bringing a change in the weather, and the leaves had begun to turn colors and fall from the trees. Many of Fred's patients, especially young children and their families, had come down with colds and chest congestion. Some of his older client customers, especially old men whose teeth were falling out, had not seen a doctor in years; many could not afford one. He saw one old man who had never been to a doctor in his entire life and had arthritis so bad that he was unable to move, especially during the morning hours. His son had persuaded his father to see the young Dr. Juelson, and had even smuggled two whiskey bottles from Reynosa as a gift for him and Fred. On many other occasions, Fred spent his time away from the clinic in his 1926 black, four-door Packard with his trusted black medical bag, making house calls. He was often summoned on emergencies, usually women in childbirth, or for farming and ranching accidents.

On one occasion, Fred was surprised to have as a patient a young white woman by the name of Emily Ferguson, who was suffering from a chest cold. Up to this point, his visitors had only been Mexican-American people of all ages. After carefully checking her age on the chart, which said eighteen, Fred became instantly smitten by the beautiful, blonde, blue-eyed Emily with a shapely figure and a nice bosom. She instantly undressed with no modesty, taking her blouse off, exposing each of her breasts, hot with promise, without any effort.

"Does your chest hurt?" Fred asked, distracted by her beauty as she lay on the examining table with her pointed nipples staring up at him. He stood breathless and bent over her and began examining her with his stethoscope, listening for any congestion in her lungs.

It did not take long before she circled her arms around his neck and pulled him toward her, his face to her lips. The wild response sent him completely out of control, causing him to forget his profession. The passionate examination took over an hour. When he was finally finished, he asked her if he could see her again on a personal basis, for she was a dream come true. He was completely taken by her and had not encountered anything like this in all the years of his medical practice. He wanted her more than ever, even though this was against all medical practice, ethics, and codes.

Emily wanted very much to see him, especially at night when they could be together and embrace more discreetly. She had planned the seduction all along and was very pleased with herself, for she had accomplished her goal, knowing that Fred was single, handsome, with a wonderful profession, a name, lots of money—a good catch.

"Name the time and place," she coquettishly replied.

"May I pick you up at your home? Do you live here?" Fred questioned, trying to find out more about who she was and where she came from. He loved the devil-may-care attitude of this young, forbidden girl—she was every man's dream. She had excited him with her wild passionate pleasures. He found himself drained and out of breath.

"No! Meet me at the park," she said brusquely, and gave him a sober look. "You can pick me up, and we can go somewhere in your car. I live with my father on a farm close to La Feria. A rancher neighbor brought me to Mercedes so that I could spend time with my sister and her children. She does not know that I was coming to see you. And if my father finds out, he'll have me whipped for seeing a Mexican doctor. We will have to be careful and discreet, so that nobody sees us. I'll wait for you around seven tomorrow."

He gave her a bottle of red syrup to take by mouth three times a day, and told her if the cough persisted, he needed to see her again. She returned every other day after closing hours to see him, when he did not pick her up in his car. The exciting affair continued off and on for many months.

On certain days, Fred closed the office early; trying to get more time for himself and re-fusing to let his mind get caught up in his medical work. Emily would show up and wait until the last patient left. She and Fred would spend hours together locked up in the examination room, where low voices could be heard and the windows would get fogged up. This caught the attention of Victoria, whose hawk-eyes never missed anything. "Who is this girl you're keeping company with?" she questioned, mystified and concerned. "Do you know who her parents are, and where she comes from? Fred, you have to be real careful who you're dealing with, especially with a *gringa*. That will cause gossip in this town. The people in this area love a scandal and watch for any mistakes the Juelson family makes and *ay qué dirán?* Father had to go through quite an ordeal to get established in this town and earn respect."

She changed the tone of the conversation. "I've invited the Castillo family from the Castillo ranch in McAllen to join us for dinner this evening. They want you to meet their daughter, the beautiful eighteen-year-old Catalina. She is very suitable, a perfect match for our family. As your sister, I have been quite concerned. It is time for you to find a wife, get married, and have children. The family is worried that you are too occupied with your profession."

"*Manita*, I hope you're not trying to find a wife for me. I'm a grown man and can find my own woman," Fred replied with confidence in himself, and obviously annoyed.

"Apparently you are not in your right senses," responded Victoria, exasperated. "For your own protection, I had the girl you call Emily checked out. Emily is not her name. She is lying.

She comes from a very trashy background. Her mother disappeared several years ago. The neighbors around them know little about them, except that the husband had routinely beaten and abused his wife. The neighbors could hear her scream but were afraid to interfere. Then one day, they noticed that the wife was not around, imagine that!"

Victoria paused and then continued. "The girl you call Emily's real name is Martha, and she is related to Otto Foster. Remember him, Uncle Howard's buddy? The two were in jail together until Howard died—remember? The German traitor, doing his scientific research on insects and boll weevils hoping to destroy our cotton crops? He is still serving time in federal prison, and the government is trying to decide what to do with him, now that the war with Germany is over."

Fred blinked and took a deep breath. He looked away from Victoria, not knowing whether to believe her, and not knowing how to respond. "*Manita,* I will handle this. I will speak to Emily—Martha—whatever her name is, and get the story straight."

"Can you see the whole picture?" She said in a cynical tone of voice. "You're a big boy now and should know better. I'm only looking out for you, and I don't want to see you bring dishonor to your profession. I've read the cards for you, and I saw deception, treachery, and trouble—and there is more than one person involved. These people know about you and have been planning something. At this moment, I do not know exactly what this lying Emily is up to, or what her intentions are, but the cards indicated that more than one person is involved, and they want revenge."

Fred stood there in a daze, not knowing what to do next. He was obsessed with the girl called Emily, and the information had stunned him. At this point, he didn't know quite what to do with it. Victoria was more like his mother, and he knew her worries were for his own best interests. He should have known better; after all, he was going against the medical code of ethics, since Emily was his patient. He had to be especially careful not to tarnish the family name.

"Revenge for what?" he asked finally. He had not done anything that he considered wrong. He was a young man in the prime of life whose hormones naturally raged.

That evening, Fred was still ill at ease and lost in thought. He stayed home and had changed from his white physician's coat to a dark navy blue, Italian silk suit. He had to admit he looked dashing. He admired himself in the mirror as he tied his patterned silk tie around his collar with his delicate hands. He was taller than the average Mexican-American individual and, as a matter of fact, taller than the average man. He was handsome and graceful and, with his gray eyes and romantic ways, he could charm the pants off any willing woman.

He seemed pleased with the planned evening meal and enjoyed meeting the charming Castillo family. They had brought as the customary gift to their hosts a large basket of imported wines, chocolates, nuts, and cans of salmon and other fish. *Señor* Castillo, a distinguished looking gentleman with black hair graying at his temples, spoke very eloquently. He was an intelligent man, educated in the city of Veracruz, and had lived many years in Texas before the Mexican raids. The Castillos had been very successful as established merchants in McAllen. They had a large store that supplied clothing, shoes, and groceries to the

Mexican-American families from the surrounding area. *Señora* Castillo seemed solicitous and kind, and was very attractive, with large green eyes, and black hair arranged on top of her head. Sparkling diamond earrings and a brooch adorned her stylish gown.

Fred was staggered by the exotic beauty of Catalina Castillo. *Victoria knows how to pick them!* He thought. The petite girl had an hourglass figure, with beautiful black hair down to her waist, and large green eyes, much like her mother's. She wore a long, black, lace gown scooped in front to display some cleavage and her light delicate skin. A diamond brooch on her right shoulder and two small diamond earrings completed her stunning look.

The two families were quick to notice the subtle glances winging their way between the young couple across the dining table; they were all careful in their conversation, each aware of the chemistry at work between the charismatic Fred and the lovely Catalina.

Fred's insides turned to mush. Catalina smiled serenely, and her appearance reminded him how his mother must have looked when his father fell in love with her and decided to marry her. The only difference was that his mother was taller, leaner, and her eyes were dark. He was impressed with Catalina's glossy, light-pink complexion, large beautiful eyes, and long, thick eyelashes. She was like a rare and delicate blooming orchid kept hidden in the shade and away from ordinary men full of temptations.

Occasionally loud bangs could be heard from the back of the house. The guests would stare at one another in question while eating. *Señora* Castillo's eyes would widen and stare at Gloria Hinojosa, while *Señor* Castillo's eyebrows would rise, and Catalina would blink and blush.

"I apologize," remarked *Don* Federico trying to keep a calm demeanor. He patted his mouth with his dinner napkin, looking straight into *Don* Castillo's eyes. "My sister is sick, an invalid, and lives with us. The only way she can get attention is by hitting the walls. I will send one of the servants to see about her." He nodded toward Victoria and asked her to have one of the servants check on his sister. Mexican families were responsible for their elders and took care of them, regardless of their sacrifice.

Victoria excused herself and said she would be right back. As she walked the long hallway she realized how upset she was becoming over her mad aunt, with her incessant screaming and wild surprises, which were getting out of hand. Her behavior was wearing on everyone's nerves and unbalancing everyone's schedule. She was afraid to have guests or friends over for any length of time for fear of their finding out that Josie was insane, something which would reflect on their family's name and honor. But Josie was her father's only living relative, and half of Spanish Acres had been bequeathed to her. One day, though, Victoria would inherit all of the property, and she was going to run the land, the cotton, and the oil field her own way!

When she returned, she motioned to Fred to come out into the hall.

Fred immediately excused himself and joined Victoria in the hall, noticing the disturbed expression on her face.

"You're going to have to sedate her," whispered Victoria. "We simply cannot put up with her like this all the time, especially when we have company."

"What's wrong with her now?" asked Fred, concerned. "Has she been given her late meal?"

"Of course, she has!" snapped Victoria. "She has it plastered all over the walls and has messed the bed and used her hands to wipe it all over the sheets and covers. The servants and the nurse are cleaning everything up at this moment. They left her alone for several minutes while they were eating and this is what happened."

"I'll get my medical bag," replied Fred in his calm, good-natured way.

The rest of the evening went smoothly, as the family enjoyed the political rhetoric and discussed current events. All shared the excitement of the coming changes promised in the modern age, while they sipped on the gifted wines from crystal goblets.

Later, the men stepped outside onto the porch, sharing brandy and smoking Cuban cigars, enjoying the magnificent sunset. Victoria, Grandmother Gloria, and *Señora* Castillo disappeared into the parlor to discuss women's rights issues, quilt patterns, and new recipes for making orange pineapple marmalade.

Fred and Catalina walked outside into the lush patio, drinks in hand, laughing and conversing as though they'd known each other forever.

CHAPTER 36

The next week, in the late evening after all his patients were gone, Fred confronted the girl named Emily in his office. He mentioned that the family had investigated her, and she needed to tell the truth. Insulted by Fred's remarks, she did admit that her name was Martha, but she went by Emily. Her full name was Martha Emily Ferguson, and Otto Foster was a distant relative, by adoption. Not completely telling him the whole truth, she made up the story that while downtown, she had overheard several men who were talking about Fred and how important his father was to the community. "They said that if it hadn't been for your grandfather that you people wouldn't be anything. They said your chicken-shit grandfather was a crooked, thievin', shrewd, businessman, and would sell his mother down the river for a dollar, since there was a possibility that you people had Jewish blood." She also admitted that the men who were talking were all white men who envied the Juelson family because of their being Mexican-Americans and because of all the money they had acquired.

Fred, disturbed by what Emily had said and by Victoria's stern conviction, had to swallow his pride. He decided not to see her again. "It is best not to come around here anymore," he said with a commanding authority. "You are right! I am a Mexican-American. There are other doctors in the area that would love to take you as their patient. For your safety and mine, it is best this way." He became strict and to the point. "It was nice meeting you. But I take my profession seriously, and I do not tolerate lies, and I don't want an embarrassing scandal to come to our family." He turned a cold shoulder, ignored her, and continued looking into his microscope and examining bacterial specimens lying on the table.

"You cannot dump me like this!" Emily yelled. "You and I had something special going—you told me you loved me! Just think of all the wonderful sex we had, and how you were able to completely satisfy me—how you said you never wanted it to end!"

"Yes, I know all that, but that was before I knew you lied," Fred replied evenly. "I do not like your, foolish pranks."

"You dirty Mexican! I've heard that you Mexicans are all the same—love 'em and leave 'em! Is what ya'll do! You're going to pay for this! You owe me something! My father will see that you get yours, you asshole! You cowardly bastard!" she continued, becoming hysterical.

Her face was ugly and twisted with rage, and she began throwing his books and kicking anything in her way.

Fred managed to get a hold of her arm, and jerked, dragged, and pushed her out the door. "Because I'm a dirty Mexican-American, you need to go. It's dangerous for you to be here," he replied, vexed and looking her straight in the eye. "It is best not to see each other. And I do not owe you anything. You're the one that was sick and came to see me, remember?" Fred slammed the door hard and locked it, then moved to the window, where he watched Emily stomp down the sidewalk in her high heels toward the palms area of the park, still crying and screaming epithets. "You dirty Mexican bastard!"

He watched until she disappeared among the tall bushes and trees and then questioned himself on his reactions to the criticism and puzzled over his feelings. He paced the floor and sat absently eyeing his bacterial specimens, but looking past them, deep in thought. He was provoked by what she said and began wondering what she meant by *my father will see that you get yours!* What did she mean by that? Had her father planned this? She was an adopted girl, he had gathered, but he could not make the connection. He remembered her mentioning earlier that if her father found out that she was seeing a Mexican doctor, he would whip her. Fred knew something was not right. She was not telling the whole truth. He was glad now that he had made the final decision not to see her again. He would avoid that excruciating tension in his life. Victoria was right! She was always right.

In the following weeks, Fred and Catalina strolled around the palm park together when the Castillos joined the family for their weekly dinner and visit. At other times, Fred would make an exodus from his sick patients and find time to visit the family at their *ranchito* near McAllen. There was talk in the Castillo and the Juelson families of the couple's engagement and future marriage. The mixed ethnic group in Mercedes had become a hotbed of gossip and scandals, and when Fred and Catalina sauntered around the park, the people would whisper among themselves, while others would admire the handsome couple.

Bad news came the following week. The mournful *Lechuzas* had been circling around Spanish Acres, and dear ol' Manuel, who hadn't drawn a sober breath in sixty years, died, probably from a corrupted, wasted liver from drinking too much. Manuel, fearing that some-day he might run out of liquor, had stashed enough bottles around the place to sink a battle-ship. Many weeks and months later, bottles were still being found. Yo-Yo, especially, would sorely miss his ol' drinking buddy. The funeral was small, among the families at Spanish Acres and a few others who knew him. He would be missed the most by *Don* Federico, who had known him the longest. He was buried next to Mamá Maria in the Juelson cemetery. Victoria sobbed for a week, since he had been a part of her life since she was a child and was one of her favorite people. Carlos, now a young man of twenty-six, was not present for the funeral, since he was in San Antonio handling the sale of the Juelson's cattle.

One day Emma, all excited, called Victoria on their chattering, ten-way Southern Bell party line. She had gotten a letter informing her that Dr. Benjamin Burr had retired, sold everything in Houston, and was moving to Mercedes. Anytime the phone rang, everyone on the party line picked up the phone and listened in on the conversations of others. It was a hotline for steamy mudslinging, and within hours, the whole community had heard the news. Unperturbed, Emma began planning for his arrival. She painted the bedrooms and cleaned the whole house and bought new rugs and furniture. Dr. Burr was coming to Emma's house and moving right in. This not only raised eyebrows in the community, but Felicia and Dan, who now had three youngsters, were equally astonished. Emma's house was getting crowded.

The times were changing and it was an opportune time for Dan Land to start building his own home for Felicia and his family. *Don* Federico sold the couple several acres of vacant land across the street from his property, and immediately construction began on a beautiful three-story home. Victoria was overjoyed, since they would only be a step away from seeing one another, and she and Felicia could raise their children together.

The news that Dr. Burr was coming to live in Mercedes pleased Dr. Fred, who had more than enough patients to go around.

Dr. Burr seemed to fit right in and became very accommodating to everyone around him. He assisted Fred with hard-to-diagnose cases, and was there to take over the office when Fred needed to travel to visit his homebound patients and on emergencies. In Emma's household, there was never a dull moment, as he would recommend solutions for everyone's ailments. Within two months of having the doctor move in, the couple decided that it was more convenient to get married than to have the whole community pointing fingers and whispering about their scandalous behavior right in front of them.

The small wedding reception held for the immediate families was a joyous occasion, as it also presented an opportunity for everyone to see Jaime and John. The twins congratulated Fred for finishing his studies and were impressed by his medical office and his roster of patients. They always knew that Fred was smart and would be very successful in the medical profession. They were also pleased that Carlos was successfully taking over the family cattle empire. Jamie had become an attorney in Austin, and John, who lived in San Antonio, was an engineer. "If you ever need an attorney," Jamie said with a wink before he left, "just give me a chime. I work in a corporate office with ten other lawyers, each specializing in their own legal field."

⌘ ⌘ ⌘

One chilly, rainy night in the middle of January, when all the patients had been treated and had left his office, Fred remained, spending hours studying a certain virus infection from a woman patient who had sores in her ears and now on her eyelids. It was completely baffling him. No matter what he had prescribed for it, the virus kept eating at her and was getting worse. He had tried treating it with powerful chemical ingredients he had at hand, but nothing had worked. It only kept reproducing. Wondering if he could ask Dr. Burr's advice, he got up from his desk and started to dial the wall phone next to the window. At the same time, he thought he saw a dark shadow outside the window, but dismissed it as something blowing in the wind. Then he saw movement again and stayed near the window.

Hearing a noise outside his door, Fred hung the phone up and went to the door to investigate. He opened it to find Emily standing there, soaked and shivering, her blonde hair dangling and dripping around her shoulders, her clothes drenched. He had never expected to see her again.

"What are you doing here?" he questioned, as he led her inside the office. He had not seen her in several months. His first thought was to get a warm blanket to cover her up, and he found one immediately. "You're all wet and going to catch a cold!" He wrapped the blanket around her shivering body and sat her down in a chair near his desk. Baffled at her presence, he asked again, "What brings you here at this hour and in this weather?"

"Fred," she spoke nervously, looking at him with a solemn but anxious gaze, "I need to talk to you. I need to tell you something. I'm in trouble, and you need to know about it. I'm sorry for the name calling."

"Nah, go ahead," answered Fred, dismissing her apology with a wave of his hand. "I'm listening." He watched her expression change from frustration to fear. "What's wrong?" he asked kindly.

"I need to start from the beginning. My stepfather, Bill Wild, threatened me and made me pretend that I was ill. He ordered me to go to your office and get acquainted with you. He also ordered me to have sexual intercourse and to see how far I could go with you. Mind you, I did have a cough. Remember?" She spoke as if she were a young innocent, simpleton girl afraid of the consequences and wanting help defuse the problem that she had created.

"What a minute! I'm not quite sure how I'm involved. So, tell me, what was the reason he threatened you?" He knew Emily was not educated, and with little schooling, she had trouble explaining things. Fred studied her intently as she continued revealing her story.

"My stepfather and a Mr. Hanson have become good friends. After listening to Mr. Hanson telling his story—and I've heard it over and over again—he apparently hates your father for what he did to him years ago in Mexico, and he's trying to get even by getting to you. Mr. Hanson also became angry when he heard that you are the one who uncovered Otto's insect farm and blabbed it to the officials. Judge Ale was Mr. Hanson's good friend and had been helping him secretly, all the time he was a fugitive in Mexico. After hearing what happened to Judge Ale, Mr. Hanson began plotting with my stepfather, waving dollar bills in his face. He hates the whole Juelson family. He began using me as a scapegoat, to get to you and get even with your father by doing something terrible—I don't know what. They never told me their plans. All they did was used me," she said sadly.

"Wait a minute," interrupted Fred. "Hanson, the ex-Texas Ranger, is here in Texas?"

"Yes. He was pardoned by the governor of Texas months ago and is living in a shack in La Feria."

"So tell me, you talked about Otto. How are you and Otto related?" asked Fred becoming curious and more concerned, trying to grasp the whole detailed picture of the plot.

"Otto is my step-grandfather. I was adopted by his daughter, Mary Ferguson, and then given to one of Mary's cousins. That's why I go by the last name of Ferguson. So what were you saying about Mr. Hanson?"

"Hanson is a murderer, a greedy ass. He has no feelings. He will kill anyone who gets in his way. All he thinks of is money, and how he is going to get it. He was supposed to be my grandfather's friend, but he killed him for his gold mine in Monterrey. He's a Mexican-hater and probably involved now with the Klan."

"Yes! I've heard Mr. Hanson talking about the men in white robes and how he disguises himself," explained Emily, still shivering and wiping her eyes with a towel. "There are many Klan members in the Valley and many in Harlingen, especially the Rangers. I've heard Mr. Hanson talk about them many times."

"Hanson has killed so many Mexicans here in the Valley, and even a Pinkerton detective, but nobody can prove anything, so he's gotten away with it so far. My father turned him in to the authorities in Mexico for killing a Mexican man there, and he thought he had put Hanson in a Mexican jail for good, but apparently the devil got lucky. He deserves to be locked up, with the keys thrown away, and he should not be here in Texas. So, what do your stepfather and Hanson have to do with me?"

"Mr. Hanson is manipulating Bill, who is supposedly his friend, while they drink together." Emily rambled on. "Hanson took a liking to me and offered my stepfather money to have me sleep with him. My stepfather went right along, seeing the opportunity for easy money, since he thinks women are only for sex. Mr. Hanson, of course, is sexually different. I never got used to it and I hated it, but it was better sleeping with him, in his dirty rundown shack, than with Bill—he's been sexually abusing me since I came of age. I do not know what happened to my adopted mother, but she's not around anymore. She used to protect me from him, but he beat her all the time. After she left, it became a nightmare for me and real convenient for Bill—he would not leave me alone sexually. When I refused, he took pleasure in beating me with his horsewhip and, while I was still hurting, crying and weak, he would rape me anyway. I had no other choice but to go along with his desires. It was easier that way, since I had no other person to turn to."

Fred kept eyeing her and knew, from Victoria's investigation, that she was telling the truth. He felt that Emily was in danger and that was the reason she was afraid. He remembered seeing bruises on her body, which only gave more credit to her story. A feeling of compassion overtook him, knowing that it must have been horrible for a child not to be loved, and to be given away and then abused. And no doubt, such treatment would have a terrible impact on a child when they became an adult.

Emily wiped her eyes and continued, "Hanson convinced my stepfather, since I was such a hot piece of ass, as he put it, to use me as a backdoor arrangement to get to you. Hanson saw the opportunity in me and offered my adopted father plenty of money to have me do their dirty plan. It was then that my stepfather ordered me to seduce you or he'd kill me. Mr. Hanson told my stepfather that you were going to suffer like he did. He said he was going to enjoy watching your father suffer in agony by destroying you and your profession, and bringing you and your family down to the dirt, where all Mexicans should be." She talked fast and nervously, wiping her eyes.

"The Mexican-hater, Hanson, killed my grandfather in his greed. What happened to him in Mexico was his fault and he got caught! It exposed him for what he really is—a murderer!" Fred was livid.

Emily continued, "Mr. Hanson said he hates you and your father because of losing his Texas Rangers job and rotting in the Mexican jail, living like a beggar in the border towns, and sleeping in the dirty streets. He said he was going to make you pay and see how your rich, arrogant, SOB father liked it. He said that I had to do what he said or else—"

"Which was—?"

"To have me steal the .38 special revolver with your name on it, the one that was in your holster on top of those shelves." She pointed to the shelf above Fred's head. "I was ordered by my stepfather, who was told by Mr. Hanson, to steal it when you were not looking. At first, I thought it would be fun, but after you caught me in the lie, and you didn't want any part of me anymore, I got worried and began thinking."

"My gun, the one that Dad gave me when I graduated from high school? You took my .38 revolver? For what reason?" Fred was furious. He got up from his desk and reached for the holster on the top shelf and found it empty. He wanted to lash out at the girl, forgetting that he felt sorry for her and wanted to help her. He felt betrayed. Controlling his temper, he asked instead, "Why?"

"I'm afraid now," Emily said, starting to cry again. "They are going to kill me. I'm sorry, Fred. I did wrong and I've hurt you. I've felt so guilty about what I said to you. What I did was wrong." She sobbed and sobbed, with tears running down her cheeks. "I had to come over and tell you the truth before it was too late, before my stepfather finds out I'm here, blabbing my guts out and confessing to you their plans."

"So where's my gun now—who has it?" Fred snapped. "What the hell do they want with my gun? What are they going to do with it?"

Emily answered hysterically, "I don't know!" She was shaking with fear and wailing. "What are guns for," she exclaimed, "if not to kill someone? They are planning something terrible!" Emily continued sobbing, burying her face in her hands. "I should have killed my stepfather with the gun, while I had the chance."

Overcome by guilt and remorse, Fred's thoughts went haywire. This was the stupid, ignorant girl he was having sex with, the woman he had desired and lusted over, having wet dreams. This was the trashy girl sleeping with her stepfather and the hated Hanson, while he was having seconds. His blood boiled. What was he thinking? He should have realized the consequences it would bring. He thought of Victoria and how right she always was, telling him, *there is more than one.* Who was Hanson going to kill? Then it hit him like a ton of bricks—Father!

Fred, shaken and vexed, kept his thoughts to himself. He got up from his desk and began dialing the phone to speak to Victoria. He had to be careful with his words, for the whole gossiping community that was always picking up the phone lines would be listening.

"*Manita,*" he said. "Can you come over to my office? I have something I need to show you."

Victoria came quickly, recognizing the urgency in Fred's voice. She left her dipping wet umbrella outside on the porch, entered, and shook the rain from her clothes and pulled the scarf from her head. "What did you want to show me?" she asked Fred, whose face was ashen. She turned and viewed a shivering Emily sitting with the blanket around her. "What the hell is she doing here?" She caught the drift from Fred's expression and said, "What's going on?" Recalling what she had read in the fortune cards earlier, she became instantly concerned.

Emily told her story while Victoria listened intently. Fred sat nervously doodling on a piece of paper on his desk and knew that his sister, like a keg of dynamite, was getting ready to explode.

"Why you dirty, bitch!" Victoria shouted in Emily's face, quelling a maddening urge to hit her. "What was your reward? What were you trying to get from us?"

"*Manita*," said Fred, getting up from his chair and addressing Victoria. "Please, let's not make this any worse than it already is. Emily is sorry for what she did, what she was forced to do. She's full of guilt and has already confessed. She's in extreme danger for coming all the way here and telling us the truth."

"I cannot believe that you are defending her, Fred." Victoria stormed, turning toward her brother in a tantrum. "She was forced to—my butt! Did someone put a gun to her head? Hell no! Did she enjoy the sex with you? Hell yes!" She paced the floor, her hands flailing. "After all, they got your gun with your name, and Father is the target. I hope you enjoyed your sexual behavior for the price of our father's head!"

"Wait a minute, *Manita*!" Fred thundered. "I remembered you having your little secrets, too. Who's calling the kettle black? And guess who's kept quiet all these years regarding your nasty little skeleton in the closet!"

"All right," Victoria conceded. She rubbed her forehead and paced the floor again in total disgust. "Let's not bring out all our dirty laundry. We have to think this thing out. If Emily is in danger, then she better stay here, until we find a way of getting your gun back. And Father has to be notified. We cannot go to the sheriff, and Lord knows we can't tell the Texas Rangers that your gun was stolen. We'd have to explain the whole sordid story, and it would definitely bring scandal to our family, once everyone found out."

"I'm not wanted here," said Emily in between a whimpering fit of sobs, feeling sorry for herself and fearing the vengeful look that had settled on Victoria's face.

"That's right! You are not wanted in our house," stated Victoria, having no sympathy for the lame-brained girl who could not think for herself, being controlled by two abusers. "But for this night you're stuck with us. You're going to stay here in the office, until we figure out what we are going to do."

That night, arrangements were made for clean, dry clothes, a cot, linens, pillows and blankets to be brought from the main house so Emily could sleep in one of Fred's medical examination rooms.

The following morning, breakfast was prepared and taken to Emily, but the servant returned with the food tray, saying the bed was empty and the *gringa* was gone.

⌘ ⌘ ⌘

Don Federico returned from Spanish Acres that evening and was shocked to hear that Bernard Hanson was living in the Valley, and he reacted nervously to the news about Fred's gun. Later, after he and Victoria had engaged in a full-fledged ruckus with Fred that had disturbed the entire household, all had gone to bed with frayed nerves. It was getting close to midnight and the mansion finally seemed quiet and peaceful, with the children and servants asleep and dotty Aunt Josie sedated.

After drinking a glass of red wine, Victoria, still unable to sleep, decided to crochet some doilies, hoping it would calm her nerves. She had brought her basket of needlework and put her feet up on a velvet ottoman in the main living room of the house. Before long, she became sleepy and dozed off, with a needle hook still in her hand on her lap.

She was asleep for how long, she didn't remember, but she heard the large clock out in the foyer striking twelve. A different sound down the long hall startled her, and in her imagination, she thought she saw a hulking shadow in the dimness of the soft light. She cleared her eyes, but something was still there. It seemed to be the dark figure of a large dog resembling—a black wolf? It was standing in the murky light of the hallway, its large bright eyes staring at her. The animal stalked slowly into the living room and drew closer.

Victoria thought she was dreaming but quickly realized that it was real. She stiffened with fright, stupefied and afraid to move. She kept her eyes on the black wolf now coming toward her. She felt the needle in her hand and decided she would use it if the creature got too close. She saw its eyes, bright like two lit lanterns, and a full mouth of sharp white teeth. She felt her blood run cold and the hair on the back of her neck stand up. Her eyes blinked nervously, and her heart nearly pounded out of her chest in fear. The animal was huge and kept coming toward her, and then circled around her. As it did so, she could feel it breathing and suddenly sensed a benevolent presence. The wolf sniffed her and then licked her cheek, as if it were a sign of approval. Then, something startling happened.

It spoke: "Victoria! Don't you remember me?"

"*Doña* Adela!" Victoria answered in a cold sweat and staring into the wolf's eyes. "You're not dead?" Letting out a ragged sigh of relief, she placed both hands to her chest as if to contain her pounding heart. She stood up, dropping the needle to the floor. "*Dios mío!*"

"Did you think I was going to live forever? Death is only a moment. It's only the passing into a different dimension. I'm a spirit now. I have no pain, I have no sorrow. I have wished it that way and was granted to be the spirit of the wolf because of all the good deeds I performed while in the flesh."

"*Doña* Adela, please tell me how you died and who killed you! All of the families at Spanish Acres and I mourned your loss and have missed you so terribly."

"Who killed me? The same white men who killed your grandfather! The ex-Texas Ranger, *El Rinche,* and his murderous sidekick friend surprised me in my home and dragged me outside. They thought I had silver and gold coins stashed away. They wanted it. Thank goodness, Roberto was hiding in the *brasada.*"

"Hanson! Why, of course," gasped Victoria, horrified. "Who else would it have been?"

"He used another friend to help him with the stolen dynamite from the oil wells. Hanson killed his partner too, later in Mexico, to keep him quiet," replied the large wolf. "It's the same man who wants to get to your brother, Fred. I know that you have thought of me and wanted answers, especially about your brother. Yes, I'm afraid he is in danger. He needs guidance from the unseen spirit world. Fred has done good deeds, especially for the poor."

"What do you mean, Fred is in danger?" Victoria begged her.

"Because of things your grandfather did, your father and now Fred are going to pay for those deeds. There is a terrible plot that several white men have against your father, and Fred is going to be blamed for those actions. You must light three white candles and say the prayer that I once taught you for a miracle for seven days straight. You cannot break the cycle, or you'll have to start all over again for another seven days. You need to make a figure of *el Rinche* and then burn it during the full moon, and also a black candle to get rid of him."

"Fred is going to get married soon. Nothing can happen to him to now," Victoria cried. "He has his career and is happy. Nobody can harm him or my father. I'll see to that! However, I'll burn the candles and do what I have to do."

"We will see!" *Doña* Adela answered. "He will never marry this girl! The fortune cards should give you many of the answers you need. If you need my special help, when the clock strikes twelve at midnight, call for me, and I will come to you in the spirit. Until then, I must go into the night and help others, appearing in their dreams."

"*Doña* Adela," Victoria called out, wanting to ask more questions, but the wolf had vanished. She stood alone in the darkness talking to herself and thinking that perhaps it had been a wild nightmarish dream. Was she going out of her mind? After all, madness did run in the family! There was the lingering smell of death, which finally convinced her of what had occurred was real. She would keep the secret to herself, her own special secret, since nobody would believe her anyway, and she could call upon *Doña* Adela on any given midnight for help. She would burn the candles and say the prayers, but make a figure of Hanson? She didn't think that was necessary.

Soon, arrangements were being made for Fred and Catalina's marriage, and the guest list of important people was being prepared. Both families had relatives on either side of the river, so invitations, as a custom, were to be mailed out two months early for families having to travel long distances. *Don* Federico was getting an architect ready to build Fred and his bride a fancy new home, the finest in the land, regardless of cost. The couple could choose any plot from five to twenty acres, any place they would prefer to live. *Don* Federico was going to see that Fred and Catalina had the very best in their married life.

On that same evening, as the rainy season had started and the rain pummeled the roof of the house, the doorbell rang. There was a commotion in the foyer with the servants and loud inflamed talk could be heard. Strange men in uniforms with badges on their chests and guns in their holsters, stood there dripping wet, demanding to see Fred.

"What is this all about?" questioned *Don* Federico, coming out of his library, where he had taken refuge from the ladies and all the wedding plans. "What do you want with my son, Fred?"

Pat Marshall, the head of Texas Rangers located in Weslaco, answered, "Senator, we found your son's gun. Is this it?" He showed *Don* Federico the .38 Smith and Wesson handgun with Fred's name inscribed on the grip.

"Why, yes, that's my son's gun. I personally gave it to him when he graduated from high school."

"How touching!" answered one of the officers in a sarcastic tone of voice.

"Where was it?" inquired the *Don*, becoming disturbed by their rude attitude, "and what is this all about?"

"That's why we need to talk to your son. Where is he? We need some answers." The Texas Ranger's piercing eyes darted around the interior of the house in all directions.

"What does all this have to do with Fred?" the *Don* repeated bluntly.

"It was found next to the body of one Martha Emily Ferguson," Marshall went on. "We want to ask him some questions, bring him down to headquarters. Where is Dr. Juelson now?"

Don Federico was totally confused. "A body, you said? Found dead, with Fred's gun nearby? Impossible!"

"Hardly," replied a smug rookie officer. "When you find a dead girl's body and a gun with the name of the owner on it, it's hard to miss the obvious," he said curtly, so cocky and sure of himself. They had Fred already convicted of the murder.

Don Federico was momentarily speechless and felt the blood drain from his face. He touched his chest as he felt a sudden pressure erupt, as if kerosene had been thrown into burning ashes, and his left arm was going numb. His heart felt as if was being crushed. The *Don* needed to sit down. Instead, he calmly replied, "Fred is out on a call. He's delivering a baby at one of the *ranchitos* west of Weslaco. If you men want to wait in the living room until he returns, you can do so."

"I don't think so, Senator," replied the head Texas Ranger, adjusting his jacket and donning his gloves. "We will leave for now and come back later. We need to talk to Fred about this girl. We got word that your son was courting her. Lots of people saw them together, you know," he said, clearing his throat. "This girl had repeatedly told everybody that Fred was going to marry her. We'll keep the gun for evidence, and we'll be back in a few hours."

Attracted by the noisy intrusion, Victoria and the others had stood and listened from the side hall. They all heard what the Ranger had said. Catalina began crying, and her mother tried to comfort her. Emma, Felicia and Grandmother Gloria all embraced Catalina and her mother.

"Don't pay any attention to what they are saying," Emma said dryly. "They are all liars."

Señora Castillo's face was somber and she became withdrawn. She asked for her shawl and Catalina's wrap-around mantilla. "We must leave. It's getting late and it's a long drive back to

McAllen," she said, very quietly and gracefully. Catalina's face reflected the distressing feeling that this whole dream of marriage to Fred Juelson had been too good to be true. The two women left, and did not say when they would return. The rest stood around breathing hard and thinking to themselves that a horrendous scandal was about to erupt.

Emma found a chair in the living room and began complaining, predicting what could happen. "Those *malditos Rinches*, if they catch Fred, they will kill him on the spot! I can't believe that those idiots think Fred would kill somebody just because they found his stolen gun. They are blaming him for the murder of a no-good trashy woman. *Los Rinches* will find any excuse to accuse Fred because of who he is." Her voice echoed the anger throughout the mansion.

As the atmosphere in the house descended into melancholy, *Señora* Del Calderóne grabbed her shawl and decided to leave before it got too dark. *Don* Federico apologized to her and thanked her for helping with the invitations, then joined the other ladies in the living room. The disturbing events of the evening were etched on his face. Grandmother Gloria looked grim and sat quietly on a sofa viewing the palms park from the window. The wonderful prospect of a happy marriage was turning into a horribly troubling calamity instead.

Felicia whispered to Victoria. "I'll go get Dan to drive over to the *ranchito* where Fred is and tell him what's happening. The Rangers are sitting, with their windshield wipers on, watching and waiting on the opposite side of the road. It's the only road coming from Weslaco."

"Wait a minute!" Victoria answered. Her head was spinning, and her brain was in a fog, but she was trying to think how to best help and warn her brother. The Rangers were definitely watching the house for any activity. "I'll go over to your house and get Dan. We'll drive south on the Old Military Road and take the long way around, without *los Rinches* seeing us." She spoke with panicked urgency.

Don Federico spoke up: "Victoria, take the money bag from my desk and give it to Fred—Lord knows, he's going to need it! There must be a thousand dollars in there that he'll need to get away from here, and stay away for a while. Just so *los Rinches* don't get their hands on him."

"Father, where?" Victoria's eyes widened with alarm. "Where will he go? Where can he find shelter in the middle of the night?"

"Across the border into Mexico," answered the *Don*, wheezing and gasping for breath. "There he'll be safe, until we can clear this matter up. Emma is right—if *los Rinches* arrest Fred, he won't have a chance to clear his name. I don't want my son to die at their hands, like so many others, without any explanation. I can tell you right now that this is Hanson's revenge. He planned it that way, by having someone steal Fred's gun, and frame him for murder. These allegations are going to be hard to disprove."

Don Federico sat down in the nearest chair, holding his chest. "This is the way he used to operate in the old days—it was one of his favorite tricks. He would accuse some poor Mexican of any wrongdoing, and then scare him to death with vile threats, and the Mexican would give him anything he asked for, even his land. Fred is going to get away into Mexico, and we are going to clear his name, even if I have to travel to the state capital building in Austin to do so."

"Papá, Fred is going to lose everything—the profession he wanted all of his life, his good name, his prestige and honor," cried Victoria. "What about his marriage?" She stood and gulped for air, not believing the nightmare that was sprouting.

"It's better to lose material things than your life," said the *Don*. "For the moment, I have to do what is best for Fred, without getting him killed by the Goddamn Rangers. Give Fred the money, Victoria, and get rid of his car once he reaches the border. Tell Fred to find shelter with the Solis family in Reynosa. They are your cousins from your mother's side of the family and will see that he is taken care of. I will repay them as soon as I can. Tell Fred that I will try to get in touch with him later. Meanwhile, I'll call Canalo in Brownsville and get his advice."

The next day, Canalo replied in a telegram addressed to the Dan Land home as a precaution. His advice was for Fred to stay put in Reynosa, or maybe Matamoros, a bigger city, with less danger of being recognized. Mexico would be a safe refuge for him until the investigation cleared him of any wrongdoing.

CHAPTER 37

It must have been past midnight, in a soggy steady downpour. The disguise that Victoria and Dan had brought Fred had worked; camouflaged in a worn-out coat and a cap, he crossed the newly built wooden bridge into Reynosa, Mexico. They had found him as he was heading down the muddy road coming from the *ranchito*, where they informed him of the murderous tale told by the Rangers. The two cars followed one another through the damp wet night to the bridge crossing into Reynosa. Handing Fred the moneybag, Victoria informed him that *Don* Federico wanted him to stay with the Solis's until he was given later instructions. The *Don* would get in touch with the Solis cousins later. It was the same hacienda where Victoria and Ricardo had their wedding reception several years ago. Fred, still in shock, kept saying he was innocent. And what about Catalina? What would she say? Victoria told him that it was for his own good to go into hiding. Their father's orders were he must escape and save himself. As for Catalina, she now knew everything! Their marriage would have to wait.

Victoria drove Fred's car and dumped it into the deepest part of the Rio Grande River several miles southeast on the Military Road, where the Rio Grande River separated, forming an island like a crooked stick called *El Horcón*. She stood in the drizzling rain and watched as the car slowly spun in a whirlpool and finally sank. From there, Dan drove her back over rural roads to Mercedes. It was now around three-thirty in the morning, and the tension in the household was at its highest peak. *Don* Federico was suffering with chest pains and had not slept that night.

The next morning, local newspaper people were knocking on the door of the Juelson mansion and asking questions. While the two doctors, Hedrick and Burr, were leaving the premises, all the reporters were asking if Fred had returned, and others were querying and concerned about *Don* Federico's illness. Little was said, only that Fred had not returned and the household was worried. *Don* Federico had been sedated and was now resting comfortably. Dr. Burr replaced Fred temporarily while messages were being sent to the Indian doctor, White Eagle, in Oklahoma, asking him if he wanted to attend and help the doctor in the Valley until another doctor could be found for the booming business. At the clinic, people needing medical attention were already in line inquiring as to the whereabouts of *El Doctor Fred*.

TERRI RAGSDALE

The headline story on the front page was full of accusations that Dr. Fred Juelson was the suspect in the killing of a white woman, as his gun inscribed with his name was found near her body, and of course his disappearance was highly suspicious. Later, a hefty reward was offered for information on the whereabouts of Dr. Juelson. The Texas Rangers and the sheriff were all busy getting information and leaving posters trying to locate Fred. The car had not been found. Occasionally, one of the Ranger cars could be viewed some distance from the Juelson mansion. They sat for days, two at a time, on the road coming from Weslaco, waiting to see if they caught any glimpse of Fred.

Meanwhile in Reynosa, Fred, now a fugitive, found shelter with the gracious Solis family, who were more than honored to have him as their guest on their two hundred-acre ranch south of Reynosa. Fred was quickly back in business, as there was always a line of people, including the members of the Solis family, their *vaqueros* and their families, malnourished, ailing children, and women who had been abused and beaten—all wanting medical help and advice. And as always, Fred, ever good-hearted and grateful for having a place to stay, went right to work and tried not to worry about the complications that were taking place across the river in Mercedes.

Out in the patio in the evenings, and in the lonely hours of the night, he would listen to the beautiful Mexican love songs sung by the resident *vaqueros* sitting around campfires on the grounds. But as the days progressed, he started to feel melancholy and guilty, thinking of his clientele across the border, his family, his courtship to Catalina, and his future marriage. Sweet memories began crowding in on him. He wondered about his father and all of the sacrifice made for him to become successful, and now his life had become a total failure. Occasionally, *Señor* Solis would bring newspapers from across the river full of articles insinuating that Fred was the killer. All were asking, where is the mysterious car? And where is he hiding?

Up to this time, Fred was so involved in his medical activities; he was totally unaware of the turmoil of the restless Mexican citizens' *Cristero Rebellion* movement that was happening in Mexico. During the year of 1928, Alvaro Obregón, newly elected president of Mexico, had been assassinated because of his hatred of the Catholic Church, since all convents and Catholic schools had been closed and church properties had been confiscated. Many of the illiterate Mexican citizens were convinced that Obregón was the antichrist, and a Catholic zealot determined to kill Obregón was successful. Riots were taking place in many cities of Mexico, including Reynosa, demanding justice for the Catholic Church. Pasual Ortiz Rubio was elected to complete Obregon's term. During that same year, Republican Herbert Hoover was elected the thirty-first President of the United States.

Carlos had returned to Spanish Acres from San Antonio, with a good sale on the cattle and got word from Victoria to come home to Mercedes to be with his father who was ill. Not only did Carlos join his father, who was glad that the sale of the cattle had gone well, but the unpopular Mrs. McCray was also at *Don* Federico's bedside, tending to his every whim, something that enraged Victoria.

Within two weeks, White Eagle arrived by train in Mercedes with his medical bag and baggage and his bow and arrow, which he used for hunting and entertainment when he was not otherwise occupied. He was given permission to hunt on the land at Spanish Acres, when the occasion was at hand. He was received by the working members of the Juelson household, who drove him to the mansion, where he was welcomed in a gracious manner by Victoria and *Don* Federico, who had his room ready.

Replacing Fred in his own medical business office, White Eagle went right to work and spent long hours with the Mexican clientele, and many times did not finish doctoring until the middle of the night. The Indian doctor helped Dr. Burr and Dr. Hedrick from time to time and introduced several new methods of healing. He also showed them the newest drugs that had been introduced since Dr. Burr had left the Houston area.

The coming of an Indian doctor to Mercedes did not sit well with the white community, especially secret members of the KKK, who were already stealthily busy making plans, with the ex-Ranger Hanson egging the group on. While the rest of the Klan heard and read about the mystery of the dead girl, Hanson was glad that there was no Mexican doctor around. They had tolerated Fred, a Mexican doctor, far too long, because of his father's influence and money, but an Indian doctor? That was outrageous and something had to be done.

Early in the spring of 1929, on a cloudless night with a shining full moon, White Eagle was working late in the lab when he saw several shadowy figures outside the clinic with lit torches. He grabbed his bow and arrow and exited out the back of the building.

The torches outside in the yard caught Victoria's eye, too. Already the victim of jumpy nerves, she called it to Carlos's attention. He viewed the activity from their dining room window and shouted for his father to come. After viewing the scene, *Don* Federico immediately ordered Chico and his work crew to get their guns and rifles.

Don Federico, Carlos, Victoria, and the rest of the crew sneaked from the back of the mansion, outside among the shrubs and palms trees, while two Texas Rangers arrived on the scene, one with a gun, the other with a double-barreled shotgun, both waiting to see what was going to develop.

From behind the group of seven white-hooded men, who were carrying torches and ropes, came the voice of the young, cocky Ranger, "What's going on here? You forgetting this is Texas, not Mississippi, and that you're stepping on private property?"

"What is it to you? Whose side are you on?" replied one of the masked men. "There's an Indian in there that needs killin'. And in this state you can get away with almost anything."

"Stop, and no, you cannot," stated the other Ranger. "What the hell has the Indian done to you, anyway?" he asked, pointing his gun towards the vigilante group that was trying to scatter around the buildings with their torches. "Get over here!" he bellowed to them, "or I'll shoot! I'll shoot to kill!" he shouted, but two managed to disappear to the back of the clinic, among the bushes and palms.

"What are you, a Mexican and Indian lover? They need to be done away with! What the hell are we paying you bastards for anyway?" replied one of the gutsy hooded men holding a rope. He started to advance, but changed his mind and stayed put. The double-barreled shotgun was aiming at him.

"Enough of that," said the other plucky Ranger, waving his gun. "You men need to git the hell off this land and go. There's been enough killin' already, and we are here to uphold the law!" He turned around suddenly surprise, for behind him he heard the clicking of rifles.

In the brightness of the moonlight, *Don* Federico and the rest of the crew stood and pointed their weapons toward the masked men. "Is that you, Milton?" the *Don* asked, angling his rifle toward the belligerent hooded figure. "I thought your voice sounded familiar."

"Yeah, well what of it?" Milton answered. "And what do you plan to do about it? Did you pay these bastard Rangers to protect your land?"

"Damn cowards!" shouted Carlos. "All of you hiding in those ridiculous masks. Why not show your face like a real man?" The rest of the Mexican crew began taunting them saying, "*Si! Si!* Take your masks off!" They laughed, "*Eh, eh!* C'mon!"

"Get off my land. You got a lot of balls, coming to my property, at night and uninvited," admonished *Don* Federico. "People have gotten killed for this kind of intrusion and trespassing on private property. And what the hell have I done to you that you feel you need to come onto my premises like hooded creeps and burn your damn crosses?"

Instantly, there was a whistling sound through the air, along with sounds of a scuffle and a loud noise coming from in back of the medical clinic. An arrow had struck one of the hooded men in his upper left thigh, and he rushed out from the back of the building screaming and holding onto his leg and hollering for help. He had tossed his torch against the corner of the building, and it was now on fire. Milton and the rest of the hooded men dropped their ropes and guns and rushed to help the crippled, crying individual.

"David!" cried ol' man Milton, knowing that his son was the one that had been wounded with an arrow in his leg. "Gawddamn!" he said, viewing the medical building that was going up in flames. "Let's get the hell out of here!"

"Wait a minute!" the Ranger called out. "All of you men are under arrest!" Four of the men ran and scattered in different directions and slipped off their masks. The companion Ranger ran after them. Shots were fired. One of them slipped and fell to the cold gravel road and began cussing Milton for his ideas before he was arrested.

Although *Don* Federico's men made a valiant effort to quell the fire, it was too late. The flames quickly devoured the entire building. It had been more like another curse. Fred was gone, and there was nothing to save. *Don* Federico felt his world crashing, and his family coming apart, and yet, there was nothing he could do now but wait. Wait until Fred was free. Wait until he could see his son again.

By that time, Dan Land and Felicia had arrived on the premises and stood next to Victoria and *Don* Federico watching in horror. Fred's predicament had brought difficulty and tragedy to everyone. Even in the middle of the night, word had spread rapidly, especially along the phone lines, that fire was destroying the Mexican medical clinic. Several influential Mexican-American businessmen from across the tracks showed up with their wagons, willing to help in any way they could. They were also afraid of similar incidents happening to their own small businesses.

In the months that followed, White Eagle returned to Oklahoma. Not much was left of the clinic. Rubble was cleared, but the medical building was never rebuilt. The incident on *Don* Federico's property was never reported, nor was any criminal indictment ever issued, as the Texas Rangers continued to keep vigil on the Juelson mansion and occasionally asked questions. David Milton limped the rest of his life and hated and cursed the Indians, the Mexicans, and any other ethnic group to his dying day. The secret members of the KKK went on discriminating and destroying other Mexican properties and lives, but evil never wins, because truth is righteous.

Six months later, Milton's warehouse and building went up in flames, and he lost everything. Months later, Garcia's grocery store across the tracks was torched and several other Mexican shops were destroyed during the night.

It was also in the middle of March of the same year that a gruesome murder was committed in the newly built town of Edcouch, northwest of Mercedes. Claude Kelly, son-in-law of the founder of the town, was hacked to death while sleeping in his father-in-law's home.

Terror swept and spread throughout the smaller communities. Demanding they find the murderer, Mr. Edward Couch hired several detectives to investigate, including several of the Texas Rangers. During this time, Couch was a candidate for County Judge and was disliked by politically opposed groups throughout the area. The Texas Rangers figured out that Couch was the intended victim, and his son-in-law had been at the wrong place at the wrong time. It became common for prominent people and leaders to arm themselves and guard their homes and families. Vigilantes took up arms and began investigating the workers and field hands. Nothing was taken and it was not considered robbery.

Every Mexican was a suspect, and every one that talked about or even mentioned the Claude Kelly incident was dragged in by the Texas Rangers for heavy questioning. On one occasion, an overly zealous, talkative drunk who mentioned he knew the killer was hauled in, tortured, and later found dead. The case went unsolved and as the years went by, the papers were shoved into the cold files.

⌘   ⌘   ⌘

In Mexico, the mood was threatening, with many militant Catholic zealots everywhere surrounding the cities. *Señor* Solis and his family were almost killed when a bomb was thrown at the Solis business. Luckily, no one was hurt. A note had followed to get rid of the "giant doctor," as they now referred to Fred.

Clandestine messages were being sent by Dan Land to *Señor* Solis and then given to Fred. All incoming mail to the Juelson residency was being inspected by special agents, so the family was careful not to repeat any information. Fred had gotten word from his father, via *Señor* Solis, to leave the hacienda and travel to Matamoros. Victoria had found out from Emma that she had accidentally mentioned to Yolanda where Fred was hiding. Secrets were hard to keep. And the greedy Yolanda, knowing that a price was on Fred's head, would automatically inform the authorities for the money.

In the middle of night, gracious goodbyes were exchanged, and Fred was driven out of town in a worn-out Ford truck used by the Solis's hacienda field workers and taken down the road that led to Matamoros. Within three hours, the slow Fork truck finally entered the sleeping city of Matamoros. Across the border, on the other side of the Rio Grande River, they could see the shimmering lights of Brownsville, Texas.

Fred planned to reside in Matamoros until given further orders by his father. But no sooner had he found shelter in the home of the Solis's friends, when several uniformed policemen accosted and questioned him. He was taken to the local jail and booked on charges of using Mexico as a refugee encampment. Fred was interrogated during the course of the night, where one policeman after another took turns asking him questions; up to this point, he had not slept.

The following morning, Fred was driven west of Matamoros to a prison, a large gloomy, stone building once used by *General* Manuel Mier. There he was ushered into an office with a large desk, behind which sat a high-ranking lieutenant, with gold medals strung across his chest, wearing tall black boots and dark sunglasses. He glared at Fred for a long time. When he did speak, he implied that a man of high stature had informed them of his arrival in their city. Fred found out later that it was *Señor* Del Calderóne, who was still living in Matamoros. How did *Señor* Del Calderóne know? Who had informed him that Fred was coming to Matamoros?

He was shown a poster with his picture on it and told to confess to the killing of Emily Ferguson. When he denied any wrongdoing, he was slapped around. Why did they care in Mexico? There had been real killer renegades from the United States living in Mexico, and nobody cared. Why was he so important to them?

Next, Fred was stripped of his clothing. The little money he had left was taken. He was whipped and tortured, and ordered to sign a confession of violating Mexican laws. Fred refused. He declared he was innocent, only helping the poor people. The policemen standing in the dirty office laughed. Fred was given cold tortillas to eat and water to drink, the only food that kept him alive. In his lonely hours spent in the cold cell, he kept thinking of who had informed *Señor* Del Calderóne. He learned there was a large reward being offered by *gringos* across the river. If Fred was so valuable on the other side of the river, the officers would hold him for ransom and have the *Americanos* pay them more *dinero*.

Within several days, the lieutenant had inquired and found out that Fred was a doctor and came from a rich, prosperous family and presumed that his father, the former Goodwill Ambassador to Mexico, would probably be willing to pitch them hundreds of dollars under the table to keep Fred alive. All of the smart officers in the prison worked the system and played two against each other. It had always been done, and it had always worked before.

By the time the news of Fred's capture had broken in Mercedes, *Don* Federico was being given nitroglycerin pills to put under his tongue each time he had a chest pain. Extremely upset at the news of Fred's incarceration, Victoria and Carlos made arrangements to visit him at the prison in Matamoros.

Upon reaching Matamoros, the duo had to rely on Victoria's tough, uncompromising attitude to get the officers' attention to be able to see and speak with Fred. The older gracious head *General* found Victoria to be so amusing and so attractive that he wanted her to return again so she could be his guest. He had never met a woman who was so vivacious, so headstrong, and heated with so much passion. He said this with a loud sigh while kissing her hand. He had never seen such beauty. Had chivalry returned?

I'll be his guest with a bullet in his head, she kept thinking. So by the time she and Carlos were allowed to visit Fred, they were appalled with the conditions at the prison. There were long passageways of noisy rows of cells filled with killers, thieves, and dope dealers clinging and hanging onto the cell bars, and the odors were disturbing. The inmates urinated in their cells and on the walls. The hideous smell was so terribly offensive that Victoria and Carlos had to put their hands over their noses. At the far end of one of the halls, Fred lay in a cold, wet cell, on a dirty wire cot, thin, weak and appearing malnourished. His face was black and blue. His eyes were full of despair. His clothes were dirty and torn.

"My God!" Victoria cried. "What have they done to you?" She hung on to the cell bars with a sickening pity, reaching out to her brother in an act of kindness, with tears falling from her eyes. She began shaking. "We're going to get you out of this hell!" she stormed. "We're going to do everything we can, and as soon as possible!"

From inside his cell, Fred began asking questions: "How is father doing? What have you heard from Catalina?" And then he told them how Ricardo's father, *Señor* Del Calderóne, had informed the officers of his coming to Matamoros. "How did he know? How was he informed?" Victoria and Carlos glanced at each other. They would get busy investigating.

While returning home, Carlos kept his eyes on the road, not saying a word. It was a long, lonely road. He was aware of the depth of Victoria's outrage and anger—she had done her share of crying in the last twenty miles. "I know what you're thinking!" He finally sounded off. "Don't do anything foolish! Let the lawyers and the two countries do their international arguing—that's why we're paying them a high price. Forget any stupid ideas you might have to get Fred out of prison."

"I can't stand it," Victoria said, blowing her nose on her lace handkerchief. "Fred needs clean clothes and food, and Lord knows, so does everyone in that prison. It's so pitiful!" She began concentrating and frown lines were forming on her forehead. "I can't for the life of me figure out how Ricardo's father heard about Fred."

"We'll find out sooner or later," replied Carlos, focusing his eyes on the road ahead.

When they got home, Victoria went into a trance. And sure enough, it was Yolanda who had informed Ricardo, and he had informed his father in Matamoros.

Within a week, Victoria's cleverness and maternal instincts had orchestrated a truckload of dry goods, including rice, pinto beans, and large cans of vegetables and fruits, along with blankets and clothing. On the other side, crossing the newly built bridge into Rio Rico, she bribed the Mexicans guards, pacifying them at the port called *mordida*, by giving them money, food, and clothes to let her pass through, which they were more than willing to do.

In Matamoros, the officers were delighted to see the coquettish Victoria every week coming with the commodities, which they all enjoyed. The officers were all getting to know her personally and called her by her first name. They were smitten with her, and Victoria was happy to share the bounty with them. They felt extremely lucky to have Dr. Fred as a prisoner, with all of the attention and free handouts they were receiving. They realized he was becoming an asset to them.

Several packages were brought from the medical clinic, which had been delivered four days after the fire. Many of the medical supplies were alcohol, chloroform, cotton swaps, injections, and several drugs including syrups, all quite welcome to the attending doctor that only came once a month, mostly to sign death certificates. One or two prisoners ended up dying every month, and their bodies were taken in a van and dumped in the Gulf, where hungry sharks would quite successfully clean up the evidence.

Victoria was becoming a regular visitor and things were starting to go in Fred's universal favor as he was given liberty to roam freely around inside the prison walls and help the sickly patients; however, he was kept under close supervision by the guards. He was appalled by the gruesome conditions and the horrible treatment of the prisoners. He was also aware that the majority of the prisoners were cold, murderous killers, but Fred, seeing the world through kindly eyes and wanting to heal people, only saw them as human beings.

The kitchen area was the worst. Nothing was ever cleaned. Slop was being fed to all of them, and nothing, not even the water, was boiled. Most of them had fleas and lice, dysentery, and many coughed throughout the night from colds or tuberculosis, a contagious disease. It was worse during the summer months, with the unbearable heat and the flies and mosquitoes.

Having overheard *Capitán* Gutierrez telling another guard of his newborn child crying all the time, Fred asked from his cell, "What is wrong with your baby?" he questioned with sincere concern.

"The child cries all the time and will not eat. He did not take to his mother's breast milk, and we gave him cow's milk, and that made it even worse. The household is pulling their hair out. I had to go across the street to my cousin's home to get any sleep."

"Buy goat milk. Bring it to a soft boil and let it cool. Many infants are hypersensitive to cow's milk and are allergic to it. Let me know how that works out."

Within two days, *Capitán* Gutierrez walked in to Fred's cell and was delighted to inform him that the infant was now eating and sleeping comfortably. He whispered to Fred, if there was anything he could do for him, to let him know.

"Glad you mentioned that," Fred replied. "I would like to join the men with the van who drive the bodies out to the ocean. I want to make sure they are medically dead, so I'll feel better."

"You think that they are still alive when we throw them into the sea?" *El Capitán* threw back his head and guffawed. "I normally have to get permission from the old generals, but all of them are gone to Mexico City for the rest of the year, leaving me in command. They will not return until after the *Posadas*," he replied, mulling over Fred's request. He was fond of Fred and grateful for his help with his son's health. He pondered a moment, gave Fred a penetrating glance while rubbing his chin, and then said, "It would probably be a good idea. I'll make an order on that. It's done!" *Capitán* Gutierrez stated. "We'll have you join the driver on his runs."

Fred continued to live in the Matamoros prison for many months. He was kept alive by the food that Victoria was bringing. His natural instinct, being a humanitarian, was to do whatever he could for the many sickly inmates. As for the corpses, if the families did not claim them quickly, Fred and the van driver would make the runs at night with three or more cadavers and dump them into the ocean, a delicatessen to the sharks. He continually checked and studied the exits and the schedule of the indolent officers, who took their jobs for granted and did not care about the condition of the inmates.

Three prisoners in the adjoining cells had long been planning an escape, and they offered Fred the opportunity to go with them, knowing he was a medic and had an "in" with *Capitán* Gutierrez. One of them had overheard *Capitán* Gutierrez asking Fred how he could help him, and the inmate decided that presented an opportunity for all of them.

"Next week the full moon will be at its peak. What do you say if you joined us and helped us in escaping from this dirty, filthy place while you're on the funeral van? We can help each other," said the murderous, cold-blooded one, who had been accused of killing his pregnant wife, two children, and his in-laws. "We're all in here for life. We're all doomed to die in this rotten place if we don't escape from this hellhole. We have no other choice."

"It looks to me like it might be a little difficult," replied Fred, "but what are your plans, anyway?"

"We have heard that *Capitán* Gutierrez is on duty for the rest of the year. While the *Capitán* is in charge on those nights, he is very congenial to all of us. He always opens the cells and lets us roam around, and usually they do not pay any attention to the inmates. The *Capitán* plays cards with the guards, and they drink until the wee hours of the morning."

"We will have to plan this carefully and watch everything that's going on," answered Fred, encouraged. For the first time, he felt there was a possibility.

On Victoria's return, Fred informed her of their plans. She told him that it had occurred to her once or twice, but she was afraid, since Carlos had forbidden her to try anything. She declared that the attorneys were taking their own sweet time even though they were being paid a high price to handle international matters. The federal courts were planning extradition, but were not having any luck, since the Mexican government was not complying with their laws. She cried, cautioning Fred that, with all the high stone walls and guards, it would not be an easy place to escape from. And where would he go? He could not go back into Texas, and Mexico was not the safest place to live either.

Fred, all excited, replied. "You remember *Señor* Castillo telling us how beautiful Veracruz was? Well, I think I'm going to try and make my way to that area."

"How will we know? Father is going to die in agony wanting to know where you are. How soon will you know, and how soon will you contact us?" Victoria pleaded, crying and shaking her head.

"Only time will tell! I'll write to Felicia or Dan, since nobody suspects them of anything. I will contact them and let them know where I end up."

Victoria embraced him. "I will pray for your safety every day. *Manito*, go with God! I'm just hoping that Father will be able to handle all of this."

⌘　⌘　⌘

The night of the full moon was set as the time for the escape, and everything seemed to be going according to plan. The guards and *Capitán* Gutierrez began playing Mexican poker and bidding large amount of *pesos* and drinking hard tequila and not paying any attention to the inmate's actions. Earlier in the day, Fred had advised *Capitán* Gutierrez that another man had died of an infectious disease and it was wise to dump him as soon as possible, so he had been given the go-ahead for the van to head for the sea. They would leave within the next hour.

"What did the prisoner die of?" asked one of the guards.

"Cholera," was the answer. "And we may have more." He might as well have said "fire," for nobody even flinched and went on bidding on the cards and drinking tequila.

The cells were open and one at a time, each murderous inmate scurried along the dark halls. When the three were finally united, they stood behind a large arched pillar and watched the van, while two guards loaded the remains. They kept an eye on Fred's movements. The two guards went inside the lighted quarters and closed the door. The signal had been to light a cigarette so that Fred would know that they were waiting. Fred turned around and noticed the flame from the corner of his eye. When the van was getting ready to leave, Fred advised the driver that he would get in the back with the dead bodies, until they got to the ocean where they could be disposed of. The driver nodded and started the vehicle. Fred went to the back of van and opened the door, looked both ways, and summoned the three inmates to climb into the back. Inside, Fred indicated with his index finger against his mouth not to talk. They nodded. Fred then gave the go ahead to the driver with several thumps on the inside of the van.

The drive was long and tedious. It must have taken more than two hours over a bumpy, winding, uneven road heading east to the coastline. The moon shone brilliantly, making the drive more visible along the tedious route. Finally, the gears shifted and the van began slowing down; it rumbled and shook and came to a complete stop. Fred opened the back door, and the three inmates, one at a time, rolled out and hid among the tall grass and mangrove shrubs that grew close to the sea. The three waited until Fred and the driver dumped the dead bodies into the splashing waves that were crashing against the shore. The driver walked back to the vehicle and stood beside it, smoking a cigarette.

Fred paused and took a deep breath. The ocean smelled of fresh air and freedom. Harbor lights were visible from across the border at Port Isabel in Texas, and in the moonlight, he could make out small boats along docks jutting out into the sea nearby. He was a romantic and a reflective dreamer, and his thoughts turned to his happier early years, as he watched the dark waves roll in and deposit their foam on the shore.

He sighed and turned back toward the van, becoming immediately aware of the sounds of a scuffle. He was horrified to discover that the three killers had ganged up on the driver from behind and had slit his throat with a sharp, handmade object.

The driver made a gurgling sound and fell to the ground holding his throat, as blood spurted out.

Fred rushed over, furious. "We weren't planning to kill the driver—he has nothing to do with us!" Panicky, he tried to save the dying man who was still struggling and fighting for his next breath as he lay on the damp grass. When Fred knelt down, tying to save him, the dying driver grabbed Fred's arm in desperation, unfastening Fred's watch. The watch fell unnoticed and disappeared in the high wet grass. "This is monstrous!" Fred yelled at the inmates he had helped. "Killing a human being for the sake of escaping is unthinkable!"

"Do you want to die also, doctor?" replied one of the cold-blooded killers in a state of rage and hatred, hovering over him with the murder weapon still in his hand.

"Are you coming with us?" asked the other one, taking the keys from the dead guard, as the other two murderers began dragging his body toward the sea. "Come! We are driving a long ways from here, and we will dump the van along the way."

"No!" was Fred's firm replying. Instinctively, he knew his life was also in danger. He knew he was next. He was afraid of these three men and knew that if he traveled with them, somewhere he too would be killed when they found the opportunity. "Leave me here. I will stay here and deal with my fate. I will try to escape back across the border."

"Have it your way," said the younger escapee, seemingly proud of what they had done. "We are free now, and nobody is going to take us alive."

The other two quickly returned from dumping the driver's body. "*Gracias, Compadre!* It's been nice knowing you!" said the older man. "You are going to have a hard time explaining to the prison guards what happened, if they catch you. But, of course, you will never live to tell the tale, since they will shoot you first!" He shouted to the others, "*Vámonos, ándale!*"

"I'll take my chances," said Fred, still shaken by the grisly murder. He grieved for the guard and felt guilty for not being able to save his life.

Within minutes, the three murderers jumped in the van, turned it around, and drove off without the headlights on. Fred felt empty and betrayed. In his naiveté, he never dreamed that this would happen. He was lost at the end of the isthmus in the middle of the night and would have to fend for himself.

He studied what he could see in the brightness of the full moon. He looked around to the northern end, where he had seen the shadows of small boats and several small rafts tied up at the docks. He began walking in that direction, hoping to find a boat he could take. He walked and walked, stumbling over rocks, through thorn bushes and marsh, and finally reached the dock area. He could smell the ocean and heard the sounds of the rippling surf. Staying hidden in the tall marsh scrubs, he studied the dock for any movement. With the brilliance of the moon, he could make out a small boat with fishing gear, two oars, and some kind of supplies on board. He looked around again, watching for any activity. He stood for a few minutes with his feet getting wet from the marshy ground, and then approached the boat by way of the dock. He untied the rope from the dock, crawled into the boat, and lifted the small anchor.

It was high tide, and the boat began to drift, making it possible to get into the channel that entered an enormous gulf of water. There was enough brightness of the moon that he was able to see the shadows of the island. He began using the oars on each side, aiming the boat toward the sea. The tide was going out, and the boat floated out into the wide ocean, into the dark abyss. He did not know where he was going, but he knew that he was free. He could see the waves hitting against the boat, rocking it, but he kept on rowing. He rowed until his arms ached, but he kept on going, trying to keep his eyes open and concentrating on controlling the boat. He had to free himself from the horrible injustices and get away from the dreadful prison. Although a sense of guilt had overtaken him, he knew he was innocent, and somehow the truth would eventually be told.

Fred did not remember when he fell asleep; perhaps it was due to the constant rocking of the boat, the murderous incident of the driver, the adrenalin rush during his flight, or just plain exhaustion. He woke up in the brightness of the morning sun and was immediately besieged by the incredible nightmare in which he found himself. He was not sure where his mysterious cruise was heading, or the consequences that it would bring. He was free, but not entirely free, for he was surrounded by water.

While sitting in the boat in the bright morning light, he inspected the small craft. On top there was a long pole and a small tarp for protection from the brutal rays of the sun that would come later in the day. His delicate hands were red and raw, and his striped cotton shirt was torn on the right side. He realized that somewhere in the middle of the night he had lost his watch and would not be able to tell time. What did it matter now? His pants had been torn and ripped by the thorn bushes. He removed his shoes and socks that were still wet from the night before and realized his feet were red and swollen from the long walk down to the dock.

There was a calm stillness in the ocean as the small crested waves rocked the boat. He presumed he was heading southeast, into the Tropic of Cancer. There was no land in sight, only water that completely surrounded him, and he felt engulfed by the immense energy of the ocean. He knew he was out in deep water. The sun was now at mid-heaven, showing through a cloudy mist of fog. His stomach began to churn. In the bottom of the stolen boat were several aluminum buckets, one with some kind of stinky material used for bait, and one that had water, or what looked like water. It had probably been sitting around for a couple of days, but he did not care. His throat was getting dry, his mouth parched, yearning for cool water. He began drinking some of the stale liquid and made an ugly face at the taste. He found several dried corn tortillas in a closed tin container and ate two. He had never eaten anything more delicious in his whole life. He wanted to cry in his desperate, lonely condition, but he was grateful he was free.

On the second day, he woke to the sounds of blowing, hissing, playful porpoises dancing in the dark, blue-green water. They had surrounded the small boat and followed him while he rowed until the afternoon light. They entertained him for many hours, jumping, rolling, and dipping into the sea, making things appear normal and natural. He recognized the intelligence of the gracious mammals that were so joyously happy. *Why would anyone want to kill these beautiful animals?* He thought. He watched them for hours until they disappeared into the deep water. He ate two more of the tortillas and drank some of the water and realized he was running low. When he needed to, he stood up and urinated into the sea. If he was going to stay on the boat, he needed to find fresh water to drink. In these conditions, he would become dehydrated very fast without even realizing it, and sometimes the body did not give warning until it was too late. Fred also knew that he was sailing straight south, because the sun had been on his left side most of the day, until it began going down on his right.

The sun looked like a gigantic red ball of fire in the western sky, dipping slowly through a diffusion of blood-hued atmosphere, and then it was twilight. Soon he was, once again, subjected to a dark void. He could hear and feel the waves smash against the keel, as a strong gale coming from the east rocked the boat. He could hear the flapping of the overhead tarp hitting the side of the boat. Occasionally he would hear the foghorns sounding in the faraway distance and the loud horns of big vessels headed for the ports of Brownsville or Houston. Fred felt the wind becoming stronger and could smell rain. He needed to make sure the buckets were turned upright in order to preserve the precious rainwater. As the wind began to blow harder, the temperature dropped, and Fred could feel it in his bones. His torn shirt was too thin and the worn out jacket he'd found in the boat was too small, but he wrapped it around him anyway. He held onto the oars more tightly, as the boat was rocked and tossed around. By the time the storm subsided, he was so exhausted that he finally closed his eyes and slept a while.

A drizzling rain and strong trade wind woke him up the next day. He could not remember how many days he had been afloat, but he was beginning to get weak, He lived with constant hunger pains as his empty stomach complained. He would have enough water if the buckets would hold the downpour, but he needed to find some kind of nourishment. All around him was the unending sea, and he knew the sea contained minerals and food and was a treasure in itself. He remembered the bait and some of the fishing lines. If he had enough courage to smell the rotten meat and adjust the hooks, maybe he would be able to snag something. He had to do it, if he was going to survive. He had only one dried tortilla left, and it would have to last until he found some other kind of nourishment.

In the oncoming rain, he turned his head as far away from the bait bucket as he could, took in a deep breath, and held it, not wanting to inhale the fetid smell. He reached into the stinky mess and placed a piece of it on a hook. He dropped it into the water and waited. While holding onto the line, he washed his hands in the ocean current and noticed green kelp floating on top of the water. He knew that kelp was rich in minerals and contained nutrients that contributed to life in the ocean. He began picking it up and eating it. At first, it was hard to consume the slimy, salty substance, but his hunger had become vicious and difficult to bear. He ate like a glutton. He realized that kelp normally grew close to land, but he still had not seen any sign of dry land. He figured he was somewhere off the coast of Mexico.

Within an hour, he dropped the line in deeper, as far as it would go. He wrapped it around the pole, letting the bait drag many fathoms below.

In his long wait, he watched the flying fish that were in abundance in the ocean waters, and the terns that flew and dipped themselves into the waves so gracefully. Downhearted and sick in his mind, he began wondering about his father, Carlos, Victoria, and Catalina, and what had transpired since his escape. Perhaps his life would end here, in this tiny boat, lost at sea. If this ended with his death, nobody would know the real truth of what had happened in his escape.

He spiraled downward into a melancholy mood, and his dark thoughts tormented him. He viewed the water as far as his eyes could see and noticed how the sea and sky touched in a great union, but yet were so far apart. He understood how sailors became disoriented and lost and were never heard from again. *Dear Lord*, he asked out loud: "Is this what your intentions are, for me to die out here in the ocean? Is this what I have come to, never really having experienced life? I wanted to do so much. I wanted to help the poor and disadvantaged people, and I still feel I have not been able to accomplish my full potential." Dispirited and demoralized, Fred had tears in his eyes and used his dirty, wet shirt to wipe his nose. He was desolate, lonely and hungry, floating on the sea of desperation. If his family could see him now, they would surely die.

No sooner had he said that out loud, when he felt a jerk on the line trailing in the water. He quickly pulled it up, his excitement building, cutting his hand with the wire and oozed blood. With the drizzled rain the blood washed and disappeared into the ocean waves. The catch was a five-pound tuna, which in Fred's voracious hunger; he began eating it alive, even as it kept flopping out of his hands. His teeth cut into the fresh white flesh, and he gorged himself, not stopping until he had satisfied his massive hunger. He threw the remains into the sea and drank some of the rainwater. *Funny*, he thought, *what humans will do if they are thirsty and hungry enough*. He never thought he would sink to this level of survival.

He decided he should try and catch another fish for his next meal and baited the hook again and dropped it down as far as it would go. His thoughts now centered only on his next meal and it became a game, a curious challenge, taking up most of his time. And he had all the time in the world.

Several hours later and in the midst of rain, Fred began noticing movement in the water around the boat. His worst fears were confirmed: Sharks! Several purple-gray fins circled the boat and were getting too close for comfort. One of them slid underneath and touched the boat, rocking it. Up to now, Fred had not felt any fear, but now the hair on the back of his neck stood up and he was apprehensive. His eyes and thoughts concentrated on the circling sharks, and he paid close attention to what they were doing. Then, the fishing line snagged and moved, and he began reeling it in, anticipating a large fish on the hook. Immediately, there was a great confusion of movement among the sharks as they began attacking his catch. Desperate to save his next meal from the predators, Fred grabbed one of the wooden oars and began beating the sharks. "Go and get your own!" he shouted. "There are plenty of fish out in the Gulf! I'm hungry, and this one is mine!"

By the time the sharks gave up and swam away, Fred, weak and exhausted, pulled in what was left of his fish. It was the skeletal remains of what was once a medium-sized fish, perhaps a young marlin with its long, blue beak and fins. There was some meat still hanging in torn pieces, and he used a tin can edge to cut slices and began spreading the flesh on the top of the buckets to dry. He would have enough for the next meal. He had collected rainwater to drink and had also some kelp to use as greens, although it was so salty, it made him thirsty.

Several days went by, and the rain kept coming down harder, and the trade winds grew. Fred had eaten the last of the fish. He figured he had been afloat for over a week, and he knew that he would eventually hit land somewhere, or at least come close to it.

As another night fell and another gloomy, pewter-gray day came with the rains pouring down more severely, there was not a dry place in the small boat. The winds blew hard and the waves were become bigger and higher, pushing the boat ever southward. Fred was soaked to the bone. The afternoon turned dark, and the dark purple clouds indicated they were heavy with rain. Fred found himself in the middle of a tropical storm. The gale winds blew ever more forcefully, rocking the small vessel from side to side. Oversized waves attacked the boat, and it was all that Fred could do to hold onto the sides. Flashes of lightning loomed across the sky in a terrifying display of electrical energy. The winds increased, creating immense, destructive waves, rocking and pummeling the boat and Fred like a toy. The Gulf rose to terrible heights, pushing water into the boat. Fred tried using one of the buckets to scoop up the seawater, but it poured in quicker then he could bail. Terrified, he thought the sea was going to take him after all. He could do nothing but hang on and pray.

In the dark misty atmosphere, Fred had not noticed that he was coming close to the outskirts of an island. The swells elevated as they approached the coast and crashed against the rocky shore. The heightened waves reached up to forty feet into the air and suddenly flung the small boat into the rocks, sending Fred into the ocean, fighting for his life. He tried to swim, but it was fruitless against the strength of the waves. He tried to remember to hold his breath and fill his lungs full of air each time the sea would spit him up. He did that several times, as the Gulf swallowed him time and time again. The ocean was too powerful, and in his weak condition, he began giving up. Somewhere in between his gulps for air and his struggles to swim, he said to himself, *you win Mr. Gulf—I give my life to you.* His head hit an object, and he lost consciousness and began sinking slowly toward the bottom of the sea.

CHAPTER 38

For the next two weeks, Fred was not able to ascertain where he was. All he remembered was confusion and people talking in Spanish. He remembered a kindly old man and woman feeding him some kind of delicious soup and periodically talking to him. He would come to realize, weeks later, the soup was sea turtle soup.

"Ay!" she would say. "You are so light-complexioned and so big and tall. You need to eat more soup so that you will get well, and maybe we can all know the mystery of where you came from."

As the weeks passed, he became strong enough to sit up on the grass cot where he had been sleeping. He was wrapped with banana leaves, since crawling crabs had bitten him while he was lying on the sandy beach and had left large sores all over his body, especially his arms and legs. Papaya juice had been used as a salve, taking away the sting and the redness from the sores.

One day, several older men from the main village up the road came into the hut and began asking questions.

"This couple found you washed up on the beach. All of us on this island want to know who you are and what brought you to our land. We have all been curious, since our Savior, *El Señor de Tampico-Alto*, was also found on our shores, the same way we found you."

The old man was referring to a crucifix that was found on the same spot over two hundred and fifty years before. They had built a church for the icon and added the name of *"El Señor"* to the small village. Perhaps that was the only point of interest in the area. The natives, being superstitious, recalled the tribal legend of the Aztecs, about the tall, blond-haired, blue-eyed god named *Quetzalcóatl*, meaning "feathered serpent" that departed into the sea, promising he would return. However, the Indians confused the promise, and when Cortez showed up on the shores of Veracruz years later, he was considered a descendant of the same great god returning, a mistake which later led to the destruction of the Aztec Empire.

In the same way, the tall, fair, and handsome Fred Juelson, to the puzzled and superstitious natives, was considered some kind of an omen, but they did not know whether for good or evil.

"I am from the United States—Texas," answered Fred weakly.

"What brought you to our land? What is your name?" asked the prying old man.

Fred hesitated, remembering what his father had advised him—to tell the truth no matter what. But he restrained himself; he was taking a chance in divulging the truth of his life. He was free now and he didn't want them to know that he had escaped from prison. He discreetly decided to change his name and not take any more chances. These people were unaware that his name was on the front headlines of every paper in the country.

Remembering the doctor from Reynosa who had been killed several years ago, he replied calmly, "My name is Dr. Cantu," but he felt guilty for lying, even though it was his only chance of survival. "Dr. Federico Cantu."

"Did you say doctor?" All in the group smiled with humility and joy. "Our prayers have been answered by *El Señor de Tampico-Alto!* We have been praying for a doctor for many years. Father Gonzales will not believe this! What a miracle!" Three of the old men took off their hats and got on their knees and crossed themselves, thinking Fred had come like the savior in the living flesh.

"There is one doctor who comes once or twice a year to our village, but we have not seen him for many months," said the only young man that had come with the elders. "Father Gonzales will be thrilled to see you!"

"What's the doctor's name and where does he come from?"

"He's a young doctor in his thirties, we believe. His name is Dr. Terán, and I think his first name is Antonio. Yes, I think its Dr. Antonio Terán. He lives in the city of Tampico across the Rio Panuco river to the northwest. He was studying the vegetation that the people here use to heal the sick."

"What do you call this place?" questioned Fred.

"This place is called Tampico-Alto, in the state of Veracruz. We are divided by the Rio Panuco that flows out into the gulf. The city of Tampico is located to the northwest in the state of Tamaulipas. We will come and take you to Father Gonzales when you feel better. Tampico-Alto is several miles up the dirt road. He will be pleased to see you. *El Señor de Tampico-Alto* has answered our prayers." They were all smiling and very pleased, knowing that miracles can happen and that their prayers had been fervent enough to bring a savior who had come to rescue the weak and sick among them.

Before long, Fred's health improved and he was promoted from the grass cot to a hammock. He was given a loose, white Panama shirt that was big and long enough to fit him. He was also honored with a pair of leather sandals too small for his big feet, and a worn-out straw hat with many holes in it. The pants that he had arrived in were washed and mended by the kindly old woman who had nursed him back to health. He had bathed and had shaved with a sharp knife the old fisherman used for cutting up his fish. They offered him their old donkey to take him up to the village. He mounted the animal and laughed, as did they, since his long legs caused his feet to drag the ground. Fred was grateful for everything and promised to repay them all a thousand times.

The little village of Tampico-Alto was several miles up a dirt road bordered by stately coconut palms, guava shrubs, figs, and groves of banana, mango, lemon and orange trees.

There was vegetation of every kind, with clinging bougainvilleas and yellow mimosa flowers, making it a perfect paradise above the shores of the Gulf.

He was getting away from pesky, hungry, tormenting insects: the sand flies which could trigger a leprosy type disease; horse flies that could inflict a form of blood disease; and black flies that caused blindness if not treated properly. This was mosquito country, and they were big enough to screw a grown chicken and inject malaria into a person's system, or other mosquito-borne plagues like dengue fever and yellow fever.

It was a small fishing village with dogs and naked children playing everywhere. In the center was the main attraction, the Church of *El Señor de Tampico-Alto*, with its tower up top that enclosed a large bell. Around the village were many picturesque mud huts with thatched roofs, and several adobes with wooden, mud plastered, picket fences. Donkeys intermingled with hundreds of goats, chickens, and pigs, while dogs scampered around the streets, barking and playing with the children.

The shrubs and bright colored flowers of hibiscus and gardenia were extremely dense and high, to the point of obscuring many of the homes. A young, barefoot girl about ten, carrying her naked baby brother on her hip, stood mesmerized and observed Fred as he passed by. Nearby, a mangy, rickety dog humped a mangy, half-starved bitch in full view.

Inside the church was the largest crucifix Fred had ever seen—a breathtaking Christ covering the whole altar wall. Below the hanging Christ, on the large altar, were hundreds of items that people from all over Mexico and the surrounding area, grateful for *El Señor's* great miracles, had brought in payment for his favors. Pictures of people and small children of different nationalities were lined up side by side. All represented miracles that the patrons had asked for, and prayers that had been answered time and time again. Fred stood in awe viewing all of the good works.

An overwhelming spiritual awareness overtook Fred as he stood gazing at the high altar, and a feeling of humility overpowered him. He was grateful he was alive and perhaps had been guided into this hidden, unknown paradise by simple divine destiny. So taken was he by an almost overpowering force, that his knees buckled, and he knelt on the steps of the altar before the Christ. He took off his straw hat, his eyes fixed on the agonizing face of the figure on the crucifix. He felt humbled and full of devotion to be in His presence and felt as if he were only a grain of sand upon an infinite beach. He wondered if other visitors felt the same way when viewing the Christ.

He crossed himself and thought of his religious mother. "Heavenly Father," he spoke aloud without thinking, in an almost hypnotic state. "Please forgive my transgressions and the things that I have done to offend you. I must have done something terrible and am being punished for it, to be sent through so much hardship to this place. Please guide me to do good works and to continue to help the people in this village—"

"—and good works we need in this place, Dr. Cantu." Father Gonzales answered and greeted him, coming up the aisle behind him. The priest had already learned of his near tragic encounter with the sea from the excited, gossiping inhabitants of the village.

Surprised, Fred immediately stood up, straw hat in hand, and greeted the priest.

Coming from Spanish blood, handsome Father Gonzales was in his early forties, a dedicated priest with a light complexion, black hair, and light-colored eyes. He was wearing the customary long, black cassock. He was steadfast in his convictions, which kept him busy performing daily Mass and hundreds of baptisms and confirmations, not counting the number of people he counseled. Mostly of Spanish descent, the people of the village were mixed with Mayan and other Indian blood. He saw his labors coming to fruition among his congregation, who were growing and maturing from a stubborn, uneducated, ignorant people into a population who could read and write and determine their own affairs.

In his small ministry and mission kingdom, Father Gonzales was assisted by two older nuns who taught English and Spanish to the children who wanted to come to their three-class school on the grounds of the church. There were many other buildings around the church, including living quarters for the priest and separate quarters for the nuns.

It was getting close to the great *Posadas* celebration, which was one of the most important activities of the year. In preparation, a group of young girls were rehearsing the songs that were sung inside each home and during the final celebration that took place inside the church. The singing was being led by a nun, who smiled at Fred as he peeked his head in the door of the rectory, viewing the group of young girls, whose eyes were full of excitement. Several giggled shyly and put their hands to their mouths when they saw Fred looking at them.

This was the land of *fiestas*. Everyone who lived in this small community was a devout Catholic, each with his or her own saint's day, and they took part in the celebration parties, sometimes once a week. It motivated each individual by bringing music, dancing, friendship, communication, and passion to the people of this isolated village.

"Do you have any mail coming into your village?" Fred asked the priest. "Do you have any newspapers that are delivered here?" He was being cautious, for it had been many weeks now since he had left the rotten prison in Matamoros, and he wanted some answers about his situation. He also wanted to find a way to inform his family in Texas without arousing the suspicion of the people or the priest in the village, or anyone across the border.

"No, my son," replied Father Gonzales. "This is a very poor village, and the only information we get is from Tampico across the river. Sometimes weekly vendors bringing items to sell will have news of what is happening in the outside world. I have not seen the bishop who comes from Mexico City to bring me instructions of the church for many years now. I have lost contact since the Catholic Rebellion. As you can tell, we are very limited in what we have. No phones, no radios, no newspapers. Here, we are at peace with nature, the sea, and our holy commandments of the church." He paused, then added, "And with the people who want to stay and live here."

"I see." answered Fred, trying to sound casual. "So if I want to send a letter or a telegram, I will have to travel to the city of Tampico, across the river, and take a ferry."

Father Gonzales stood back and eyed him intently. "That is correct," he answered, deciding not to inquire about his circumstances. "Whatever great sins you have, they shall be forgiven, my son. Turn to our savior, *El Señor de Tampico-Alto*, and he will answer all prayers, no matter how large or small your sins have been, and everything will turn as white as snow.

El Señor knows that each of his children must suffer to become stronger and later serve his other lost sheep." The priest gazed at him in his infinite kindness, knowing that there was a long story behind the tall man he was addressing, but he never dared to question him. He saw each individual as a good soul, and each had a purpose in life. "How long do you plan to stay with us? Your coming has been prophesied for many years by the people of this village."

"I'm honored," Fred answered, touched by his simplicity and kindness. "I will try to set up a practice as soon as I can find a place to do so."

"Here, on the church grounds, is the center of all activities in this community. We can make room for you and get you some help." His eyes lit up, as he saw that a miracle was beginning to unfold.

"Get me help?" Fred questioned in amazement.

"Why yes, we have many young girls in the village who would be interested in helping out in whatever way they can. We can empty one of the classrooms for you. How soon can you start?"

"First, I'll have to find some money to get the medicine that I need and buy the supplies for running a medical clinic. I'll have to travel to Tampico to buy the things that I need."

"Do not worry, my son. With God's help, nothing is impossible. We will find the money that is needed for you to get started. We have a little money here in the church, and we will find one of the members of the community to drive you across the river." Father Gonzales turned to view the group of young girls leaving the rectory. Catching the eye of one of the older girls, he called her name.

Maria Dolores Gariby was beautiful; light complexioned, with all the features coming from Spanish blood. She stood five-feet-five, with a slender figure, brownish hair down to her waist, and soft brown eyes. Coming over, she blushed immediately, and in her shyness, looked toward the floor, avoiding eye contact with Fred.

"Dolores, meet your doctor! Remember, it was you who asked in your prayers for a doctor to come into our village? Well, here he is! Your prayers, my daughter, have been answered. Dr. Federico Cantu, meet Dolores."

Flustered and embarrassed, Dolores extended her right hand to Fred. She stood enthralled, looking at the handsome, tall individual with torn and mended jeans and worn out leather sandals, and the poor little donkey patiently waiting outside. She thought it was a wonder the donkey hadn't thrown him off while riding, dragging his long legs. She wanted to laugh—he looked more like a first class beggar than a doctor.

Father Gonzales was pleased and spoke, addressing Dolores, "I have mentioned to Dr. Cantu that you would be willing to assist him when he starts building his medical practice here on the church grounds."

She was still in a state of dazed stupor. "Yes, I will be more than willing," she answered shyly, then turned and left rapidly, meeting the other girls who were waiting for her to walk home. She did not want to disrespect Father Gonzales by saying no. She had never been more embarrassed in her life, but she wanted to tell her surprised parents that her prayers had been answered. The girls walked home laughing and giggling.

"Now you have the help you need, and we can get more from the nuns, if necessary."

"She is very beautiful. Tell me about her," Fred asked, mesmerized.

"Her father, Venustiano Gariby came from Zaragoza, España, and has lived in this area for many years. He is a much respected landowner of a sugar cane plantation and also owns hundred of goats. They donate much meat and goat cheese to the church and to other needy people in the area. They have many children and are very dedicated to *El Señor de Tampico-Alto*. Dolores is their oldest daughter and spends most of her time helping the nuns in the classrooms and helping the sick. She devotes much of her time to the Church and sings in the choir."

⌘ ⌘ ⌘

In December the celebration of *las Posadas* went on for over a week, where everyone visited each other's homes with their own displayed version of Mary, Joseph, and Baby Jesus, and shared their food with prayer and singing. Midnight Mass was celebrated the night of December 24th, but Christmas was not celebrated as it was in the United States. The giving of gifts was celebrated in January, known as *Los Tres Reyes,* and the presents were put inside the children's shoes that were left out that night.

Inspired, Father Gonzales and the nuns kept busy buying the necessities for running a medical practice, as well as cleaning and painting the inside of the designated room.

Fred took advantage of some of the money that Father Gonzales had given him and, while in the port of Tampico buying cases of chloroform, alcohol, and cotton swabs, he ended up with sufficient money to send a telegram to Felicia, who was the safest person to notify his father and sister in Texas. The message was short, informing them that he was fine and would explain later what had taken place in the last three months. He gave no return address. Any return messages would be left at the telegraph office in Tampico, and he would pick them up later.

It was in Tampico that Fred realized that something terrible had happened to the economy in the United States by the way the merchants talked of the American dollar. Not understanding the full impact, he picked up several newspapers and was startled to learn that the stock market had collapsed. He was appalled because all of his money that he had saved throughout his medical practice had been invested. His father had owned several hundred stocks in the oil companies and had all his money invested in several depositories. He also learned that the banks were closing their doors and people throughout the U.S. were losing everything; many were committing suicide, especially rich investors. He stood shaken, wondering what was going to happen in Texas and to his family's future. Starting from scratch in the medical field in a small village with nothing to go on but faith was going to take an even bigger miracle than he thought!

Returning to the village, Fred retreated in self-introspection and refused to converse with anyone. His conscience was beginning to bother him, as he was leading a good life like few had ever experienced, at a time when others were apparently encountering serious trouble back home. His thoughts were going through a critical, unbridled moment of despair and truth. If he was going to stay in this village, a matter in which he had no choice, he would have to reassess his self-tormented life in a humble way and think things through. He prayed for guidance.

It was a time of miracles and faith, and the following day, Antonio Terán arrived in the village in a battered, noisy, old Ford Roadster, anxious to meet Fred. The two formed an immediate and harmonious mutual friendship, since their thinking regarding their profession was in agreement. Dr. Terán was brown-skinned, with brown hair and eyes, and nice white teeth, beautifully displayed when he laughed, which was often. He was medium in stature, slender, and handsome in his own manly way, and exhibited a very optimistic humor. He had studied medicine in Europe and had gone to school in Mexico City. He was a humanitarian with enormous empathy for the sick and poor. He was an intelligent, charming young newlywed residing in the oil city of Tampico close to the shores of the Rio Panuco. He was in tune with Father Gonzales and had been pleading for a medical facility in the village, but never considered making his residence in the small community, for it did not offer the facilities needed for an ambitious, upcoming young doctor.

"Come and stay with my wife and me in Tampico," he said. "You will love my wife Teresa, who is very kind and loves company. She gets very lonely, since I'm working in my medical office and gone most of the day. Come and join me downtown so I can show you my clinic. We have several students and many young men there learning this profession. And you are more than welcome to use any of my instruments. I have an extra stethoscope and a microscope that you can borrow and several other instruments that I'm not using that you can have for your office."

"Thank you! I sure can use all of them. I'll come down when I buy supplies next week," answered Fred happily. With his new friend, and his new medical practice, life was beginning to offer welcome and challenging possibilities. Meeting Dr. Terán would represent a turning point in his life.

For the time being, Fred would have to concentrate and devote his skills to the charming, dreamy village of lavish gardens, grass-hut bungalows, moonlit fiestas, and strolling marimba bands, where the people were easy going and humble. The natives' only thoughts were of their three-course meals, which might explain the prevalence of obesity. They ate heavy meals and rested in their siestas and enjoyed the music and the environment. They never hurried anywhere or breathed hard from rushing about. It was a heavenly paradise.

On a sunny afternoon, Fred strolled down to the shore close to where the old man and woman had found him washed up on the beach. He wanted to be alone and think, since he was drenched in his own sadness of loss, and the sound of the ocean always gave him intuitive insights. He sat on the sandy bank hugging his knees and viewing from a distance several girls wearing straw hats and a young boy swimming down below in the surf. The girls carried a wicker basket and were finding many of the larger blue crabs that were in abundance in this part of the Gulf. The girls waded with their skirts wrapped around their legs, while they splashed through the shallow, blue-green water. He sat quietly so as not to disturb anyone and enjoyed the trade winds blowing around him. He tried to piece together his anguished and sometimes overwhelming life, hoping he might heal in the silence. He closed his eyes and rested his chin on his knees.

Fred should have paid more attention to where he was sitting, for it was near the entrance of a red anthill. The huge red ants in this area were vicious and hostile and would attack any intruder coming anywhere near their domain. Their sting was brutal and painful—worse than the biting crabs. The nerve of anyone sitting on top of their home was unforgivable, especially when anyone could have sat anywhere else on the thousand-mile seashore. How rude of him!

Almost immediately, Fred felt the stings of the ants. He had a million of them crawling underneath his clothes, all over his legs and body, on his arms and his neck. His body and soul awoke with a start. He stood up and yelled, with his arms in the air, and ran toward the water, stumbling over scattered stones. His actions caught the attention of the spectators, making the girls and the young boy look up, startled.

Like a pro in the 200-meter, he dived into the water as if his life depended on it, into the oncoming waves. Coming up to the surface on his next breath, he treaded water while he rubbed his arms and legs.

The young boy and the three girls with their straw hats and basket of blue crabs giggled. They thought the tall man had lost his mind and was making a fool of himself. As the four-some stood there laughing at him, Fred discovered that one of the girls was the beautiful Dolores, and the others were her younger sisters. The young boy bobbed with Fred in the oncoming waves, gawking at him and smiling, while the girls stood and laughed. Fred felt his face flush. He was so embarrassed that he decided, *what the hell*, so he joined them and began laughing too.

Later in the afternoon, as the three nuns and Father Gonzales were putting alcohol and cotton pads around Fred's legs and arms, Dolores and her younger brother, Juan, showed up, surprising all of the Florence Nightingale healing group. She asked Fred and Father Gonzales to join her family for dinner. There was no doubt—the main course was going to be crabs!

The ten-minute walk from the church led to a dirt path leading to the one-level Gariby home. The large adobe house was made of plastered mud and clay, painted over with a mustard yellow color, which was barely visible from the distant road through the green shrubs that covered the landscape. Father Gonzales guided Fred around the house along a narrow path shaded by flowering vines.

Fred was anxious to meet all of the family. *El Señor* Gariby was a short blond-headed, blue-eyed Spaniard. He was very gracious and seemed honored to have Fred as their guest in their twenty-room home. His charming wife, *Señora* Carlotta, was fair-skinned, short and heavy, with light brown hair and dark eyes, and seemed genuinely glad to have Fred as well. Among the six children were the three girls—Dolores and two younger sisters Gloria and Estella—and three younger boys, Juan, Lupe and Chaño, who were the pride of *Señor* Gariby. The men in Mexico took pride in their sons, who were deemed more valuable than girls.

ROOTS OF INDIFFERENCE

There were also two other small children of Indian descent whom the Gariby family had adopted. In addition, there were twin spinster aunts, Niña and Piña—*Tías*—who lived with them. Everyone sat at the large wicker dining room table, which was outside next to the kitchen. In the middle of the table was a large bowl of different fruits: bananas, oranges and coconut from their own orchards.

The patio was open, with surrounding high arches, and colorful talking parrots in large wicker cages. The floors were inlaid with colorful homemade tiles mixed with a variety of polished stones. Throughout were lavish green vines of purple bougainvilleas and yellow mariposa flowers. The vines extended to the outside open kitchen, where three short, heavy, Indian women were busy forming round balls of fresh masa and making tortillas on top of an open adobe oven. Next to the outside kitchen was a water pump, whose water flowed into a large pond full of water lilies and colorful fish. Hanging along the kitchen walls were bundles of garlic bulbs and red chilies, and pieces of drying goat meat were draped over lines fastened from the kitchen to a gnarled old plum tree in the yard. The drying meat brought in hordes of uninvited, happy-go-lucky flies. The yard was full of clucking chickens and quacking ducks, wandering goats, barking dogs, and occasionally small pigs. To the back of the adobe house were several small thatched-roof shacks, where large canteens stored the goat milk, which would later be made into cheese. Large *ahuehuete* trees shaded the area, with hammocks tied from one to the other, while another held a long rope children's swing.

In the distance were lush gardens of corn and squash, and farther beyond were acres full of tobacco plants, and coffee, banana, mango and avocados trees, as well as tall stalks of sugar cane ready to be cut and made into *piloncillo*. It was truly a lost, hidden paradise. How could anyone ask for more?

Everyone laughed and talked freely around the large table, especially the younger adolescent boys who bullied and teased one another. The stern looking *Senor* Gariby sat like a noble grandee surrounded by his family, but yet, he was a lenient pacifistic who would not punish his children when they got out of hand. Instead, his face muscles would twitch, or he would motion with his head, or flash a stern glance from his diplomatic eyes, or move his fingers. The *Señor* became a living, breathing ventriloquist dummy, and the funny part was, the children understood.

On the contrary, *La Señora* sat staunch and stern, with several very long, thin sticks close at hand, which she did not hesitate to use on the ornery boys. Although they employed different disciplinary tactics, it was obvious the two strong-willed parents loved their children, and they were extremely grateful that a doctor was going to be living among them.

The girls giggled and eyed Fred closely. Everyone in the household had heard about the incident with the ants, since it had been repeated several times among the children, the twin *tías*, and the tortilla makers, but they had all been harshly tongue-lashed and warned by Dolores not to mention it.

When the crab dish was brought in by one of the *tías*, everyone made a grab for the wooden spoon in the large pottery bowl painted with colorful flowers. It seemed to Fred that little etiquette had been taught in the way of table manners. The crabmeat had been cooked into a casserole with a cornmeal stuffing, onions, celery, and spices. Fred found it totally delicious. He had not had a full meal in years, nor had he been among a cheerful, close family such as this one. He yearned for the warm stability and security that came with a joyful family. He found the lavish meal and everything in the household wonderful, and he savored it all.

The drink served was a very tasty liquid, called *pulqué*. Slices from the pineapple skin fermented in the hot climate for about two weeks in wooden barrels, sugar and yeast was added. With cubes of ice, the drink was very refreshing, although it had a kick. Drinking too much of the *pulqué* was known to affect a person's balance hours later.

As the evening progressed, a small band of musicians began playing favorite songs from the region, utilizing *marimbas* and *maracas*, which brought a refreshing sound to the ears and a certain joy energizing every part of one's body, making everyone want to get up and dance.

While Fred sat and talked with the family, he realized they were not unlike the rest of the village people, so humble and giving, so easy-going and innocent of any intrusion from the outside world. They were also very set in their ways of thinking and believed completely in the blessings from the Catholic Church. There was no thought of rebellion here.

The natives were also highly superstitious; they observed the weather and signs from the sky as prophesy. Everything had a time and a purpose. If a bird hit your glass window and died, it became a sign of death, and most likely that of a relative. The cleaning of the floors was done early in the morning with a broom, and the house was always swept out from the front door to the back, and then sprinkled with holy water. If a black cat ran across your path, you needed to turn and go another direction. Finding a spider inside your home could be good or bad, depending on the color of the creature: if light-colored, it was considered good luck, if black, bad news. Meteors or shooting stars were signs of good luck and could indicate that a special wish would eventually come true. A groom was never supposed to see his future wife in her wedding dress; it was considered bad luck and the wedding would never take place. The list of superstitions went on and on.

When the evening ended, *Señor* Gariby graciously invited Fred to stay in his residence, since they had plenty of room in their large home. From there it would be easy for him to walk to his medical clinic, rather than having to come from the seashore where he had been living with the couple who had rescued him. And the fact that Dolores had promised to help him would make it convenient for everyone. Before the two men said their goodbyes, *Señor* Gariby told Fred that he would find suitable clothes for him to wear. However, there was the problem of his large feet, which resembled sailboats. Mexican people had small feet, but Fred's were a much bigger size, and it would be hard finding shoes that large.

In less than a day, Fred said *adiós* to the old man and woman by the seashore and moved in with the Gariby family. He had been promoted. Things were looking up, from a grassy cot to a real bed with a mattress, and in his own bedroom. He had few possessions except for the ragged clothes on his back and the worn-out shoes he had come with.

The longer Fred stayed in the village, the more he became captivated with the people living there. For the first time, because of his altruistic thinking, he felt a personal empowerment toward the natives, with gratitude and a strong obligation. There was a sense of stability in the adobe house he would call home. There was no opulence, or magnificence, but here, warm gatherings took place, people shared their joys and sorrows, and laughing, happy children lived and played.

Within the coming weeks, Fred began to examine sick children and consulted the native wives in his one room clinic next to the church. He lacked many supplies, but he managed with what little he had, until he was able to order more. Energetic and beautiful Dolores was always there, so willing and pleasant, to assist him in cleaning wounds, handing him scissors and bandages, and helping in the sterilizing of instruments. Most of the ailments were common dysentery, acute bronchitis, and ear infections. But many of the children had head lice. Some had ringworms, pinworms, hookworms, or threadworms; others with yellowish skin were harboring parasites that affected their growth and weight. Some were covered with skin lesions caused by the bite of the sand fly, which caused a disease called "leishmaniasis." Other children suffered from *trachoma*, infection of the eyes, brought on by small flies and if not treated with sulfonamide, would cause blindness.

Fred had a problem making the local women understand the necessity of boiling their drinking water. Most of them were also anemic, for which he would normally recommend blackstrap molasses, since it was so rich in iron. The local sugar cane was boiled to make the molasses to put in milk. Cow and goat milk needed to be heated to a certain degree to kill bacteria, and then cooled. The sessions went on and on, with Fred constantly trying to educate the mothers with young children about proper hygiene and nutrition. He would give each attending mother a bar of soap to use for washing. Quinine was used to treat malaria; aspirin came from the willow bark; and salvarsan was used to treat syphilis.

As the weeks and months passed, Fred would occasionally visit Dr. Terán and his wife in Tampico, making the trip for supplies and information. He had visited the telegraph office several times, but had not as yet received a return message. He was reassured by the clerks that messages sent between foreign countries usually took longer, but the long delay began to worry Fred.

When the torrential rains came, which were often and lasted for days, he would find himself restless and would travel across the Rio Panuco. He would ask one of the natives to drive him to Tampico and would then find a ride home after spending a day or two with the Teráns. Normally, Dr. Terán would send him back with several boxes full of donated medical supplies.

One evening, while eating dinner at Dr. Terán's upscale home overlooking the Gulf, the gracious *Señora* Terán suggested that Fred use their mailing address, since no mail was received in Tampico-Alto, and she knew how difficult it was to live in a small village with no communication. The tall *Señora* Terán was not a pretty woman, but her gentleness and kindness more than made up for her lack of beauty. Her high cheekbones and black hair and eyes indicated part Indian blood in her heritage, and her disposition was that of a very strong-willed individual. According to Dr. Terán, it was her family's money from large agricultural estates south of Mexico City that had put him through medical school.

That same evening, Dr. Terán showed Fred a Mexican magazine from Monterrey featuring headlines relating that Juan Alvarez, the popular former physician, was going to run for governor of Tamaulipas in the next election.

"See what's ahead for doctors," he said, chuckling. "I guess after I get fed up with doctoring, maybe I, too, will run for office."

Señora Terán grinned and shook her head while gathering up the dishes, saying, "You'll do no such thing!" She laughed and disappeared into the kitchen.

Fred's eyes widened after reading the optimistic column from the magazine showing Juan's picture taken in an elaborate office full of books and wall paintings by known artists. He laid the magazine down and stared at it for the longest time, then spoke: "He was my idol when I was young. He hasn't changed much—he's beginning to go gray at the temples, but he's as handsome as ever."

"You know him?" Dr. Terán inquired with surprise.

Señora Terán returned from the kitchen and sat listening to the conversation.

"Yes. I've known Juan since he came to our home in Spanish Acres a long time ago. I must have been about ten years old. As a matter of fact, it was Juan who gave me the urge and inspiration to become a doctor. My sister, Victoria, had high hopes of marrying him, but instead ended up marrying somebody else—unfortunately, a man she hates. She displayed an interest in Juan while growing up, but she was forbidden to have anything to do with him. However, during her education in Monterrey, she ended up meeting Juan again, getting pregnant, and having his child. It's a long story," he said, expelling a deep sigh.

"How interesting," *Señora* Terán commented. "Spanish Acres sounds so romantic. Was that your home in Texas?" Her husband eyed her sharply at this questioning.

Fred's eyes became filled with tears, and he swallowed hard but did not answer *Señora* Terán right away. He stared out the window, momentarily lost in thought, and then, in a moment of guilt, depression, and weakness, he began to tell the Teráns his life story. It was a moment of truth and a critical period of reassessment in his life. It was for the best. The Teráns had been wonderful to him, always willing to help him, giving him guidance, medical instruments, and everything to assist him, and they had never asked questions about who he was. It was the only honest and sincere thing to do—to tell them the whole truth.

It was then that Fred launched into his fascinating story: the arrival of Juan Alvarez and the Revolution with Madero; his family status; his diplomat father; his academic school life; his successful medical career; how he had been accused of killing a young woman; having to leave his fiancée and flee the county; and bringing to light who he really was, and how mysteriously, perhaps for a purpose, he had appeared in Tampico-Alto. Occasionally, he would wipe his eyes with a napkin from the table. After talking without stopping for an hour, he paused, fearing he had sabotaged their friendship. Why would they want anything to do with him now? Sinking once again into self-pity, he thought his life was ruined.

"I want to thank you both for your kindness and for being my friends, giving me the opportunity to open a medical practice in Tampico-Alto, and for your hospitality. I'm a fugitive from the United States, and it's all right if the both of you don't want me to come around. I will understand."

Sobbing quietly, *Señora* Terán came over to Fred and hugged him with compassion, then wiped the tears from her eyes. She had never felt more humble. "I'm sorry," she said, "We did not mean to pry."

Dr. Terán was obviously caught off guard. He knew that there was a story to tell when he first laid eyes on Fred, but he still had a good feeling about their friendship. He stepped up and gave Fred a warm *abrazo*. "We do not want you to feel that way," Dr. Terán said sincerely. "Whatever happened in Texas is not our concern. We have heard about the terrible things that have happened in South Texas. This is Mexico, and many good changes are coming into our country, especially in medicine. A new discovery called penicillin, a drug to fight infections, will save many lives. My wife and I have become very fond of you, and we want you to stay in Mexico and be our friend. We want to help you any way we can to make your life better."

For the first time in many months, Fred felt as if the whole world had been lifted off his shoulders. "I can't thank you enough," he said softly. "I knew I would eventually have to tell you folks the true story, but I can't find it in me to tell the people in Tampico-Alto. They would see me as a charlatan."

"Don't worry about that. They all seem to like you and are happy that you help them with their ailments. For you to be their friend is all they want." Dr. Terán smiled charitably. "Now forget it, and let go of your despair and nostalgia. Release your regrets and fears. This is a new life. Relax, this is Mexico. We are your friends, *compadre!* I've heard worse stories. If we all get our heads together, we will elect Juan Alvarez as the new governor of Tamaulipas."

⌘ ⌘ ⌘

Changes were coming into Mexico as new presidential candidates were bringing fresh new ideas in education and land distribution. Pasual Ortiz Rubio was still president of Mexico, although he had several attempts on his life since he took office after Obregon's assassination. But Plutarco Elias Calles, the previous president, still controlled the paramount political power in Mexico.

In the middle of the summer, President Hoover signed the Hawley-Smoot Tariff Act, eventually weakening the already failing U.S. economy by raising tariffs to historically high rates and provoking the foreign market to drastically curtail foreign trade. It became a perilous era for trade. Unemployment rose into the millions and brought soup lines to the larger cities to feed the poor. The lower and middle class people were starving. Vendors appeared on main streets selling their fruits and vegetables for pennies. Con artists were inventing underhanded, get-rich-quick schemes, taking people's money and hightailing it to other towns. To make things worse, in the Midwest, where drought occurred, dust storms arose, making the poor pick up their belongings and head for California, where people were needed to work in the orchards and fields. The production index fell to the lowest in history, and the banking industry collapsed, exceeding many millions of dollars and sinking the Depression to its very lowest. The unfavorable Hoover was making a desperate last-ditch effort for his coming re-election in the mist of the Depression, and Prohibition became unpopular with the common man, who was desperately trying to bring food home to his hungry family.

In Europe, rumors of another war spread, as the Nazi party placed second in the German elections. Adolph Hitler started to become a household name, with rumors of a new military empire rising in Germany, and Stalin's cruel form of Communism in Russia was also becoming known to the world.

After his visits with Dr. and *Señora* Terán, Fred would return to the Gariby home feeling more inspired and with more medical knowledge each time, and with medical supplies he needed to keep people from dying of common diseases. The young doctor was becoming recognized and respected from word of mouth within the area that included several small towns beyond Tampico-Alto. More people from the surrounding villages were starting to come to church for spiritual healing, and for medical healing from Fred. He was starting to feel like himself again, but without the comforts he once had at his home in Texas. He began to regain his self-worth as a doctor and began spreading his wings, feeling more confident in his profession. And the natives all loved him, nicknaming him *El Jirafe,* The Giraffe, because of his stature.

A small store was opened on the opposite side of the church building, which sold holy water, goat cheeses, fruit drinks, and small trinkets made from seashells with the inscription of *El Señor de Tampico-alto.* It became prosperous and brought in needed revenue to the church and to the villagers.

In the months that followed, Fred delivered half a dozen babies to several households in Tampico-Alto. When he was free from his regular patients, he would walk with his black bag full of medicine and visit each of the little babies and their mothers to check on their condition. Each hut was almost identical, landscaped with gardens full of flowering vines, jacaranda, rubber tree plants, figs, blue and scarlet plumería, and many white and pink oleander bushes.

The thatched roof huts, called *jacales,* had floors of packed mud, and water had to be carried in buckets from the nearby streams. Having an outhouse was a luxury. The majority of the huts had no lavatory or washbasin, but inside were elaborate shrines and pictures of saints, with lit candles, and each had its own purpose called *Los Santos qué Curan,* the Curing Saints: *St. Anthonio* would be buried to help locate a lost object; *St. Benito,* the black saint, was for people of mixed Negro blood, giving them courage and hope; *St. Martin Caballero* was asked for money or love; *San Martin de Porres* and *San Judas Takeo* were prayed to for the impossible; and, of course, there was always *La Virgen de Guadalupe,* the Patron Saint of Mexico. The most often called on saint was *St. Ramon,* who worked overtime, for he was the saint for stopping gossip and was used almost daily. He would be turned upside down with a peso taped to his face, stopping any slander that was running around the village. When the gossip stopped, he was put right side up again. *Saint Ramon* was doomed from the very beginning, since he spent most of his time with his head down and his feet up.

At one time, one of the inquisitive young mothers asked Fred why he was not married and told him that she would make penance to *St. Martin Caballero* or *El Señor de Tampico-Alto* to find him a wife. Fred laughed and told her not to bother in her deep sacrifice, which he was perfectly content with the way his life was. The young mother was concerned, shaking her finger and telling him that a man without a family was a disgrace to society, and such a handsome man should consider getting married and having many children. Fred chuckled again and said he was not aware of any available women in the area who were seriously looking for a husband.

No sooner said than done. In the coming week, one morning following Mass, over twenty young girls and two older widow women were in line, like pilgrims to a shrine, and almost knocked down the door to his medical clinic, wanting him to check them over! They were all in a conspiracy to see that he picked the right woman and got married. The news had spread like hungry cockroaches when light shone in the kitchen and had mushroomed to all parts of the village and beyond. The feisty Dolores, having a mind of her own, saw all of the hopeful women wanting Fred for their husband and was infuriated. She dropped everything, defying the rules, took her white apron off, and walked home. The rest of the day was busy and frustrating for Fred alone. He had no help with all of the sick children and romantic women around him, until two laughing nuns came to his rescue. With great relief, he told them, "I felt like a one-armed paper-hanger."

At the Gariby home that evening, Fred sat like a lump at the dinner table, feeling like a fool and trying to analyze the mysterious events of the day. He asked of the two *tías*, busy getting his meal, "Where's Dolores? When he got no answer, he asked, "Where's *Señor* Gariby?"

"The children are with Dolores at the beach picking up clams and seashells to make necklaces to sell at the shop. They should be home before it gets dark," replied one of the unsympathetic aunts. "*Señor* Gariby has already eaten and is out in the fields cutting the sugar cane with several of the village men." She went on with her kitchen duties and moments later reached inside her apron pocket, handing him a note. "One of the messengers from Tampico brought this message from Dr. Terán." Fred read it, and after eating his dinner, he went to his sleeping quarters.

The following day found Fred in the busy city of Tampico close to the *Catedral de la Inmaculada Concepción,* and high-walled homes with gazebos made of iron, and streets with names of Colon, Olmos, Díaz-Mirón, and Hidalgo Avenue. All around Tampico were lakes and inlets of ocean water surrounding the city that smelled of dampness and of petroleum. He had checked the telegraph office with no results and sent yet another message to Felicia in Mercedes, hoping he would get an answer back to the Terán's home.

During World War I in Europe, many foreign investors had gotten away from the cold weather and devastation and had traveled to Mexico to live in the warm, temperate climate.

Many wealthy German residents lived along the north side of the new developing city, in an area called *Ciudad Madero*. There were also many Arabs who were successful merchants, bringing a rich culture and also colorful, beautifully crafted rugs. They also sold gold jewelry and pottery and traded with the Mexican merchants for their own commodities. Many had bought property and built beautiful homes along the shorelines.

That evening, while staying with the Teráns, Fred was introduced to several German doctors who were specializing in plants and herbs. The Teráns had brought together a number of European doctors who were investing in a large company that was developing drugs from the common *yerbas* found in Mexico. A doctor by the name of Samuel Krog referred to himself as a phytosociologist and was a leading researcher in the use of herbs. A tall man with blond hair and deep blue eyes, he had been living in Tampico for the past several years. Ever since the war with Germany had been resolved, he had been studying the uses of many native plants.

The other German was Andre Steinhoff, a medium-sized man with thick glasses and considerably older then the rest of the doctors, with salt and pepper hair, and candid hazel eyes. Steinhoff was very reserved, extremely intelligent, and spoke with few words; he sat quietly in a corner with a drink in his hand, studying the individuals as if he were characterizing them in a novel. There were several other wealthy German businessmen, who owned companies in Tampico and wanted to invest in the new research.

Fred was introduced to all of them by Dr. Terán, who told them that he was a bachelor from the United States and was making his home now in Tampico-Alto, a small village across the Rio Panuco, doing research and helping with the poor in that village. He also mentioned how successful Fred had been and how much the people there liked him.

As the conference began, Samuel Krog told the group that he had invested in the Krog-Stein-Mex Company, which was working to discover new drugs that would be important and beneficial to mankind. Krog informed the group that Aztec manuscripts, which gave the name and uses for each plant, had been found in a lost cave below Mexico City. It had taken years to complete the translation, but now they had all the formulas. The German doctor commented on the fact that many of the Aztecs in the New World were further advanced in medicine than the rest of the world. Mexico was the crown jewel of medicine, with so many beneficial plants and herbs available. In his comment, Krog said that it was more convenient doing business in Mexico, since the *Instituto Médico Nacional* in Mexico City did not investigate or poke their noses into any of their findings. He then pleaded with the rest of the group to invest in the newly formed company.

While Fred mingled with the German doctors, he enjoyed a large spread of foods that he was not accustomed to, but which were delicious and new to his palate. It was an enjoyable social evening mixed with intelligent conversation. He got caught up in the subject at hand and was able to relate to Krog his knowledge of plants and herbs that he had learned as a young lad in Texas.

As the evening came to an end, Fred was asked by Samuel Krog, who was championing and promoting the whole campaign, if he would like to join them in their company doing research. He stated that Fred would have to move to Tampico, since the manufacturing company was being built close to the Gulf and away from the rest of the city, giving them more room to expand.

"Thank you very much for asking me." Caught in a dilemma between the need of the people of Tampico-Alto and his beckoning future, Fred graciously replied, "I'm going to have to think it over, since I have a responsibility to the villagers in Tampico-Alto."

Krog responded, "Take your time. You can do research here three days a week and the rest you can spend treating the people of the village. You can't lose. You'll have a future with us here, and we would certainly enjoy having you. Let me know. You're welcome to join us. As for money, we can talk about that later."

Fred departed after thanking the German doctors and the Teráns. He mind was spinning. He could hardly believe his good luck, being offered a job with a foreign research company and earning money, both of which interested him. He had not had any income to speak of, and he was desperate to earn some. With money, he could help so many people in more ways. He started to gain his old confidence back and feel like himself again. But, in the back of his mind, he was always looking over his shoulder for fear of being discovered. He would ask the Gariby family how they felt about his job offer. He loved the little village, and he had fallen in love with Dolores and did not want to move away from her family. But he cherished the idea of using the Germans' instruments at their expense, since he had few, and he could do his own research for the villagers of Tampico-Alto. *Why not?*

The evening meal at the Gariby home consisted of grilled fish caught in the Gulf, *fideo*, a thin spaghetti fried with tomatoes and spices, and garbanzos cooked in butter and goat cheese. Dolores, who sat across from Fred at the dining table, ignored him and hadn't spoken a word. When the supper ended and the children, the goats, the chickens, and the dogs, and one small pig had gone outside, Fred began to explain to the Garibys that there was the possibility of his moving to Tampico. He told them about the job with the foreign company, and that he thought he might accept it. He also asked about the possibility of Dolores coming with him to Tampico. He did not want to be alone—he had been lonely too long.

Dolores glanced up and seemed delighted—her prayers to *El Señor de Tampico-Alto* had been answered. She smiled happily, with blinking, dancing eyes.

Her parents looked startled, as if a jungle monkey had backed up to their faces and farted. "You're talking of marrying Dolores," commented *Señor* Gariby, gathering his thoughts and being a sound thinker. He eyed Fred over the rims of his eyeglasses.

Señora Gariby, while sitting with her legs propped up, chuckled nervously.

Fred did not answer right away, but went into a long explanation of how he had missed Dolores when she had left him alone at the office, and how difficult it was to handle all of the sick children by himself. "I don't want to marry right away, since I have to start building my profession and begin making money to support a wife. I wanted to ask for Dolores's hand to be my wife, with your permission and your blessing, in the near future. This way we can be together and plan our life together."

"Dolores will not be permitted to be running around alone in Tampico without an escort," stated *Señora Gariby* firmly. "She can stay here and help you in your practice, but not in Tampico."

Dolores heard her mother's stern edict and left the room crying. One of the concerned aunties followed Dolores to her room.

Señor Gariby sat like a statue, rubbing his chin, and did not answer.

"We need to know when this marriage is going to take place. There is a lot of work in planning a wedding," commented *Señora* Gariby, taking it all in stride, since she never lifted a finger, and had everyone doing her chores, especially the *tías. Señora* Gariby was pleased that Dolores did not find herself a husband from the *Plaza del Paseo,* an old Spanish custom, where girls strolled clockwise and the young gentlemen counterclockwise on a Saturday night, among the lanterns on the Plaza, taking a chance on finding a reliable husband that way.

After some thought, Fred took the Germans up on their offer, and soon after, he received his first envelope of several hundred Mexican pesos. With the help of the Teráns, he was able to find himself a small kitchenette in Tampico, close to the research building. He bought a used, brown Packard jalopy, perhaps stolen and brought in from the border, along with several suits, and a pair of custom made shoes to fit his big feet. During his shopping spree, Fred did not forget the kindly old man and woman who had rescued him, and he purchased things for them. For Dolores, he bought a pair of ruby earrings, with the promise of buying an engagement ring later.

He spent Monday through Wednesday in the laboratory, which was cloaked in secrecy, with foreign-speaking chemists, pharmacists, and physicists, all dressed in white coats. Since he was able to come and go as he pleased during the week, he had been given the key to the locker where the white coats were kept.

All seven floors, all of the rooms, and all of the corridors were heavily guarded by German security aides with revolvers at their sides. The well-equipped pharmaceutical experimental area occupied the main floor, with experiments being conducted in other rooms, but only special people had keys to enter those rooms. This was only one of the many buildings that made up the complex.

All of the researchers were Germans and spoke little Spanish. Fred was told by the janitor, a man called Hans—who smoked heavily and often had coffee with him—that at night all of the outside lights were turned on and half a dozen Dobermans and German shepherd dogs, trained to kill, roamed the complex to deter intruders.

Hundreds of weeds and plants were being introduced and analyzed for their beneficial uses. After the herbs were separated and cleaned, they were dried, and then crushed and made into capsules or liquids. Hundreds of Mexican men were employed in shipping the products on large vessels to South America, Australia, Europe, and Canada, but largely to Germany. The company was soon getting hundreds of responses expressing how wonderful the products were.

ROOTS OF INDIFFERENCE

The Krog-Stein-Mex Company was being recognized as one of the leading pharmaceutical industries in the world, and it kept expanding, making millions; however, the products were not being endorsed by the U.S. Food and Drug Administration.

The rest of the divided week Fred spent in Tampico-Alto with Father Gonzales and his villagers. Each day there would be a long line of people waiting for help. On many occasions he would conceal the microscopic glass strips from Krog-Stein-Mex, hide them under his coat, and take them to the village to do research in his own clinic, hoping to find cures for different diseases. Fred loved his job with Krog-Stein-Mex and the generous remuneration— it was more than he had ever anticipated.

Dolores would secretly join him on his trips and would stay in their small apartment, fixing it up by sewing curtains and adding small conveniences. She would explain to her mother that she was buying supplies for his practice and spending the time with *Señora* Terán. On the days that she did indeed spend the whole day with *Señora* Terán, while waiting for Fred's return, the two women would take the trolley downtown and visit the food markets and venture into many shops of interest, especially the fabric store, since Dolores enjoyed sewing and was busy planning her wedding.

Knowing that they were planning their future together, Fred and Dolores often made passionate love. Dolores had been warned by her mother that she was forbidden to be alone in Tampico, without the spying eyes of *las tías.* But Dolores rebelled. She was in love and had disobeyed her mother many times, because she wanted to be with Fred. And the tall, handsome doctor was also very convincing and reassuring about their relationship. He loved her and wanted her with him.

Many times they would spend a full day going to *Miramar,* the beach along the coast of Tampico. Other days the couple would shop in downtown Tampico and travel to the busy boat docks to buy seafood. When alone, they loved to listen to the beautiful, tear-jerking songs from *El Trío Del Los Panchos* on the radio.

⌘　⌘　⌘

Propaganda in the Mexican headlines in 1933 was always describing the terrible conditions occurring in the United States and the terrible financial failures of the country. Stocks declined and commodities dropped; companies failed and fortunes were lost. People were fighting over jobs and fighting over food that was thrown into garbage cans. Millions of people wandered around the country, hungry and without hope, and many were evicted from their farms. Labor unions across the country demanded better working conditions and pay in factories. Franklin Delano Roosevelt had been elected president, and his wife Eleanor was already busy distributing millions of dollars in cash to the destitute, helping them with food, clothes, and shelter.

Hobos traveling on trains were being killed when caught by train detectives. Several songwriters like Woody Guthrie, who wrote *This Land Is My Land,* rode the weary rails on top of the railroad cars, making up sad songs of the times. Jimmy Rogers traveled the lonesome railroad tracks also and wrote many memorable songs.

The Depression also brought out a different breed of criminal—the "desperate ones," as they were called. To the hungry hoards, they were considered heroes, while to the authorities; they were "Public Enemy Number One." Bonnie and Clyde came to notoriety, robbing banks and driving fast cars to get away. Notorious John Dillinger, Pretty Boy Floyd, Baby Face Nelson, Machine Gun Kelly, and so many others lived a life of crime and were eventually gunned down by law enforcement.

With so many white Americans suffering, it was not surprising that they turned their attention to the Mexican-American people, who said little and lived quietly along the border. There were angry complaints from the white people to the Representatives and to the Congress of the United States, claiming that the Mexican people took their jobs away and also stole from them. It was ironic, since the average Mexican-American man was uneducated and accustomed to doing the hard menial jobs, especially field work, that the majority of the educated people would not touch. But, there had to be someone to blame, especially during the terrible times of the Depression.

In Texas, the federal authorities did not take long to react. They were kept busy deporting hundreds of Mexican families. Once again, the Mexican-American people were living in constant fear; they were the silent ones, without voice and without justice. Ironically, many of the people were American citizens, and in time, all moved back into Texas.

CHAPTER 39

The Mexican elections, which had always been tainted with violence, took a different turn with the new presidential outcome. In 1934, Lázaro Cárdenas, governor of Michoacán, a man known for his honesty, became President of Mexico and transcended the traditional role. He wanted to be like the common people of Mexico and wore business suits instead of a military uniform.

In the same election year in Mexico, Juan Alvarez won by a landside and became governor of the state of Tamaulipas, moving to Ciudad Victoria, which was the state capital. He rapidly initiated many changes, sharing the same ideas as the new president.

Fred's life in Mexico was wonderful, and he felt he had made a difference. He had a fabulous part-time job and had Dolores, whom he loved and adored. They would be married in the near future. It was hard to believe that several years back, he had starved and ate raw fish in a stolen boat going nowhere and did not think he was going to live. Up to this point, he had not received one word from his family in Texas. In the back of his mind, he missed everyone terribly and wondered and worried about their situation.

In the summer of 1935, after working for a year and a half with the Germans in Tampico, he had been rewarded with almost a degree's worth of lessons in chemical and plant research. Samuel Krog was pleased with Fred and favored him. At the end of one workday, Fred was ready to leave and go visit the Teráns when he was summoned by Krog and ushered by one of the guards into his opulent office. He entered the large elaborate room, surrounded by windows overlooking the waves of the Gulf of Mexico. The room was beautifully appointed, with plush carpet, priceless paintings on the walls, and a full-service bar.

"Take a seat, Fred," Krog ordered, pointing with his pipe to one of the sofas. "Would you like some coffee?" Krog was in his late sixties, with graying hair. In his youth he had been a very handsome man, who, along with his intelligence, presented a commanding presence, but he seemed cynical, with hidden secrets, and was rumored to have a dark, mysterious past. He was single, but talk was that he was living with a seventeen-year-old mistress from Spain. In the pharmaceutical lab, the Germans chuckled as they related that Krog had the girl kidnapped and had hidden her away in his newly built mansion somewhere up the coast.

"Yes, thank you," answered Fred, as he watched Krog pour black coffee into a white china cup and hand it to him. "Thank you," he replied humbly, but in the back of his mind, he waited for a surprise. He had never trusted Krog—there was something about the man that made him nervous.

"We are all hoping that you are enjoying your job."

"Why yes, very much so," Fred replied.

"We have been hearing good reports from you at the laboratory, and it seems that everyone in the research office trusts you and likes you a lot," he said, as his pipe smoke circled upwards toward the ceiling. "We are very pleased with your introduction of the South American plant, *Curare*, and we are discovering more and more uses for it every day. The head scientist was elated last week to discover that its extract increases urination, reduces fever, blocks pain, and treats testicular inflammation, especially an enlarged prostate. Imagine how it will help the male population. Imagine what it will do for people in pain." Pleased with those prospects, Samuel Krog's eyes lit up. But he was also thinking of the millions of dollars that Krog-Stein-Mex was bringing in. Already, the company had bought half a dozen shipping vessels and transported millions of cases of the bottled capsules to many of the world's countries. The company had proven to be a lucrative venture, and the two owners and the majority of the researchers, scientists, and chemists drove fancy imported German Duisenbergs.

"Thank you," replied Fred, "but you also have to be very careful with *Curare*. Giving the right dosage works wonders, but too much could cause problems. One could become paralyzed." He was trying to project the pros and cons of the drug, but he was not revealing the complete effect of the other ingredients. That information they would have to discover for themselves.

"Yes, of course. The scientists have plenty of time to figure that out," Krog answered confidently. "However, the reason that I called you into my office is that we would like to make you a proposal. The company would like to double the amount of money that you are now receiving, and we wondered if you would like to travel for our company. You speak Spanish fluently and have the intelligence to sell." He rubbed his hands together enthusiastically, envisioning more profits.

There was a long pause as he gave Fred a chance to assimilate his words, but he could not help but notice Fred's perplexed reaction. Krog continued, "The traveling would be to the bigger cities, where purchasing is done in larger quantities that are more profitable for us. You, of course, would have to leave the research office group. We would provide an office for you—"

"And become a salesman? A traveling salesman?" remarked Fred, surprised and disappointed. This was not the reason he had taken on the job. Perspiration popped out on his face, and his heart pounded. "You need to remember, Mr. Krog, I'm a humble, simple doctor, not a promoter of products, and I have given my solemn oath to the villagers of Tampico-Alto to heal them. I cannot leave this area. I need to stay with the people. I love the little village. I took on working with your company because of my interest in research." He wanted to say that medicine was given by God for healing, not to make millions for greedy people, but he refrained.

With those words, Krog became somewhat hostile, thinking that this was the chance of a lifetime, and anyone in their right mind would surely leap at the opportunity! His cool demeanor and personality completely changed; his voice hardened. "How long do you plan to live in that rotten village, with those uneducated, tribal Mexicans? How long do you plan to stay in Mexico? He began cursing in the German language. He was scowling, with a stormy look in his eyes that was alarming. The German executive began puffing his expensive pipe harder, as he glared at Fred through his spectacles.

"Because those uneducated, tribal villagers, those poor people, saved my life and fed me and took care of me when I was sick, and because I have compassion for the needy and disenfranchised," Fred replied. He grabbed his attaché case and hat and stood up. "Money is a commodity and really not that important to me. I plan to return to the United States when the time is right; when I have done all of the right things, the good things that I have planned to do. Sorry, but I will have to pass on your offer."

"Enough!" Krog stormed. "There is depression in that country. Have you not seen the propaganda in the Mexican headlines? You should hear what the Germans have predicted, especially Chancellor Hitler. The United States is doomed, and people are starving to death. Here, with our company, you have an opportunity to grow and enrich yourself. With all of the money that we are offering, you could live like a king. We are offering you the universe carte blanche—I do not understand!" he bellowed, and rose up from his chair, swearing again in German. "Let me know if you change your mind," he said, and turned his back on Fred as sign of disrespect, and began fussing with the phone. "That is all," he said, not facing him. "You may leave. I may call on you later."

As Fred left the office, he heard the phone ring at the receptionist desk in the foyer. The call was from Herr Samuel Krog to the officer's answering station. He heard the receptionist say, "Yes, Herr Krog, I will get the report right away and get the Intelligent Committee Officers to check on the last name. It was 'Cantu,' did you say?"

Fred left the office drained and felt like a fool for refusing Krog's offer, not knowing if he had a job to return to the following week. If they investigated, they would find the real Dr. Cantu was a physician from Reynosa, but was twenty years older and long dead. Fred was a wanted man in Mexico, a fugitive. On so many occasions, especially in Tampico when he visited the Teráns, he had a habit of looking behind him, hoping that no one recognized him. He was always paranoid and fearful, afraid of being arrested again.

Fred found his way to the residence of the Teráns, who were not expecting him. *Señora* Terán was thrilled to see him and held the door open. "Fred," she said in a whispering tone. "You have visitors, people from the United States, waiting for you in the family room." He remembered that the last message he had mailed to Texas was from the Terán residence.

He asked, "From the United States?" He was shocked and didn't know if his heart could stand another surprise. He rushed in and found Dan Land and Luis Martin, Victoria's son, now grown, standing in the middle of the room! It was a memorable moment, and they all embraced in a huddle and wept.

Fred finally got a grip on himself after the long hugs and sobs. Dan Land informed him that they had never received any messages, that there had been no word until a month ago. Perhaps poor communication lines were at fault, nobody knew. They had had several hurricanes hit the Rio Grande Valley, especially the bad one in 1933 that destroyed many of the lines, and always took a long time to repair anything.

Dan Land sat down and tried to explain the events that had transpired during the years of his absence. He informed Fred that everyone at the Matamoros prison, and his family as well, thought he was dead. The guards thought both he and the driver were killed by the fugitives that had fled with the van, and that they had been thrown into the sea. The guards found his watch on the ground the following day and gave it to Victoria. A week later, the fugitives were caught and killed instantly on their way to Monterrey, before they had a chance to talk. Since they never revealed anything, nobody knew what had happened. "However, your sister never believed you were dead and kept repeating it to *Don* Federico," he said.

Fred was overwhelmed by emotion and excitement.

"And we have good news! Your father and Victoria, with the help of several well-known attorneys, are still in conference with the State Representatives in Austin to get your name cleared. Emily's stepfather, who was shot and killed by Bernard Hanson, had confessed on his deathbed that it was he and Hanson who had killed the girl with your gun, because she was going to the authorities on your behalf. Meanwhile, Hanson has fled and is a fugitive again. Nobody knows where he has gone. The authorities are searching for him, wanting answers. There was a big article in the newspaper about the case being reopened in Hidalgo County to clear your name."

Barely able to speak in his jubilation, Fred's first words were: "How's my father? How's Victoria? Carlos? And what were their reactions to finally getting my telegram?"

"Everybody was thrilled and excited." Dan searched for the right words. "Your father was thrilled, and, as a matter of fact, started to feel better and is beginning to talk more. Victoria is fine, with another son, Danny, now three years old. Carlos is also doing fine. Everyone is anxious to see you after getting your message."

Noticing Dan's uneasiness and his facial expression, Fred questioned him. "What's wrong with father? He observed his nephew Luis Martin shudder slightly and drop his gaze to the floor.

"Well, I guess you didn't know." Dan's expression turned from jovial to sad. "We were all affected by what happened to you. Your father took it real hard and had a bad stoke—a critical one. This was after the prison authorities in Matamoros pronounced you dead. It has taken time. At first he could not speak, but with therapy and encouragement from friends and family, he is now talking some. *El Guapo* Jim and Tomas Canalo from Brownsville visit him quite often. Last year Marshall Bishop from Austin was one of his guests, giving him support and comfort. We had another surprise, too, from White Eagle, who came from Oklahoma to visit your father and stayed for a week. They both enjoyed each other's company. And your sister Victoria is doing fine. She keeps real busy, taking care of everyone, especially your father, all of her children, and Aunt Josie.

There was a long pause. "I had no other choice," remarked Fred, shaking, and in tears again. "I had to escape, my life was at stake." He turned to view Luis Martin, who was going to be twenty-two years old, tall and handsome, so resembling Juan Alvarez, with his large green eyes and striking features. Fred wondered if he knew who his real father was—an important man, now governor of Tamaulipas.

The kindly *Señora* Terán graciously excused herself so that the men could talk privately among themselves, catching up with the past years. She busied herself in the kitchen and once brought in a tray with tall glasses of cold refreshments.

Presently, Dr. Terán, having been informed by his wife in another room that Fred had guests from Texas, walked into the room. He began introducing himself to the two men.

The men spent the next couple of hours talking around the kitchen table while having supper with the Teráns and discussing the conditions in the United States, Texas, and the Rio Grande Valley. It was Dan Land who feared trouble was fomenting around the world. He had brought the *Brownsville Herald* with articles explaining that trouble was brewing in Europe once again, and that Adolph Hitler, the German Chancellor, had organized the Nazi Party and was turning Germany into a police state. However, at the same time, Hitler was busy expressing his strong desire for peace throughout the world. The *Sturmabteilung*, called the S.A., began arresting people opposing Hitler's power. Many were shot to death. The general public in the Western hemisphere lacked the awareness of the evils lurking beneath the surface.

That evening, nerves were all in high tension, as Fred told Dr. Terán that there was the possibility of him having to leave Krog-Stein-Mex Company. He related what had taken place that afternoon in Krog's office. "I'm being investigated. They are going to find out about me, sooner or later."

This concerned Dr. Terán, since he had a large amount of his wife's investments in Krog-Stein-Mex Company. Hearing what Dan Land was saying about the happenings in Europe, and especially Germany, it immediately created apprehension.

"No doubt, the United States knows more of what's happening in the world than is reported in the newspaper here in Mexico," said Dr. Terán, worried. "I'm treating a patient who came in from exposure to powder burns on his hands and arms. He works nights at Krog-Stein-Mex, on the shipping docks, and loads boxes onto the German ships. It's funny, but he said at the end of the building, toward the ocean where they load the shipments onto ships, it was full of rifles, guns, ammunition, and boxes of gunpowder. When he returns to the clinic, I'll ask him more questions," he said somberly.

Fred and Dr. Terán were both surprised by this information. They thought that Krog-Stein-Mex Company only exported pharmaceutical and plant products. They glanced at each other and shrugged their shoulders.

During the next few days, Fred invited Dan and Luis Martin to spend the rest of the week in Tampico-Alto, where they could meet the wonderful people who had transformed his life, and view the beautiful landscape, and walk the magnificent seashores. They would also meet Dolores, her family, Father Gonzales and the nuns, and find inspiration in the church of *El Señor de Tampico-Alto* and its little community.

On the road to Tampico-Alto, Fred drove and casually asked Dan about Catalina. His torch no longer burned for her, since he now had Dolores, but he was curious.

Dan said, "She came around a couple of times, according to what Felicia said. She wanted to know about your disappearance. She did come for a while, but not anymore. I think your father still deals with *Señor* Castillo, concerning their bulls." Dan had been instructed by Victoria not to repeat the information that eight months after Fred left the Valley, Catalina gave birth to a baby girl. Dan continued, "I think Victoria mentioned her getting married some time back. I don't know for sure."

Fred was silent, but he understood Catalina's thinking. He kept telling himself, *why should she have waited, if he were supposedly dead?*

"And Victoria has another boy? How wonderful," he said, regretting that he was unable to see any of them.

Luis Martin sat in the back seat, peering from the window of the Packard, enthralled with the scenery, especially the ships sounding their loud foghorns.

Meanwhile, Fred was brought up to date on the scandalous gossip from Mercedes. Carlos had gotten married to a lovely girl named Mary from Sebastian, Texas, and they were now living at Spanish Acres, taking care of the large mansion, helping with the cattle, and clearing acres of land for the production of more cotton. Dan and Felicia had two sons and a daughter and were enjoying their new home. Emma had gotten considerably larger, more cantankerous, and was having trouble with her sugar highs and lows, driving Dr. Benjamin Burr crazy. Ricardo traveled back and forth across the river to see Victoria occasionally and to collect his yearly income from the cotton. He preferred Monterrey and lived there with his mother. Ricardo's father, *Señor* Del Calderóne, and Bruno Pue were murdered in Matamoros, shot in the head, execution-style. The killers had never been found. Rumors were that it was his young mistress's family, since he used to beat her up all the time, but this had never been confirmed. Grandmother Gloria was getting old and forgetful. Mrs. McCray was still trying to coerce *Don* Federico into getting married. The last word was that Magdalena was terminally ill, which surprised Fred, since she was married to Dr. Juan Alvarez.

Dan Land and Luis Martin left after three days in Tampico-Alto. They had enjoyed their trip to the port city and Veracruz. Dan's last word as the two men left on the train back to Matamoros was, "Don't be surprised if Victoria shows up here in Tampico to see you!"

Fred stood for a long time watching the train disappear into the distance, his eyes misting with tears. He wanted to see his family, especially his sickly father. But, for the moment, he would have to wait patiently until he was legally freed, and in the meantime, do what he knew best—heal people.

CHAPTER 40

Fred returned to Krog-Stein-Mex the following week, pretending that nothing had happened, and kept working his normal days and hours at the laboratory under tight security. There were new people working whom he did not recognize. Hans was gone from his janitorial position and had not been seen for some time. There was a difference in attitude among the scientists and co-workers at the laboratory—a sense of restlessness and nervousness prompting each one of them not to say a word. Fred kept to himself and did his job. However, he suffered due to the cloud of suspicion he sensed under the watchful eyes of co-workers. Fred wisely said nothing.

At the end of this workday, he picked up his attaché case and left. He stopped at his mailbox and checked his mail, hoping for something from Texas. He picked up several Mexican newspapers and sat down at a busy sidewalk *café* and ordered coffee.

The headlines from the United States sensationalized the murder trial of Bruno Hauptman, who was accused of kidnapping and killing the baby son of aviator icon Charles Lindbergh. In other world news, Spain was in torment with the fighting between the Republicans and the rebel Nationalists destroying churches and killing nuns and priests. England was still trying to get over Edward's abdication to the throne of England. He married Wallis Simpson, in Paris, France, a woman married and divorced twice, creating a storm of controversy throughout the world.

Mexican reporters, who were learning of the problems in Europe, were becoming curious, especially with the threat coming from Germany. President Hindenburg had died the year before, and Hitler declared himself Fuhrer, the leader of the Third Reich. It did not take long for Hitler to take over Germany, arresting Communists, Socialists, and anyone who opposed his views by torturing and killing them; he also began burning books. His main concern was getting rid of the Jewish people as a race, blaming the Jews for all the problems of the world. With Hitler's view and orders, he started to convince the rest of the German people to think of themselves as the one white race—a superior race. He began giving orders to isolate the Jewish people and strip them of any civil rights. He removed them from any social or political activities, thus beginning the Nazi terror. This strategy would force them to close their businesses and starve; he branded them with the Star of David and separated them and displayed them like lambs. And, like lambs to the slaughter, they would all go.

Nazism was beginning to become evident in Mexico, too, as the swastika was brazenly displayed throughout the Krog-Stein-Mex Company.

While reading the news, it finally dawned on Fred that all the happenings with Hitler in Germany were also influencing his co-workers at the laboratory where he worked. They were all Germans.

Absorbed in his reading, and drinking a cup of coffee, he had his back to the busy street. He felt a tap on his shoulder. It startled him, and he looked around. There stood Hans like the angel of death. He was wearing a dark cap around his soft blond hair and his bright blue eyes portrayed a scared and worried look. He stood like a statue but was shaking with fright.

"Hans!" said Fred, getting up with a smile and extending his hand. "Have a seat. I haven't seen you for a while. Where have you been?" He gestured for Hans to sit down.

"I don't work there anymore," he said bluntly, taking a seat on the opposite side of the small round table. "And if you were smart, you would leave too."

Fred frowned "Why, Hans? What happened? Why did you leave?"

"They are doing things in that laboratory that are not human," he said. "Being a janitor, I was able to snoop around, and I heard things, and I saw it with my own eyes." He spoke as if he were horrified. "They are killing people in the East B laboratory where you work. The worst part is that they know I was aware of everything. The scientists are experimenting and giving injections to poor, homeless men who do not have families and no one to claim them. When they die, they take the body parts out of their bodies and put them into others. Some of the organs are being shipped to heaven knows where."

"Of course, that happens all the time in medicine. That's how I learned how to be a doctor. But organs being shipped out! Hmmm! Maybe they are being shipped out to Guadalajara, which is the largest medical hospital in Mexico doing research. That takes place in all hospitals," Fred assured him.

"Fred!" he said harshly. "Three weeks ago, I was getting my money envelope at the cash register. I had not informed them that it was my last week, so it was taking longer to get my money. I sat quietly on a low chair while I waited, and nobody saw me. I overheard the commander talking about you to three investigators in uniform. The conversation was about you being investigated."

"Oh!"

"They were saying that your last name was not the name you were using. That you were going by a false name. And that your real name was Juelson—and it was Jewish. They hate the Jews, you know. I'm part Jew myself, on my mother's side. They do not know that." He laughed, as if the joke was on the Krog-Stein-Mex Company. "I have never been back, but I still have the keys to get in and out of the laboratory. I want to give them to you. See for yourself. You might need them." He placed them on the table.

"So they know about me?" said Fred. "They know that my last name is Juelson?"

"I'd get the hell out of there real fast, like I did," said Hans, nodding. "I have a job and started work on the shipping docks. I like it very much. And you could get a job anywhere in this city." Hans looked up and saw a dark car parked around the corner of Olmos and Díaz Street with its motor running.

"Hans, I haven't done anything! Why would I want to run?"

"They think you are a Jew, because of your last name! Don't you see what I mean? The Germans kill Jews!"

"That doesn't mean anything to me. I'm not Jewish. And this is Mexico, not Germany."

"For God sakes," Hans said. "You do not understand! Your name, silly, it's Jewish!"

Hans glanced over his shoulder and occasionally got close to Fred's face and whispered. Then suddenly, his face became paralyzed with fear, and he sat frozen for a minute in time.

"They're after me and have found me!" he said anxiously, and stood up. "He quickly lowered his head, trying to hide his face under the bill of his dark cap, and dashed off down the busy sidewalk, getting lost in the crowd.

"Wait!" Fred said, surprised. "Who? Who's after you?" He noticed the car begin to move and follow Hans as he hurried down the sidewalk. Fred managed to glance at the license plate, but only got MM8021 and could not get the rest of the numbers before the vehicle disappeared in traffic. He noticed the keys belonging to the Krog-Stein-Mex Company lying on the table. He picked them up and put them in his attaché case.

On the way to the Terán's home, Fred had time to think and wonder what the real truth was behind Hans' story. He knew that Hans seemed genuinely interested in their friendship and would not have given him the keys otherwise. Full of concern, his thoughts took a different twist—he wondered what was going on in laboratory B at the back of the main building. It was the building that only authorized people were allowed to enter. He had the keys, and in the coming weeks he might be able to see for himself.

Fred found Dr. and *Señora* Terán excited when he reached their home. Dr. Terán had been offered a better paying medical job in Mexico City, which pleased *la Señora*, being close to her parents.

"Imagine, I'll be making double the amount in Mexico City, and I'll have the chance to get my degree, specializing as a heart surgeon. It will complete my heart's desire!" He laughed at his joke and could see that *Señora* Terán was thrilled by the news.

Fred was happy for the couple, but he explained about the events that had taken place that day. He told them of Hans, how scared he was, and the keys. Their facial expressions went from joyous to one of concern.

Dr. Terán said, "I'm going to try and get my money back from Krog-Stein-Mex Company before I leave for Mexico City. I've been getting an uncomfortable feeling about them. I think there is something terrible going on—people are talking. I've had workers and other investors talking about the foreign company, and they do not seem pleased. There's talk about the Germans and their Fuhrer. You might have to travel with us to Mexico City, Fred, and—" He stopped in the middle of his sentence as a thought came to him. "Quit!" he blurted out. "Leave Krog-Stein-Mex Company and come with us! I'll find you a job in the clinics in

Mexico City! And bring Dolores, she'll love the capital. Who knows, we may be in for some rough times ahead, especially living so close to a port city."

Later that evening, Fred returned to Tampico-Alto. He was happy to be home with Dolores and her affable family and glad to see his patients. When the couple was alone, Fred began explaining the events of the day and the reason he would have to leave the German company. He asked Dolores if she would want to live with him in Mexico City.

Shaking her head, she replied, "I cannot leave my parents. Mother is at an age where she needs all of my attention, and she needs help raising the rest of the children." She went on making excuses. The fact was that Dolores was fiercely independent within her own class of people, but she felt awkward in social settings with higher-up groups of society and did not want to leave her home base. The strong family bond forbade her leaving her parents, and leaving her church and her familiar surroundings was out of the question.

"Then the wedding will have to wait."

In the following weeks, Dr. Terán, in the middle of packing his medical supplies, kept hounding Fred to leave with them for the capital.

Fred, in turn, tried to convince Dolores to travel with him to Mexico City. But Dolores was adamant. She did not want to leave her parents.

Fred teased her, "If I leave, I may not be back."

Dolores laughed, with a mischievous twinkle in her eye. "Go, see if I care."

Headlines in the Tampico newspaper soon reported that a body had been found along the Laguna de Tamiahua shoreline. Later it was revealed the body was that of Hans. It made the hair on the back of Fred's neck stand up and brought a chill of fear.

At Krog-Stein-Mex Company, Fred, still distressed, wondered who had killed Hans and why? *Was it that Hans knew too much about the German company? Why was Hans so scared, and what did the black car that was following him want from him?* Millions of questions were going through his mind. He wished he would have gotten more information from Hans at the sidewalk cafe. The keys were in his attaché case, and he had already gotten paid for the week. His curiosity soon won out. Lucky for him, the majority of the Germans were celebrating Stein's birthday, and all were in the main conference room with a large cake and ice cream.

At certain times of the day, when the guards changed positions and were gone for an hour or so, it was the perfect time to walk down the long corridor unnoticed. Glancing both ways, Fred was able to enter laboratory B with the keys that Hans had given him, and to his amazement, the room was empty, without a soul working. Inside there were counters with glass containers full of liquid drugs and powders, and papers in German handwriting on the findings and conclusions of experimental research. There were hundreds of glass bottles sitting on the counters, and inside were dead fetuses and human brains. Apparently, experiments were being conducted to help improve care in pregnancy, and in the human brain, perhaps to help neurotic or psychiatric problems. *Where are they getting all of these? The Germans must be paying the surrounding hospitals to provide them with everything,* Fred thought.

There were cages of live tropical birds, rabbits, white rats, snakes, and mice. He stood in shock for several minutes and viewed all of this and then, from a room further inside, he heard a strange noise and headed to investigate. The door was open, but he was being lured by an odor that was overwhelming.

Inside were three men, and two were moaning. By the look of the clothes they wore and by the fetid smell, they were probably homeless bums. All three sat next to the wall and were hooked into some kind of wiring. One was getting a white transparent liquid put into his veins from a machine that was plugged into the wall. When they saw Fred walk in, one screamed in fear. The other one began begging. "Please help me!" he said, his voice hoarse from wailing.

Horrified at these inhumane acts, Fred looked stricken and checked the contents of the liquid to see what was being put into their bodies. He was correct in guessing one of the chemicals. The man who was unconscious was being given *Curare*, which was deadly if given too much. They were doing human experiments to see how much *Curare* it would require to die! The other live one was being injected with liquid penicillin, used for infection or venereal disease. Fred's heart pounded from fear, but he quickly unplugged each man. He touched the throat pulse on the man who was limp and decided he was already dead. He had been given a chemical warfare poison. *Hans was right,* he told himself in abhorrence. He had to act quickly. Finding bandages on the shelves, he wrapped them around the two men's arms to stop the bleeding.

He faced the two bums who were startled and shaky. They seemed grateful, and he repeated in a whispering tone for them to be quiet while they got away. "Come with me and I will drive you to the nearest police station," he said softly. They nodded and picked themselves up, as they were willing to do anything to get away from the torturing hell.

While he was still in B laboratory, Fred gathered up as many of the papers that contained scribbled information as he could and stuffed them in his attaché case. He took bottles of pills and powders, and all of the written information on certain drugs and put them in his side pockets. He got the other two men, now standing, to help him gather some of the written manuscripts for them to take with them as evidence. He picked up his attaché case, and the three took off down the hallway and out the exit doors. Luckily, no one saw them leave. He did not care, since he had become convinced since Hans' death that this would be his last day there. His feeling of outrage against the German company and their greed was enough for him to end his employment. There were many other places he could work.

It was a twenty-minute drive to the downtown police station in the middle of Tampico. Down the road, Fred's hands and body shook like Mexican jumping beans as he gripped the steering wheel of the car. He was still reeling from the horrible laboratory incident and the experiments being conducted. The two men told their story as he drove. One was sitting in the front and the other in the back. The odiferous bum in front was the most talkative. Fred lowered the window on his side to get a whiff of fresh air. The smell was overwhelming; apparently, they had both crapped and peed in their pants. How many times, he dared not ask.

The bum in the front seat was named Adán. He had a large mouth displaying missing front teeth. The one in the back was Pedro. He was short and stocky, with dark hair and blazing black eyes. They never revealed their last names. They did not know the name of the one who had died in the laboratory, for they had never gotten formally acquainted.

According to the story the poor souls told, two individuals in a black car had offered them money to assist in laboratory drug testing. Being destitute, the three had enthusiastically complied, seeing it as an opportunity. The mysterious individuals had promised them cocaine and morphine to satisfy their addictions. They were told that after a couple of days testing, they would be released back into society and get paid.

What the two individuals in the black car did not tell them was that there were certain dangerous risks in this type of adventure, and they might never live to tell anyone. It was true that the Krog-Stein-Mex Company was doing research; however, the three individuals were drug addicts, and the German company was known in the city of Tampico as doing research only with herbs and plants. Apparently Krog-Stein-Mex Company had hired the two individuals to lure bums to conduct illegal, clandestine scientific research without anybody knowing the results. The unknown characters in the black car were being paid under the table for each bum they enticed and dragged in. If they died, it was unfortunate—their bodies were disposed of secretly.

Raging mad, Fred was disgusted by the Germans—cowardly brutes doing this to poor illiterate people, desperate to survive. He was also thinking of himself and his own future, since he was still a fugitive and had not been cleared within the United States. Walking into the *policía* with the two bums and the German papers would stir questions; however, it had to be done. Krog-Stein-Mex Company had to be exposed. He had to sacrifice to stand up for what was right.

After the two men hurriedly showered and shaved in a downtown flophouse and had their clothes washed and dried, they ate a quick meal from a sidewalk taco stand. Several hours later, they walked into the headquarters of el *Estación de Policía*.

The old, ratty, brick building had been a government compound during the Díaz regime, but now maintained one hundred uniformed policemen on the busy downtown streets, where train stations and trolley cars, busses, trucks, and cars ran through its noisy, clogged streets. Fumes of crude gasoline and burning oil infiltrated lungs and nostrils. Everywhere tall billboards showed pictures of a pretty, smiling lady drinking Coca-Cola, and others displayed several cowboys smoking Camel or Lucky Strike cigarettes.

Strange people scurried in and out of the old, dark police building. The odor of stale cigarettes and smoke filled the rooms, as noisy chattering echoed throughout the entire building. Hysterical people were talking loudly; others were crying; phones rang; and manual typewriters were busy clicking away in closed rooms.

It was the same old story of a metropolis—a busy, port city dealing with days and nights of complete mayhem. Perhaps the *numero uno* problem was knife stabbings from heavy drinking; second, jealous husbands beating and killing their wives. The rest were gun wounds, burglaries, rape, and other violent assaults, but with so many foreigners coming from elsewhere to the port city, these were becoming more widespread.

ROOTS OF INDIFFERENCE

The three men were introduced to Pablo Rubio, first pictured in the *Tampico Headlines* as the head of intelligence, a forty-year-old man with shiny, dark hair combed back and who displayed a bushy, walrus mustache from ear to ear, and flashing dark eyes that were never still. He was extremely polite, astute, and a prudent man of medium height, wearing a white Panama shirt. It surprised Fred that Rubio was not wearing a uniform. The average individual who viewed him would have never suspected that he was into police work.

Detective Rubio led Fred, Adán, and Pedro down a long corridor with cracked, uneven, dirty tile to the back of the large brick building with high ceilings, peeling paint, and bleached-out walls. A noisy ceiling fan revolved crankily inside Rubio's room. The three sat on hard wooden chairs and faced the ambitious, intelligent Rubio, who sat behind his desk.

The interrogation lasted two hours, with questions and answers, primarily of the nervous, drug-addicted bums, who were offered cigarettes and smoked like chimneys and still reeked, although they had recently bathed. Still, several whiffs of caked shit lingered.

The two told the same story over and over again, about the lies told them, and how the third one was left dead in the laboratory. All three sat nervously eying Rubio, while the detective studied them with penetrating stares, looked down, and scribbled on a pad of paper, getting all of the details.

Rubio had gotten all of the information about Fred's employment at the German Company and then informed him that the Krog-Stein-Mex Company was already being looked at with suspicion for other incidents, but he did not go into details. He was grateful, he told Fred, for what he did in bringing the two men to tell their story. He was going to see about the dead man left at the research building and would be investigating the firm more closely. Rubio explained to Fred that the port of Tampico had many addicts and derelicts, and in their desperation, they were easily lured from the downtown area.

The detective also added that he was going to investigate the mysterious men in the black car. Stories were being spread around the homeless on the waterfront, at the dock port, and in the lower part of Tampico, where the poor addicts and derelicts roamed. Giving Fred a firm look, he said he already had several written reports of problems regarding the occupants in the mysterious black car.

At that moment, Fred remembered the incident with Hans several weeks prior and told Pablo Rubio of it. He gave him the license plate numbers of the black car. In his excitement, he had completely forgotten about them. He related what Hans had told him about the Krog-Stein-Mex Company, and after hearing about the janitor's death weeks later, he was convinced there had to be some truth to his story. Fred informed Rubio that Hans had told him that human body parts were being exported.

Fred added in his conversation to Rubio that he had quit the German Company and was on his way to Mexico City. He produced the keys Hans had given him and tossed them to the detective. He opened his attaché case, which was full of papers, bottles, and pills, and handed him the German manuscripts, thinking Rubio might be able to use them as evidence.

Rubio's thoughts spiraled nervously in all directions while examining the German papers. He was afraid this would open a can of worms, creating a worldwide incident, and he didn't quite know how he would approach this with his high commanders, who were being bribed with much *dinero*. Politics came to mind. *Those damn politics*, he thought. The Germans paid the city of Tampico an enormous amount of money to do business here, and half of that money went into their pockets. Without that revenue, the city would suffer; people would be upset and accuse the city fathers of corruption. There was another problem: derelicts and addicts were not on the city's top priority list. Rubio wanted to become famous, popular, and well known. He would have to find a subtle way of investigating the German Company. There were ways.

Fred looked at his watch. He got up from his chair to leave his two drug-addict buddies to explain how they had gotten into the German company in the first place. The two bums cried and hugged Fred, not wanting to see him leave, viewing him as their coming savior. It was a touching moment. Fred gave each one some pesos and told them to take care of themselves. He also gave Rubio some money to see that the two bums were taken care of. With a warm handshake from the detective, Fred left to get his belongings and depart for Mexico City.

He closed his mailbox, and then paid the old lady who managed the apartment, taking most of his possessions with him, and headed for Tampico-Alto.

In the village, Fred said his good-byes to Father Gonzales and the nuns, who were shocked when he told them what, had happened at the Krog-Stein-Mex Company involving the three bums. Fred told them that there was probably going to be an investigation into the German company for the horribly inhumane things they were doing, especially experimenting with human lives. He said that everything had been turned over to the Tampico police.

"Don't worry, my son," Father Gonzales replied. "*El Señor* knows what is best for you and he will be with you. Go in peace. We will be praying for your safety. I will inform your patients that you will be gone for a while, but will return. The nuns and I will keep your office open and safe. Perhaps there will be a wedding when you return?"

Fred told them that he was going to spend several months in Mexico City with Dr. Terán, doing research and study, but would return, as soon as the stormy black clouds of the German company passed over and dissipated. Then, he headed to the Gariby's home to pick up his clothes and kiss Dolores farewell.

The Garibys, Dolores, and the two *tías* were all sad as they bid him farewell.

Within three hours that night, he traveled back toward the bright neon lights of Tampico again, to meet with Dr. Terán and journey to Mexico City.

⌘　⌘　⌘

A whole month had gone by and Dolores had received only one letter from Fred. In his written notes, he stated how busy he had been, and how much he had missed her. He wrote how he missed the small village of Tampico-Alto, and Father Gonzales, and all of its inhabitants. He was doing well in the capital city, studying and staying with the Teráns, but he was lonely. In the next week, he would travel south of Mexico City with the Teráns to meet *La Señora's* family, who lived several hundred *kilómetros* away in Morelos. He was going to do research in the small villages. He would write to her as soon as he got paper and pen and got settled.

Dolores wanted to tell him the good news that she was pregnant. Finding herself in a pickle, and in her desperate moments, she came to the reality of what was happening. She confessed to her mother, who had fussed at her many times and had always been against her spending time alone with Fred. But, after a short time, *La Señora* Gariby reconsidered and entertained thoughts of the wonderful blessing of a grandchild, giving into Dolores's happiness. *Señora* Gariby and the two *tías* were extremely happy and could hardly wait until Fred returned. Everything had to be kept as a family secret without any of the gossiping villagers knowing anything about it.

There was going to be a wedding.

CHAPTER 41

The Depression had taken a toll on Mercedes, the Rio Grande Valley, and the state of Texas. Franklin Delano Roosevelt had been re-elected president in a landslide and was busy bringing in the second New Deal. He was facing a grave national crisis with the American economy on its knees. Horrible headline stories coming out of Europe and Japan were getting hard to deal with.

After Dan Land and Luis Martin brought home the good news about Fred, Victoria and *Don* Federico were busy with the state legislators trying to free Fred from the false accusations against him. They were paying an enormous price to several attorneys, who were busy delegating the affairs to the Department of Justice so Fred could return home to the United States.

The Depression had claimed large portions of the prominent Juelson family fortune. One oil well went completely dry, and the machines and pumps were left to the elements. The two other wells were doing very little, and the expenses were very high. There were other losses within the last seven years—hundreds of their cattle had to be shot and buried due to a disease. Some suspected mad cow, others suspected spotted fever, and yet no one knew the answer. Many of *Don* Federico's favorite Brahma bulls were destroyed; few were spared.

Clearing hundreds of acres for the production of cotton became costly and depleted the funds deposited for feeding and paying the workers and their families to work the many cotton fields. Another expense was buying machinery and chemicals, to prevent the boll weevils from destroying the cotton plants. The banking deposit box, which contained silver and gold coins, was kept in a safe in *Don* Federico's library, since most of the banks were closed. Much of the bartering of food and supplies was done across the border.

Hundreds of Mexican-American families moved and migrated north toward the larger cities, abandoning their homes and properties to the eroding weather. The Mercedes school district was also having problems because the interest due on the school bonds was not met, although taxpayers were giving according to their means to keep the school open. Teachers went without pay for a length of time. The land of the old South school was sold, trying to meet its obligations. Many were unable to pay taxes, and their property was being foreclosed on. The majority of the properties belonged to Mexican people who were unable to come up with the money, and they complained to *Don* Federico, not knowing what else to do.

On one occasion, *Don* Federico stood at the steps of the Hidalgo County Court House and bid on some of his Mexican friends' homes. He stood for hours bidding, until he bought them, later giving them the title to their property, having paid for everything. They were eternally grateful. He was their hero.

However, even with the tough times, Victoria had been coasting along quite comfortably on the Juelson fortune with Fred gone and pronounced dead. With *Don* Federico's ill health, she took advantage and borrowed secretly against Fred's inheritance, believing she had time to repay it, and knowing all along that Fred was not dead; it had been confirmed in her meditations and consultations with the dead *Doña* Adela, who continued to appear at midnight as the black wolf.

Carlos had been the loyal son who had sacrificed his education by staying close to his father's side and pleasing him, and so willingly took orders from Victoria for the sake of the family honor and pride. He worshipped his sister, for Victoria was more like his mother, and he would do anything she asked. He had cushioned himself financially and preferred to live at Spanish Acres and care for the land and the workers. Carlos was the sensitive, silent one in the family; he never asked any questions and had kept out of family confrontations, especially over money.

The *Don* had ordered legal papers made up, putting Victoria in control of the entire estate; she had finally convinced him to let her become half heir to the Juelson's legacy, since she was already prudently taking care of the books for the Juelson cattle empire, the oil ledgers, the cotton bookkeeping, and other money affairs. Aunt Josie was the other half. *Don* Federico knew that if anything happened to him, Victoria was smart and would take care of her children, and Carlos and his family and would see that Spanish Acres would be administered properly.

The Depression had also brought dispirited thoughts to Victoria. She felt swindled out of love by being betrothed to a man she hated. She had wasted so many years yearning for the only man she ever wanted, the only man who had conquered her and loved her, and that man was Juan Alvarez. This life-long depression caused her to become bitter and hateful, wanting to strike like a rattler at the least provocation. Occasionally she dissolved into crying bouts and wouldn't eat for days at a time. She would appear red-eyed and with a swollen face and would calmly tell the household, "Oh, don't pay any attention to me, it's nothing."

Occasionally, a surprising letter would arrive from Juan, telling her how much he loved her, and how they'd soon be together again.

She replied quickly that *he knew what to do.*

She had Luis Martin, who looked just like Juan, to remind her daily of his past affection. Finally, Victoria's maternal instincts had made up her mind—she was going to make arrangements to go get Fred in Mexico as soon as they got word of his freedom. When she traveled there, she would stop in Ciudad Victoria and visit with Juan, now the governor of

Tamaulipas. Word had come from Ricardo in Monterrey that Magdalena was gravely ill, and that Juan and *Señora* Del Calderóne were very concerned.

However, there were obstacles to be taken care of before she could travel. Victoria felt overwhelmed by the daily burden of giving orders to the household in Mercedes as well as at Spanish Acres. Then there was the dilemma of Aunt Josie, who had gotten incredibly worse and needed continual attention. Her grandmother Gloria was getting older, hard of hearing, and needed care. Her father, the great *Don*, was getting slower and needed constant reminding. There were her children, all being raised only by her, since Ricardo continued to live his bachelor life in Monterrey. But the bookkeeping business could wait for a month, and Carlos would take care of the cattle and the upcoming production of the cotton. She would plan to go during the slow time of year, between January and April.

Ricardo never failed to show up to collect his money once a year during the fall after harvesting the cotton. Victoria always protested. She hated him as a person and was never prepared for him when he made his yearly appearance in Texas. His main ambition was money, but in the last five years, with the Depression, there had been little cash to give out. Although Victoria wanted to, the thought of divorcing him was out of the question—it would only bring another scandal to the already disgraced family.

Finally, in early 1937, word came in a registered letter from the State Capital in Austin, announcing that Fred Juelson was officially vindicated, found innocent, and was free to return to the United States, signed by Governor James Allred of Texas. There was a huge family celebration at the big house, including Emma and Dr. Burr, with Felicia and Dan, and all of their children, Grandmother Gloria, and even Mrs. McCray. There were many other families who were pleased to honor them, especially members of the gossiping hen's society and the Catholic praying members who had known the Juelson family for so many years.

In the midst of all the rejoicing, several owls were seen circling, whistling outside the mansion, instilling fear and apprehension in the household workers.

On an early foggy morning late in February, Carlos was driving a large truckload of twenty Mexican workers from Mercedes to Spanish Acres. Along with the workers, his truck contained hundreds of pounds of cotton seeds and chemicals for the soil. The timing was set to begin plowing the land, getting it ready for cotton planting. It had rained for two days straight, and finally the storm had stopped and had left the soil wet and damp. In order for him to get to Spanish Acres, he had to stop at the small town of La Villa, which had developed a railroad station. The train tracks headed east into the newly organized towns of Donna and Edcouch.

There was no railroad-crossing warning. In the still cold morning, the side-windows of his large field truck were closed and frosted over with condensation, as he listened to the radio's weather report, and the busy windshield wipers cleared the hazy windshield. Slowing down, the truck became stuck on the railroad tracks, and Carlos nervously tried shifting the vehicle into a lower gear. In the heavy mist, he did not see the train coming. He never felt the impact. The train hit the truck on the passenger's side, sending all nineteen workers sitting in the back of the truck flying in all directions. The noise of the crash and the appalling screams of the injured men woke the sleeping community and jolted them into action. The train finally screeched to a complete stop several hundred yards down the tracks. Carlos and the field worker sitting on the passenger side of the truck were killed instantly. All of the workers in the back were hurt, with scrapes, lacerations, bruises, and broken bones, but they were lucky to be alive.

The news traveled fast like a windblown, blazing firestorm. The telephone rang early in the morning at the mansion in Mercedes. Victoria answered. There was a long silence, then a loud scream that echoed throughout the house and died in an agonizing moan.

The funeral was grim. Hundreds of people around the Rio Grande Valley came to pay their respects. Carlos was buried at the Mercedes Catholic cemetery northwest of town. His wife Mary sat dumbfounded in front of the casket with a black mantilla covering her head, as tears rolled down her cheeks. Their two children, Carlos Jr., five years old, and one-year-old Mary Frances, sat next to her, not understanding all of the commotion. Mary was still in shock, facing the grim reality of not knowing what she was going to do with her life, or how she was going to raise her children. Many friends comforted her, as they also comforted Victoria, who was dressed in black, and the *Don* in his dark three-piece suit. The burial of the farm worker who had been sitting beside Carlos was conducted the following day.

This latest tragedy was just about all that *Don* Federico's heavy, despairing heart could stand, but he would see that Mary and her two children were taken care of. He kept asking himself why his golden life had become so sorrowful. He questioned himself in guilt-ridden anguish as to what he had done to cause so much sadness and despair. It had all been a terrible tragedy, and losing his sons was unbearable and inconceivable. But at least Fred was still alive, although unreachable somewhere in Mexico. He would return—someday. It was wishful thinking, but *Don* Federico hoped Fred would return before he died. He wiped his swollen, red eyes and wheezed, gasping for breath.

The front door of the mansion was hung with a large, dark wreath. All the mirrors were covered with dark cloths. After the funeral, Victoria became withdrawn and hid herself in her bedroom; she could not bear to think that Carlos, her wonderful brother, was dead and gone. He had been like one of her children and was so attentive to her. For days and weeks she was absent from the public, and when she did show her presence, it was like an aura of doom and gloom had pervaded her spirit. Her face looked even more drawn and pale contrasted against the black attire she wore from head to toe. Her attitude was haughty and she ate very little. The housemaids, and Felicia and Dan, would take turns helping out, bringing in Mexican casseroles even though they had their hands full with Emma and their own children. Carlos's death had been like a wicked curse—a poker hand, black spades dealt in a bad round. Victoria had no other choice but to postpone her travel plans.

In the following two months, Victoria had to rely on her strong will to snap out of her doldrums. She was determined to find someone who would help her manage the fields, machinery, and crops. With Carlos gone, someone had to work out in the fields instructing the workers and working the heavy machinery. The first person that came to mind was Pepito, the son of Miguel and Ellen, now in his late thirties and still living at Spanish Quarters. She would have to travel to Spanish Acres and make arrangements.

Roy was getting older, as were so many of the *vaqueros* who still lived there and cared for the cattle. Much of the milk, cheese, and butter were being sold to the local Mexican grocers in the smaller communities. Memo and José, who now drove a small Ford van, would deliver to the surrounding *ranchitos* on a daily basis. Cattle were slaughtered twice a week, split in half, and hung for several days; these were also sold to the local Mexican people and many of the adjoining small business proprietors.

By the end of March, the letter that Victoria had mailed to Fred in Tampico was returned. It was stamped "cancelled" in Spanish on the outside of the envelope. This puzzled *Don* Federico and became a concern to Victoria. In their grief, the two had no other alternative but to wait until they received confirmation of Fred's whereabouts.

During her visit to Spanish Acres, Victoria talked to Pepito and was alarmed to hear about the mystery of Yolanda's long absence. Yolanda was Pepitos oldest sister, and the family had been proud of her, being so astute in acquiring ownership of Spanish Quarters from the Juelson estate. Nobody in Spanish Acres had seen her. "She now spends most of her time in Monterrey, México," Pepito told her.

"And just what is she doing in Monterrey? Who is she staying with?" she asked, knowing the answer before she even heard it.

The answer came back quickly: "With the Del Calderóne family, of course."

Forgetting about her bereavement, Victoria went into a petulant rage. *The bitch and the bastard!* She thought, with hate seething inside of her. *My own supposed husband with that hateful puta, Yolanda!* The two had been planning something all this time behind her back, but she was not surprised. They were planning to take over Spanish Acres! No wonder Ricardo was so interested in the land she owned and was advising Yolanda on the legal aspects of the property all this time. She'd fix him. She'd fix the two of 'em. The bastard! Her Juelson blood boiled. It was amazing how her anger triggered and controlled her emotions, making her want to quickly act.

Pepito was startled when he saw Victoria's reactions. She was worse than a pregnant rattler with an impacted tooth, and he wanted no part of working for her. He refused and decided to concoct a story of leaving for Houston in the following weeks.

Victoria did not remember how she returned to Mercedes. She hit the door cussing. There was more news, a letter stamped from Monterrey, with Ricardo's handwriting informing them that Magdalena had died from some strange ailment that no one could cure. At first, she felt sorry for the dead Magdalena and the family, but she had expected it. Minutes zoomed; her mind began spiraling, thinking of Ricardo and Yolanda making a fool of her and her family all this time.

Fuming, Victoria began making arrangements for her trip and did not care whether it would hair-lip every Goddamn cow in Texas. *Don* Federico was not surprised in hearing Victoria's theory on Yolanda and Ricardo's scheming escapades, knowing, Ricardo's craftiness' and Yolanda's ill-morals. Uncertain of what to say, he began chewing the inside of his cheek as he smoked his pipe, his eyes steely. Victoria called Felicia and told her the story. In thirty minutes, Felicia, who also had her hands full, but with concern, showed up, still wiping her hands on her apron, trying to calm her cousin in her raging tantrum. Victoria swore as she threw clothes, undergarments, hats, and gloves into several train trunks. Shoes were scattered everywhere in the bedroom. In anger, she had a lovely habit of throwing things, and shoes were handy and very appropriate—she had over a hundred pair.

Victoria hired several more servants and wasted no time in giving orders to the household. During the Depression, workers could be bought for a dime a dozen, and in no time she had hired ten maids. Her instructions were to care for her three-year old son and help out with the rest of the household chores. The cotton planting at Spanish Acres would have to wait. She would make other arrangements when she returned from her trip; there was still plenty of time.

Within two days, she arrived in Monterrey. After descending from the train; she ordered the cab driver to take her to the most expensive and fanciest hotel in the heart of the beautiful silver mining city. The cab driver drove her to the elegant El Gran Hotel Ancira, located in the downtown Monterrey's Zona Rosa. The hotel was what Victoria had expected: beautiful, built in 1912, in French architectural style. All of the décor was French imported *marqueterie* furniture and accessories. It had the classical marbled floors and winding staircase. There were several exquisite shops inside the Gran hotel, ideal for shopping.

That afternoon, after reading Monterrey's news and informing herself about the funeral service for Magdalena, Victoria shopped for a white gown in the lobby of one the finest Italian shops in the Gran Hotel. She also purchased a long, blonde wig, expensive perfume, and dark glasses, and put them on. She looked like a million dollar woman. She walked out onto the sidewalk, not wanting anyone to recognize her.

She had plans. Walking along the unfamiliar Monterrey streets, she was a woman on a mission. First, she wanted to uncloak the two lovers, slap her husband, and knock Yolanda into kingdom come! Her unscrupulous, womanizer husband had used her to get the family's money, and had became a married bachelor, doing what he pleased, with no responsibilities. Second, was the bitch Yolanda, who was his mistress, going around enjoying vacations, with the cotton money the Juelsons had work so hard for. Victoria would give new meaning to the old saying "Hell hath no fury like a woman scorned." Her mind stewed as she walked. She came upon the *cathedral* where Magdalena's funeral was going to take place the next morning. She studied it and went inside. Perhaps she would light a white candle. Maybe it would save her soul.

Early the next morning, Victoria, completely disguised with her blonde wig, black glasses, and a black lace mantilla over her head, slipped into the church. She found a seat next to the adjoining room where the casket was being viewed. From that area she could view the attendance and watch the movements of each individual. Slowly, each individual dressed in black, lined up and hovered over Magdalena lying in her casket. Tears flowed down their faces, and they used their white handkerchiefs to wipe their noses and eyes as they walked in an attitude of dutiful respect.

There were few people present, mostly family and some who knew the Del Calderóne family. She was surprised to see the revolutionist, Luis Del Calderóne, who had outlived the Revolution and now limped with a cane. Next to him was Amparo with white hair, looking older, but still attractive. Victoria recognized Yolanda from a distance, playing the part of Ricardo's partner. She watched her husband being so attentive to her, with his arm around her as they both viewed his sister's body in her casket, and with copious tears flowing from their eyes. *How touching*, Victoria thought.

Three heavy-set, older women dressed in dark clothing and hats sat in the front row. Victoria sat behind them and listened to their conversation. They were very talkative and gossiped and conversed among themselves about how Magdalena had died. They talked about the bereaved, handsome husband, now governor of Tamaulipas.

"The well-known doctor of Monterrey couldn't save her as she lay in her bedroom quarters for months," said the lady on the left.

"He didn't know what was wrong. He tried everything to save her. He loved her so much," said one of the other ladies.

They also discussed Magdalena's brother, Ricardo, who was so dutiful to his mother after her husband, the jackass *El General* Calderóne was found murdered. "The girl with him is from Texas, not his wife, I was told, but he is so smitten by her. She comes from Texas and spends many weeks at a time with him and his mother. Ricardo is so appreciative. I was told he buys her the most beautiful jewelry from the French shops at the fancy hotel Gran Ancira. She is wearing a beautiful opal necklace that *Señora* Calderóne gave her. They make such a fine couple, don't you think?"

"Where is Ricardo's wife?" asked the lady sitting in the middle.

"I have never seen her, but Ricardo brags about her all the time and all their money. He talks as if she, whoever she is, does not care what he does and gives him all the money he wants."

The lady on the right said: "How lucky! Who wouldn't want it that way? And why would he want to divorce the rich Texas wife?" The three snickered and lowered their heads.

Victoria was aghast. She wanted to voice her opinion. She wanted to tell them that Ricardo was less than a manipulating parasitic worm, the worst breathing, crawling creature that ever lived. She wanted to tell them who she was, but decided to stay calm and patient— not her strongest virtues—and listen.

He buys her beautiful expensive jewelry from the French jewelry shops. She is wearing a beautiful opal necklace that Señora Calderóne gave her. The words echoed in her brain. *Ricardo brags about her all the time, and she gives him all the money he wants.* It made Victoria's blood boil with contempt, making her head feel like it was about to explode. Her mother-in-law was in cahoots with Ricardo and going around giving opal necklaces to his son's lovers? She had received an opal necklace from *Señora* Calderóne on her birthday. The opals were becoming a curse, a devious power play, and she would get rid of the necklace she had stored away.

Victoria gritted her teeth and snarled in her soul, realizing that she was in a snake pit situation and had to play her cards right. She would turn the screws from both ends in her aggressive rage, but she would do it in her own cunning way. Her mind spiraled: *He buys her beautiful expensive jewelry from the Gran Ancira Hotel. Was it coincidental that that was the hotel in which she was staying?*

Toward the end of the long funeral service, the Bishop finally blessed the corpse by sprinkling holy water inside and closed the casket. The nuns upstairs sang Latin hymns and left everyone feeling spiritual. The immediate family began gathering in front of the cathedral and expressing their gratitude to those who came to the services.

Victoria sat quietly observing. She noticed a young girl, who looked to be about fifteen years old, in a navy-blue organdy dress, crying at the casket, sobbing hard. It was then that Victoria realized that the girl must be Juan's daughter. She got up and hugged her. As she did so, Victoria felt the energy of someone behind her. She turned and looked up. There stood the bereaved Juan, older, with white hair at both temples, but still devastatingly handsome.

"Thank you," he said, not realizing who she was. "Thank you for being so kind to my daughter in this time of sorrow and loss." He bent down and kissed his daughter on her forehead. "She needs all the love that people can give her," he said, as he straightened himself up and faced her. For a few seconds, Juan's eyes narrowed as he tried to recognize Victoria. His daughter left to be with the other family members.

Victoria stood frozen behind her dark glasses, not knowing what to say. Finally, not being able to contain herself in the presence of the only man she ever loved, she looked around, making sure nobody was near them, and found the courage to speak.

"Juan!" She finally said, removing her dark glasses.

Juan leaned closer and his eyes opened wider. He viewed her up and down and then exclaimed, "Victoria!" There was a long pause. "Is it possible that it's you?"

There was a long lingering moment of silence from Juan as he hesitated to hug and kiss her. He would have never known who she was until he took a good look. "I did not recognize you! You do look beautiful in your blonde getup. Where are you staying?"

"The Gran Hotel Ancira," she said in a low voice. "Tonight, maybe have dinner?"

"Tonight, of course," he said. "It will be late after saying *adiós* to the many guests at my home, but we'll have dinner. We have a lot to talk about."

While standing so close to Juan, Victoria's heart pumped so fast that it felt like it was coming out of her chest. She bristled when she saw her husband, the Casanova, with Yolanda, holding hands and coming in their direction. She could not let them recognize her, so she put her dark glass back on. Victoria excused herself, saying to Juan, "Tonight!" and held her lace-mantilla close to her face. Juan acknowledged by nodding his head. As she left the church, she heard Ricardo asking Juan who she was. "A patient of mine," said Juan. "A very old friend of mine. I've known her for many years."

Victoria ordered the taxi driver to take her to the oldest part of town, which was called *Barrio Antiguo*, where the marketplace was located. She was looking for a special shop. Many of the buildings had been destroyed by the Mexican Revolution, but the majority of them were being renovated and re-opened. As she walked down the long, narrow cobblestone streets, she enjoyed mixing with the throngs of native people. Many with little stands were selling fruits, vegetables, and homemade trinkets of all kinds. Other stands were selling tacos, tamales, and fruit beverages. Many shops offered silver jewelry from the silver mines up in the mountains; others sold clothes, boots, and colorful serapes. She came upon an older woman dressed in black selling strings of fresh garlic and asked her a question. The old woman pointed out a small shop down an alley in the next block.

Inside the little run-down shop were two older women who were busy creating home-made rag dolls on a foot-pedal Singer sewing machine. When Victoria left the shop some time later, she walked away with a small paper package. She hurried to the end of the street and waved down a taxi to drive her back to the Gran Hotel Ancira.

Safe inside the hotel, she took the package up to her room and changed her clothes, trading her black outfit for a flowery, low-cut dress that flattered her ample bosom, and then donned her disguise. She took the elevator to the ground floor and began walking down the marble corridors, viewing the beautiful French shops featuring clothes and expensive jewelry. She entered the most elaborate jewelry shop in the hotel lobby.

She was marveling at the beautiful artistic designs of rings, bracelets, and earrings set with brilliant diamonds, emeralds, and rubies in the display cases, when an old man appeared from the back of the shop. "Is there anything I can help you with? He looked her over and sighed with delight. "The jewelry is very exquisite, and someone like you deserves to wear the best. May I show you any of this fine jewelry? Can we put any of the rings on your fingers?" He was charming, and definitely a promoter and a salesman.

Victoria chuckled. She blinked her eyes coyly at him and bent down exposing her cleavage as she viewed the display, trying to choose the most expensive set. "Let me see—"

The old man averted his eyes. He was obviously flustered but wanted to help her buy the most expensive stones. "Look at this ring with three-carat diamonds, and in the middle, a four-carat emerald from Columbia, costing many pesos," he said. "It is the most expensive ring we have." He eyed her again and was very attentive. "Whom might I be speaking with?" he asked.

Victoria lowered her head and batted her eyelashes again. "Are you acquainted with the family of Del Calderóne?" she asked snobbishly, turning away to view other jewelry.

"Why! Of course!" he said, smiling broadly. "We have designed several pieces for Ricardo for his—"

Victoria turned and faced the old man and smiled sweetly at him.

"You must be—"

"Why, yes! Ricardo has sent me to pick up any pieces I want, and as many as I want." She laughed, giddy with her deception.

The old man took her hand and kissed it several times, sighing each time. With joy, he gently put the ring on Victoria's finger, enjoying the connection with her—with the ring, her fingers, her hands, her body, her shapely figure, and general loveliness. Ah, yes. She was a dream come true.

"I will take the ring," she said admiring it on her finger. She brought her hand up to her face, and looked into the reflecting mirrors on the walls. "I would also like some earrings and perhaps a nice necklace with some impressive stones," she replied. "We have a nice dinner party to attend, and I would like to look important, extraordinary, especially with the beautiful white gown I will be wearing."

The old man jumped into action, immediately zeroing in on the opportunity to show her the most expensive necklaces he had in the shop. He began opening one velvet box after another, displaying exquisite stones of all kinds. "Any one of the necklaces would be very appropriate with a white dress," he suggested. "As a matter of fact, I have this diamond set with a necklace and earrings to match. This would probably be more appropriate. It goes with everything you might want to wear."

Victoria took her time. She was pretending to ponder and brought her finger to her chin as though concentrating. Finally, after letting the old man stew for a bit, she decided to take the diamond set. "Yes! I believe you are right. I'm so glad I decided to come to your place and shop. Ricardo will be thrilled with the items I picked. He asked that you mail him the bill."

"Why, of course! We have been doing business with the Del Calderóne family for a long time," answered the old man, smiling happily. "We are always honored to be of service. Ricardo and his mother shop here regularly. I cannot thank you enough for coming in and buying this beautiful jewelry. I do think Ricardo will be pleased."

"He is going to be thrilled. I can hardly wait to show him," Victoria said with a radiant smile. "He is going to jump up and down with pleasure, especially when he sees the necklace around my neck," she said, spreading her hands over her bosom. But her thought was: *I can just see him jumping up and down, with anger, when he receives the bill!*

"I have never seen a more perfect neck," said the old man, who closed his eyes in ecstasy, either with admiration for Victoria, or for the large sale that he had just made. "I will wrap these boxes right away for you. We will mail Ricardo the bill. I know he will be in as soon as possible to pay for the merchandise. I know he has been quite successful as an engineer designing many of the new buildings in the city."

The old man soon had her purchases wrapped and placed in a bag for her. Victoria thanked him graciously, kissed the old man on the cheek, and walked out. "Ricardo will be in real soon," she told him, smiling from ear to ear, "as soon as you send him the bill." *I'll just bet he will!* She thought to herself and laughed inwardly.

Late that evening, Victoria donned her long, white evening gown and her new diamond necklace and earrings, and admired herself in the full-length mirror.

There was a knock on the door, and in walked Juan Alvarez.

The night was unforgettable. Juan complimented her on her stunning appearance. They ordered their meal and had it delivered to the hotel room. They talked for hours, reminiscing about their long history together, up until the time he married Magdalena and brought her to Monterrey. They shared tears over each of their family's deaths and losses. She told him about her father's illnesses, and Carlos and Fred's tragedies.

They dined and danced in the balcony, to the music of *Amapola* and *Stardust*, from the musicians playing below the courtyard. Juan suddenly swooped Victoria up and carried her to the large, four-poster bed. He slowly undressed her and laid her on the bed, then removed his own clothes. It had been a long time since the two had had any love, and they wasted no time. He took her in his arms and kissed her mouth lustfully, beginning with French kisses. His hands caressed her breasts and started their foreplay as her body responded, igniting the passion and fire of desire they both wanted. He made love to her like he had never before, exploring her body and giving her every pleasure. Their mutual climax erupted in a momentous fireworks display.

The couple made love all night long and in between their hard breathing, they lay there talking and aching with nostalgia. Juan confessed he had never loved anyone else. And Victoria in return told him the same thing. Thinking back over the long years of separation, they discussed their misery without each other's companionship. They now promised to be together forever.

Victoria suddenly interrupted their reverie. "Was it the magic black mushrooms?"

"Yes, and nobody suspected anything," Juan answered. "I received your package about ten months ago and used them in hot teas. You need to use them on Ricardo. It's a slow process that takes time—the poison has to build up in the system. The Del Calderónes love mushrooms, but you have to be careful. You need to have a dish ready for Ricardo when he returns to Texas. He has been making a fool of you all these years with Yolanda. I have heard him brag in front of Magdalena and laugh about all the money he has taken from your family, and how he used it foolishly."

"I am slowly finding all this out," she said, pretending she did not know. "I had to come in disguise and see for myself, in spite of being in mourning for my own brother."

"Let's make this the best night of those long lost years," said Juan. "Lord knows how I have missed you. We'll still have to keep in touch, but secretly."

The rest of the night was glorious. They made love until the morning sun's rays glowed through the curtains. When Juan left, his last words were, "Until we meet again, my love. I'll write you!"

The following day, Victoria, with a wide smile on her face, found her way aboard the train back to Texas. Leaving Juan was hard to bear, and with such a memorable night, she could not keep from thinking about him. Soon, they would be together. They would be together—forever.

She also kept thinking, *The Devil has a sense of humor, too! I wonder how Ricardo is going to react when he finds out a mysterious woman posed as his mistress Yolanda and walked away with over forty thousand dollars worth of jewelry!* The arrogant, pompous ass would eventually have a payback for being such a Romeo and a hot lover. *He deserved it,* she thought, *and more. That will teach him not to steal from my family and, as for Miss fat-ass tamales, Yolanda, I will deal with her later!* She would immediately get to work and start the curses using the dolls she had purchased. *Thank you, Señora Adela!*

Back in Mercedes, Victoria was surprised to find Luis Martin had completely taken over the job of managing the field hands at Spanish Acres. He had hired some workers and had used some of the working hands at the ranch. She was shocked to see that Yolanda's son Antonio was working hand in hand with Luis, and they had become good friends. It was never confirmed that Antonio was Juan's son, and he did not look like him. Yolanda never told who the father was, because the night of Victoria's celebration, she had slept with more than one—Juan had been the encore, the icing on the cake.

On her return from Spanish Acres, there was a much anticipated letter from Fred. Apparently, he had traveled to Mexico City with his doctor friend and his wife and while there, had fallen terribly ill with a bad case of malaria, or yellow fever—nobody knew for sure what he had—which had caused him to have terrible high fevers, and it had taken him months to recuperate. He was beginning to get on his feet after losing weight and was working on the laboratory research that he had once started. In his letter, Fred stated that he was going to marry a beautiful village girl he had met in Tampico-Alto, when he returned from Mexico City. Fred wrote that the family would have to accept her, when he brought her back to Texas. His statement came as a complete surprise. He also mentioned that circumstances had caused him to leave Tampico, and he would explain later.

It had been an interesting day, a day of surprises, thought Victoria, as she puzzled over the letter. Fred sounded like he had changed in many ways. He was now demanding and giving orders to the family? Marrying a peasant girl? It hit her like hot coals going through her system. He would marry a common peasant and bring her to Mercedes, to their home? This scenario would not be compatible with their social status. What was Fred thinking?

Victoria voiced her concerns to her father. "This may present problems, especially when Fred returns with a peasant girl as his bride and has to answer to everyone."

"It's nobody's Goddamn business what Fred does with his life!" replied *Don* Federico, getting crotchety in his old age. He was sitting in his comfortable rocking chair smoking his pipe, with his boots on, and his Stetson hat still on his head, listening to the radio in their living room. "If Fred marries a peasant Mexican girl, that's his business, and it's nobody's damn business what he does. He does not have to answer to any son-of-a-bitch here. Have you forgotten that it was the dang-blasted people in this town who sent him away? All we care is that he returns home where he belongs."

That's just like Father, thought Victoria, with her lips pursed. She felt intimidated by his remarks. *Always protecting Fred, since he never did anything wrong. Yet in my case, I have to do everything in hiding or suffer the consequences.*

There was a return address on the envelope and Victoria immediately wrote Fred back and told him about the loss of Carlos and how tragically he had died.

⌘   ⌘   ⌘

The war in Europe had gotten worse and headlines showed escalating problems with Germany. President Roosevelt, busy with his New Second Deal Policy, was trying to bring the country out of the grips of the Depression. In stabilizing the economy, he banned the private ownership of gold. The majority of people, afraid of banks, had begun hiding and hoarding their coins. The State of Texas had a dilemma trying to elect a new governor, since James Allred's second term was up for grabs. Billboards and signs grew overnight along the highways, displaying the candidates.

ROOTS OF INDIFFERENCE

The following year, W. Lee O'Daniel, called Pappy, won the gubernatorial election in what was considered one of the greatest upsets in Texas history. O'Daniel, who had his own religious radio program, was also a song writer and helped popularize Western swing music. He was known for saying, "Please pass the biscuits." About that same time, Bob Wills came out with *San Antonio Rose.*

Mercedes was still the typical peaceful town, with newly renovated streets adorned with new streetlights and palms on all the main streets. The new Highway 83 crossed the town, dividing the Juelson property. *Don* Federico had given up some property rights to make way for it. With a fresh and more lenient City Council, and with the Mexican-American people offering to buy some of his land, *Don* Federico began subdividing his land among them. One of them was the Villarreal family, who bought two lots across the highway from the Juelson mansion. They transported vegetables and citrus raised in the Valley to Dallas and Houston, and brought back fruit that normally was not grown close to the border. Ol' man Villarreal quickly set up a small grocery store with his fruits displayed outside, enticing the drive-bys, and became very prosperous. The Saldaña family made a bargain with *Don* Federico and bought a lot south of his property. To the east side the Lara family began building their home. Another family, the Garcias, built a small, religious novelty shop, selling candles and statues of patron saints. The Cantus set up a Mexican café on Highway 83 and became very successful. The Gonzales started several service stations and a mechanic shop, where they would repair cars and wash them.

People were buying appliances, making the housewives job easier. One in particular was the newest, electric, wringer washing machine, and Oxydol was the detergent of choice, packed with gifts inside the box. But Mexico was still the place to buy coffee, flour, and sugar.

In May, shocking headlines told how thirty-six people died when the German LZI92 Hindenburg caught fire while landing at the Lakehurst Naval Air Station, in New Jersey. Many rumored that it had been sabotaged.

In June of that year, everyone had come home that evening tired and sweating from the fields to hear the Joe Lewis fight with the German, Max Schmeling.

In this epoch of time, when Mexicans, Indians, and Negroes were ostracized and hated and still being burned out, lynched, and discriminated against, the winds of change were beginning to blow. The boxer Joe Lewis represented the poor, deprived, oppressed Mexicans, Indians, and blacks, who could relate to him. Schmeling represented the "Master race," the smart-alec Germans who thought they were superior to everyone else. It personified the fight between good and evil, a fight for the rightfully deserved final justice.

When the final blow came, Joe Lewis knocked Max Schmeling out and won the fight. Joe Lewis became the heavyweight champion of the world, and to the minority people there was a sense of fairness. There was a God. That night, within the Mexican *barrios*, joyous shouts could be heard in homes, bars, and *cantinas* from small boys to old men. Joe Lewis represented everyone's justice. It taught people as a whole, regardless of race and who they were, by working hard for what they believed, they could finally reach their goals. It gave a sense of hope and strength to the Mexican-American young people, encouraging them not to give up on what they believed in.

Still, the Mercedes school district was brewing with indifference and conspiracy. The school on Hidalgo Street that had taught the majority of Mexican children for so many years had been torn down, and in September school was going to start. This became a headache for the white school administrators who ran the educational district. Funds were low, and it had become mandatory by the State of Texas and by the federal government to teach each child that was registered, regardless of race. After World War I, there had been an enormous baby boom in Mercedes. There were more Mexican-American children than there were whites, and the majority of them were coming from across the tracks to be taught.

Some of the Mexican children attended the private parochial Lady of Mercy School run by the sisters, which was expensive for the average family, but the schooling only went to the sixth grade. After the sixth grade, the Mexican children had no choice but to attend the only white public school available, which was the Graham School, south of town. Because of the Jim Crow laws, classes were crowded and segregated. The Mexican children attended the Mexican class; the white children went to the white class. There were two rooms for each class starting from the first grade. The white teachers who were assigned to teach the Mexican classroom felt those children were less important, and they were often treated with cruel and harsh discipline. In many cases, they would spank the Mexican child for voicing their opinion. They would say degrading and discriminatory things to the students, with a wooden paddle in view of the class to intimidate them, creating fear and driving them to silence. It squelched the desire for education and held them back academically.

The Jim Crow laws affected even the smallest child. They were instructed from an early age not to mix with the whites, even in school activities; it was hurtful and generated mistrust in the vulnerable and impressionable children only beginning to form their identities. But that was the white men's law, and since the Anglos were always right and had control of everything, the Mexican-Americans had to comply and go along quietly in bondage. It was the law of oppression robbing them of any dignity that they had, fulfilling the scripture of ugly tradition—racism.

Many children did not return to school, especially the boys, when they reached working age. They worked helping their fathers, out in the fields, in tomato patches, in melon tracts, picking cotton, and in packing plants and barns, earning money for their families.

It was too hard to learn in school and too difficult to do homework, since homework was given as a punishment and came with the swift indignity of the belt for not completing their lessons the preceding day. The spankings were frightening and hurtful for a young pupil. It was a way of suppression, of holding them back, never allowing them to reach their full potential. The children would rather work out in the fields with their parents, where they felt safe and more secure.

When an outbreak of head lice occurred in the school classrooms, the Mexican-American children were blamed and told not to return; they were given a slip of paper for their parents.

ROOTS OF INDIFFERENCE

The majority of the parents could not read or write. They had to have an approval slip from the doctor to admit them back. Embarrassed, many did not return.

Ironically, something happened, as it always does. The bubble hit home and burst.

Maria Theresa, Victoria's daughter, who had nearly completed high school, was accused of having head lice and given the ominous slip of paper to give to her parents. She came home crying from embarrassment, and it jangled the sensitive nerves of the entire household. This was in itself a terrible lie and an unforgivable mistake.

Don Federico was listening to *The Amos and Andy Show,* which came on the radio every weekday evening, when he heard the news. *Head lice!* He thought. *There are no varmints or head lice in this household!* This was his beloved granddaughter, and just because she had a Mexican last name, she became a victim of the bigoted school. "Surely the school counsel doesn't want me to show my face," he said, bristling. "I'll tell them a thing or two! Have they forgotten who helped organized the damn school district in the first place? How quickly they forget all the dang-blasted money I've given the school, and all of my dedicated time and effort. They're not getting any more! They can go to their damn cash register and hit the 'no sale' sign and cut the crap." He chomped on his Cuban cigar in disgust.

His indignation was nothing compared to Victoria's. "How dare them!" she said, seething. "Tomorrow I will pay them a visit!" And she did—like a rattler with an impacted tooth. She stormed into the main office and addressed the principal, an old man, with thick glasses and cold watery eyes, and handed him the note. "Can you explain this?" she said, drumming her fingers on the counter top.

The principal looked at her and rudely replied, "Well, it reads, just what it says. Can't you read, lady?" His voice boomed loud enough for everyone to hear.

"This Del Calderóne girl has lice on her head. And we do not allow them back in the school. They will infect the rest of the children. And who are you?" he asked, looking over the rim of his glasses, ice dripping from his dead-set eyes fixed on Victoria.

There was a long silence. They eyed each other, as tensions built and sparks flew.

"Does the name Juelson sound familiar?" stormed Victoria. "Does the Juelson name have any meaning in this shitty school?"

"Oh, dear," he said, startled when he heard the Juelson's name. He began quivering. They had made a mistake all right. His voice lowered an octave, down to earth, radio smooth. "I did not know she was your daughter. I've known *Don* Federico for many years, and if it hadn't been for his money, this school would not be operating." Mr. Principle's attitude immediately changed, expressing a smile of reassurance after his kindly remarks about her father.

Victoria wasn't impressed. "The school will have even more problems now, since my father is refusing, on my behalf, not to hand over any more money to this lousy school. Wait until the school district hears about this—how your teachers target innocent Mexican children and intimidate them into not returning. And, by the way," raged Victoria, in a demonic attitude. "Who inspected my daughter's hair and lied about the results?"

The old man fumbled with the piece of paper in his hands. His legs wobbled; they were becoming noodles. He finally had to speak. "The young Mrs. Gray," he said. "It could be possible that Mrs. Gray overlooked her inspection and handed the note to your daughter by mistake," he replied nervously.

"Oh, I'm not buying this," Victoria fumed. "The reason my daughter was targeted was because she has a Mexican last name—bottom line, main reason! My daughter will not return to this crappy school!"

"I truly apologize. I will talk to Mrs. Gray. But I'm sure she just made a mistake," he replied.

It was surprising the importance and value of money, and how the power of money and greed could control people's behavior. Having money gave you power, and everyone in the end finally had a price.

After days of hearing Victoria fume and fuss, *Don* Federico made it a point to attend the next school district meeting to heatedly discuss the incident with the members. Three of them were white, high-brow bankers, and associates of the Rotary Club, the Kiwanis Club, and the Lions Club, of which *Don* Federico was also a member and had held offices. There were others attending, all white men, who were small businessmen, from bakers to grocery store owners and retailers, and who had their own children in the schools.

The majority listened with arrogance to his speech with their hypocritical attitude, eyeing one another with an indifferent posture. The undaunted *Don* Federico stood in front of them, elegant, eloquent, and articulate, as he explained, with a silver tongue, how the incident of the head lice notice had erupted into a critical decision on his part. The bottom line—it was a lie. His granddaughter did not have lice. Yes, it was an embarrassment. Yes, it was a slap in the family's face. And yes, having head lice was a problem. But the school had gone overboard in handing out slips of paper, inappropriately using their authority because the children had Mexican last names, regardless if the child was infected or not. The school would not admit it, but it was the truth. The final conclusion, he said, was that it was a racial issue. He told them that being racist never won anything. It deprived little children who were victims of an unjust society, causing hurt and anger for the rest of their lives.

He told them that perhaps it was going to take something more drastic before the evil South would come to grips with the understanding that separating classes of people would never work, because it was not just. Truth and understanding was the only way to communicate with one another. The hateful Jim Crow laws that were the rule of law all these years were going to come to an end some day. Perhaps it was going to take the United States Congress and the Supreme Court to wake up and discipline the states and counties to correct their terrible mistakes.

When the staunch *Don* Federico finished his argument, he silently walked away. In the audience not a sound could be heard, and none of the surprised, shaken and chagrined businessmen said a word. It marked a historical event for the town of Mercedes.

"Something more drastic" did not occur immediately. Changes did not happen right away, not that year, nor the following year in the school district or in the region. It would take years of long suffering and continuing arguments by sensitive and just educators who saw that changes had to be made, especially when dealing with '*roots of indifference*,' with the Mexican-Americans. Something was done— thirty years later, from a peaceful, fearless black leader who preached that only through *truth* and *love* would win people, and initiated the Civil Rights Law of 1964. It was the great Dr. Martin Luther King, Jr. who transformed the course of history for all.

Maria Theresa did not return to the school. Victoria hired a special woman tutor to complete her studies at home and made arrangements to send her the following September to study at Lady of the Lake in San Antonio, Texas. They did not hear any more from the Principal, and the funds being given to the school ceased. The following school year, the young Mrs. Gray did not return to the Mercedes school district. *Don* Federico was always a hero and loved among the Mexican people for his honesty and sincere justice, but he continued to be despised among the high and mighty white businessmen.

It was around this time that a telegram arrived from Monterrey that *Señora* Del Calderóne had died from an apparent heart attack. Victoria did not find it in her heart to attend the funeral, but sent flowers to Ricardo in condolence. A month later, the longtime house servant, Ophelia, died and was buried in the Juelson cemetery.

The saying goes: when it rains, it pours, and shit happens. Problems started to occur with the land at Spanish Acres. Apparently, Yolanda Garcia had returned from being with Mr. Romeo in Monterrey. She had gotten greedy and wanted more of the land; all along, she was being coached by Ricardo, who knew the laws in Texas. She began investigating in Hidalgo County Courts the boundaries between hers and the Juelson's land. As a result, she became involved in legal allegations and created a stir among the Juelson clan. Yolanda possessed old legal papers given to her by George Juelson many years before, which would apparently stand up in court.

The Hidalgo County Court began mailing registered letters to *Don* Federico questioning the boundaries because of land development around his property. Taxes were being raised, and easement for the development of public roads and the North Floodway was being sought around the Spanish Acres region. *Don* Federico hired Attorney Canalo, who had retired from public office but was busy forming the LULAC meeting on human relations.

Canalo drove from Brownsville and began investigating the legal court papers at the Hidalgo County Courts in Edinburg. He found several mistakes in the legal paperwork on the boundaries of the land tracts, and finally, after many months of bitter litigation with Yolanda and the Garcia family, the result was drastic losses of the Juelson fortune. The courts and attorneys were eating up the family estate.

Finally in 1939, everything unraveled.

Yolanda was given a large portion of land, over forty acres north of Spanish Acres— land full of cactus, alkali, and heavy thickets of undergrowth, which was still undeveloped and never used. Yolanda's father Miguel was immediately fired by Victoria and was told to get the hell out, and not to set foot in Spanish Acres again, creating a heated feud on each side of the boundary line. Victoria made her demands known: "If any of your damn-blasted family even comes close," she said, "I'll shoot to kill."

There was still plenty of land for raising cotton and plenty of acres for the cattle to roam as long as there was water. After the confusing battle of boundaries was splashed across the headlines all over the South Texas region, there were offers from several rich buyers in Houston and Dallas who were interested in buying Spanish Acres. Whether their motives were for recreation or for oil, nobody really knew. Oil was of great interest and had been discovered all around the region.

Months later, while staying and working at Spanish Acres, Victoria looked like a *campesina* out in the cotton fields in her straw hat, overalls, and cotton jacket. She was overseeing the work—the plowing, watering, and fertilizing—and making notes in her book, working alongside three hundred cotton pickers. She noticed from a distance, behind her dark sunglasses, none other than Yolanda walking to the pond where the giant Montezuma cypress tree grew.

Yolanda had not been seen since the funeral of Ricardo's sister and was absent from the court proceedings. Victoria watched as she dipped her feet into the still water, perhaps to cool herself from the summer heat. But it was not Yolanda's property. How dare she? She had no business trespassing on Spanish Acres land—they had been sternly warned!

Victoria wondered if Yolanda was scheming some way to control the water rights, which were a scarce commodity in this part of the region. The pond was created from an early spring back in 1840 during her grandfather's time. Victoria remembered, as a little girl, the story told by her grandfather: *Doña* Adela's father, the old Indian water witcher had taken a forked willow tree branch that had buried itself into the rich black soil. They had dug deep and created the pond that had lasted all these years. Yolanda was sleeping with everyone even then, including Victoria's grandfather, convincing him to sign papers of ownership over to her, the two-timing slut. She was probably hoping before long to walk away with everything. *Well!* Victoria decided. *It isn't going to happen!*

Within the week, Yolanda was found dead, floating face down in the pond, by two *vaqueros* early at dawn. Drowning was the final word. Nobody knew why she had been at the Spanish Acres pond. What business did she have there? Her life was so happy now that she had acquired her property. Why? She had so many plans for her land. These were the many questions from the working *vaqueros* and the household, who were all stunned. Emma was astonished, for she thought Yolanda had what it took to make it in this world. She had so many ideas. She was so talented. Felicia was bewildered. It was said that Ricardo was beside himself.

Victoria raised her eyebrows and shrugged her shoulders. "She knew better than to trespass. Only the Shadow knows," she said, alluding to the popular radio program that aired on late night radio.

Headlines in September, 1939, reported the German army had invaded the country of Poland. Over three million Jews were being rounded up; many had died from hunger and disease. What were they up to? And where were they putting all the Jewish people? These were the questions being asked by the American people—and was the United States going to get involved?

ROOTS OF INDIFFERENCE

It was also in 1939 that *Gone with the Wind* became the most successful film of all time. Steinbeck's *Grapes of Wrath* movie that dealt with life during the Depression, and the children's movie, *The Wizard of Oz* hit the screen, with Judy Garland making her singing debut.

That same year elections for President of Mexico were being held. After being governor of Tamaulipas, Juan Alvarez put his hat in the ring and began campaigning. The plot thickened as Juan was running against tough *hombres* like Ávila Camacho.

In the late fall of 1939, letters received from Fred, who once again resided in Tampico, were disturbing and raised all kinds of suspicions regarding the Germans. In his letter, Fred conveyed that they were infiltrating the country and had deployed submarines along the Gulf coast. He also said that the Krog-Stein-Mex Company was closed due to allegations of cruelty and other terrible charges he would rather not mention at the moment. He wrote that his former employer, Krog, had committed suicide, and his partner, Stein, had gone back to Germany. He said his medical clinic there had been destroyed by the Germans, and all the people were afraid.

Fred told them he was busy rebuilding the clinic and was making terrific strides in the advancement of medicine. He also said how happy he was with his beautiful two-year-old daughter named Maria Venus, who had light gray eyes, a face full of freckles, and resembled their grandfather George, an attribute that disturbed Victoria. And he had another surprise for them—Dolores was expecting another child in the coming year. He stated he wanted to come back to Texas but was going to wait until the child was born. He was hoping for a boy. He was arranging legal papers for Dolores with the immigration department in Brownsville, but all of the legal rhetoric and correspondence was taking a long time.

In April of 1940, another baby girl was born to Dolores, and she and Fred named the child Ana Maria. The child was born breech, and Dolores had gone through a long hard labor. The baby girl had digestive problems and had trouble eating. Finally, after the second day, she was given goat's milk. And there was another problem. The baby girl had an infection on the right side of her face that would not heal. Months passed, and Fred went into intensive research trying to find the cure, but there was none. It was considered an unknown virus, and the child would probably have to live with it for the rest of her life.

In the middle of summer, the other old servant, Olivia, died and was buried next to Ophelia in the Juelson cemetery.

In the same year, headlines from the Mexican political newspapers stated that Juan Alvarez had lost the Mexican presidential election and had fled to Cuba for protection, having received several threats on his life. Apparently he was protesting against alleged election irregularities and feared the more powerful and aggressive Camacho, who would entertain no challenge to his becoming President of Mexico. Victoria became fearful for Juan's safety.

President Franklin Roosevelt's second term was busy working with a special session of Congress trying his best to bring the country out of the long crisis. He set up the Agricultural Administration to help farmers, insured banks, regulated the stock market, subsidized homes and mortgage payments. The Workers Compensation Act provided unemployment compensation, and a new program called Social Security offered help for the elderly. He had been getting encouraging results in bringing prosperity back to the country.

The economy started to see a silver lining. People found jobs, and many worked in factories, bought homes, and were able to feed their families. In Europe, England and France were at war with the Germans, but the United States had remained neutral; however, it was giving foreign aid to those countries. Seeing the problems overseas, Congress enacted a draft for the military service.

Then, on December 7, 1941, the unthinkable happened, as if the United States did not have enough problems to solve, with the country barely coming out of the Depression. While Texans listened to their radio early in the morning to Texas swing music, getting ready for their church services, and the Mexican-Americans listened to *Jorge Negrete, Los Trío Calaveras, Pedro Infante,* and *Dos Arbolitos,* then came the shocking news: the Japanese had attacked Pearl Harbor. Four days later, as the United States was still in a state of shock, Germany and Italy aligned with Japan and declared war on the United States. Immediately President Roosevelt exercised his powers as Commander-in-Chief and began mobilizing for the unwanted war. Within months all hell broke loose as young, enthusiastic men from the two different races were in long lines signing up to fight for the United States. Billboards were going up all over the country with Uncle Sam displaying the sign, "Uncle Sam needs you," and flyers were being distributed and dropped from planes. Buying war bonds to help fund the war became popular. Gasoline, flour, coffee and sugar were being rationed, and silk stockings were hard to find. Texas had a new governor, Coke R. Stevenson, since Pappy O'Daniels resigned to become a United States Senator.

A sense of despair and fear ran through everyone. Was the world coming to an end? Every family with eligible sons panicked, including Victoria, who was like a mother hen protecting her chicks. Those young boys who were available to go to war had to be eighteen years old and up, in good health, and not enrolled in school. Luis Martin was already studying engineering at a school across the border in Monterrey; Aaron was twenty-two, but was in school in Austin, Texas, studying accounting; Danny was still too young. There were Felicia and Dan Land's children, especially Stewart, who was going on twenty-three and perfect for the draft, and the next son, James, who was going on eighteen. They would feel the brunt of war. There were several attempts to telephone Fred in Tampico, but they were unsuccessful. Several telegrams were sent to Tampico-Alto, which now had communications services. And yet no answer came from Fred. *Don* Federico, in a mad frenzy, insisted that Fred return to the United States as soon as possible.

The following spring, Luis Martin, continuing his education in a sophisticated technological school in Monterrey, telegraphed Victoria with bad news. Apparently, while Ricardo was working on a modern high-rise building in the downtown, he was hit in the head by a large steel girder. And the accident had left him paralyzed and in the hospital. Luis Martin had always thought Ricardo was his father, but before he left for school in Monterrey, Victoria finally broke down and told him the truth, since it was best. It left hard sentiments all around.

Victoria refused to travel to Monterrey and quickly responded to Luis Martin to keep in touch with her on Ricardo's outcome. She told him that she was in the middle of planting the cotton and could not leave the area. She emphasized that his education depended on the cotton profit. *Maybe all of the women in Monterrey who thought Ricardo was so wonderful will take care of him,* she thought. *Apparently, the special voodoo dolls and candles worked—thank you, Doña Adela!* There was still one doll left, and she would start working on it next. It was meant for a certain ex-Texas Ranger.

⌘   ⌘   ⌘

A month later, Ricardo died. Needless to say, Victoria did not attend the funeral.

Months passed and Victoria kept busy with the development of the *labores* and the smooth running of the machinery out in the cotton fields. She kept books on the number of pounds each worker picked, for which they received one cent a pound. She stayed overnight at Spanish Acres on Fridays so that on Saturday afternoon the workers would be paid in cash for the weekly quota, and then she completed her bookkeeping, after seeing that the trucks were driven to the Mercedes cotton gin. She then would return home to Mercedes. Victoria's other purpose was to see that Mary and her children, who still lived at Spanish Acres, had enough provisions. She was amazed how big Carlos's children were getting. They would be attending the Edcouch-Elsa school district, and during the school year would ride the bus.

But on this special day, in the warmest of windy June, Victoria did not return to Mercedes. After working all day out in the blistering sun, she paid the workers and wearily went to the Spanish Acres mansion to clean up and eat dinner with Mary and the children.

Mary, in a happy state of jubilation, announced she had a surprise for her.

"A surprise?" answered Victoria, exhausted, taking her hat, gloves, cotton jacket and sunglasses off in the vestibule. She noticed Roy looking much older, as he limped around helping Mary. Soledad, with salt and pepper hair, showed signs of aging as well. She was busy helping prepare a quail dinner with all of the festive ingredients of a banquet. Victoria excused herself to go upstairs to wash and put on clean clothes.

When she retuned to the kitchen area, she was still curious. "Now what was the surprise you wanted to tell me?" she asked Mary, while straightening her blouse. "Nothing surprises me anymore." She noticed the silence on everyone's lips. Nobody said a word, or even dared to look at her. Several seconds ticked by, and then it was Roy who rubbed his chin and spoke: "Let's go into da eatin' area."

Sitting at the dining room table was Juan Alvarez, wearing a white Panama shirt and looking at her with adoring eyes. Victoria screamed and brought her hands to her face and gasped. She could feel her heart beating faster. Juan got up and embraced her. Everybody smiled and then laughed and clapped their hands. What a surprise!

"I'm here to stay, *mí Chula*," he said, "to stay forever with you." He hugged her and kissed her cheeks. "*Mí Vida!* We will live together—forever."

Victoria sat down and cried. She remembered *Doña* Adela telling her in her last meditation, which was yesterday, *Juan will return. He will come back to live with you. Remember he is on the run from the Mexican government and needs a safe haven. He will find it with you.* Victoria also remembered telling *Doña* Adela, *It's impossible!*

CHAPTER 42

On an early June morning in 1942, at the Mercedes train depot, Fred stood frazzled from a two day trip from Tampico with his two little girls, each now holding onto a leg, waiting for the Juelson car to pick them up. When Victoria arrived, she hugged Fred for the longest time, with tears in her eyes. Juan, looking older and even grayer, joyfully hugged him, happy to see him again. *Don* Federico, looking thinner, more bald, and pale, was not able to contain his own tears of wonderment. He also embraced his son, not wanting to let him go.

Victoria glanced apprehensively at the two little girls, trying to decide whether to hold them or not. They reminded her of two, just-hatched, orphan birds—helpless. She was not pleased in seeing them and wondered what the rest of society was going to say. Fred had been the golden boy, and so much had been expected of him, and now this.

Victoria remained aloof and toyed with the thought of pretending, but they were her nieces, and there was nothing she could do about it. Any unkind words coming from her mouth would only hurt Fred. She and the family would have to put up with them, and she had to watch what she said. She finally picked up two-year-old Ana Maria, who was snotty nosed and crying, afraid of all the commotion and all the strange people. She only bawled louder, prompted by the brusqueness of Victoria's attitude.

"Easy with her," said Fred. "Be careful, those are my two little girls. They are tired and hungry. They have come a long way, and they miss their mother." And Fred added, "It's little Ana Maria who is more attached and cries more for Dolores."

Victoria came to her senses and realized her abruptness and reached for five-year-old Maria Venus, who was shy and nervous. But the child recoiled, rejecting her, as if she felt something strange about Victoria, and she hugged her father's leg ever more tightly. Fred reassured Maria Venus and led her to the car. He held Ana Maria, patting her back, and calmed her down while the driver drove them home. And where was Dolores? That was the big question. Come to find out, Dolores was unable to come to the United States until her visa was cleared, and that would perhaps take a couple of years. And it was a good thing, since the hen-house wagging tongue society was ready to start slinging mud. "You should have smuggled her into the country," remarked Victoria, halfway serious. "Since the closing of the borders and the new immigration law, the Mexican *coyotes* are busy reaping hundreds of dollars by crossing Mexicans over illegally."

"Oh, no, things must be done legally, according to the law," commented *Don* Federico.

For the next two months, hundreds of Fred's previous patients and friends came to the mansion and welcomed him back with great respect. Fred's heart was conflicted; he was happy being home with his father and Victoria, but his life was at a crossroads. He had changed so much. He wanted to be in Tampico-Alto with Dolores and his clinic, where he was needed, and where people appreciated him for his integrity.

Weeks afterward, Fred brought himself to ask questions about things that had happened since he had left. With his heart broken over Carlos's death, he asked again how he had died and wondered why? He eventually would go to Spanish Acres and meet Mary and Carlos's lovely children. Fred also questioned the health of *Don* Federico, who was getting forgetful and would swear a lot, and often repeated the same story over and over again. He was also concerned about Aunt Josie, who was still creating a ruckus within the household.

Fred saw how the town of Mercedes had been transformed with so many new shops and businesses exploding along the highway. However, the white downtown business-men had not changed in their prejudices. They were still bold and certain in their usual double-standard ways. The Mexicans-American still did business in the Mexican *bar-rios*, and the whites stayed in their section. He was deeply hurt when he walked into the downtown, among the white neighborhood shops, wanting to greet people, and found himself completely shunned, with most turning their backs on him. It profoundly hurt and dismayed him.

Fred and Victoria spent many hours catching up on different subjects; so much had altered in his absence. Aaron, after his schooling, got a job with an accounting firm and mar-ried a beautiful girl from Monterrey and were now living in Houston. Fred mentioned to Victoria one main reason he'd returned after war was declared was that a week before, he had sewn up several wounded German soldiers. With a gun being pointed at his head, he had no other choice. The Germans had submarines all along the shores of Tampico. He was fright-ened for his children and thought it best to bring them to the United States. He also saw how happy Victoria was with Juan and how she had finally fulfilled her dream of their being together. After hearing Juan's story, Fred understood his having to flee Mexico; it brought back his own ugly memories.

The country was at war, and realizing, with his shady background, no medical profession would hire him, he was deeply saddened. He had to come up with some form of employ-ment, if he were going to support his family. His two little girls would have to stay at the mansion, and would have Victoria and the rest of his family raise them, until Dolores was able to join him later.

In a short time, Fred found himself feeling disillusioned at having returned home to Mercedes, and he became restless and did not stay in the town for very long. With the toss of the dice, he was fortunate to have found work in Brownsville, doing bookkeeping and keeping account ledgers for a large shipping company. He stayed five days a week in a lodging area and returned home on the weekends. It was a rat-shit salary, but it was a job. Saturday and Sunday were the only days he was able to spend time with little Ana and Maria.

Victoria and *Don* Federico bought him a new car that gave him the opportunity to travel back and forth to work. His vehicle also gave him the freedom to roam. On several occasions, with his restless mind and loneliness, he would drive to Spanish Acres with his two little girls to spend time with the older *vaqueros*, Roy, Soledad, Mary, and her two children. It was fun for the two girls seeing the many animals at the ranch.

One particular Saturday, he drove the winding curves of the paved road, and before coming to La Villa, he stopped the car and listened to the sounds of the wind, and with his usual curiously, studied the changes in the landscape. The area was now called Sunrise Hill, where thousands of acres of citrus trees had been planted in an area that years ago had belonged to a *ranchero* friend of *Don* Federico.

Fred marveled at the beautiful scenery and all the changes that had come about since he had left this area. It had stormed and drizzled rain the night before, and throughout the countryside there were puddles of water on the ground and on the gravel road.

After driving through the town of La Villa, within half an hour, he was into Juelson territory, the area he was most accustomed to, and where he had grown up. As he was getting closer to Spanish Acres, along the old La Sal Road, he became aware that his two children were quieter and had fallen asleep on the back seat. Up ahead he noticed a medium-sized, dark lump next to the road, but the object, upon seeing him, rapidly disappeared into the undergrowth in the area that was once *Doña* Adela's abode.

Fred slowed down and rolled the window down. He was curious, and, on impulse, he turned into *la bruja's* old place. The road was a lonely dirt trail that perhaps only the *vaqueros*, cotton field workers, or the riggers from the oil field occasionally used. Both sides of the road were impenetrable, with mesquite, thick undergrowth, chaparral, tall cottonwood trees, and many dried, tangled bushes had lived and died and had revitalized the following year in the same spot again. There were a hundred different varieties of the unwanted cacti that persisted to this day.

As he was about to circle into the tract where *Doña* Adela once lived, he noticed an old, faded blue Ford pickup parked inside the lot. He turned the engine off and sat in his car and watched to see if there was any movement. Only silence. Among the trees was only the chirping of the mockingbirds, and the wind that consistently blew, and the angry echoing cries of the black birds flying and circling around.

Finally, after several minutes went by, and since this was their land, Fred decided to step out of his car and check on the whereabouts of the driver of the Ford truck. He felt the truck's hood, and it was still warm. He walked onto the property, stepping on wet, soggy stones, broken glass, and burned wooden boards still scattered about from the explosion that had wrecked the house. Tall grass and sprawling weeds had taken over. The area had been cleared from the old house, but there was still plenty of debris lying on the ground, and there still remained parts of a tumbled-down chimney and the sagging remnants of the dilapidated barn and shed.

Getting closer, he heard a noise coming from yards outside the old barn. He walked over and peered through a crack in the rotted boards of the only wall left intact. A large, brawny man wearing overalls and a straw hat was using a wooden-handled metal pick to dig through the rich, dark ground. Fred frowned and wondered for a moment what the man was doing and what business he had digging in this area that was spiritually forbidden by the Mexican people, who would not think of coming close to this spot. It was considered haunted. And what was the fleeting dark shape that he had seen on the road? Did it have anything to do with this scene before him?

He kept a close watch through the hole, trying to recognize the person, hoping to view his facial features. From that distance, Fred could not tell. Suddenly, the large man stopped and knelt down. He had found something, which he began pulling from the earth. The *hombre* seemed overjoyed with the large object in his hands and was unaware of anyone else's presence. Fred was hesitant to make himself known and kept straining his eyes to determine what the object was that held the attention of the stranger. He was ready to come forward and ask questions— when he was distracted by a sudden movement in the nearby west undergrowth.

From the dense growth of cactus, mesquite, and brushy undergrowth, a small dwarf figure appeared and stood silently over the big man, who was kneeling down, brushing the dirt off of a small tin trunk.

Fred eyed the small figure and instantly recognized him, his eyes growing wide. It was Roberto! He was alive! Everyone around Spanish Acres thought Roberto had died sometime out in the *brasada.* But, this was his home, and deformed and disfigured as he was, Roberto still claimed his grounds, haunted or not. Fred stood petrified with horror as he watched the scene before him unfold.

Roberto gripped in one hand a large, dried mesquite limb ripped to a sharp point, and he quickly plunged it into the side of the large man's neck. The enormous man jumped to his feet, growling in pain and cussing, his epithets echoing throughout the *brasada.* He turned to face Roberto, surprise and terror in his eyes. His face twisted in pain, and he wrapped his beefy hands around his throat as blood spurted higher and higher. He was still standing, but became wobbly, then fell to his knees. Roberto circled around him, grabbed the pick from the ground, and plunged it into the man's back. The big man let out another strangled cry, but he was not giving up easily. He reached into his pants with one bloody hand, pulled out a pistol, and began shooting randomly—one shot, two shots, three—the last one hitting Roberto in the stomach. Eventually, the man dropped the gun and rolled over onto the ground.

Roberto, holding his stomach, fell to his knees groaning.

Without thinking, Fred ran toward Roberto. He was still alive, but gravely wounded. The burly, strapping man lay sprawled and moaning on the damp ground. Fred kneeled and felt the pulse on the man as blood kept spurting from the punctured artery in his neck. The injured man was fighting back death and struggling to speak. "…I should have known," he uttered, glaring at Fred, "…gaw'd…damn! …Trying to kill Juelson…had a trap for me!"

Gasping and breathing hard, he gurgled, "...the son-of-a-bitch, Juelson...he finally won!" His body went into spasms; he rolled his eyes, and died.

Fred's instincts told him it was the ex-Texas Ranger Hanson. Apparently he had been planning to kill his father, waiting for the chance, hiding around *Doña* Adela's place, with nobody aware of his plans. Next to the body of Hanson was a corroded tin chest covered with damp clay—he never had a chance to open and enjoy his pirate's hoard.

Fred leaned over to examine Roberto, who was lying on the ground holding his bloody stomach. The bullet had penetrated the lower part of his abdomen and was still lodged there. The bullet had to be taken out. Fred panicked. He had forgotten about his two girls sleeping in the car, and he needed to check on them. When he turned to go, he was surprised to find Maria Venus standing there wide-awake and white as a sheet. She had gotten out of the car and perhaps had witnessed the whole scene. She started to cry hysterically when Fred picked her up.

Dear God! Fred prayed, *I have to help Roberto!* His first thought was to get Maria Venus calmed and back inside the car and then try and get Roberto into the front seat and drive him to Spanish Acres, only a couple of miles away.

Half an hour later, Roberto was taken inside by Roy and several other *vaqueros*, who saw Fred driving madly up the road and honking wildly—he had not taken his hand off the horn since he had entered the long Spanish Acres driveway.

Fred did not have to explain—everything was bloody from the car seat to his white shirt and pants. The hero Roberto was taken to a cot close to the kitchen. Soledad and Mary comforted Maria Venus, who was still in shock and continued crying, and took care of Ana Maria, who had just woken up from all the noise.

With the help of Roy, the *vaqueros*, and the usual chloroform, alcohol, cotton, and a sharp knife, Fred extracted the bullet from Roberto, who could only moan; he had never talked in his life. The stink coming from his hideous body made a maggot want to barf, but the filthy little man was a hero.

There were no phones at Spanish Acres. Fred handed Mary the keys to his car and asked her to drive to La Villa, where there was a phone in the office of the train station, and call Victoria in Mercedes. "Have Victoria bring Dad and Juan," Fred frantically insisted. "But be careful what you say to her. Don't mention anything about this incident. Don't say any more, since everybody and their dog is listening on the phone. Tell Victoria to get here as soon as possible. She is going to start asking you questions, but tell her to just get over here, quickly! I will explain later. She will understand."

Within the next three hours, *Don* Federico, Victoria, and Juan were at Spanish Acres. Fred had explained everything and had gone over the whole story while holding Maria Venus to his shoulder and rocking her after Soledad had given her some *manzanilla* tea. Several of the *vaqueros* had brought the body of the dead man in the back of their flatbed truck. One of the *vaqueros* drove the old Ford pickup and hid it behind the barn.

Outdoors in the late afternoon as the twilight was touching earth; *Don* Federico shivered in shock as he took one look at the burly man lying on the flatbed truck and gasped.

"It's Goddamn Hanson! The mother of Satan," he said, almost out of breath. "It's him! He's heavier, grayer and uglier than I remember, but it's him, all right, and the murderous, master *Diablo* has finally gotten his due. I can now rest in peace. I cannot believe it!" *Don* Federico was relieved. He knew that Hanson was trying to kill him, plotting all along, and waiting for the chance. "All these years, and all it took was one little deformed man, so insignificant, but yet so heroic," he said, shaking his head. "Roberto has got to live, and I will reward him a hundred times over. He will need taking care of— his teeth, clothes, and food." He paused and reflected on the gruesome event. "Of course, it all makes sense now. He probably witnessed his mother's death and was protecting his property and his mother's possessions."

"It's hard to believe," said Juan. "Sometimes that's the way it happens. So now, what are we going to do with the body? We need to call the sheriff."

"No!" exclaimed Victoria frantically. "They must never know of Hanson's death. If we call the sheriff, they are going to think we killed him. It will look very suspicious. Remember, *Los Rinches* never did anything about Hanson's evilness. Think!" Victoria suggested to everyone listening. "Hanson framed Fred because of Dad. Now Fred's back, and all of a sudden Hanson shows up dead on our property? Yes, it was circumstantial, but nobody is going to believe that story. And what about Roberto? We cannot explain about Roberto. Roberto is part of Spanish Acres, and we are part of Roberto."

Her words were truer than she knew. "Victoria is right," agreed *Don* Federico. He did not want to tell them what *la bruja, Doña* Adela, had told him in confidence so many years ago. It would be too painful. The secret that he had carried with him with agonizing understanding and finally compromised, coming to terms with the reality that Roberto was his half-brother. All along, Roberto probably knew this too and understood, in his own little *brasada* world. *Doña* Adela, sometime while he was growing up, had told him the truth to make him feel he was part of the Spanish Acres family. That was the reason Roberto had saved *Don* Federico's life when he had the buggy accident out in the *brasada*. And the main reason he would roam around protecting the land, because it was his land, and all along had been his.

Don Federico still could not come to terms with telling Fred and Victoria the other secret, the one about their ancestry. Not at this time. It was too shocking. He would tell them later.

The corroded tin trunk was full of coins; five, ten and twenty-dollar gold pieces that *Doña* Adela had been saving, perhaps for a rainy day. There were many rainy days in this part of the country, and *Don* Federico would see that Roberto received the money.

He went to check on Roberto where he was lying on the cot. He got a chair and sat close to him. "Roberto, you are home now," he told him. "You will be safe here. This is your home for as long as you want it to be," the *Don* said sincerely. He smiled at the outcast little man and patted his gnarled hand.

Roberto looked at him with an anguished look in his eyes; his face was so deformed and crinkled, his hair was white, and his threadbare clothes were hanging on his small frame. It took a couple of minutes before anything registered with him, but finally he smiled and tenderly touched *Don* Federico's hand as a sign of the bond between them.

ROOTS OF INDIFFERENCE

With a lump in his throat, *Don* Federico spent close to an hour with Roberto, reassuring him of his welcome to stay. Later, as a gamut of emotions surfaced, he showed up red-eyed, and informed the others, "We'll get rid of Hanson's body. The truck will be destroyed and taken apart, piece-by-piece. We'll hear no more about this. And no more will be spoken of this incident. *Mañana* will come, for there will be many more *mañanas*."

It was never revealed how the body of the ex-Texas Ranger Hanson was disposed of. The knowledge was surrendered to the *vaqueros'* code of silence and was never repeated again. Each *vaquero* carried it to his grave.

⌘   ⌘   ⌘

A balmy wind awoke the old man from his sleeping trance. Fred looked around the park in a half-dazed stare and glanced at his watch. It was getting dark as the reddish- orange sun slanted to the west over the tops of the trees. He noticed the small black dog had cuddled on the ground next to his feet. His memory was starting to fail, but like a shot of oxygen to his half-conscious thoughts, he began questioning where his children were.

His mind was muddled and disoriented by age and forgetfulness, and he was having trouble remembering the ugly, painful ghosts of happenings in the past, so many years back.

He recalled returning to Tampico-Alto to get Dolores. She was pregnant again and, having no other choice, Fred stayed until the baby was born. It was another girl, christened Francisca, in honor of his mother. Two years after Fred and his two daughters had come to the United States without her, Dolores got her visa, and the family was able to be together in Texas.

Don Federico Juelson died from heart failure in 1945, shortly after Fred brought Dolores to Texas.

Fred remembered how he had felt cheated, and his mind had snapped from depression, not being able to continue as a physician in Texas because of racially biased people, even though he had been declared innocent of any crime. He wondered if a curse had been put on him for having married Dolores. Victoria had always disapproved of his marrying her and seemed repulsed by their children, mistreating them when they were in her care. It had been more painful for little Ana, mistreating her more than Maria Venus who was shy, silent and afraid.

Fred knew he was never the same after coming back to the United States, and he always blamed the cruelty of the bigoted people who had accused him of the crime he didn't commit, ruining his career and his life. He always felt that his '*roots of indifference*' were the basis of everything that had happened—greed for money and power—culture and traditions. He was always aware of, and resented, the sense of entrapment that dwelled within him.

In Texas, he was a branded man; in Mexico he was a healer, and to the local natives there—he was their hero. Going back became a loud siren call, with an urgency to become useful again. It was true what the people of the village of Tampico-Alto said about their water: if you drink it, you will come back.

He regretted that, after many years of being disillusioned with their marriage, Dolores became discontented with his unpredictable ways and impetuous behavior, and with Victoria always interfering and finding ways of hurting her and her children. In the end, she had filed for divorce, but stayed in Texas and raised their seven children.

Brokenhearted from his father's death and his failed marriage, and with nowhere else to go, Fred returned alone in 1955 to Tampico-Alto, fulfilling his dream as a physician. He grew old there, where he was important and of service and a champion to the native peoples. He built a new clinic and devoted himself to healing others. He would occasionally cross the border into Texas for a visit, always returning to Mexico with boxes full of second-hand clothes for the poor.

His departure into Mexico was like the ocean waves that came ashore, but each time drifted spatially out and stayed longer, like the endless sea's abyss. And finally, this last farewell trip had taken many years to materialize.

So now, with tears in his eyes, Fred gathered up his heavy old suitcase and the rope-bound cloth bag. He was getting old, disoriented and hurting. All he wanted was to reach his folks' home on Georgia Street. He called for the little dog, which he had named Blackie, seemingly appropriate. "Blackie," he said, "you and I have a lot in common. We both had a mother that once loved us. We both are roamers and adventurers. We were once young and handsome, but now we are old, wrinkled, and ugly, and without a home. We are both gypsies, so come along, ol' buddy."

Limping slightly, Fred began walking, his once tall frame half-bent carrying his heavy bags. He noticed children from afar running up to meet him on the sidewalk, Victoria's grandchildren and many other nieces and nephews, who were all expecting him. He looked back to see if Blackie was coming, but sadly, the little black dog had hesitated and had stayed in the park.

The walk from the park to his old home wasn't far, but it seemed like an eternity; it was a huge effort for his failing body. Now and then, he would stop to rest and turn around, calling Blackie's name, wanting to help the animal. Finally, his heart rejoiced seeing the black dog coming after him. He stood and rested again until the little fellow caught up with him. He was going to take him home, care for him, feed him, and heal him. After all, hadn't it always been his good nature to help and to heal?

The sun was like an enchantment finally going down and disappearing among the arboreal palms, and Fred thought how it resembled the course of his life—a brilliant sunset of fiery red-orange, yet not knowing if there would be any more *mañanas* for him. Somewhere on the breeze he heard the farewell song *Las Golondrinas—The Swallows*—being sung.

Fred hoped that, through the years, things had changed in the Rio Grande Valley, especially regarding the hatred and discrimination that had held the Mexican-American people back. The virtue within each person seemed lost in the evils that humans do. He prophesied that one day, long after he was dead and gone, everyone would have blood cells from each different race. That the world one day would be all one race, where all would have the same skin color, but would be a long ways into the future. Skin color seemed so important today, but it would not be tomorrow. There would be many tomorrows, and things were going to be different then. Many changes were coming in medicine and technology.

Finally with great effort, Fred reached his final destination, his late parents' home, with ten children surrounding him, all wanting to pet the little black dog. There was a nice supper celebration in his honor later in the evening, giving him the opportunity to see all of his old acquaintances and the newly born.

Fred saw to it that Blackie was taken care of, with plenty of food and water.

Hours later, when the house was silent, and he was getting ready to go up to bed, he approached *Doña* Panchita, the lady who had been Victoria's loyal servant for many years before she died.

"How did Victoria die?" Fred asked inquisitively. He needed to know.

"Ay, Dr. Juelson!" cried the old gray-haired woman. "She died in her sleep during the night," she replied, choking back tears. "The doctor said it was a heart attack. She didn't want to live after her beloved Juan died five years ago. They had loved each other so much. But… it was very strange," she said, hesitantly. "That morning…it was amazing what I found on your dead sister's bed."

"Strange?"

"The sheets, the pillow cases, all were covered with what looked like black dog fur."

"Dog fur?" replied Fred, puzzled.

"Yes. And to tell you the truth, right before midnight, there was an eerie howl that seemed to come from her bedroom, almost like the howl of a dog. Funny," she said, shaking her head. "We do not have any dogs in this household."

⌘ ⌘ ⌘

Fred died three years later, finally coming to peace with his life. His ashes were cast into the waters that flow into the Gulf of Mexico from the majestic Rio Grande River, the river separating his two beloved countries, divided like his soul, representing his life.

⌘ ⌘ ⌘

Fred's river of life was a journey that started as a little, bubbling, sparkling, spring full of life. His youth promised endless strength, and becoming a torrent flowing liveliness into a larger stream. From its current it gained energy and traveled onward with determination. Beyond its limited perceptions, it saw the beauty of his garden purpose, the meadows and plains, the wildflowers on its banks, the grass and trees.

Tormenting storms gave his essence a powerful momentum that caused it to crash against the rocks, but it traveled and grew, moving onward in a flow that embraced the splendor of heaven and earth and the changes of the seasons.

TERRI RAGSDALE

His spirit endured life's twist and turns, its obstacles and rocky impediments along the way, and gathered and captured life's experiences, failures, wisdom, human kindness, knowledge, forgiveness and perhaps the greatest of all—love—and then waved goodbye forever. Empowered by his splendid journey, relentlessly reaching for its final destination, it delivered his soul to a better place, to *the endless sea*.

AUTHOR'S NOTE

This is a work of fiction, but the truths it reveals ache to be told. The region of the Lower Rio Grande of South Texas does exist. The little *ranchitos* that were once prevalent throughout the region have become towns and cities. The Mexican Revolution did take place and affected all of the communities along both sides of the border. The Mexican-American people lived and died and told of the many horrible incidents that took place in their lives; many still remember.

Centuries of subjugated dominance in a land saturated with so much bigotry, prejudice, and injustice are now witnessing the birth of a social identity of a proud race, after years of repression and humiliation. Years of silent fear now yearn to speak out.

The research encompassed eighteen years of living with, talking to, and taking notes from the Mexican-American people of South Texas and utilizing documents, newspapers, and original sources. I lay no claim to the accuracy where the main characters names have been changed, to protect the living relatives.

The story does not end here…another book to come will tell the tale of Fred's children.

TERRI RAGSDALE